EYE O

LIE DOV

Ken Follett was only twenty-seven when he wrote *Eye of the Needle,* the award-winning novel which became an international bestseller and a distinguished film. Before that he had been a newspaper reporter and a publishing executive after studying philosophy at University College, London.

He has since written many equally successful novels and the non-fiction bestseller *On Wings of Eagles.*

Ken Follett lives with his family in Stevenage and London.

Visit the Ken Follett website at
http://www.ken-follett.com

KEN FOLLETT

EYE OF
THE NEEDLE
&
LIE DOWN
WITH LIONS

PAN BOOKS

Eye of the Needle first published in Great Britain 1978 by Futura Publications Ltd
Lie Down with Lions first published in Great Britain 1985 by Hamish Hamilton

This omnibus edition published 2002 by Pan Books
an imprint of Pan Macmillan Ltd
Pan Macmillan, 20 New Wharf Road, London N1 9RR
Basingstoke and Oxford
Associated companies throughout the world
www.panmacmillan.com

ISBN 0 330 41507 7

1 3 5 7 9 8 6 4 2

A CIP catalogue record for this book is available from
the British Library.

Typeset by CentraCet, Cambridge
Printed and bound in Great Britain by
Mackays of Chatham plc, Chatham, Kent

EYE OF THE NEEDLE

My thanks to Malcolm Hulke for invaluable help, generously given.

The Germans were almost completely
deceived – only Hitler guessed
right, and he hesitated to back his
hunch . . .

A. J. P. Taylor
English History 1914–1945

PREFACE

Early in 1944 German Intelligence was piecing together evidence of a huge army in south-eastern England. Reconnaissance planes brought back photographs of barracks and airfields and fleets of ships in the Wash; General George S. Patton was seen in his unmistakable pink jodhpurs walking his white bulldog; there were bursts of wireless activity, signals between regiments, in the area; confirming signs were reported by German spies in Britain.

There was no army, of course. The ships were rubber-and-timber fakes, the barracks no more real than a movie set; Patton did not have a single man under his command; the radio signals were meaningless; the spies were double agents.

The object was to fool the enemy into preparing for an invasion via the Pas de Calais, so that on D-Day the Normandy assault would have the advantage of surprise.

It was a huge, near-impossible deception. Literally thousands of people were involved in perpetrating the trick. It would have been a miracle if none of Hitler's spies ever got to know about it.

Were there any spies? At the time people thought

they were surrounded by what were then called Fifth
Columnists. After the war a myth grew up that MI5 had
rounded up the lot by Christmas 1939. The truth seems
to be that there were very few: MI5 did capture nearly
all of them.

But it only needs one . . .

We know that the Germans saw the signs they were
meant to see in East Anglia. We also know that they
suspected a trick. And we know that they tried very
hard to discover the truth.

That much is history, and I have discovered no facts
that aren't already in history books. What follows is
fiction.

Still and all, I think something like this must have
happened . . .

Camberley, Surrey
June 1977

Part One

Part One

CHAPTER ONE

I T WAS the coldest winter for forty-five years. Villages in the English countryside were cut off by the snow, and the Thames froze over. One day in January the Glasgow to London train arrived at Euston twenty-four hours late. The snow and the blackout combined to make motoring perilous: road accidents doubled, and people told jokes about how it was more risky to drive an Austin Seven along Piccadilly at night than to take a tank across the Siegfried Line.

Then, when the spring came, it was glorious. Barrage balloons floated majestically in bright blue skies, and soldiers on leave flirted with girls in sleeveless dresses on the streets of London.

The city did not look much like the capital of a nation at war. There were signs, of course; and Henry Faber, cycling from Waterloo Station toward Highgate, noted them: piles of sandbags outside important public buildings, Anderson shelters in suburban gardens, propaganda posters about evacuation and Air Raid Precautions. Faber watched such things – he was considerably more observant than the average railway clerk. He saw crowds of children in the parks, and concluded that evacuation had been a failure. He marked the number of motor cars on the road, despite petrol rationing; and he read about the new models announced by the motor manufacturers. He knew the significance of night-shift workers pouring into factories where, only months previously, there had been hardly enough work for the day shift. Most of all he monitored the movement of troops around Britain's railway network: all the paperwork passed through his office. One could learn a lot from that paperwork. Today, for example, he had rubber-stamped a batch of forms which led him to believe that a new Expeditionary Force was being gathered. He was fairly sure that it would have a complement of about 100,000 men, and that it was for Finland.

There were signs, yes; but there was something jokey about it all. Radio shows satirised the red tape of wartime regulations, there was community singing in the air-raid shelters, and fashionable women carried their gas masks in couturier-designed containers. They talked about the Bore War. It was at once larger-than-life and trivial, like a moving-picture show. All the air-raid warnings, without exception, had been false alarms.

Faber had a different point of view – but then, he was a different kind of person.

He steered his cycle into Archway Road and leaned forward a little to take the uphill slope, his long legs pumping as tirelessly as the pistons of a railway engine. He was very fit for his age, which was thirty-nine, although he lied about it: he lied about most things, as a safety precaution.

4

He began to perspire as he climbed the hill into Highgate. The building in which he lived was one of the highest in London, which was why he chose to live there. It was a Victorian brick house at one end of a terrace of six. The houses were high, narrow and dark, like the minds of the men for whom they had been built. Each had three storeys plus a basement with a servants' entrance – the English middle class of the nineteenth century insisted on a servants' entrance, even if they had no servants. Faber was a cynic about the English.

Number six had been owned by Mr Harold Garden, of Garden's Tea And Coffee, a small company which went broke in the Slump. Having lived by the principle that insolvency is a mortal sin, the bankrupt Mr Garden had no option but to die. The house was all he bequeathed to his widow, who was then obliged to take in lodgers. She enjoyed being a landlady, although the etiquette of her social circle demanded that she pretend to be a little ashamed of it. Faber had a room on the top floor with a dormer window. He lived there from Monday to Friday, and told Mrs Garden that he spent weekends with his mother in Erith. In fact he had another landlady in Blackheath who called him Mr Baker and believed he was a travelling salesman for a stationery manufacturer and spent all week on the road.

He wheeled his cycle up the garden path under the disapproving frown of the tall front-room windows. He put it in the shed and padlocked it to the lawn-mower – it was against the law to leave a vehicle unlocked. The seed potatoes in boxes all around the shed were sprouting. Mrs Garden had turned her flower beds over to vegetables for the war effort.

Faber entered the house, hung his hat on the hall-stand, washed his hands and went in to tea.

Three of the other lodgers were already eating: a pimply boy from Yorkshire who was trying to get into the Army; a confectionery salesman with receding sandy hair; and a retired naval officer who, Faber was convinced, was a degenerate. Faber nodded to them and sat down.

The salesman was telling a joke. 'So the Squadron-Leader says, "You're back early!" and the pilot turns round and says, "Yes, I dropped my leaflets in bundles, wasn't that right?" so the Squadron-Leader says, "Good God! You might've hurt somebody!"'

The naval officer cackled and Faber smiled. Mrs Garden came in with a teapot. 'Good evening, Mr Faber. We started without you – I hope you don't mind.'

Faber spread margarine thinly on a slice of whole-meal bread, and momentarily yearned for a fat sausage. 'Your seed potatoes are ready to plant,' he told her.

Faber hurried through his tea. The others were arguing over whether Chamberlain should be sacked and replaced by Churchill. Mrs Garden kept voicing opinions then looking at Faber for a reaction. She was a blowsy woman, a little overweight. About Faber's age, she wore the clothes of a woman of thirty, and he guessed she wanted another husband. He kept out of the discussion.

Mrs Garden turned on the radio. It hummed for a while, then an announcer said: 'This is the BBC Home Service. *It's That Man Again!*'

Faber had heard the show. It regularly featured a German spy called Funf. He excused himself and went up to his room.

Mrs Garden was left alone after *It's That Man Again*: the naval officer went to the pub with the salesman, and the boy from Yorkshire, who was religious, went to a prayer meeting. She sat in the parlour with a small glass of gin, looking at the blackout curtains and thinking about Mr Faber. She wished he wouldn't spend so much time in his room. She needed company, and he was the kind of company she needed.

Such thoughts made her feel guilty. To assuage the guilt she thought of Mr Garden. Her memories were familiar but blurred, like an old print of a movie with worn sprocket-holes and an indistinct soundtrack; so that, although she could easily remember what it was like to have him here in the room with her, it was difficult to imagine his face, or the clothes he might be wearing, or the comment he would make on the day's war news. He had been a small, dapper man, successful in business when he was lucky and unsuccessful when he was not, undemonstrative in public and insatiably affectionate in bed. She had loved him a lot. There would be many women in her position if this war ever got going properly. She poured another drink.

Mr Faber was a quiet one – that was the trouble. He didn't seem to have any vices. He didn't smoke, she had never smelled drink on his breath, and he spent every evening in his room, listening to classical music on his radio. He read a lot of newspapers and went for long walks. She suspected he was quite clever, despite his humble job: his contributions to the conversation in the dining-room were always a shade more thoughtful than anyone else's. He surely could get a better job if he tried. He seemed not to give himself the chance he deserved.

It was the same with his appearance. He was a fine figure of a man: tall, quite heavy around the neck and shoulders, not a bit fat, with long legs. And he had a strong face, with a high forehead and a long jaw and bright blue eyes; not pretty, like a film star, but the kind of face that appealed to a woman. Except for the mouth – that was small and thin, and she could imagine him being cruel. Mr Garden had been incapable of cruelty.

And yet at first sight he was not the kind of man a woman would look at twice. The trousers of his old worn suit were never pressed – she would have done that for him, and gladly, but he never asked – and he always wore a shabby raincoat and a flat docker's cap. He had no moustache, and his hair was trimmed short every fortnight. It was as if he wanted to look like a nonentity.

He needed a woman, there was no doubt of that. She wondered for a moment whether he might be what people called effeminate, but she dismissed the idea quickly. He needed a wife to smarten him up and give him ambition. She needed a man to keep her company and for – well, love.

Yet he never made a move. Sometimes she could scream with frustration. She was sure she was attractive. She looked in a mirror as she poured another gin. She had a nice face, and fair curly hair, and there was something for a man to get hold of . . . She giggled at that thought. She must be getting tiddly.

She sipped her drink and considered whether *she* ought to make the first move. Mr Faber was obviously shy – chronically shy. He wasn't sexless – she could tell by the look in his eyes on the two occasions he had seen her in her nightdress. Perhaps she could overcome his shyness by being brazen. What did she have to lose? She tried imagining the worst, just to see what it felt like. Suppose he rejected her. Well, it would be embarrassing – even humiliating. It would be a blow to her pride. But nobody else need know it had happened. He would just have to leave.

The thought of rejection had put her off the whole idea. She got to her feet slowly, thinking: I'm just not the brazen type. It was bedtime. If she had one more gin in bed she would be able to sleep. She took the bottle upstairs.

Her bedroom was below Mr Faber's, and she could hear violin music from his radio as she undressed. She put on a new nightdress – pink, with an embroidered neckline, and no one to see it! – and made her last drink. She wondered what Mr Faber looked like undressed. He would have a flat stomach, and hairs on his nipples, and you would be able to see his ribs, because he was slim. He probably had a small bottom. She giggled again, thinking: I'm a disgrace.

She took her drink to bed and picked up her book, but it was too much effort to focus on the print. Besides, she was bored with vicarious romance. Stories about dangerous love affairs were fine when you yourself had a perfectly safe love affair with your husband, but a woman needed more than Barbara Cartland. She sipped her gin, and wished Mr Faber would turn the radio off. It was like trying to sleep at a tea-dance!

She could, of course, ask him to turn it off. She looked at her bedside clock: it was past ten. She could put on her dressing-gown, which matched the night-dress, and just comb her hair a little, then step into her slippers – quite dainty, with a pattern of roses – and just pop up the stairs to the next landing, and just, well, tap on his door. He would open it, perhaps wearing his trousers and singlet, and then he would *look* at her the way he had *looked* when he saw her in her nightdress on the way to the bathroom . . .

'Silly old fool,' she said to herself aloud. 'You're just making excuses to go up there.'

And then she wondered why she needed excuses. She was a mature adult, and it was her house, and in ten years she had not met another man who was just right for her, and what the *hell,* she needed to feel someone strong and hard and hairy on top of her, squeezing her breasts and panting in her ear and parting her thighs with his broad flat hands, for tomorrow the gas bombs might come over from Germany and they would all die choking and gasp-ing and poisoned and she would have lost her last chance.

So she drained her glass, and got out of bed, and put on her dressing-gown, and just combed her hair a little, and stepped into her slippers, and picked up her bunch of keys in case he had locked the door and couldn't hear her knock above the sound of the radio.

There was nobody on the landing. She found the stairs in the darkness. She intended to step over the stair that creaked, but she stumbled on the loose carpet and trod on it heavily; but it seemed that nobody heard, so she went on up and tapped on the door at the top. She tried it gently. It was locked.

The radio was turned down, and Mr Faber called out: 'Yes?'

He was well-spoken: not cockney, or foreign – not anything, really, just a pleasantly neutral voice.

She said: 'Can I have a word with you?'

He seemed to hesitate, then he said: 'I'm undressed.'

'So am I,' she giggled, and she opened the door with her duplicate key. He was standing in front of the radio with some kind of screwdriver in his hand. He wore his trousers and *no* singlet. His face was white and he looked scared to death.

She stepped inside and closed the door behind her, not knowing what to say. Suddenly she remembered a line from an American film, and she said: 'Would you buy a lonely girl a drink?' It was silly, really, because she knew he had no drink in his room, and she certainly wasn't dressed to go out; but it sounded vampish.

It seemed to have the desired effect. Without speaking, he came slowly toward her. He *did* have hair on his

11

nipples. She took a step forward, and then his arms went around her, and she closed her eyes and turned up her face, and he kissed her, and she moved slightly in his arms, and then there was a terrible, awful, unbearable *sharp* pain in her back and she opened her mouth to scream.

He had heard her stumble on the stairs. If she'd waited another minute he would have had the radio transmitter back in its case and the code books in the drawer and there would have been no need for her to die. But before he could conceal the evidence he had heard her key in the lock, and when she opened the door the stiletto had been in his hand.

Because she moved slightly in his arms, Faber missed her heart with the first jab of the weapon, and he had to thrust his fingers down her throat to stop her crying out. He jabbed again, but she moved again and the blade struck a rib and merely slashed her superficially. Then the blood was spurting and he knew it would not be a clean kill, it never was when you missed with the first stroke.

She was wriggling too much to be killed with a jab now. Keeping his fingers in her mouth, he gripped her jaw with his thumb and pushed her back against the door. Her head hit the woodwork with a loud bump, and he wished he had not turned the radio down, but how could he have expected this?

He hesitated before killing her, because it would be much better if she died on the bed – better for the

cover-up which was already taking shape in his mind –
but he could not be sure of getting her that far in
silence. He tightened his hold on her jaw, kept her
head still by jamming it against the door, and brought
the stiletto around in a wide slashing arc that ripped
away most of her throat, for the stiletto was not a
slashing knife and the throat was not Faber's favoured
target.

He jumped back to avoid the first horrible gush of
blood, then stepped forward again to catch her before
she hit the floor. He dragged her to the bed, trying not
to look at her neck, and laid her down.

He had killed before, so he expected the reaction: it
always came as soon as he felt safe. He went over to the
sink in the corner of the room and waited for it. He
could see his face in the little shaving mirror. He was
white, and his eyes were staring. He looked at himself
and thought: *Killer.* Then he threw up.

When that was over he felt better. He could go to
work now. He knew what he had to do: the details had
come to him even while he was killing her.

He washed his face, brushed his teeth, and cleaned
the washbasin. Then he sat down at the table beside his
radio. He looked at his notebook, found his place, and
began tapping the key. It was a long message, about the
mustering of an army for Finland, and he had been
half way through when he was interrupted. It was
written down in cipher on the pad. When he had
completed it he signed off with: 'Regards to Willi.'

The transmitter packed away neatly into a specially
designed suitcase. Faber put the rest of his possessions

into a second case. He took off his trousers and sponged the bloodstains, then washed himself all over.

At last he looked at the corpse.

He was able to be cold about her now. It was wartime; they were enemies: if he had not killed her, she would have caused his death. She had been a threat, and all he felt now was relief that the threat had been nullified. She should not have frightened him.

Nevertheless, his last task was distasteful. He opened her robe and lifted her nightdress, pulling it up around her waist. She was wearing knickers. He tore them, so that the hair of her pubis was visible. Poor woman: she had wanted only to seduce him. But he could not have got her out of the room without her seeing the transmitter; and the British propaganda had made these people alert for spies – ridiculously so: if the Abwehr had as many agents as the newspapers made out then the British would have lost the war already.

He stepped back and looked at her with his head on one side. There was something wrong. He tried to think like a sex maniac. If I were crazed with lust for a woman like Una Garden, and I killed her just so that I could have my way with her, what would I then do?

Of course: that kind of lunatic would want to look at her breasts. Faber leaned over the body, gripped the neckline of the nightdress, and ripped it to the waist. Her large breasts sagged sideways.

The police doctor would soon discover that she had not been raped, but Faber did not think that mattered. He had taken a criminology course at Heidelberg, and he knew that many sexual assaults were not consum-

mated. Besides, he could not have carried the deception that far, not even for the Fatherland. He was not
in the SS. Some of *them* would queue up to rape the
corpse . . . He put the thought out of his mind.

He washed his hands again and got dressed. It was
almost midnight. He would wait an hour before leaving:
it would be safer later.

He sat down to think about how he had gone
wrong.

There was no question that he had made a mistake.
If his cover were perfect, he would be totally secure. If
he were totally secure no one could discover his secret.
Mrs Garden had discovered his secret – or rather, she
would have if she had lived a few seconds longer –
therefore he had not been totally secure, therefore
his cover was not perfect, therefore he had made a
mistake.

He should have put a bolt on the door. Better to be
thought chronically shy than to have landladies with
duplicate keys sneaking in at night in their bedwear.

That was the surface error. The deep flaw was that
he was too eligible to be a bachelor. He thought this
with irritation, not conceit. He knew that he was a
pleasant, attractive man, and that there was no apparent
reason why he should be single. He turned his mind
to thinking up a cover that would explain this without inviting advances from the Mrs Gardens of this
world.

He ought to be able to find inspiration in his real
personality. Why *was* he single? He stirred uneasily: he
did not like mirrors. The answer was simple. He was

single because of his profession. If there were deeper reasons, he did not want to know them.

He would have to spend tonight in the open. Highgate Wood would do. In the morning he would take his suitcases to a railway station left-luggage office, then tomorrow evening he would go to his room in Blackheath.

He would shift to his second identity. He had little fear of being caught by the police. The commercial traveller who occupied the room at Blackheath on weekends looked rather different from the railway clerk who had killed his landlady. The Blackheath persona was expansive, vulgar and flashy. He wore loud ties, bought rounds of drinks, and combed his hair differently. The police would circulate a description of a shabby little pervert who would not say boo to a goose until he was inflamed with lust, and no one would look twice at the handsome salesman in the striped suit who was obviously the type that was more or less permanently inflamed with lust and did not have to kill women to get them to show him their breasts.

He would have to set up another identity – he always kept at least two. He needed a new job, fresh papers – passport, identity card, ration book, birth certificate. It was all so *risky*. Damn Mrs Garden. Why couldn't she have drunk herself to sleep as usual?

It was one o'clock. Faber took a last look around the room. He was not concerned about leaving clues – his fingerprints were obviously all over the house, and there would be no doubt in anyone's mind about who was the murderer. Nor did he feel any sentiment about leaving the place that had been his home for two years: he had never thought of it as home. He had never thought of anywhere as home.

He would always think of this as the place where he had learned to put a bolt on a door.

He turned out the light, picked up his cases, and crept down the stairs and out of the door into the night.

CHAPTER TWO

Henry II was a remarkable king. In an age when the term 'flying visit' had not yet been coined, he flitted between England and France with such rapidity that he was credited with magical powers; a rumour which, understandably, he did nothing to suppress. In 1173 – either the June or the September, depending upon which secondary source one favours – he arrived in England and left for France again so quickly that no contemporary writer ever found out about it. Later historians discovered the record of his expenditure in the Pipe Rolls. At the time his kingdom was under attack by his sons at its northern and southern extremes – the Scottish border and the South of France. But what, precisely, was the purpose of his visit? Whom did he see? Why was it secret, when the myth of his magical speed was worth an army? What did he accomplish?

This was the problem that taxed Percival Godliman in the summer of 1940, when Hitler's armies swept across the French cornfields like a scythe, and the British poured out of the Dunkirk bottleneck in bloody disarray.

Professor Godliman knew more about the Middle

Ages than any man alive. His book on the Black Death had upended every convention of medievalism; it had also been a bestseller and published as a Penguin. With that behind him he had turned to a slightly earlier and even more intractable period.

At 12.30 on a splendid June day in London, a secretary found Godliman hunched over an illuminated manuscript, laboriously translating its medieval Latin, making notes in his own even less legible handwriting. The secretary, who was planning to eat her lunch in the garden of Gordon Square, did not like the manuscript room because it smelled dead. You needed so many keys to get in there, it might as well have been a tomb.

Godliman stood at a lectern, perched on one leg like a bird, his face lit bleakly by a spotlight above: he might have been the ghost of the monk who wrote the book, standing a cold vigil over his precious chronicle. The girl cleared her throat and waited for him to notice her. She saw a short man in his fifties, with round shoulders and weak eyesight, wearing a tweed suit. She knew he could be perfectly sensible once you dragged him out of the Middle Ages. She coughed again and said: 'Professor Godliman?'

He looked up, and when he saw her he smiled, and then he did not look like a ghost, more like someone's dotty father. 'Hello!' he said, in an astonished tone, as if he had just met his next-door neighbour in the middle of the Sahara Desert.

'You asked me to remind you that you have lunch at the Savoy with Colonel Terry.'

'Oh, yes.' He took his watch out of his waistcoat

pocket and peered at it. 'If I'm going to walk it, I'd better leave now.'

She nodded. 'I brought your gas mask.'

'You are thoughtful!' He smiled again, and she decided he looked quite nice. He took the mask from her and said: 'Do I need my coat?'

'You didn't wear one this morning. It's quite warm. Shall I lock up after you?'

'Thank you, thank you.' He jammed his notebook into his jacket pocket and went out.

The secretary looked around, shivered, and followed him.

Colonel Andrew Terry was a red-faced Scot, pauper-thin from a lifetime of heavy smoking, with sparse dark-blond hair thickly brilliantined. Godliman found him at a corner table in the Savoy Grill, wearing civilian clothes. There were three cigarette stubs in the ashtray. He stood up to shake hands.

Godliman said: 'Morning, Uncle Andrew.' Terry was his mother's baby brother.

'How are you, Percy?'

'I'm writing a book about the Plantagenets.' Godliman sat down.

'Are your manuscripts still in London? I'm surprised.'

'Why?'

Terry lit another cigarette. 'Move them to the country in case of bombing.'

'Should I?'

'Half the National Gallery has been shoved into a bloody big hole in the ground somewhere up in Wales. Young Kenneth Clark is quicker off the mark than you. Might be sensible to take yourself off out of it too, while you're about it. I don't suppose you've many students left.'

'That's true.' Godliman took a menu from a waiter and said: 'I don't want a drink.'

Terry did not look at his menu. 'Seriously, Percy, why are you still in Town?'

Godliman's eyes seemed to clear, like the image on a screen when the projector is focused, as if he had to think for the first time since he walked in. 'It's all right for children to leave, and national institutions like Bertrand Russell. But for me – well, it's a bit like running away and letting other people fight for you. I realize that's not a strictly logical argument. It's a matter of sentiment, not logic.'

Terry smiled the smile of one whose expectations have been fulfilled. But he dropped the subject and looked at the menu. After a moment he said: 'Good God. *Le Lord Woolton Pie.*'

Godliman grinned. 'I'm sure it's still just potatoes and vegetables.'

When they had ordered, Terry said: 'What do you think of our new Prime Minister?'

'The man's an ass. But then, Hitler's a fool, and look how well he's doing. You?'

'We can live with Winston. At least he's bellicose.'

Godliman raised his eyebrows. '"We?" Are you back in the game?'

'I never really left it, you know.'

'But you said—'

'Percy. Can't you think of a department whose staff all say they don't work for the Army?'

'Well, I'm damned. All this time . . .'

Their first course came, and they started a bottle of white Bordeaux. Godliman ate potted salmon and looked pensive.

Eventually Terry said: 'Thinking about the last lot?'

Godliman nodded. 'Young days, you know. Terrible time.' But his tone was wistful.

'This war isn't the same at all. My chaps don't go behind enemy lines and count bivouacs like you did. Well, they do, but that side of things is much less important this time. Nowadays we just listen to the wireless.'

'Don't they broadcast in code?'

Terry shrugged. 'Codes can be broken. Candidly, we get to know just about everything we need these days.'

Godliman glanced around, but there was no one within earshot, and it was not for him to tell Terry that careless talk costs lives.

Terry went on: 'In fact my job is to make sure *they* don't have the information they need about *us*.'

They both had chicken pie to follow. There was no beef on the menu. Godliman fell silent, but Terry talked on.

'Canaris is a funny chap, you know. Admiral Wilhelm Canaris, head of the Abwehr. I met him before this lot started. Likes England. My guess is he's none too fond of Hitler. Anyway, we know he's been told to mount a major intelligence operation against us, in preparation for the invasion – but he's not doing much. We arrested their best man in England the day after war broke out. He's in Wandsworth prison now. Useless people, Canaris's spies. Old ladies in boarding-houses, mad Fascists, petty criminals—'

Godliman said: 'Look here, old boy, this is too much.' He trembled slightly with a mixture of anger and incomprehension. 'All this stuff is secret. I don't want to know!'

Terry was unperturbed. 'Would you like something else?' he offered. 'I'm having chocolate ice-cream.'

Godliman stood up. 'I don't think so. I'm going to go back to my work, if you don't mind.'

Terry looked up at him coolly. 'The world can wait for your reappraisal of the Plantagenets, Percy. There's a war on, dear boy. I want you to work for me.'

Godliman stared down at him for a long moment. 'What on earth would I do?'

Terry smiled wolfishly. 'Catch spies.'

Walking back to the college, Godliman felt depressed despite the weather. He would accept Colonel Terry's offer: no doubt about that. His country was at war; it was a just war; and if he was too old to fight, he was still young enough to help.

But the thought of leaving his work – and for how many years? – depressed him. He loved history, and he had been totally absorbed in medieval England since the death of his wife ten years ago. He liked the unravelling of mysteries, the discovery of faint clues, the resolution of contradictions, the unmasking of lies and propaganda and myth. His new book would be the best on its subject written in the last hundred years, and there would not be one to equal it for another century. It had ruled his life for so long that the thought of abandoning it was almost unreal, as difficult to digest as the discovery that one is an orphan and no relation at all to the people one has always called Mother and Father.

An air-raid warning stridently interrupted his thoughts. He contemplated ignoring it: so many people did now, and he was only ten minutes' walk from the college. But he had no real reason to return to his study – he knew he would do no more work today. So he hurried into a Tube station and joined the solid mass of Londoners crowding down the staircases and on to the grimy platform. He stood close to the wall, staring at a Bovril poster, and thought: But it's not just the things I'm leaving behind.

Going back into the game depressed him, too. There were some things he liked about it: the importance of *little* things, the value of simply being clever, the meticulousness, the guesswork. But he hated the blackmail and the treachery, the deceit, the desperation, and the way one always stabbed the enemy in the back.

The platform was becoming more crowded. Godliman sat down while there was still room, and found himself leaning against a man in bus-driver's uniform. The man smiled and said: 'Oh to be in England, now that summer's here. Know who said that?'

'Now that April's there,' Godliman corrected him. 'It was Browning.'

'I heard it was Adolf Hitler,' the driver said. A woman next to him squealed with laughter, and he turned his attention to her. 'Did you hear what the evacuee said to the farmer's wife?'

Godliman tuned out and remembered an April when he had longed for England, crouching on a high branch of a plane tree, peering through a cold mist across a French valley behind the German lines. He could see nothing but vague dark shapes, even through his telescope, and he was about to slide down and walk a mile or so farther when three German soldiers came from nowhere to sit around the base of the tree and smoke. After a while they took out cards and began to play, and young Percival Godliman realized they had found a way of skiving off and were here for the day. He stayed in the tree, hardly moving, until he began to shiver and his muscles knotted with cramp and his bladder felt as if it would burst. Then he took out his revolver and shot the three of them, one after another, through the tops of their close-cropped heads. And three people, laughing and cursing and gambling their pay, had simply ceased to exist. It was the first time he killed, and all he could think was: Just because I had to pee.

Godliman shifted on the cold concrete of the station platform and let the memory fade away. There was a warm wind from the tunnel and a train came in. The people who got off found spaces and settled to wait. Godliman listened to the voices.

'Did you hear Churchill on the wireless? We was listening in at the Duke of Wellington. Old Jack Thornton cried. Silly old bugger . . .'

'From what I can gather Kathy's boy's in a stately home and got his own footman! My Alfie milks the cow . . .'

'Haven't had fillet steak on the menu for so long I've forgotton the bally taste . . . wine committee saw the war coming and bought in twenty thousand dozen, thank God . . .'

'Yes, a quiet wedding, but what's the point in waiting when you don't know what the next day's going to bring?'

'They call it Spring, Ma, he says to me, and they have one down here every year . . .'

'She's pregnant again, you know . . . yes, thirteen years since the last . . . I thought I'd found out what was causing it!'

'No, Peter never came back from Dunkirk . . .'

The bus driver offered him a cigarette. Godliman refused, and took out his pipe. Someone started to sing.

> *A blackout warden passing yelled*
> *'Ma, pull down that blind—*
> *Just look at what you're showing,' and we*
> *Shouted 'Never mind.' Oh!*
> *Knees up Mother Brown . . .*

The song spread through the crowd until everyone was singing. Godliman joined in, knowing that this was a nation losing a war and singing to hide its fear, as a

26

man will whistle past the graveyard at night; knowing that the sudden affection he felt for London and Londoners was an ephemeral sentiment, akin to mob hysteria; mistrusting the voice inside him which said 'This, this is what the war is about, this is what makes it worth fighting'; knowing but not caring, because for the first time in so many years he was feeling the sheer physical thrill of comradeship and he liked it.

When the all-clear sounded they went singing up the staircases and into the street, and Godliman found a phone box and called Colonel Terry to ask how soon he could start.

CHAPTER THREE

THE SMALL country church was old and very beautiful. A dry-stone wall enclosed a graveyard where wild flowers grew. The church itself had been there – well, bits of it had – the last time Britain was invaded, almost a millennium ago. The north wall of the nave, several feet thick and pierced with only two tiny windows, could remember that last invasion; it had been built when churches were places of physical as well as spiritual sanctuary, and the little round-headed windows were better for shooting arrows out of than for letting the Lord's sunshine in. Indeed, the Local Defence Volunteers had detailed plans for using the church if and when the current bunch of European thugs crossed the Channel.

But no jackboots sounded in the tiled choir in this August of 1940; not yet. The sun glowed through stained-glass windows which had survived Cromwell's iconoclasts and Henry VIII's greed, and the roof resounded to the notes of an organ which had yet to yield to woodworm and dry rot.

It was a lovely wedding. Lucy wore white, of course; and her five sisters were bridesmaids in apricot dresses. David wore the Mess uniform of a Flying Officer in the

28

Royal Air Force, all crisp and new for it was the first time he had put it on. They sang Psalm 23, The Lord's My Shepherd, to the tune *Crimond*.

Lucy's father looked proud, as a man will on the day his eldest and most beautiful daughter marries a fine boy in a uniform. He was a farmer, but it was a long time since he had sat on a tractor: he rented out his arable land and used the rent to raise racehorses, although this winter of course his pasture would go under the plough and potatoes would be planted. Although he was really more gentleman than farmer, he nevertheless had the open-air skin, the deep chest, and the big stubby hands of agricultural people. Most of the men on that side of the church bore him a resemblance: barrel-chested men, with weathered red faces, those not in tail coats favouring tweed suits and stout shoes.

The bridesmaids had something of that look, too; they were country girls. But the bride was like her mother. Her hair was a dark, dark red, long and thick, shining and glorious, and she had wide-apart amber eyes set in an oval face; and when she looked at the vicar with that clear, direct gaze and said 'I will' in that firm, clear voice, the vicar was startled and thought, 'By God she means it!' which was an odd thought for a vicar to have in the middle of a wedding.

The family on the other side of the nave had a certain look about them, too. David's father was a lawyer: his permanent frown was a professional affectation, and concealed a sunny nature. (He had been a Major in the Army in the last war, and thought all this business about the RAF and war in the air was a fad which would soon pass.) But nobody looked like him, not even his son who stood now at the altar promising to love his wife until death, which might not be far away, God forbid. No, they all looked like David's mother, who sat beside her husband now, with almost-black hair, dark skin and long, slender limbs.

David was the tallest of the lot. He had broken high-jump records last year at Cambridge University. He was rather too good-looking for a man – his face would have been feminine were it not for the dark, ineradicable shadow of a heavy beard. He shaved twice a day. He had long eyelashes, and he looked intelligent, as he was, and sensitive, which he was not.

It was idyllic: two happy, handsome people, children of solid, comfortably off, backbone-of-England type families, getting married in a country church in the finest summer weather Britain can offer.

When they were pronounced man and wife both mothers were dry-eyed, and both the fathers cried.

Kissing the bride was a barbarous custom, Lucy thought as yet another middle-aged pair of champagne-wet lips smeared her cheek. It was probably descended from even more barbarous customs in the Dark Ages, when every man in the tribe was allowed to – well, anyway, it was time we got properly civilized and dropped the whole business.

She had known she would not like this part of the

wedding. She liked champagne, but she was not crazy about chicken drumsticks or dollops of caviar on squares of cold toast, and as for the speeches and the photographs and the honeymoon jokes, well . . . But it could have been worse. If it had been peacetime Father would have hired the Albert Hall.

So far nine people had said, 'May all your troubles be little ones,' and one person, with scarcely more originality, had said, 'I want to see more than a fence running around your garden.' Lucy had shaken count-less hands and pretended not to hear remarks like, 'I wouldn't mind being in David's pyjamas tonight.' David had made a speech in which he thanked Lucy's parents for giving him their daughter, as if she were an inani-mate object to be gift-wrapped in white satin and presented to the most deserving applicant. Lucy's father had been crass enough to say that he was not losing a daughter but gaining a son. It was all hopelessly gaga, but one did it for one's parents.

A distant uncle loomed up from the direction of the bar, swaying slightly, and Lucy repressed a shudder. She introduced him to her husband. 'David, this is Uncle Norman.'

Uncle Norman pumped David's bony hand. 'Well, m'boy, when do you take up your commission?'

'Tomorrow, sir.'

'What, no honeymoon?'

'Just twenty-four hours.'

'But you've only just finished your training, so I gather.'

'Yes, but I could fly before, you know. I learned at Cambridge. Besides, with all this going on they can't spare pilots. I expect I shall be in the air tomorrow.'

Lucy said quietly: 'David, don't,' but she was ignored.

'What'll you fly?' Uncle Norman asked with school-boy enthusiasm.

'Spitfire. I saw her yesterday. She's a lovely kite.' David had consciously adopted all the RAF slang, kites and crates and the drink and bandits at two o'clock. 'She's got eight guns, she does three hundred and fifty knots, and she'll turn around in a shoebox.'

'Marvellous, marvellous. You boys are certainly knocking the stuffing out of the Luftwaffe, what?'

'We got sixty yesterday for eleven of our own,' David said, as proudly as if he had shot them all down himself. 'The day before, when they had a go at Yorkshire, we sent the bally lot back to Norway with their tails between their legs – and we didn't lose a single kite!'

Uncle Norman gripped David's shoulder with tipsy fervour. 'Never,' he quoted pompously, 'was so much owed by so many to so few. Churchill said that the other day.'

David tried a modest grin. 'He must have been talking about the mess bills.'

Lucy hated the way they trivialized bloodshed and destruction. She said: 'David, we should go and change now.'

They went in separate cars to Lucy's home. Her mother helped her out of the wedding dress and said: 'Now, my dear, I don't quite know what you're expecting tonight, but you ought to know—'

'Oh, mother, don't be embarrassing,' Lucy interrupted. 'You're about ten years too late to tell me the
facts of life. This *is* 1940, you know!'

Her mother coloured slightly. 'Very well, dear,' she
said mildly. 'But if there is anything you want to talk
about, later on . . .'

It occurred to Lucy that to say things like this cost
her mother considerable effort, and she regretted her
sharp reply. 'Thank you,' she said. She touched her
mother's hand. 'I will.'

'I'll leave you to it, then. Call me if you want
anything.' She kissed Lucy's cheek and went out.

Lucy sat at the dressing-table in her slip and began
to brush her hair. She knew exactly what to expect
tonight. She felt a faint glow of pleasure as she
remembered.

It was a well-planned seduction, although at the time
it did not occur to Lucy that David might have plotted
every move beforehand.

It happened in June, a year after they had met at the
Glad Rag Ball. They were seeing each other every week
by this time, and David had spent part of the Easter
vacation with Lucy's people. Mother and Father
approved of him: he was handsome, clever and gentlemanly, and he came from precisely the same stratum of
society as they did. Father thought he was a shade too
opinionated, but Mother said the landed gentry had
been saying that about undergraduates for six hundred
years, and *she* thought David would be kind to his wife,
which was the most important thing in the long run. So
in June Lucy went to David's family home for a weekend.

The place was a Victorian copy of an eighteenth-century grange, a square-shaped house with nine bedrooms and a terrace with a vista. What impressed Lucy about it was the realization that the people who planted the garden must have known they would be long dead before it reached maturity. The atmosphere was very easy, and the two of them drank beer on the terrace in the afternoon sunshine. That was when David told her that he had been accepted for officer training in the RAF, along with four pals from the university flying club. He wanted to be a fighter pilot.

'I can fly all right,' he said, 'and they'll need people once this war gets going – they say it'll be won and lost in the air, this time.'

'Aren't you afraid?' she said quietly.

'Not a bit,' he said. Then he covered his eyes with his hand and said: 'Yes, I am.'

She thought he was very brave, and held his hand.

A little later they put on swimming costumes and went down to the lake. The water was clear and cool, but the sun was still strong and the air was warm. They splashed about gleefully, as if they knew this was the end of their childhood.

'Are you a good swimmer?' he asked her.

'Better than you!'

'All right. Race you to the island.'

She shaded her eyes to look into the sun. She held the pose for a minute, pretending she did not know how desirable she was in her wet swimsuit with her arms raised and her shoulders back. The island was a small patch of bushes and trees about three hundred yards away, in the centre of the lake.

She dropped her hands, shouted 'Go!', and struck out in a fast crawl.

David won, of course, with his long arms and legs. Lucy found herself in difficulty when she was still fifty yards from the island. She switched to breaststroke, but she was too exhausted even for that, and she had to roll over on to her back and float. David, who was already sitting on the bank blowing like a walrus, slipped back into the water and swam to meet her. He got behind her, held her beneath the arms in the correct lifesaving position, and pulled her slowly to the shore. His hands were just below her breasts.

'I'm enjoying this,' he said, and she giggled despite her breathlessness.

A few moments later he said: 'I suppose I might as well tell you.'

'What?' she panted.

'The lake is only four feet deep.'

'You rogue!' She wriggled out of his arms, spluttering and laughing, and found her footing.

He took her hand and led her out of the water and through the trees. He pointed to an old wooden rowing-boat, rotting upside-down beneath a hawthorn. 'When I was a boy I used to row out here in that, with one of Papa's pipes, a box of matches, and a pinch of tobacco in a twist of paper. This is where I used to smoke it.'

They were in a clearing, completely surrounded by

bushes. The turf underfoot was clean and springy. Lucy flopped on the ground.

'We'll swim back slowly,' David said.

'Let's not even talk about it just yet,' she replied.

He sat beside her and kissed her, then pushed her gently backwards until she was lying down. He stroked her hip and kissed her throat, and soon she stopped shivering. When he laid his hand gently, nervously, on the soft mound between her legs, she arched upwards, willing him to press harder. She pulled his face to hers and kissed him open-mouthed and wetly. His hands went to the straps of her swimsuit, and he pulled them down over her shoulders. She said: 'No.'

He buried his face between her breasts. 'Lucy, please.'

'No.'

He looked at her. 'It might be my last chance.'

She rolled away from him and stood up. Then, because of the war, and because of the pleading look on his flushed young face, and because of the glow inside her which would not go away, she took off her costume with one swift movement, and removed her swimming-cap so that her dark red hair shook out over her shoulders, and knelt in front of him, taking his face in her hands and guiding his lips to her breast.

She lost her virginity painlessly, enthusiastically, and only a little too quickly.

The spice of guilt made the memory more pleasant, not less. If it had been a well-planned seduction then she had been a willing, not to say eager, victim, especially at the end.

She began to dress in her going-away outfit. She had startled him a couple of times, that afternoon on the island: once when she wanted him to kiss her breasts, and again when she had guided him inside her with her hands. Apparently such things did not happen in the books he read. Like most of her friends, Lucy read D. H. Lawrence for information about sex. She believed in his choreography and mistrusted the noises-off: the things his people did to one another sounded nice, but not that nice; she was not expecting trumpets and thunderstorms and the clash of cymbals at her sexual awakening.

David was a little more ignorant than she; but he was gentle, and he took pleasure in her pleasure, and she was sure that was the important thing.

They had done it only once since the first time. Exactly a week before their wedding they had made love again, and it caused their first row.

This time it was at her parents' house, in the morning after everyone else had left. He came to her room in his dressing-gown and got into bed with her. She almost changed her mind about Lawrence's trumpets and cymbals. David got out of bed immediately afterwards.

'Don't go,' she said.

'Somebody might come in.'

'I'll chance it. Come back to bed.' She was warm and drowsy and comfortable, and she wanted him beside her.

He put on his dressing-gown. 'It makes me nervous.'

'You weren't nervous five minutes ago.' She reached for him. 'Lie with me. I want to get to know your body.'

'My God, you're brazen.'

She looked at him to see whether he was joking, and when she realized he was not, she became angry. '*Just* what the *hell* does *that* mean?'

'You're just not . . . ladylike!'

'What a *stupid* thing to say—'

'You act like a – a – tart.'

She flounced out of bed, naked and furious, her lovely breasts heaving with rage. 'Just how much do you know about tarts?'

'Nothing!'

'How much do you know about women?'

'I know how a virgin is supposed to behave!'

'I am . . . I was . . . until I met you . . .' She sat on the edge of the bed and burst into tears.

That was the end of the quarrel, of course. David put his arms around her and said: 'I'm sorry, sorry, sorry. You're the first one for me, too, and I don't know what to expect, and I feel confused . . . I mean, nobody tells you anything about this, do they?'

She snuffled and shook her head in agreement, and it occurred to her that what was *really* unnerving him was the knowledge that in eight days' time he had to take off in a flimsy aircraft and fight for his life above the clouds; so she forgave him, and he dried her tears, and they got back into bed and held each other tightly for courage.

Lucy told her friend Joanna about the row, saying it was over a dress David thought to be brazen. Joanna said that couples always quarrelled before the wedding, usually the night before: it was the last chance to test the strength of their love.

She was just about ready. She examined herself in a full-length mirror. Her suit was faintly military, with square shoulders and epaulettes, but the blouse beneath it was feminine, for balance. Her hair fell in sausage curls beneath a natty pill-box hat. It would not have been right to go away gorgeously dressed, not this year; but she felt she had achieved the kind of briskly practical, yet attractive, look which was rapidly becoming fashionable.

David was waiting for her in the hall. He kissed her and said: 'You look wonderful, Mrs Rose.'

They were driven back to the reception to say goodbye to everyone, before leaving to spend the night in London, at Claridge's; then David would drive on to Biggin Hill and Lucy would come home again. She was going to live with her parents: she had the use of a cottage for when David was on leave.

There was another half-hour of handshakes and kisses, then they went out to the car. Some of David's cousins had got at his open-top MG. There were tin cans and an old boot tied to the bumpers with string, the running-boards were awash with confetti, and 'Just Married' was scrawled all over the paintwork in bright red lipstick.

They drove away, smiling and waving, the guests filling the street behind them. A mile down the road they stopped and cleaned up the car.

It was dusk when they got going again. David's

headlights were fitted with blackout masks, but he drove very fast just the same. Lucy felt very happy.

David said: 'There's a bottle of bubbly in the glove box.'

Lucy opened the compartment and found the champagne and two glasses carefully wrapped in tissue paper. It was still quite cold. The cork came out with a loud pop and shot off into the night. David lit a cigarette while Lucy poured the wine.

'We're going to be late for supper,' he said.

'Who cares?' She handed him a glass.

She was too tired to drink, really. She became sleepy. The car seemed to be going terribly fast. She let David have most of the champagne. He began to whistle *St Louis Blues.*

Driving through England in the blackout was a weird experience. One missed lights which one hadn't realized were there before the war: lights in cottage porches and farmhouse windows, lights on cathedral spires and inn signs, and – most of all – the luminous glow, low in the distant sky, of the thousand lights of a nearby town. Even if one had been able to see, there were no signposts to look at: they had been removed to confuse the German parachutists who were expected any day. (Just a few days ago in the Midlands farmers had found parachutes, radios and maps; but since there were no footprints leading away from the objects, it had been concluded that no men had landed, and the whole thing was a feeble Nazi attempt to panic the population.) Anyway, David knew the way to London.

They climbed a long hill. The little sports car took it

nimbly. Lucy gazed through half-closed eyes at the blackness ahead. The downside of the hill was steep and winding. Lucy heard the distant roar of an approaching lorry.

The MG's tyres squealed as David raced around the bends. 'I think you're going too fast,' Lucy said mildly.

The back of the car skidded on a left-hander. David changed down, afraid to brake in case he skidded again. On either side, the hedgerows were dimly picked out by the shaded headlights. There was a sharp right-hand bend, and David lost the back again. The curve seemed to go on and on forever. The little car slid sideways and turned through 180 degrees, so that it was going backwards; then continued to turn in the same direction.

Lucy screamed: 'David!'

The moon came out suddenly, and they saw the lorry. It was struggling up the hill at a snail's pace, with thick smoke, made silvery by the moonlight, pouring from its snout-shaped bonnet. Lucy glimpsed the driver's face, even his cloth cap and his moustache; his mouth was open in terror as he stood on his brakes.

The car was travelling forward again now. There was just room to pass the lorry if David could regain control of the car. He heaved the steering wheel over and touched the accelerator. It was a mistake.

The car and the lorry collided head-on.

CHAPTER FOUR

FOREIGNERS HAVE spies: Britain has Military
Intelligence. As if that were not euphemism
enough, it is abbreviated to MI. In 1940, MI was part of
the War Office. It was spreading like couch grass at the
time – not surprisingly – and its different sections were
known by numbers: MI9 ran the escape routes from
prisoner-of-war camps through Occupied Europe to
neutral countries; MI8 monitored enemy wireless
traffic, and was of more value than six regiments; MI6
sent agents into France.

It was MI5 that Professor Percival Godliman joined
in the autumn of 1940. He turned up at the War Office
in Whitehall on a cold September morning after a
night spent putting out fires all over the East End:
the Blitz was at its height and he was an Auxiliary
Fireman.

Military Intelligence was run by soldiers in peacetime, when – in Godliman's opinion – espionage made
no difference to anything anyhow; but now, he found,
it was populated by amateurs, and he was delighted to
discover that he knew half the people in MI5. On his
first day he met a barrister who was a member of his
club, an art historian with whom he had been to

college, an archivist from his own university, and his favourite writer of detective stories.

He was shown into Colonel Terry's office at ten a.m. Terry had been there for several hours: there were two empty cigarette packets in the waste-paper bin.

Godliman said: 'Should I call you "Sir" now?'

'There's not much bull around here, Percy. "Uncle Andrew" will do fine. Sit down.'

All the same, there was a briskness about Terry which had not been present when they had lunch at the Savoy. Godliman noticed that he did not smile, and his attention kept wandering to a pile of unread signals on the desk.

Terry looked at his watch and said: 'I'm going to put you in the picture, briefly – finish the lecture I started over lunch.'

Godliman smiled. 'This time I won't get up on my high horse.'

Terry lit another cigarette.

Canaris's spies in Britain were useless people (Terry resumed, as if their conversation had been interrupted five minutes rather than three months ago). Dorothy O'Grady was typical: we caught her cutting military telephone wires on the Isle of Wight. She was writing letters to Portugal in the kind of secret ink you buy in joke shops.

A new wave of spies began in September. Their task was to reconnoitre Britain in preparation for the invasion: to map beaches suitable for landings, fields and roads which could be used by troop-carrying gliders, tank traps and road blocks and barbed-wire obstacles.

They seem to have been badly selected, hastily mustered, inadequately trained and poorly equipped. Typical were the four who came over on the night of 2–3 September: Meier, Kieboom, Pons and Waldberg. Kieboom and Pons landed at dawn near Hythe, and were arrested by Private Tollervey of the Somerset Light Infantry, who came upon them in the sand-dunes tucking in to a dirty great *wurst.*

Waldberg actually managed to send a signal to Hamburg:

ARRIVED SAFELY. DOCUMENT DESTROYED. ENGLISH
PATROL 200 METRES FROM COAST. BEACH WITH
BROWN NETS AND RAILWAY SLEEPERS AT A DIS-
TANCE OF 50 METRES. NO MINES. FEW SOLDIERS.
UNFINISHED BLOCK-HOUSE. NEW ROAD. WALDBERG.

Clearly he did not know where he was, nor did he even have a code name. The quality of his briefing is indicated by the fact that he knew nothing of English licensing laws: he went into a pub at nine o'clock in the morning and asked for a quart of cider.

(Godliman laughed at this, and Terry said: 'Wait – it gets funnier.')

The landlord told Waldberg to come back at ten. He could spend the hour looking at the village church, he suggested. Amazingly, Waldberg was back at ten sharp, whereupon two policemen on bicycles arrested him.

('It's like a script for *It's That Man Again,*' said Godliman.)

Meier was found a few hours later. Eleven more

agents were picked up over the next few weeks, most of them within hours of landing on British soil. Almost all of them were destined for the scaffold.

('*Almost* all?' said Godliman. Terry said: 'Yes. A couple have been handed over to our section B-1(a). I'll come back to that in a minute.')

Others landed in Eire. One was Ernst Weber-Drohl, a well-known acrobat who had two illegitimate children in Ireland – he had toured music-halls there as 'The World's Strongest Man'. He was arrested by the Garda Siochania, fined three pounds, and turned over to B-1(a).

Another was Hermann Goetz, who parachuted into Ulster instead of Eire by mistake, was robbed by the IRA, swam the Boyne in his fur underwear, and eventually swallowed his suicide pill. He had a torch marked 'Made in Dresden'.

('If it's so easy to pick these bunglers up,' Terry said, 'why are we taking on brainy types like yourself to catch them? Two reasons. One: we've got no way of knowing how many we *haven't* picked up. Two: it's what we do with the ones we don't hang that matters. This is where B-1(a) comes in. But to explain that I have to go back to 1936.')

Alfred George Owens was an electrical engineer with a company that had a few government contracts. He visited Germany several times during the thirties, and voluntarily gave to the Admiralty odd bits of technical information he picked up there. Eventually Naval Intelligence passed him on to MI6 who began to develop him as an agent. The Abwehr recruited him at about the same time, as MI6 discovered when they intercepted a letter from him to a known German cover address. Clearly he was a man totally without loyalty: he just wanted to be a spy. We called him 'Snow'; the Germans called him 'Johnny'.

In January 1939 Snow got a letter containing (i) instructions for the use of a wireless transmitter and (ii) a ticket for the cloakroom at Victoria Station.

He was arrested the day after war broke out, and he and his transmitter (which he had picked up, in a suitcase, when he presented the cloakroom ticket) were locked up in Wandsworth Prison. He continued to communicate with Hamburg, but now all the messages were written by section B-1(a) of MI5.

The Abwehr put him in touch with two more German agents in England, whom we immediately nabbed. They also gave him a code and detailed wireless procedure, all of which was invaluable.

Snow was followed by Charlie, Rainbow, Summer, Biscuit, and eventually a small army of enemy spies, all in regular contact with Canaris, all apparently trusted by him, and all totally controlled by the British counter-intelligence apparatus.

At that point MI5 began dimly to glimpse an awesome and tantalizing prospect: with a bit of luck, *they could control and manipulate the entire German espionage network in Britain.*

'Turning agents into double agents instead of hanging them has two crucial advantages,' Terry wound up. 'Since the enemy thinks his spies are still active, he doesn't try to replace them with others who may not get caught. And, since *we* are supplying the information the spies tell their controllers, we can deceive the enemy and mislead his strategists.'

'It can't be that easy,' said Godliman.

'Certainly not.' Terry opened a window to let out the fug of cigarette and pipe smoke. 'To work, the system has to be very nearly total. If there is any substantial number of genuine agents here, their information will contradict that of the double agents and the Abwehr will smell a rat.'

'It sounds tremendously exciting,' Godliman said. His pipe had gone out.

Terry smiled for the first time that morning. 'The people here will tell you it's hard work – long hours, high tension, frustration – but yes, of course it's exciting.' He looked at his watch. 'Now I want you to meet a very bright young member of my staff. Let me walk you to his office.'

They went out of the room, up some stairs, and along several corridors. 'His name is Frederick Bloggs, and he gets annoyed if you make jokes about it,' Terry continued. 'We pinched him from Scotland Yard – he was an inspector with Special Branch. If you need arms and legs, use his. You'll rank above him, but I shouldn't make too much of that – we don't, here. I suppose I hardly need to say that to you.'

They entered a small, bare room which looked out on to a blank wall. There was no carpet. A photograph of a pretty girl hung on the wall, and there was a pair of handcuffs on the hat-stand.

Terry said: 'Frederick Bloggs, Percival Godliman. I'll leave you to it.'

The man behind the desk was blond, stocky and short – he must have been only just tall enough to get into the police force, Godliman thought. His tie was an eyesore, but he had a pleasant, open face and an attractive grin. His handshake was firm.

He said: 'Tell you what, Percy – I was just going to nip home for lunch – why don't you come along? The wife makes a lovely sausage and chips.' He had a broad cockney accent.

Sausage and chips was not Godliman's favourite meal, but he went along. They walked to Trafalgar Square and caught a bus to Hoxton. Bloggs said: 'I married a wonderful girl, but she can't cook for nuts. I have sausage and chips every day.'

East London was still smoking from the previous night's air raid. They passed groups of firemen and volunteers digging through rubble, playing hoses over dying fires, and clearing debris from the streets. They saw an old man carry a precious radio out of a half-ruined house.

Godliman made conversation. 'So we're to catch spies together.'

'We'll have a go, Perce.'

Bloggs's home was a three-bedroom semi in a street of exactly similar houses. The tiny front gardens were all being used to grow vegetables. Mrs Bloggs was the pretty girl in the photograph on the office wall. She looked tired. Bloggs said: 'She drives an ambulance during the raids, don't you, love?' He was proud of her. Her name was Christine.

She said: 'Every morning when I come home I wonder if the house will still be here.'

'Notice it's the house she's worried about, not me,' Bloggs said.

Godliman picked up a medal in a presentation case from the mantelpiece. 'How did you get this?'

Christine answered. 'He took a shotgun off a villain who was robbing a post office.'

'You're quite a pair,' Godliman said.

'You married, Percy?' Bloggs asked.

'I'm a widower.'

'Sorry.'

'My wife died of tuberculosis in 1930. We never had any children.'

'We're not having any yet,' Bloggs said. 'Not while the world's in this state.'

Christine said: 'Oh, Fred, he's not interested in that!' She went out to the kitchen.

They sat around a square table in the centre of the room to eat. Bloggs was touched by this couple and the domestic scene, and found himself thinking of his Eleanor. That was unusual: he had been immune to sentiment for some years. Perhaps the nerves were coming alive again, at last. War did funny things.

Christine's cooking was truly awful. The sausages were burned. Bloggs drowned his meal in tomato ketchup, and Godliman cheerfully followed suit.

When they got back to Whitehall Bloggs showed Godliman the file on unidentified enemy agents still thought to be operating in Britain.

There were three sources of information about such

people. The first was the immigration records of the Home Office. Passport control had long been an arm of Military Intelligence, and there was a list – going back to the last war – of aliens who had entered the country but had not left or been accounted for in other ways, such as death or naturalization. At the outbreak of war they had all gone before tribunals which classified them in three groups. At first only 'A' class aliens were interned; but by July of 1940, after some scaremongering by Fleet Street, the 'B' and 'C' classes were taken out of circulation. There was a small number of immigrants who could not be located, and it was a fair assumption that some of them were spies.

Their papers were in Bloggs's file.

The second source was wireless transmissions. Section C of MI8 scanned the airwaves nightly, recorded everything they did not know for certain to be ours, and passed it to the Government Code and Cypher School. This outfit, which had recently been moved from London's Berkeley Street to a country house at Bletchley Park, was not a school at all but a collection of chess champions, musicians, mathematicians and crossword-puzzle enthusiasts dedicated to the belief that if a man could invent a code a man could crack it. Signals originating in the UK which could not be accounted for by any of the Services were assumed to be messages from spies.

The decoded messages were in Bloggs's file.

Finally there were the double agents; but their value was largely hoped-for rather than actual. Messages to them from the Abwehr had warned of several incoming agents, and had given away one resident spy – Mrs Matilda Krafft of Bournemouth, who had sent money to Snow by post and was subsequently incarcerated in Holloway prison. But the doubles had not been able to reveal the identity or location of the kind of quietly effective professional spies who are most valuable to a secret intelligence service. No one doubted that there were such people. There were clues: someone, for example, had brought Snow's transmitter over from Germany and deposited it in the cloakroom at Victoria Station for him to collect. But either the Abwehr or the spies themselves were too cautious to be caught by the doubles.

However, the clues were in Bloggs's file.

Other sources were being developed: the boffins were working to improve methods of triangulation (the directional pin-pointing of radio transmitters); and MI6 were trying to rebuild the networks of agents in Europe which had sunk beneath the tidal wave of Hitler's armies.

What little information there was, was in Bloggs's file.

'It can be infuriating at times,' he told Godliman. 'Look at this.'

He took from the file a long radio intercept about British plans for an expeditionary force for Finland. 'This was picked up early in the year. The information is impeccable. They were trying to get a fix on him when he broke off in the middle, for no apparent reason – perhaps he was interrupted. He resumed a few minutes later, but he was off the air again before our boys had a chance to plug in.'

Godliman said: 'What's this – "Regards to Willi"?'

51

'Now, that's important,' said Bloggs. He was getting enthusiastic. 'Here's a scrap of another message, quite recent. Look – "Regards to Willi". This time there was a reply. He's addressed as "Die Nadel".'

'The Needle.'

'This bloke's a pro. Look at his messages: terse, economical, but detailed and completely unambiguous.'

Godliman studied the fragment of the second message. 'It appears to be about the effects of the bombing.'

'He's obviously toured the East End. A pro, a pro.'

'What else do we know about Die Nadel?'

Bloggs's expression of youthful eagerness collapsed comically. 'That's it, I'm afraid.'

'His code name is Die Nadel, he signs off "Regards to Willi", and he has good information – and that's it?'

''Fraid so.'

Godliman sat on the edge of the desk and stared out of the window. On the wall of the opposite building, underneath an ornate windowsill, he could see the nest of a house-marten. 'On that basis, what chance have we of catching him?'

Bloggs shrugged. 'On that basis, none at all.'

CHAPTER FIVE

I T IS for places like this that the word 'bleak' has
been invented.

The island is a J-shaped lump of rock rising sullenly
out of the North Sea. It lies on the map like the top
half of a broken walking-stick; parallel with the equator
but a long, long way north; its curved handle toward
Aberdeen, its broken, jagged stump pointing threateningly at distant Denmark. It is ten miles long.

Around most of its coast the cliffs rise out of the cold
sea without the courtesy of a beach. Angered by this
rudeness the waves pound on the rock in impotent
rage; a ten-thousand-year fit of bad temper which the
island ignores with impunity.

In the cup of the J the sea is calmer, for there it has
provided itself with a more pleasant reception. Its tides
have thrown into that cup so much sand and seaweed,
driftwood and pebbles and seashells, that there is now,
between the foot of the cliff and the water's edge, a
crescent of something closely resembling dry land, a
more-or-less beach.

Each summer the vegetation at the top of the cliff
drops a handful of seeds on to the beach, the way a rich
man throws loose change to beggars. If the winter is

mild and the spring comes early, a few of the seeds take feeble root; but they are never healthy enough to flower themselves and spread their own seeds, so the beach exists from year to year on handouts.

On the land itself, the proper land, held out of the sea's reach by the cliffs, green things do grow and multiply. The vegetation is mostly coarse grass, only just good enough to nourish the few bony sheep, but tough enough to bind the topsoil to the island's bedrock. There are some bushes, all thorny, which provide homes for rabbits; and a brave stand of conifers on the leeward slope of the hill at the eastern end.

The higher land is ruled by heather. Every few years the man – yes, there is a man here – the man sets fire to the heather, and then the grass will grow and the sheep can graze here too; but after a couple of years the heather comes back, God knows from where, and drives the sheep away until the man burns it again.

The rabbits are here because they were born here; the sheep are here because they were brought here; and the man is here to look after the sheep; but the birds are here because they like it. There are hundreds of thousands of them: long-legged rock pipits whistling *peep peep peep* as they soar and *pe-pe-pe-pe* as they dive like a Spitfire coming at a Messerschmitt out of the sun; corncrakes, which the man rarely sees, but he knows they are there because their bark keeps him awake at night; ravens and carrion crows and kittiwakes and *countless* gulls; and a pair of golden eagles which the man shoots at when he sees them, for he *knows* – regardless of what naturalists and experts from Edinburgh may tell him – that they *do* prey upon live lambs and not just the carcases of those already dead.

The island's most constant visitor is the wind. It comes mostly from the north-east, from *really* cold places where there are fiords and glaciers and icebergs; often bringing with it unwelcome gifts of snow and driving rain and cold, cold mist; sometimes arriving empty-handed, just to howl and whoop and raise hell, tearing up bushes and bending trees and whipping the intemperate ocean into fresh paroxysms of foam-flecked rage. It is tireless, this wind; and that is its mistake. If it came occasionally it could take the island by surprise and do some real damage; but because it is almost always here, the island has learned to live with it. The plants put down deep roots, and the rabbits hide far inside the thickets, and the trees grow up with their backs ready-bent for the flogging, and the birds nest on sheltered ledges, and the man's house is sturdy and squat, built with a craftsmanship that knows this wind of old.

This house is made of big grey stones and grey slates, the colour of the sea. It has small windows and close-fitting doors and a chimney in its pine end. It stands at the top of the hill at the eastern end of the island, close to the splintered stub of the broken walking-stick. It crowns the hill, defying the wind and the rain, not out of bravado but so that the man can see the sheep

There is another house, very similar, ten miles away at the opposite end of the island near the more-or-less beach; but nobody lives there. There was once another man. He thought he knew better than the island; he thought he could grow oats and potatoes and keep a few cows. He battled for three years with the wind and the cold and the soil before he admitted he was wrong. When he had gone, nobody wanted his home.

This is a hard place. Only hard things survive here: hard rock, coarse grass, tough sheep, savage birds, sturdy houses and strong men. Hard things and cold things, and cruel and bitter and pointed things, rugged and slow-moving and determined things; things as cold and hard and ruthless as the island itself.

It is for places like this that the word 'bleak' has been invented.

'It's called Storm Island,' said Alfred Rose. 'I think you're going to like it.'

David and Lucy Rose sat in the prow of the fishing-boat and looked across the choppy water. It was a fine November day, cold and breezy yet clear and dry. A weak sun sparkled off the wavelets.

'I bought it in 1926,' Papa Rose continued, 'when we thought there was going to be a revolution and we'd need somewhere to hide from the working class. It's just the place for a convalescence.'

Lucy thought he was being suspiciously hearty, but she had to admit it looked lovely: all windblown and natural and fresh. And it made sense, this move. They had to get away from their parents and make a new start at being married; and there was no point in moving to a city to be bombed, when neither of them was really well enough to help; and then David's father had revealed that he owned an island off the coast of Scotland, and it seemed too good to be true.

'I own the sheep, too,' Papa Rose said. 'Shearers come over from the mainland each spring, and the wool brings in just about enough money to pay Tom McAvity's wages. Old Tom's the shepherd.'

'How old is he?' Lucy asked.

'Good Lord, he must be – oh, seventy?'

'I suppose he's eccentric.' The boat turned into the bay, and Lucy could see two small figures on the jetty: a man and a dog.

'Eccentric? No more than you'd be if you'd lived alone for twenty years. He talks to his dog.'

Lucy turned to the skipper of the small boat. 'How often do you call?'

'Once a fortnight, missus. I bring Tom's shopping, which isna much, and his mail, which is even less. You just give me your list, every other Monday, and if it can be bought in Aberdeen I'll bring it.'

He cut the motor and threw a rope to Tom. The dog barked and ran around in circles, beside himself with excitement. Lucy put one foot on the gunwale and sprang out on to the jetty.

Tom took her hand. He had a face of leather and a huge briar pipe with a lid. He was shorter than she, but wide, and he looked ridiculously healthy. He wore the hairiest tweed jacket she had ever seen, with a knitted sweater that must have been made by an elderly sister somewhere, plus a checked cap and army boots. His nose was huge, red and veined. 'Pleased to meet you,' he said politely, as if she was his ninth visitor today instead of the first human face he had seen in fourteen days.

'Here y'are, Tom,' said the skipper. He handed two cardboard boxes out of the boat. 'No eggs this time, but here's a letter from Devon.'

'It'll be from ma niece.'

Lucy thought: That explains the sweater.

David was still in the boat. The skipper stood behind him and said: 'Are you ready?'

Tom and Papa Rose leaned into the boat to assist, and the three of them lifted David in his wheelchair on to the jetty.

'If I don't go now I'll have to wait a fortnight for the next bus,' Papa Rose said with a smile. 'The house has been done up quite nicely, you'll see. All your stuff is in there. Tom will show you where everything is.' He kissed Lucy, squeezed David's shoulder, and shook Tom's hand. 'Have a few months of rest and together-ness, get completely fit, then come back: there are important war jobs for both of you.'

They would not be going back, Lucy knew; not before the end of the war: but she had not told anyone about that yet.

Papa got back into the boat. It wheeled away in a tight circle. Lucy waved until it disappeared around the headland.

Tom pushed the wheelchair, so Lucy took his grocer-ies. Between the landward end of the jetty and the cliff top was a long, steep, narrow ramp rising high above the beach like a bridge. Lucy would have had trouble getting the wheelchair to the top, but Tom managed without apparent exertion.

The cottage was perfect.

It was small and grey, and sheltered from the wind by a little rise in the ground. All the woodwork was freshly painted, and a wild rose bush grew beside the doorstep. Curls of smoke rose from the chimney to be whipped away by the breeze. The tiny windows looked over the bay.

Lucy said: 'I love it!'

The interior had been cleaned and aired and painted, and there were thick rugs on the stone floors. It had four rooms: downstairs, a modernized kitchen and a living-room with a stone fireplace; upstairs, two bedrooms. One end of the house had been carefully remodelled to take modern plumbing, with a bathroom above and a kitchen extension below.

Their clothes were in the wardrobes. There were towels in the bathroom and food in the kitchen.

Tom said: 'There's something in the barn I've to show you.'

It was a shed, not a barn. It lay hidden behind the cottage, and inside it was a gleaming new jeep.

'Mr Rose says it's been specially adapted for young Mr Rose to drive,' Tom said. 'It's got automatic gears, and the throttle and brake are operated by hand. That's what he said.' He seemed to be repeating the words parrot-fashion, as if he had very little idea of what gears, brakes and throttles might be.

Lucy said: 'Isn't that super, David?'

'Top-hole. But where shall I go in it?'

Tom said: 'You're always welcome to visit me and share a pipe and a drop of whisky. I've been looking forward to having neighbours again.'

'Thank you,' said Lucy.

'This here's the generator,' Tom said, turning around and pointing. 'I've got one just the same. You put the fuel in here. It delivers alternating current.'

David said: 'That's unusual – small generators are usually direct current.'

'Aye. I don't really know the difference, but they tell me this is safer.'

'True. A shock from this would throw you across the room, but direct current would kill you.'

They went back to the cottage. Tom said: 'Well, you'll want to settle in, and I've sheep to tend, so I'll say good-day. Oh! I ought to tell you: in an emergency, I can contact the mainland by wireless radio.'

David was surprised. 'You've got a radio transmitter?'

'Aye,' Tom said proudly. 'I'm an enemy aircraft spotter in the Royal Observer Corps.'

'Ever spotted any?' David asked.

Lucy flashed her disapproval of the sarcasm in David's voice, but Tom seemed not to notice. 'Not yet,' he replied.

David said: 'Jolly good show.'

When Tom had gone Lucy said: 'He only wants to do his bit.'

'There are lots of us who *want* to do our bit,' David said bitterly. And that, Lucy reflected, was the trouble.

She dropped the subject, and wheeled her crippled husband into their new home.

When Lucy had been asked to visit the hospital psychologist, she had immediately assumed that David had brain damage. It was not so. 'All that's wrong with his head is a nasty bruise on the left temple,' the psychologist said. She went on: 'However, the loss of both his legs brings about a trauma, and there's no telling how it will affect his state of mind. Did he want very much to be a pilot?'

Lucy pondered. 'He was afraid, but I think he wanted it very badly, all the same.'

'Well, he'll need all the reassurance and support that you can give him. And patience, too: one thing we can predict is that he will be resentful and ill-tempered for a while. He needs love and rest.'

However, during their first few months on the island he seemed to want neither. He did not make love to her, perhaps because he was waiting until his injuries were fully healed. But he did not rest, either. He threw himself into the business of sheep farming, tearing about the island in his jeep with the wheelchair in the back. He built fences along the more treacherous cliffs, shot at the eagles, helped Tom train a new dog when Betsy began to go blind, and burned-off the heather; and in the spring he was out every night delivering lambs. One day he felled a great old pine tree near Tom's cottage, and spent a fortnight stripping it, hewing it into manageable logs, and carting them back to the house for firewood. He relished really hard manual labour. He learned to strap himself tightly to the chair to keep his body anchored while he wielded an axe or a mallet. He carved a pair of Indian clubs and exercised with them for hours when Tom could find nothing more for him to do. The muscles of his arms and back became grotesque, like those of men who win body-building contests.

He refused point-blank to wash dishes, cook food or clean the house.

Lucy was not unhappy. She had been afraid he might sit by the fire all day and brood over his bad luck. The way he worked was faintly worrying because it was so obsessive, but at least he was not vegetating.

She told him about the baby at Christmas.

In the morning she gave him a petrol-driven saw, and he gave her a bolt of silk. Tom came over for dinner, and they ate a wild goose he had shot. David drove the shepherd home after tea, and when he came back Lucy opened a bottle of brandy.

Then she said: 'I have another present for you, but you can't open it until May.'

He laughed. 'What on earth are you talking about? How much of that brandy did you drink while I was out?'

'I'm having a baby.'

He stared at her, and all the laughter went out of his face. 'Good God, that's all we bloody well need.'

'David!'

'Well, for God's sake . . . When the hell did it happen?'

'That's not too difficult to figure out, is it?' she said bitterly. 'It must have been a week before the wedding. It's a miracle it survived the crash.'

'Have you seen a doctor?'

'Huh – when?'

'So how do you know for sure?'

'Oh, David, don't be so boring. I know for sure because my periods have stopped and my nipples hurt and I throw up in the mornings and my waist is four inches bigger than it used to be. If you ever *looked* at me *you* would know for sure.'

'All right.'

'What's the matter with you? You're supposed to be thrilled!'

'Oh, sure. Perhaps we'll have a son, and then I can take him for walks and play football with him, and he'll grow up wanting to be like his father the war hero, a legless fucking joke!'

'Oh, David, David,' she whispered. She knelt in front of his wheelchair. 'David, don't think like that. He will respect you. He'll look up to you because you put your life together again, and because you can do the work of two men from your wheelchair, and because you carried your disability with courage and cheerfulness.'

'Don't be so damned condescending,' he snapped. 'You sound like a sanctimonious priest.'

She stood up. 'Well, don't act as if it's my fault. Men can take precautions too, you know.'

'You can't take precautions against invisible lorries in the blackout!'

That was a silly, feeble excuse, and they both knew it, so Lucy said nothing. The whole idea of Christmas seemed utterly trite now: the bits of coloured paper on the walls, and the tree in the corner, and the remains of a goose in the kitchen waiting to be thrown away – none of it had anything to do with her life. She began to wonder what she was doing on this bleak island with a man who seemed not to love her, having a baby he didn't want. Why shouldn't she – why not – well, she could . . . Then she realized she had nowhere else to go, nothing else to do with her life, nobody else to *be* other than Mrs David Rose.

Eventually David said: 'Well, I'm going to bed.' He wheeled himself to the hall and dragged himself out of the chair and up the stairs backwards. She heard him scrape across the floor, heard the bed creak as he hauled himself on to it, heard his clothes hit the corner of the room as he undressed, then heard the final groaning of the springs as he lay down and pulled the blankets up over his pyjamas.

And still she would not cry.

She looked at the brandy bottle and thought: If I drink all of this now, and have a bath, perhaps I won't be pregnant in the morning.

She thought about it for a long time, until she came to the conclusion that life without David and the island and the baby would be even worse because it would be empty.

So she did not cry, and she did not drink the brandy,

and she did not leave the island; but instead she went upstairs and got into bed, and lay awake beside her sleeping husband, listening to the wind and trying not to think, until the gulls began to call, and a grey rainy dawn crept over the North Sea and filled the little bedroom with a cold, cheerless, silver light, and then at last she went to sleep.

A kind of peace settled over her in the spring, as if all threats were postponed until after the baby was born. When the February snow had thawed she planted flowers and vegetables in the patch of ground between the kitchen door and the barn, not really believing they would grow. She cleaned the house thoroughly and told David that if he wanted it done again before August he would have to do it himself. She wrote to her mother and did a lot of knitting and ordered nappies by post. They suggested she go home to have the baby, but she knew that if she went she would never come back. She went for long walks over the moors, with a bird book under her arm, until her own weight became too much for her to carry very far. She kept the bottle of brandy in a cupboard David never used, and whenever she felt depressed she went to look at it and remind herself of what she had almost lost.

Three weeks before the baby was due, she got the boat into Aberdeen. David and Tom waved from the jetty. The sea was so rough that both she and the skipper were terrified she might give birth before they reached the mainland. She went into hospital in Aberdeen, and four weeks later brought the baby home on the same boat.

David knew none of it. He probably thought that women gave birth as easily as ewes. He was oblivious to the pain of contractions, and that awful, impossible stretching, and the soreness afterwards, and the bossy, know-all nurses who didn't want you to *touch* your baby because you weren't brisk and efficient and trained and *sterile* like they were; he just saw you go away pregnant and come back with a beautiful, white-wrapped, healthy baby boy and said: 'We'll call him Jonathan.'

They added Alfred for David's father, and Malcolm for Lucy's, and Thomas for old Tom, but they called the boy Jo, because he was too tiny for Jonathan, let alone Jonathan Alfred Malcolm Thomas Rose. David learned to give him his bottle and burp him and change his nappy, and he even dandled him in his lap occasionally, but his interest was distant, uninvolved. He had a problem-solving approach, like the nurses; it was not for him as it was for Lucy. Tom was closer to the baby than David. Lucy would not let him smoke in the room where the baby was, and the old boy would put his great briar pipe with the lid in his pocket for hours and gurgle at little Jo, or watch him kick his feet, or help Lucy bath him. Lucy suggested mildly that he might be neglecting the sheep. Tom said they did not need him to watch them feed – he would rather watch Jo feed. He carved a rattle out of driftwood and filled it with small round pebbles, and was overjoyed when Jo grabbed it and shook it, first time, without having to be shown how.

And still David and Lucy did not make love.

First there had been his injuries, and then she had been pregnant, and then she had been recovering from childbirth; but now the reasons had run out.

One night she said: 'I'm back to normal, now.'

'How do you mean?'

'After the baby. My body is normal. I've healed.'

'Oh, I see. That's good.' And he turned away.

She made sure to go up to bed with him so that he could watch her undress, but he always turned his back.

As they lay there, dozing off, she would move so that her hand, or her thigh, or her breast, brushed against him, a casual but unmistakable invitation. There was no response.

She believed firmly that there was nothing wrong with her. She wasn't a nymphomaniac: she didn't simply want sex, she wanted sex with David. She was sure that, even if there had been another man under seventy on the island, she would not have been tempted. She wasn't a sex-starved tart, she was a love-starved wife.

The crunch came on one of those nights when they lay on their backs, side by side, both wide awake, listening to the wind outside and the small sounds of Jo from the next room. It seemed to Lucy that it was time he either did it or came right out and said why not; and that he was going to avoid the issue until she forced it; and that she might as well force it now as live in miserable incomprehension any longer.

So she brushed her arm across his thighs and opened her mouth to speak – and almost cried out with shock to discover that he had an erection. So he could do it!

And he wanted to, or why else – And her hand closed triumphantly around the evidence of his desire, and she shifted closer to him, and sighed: 'David—'

He said: 'Oh, for God's sake!' He gripped her wrist and thrust her hand away from him and turned on to his side.

But this time she was not going to accept his rebuff in modest silence. She said: 'David, why not?'

'Jesus, Christ!' He threw the blankets off, swung himself to the floor, grabbed the eiderdown with one hand, and dragged himself to the door.

Lucy sat up in bed and screamed at him: 'Why not?'

Jo began to cry.

David pulled up the empty legs of his cut-off pyjama trousers, pointed to the pursed white skin of his stumps, and said: 'That's why not! That's why not!'

He slithered downstairs to sleep on the sofa, and Lucy went into the next bedroom to comfort Jo.

It took a long time to lull him back to sleep, probably because she herself was so much in need of comfort. The baby tasted the tears on her cheeks, and she wondered if he had any inkling of their meaning: wouldn't tears be one of the first things a baby came to understand? She could not bring herself to sing to him, nor could she with any sincerity murmur that everything was all right; so she held him tight and rocked him, and when *he* had soothed *her* with his warmth and his clinging, he went to sleep in her arms.

She put him back in the cot and stood looking at him for a while. There was no point in going back to bed. She could hear David's deep-sleep snoring from the living-room – he had to take powerful pills, otherwise the old pain kept him awake. Lucy needed to get right away from him, where she could neither see nor hear him, where he couldn't find her for a few hours even if he wanted to. She put on trousers and a sweater, a heavy coat and boots, and crept downstairs and out into the night.

There was a swirling mist, damp and bitterly cold, the kind the island specialized in. She put up the collar of her coat, thought about going back inside for a scarf, and decided not to. She squelched along the muddy path, welcoming the bite of the fog in her throat, the small discomfort of the weather taking her mind off the larger hurt inside her.

She reached the cliff top and walked gingerly down the steep, narrow ramp, placing her feet carefully on the slippery boards. At the bottom she jumped off on to the sand and walked to the edge of the sea.

The wind and the water were carrying on their perpetual quarrel, the wind swooping down to tease the waves and the sea hissing and spitting as it crashed against the land, the two of them doomed to bicker forever because neither could be calm while the other was there, but neither had any place else to go.

Lucy walked along the hard sand, letting the noise and the weather fill her head, until the beach ended in a sharp point where the water met the cliff, when she turned and walked back. She paced the shore all night. Toward dawn a thought came to her, unbidden: It is his way of being strong.

As it was, the thought was not much help, holding its

meaning in a tightly clenched fist. But she worked on it for a while, and the fist opened to reveal what looked like a small pearl of wisdom nestling in its palm: for perhaps David's coldness to her was of one piece with his chopping down trees, and undressing himself, and driving the jeep, and throwing the Indian clubs, and coming to live on a cold cruel island in the North Sea . . .

What was it he had said? '. . . his father the war hero, a legless joke . . .' He had something to prove, something that would sound trite if it were put into words; something he could have done as a fighter pilot, but now had to do with trees and fences and Indian clubs and a wheelchair. They wouldn't let him take the test, and he wanted to be able to say: 'I could have passed it anyway, just *look* how I can suffer.'

It was cruelly, hopelessly, screamingly unjust: he had had the courage, and he had suffered the wounds, but he could take no pride in it. If a Messerschmitt had taken his legs the wheelchair would have been like a medal, a badge of courage. But now, all his life, he would have to say: 'It was during the war – but no, I never saw any action, this was a car crash, I did my training and I was going to fight, the very next day, I had seen my kite, she was a beauty, and I *would* have been brave, I know . . .'

Yes, it was his way of being strong. And perhaps she could be strong, too. She might find ways of patching up the wreck of her life so that it would sail again. David had once been good and kind and loving, and she might now learn to wait patiently while he battled to become the complete man he used to be. She could find new hopes, new things to live for. Other women had found the strength to cope with bereavement, and bombed-out houses, and husbands in prisoner-of-war camps.

She picked up a pebble, drew back her arm, and threw it out to sea with all her might. She did not see or hear it land: it might have gone on forever, circling the earth like a satellite in a space story.

She shouted: 'I can be strong, too!'

Then she turned around and started up the ramp to the cottage. It was almost time for Jo's first feed.

CHAPTER SIX

I T LOOKED like a mansion; and, up to a point, that was what it was: a large house, in its own grounds, in the leafy town of Wohldorf just outside North Hamburg. It might have been the home of a mine owner, or a successful importer, or an industrialist. It was in fact owned by the Abwehr.

It owed its fate to the weather – not here, but two hundred miles south-east in Berlin, where atmospheric conditions were unsuitable for wireless communication with England.

It was a mansion only down to ground level. Below that were two huge concrete shelters and several million Reichsmarks worth of radio equipment. The electronics system had been put together by one Major Werner Trautmann, and he did a good job. Each hall had twenty neat little soundproofed listening posts, occupied by radio operators who could recognize a spy by the way he tapped out his message, as easily as you can recognize your mother's handwriting on an envelope.

The receiving equipment was built with quality in mind, for the transmitters that were sending the messages had been designed for compactness rather than power. Most of them were the little suitcase sets called Klamotten which had been developed by Telefunken for Admiral Wilhelm Canaris, the head of the Abwehr.

On this night the airwaves were relatively quiet, so everyone knew when Die Nadel came through. The message was taken by one of the older operators. He tapped out an acknowledgement, transcribed the signal quickly, tore the sheet off his notepad and went to the phone. He read the message over the direct line to Abwehr headquarters at Sophien Terrace in Hamburg, then he came back to his booth for a smoke.

He offered a cigarette to the youngster in the next booth, and the two of them stood together for a few minutes, leaning against the wall and smoking.

The youngster said: 'Anything?'

The older man shrugged. 'There's always *something* when he calls. But not much, this time. The Luftwaffe missed St Paul's Cathedral again.'

'No reply for him?'

'We don't think he waits for replies. He's an independent bastard, that one. Always was. I trained him in wireless, you know: and once I'd finished he thought he knew it better than me.'

The youngster was awestruck. 'You've *met* Die Nadel?'

'Oh, yes,' said the old-timer, flicking ash.

'What's he like?'

'As a drinking companion, he's about as much fun as a dead fish. I think he likes women, on the quiet, but as for sinking a few steins with the boys – forget it. All the same, he's the best agent we've got.'

'Really?'

'Definitely. Some say the best spy ever. There's a story that he spent five years working his way up in the NKVD in Russia, and ended up one of Stalin's most trusted aides . . . I don't know whether it's true, but it's the kind of thing he'd do. A real pro. And the Führer knows it.'

'Hitler knows him?'

The older man nodded. 'At one time he wanted to see all Die Nadel's signals. I don't know if he still does. Not that it would make any difference to Die Nadel. Nothing impresses that man. You know something? He looks at everybody the same way: as if he's figuring out how he'll kill you if you make a wrong move.'

'I'm glad I didn't have to train him.'

'He learned quickly, I'll give him that.'

'Good pupil?'

'The best. He worked at it twenty-four hours a day, then when he'd mastered it, he wouldn't give me a good morning. It takes him all his time to remember to salute Canaris.'

'*Ach du meine Scheisse.*'

'Oh, yes. Didn't you know – he always signs off "Regards to Willi". That's how much he cares about rank.'

'No. Regards to Willi? *Ach du meine Scheisse.*'

They finished their cigarettes, dropped them on the floor, and trod them out. Then the older man picked up the stubs and pocketed them, because smoking was not really permitted in the dugout. The radios were still quiet.

'Yes, he won't use his code name,' the older man went on. 'Von Braun gave it to him, and he's never liked it. He's never liked Von Braun either. Do you remember the time – no, it was before you joined us – Braun told Nadel to go to the airfield in Farnborough, Kent. The message came back, quick as a flash: "There is no airfield at Farnborough, Kent. There is one at Farnborough, Hampshire. Fortunately the Luftwaffe's geography is better than yours, you cunt." Just like that.'

'I suppose it's understandable. When we make mistakes we put their lives at risk.'

The older man frowned. He was the one who delivered such judgements, and he did not like his audience to weigh in with opinions of its own. 'Perhaps,' he said grudgingly.

The youngster reverted to his original wide-eyed role. 'Why doesn't he like his code name?'

'He says it has a meaning, and a code word with a meaning can give a man away. Von Braun wouldn't listen.'

'A meaning? The Needle? What does it mean?'

But at that moment the old-timer's radio chirped, and he returned quickly to his station; so the youngster never did find out.

Part Two

CHAPTER SEVEN

THE MESSAGE annoyed Faber, because it forced him to face issues which he had been avoiding.

Hamburg had made damn sure the message reached him. He had given his call-sign, and instead of the usual 'Acknowledge – proceed' they had sent back 'Make rendezvous one'.

He acknowledged the order, transmitted his report, and packed the wireless set back into its suitcase. Then he wheeled his bicycle out of Erith Marshes – his cover was that of a bird-watcher – and he got on the road to Blackheath. As he cycled back to his cramped two-room flatlet, he wondered whether to obey the order.

He had two reasons for disobedience: one professional, one personal.

The professional reason was that 'rendezvous one' was an old code, set up by Canaris back in 1937. It meant he was to go to the doorway of a certain shop between Leicester Square and Piccadilly Circus to meet another agent. The agents would recognize each other by the fact that they both carried a Bible. Then there was a patter:

'What is today's chapter?'

'One Kings thirteen.'

Then, if they were certain they were not being followed, they would agree that the chapter was 'most inspiring'. Otherwise one would say: 'I'm afraid I haven't read it yet.'

The shop doorway might not be there any more, but it was not that which troubled Faber. He thought Canaris had probably given the code to most of the bumbling amateurs who had crossed the Channel in 1940 and landed in the arms of MI5. Faber knew they had been caught because the hangings had been publicized, no doubt to reassure the public that something was being done about Fifth Columnists. They would certainly have given away secrets before they died, so the British now probably knew the old rendezvous code. If they had picked up the message from Hamburg, that shop doorway must by now be swarming with well-spoken young Englishmen carrying Bibles and practising saying 'Most inspiring' in a German accent.

The Abwehr had thrown professionalism to the wind, back in those heady days when the invasion seemed so close. Faber had not trusted Hamburg since. He would not tell them where he lived, he refused to communicate with their other agents in Britain, he varied the frequency he used for transmission without caring whether he trod all over someone else's signal.

If he had always obeyed his masters, he would not have survived so long.

At Woolwich Faber was joined by a mass of other cyclists, many of them women, as the workers came streaming out of the munitions factory at the end of the day shift. Their cheerful weariness reminded Faber of his personal reason for disobedience: he thought his side was losing the war.

They certainly were not winning. The Russians and the Americans had joined in, Africa was lost, the Italians had collapsed; the Allies must invade France this year, 1944.

Faber did not want to risk his life to no purpose.

He arrived home and put his bicycle away. While he was washing his face it dawned on him that, against all logic, he *wanted* to make the rendezvous.

It was a foolish risk, taken in a lost cause, but he was itching to get to it. And the simple reason was that he was unspeakably bored. The routine transmissions, the bird-watching, the bicycle, the boarding-house teas: it was four years since he had experienced anything remotely like action. He seemed to be in no danger whatsoever, and that made him jumpy, because he imagined invisible perils. He was happiest when every so often he could identify a threat and take steps to neutralize it.

Yes, he would make the rendezvous. But not in the way they expected.

There were still crowds in the West End of London, despite the war; Faber wondered whether it was the same in Berlin. He bought a Bible at Hatchard's bookshop in Piccadilly, and stuffed it into his inside coat pocket, out of sight. It was a mild, damp day, with intermittent drizzle, and Faber was carrying an umbrella.

This rendezvous was timed for either between nine and ten o'clock in the morning or between five and six in the afternoon, and the arrangement was that one went there every day until the other party turned up. If no contact was made for five successive days one went there on alternate days for a fortnight. After that one gave up.

Faber got to Leicester Square at ten past nine. The contact was there, in the tobacconist's doorway, with a blackbound Bible under his arm, pretending to shelter from the rain. Faber spotted him out of the corner of his eye and hurried past, head down. The man was youngish, with a blond moustache and a well-fed look. He wore a black double-breasted showerproof coat, and he was reading the *Daily Express* and chewing gum. He was not familiar.

When Faber walked by the second time on the opposite side of the street, he spotted the tail. A short, stocky man wearing the trench coat and trilby hat beloved of English plain-clothes policemen was standing just inside the foyer of an office building, looking through the glass doors across the street to the spy in the doorway.

There were two possibilities. If the agent did not know he had been rumbled, Faber had only to get him away from the rendezvous and lose the tail. However, the alternative was that the agent had been captured and the man in the doorway was a substitute, in which case neither he nor the tail must be allowed to see Faber's face.

82

Faber assumed the worst, then thought of a way to deal with it.

There was a telephone kiosk in the Square. Faber went inside and memorized the number. Then he found I Kings 13 in the Bible, tore out the page, and scribbled in the margin: 'Go to the phone box in the Square.'

He walked around the back streets behind the National Gallery until he found a small boy, aged about ten or eleven, sitting on a doorstep throwing stones at puddles.

Faber said: 'Do you know the tobacconist in the Square?'

The boy said: 'Yerst.'

'Do you like chewing-gum?'

'Yerst.'

Faber gave him the page torn from the Bible. 'There's a man in the doorway of the tobacconist's. If you give him this he'll give you some gum.'

'All right,' the boy said. He stood up. 'Is this geezer a Yank?'

Faber said: 'Yerst.'

The boy ran off. Faber followed him. As the boy approached the agent, Faber ducked into the doorway of the building opposite. The tail was still there, peering through the glass. Faber stood just outside the door, blocking the tail's view of the scene across the street, and opened his umbrella. He pretended to be struggling with it. He saw the agent give something to the boy and walk off. He ended his charade with the umbrella, and walked in the direction opposite to the way the agent had gone. He looked back over his shoulder to see the tail run into the street, looking for the vanished agent.

Faber stopped at the nearest call box and dialled the number of the kiosk in the Square. It took a few minutes to get through. At last a deep voice said: 'Hello?'

Faber said: 'What is today's chapter?'

'One Kings thirteen.'

'Most inspiring.'

'Yes, isn't it.'

The fool has no idea of the trouble he's in, Faber thought. Aloud he said: 'Well?'

'I must see you.'

'That is impossible.'

'But I must!' There was a note in the voice which Faber thought close to despair. 'The message comes from the very top – do you understand?'

Faber pretended to waver. 'All right, then. I will meet you in one week's time under the arch at Euston Station at nine a.m.'

'Can't you make it sooner?'

Faber hung up and stepped outside. Walking quickly, he rounded two corners and came within sight of the phone box in the Square. He saw the agent walking in the direction of Piccadilly. There was no sign of the tail. Faber followed the agent.

The man went into Piccadilly Circus underground station and bought a ticket to Stockwell. Faber immediately realized he could get there by a more direct route. He came out of the station, walked quickly to Leicester

Square, and got on a Northern Line train. The agent would have to change trains at Waterloo, whereas Faber's train was direct; so Faber would reach Stockwell first, or at the worst they would arrive on the same train.

In fact Faber had to wait outside the station at Stockwell for twenty-five minutes before the agent emerged. Faber followed him again. He went into a café.

There was absolutely nowhere nearby where a man could plausibly stand still for any length of time: no shop windows to gaze into, no benches to sit on or parks to walk around, no bus stops or taxi ranks or public buildings. It was a dreary, blank suburb. Faber had to walk up and down the street, always looking as if he were going somewhere, carrying on until he was just out of sight of the café then returning on the opposite side, while the agent sat in the warm, steamy café drinking tea and eating hot toast.

He came out after half an hour. Faber tailed him through a succession of residential streets. The agent knew where he was going, but was in no hurry: he walked like a man who is going home with nothing to do for the rest of the day. He did not look back, and Faber thought: Another amateur.

At last he went into a house – one of the poor, anonymous, inconspicuous lodging-houses used by spies everywhere. It had a dormer window in the roof: that would be the agent's room, high up for better wireless reception.

Faber walked past, scanning the opposite side of the

street. Yes – there. A movement behind an upstairs window, a glimpse of a jacket and tie, a watching face withdrawn: the opposition was here too. The agent must have gone to the rendezvous yesterday and allowed himself to be followed home by MI5 – unless, of course, he *was* MI5.

Faber turned the corner and walked down the next parallel street, counting the houses. Almost directly behind the place the agent had entered there was the bomb-damaged shell of what had been a pair of semi-detached houses. Good.

As he walked back to the station he felt a buzz of excitement. His step was springier, his heart beat a shade faster, and he looked around him with bright-eyed interest. It was good. The game was on.

He dressed in black that night: a woollen hat, a roll-neck sweater under a short leather flying jacket, trousers tucked into socks, rubber-soled shoes; all black. He would be almost invisible, for London, too, was blacked out.

He cycled through the quiet streets with dimmed lights, keeping off main roads. It was after midnight, and he saw no one. He left the bike a quarter of a mile away from his destination, padlocking it to the fence in a pub yard.

He went, not to the agent's house, but to the bombed-out shell in the next street. He picked his way carefully across the rubble in the front garden, entered the gaping doorway, and went through the house to the back. It was very dark. A thick screen of low cloud hid the moon and stars. Faber had to walk slowly with his hands in front of him.

He reached the end of the garden, jumped over the fence, and crossed the next two gardens. In one of the houses a dog barked for a minute.

The garden of the lodging-house was unkempt. Faber walked into a blackberry bush and stumbled. The thorns scratched his face. He ducked under a line of washing – there was enough light for him to see that.

He found the kitchen window and took from his pocket a small tool with a scoop-shaped blade. The putty around the glass was old and brittle, and already flaking away in places. After twenty minutes' silent work he took the pane out of the frame and laid it gently on the grass. He shone a torch through the empty hole to make sure there were no noisy obstacles in his way, then climbed in.

The darkened house smelled of boiled fish and disinfectant. Faber unlocked the back door – a precaution for fast escape – before entering the hall. He flashed his pencil torch on and off quickly, once. In that instant of light he took in a tiled hallway, a kidney table he must circumvent, a row of coats on hooks and a staircase, to the right, carpeted.

He climbed the stairs silently.

He was halfway across the landing to the second flight when he saw the light under the door. A split-second later there was an asthmatic cough and the sound of a toilet flushing. Faber reached the door in two strides and froze against the wall.

Light flooded the landing as the door opened. Faber slipped his stiletto out of his sleeve. The old man came out of the toilet and crossed the landing, leaving the light on. At his bedroom door he grunted, turned, and came back.

He must see me, Faber thought. He tightened his grip on the handle of his knife. The old man's half-open eyes were directed to the floor. He looked up as he reached for the light cord, and Faber almost killed him then – but the man fumbled for the switch, and Faber realized he was so sleepy he was practically sleepwalking.

The light died, the old man shuffled back to bed, and Faber breathed again.

There was only one door at the top of the second flight of stairs. Faber tried it gently. It was locked.

He took another tool from the pocket of his jacket. The noise of the cistern filling covered the sound of Faber picking the lock. He opened the door and listened.

He could hear deep, regular breathing. He stepped inside. The sound came from the opposite corner of the room. He could see nothing. He crossed the pitch-black room very slowly, feeling the air in front of him at each step, until he was beside the bed.

He had the torch in his left hand, the stiletto loose in his sleeve, and his right hand free. He switched on the torch and grabbed the sleeping man's throat in a strangling grip.

The agent's eyes snapped open, full of fear, but he could make no sound. Faber straddled the bed and sat on him. Then he whispered: 'One Kings thirteen,' and relaxed his grip.

'You!' the agent said. He peered into the torchlight, trying to see Faber's face. He rubbed his neck where Faber's hand had squeezed.

Faber hissed: 'Be still!' He shone the torch into the agent's eyes, and with his right hand drew the stiletto.

'Aren't you going to let me get up?'

'I prefer you in bed where you can do no more damage.'

'Damage? More damage?'

'You were watched in Leicester Square, you let me follow you here, and they are observing this house. Should I trust you to do anything?'

'My God, I'm sorry.'

'Why did they send you?'

'The message had to be delivered personally. The orders come from the Führer himself.' The agent stopped.

'Well? What orders?'

'I . . . have to be sure it is you.'

'How can you be sure?'

'I must see your face.'

Faber hesitated, then shone the torch at himself briefly. 'Satisfied?'

'Die Nadel,' the man breathed.

'And who are you?'

'Major Friedrich Kaldor, at your service, sir.'

'Then I should call you "Sir".'

'Oh, no, sir. You've been promoted twice in your absence. You are now a lieutenant-colonel.'

'Have they nothing better to do in Hamburg?'

'Aren't you pleased?'

'I should be pleased to go back and put Major von Braun on latrine duty.'

'May I get up, sir?'

'Certainly not. What if Major Kaldor is languishing in Wandsworth gaol, and you are a substitute, just waiting to give some kind of signal to your watching friends in the house opposite?'

'Very well.'

'So – what are these orders from Hitler himself?'

'Well, sir, the Reich believes there will be an invasion of France this year.'

'Brilliant, brilliant. Go on.'

'They believe that General Patton is massing the First United States Army Group in the part of England known as East Anglia. If that army is the invasion force, then it follows that they will attack via the Pas de Calais.'

'That makes sense. But I have seen no sign of this army of Patton's.'

'There is some doubt in the highest circles in Berlin. The Führer's astrologer—'

'What?'

'Yes, sir, he has an astrologer, who tells him to defend Normandy.'

'My God. Are things that bad there?'

'He gets plenty of earthbound advice, too. I personally believe he uses the astrologer as an excuse when he thinks the generals are wrong but he cannot fault their arguments.'

Faber sighed. He had been afraid of news like this. 'Go on.'

'Your assignment is to assess the strength of FUSAG: numbers of troops, artillery, air support—'

'I know how to measure armies, thank you.'

'Of course.' He paused. 'I am instructed to emphasize the importance of the mission, sir.'

'And you have done so. Tell me: are things that bad in Berlin?'

The agent hesitated, and said: 'No, sir. Morale is high, output of munitions increases every month, the people spit at the bombers of the RAF—'

'Never mind,' Faber interrupted him. 'I can get the propaganda from my radio.'

The younger man was silent.

Faber said: 'Do you have anything else to tell me? Officially, I mean.'

'Yes. For the duration of the assignment you have a special bolthole.'

'They *do* think it's important,' Faber said.

'You rendezvous with a U-boat in the North Sea, ten miles due east of a town called Aberdeen. Just call them in on your normal radio frequency and they will surface. As soon as you or I have told Hamburg that the orders have been passed from me to you, the route will be open. The boat will be there every Friday and Monday at six p.m. and will wait until six a.m.'

'Aberdeen is a big town. Do you have an exact map reference?'

'Yes.' The agent recited the numbers, and Faber memorized them.

'Is that everything, Major?'

'Yes, sir.'

'What do you plan to do about the gentlemen from MI5 in the house across the road?'

The agent shrugged. 'I shall have to give them the slip.'

Faber thought: It's no good. 'What are your orders for action after you have seen me? Do you have a bolthole?'

'No. I am to go to a place called Weymouth and steal a boat in which to return to France.'

That was no plan at all. So, Faber thought: Canaris knew how it would be. Very well.

He said: 'And if you are caught by the British, and tortured?'

'I have a suicide pill.'

'And you will use it?'

'Most certainly.'

Faber looked at him. 'I think you might,' he said. He placed his left hand on the agent's chest and put his weight on it, as if he were about to get off the bed. That way he was able to feel exactly where the rib cage ended and the soft belly began. He thrust the point of the stiletto in just under the ribs and stabbed upward to the heart.

The agent's eyes widened for a terror-stricken instant. A cry came to his throat but did not escape. His body convulsed. Faber pushed the stiletto an inch farther in. The eyes closed and the body went limp.

Faber said: 'You saw my face.'

CHAPTER EIGHT

'I THINK we've lost control of it,' said Percival Godliman.

Frederick Bloggs nodded agreement, and added: 'It's my fault.'

The boy looked weary, Godliman thought. He had had that look for almost a year, ever since the night they dragged the crushed remains of his wife from underneath the rubble of their bombed house in Hoxton.

'I'm not interested in apportioning blame,' Godliman said briskly. 'The fact is that something happened in Leicester Square those few seconds when you lost sight of Blondie.'

'Do you think the contact was made?'

'Possibly.'

'When we picked him up again back in Stockwell, I thought he had simply given up for the day.'

'If that were the case he would have made the rendezvous again yesterday and today.' Godliman was making patterns with matchsticks on his desk, an aid to thinking he had developed into a habit. 'Still no movement at the house?'

'Nothing. He's been in there for forty-eight hours.'

Bloggs repeated: 'It's my fault.'

'Don't be a bore, old chap,' Godliman said. 'It was my decision to let him run, so that he would lead us to someone else; and I still think it was the right move.'

Bloggs sat motionless, his expression blank, his hands in the pockets of his raincoat. 'If the contact has been made, we shouldn't delay picking Blondie up and finding out what his mission was.'

'That way we lose whatever chance we have of following Blondie to somebody really dangerous.'

'Your decision.'

Godliman had made a church with his matches. He stared at it for a moment, then took a halfpenny from his pocket and tossed it. 'Tails,' he observed. 'Give him another twenty-four hours.'

The landlord was a middle-aged Irish Republican from Lisdoonvarna, County Clare, who harboured a secret hope that the Germans would win the war and thus free the Emerald Isle from English oppression forever. He limped arthritically around the old house, collecting his weekly rents, thinking how much he would be worth if those rents were allowed to rise to their true market value. He was not a rich man – he owned only two houses, this and the smaller one in which he lived. He was permanently bad-tempered.

On the first floor he tapped on the door of the old man. This tenant was always pleased to see him. He was probably pleased to see anybody. He said: 'Hello, Mr Riley, would you like a cup of tea?'

'No time today.'

'Oh, well.' The old man handed over the money. 'I expect you've seen the kitchen window.'

'No, I didn't go in there.'

'Oh! Well, there's a pane of glass out. I patched it over with blackout curtain, but of course there is a draught.'

'Who smashed it?' the landlord asked.

'Funny thing, it ain't broke. Just lying there on the grass. I expect the old putty just gave way. I'll mend it myself, if you can get hold of a bit of putty.'

You old fool, the landlord thought. Aloud he said: 'I don't suppose it occurred to you that you might have been burgled?'

The old man looked astonished. 'I never thought of that.'

'Nobody's missing any valuables?'

'Nobody's said so to me.'

The landlord went to the door. 'All right, I'll have a look when I go down.'

The old man followed him out. 'I don't think the new bloke is in, upstairs,' he said. 'I haven't heard a sound for a couple of days.'

The landlord was sniffing. 'Has he been cooking in his room?'

'I wouldn't know, Mr Riley.'

The two of them went up the stairs. The old man said: 'He's very quiet, if he is in there.'

'Whatever he's cooking, he'll have to stop. It smells bloody awful.'

The landlord knocked on the door. There was no answer. He opened it and went in, and the old man followed him.

'Well, well, well,' the old sergeant said heartily. 'I think you've got a dead one.'

He stood in the doorway, surveying the room. 'You touched anything, Paddy?'

'No,' the landlord replied. 'And the name's Mr Riley.'

The policeman ignored this. 'Not long dead, though. I've smelled worse.' His survey took in the old chest of drawers, the suitcase on the low table, the faded square of carpet, the dirty curtains on the dormer window, and the rumpled bed in the corner. There were no signs of a struggle.

He went over to the bed. The young man's face was peaceful, his hands clasped over his chest. 'I'd say heart attack, if he wasn't so young.' There was no empty sleeping-pill bottle to indicate suicide. He picked up the leather wallet on top of the chest and looked through its contents. There was an identity card and a ration book, and a fairly thick wad of notes. 'Papers in order and he ain't been robbed.'

'He's only been here a week or so,' the landlord ventured. 'I don't know much about him at all. He came from North Wales to work in a factory.'

The sergeant observed: 'If he was as healthy as he looked he'd be in the Army.' He opened the suitcase on the table. 'Bloody hell, what's this lot?'

The landlord and the old man had edged their way into the room now. The landlord said: 'It's a radio' at the same time as the old man said: 'He's bleeding.'

'Don't touch that body!' the sergeant said.

'He's had a knife in the guts,' the old man persisted.

The sergeant gingerly lifted one of the dead hands from the chest to reveal a small patch of dried blood. 'He *was* bleeding,' he said. 'Where's the nearest phone?'

'Five doors down,' the landlord told him.

'Lock this room and stay out until I get back.'

The sergeant left the house and knocked at the door of the neighbour with the phone. A woman opened it. 'Good morning, madam. May I use your telephone?'

'Come in.' She showed him the phone, on a stand in the hall. 'What's happened – anything exciting?'

'A tenant died in a lodging-house just up the road,' he told her as he dialled.

'Murdered?' she asked, wide-eyed.

'I leave that to the experts. Hello? Superintendent Jones, please. This is Canter.' He looked at the woman. 'Might I ask you just to pop in the kitchen while I talk to my governor?'

She went, disappointed.

'Hello, Super. This body's got a knife wound and a suitcase radio.'

'What's the address again, Sarge?'

Sergeant Canter told him.

'Yes, that's the one they've been watching. This is an MI5 job, Sarge. Go to number forty-two and tell the surveillance team what you've found. I'll get on to their chief. Off you go.'

Canter thanked the woman and crossed the road. He was quite thrilled: this was only his second murder in 31 years as a Metropolitan Policeman, and it turned out to involve espionage! He might make Inspector yet.

He knocked on the door of number forty-two. It opened, and two men stood there.

Sergeant Canter said: 'Are you the secret agents from MI5?'

Bloggs arrived at the same time as a Special Branch man, Detective-Inspector Harris, whom he had known in his Scotland Yard days. Canter showed them the body.

They stood still for a moment, looking at the peaceful young face with its blond moustache.

Harris said: 'Who is he?'

'Codename Blondie,' Bloggs told him. 'We think he came in by parachute a couple of weeks ago. We picked up a radio message to another agent arranging a rendezvous. We knew the code, so we were able to watch the rendezvous. We hoped Blondie would lead us to the resident agent, who would be a much more dangerous specimen.'

'So what happened here?'

'Buggered if I know.'

Harris looked at the wound in the agent's chest. 'Stiletto?'

'Something like that. A very neat job. Under the ribs and straight up into the heart. Quick.'

'There are worse ways to die.'

Sergeant Canter said: 'Would you like to see the method of entry?'

He led them downstairs to the kitchen. They looked at the window-frame and the unbroken pane of glass lying on the lawn.

Canter said: 'Also, the lock on the bedroom door had been picked.'

They sat down at the kitchen table, and Canter made tea. Bloggs said: 'It happened the night after I lost him in Leicester Square. I fouled it all up.'

Harris said: 'Nobody's perfect.'

They drank their tea in silence for a while. Harris said: 'How are things with you, anyway? You don't drop in at the Yard.'

'Busy.'

'How's Christine?'

'Killed in the bombing.'

Harris's eyes widened. 'You poor bastard.'

'You all right?'

'Lost my brother in North Africa. Did you ever meet Johnny?'

'No.'

'He was a lad. Drink? You've never seen anything like it. Spent so much on booze, he could never afford to get married – which is just as well, the way things turned out.'

'Most people have lost somebody.'

'If you're on your own, come round our place for dinner on Sunday.'

'Thanks, I work Sundays now.'

Harris nodded. 'Well, whenever you feel like it.'

A detective-constable poked his head around the door and addressed Harris. 'Can we start bagging-up the evidence, guv?'

Harris looked at Bloggs.

'I've finished,' Bloggs said.

'All right, son, carry on,' Harris told him.

Bloggs said: 'Suppose he made contact after I lost him, and arranged for the resident agent to come here. The resident may have suspected a trap – that would explain why he came in through the window and picked the lock.'

'It makes him a devilish suspicious bastard,' Harris observed.

'That might be why we've never caught him. Anyway, he gets into Blondie's room and wakes him up. Now he knows it isn't a trap, right?'

'Right.'

'So why does he kill Blondie?'

'Maybe they quarrelled.'

'There were no signs of a struggle.'

Harris frowned into his empty cup. 'Perhaps he twigged that Blondie was being watched, and he was afraid we'd pick the boy up and make him spill the beans.'

Bloggs said: 'That makes him a ruthless bastard.'

'That might be why we've never caught him.'

'Come in. Sit down. I've just had a call from MI6. Canaris has been fired.'

Bloggs went in, sat down, and said: 'Is that good news or bad?'

'Very bad,' said Godliman. 'It's happened at the worst possible moment.'

'Do I get told why?'

Godliman looked at him through narrow eyes, then said: 'I think you need to know. At this moment we have forty double-agents broadcasting to Hamburg false information about Allied plans for the invasion of France.'

Bloggs whistled. 'I didn't know it was quite that big. I suppose the doubles say we're going in at Cherbourg, but really it will be Calais, or vice versa.'

'Something like that. Apparently I don't need to know the details. Anyway they haven't told me. However, the whole thing is in danger. We knew Canaris; we knew we had him fooled; we could have gone on fooling him. A new broom may mistrust his predecessor's agents. There's more: we've had some defections from the other side, people who could have betrayed the Abwehr's people over here if they hadn't been betrayed already. It's another reason for the Germans to begin to suspect our doubles.

'Then there's the possibility of a leak. Literally thousands of people now know about the double-cross system. There are doubles in Iceland, Canada, and Ceylon. We ran a double-cross in the Middle East.

'And we made a bad mistake last year by repatriating a German called Erich Carl. We later learned he was an Abwehr agent – a real one – and that while he was

101

in internment on the Isle of Man he may have learned about two doubles called Mutt and Jeff, and possibly a third called Tate.

'So we're skating on thin ice. If one decent Abwehr agent in Britain gets to know about Fortitude – that's the codename for the deception plan – the whole strategy will be endangered. Not to mince words, we could lose the fucking war.'

Bloggs suppressed a smile: he could remember a time when Professor Godliman did not know the meaning of such words.

The professor went on: 'The Twenty Committee has made it quite clear that they expect me to make sure there aren't any decent Abwehr agents in Britain.'

'Last week we would have been quite confident that there weren't,' Bloggs said.

'Now we know there's at least one.'

'And we let him slip through our fingers.'

'So now we have to find him again.'

'I don't know,' Bloggs said gloomily. 'We don't know what part of the country he's operating from, we haven't the faintest idea what he looks like. He's too crafty to be pinpointed by triangulation while he's transmitting – otherwise we would have nabbed him long ago. We don't even know his codename. So where do we start?'

'Unsolved crimes,' said Godliman. 'Look: a spy is bound to break the law. He forges papers, he steals petrol and ammunition, he evades checkpoints, he enters restricted areas, he takes photographs, and when people rumble him he kills them. The police are bound to get to know of some of these crimes, if the spy has been operating for any length of time. If we go through the unsolved crimes files since the war, we'll find traces.'

'Don't you realize that *most* crimes are unsolved?' Bloggs said incredulously. 'The files would fill the Albert Hall!'

Godliman shrugged. 'So, we narrow it down to London, and we start with murders.'

They found what they were looking for on the very first day of their search.

It happened to be Godliman who came across it, and at first he did not realize its significance.

It was the file on the murder of a Mrs Una Garden in Highgate in 1940. Her throat had been cut and she had been sexually molested, although not raped. She had been found in the bedroom of her lodger, with a considerable amount of alcohol in her bloodstream. The picture was fairly clear: she had had a tryst with the lodger, he had wanted to go farther than she was prepared to let him, they had quarrelled, he had killed her, and the murder had neutralized his libido. But the police had never found the lodger.

Godliman had been about to pass over the file: spies did not get involved in sexual assaults. But he was a meticulous man with records, so he read every word, and consequently discovered that the unfortunate Mrs Garden had received stiletto wounds in her back, as well as the fatal wound to her throat.

Godliman and Bloggs were on opposite sides of a wooden table in the records room at Old Scotland Yard. Godliman tossed the file across the table and said: 'I think this is it.'

Bloggs glanced through it and said: 'The stiletto.'

They signed for the file and walked the short distance to the War Office. When they returned to Godliman's room, there was a decoded signal on his desk. He read it casually, then thumped the table in excitement. 'It's him!'

Bloggs read: 'Orders received. Regards to Willi.'

'Remember him?' Godliman said. 'Die Nadel?'

'Yes,' Bloggs said hesitantly. 'The Needle. But there's not much information here.'

'Think, think! A stilletto is like a needle. It's the same man: the murder of Mrs Garden, all those signals in 1940 that we couldn't trace, the rendezvous with Blondie . . .'

'Possibly.' Bloggs looked thoughtful.

'I can prove it,' Godliman said. 'Remember the transmission about Finland that you showed me the first day I came here? The one which was interrupted?'

'Yes.' Bloggs went to the file to find it.

'If my memory serves me well, the date of that transmission is the same as the date of this murder . . . and I'll bet the time of death coincides with the interruption.'

Bloggs looked at the signal in the file. 'Right both times.'

'There!'

'He's been operating in London for at least five

years, and it's taken us until now to get on to him,' Bloggs reflected. 'He won't be easy to catch.'

Godliman suddenly looked wolfish. 'He may be clever, but he's not as clever as me,' he said tightly. 'I'm going to nail him to the fucking wall.'

Bloggs laughed out loud. 'My God, you've changed, Professor.'

Godliman said: 'Do you realize that's the first time you've laughed for a year?'

CHAPTER NINE

T HE SUPPLY boat rounded the headland and chugged into the bay at Storm Island under a blue sky. There were two women in it: one was the skipper's wife – he had been called up and now she ran the business – and the other was Lucy's mother.

Mother got out of the boat, wearing a utility suit – a mannish jacket and an above-the-knee skirt. Lucy hugged her mightily.

'Mother! What a surprise!'

'But I wrote to you.'

The letter was with the mail on the boat – Mother had forgotten that the post only came once a fortnight on Storm Island.

'Is this my grandson? Isn't he a big boy?'

Little Jo, almost three years old, turned bashful and hid behind Lucy's skirt. He was dark-haired, pretty, and tall for his age.

Mother said: 'Isn't he like his father!'

'Yes,' Lucy said. Her assent held a note of disapproval. 'You must be freezing – come up to the house. Where *did* you get that skirt?'

They picked up the groceries and began to walk up the ramp to the cliff top. Mother chattered as they went. 'It's the fashion, dear. It saves on material. But it isn't as cold as this on the mainland. Such a wind! I suppose it's all right to leave my case on the jetty – nobody to steal it! Jane is engaged to an American soldier – a white one, thank God. He comes from a place called Milwaukee, and he doesn't chew gum. Isn't that nice? I've only got four more daughters to marry off now. Your father is a Captain in the Home Guard, did I tell you? He's up half the night patrolling the common waiting for German parachutists. Uncle Stephen's warehouse was bombed – I don't know *what* he'll do, it's an Act of War or something—'

'Don't rush, Mother, you've got fourteen days to tell me the news.' Lucy laughed.

They reached the cottage. Mother said: 'Isn't this *lovely*?' They went in. 'I think this is just lovely.'

Lucy parked Mother at the kitchen table and made tea. 'Tom will get your case up. He'll be here for his lunch shortly.'

'The shepherd?'

'Yes.'

'Does he find things for David to do, then?'

Lucy laughed. 'It's the other way around. I'm sure he'll tell you all about it himself. You haven't told me why you're here.'

'My dear, it's about time I saw you. I know we're not supposed to make unnecessary journeys, but once in four years isn't extravagant, is it?'

They heard the jeep outside, and a moment later David wheeled himself in. He kissed his mother-in-law and introduced Tom.

Lucy said: 'Tom, you can earn your lunch today by bringing Mother's case up, as she carried your groceries.'

David was warming his hands at the stove. 'It's raw today.'

Mother said: 'You're really taking sheep-farming seriously, then?'

'The flock is double what it was three years ago,' David told her. 'My father never farmed this island seriously. I've fenced six miles of the cliff top, improved the grazing, and introduced modern breeding methods. Not only do we have more sheep, but each animal gives us more meat and wool.'

Mother said tentatively: 'I suppose Tom does the physical work and you give the orders.'

David laughed. 'Equal partners, Mother.'

They had hearts for lunch, and both men ate mountains of potatoes. Mother commented favourably on Jo's table manners. Afterwards David lit a cigarette and Tom stuffed his pipe.

Mother said: 'What I really want to know is when you're going to give me more grandchildren.' She smiled brightly.

There was a long silence.

'Well, I think it's wonderful, the way David copes,' said Mother.

Lucy said: 'Yes,' and again there was that note of disapproval.

They were walking along the cliff top. The wind had

dropped on the third day of Mother's visit, and it was mild enough to go out. They took Jo, dressed in a fisherman's sweater and a fur coat. They had stopped at the top of a rise to watch David, Tom and the dog herding sheep. Lucy could see in Mother's face an internal struggle as concern vied with discretion. She decided to save her mother the effort of asking.

'He doesn't love me,' she said.

Mother looked quickly to make sure Jo was out of earshot. 'I'm sure it's not that bad, dear. Different men show their love in diff—'

'Mother, we haven't been man and wife – properly – since we were married.'

'But . . .?' She indicated Jo with a nod.

'That was a week before the wedding.'

'Oh! Oh, dear.' She was shocked. 'Is it, you know, the accident?'

'Yes, but not in the way you mean. It's nothing physical. He just . . . won't.' Lucy was crying quietly, the tears trickling down her wind-browned cheeks.

'Have you talked about it?'

'I've tried. Mother, what shall I do?'

'Perhaps with time—'

'It's been almost four years!'

There was a pause. They began to walk on across the heather, into the weak afternoon sun. Jo chased gulls. Mother said: 'I almost left your father, once.'

It was Lucy's turn to be shocked. 'When?'

'It was soon after Jane was born. We weren't so well-off in those days, you know – Father was still working for his father, and there was a slump. I was expecting for the third time in three years, and it seemed that a life of having babies and making ends meet stretched out in front of me with nothing to relieve the monotony. Then I discovered he was seeing an old flame of his – Brenda Simmonds, you never knew her, she went to Basingstoke. Suddenly I asked myself what I was doing it for, and I couldn't think of a sensible answer.'

Lucy had dim, patchy memories of those days: her grandfather with a white moustache; her father, a more slender edition; extended-family meals in the great farmhouse kitchen; a lot of laughter and sunshine and animals. Even then her parents' marriage had seemed to represent solid contentment, happy permanence. She said: 'Why didn't you? Leave, I mean.'

'Oh, people just didn't, in those days. There wasn't all this divorce, and a woman couldn't get a job.'

'Women work at all sorts of things now.'

'They did in the last war, but everything changed afterwards with a bit of unemployment. I expect it will be the same this time. Men get their way, you know, generally speaking.'

'And you're glad you stayed.' It was not a question.

'People my age shouldn't make pronouncements about Life. But *my* life has been a matter of making-do, and the same goes for most of the women I know. Steadfastness always looks like a sacrifice, but usually it isn't. Anyway, I'm not going to give you advice. You wouldn't take it, and if you did you'd blame your problems on me, I expect.'

'Oh, Mother.' Lucy smiled.

110

Mother said: 'Shall we turn round? I think we've gone far enough for one day.'

In the kitchen one evening Lucy said to David: 'I'd like Mother to stay another two weeks, if she will.'

Mother was upstairs putting Jo to bed, telling him a story.

David said: 'Isn't a fortnight long enough for you to dissect my personality?'

'Don't be silly, David.'

He wheeled himself over to her chair. 'Are you telling me you don't talk about me?'

'Of course we talk about you – you're my husband.'

'What do you say to her, then?'

'Why are you so worried?' Lucy said, not without malice. 'What are you so ashamed of?'

'Damn you, I've nothing to be ashamed of. No one wants his personal life talked about by a pair of gossiping women.'

'We don't gossip about you.'

'What do you say?'

'Aren't you touchy!'

'Answer my question.'

'I say I want to leave you, and she tries to talk me out of it.'

He spun around and wheeled away. 'Tell her not to bother for my sake.'

She called: 'Do you mean that?'

He stopped. 'I don't need anybody, do you understand? I can manage alone. I'm self-sufficient.'

'And what about me?' she said quietly. 'Perhaps I need somebody.'

'What for?'

'To love me.'

Mother came in, and sensed the atmosphere. 'He's fast asleep,' she said. 'Dropped off before Cinderella got to the ball. I think I'll pack a few things, not to leave it all until tomorrow.' She went out again.

'Do you think it will ever change, David?' Lucy asked.

'I don't know what you mean.'

'Will we ever be . . . the way we were, before the wedding?'

'My legs won't grow back, if that's what you mean.'

'Oh, God, don't you know that doesn't bother me? I just want to be loved.'

David shrugged. 'That's your problem.' He went out before she started to cry.

Mother did not stay the second fortnight. Lucy walked with her down to the jetty the next day. It was raining hard, and they both wore mackintoshes. They stood in silence waiting for the boat, watching the rain pit the sea with tiny craters. Mother held Jo in her arms.

'Things will change, in time, you know,' she said. 'Four years is nothing in a marriage.'

Lucy said: 'I don't think he'll change, but there's not much I can do other than give it a chance. There's Jo, and the war, and David's disability – how can I leave?'

The boat arrived, and Lucy exchanged her mother for three boxes of groceries and five letters. The water was choppy. Mother sat in the boat's tiny cabin. They waved her around the headland. Lucy felt very lonely.

Jo began to cry. 'I don't want Gran to go away!'

'Nor do I,' said Lucy.

CHAPTER TEN

ODLIMAN AND Bloggs walked side by side along the pavement of a bomb-damaged London shopping street. They were a mismatched pair: the stooped, bird-like professor, with pebble-lensed spectacles and a pipe, not looking where he was going, taking short, scurrying steps; and the flatfooted youngster, blond and purposeful, in his detective's raincoat and melodramatic hat: a cartoon looking for a caption.

Godliman was saying: 'I think Die Nadel is well-connected.'

'Why?'

'The only way he could be so insubordinate with impunity. It's this "Regards to Willi" line. It must refer to Canaris.'

'You think he was pals with Canaris.'

'He's pals with somebody – perhaps someone more powerful than Canaris was.'

'I have the feeling this is leading somewhere.'

'People who are well-connected generally make those connections at school, or university, or staff college. Look at that.'

They were outside a shop which had a huge empty space where once there had been a plate-glass window. A rough sign, hand-painted and nailed to the window-frame, said: 'Even more open than usual.'

Bloggs laughed, and said: 'I saw one outside a bombed police station: "Be good. We are still open."'

'It's become a minor art form.'

They walked on. Bloggs said: 'So, what if Die Nadel did go to school with someone high in the Wermacht?'

'People always have their pictures taken at school. Midwinter down in the basement at Kensington – that house where MI6 used to be before the war – he's got a collection of thousands of photographs of German officers: school photos, binges in the Mess, passing-out parades, shaking hands with Adolf, newspaper pictures – everything.'

'I see,' Bloggs said. 'So if you're right, and Die Nadel has been through Germany's equivalent of Eton and Sandhurst, we've probably got a picture of him.'

'Almost certainly. Spies are notoriously camera-shy, but they don't become spies until they're well into adulthood. It will be a youthful Die Nadel that we find in Midwinter's files.'

They skirted a huge crater outside a barber's. The shop was intact, but the traditional red-and-white striped pole lay in shards on the pavement. The sign in the window said: 'We've had a close shave – come and get one yourself.'

Bloggs said: 'How will we recognize him? No one has ever seen him.'

'Yes, they have. At Mrs Garden's boarding-house in Highgate they know him quite well.'

The Victorian house stood on a hill overlooking London. It was built of red brick, and Bloggs thought it looked angry at the damage Hitler was doing to its city. It was high up; a good place from which to broadcast. Die Nadel would have lived on the top floor. Bloggs wondered what secrets the spy had transmitted to Hamburg from this place in the dark days of 1940. Map references for aircraft factories and steelworks, details of coastal defences, political gossip, gas masks and Anderson shelters and sandbags, British morale, bomb damage reports, 'Well done, boys, you got Christine Bloggs at last – ' Shut up.

The door was opened by an elderly man in a black jacket and striped trousers.

'Good morning. I'm Inspector Bloggs, from Scotland Yard. I'd like a word with the householder, please.'

Bloggs saw fear leap to the man's eyes, then a young woman appeared in the doorway and said: 'Come in, please.'

The tiled hall smelled of wax polish. Bloggs hung his hat and coat on a stand. The old man disappeared into the depths of the house, and the woman led Bloggs into a lounge. It was expensively furnished in a rich, old-fashioned way. There were bottles of whisky, gin and sherry on a trolley: all the bottles were unopened. The woman sat down on a floral armchair and crossed her legs.

116

Bloggs said: 'Why is the old man frightened of the police?'

'My father-in-law is a German Jew. He came here in 1935 to escape Hitler, and in 1940 you put him in a concentration camp. His wife killed herself at the prospect. He has just been released from the Isle of Man. He had a letter from the King, apologizing for the inconvenience to which he had been put.'

Bloggs said: 'We don't have concentration camps.'

'We invented them. In South Africa. Didn't you know? We go on about our history, but we forget bits. We're so good at blinding ourselves to unpleasant facts.'

'Perhaps it's just as well.'

'What?'

'In 1939 we blinded ourselves to the unpleasant fact that we couldn't win a war with Germany – and look what happened.'

'That's what my father-in-law says. He's not as cynical as I. What can we do to assist Scotland Yard?'

Bloggs had been enjoying the exchange, and now it was with reluctance that he turned his attention to work. 'It's about a murder that took place here four years ago.'

'So long!'

'Some new evidence may have come to light.'

'I know about it, of course. The previous owner was killed by a tenant. My husband bought the house from her executor – she had no heirs.'

'I want to trace the other people who were tenants at that time.'

'Yes.' The woman's hostility had gone, now, and her intelligent face showed the effort of recollection. 'When we arrived there were three who had been here before the murder: a retired naval officer, a salesman, and a young boy from Yorkshire. The boy joined the Army – he still writes to us. The salesman was called up, and he died at sea. I know because two of his five wives got in touch with us! And the Commander is still here.'

'Still here!' That was a piece of luck. 'I'd like to see him, please.'

'Surely.' She stood up. 'He's aged a lot. I'll take you to his room.'

They went up the carpeted stairs to the first floor. She said: 'While you're talking to him, I'll look up the last letter from the boy in the Army.' She knocked on the door. It was more than Bloggs's landlady would have done, he thought wryly.

A voice called: 'It's open,' and Bloggs went in.

The Commander sat in a chair by the window with a blanket over his knees. He wore a blazer, a collar and a tie, and spectacles. His hair was thin, his moustache grey, his skin loose and wrinkled over a face that might once have been strong. The room was the home of a man living on memories: there were paintings of sailing ships, a sextant and a telescope, and a photograph of himself as a boy aboard HMS *Winchester*.

'Look at this,' he said without turning around. 'Tell me why that chap isn't in the Navy.'

Bloggs crossed to the window. A horse-drawn baker's van was at the kerb outside the house, the elderly horse dipping into its nosebag while the deliveries were made. That 'chap' was a woman with short blonde hair in trousers. She had a magnificent bust. Bloggs laughed. 'It's a woman in trousers,' he said.

'Bless my soul, so it is!' The Commander turned around. 'Can't tell, these days, you know. Women in trousers!'

Bloggs introduced himself. 'We've reopened the case of a murder committed here in 1940. I believe you lived here at the same time as the main suspect, one Henry Faber.'

'Indeed! What can I do to help?'

'How well do you remember Faber?'

'Perfectly. Tall chap, dark hair, well-spoken, quiet. Rather shabby clothes – if you were the kind who judges by appearances, you might well mistake him. I didn't dislike him – wouldn't have minded getting to know him better, but he didn't want that. I suppose he was about your age.'

Bloggs suppressed a smile: he was used to people assuming he must be older simply because he was a detective.

The Commander added: 'I'm sure he didn't do it, you know. I know a bit about character – you can't command a ship without learning – and if that man was a sex maniac, I'm Hermann Goering.'

Bloggs suddenly connected the blonde in trousers with the mistake about his age, and the conclusion depressed him. He said: 'You know, you should always ask to see a policeman's warrant card.'

The Commander was slightly taken aback. 'All right, then, let's have it.'

Bloggs opened his wallet and folded it to display the picture of Christine. 'Here.'

The Commander studied it for a moment, then said: 'A very good likeness.'

Bloggs sighed. The old man was very nearly blind.

He stood up. 'That's all, for now,' he said. 'Thank you.'

'Any time. Whatever I can do to help. I'm not much value to England these days – you've got to be pretty useless to get invalided out of the Home Guard, you know.'

'Goodbye.' Bloggs went out.

The woman was in the hall downstairs. She handed Bloggs a letter. 'The address is a Forces box number,' she said. 'No doubt you'll be able to find out where he is.'

'You knew the Commander would be no use,' Bloggs said.

'I guessed not. But a visitor makes his day.' She opened the door.

On impulse, Bloggs said: 'Will you have dinner with me?'

A shadow crossed her face. 'My husband is still on the Isle of Man.'

'I'm sorry – I thought—'

'It's all right. I'm flattered.'

'I wanted to convince you we're not the Gestapo.'

'I know you're not. A woman alone just gets bitter.'

Bloggs said: 'I lost my wife in the bombing.'

'Then you know how it makes you hate.'

'Yes,' said Bloggs. 'It makes you hate.' He went down the steps. The door closed behind him. It had started to rain.

It had been raining then. Bloggs was late. He had been going over some new material with Godliman. Now he was hurrying, so that he would have half an hour with Christine before she went out to drive her ambulance. It was dark, and the raid had already started. The things Christine saw at night were so awful she had stopped talking about them.

Bloggs was proud of her, proud. The people she worked with said she was better than two men: she hurtled through blacked-out London, driving like a veteran, taking corners on two wheels, whistling and cracking jokes as the city turned to flame around her. Fearless, they called her. Bloggs knew better: she was terrified, but she would not let it show. He knew because he saw her eyes in the morning, when he got up and she went to bed; when her guard was down and it was over for a few hours. He knew it was not fearlessness but courage, and he was proud.

It was raining harder when he got off the bus. He pulled down his hat and put up his collar. At a kiosk he bought cigarettes for Christine: she had started smoking recently, like a lot of women. The shopkeeper would let him have only five, because of the shortage. He put them in a Woolworth's bakelite cigarette case.

A policeman stopped him and asked for his identity

card: another two minutes wasted. An ambulance passed him, similar to the one Christine drove; a requisitioned fruit lorry, painted grey.

He began to get nervous as he approached home. The explosions were sounding closer, and he could hear the aircraft clearly. The East End was in for another bruising tonight: he would sleep in the Morrison shelter. There was a big one, terribly close, and he quickened his step. He would eat his supper in the shelter, too.

He turned into his own street, saw the ambulances and the fire engines, and broke into a run.

The bomb had landed on his side of the street, around the middle. It must be close to his own home. Jesus in heaven, not us, no—

There had been a direct hit on the roof, and the house was literally flattened. He raced up to the crowd of people, neighbours and firemen and volunteers. 'Is my wife all right? Is she out? IS SHE IN THERE?'

A fireman looked at him with compassion. 'Nobody's come out of there, mate.'

Rescuers were picking over the rubble. Suddenly one of them shouted: 'Over here!' Then he said: 'Bugger me, it's Fearless Bloggs!'

Frederick dashed to where the man stood. Christine was underneath a huge chunk of brickwork. Her face was visible: the eyes were closed.

The rescuer called: 'Lifting gear, boys, sharp's the word.'

Christine moaned and stirred.

Bloggs said: 'She's alive!' He knelt down beside her

and got his hands under the edge of the lump of rubble.

The rescuer said: 'You won't shift that, son.'

The brickwork lifted.

The rescuer said: 'Strewth, you'll kill yourself,' and bent down to help.

When it was two feet off the ground they got their shoulders under it. The weight was off Christine now. A third man joined in, and a fourth. They all straightened up together.

Bloggs said: 'I'll lift her out.'

He crawled under the sloping roof of brick and cradled his wife in his arms.

Someone shouted: 'Fuck me it's slipping!'

Bloggs scurried out from under with Christine held tightly to his chest. As soon as he was clear the rescuers let go of the rubble and jumped away. It fell back to earth with a sickening thud; and when Bloggs realized that *that* had landed on Christine, he knew she was going to die.

He carried her to the ambulance, and it took off immediately. She opened her eyes again once, before she died, and said: 'You'll have to win the war without me, kiddo.'

More than a year later, as he walked downhill from Highgate into the bowl of London, with the rain on his face mingling with the tears again, he thought the woman in the spy's house had said a mighty truth: it makes you hate.

*

In war boys become men, and men become soldiers, and soldiers get promoted; and this is why Billy Parkin, aged 18, who should have been an apprentice in his father's tannery at Scarborough, was believed by the Army to be twenty-one, made up to sergeant, and given the job of leading his advance squad through a hot, dry forest toward a dusty whitewashed Italian village.

The Italians had surrendered but the Germans had not, and it was the Germans who were defending Italy against the combined British-American invasion. The Allies were going to Rome, and for Sergeant Parkin's squad it was a long walk.

They came out of the forest at the top of a hill, and lay flat on their bellies to look down on the village. Parkin got out his binoculars and said: 'What wouldn't I fookin give for a fookin cup of fookin tea.' He had taken to drinking, and cigarettes, and women, and his language was like that of soldiers everywhere. He no longer went to prayer meetings.

Some of these villages were defended and some were not. Parkin recognized that as sound tactics: you didn't know which were undefended, so you approached them all cautiously, and caution cost time.

The downside of the hill held little cover – just a few bushes – and the village began at its foot. There were a few white houses, a river with a wooden bridge, then more houses around a little piazza with a town hall and a clock tower. There was a clear line-of-sight from the tower to the bridge: if the enemy were here at all, he would be in the town hall. A few figures worked in the surrounding fields: God knew who they were. They might be genuine peasants, or any one of a host of factions: fascisti, mafia, corsos, partigianos, communisti . . . or even Germans. You didn't know whose side they would be on until the shooting started.

Parkin said: 'All right, Corporal.'

Corporal Watkins disappeared back into the forest and emerged, five minutes later, on the dirt road into the village, wearing a civilian hat and a filthy old blanket over his uniform. He stumbled, rather than walked, and over his shoulder was a bundle that could have been anything from a bag of onions to a dead rabbit. He reached the near edge of the village and vanished into the darkness of a low cottage.

After a moment he came out. Standing close to the wall, where he could not be seen from the village, he looked toward the soldiers on the hilltop and waved: one, two, three.

The squad scrambled down the hillside into the village.

Watkins said: 'All the houses empty, Sarge.'

Parkin nodded. It meant nothing.

They moved through the houses to the edge of the river. Parkin said: 'Your turn, Smiler. Swim the Mississippi here.'

Private 'Smiler' Hudson put his equipment in a neat pile, took off his helmet, boots and tunic, and slid into the narrow stream. He emerged on the far side, climbed the bank, and disappeared among the houses. This time there was a longer wait: more area to check. Finally Hudson walked back across the wooden bridge. 'If they're 'ere, they're 'iding,' he said.

He retrieved his gear and the squad crossed the bridge into the village. They kept to the sides of the street as they walked toward the piazza. A bird flew off a roof and startled Parkin. Some of the men kicked open a few doors as they passed. There was nobody.

They stood at the edge of the piazza. Parkin nodded at the town hall. 'Did you go inside the place, Smiler?'

'Yes, sir.'

'Looks like the village is ours, then.'

'Yes, sir.'

Parkin stepped forward to cross the piazza, and then the storm broke. There was a crash of rifles, and bullets hailed all around them. Someone screamed. Parkin was running, dodging, ducking. Watkins, in front of him, shouted with pain and clutched his leg: Parkin picked him up bodily. A bullet clanged off his tin hat. He raced for the nearest house, charged the door, and fell inside.

The shooting stopped. Parkin risked a peep outside. One man lay wounded in the piazza: Hudson. Rough justice. Hudson moved, and a solitary shot rang out. Then he was still. Parkin said: 'Fookin bastards.'

Watkins was doing something to his leg, cursing. Parkin said: 'Bullet still in there?'

Watkins yelled: 'Ouch!' then grinned and held something up. 'Not any more.'

Parkin looked outside again. 'They're in the clock tower,' he said. 'You wouldn't think there was room. Can't be many of them.'

'They can shoot, though.'

'Yes. They've got us pinned.' Parkin frowned. 'Got any fireworks?'

'Aye.'

'Let's have a look.' Parkin opened Watkins's pack and took out the dynamite. 'Here. Fix me a ten-second fuse.'

The others were in the house across the street. Parkin called out: 'Hey!'

A face appeared at the door. 'Sarge?'

'I'm going to throw a tomato. When I shout, give me covering fire.'

'Right.'

Parkin lit a cigarette. Watkins handed him a bundle of dynamite. Parkin shouted: 'Fire!' He lit the fuse with the cigarette, stepped into the street, drew back his arm, and threw the bomb at the clock tower. He ducked back into the house, the fire of his own men ringing in his ears. A bullet shaved the woodwork, and he caught a splinter under his chin. He heard the dynamite explode.

Before he could look, someone across the street shouted: 'Bull's-eye!'

Parkin stepped outside. The ancient clock tower had crumbled. A chime sounded incongruously as dust settled over the ruins.

Watkins said: 'You ever play cricket? That was a bloody good shot.'

Parkin walked to the centre of the piazza. There seemed to be enough human spare parts to make about three Germans. He said: 'The tower was pretty unsteady anyway. It would probably have fallen down if we'd all sneezed at it in unison.' He turned away. 'Another day, another dollar.' It was a phrase the Yanks used.

'Sarge? Radio.' It was the R/T operator.

Parkin walked back and took the handset from him. 'Sergeant Parkin.'

'Major Roberts. You're discharged from active duty as of now, Sergeant.'

'Why?' Parkin's first thought was that they had discovered his true age.

'The brass want you in London. Don't ask me why because I don't know. Leave your corporal in charge and make your way back to base. A car will meet you on the road.'

'Yes, sir.'

'The orders also say that on no account are you to risk your life. Got that?'

Parkin grinned, thinking of the clock tower and the dynamite. 'Got it.'

'All right. On your way. You lucky sod.'

Everyone had called him a boy, but they had known him before he joined the Army, Bloggs thought. There was no doubt he was a man now. He walked with confidence and grace, looked about him sharply, and was respectful without being ill-at-ease in the company of superior officers. Bloggs knew that he was lying about his age, not because of his looks or manner, but because of the small signs that appeared whenever age was mentioned – signs which Bloggs, an experienced interrogator, picked up out of habit.

He had been amused when they told him they wanted him to look at pictures. Now, in his third day in

Mr Midwinter's dusty Kensington vault, the amusement had gone and tedium had set in. What irritated him most was the no-smoking rule.

It was even more boring for Bloggs, who had to sit and watch him.

At one point Parkin said: 'You wouldn't call me back from Italy to help in a four-year-old murder case that could wait until after the war. Also, these pictures are mostly of German officers. If this case is something I should keep mum about, you'd better tell me.'

'It's something you should keep mum about,' said Bloggs.

Parkin went back to his pictures.

They were all old, mostly browned and fading. Many were out of books, magazines and newspapers. Sometimes Parkin picked up a magnifying glass Mr Midwinter had thoughtfully provided, to peer more closely at a tiny face in a group; and each time this happened Bloggs's heart raced, only to slow down when Parkin put the glass to one side and picked up the next photograph.

They went to a nearby pub for lunch. The ale was weak, like most wartime beer, but Bloggs still thought it wise to restrict young Parkin to two pints – on his own he would have sunk a gallon.

'Mr Faber was the quiet sort,' Parkin said. 'You wouldn't think he had it in him. Mind you, the landlady wasn't bad looking. And she wanted it. Looking back, I think I could have had her myself if I'd known how to go about it. There, I was, only – eighteen.'

They ate bread and cheese, and Parkin swallowed a

dozen pickled onions. When they went back, they stopped outside the house while Parkin smoked another cigarette.

'Mind you,' he said, 'he was a biggish chap, good-looking, well-spoken. We all thought he was nothing much because his clothes were poor, and he rode a bike, and he'd no money. I suppose it could have been a subtle kind of disguise.' His eyebrows were raised in a question.

'It could have been,' Bloggs said.

That afternoon Parkin found not one but three pictures of Faber.

One of them was only nine years old.

And Mr Midwinter had the negative.

Henrik Rudolph Hans von Muller-Guder ('Let's just call him Faber,' said Godliman with a laugh) was born on 26 May 1900 at a village called Oln in West Prussia. His father's family had been substantial landowners in the area for generations. His father was the second son; so was Henrik. All the second sons were Army officers. His mother, the daughter of a senior official of the Second Reich, was born and raised to be an aristocrat's wife, and that was what she was.

At the age of thirteen he went to the Karlsruhe cadet school in Baden; two years later he was transferred to the more prestigious Gross-Lichterfelde, near Berlin. Both places were hard, disciplinarian institutions where the minds of the pupils were improved with canes and cold baths and bad food. However, Henrik learned to speak English and French and studied history, and passed the Reifeprüfung with the highest mark recorded since the turn of the century. There were only three other points of note in his school career: one bitter winter he rebelled against authority to the extent of sneaking out of the school at night and walking 150 miles to his aunt's house; he broke the arm of his wrestling instructor during a practice bout; and he was flogged for insurbordination.

He served briefly as an ensign-cadet in the neutral zone of Friedrichsfeld, near Wesel, in 1920; did token officer training at the War School at Metz in 1921, and was commissioned Second Lieutenant in 1922.

('What was the phrase you used?' Godliman asked Bloggs. 'The German equivalent of Eton and Sandhurst.')

Over the next few years he did short tours of duty in half a dozen places, in the manner of one who is being groomed for the general staff. He continued to distinguish himself as an athlete, specializing in longer-distance running. He made no close friendships, never married, and refused to join the National Socialist party. His promotion to lieutenant was somewhat delayed by a vague incident involving the pregnancy of the daughter of a lieutenant-colonel in the Defence Ministry, but eventually came about in 1928. His habit of talking to superior officers as if they were equals came to be accepted as pardonable in one who was both a rising young officer and a Prussian aristocrat.

In the late twenties Admiral Wilhelm Canaris became friendly with Henrik's Uncle Otto, his father's elder brother, and spent several holidays at the family estate at Oln. In 1931 Adolf Hitler, not yet Chancellor of Germany, was a guest there.

In 1933 Henrik was promoted Captain, and went to Berlin for unspecified duties. This is the date of the last photograph.

About then, according to published information, he seems to have ceased to exist.

'We can conjecture the rest,' said Percival Godliman. 'The Abwehr trains him in wireless transmission, codes, map-making, burglary, blackmail, sabotage and silent killing. He comes to London in about 1937 with plenty of time to set himself up with a solid cover – perhaps two. His loner instincts are honed sharp by the spying game. When war breaks out, he considers himself licensed to kill.' He looked at the photograph on his desk. 'He's a handsome fellow.'

It was a picture of the running team of the 10th Hanoverian Jaeger Battalion. Faber was in the middle, holding a cup. He had a high forehead, with cropped hair; a long chin; and a small mouth decorated with a narrow moustache.

Godliman passed the picture to Billy Parkin. 'Has he changed much?'

'He looks a lot older, but that might be his . . . bearing.' He studied the photograph thoughtfully. 'His hair is longer now, and the moustache has gone.' He passed the picture back across the desk. 'But it's him, all right.'

'There are two more items in the file, both of them conjectural,' Godliman said. 'First, they say he may have gone into Intelligence in 1933 – that's the routine assumption when an officer's record just stops for no apparent reason. The second item is a rumour, unconfirmed by any reliable source, that he spent some years as a confidential advisor to Stalin, using the name Vasily Zankov.'

'That's incredible,' Bloggs said. 'I don't believe that.'

Godliman shrugged. '*Somebody* persuaded Stalin to execute the cream of his officer corps during the years Hitler rose to power.'

Bloggs shook his head, and changed the subject. 'Where do we go from here?'

Godliman considered. 'Let's have Sergeant Parkin transferred to us. He's the only man we know who has actually seen Die Nadel. Besides, he knows too much for us to risk him in the front line: he could get captured and interrogated, and give the game away. Next, make a first-class print of this photo, and have the hair thickened and the moustache obliterated by a re-touch artist. Then we can distribute copies.'

'Do we want to start a hue and cry?' Bloggs said doubtfully.

'No. For now, let's tread softly. If we put the thing in the newspapers he'll get to hear of it, and vanish. Just send the photo to police forces for the time being.'

'Is that all?'

'I think so. Unless you've got other ideas.'

Parkin cleared his throat. 'Sir?'

'Yes.'

'I really would prefer to go back to my unit. I'm not really the administrative type, if you know what I mean.'

'You're not being offered a choice, Sergeant. At this stage of the conflict, one Italian village more or less makes no difference – but this man Faber could lose us the war. As the Americans say, I'm not kidding.'

CHAPTER ELEVEN

FABER HAD gone fishing.

He was stretched out on the deck of a thirty-foot boat, enjoying the spring sunshine, moving along the canal at about three knots. One lazy hand held the tiller, the other rested on a rod which trailed its line in the water behind the boat.

He hadn't caught a thing all day.

As well as fishing, he was bird-watching – both out of interest (he was actually getting to know quite a lot about the damn birds) and as an excuse for carrying binoculars. Earlier today he had seen a kingfisher's nest.

The people at the boatyard in Norwich had been delighted to rent him the vessel for a fortnight. Business was bad: they had only two boats nowadays, and one of them had not been used since Dunkirk. Faber had haggled over the price, just for the sake of form. In the end they had thrown in a locker of tinned food.

He had bought bait in a shop nearby; the fishing tackle he had brought from London. They had observed that he had nice weather for it, and wished him good fishing. Nobody even asked to see his identity card.

So far, so good.

The difficult bit was to come. For assessing the strength of an army was difficult. First you had to find it.

In peacetime the Army would put up its own road signs to help you. Now they had taken down, not only their own but everyone else's road signs.

The simple solution would be to get in a car and follow the first military vehicle you saw until it stopped. However, Faber had no car; it was nearly impossible for a civilian to hire one; and even if you got one you couldn't get petrol for it. Besides, a civilian driving around the countryside following Army lorries and looking at Army camps was liable to be arrested.

Hence the boat.

Some years ago, before it had become illegal to sell maps, Faber had discovered that Britain had thousands of miles of inland waterways. The original network of rivers had been augmented during the nineteenth century by a spider-web of canals. In some areas there was almost as much waterway as there was road. Norfolk was one of these areas.

The boat had many advantages. On a road, a man was going somewhere: on a river he was just sailing. Sleeping in a parked car was conspicuous: sleeping in a moored boat was natural. The waterway was lonely. And who ever heard of a canal-block?

There were disadvantages. Airfields and barracks had to be near roads, but they were located without reference to access by water. Faber had to explore the countryside at night, leaving his moored boat and tramping the hillsides by moonlight, exhausting forty-mile round trips during which he could easily miss what he was looking for because of the darkness or because he simply did not have enough time to check every square mile of land.

When he returned, a couple of hours after dawn, he would sleep until midday then move on, stopping occasionally to climb a nearby hill and check the outlook. At locks, isolated farmhouses and riverside pubs he would talk to people, hoping for hints of a military presence. So far there had been none.

He was beginning to wonder whether he was in the right area. He had tried to put himself in General Patton's place, thinking: If I were planning to invade France east of the Seine from a base in eastern England, where would I locate that base? Norfolk was obvious: a vast expanse of lonely countryside, plenty of flat ground for aircraft, close to the sea for rapid departure. And the Wash was a natural place to gather a fleet of ships. However, his guesswork might be wrong for reasons unknown to him. Soon he would have to consider a rapid move across country to a new area: perhaps the Fens.

A lock appeared ahead of him, and he trimmed his sails to slow his pace. He glided gently into the lock and bumped softly against the gates. The lock-keeper's house was on the bank. Faber cupped his hands around his mouth and hallooed. Then he settled down to wait. He had learned that lock-keepers were a breed that could not be hurried. Moreover, it was tea-time, and at tea-time they could hardly be moved at all.

A woman came to the door of the house and beckoned. Faber waved back, then jumped on to the bank, tied up the boat, and went into the house. The lock-keeper was in his shirt-sleeves at the kitchen table. He said: 'Not in a hurry, are you?'

Faber smiled. 'Not at all.'

'Pour him a cup of tea, Mavis.'

'No, really,' Faber said politely.

'It's all right, we've just made a pot.'

'Thank you.' Faber sat down. The little kitchen was airy and clean, and his tea came in a pretty china cup.

'Fishing holiday?' the lock-keeper asked.

'Fishing and bird-watching,' Faber answered. 'I'm thinking of tying-up quite soon and spending a couple of days on land.'

'Oh, aye. Well, best keep to the far side of the canal, then. Restricted area this side.'

'Really? I didn't know there was Army land hereabouts.'

'Aye, it starts about half a mile from here. As to whether it's Army, I wouldn't know. They don't tell me.'

'Well, I suppose we don't need to know,' Faber said.

'Aye. Drink up, then, and I'll see you through the lock. Thanks for letting me finish my tea.'

They left the house, and Faber got into the boat and untied it. The gates behind him closed slowly, and then the keeper opened the sluices. The boat gradually sank with the level of the water in the lock, then the keeper opened the front gates.

Faber made sail and moved out. The lock-keeper waved.

He stopped again about four miles away and moored the boat to a stout tree on the bank. While he waited for night to fall he made a meal of tinned sausage-meat, dry biscuits, and bottled water. He dressed in his black clothes, put into a shoulder-bag his binoculars, camera, and copy of *Rare Birds of East Anglia*, pocketed his compass and picked up his torch. He was ready.

He doused the hurricane lamp, locked the cabin door, and jumped on to the bank. Consulting his compass by torchlight, he entered the belt of woodland alongside the canal.

He walked due south from his boat for about half a mile until he hit the fence. It was six feet high, chicken-wire, with coiled barbed wire on top. He backtracked into the wood and climbed a tall tree.

There was scattered cloud above. The moon showed through fitfully. Beyond the fence was open land, a gentle rise. Faber had done this sort of thing before, at Biggin Hill, Aldershot, and a host of military areas all over Southern England. There were two levels of security: a mobile patrol around the perimeter fence, and stationary sentries at the installations.

Both could be evaded by patience and caution.

Faber came down the tree and returned to the fence. He concealed himself behind a bush and settled down to wait.

He had to know when the mobile patrol passed this point. If they did not come until dawn, he would simply return the following night. If he was lucky, they would pass shortly. From the apparent size of the area under guard he guessed they would only make one complete tour of the fence each night.

He was lucky. Soon after ten o'clock he heard the tramp of feet, and three men marched by on the inside of the fence.

Five minutes later Faber crossed the fence.

He walked due south: when all directions are equal, a straight line is best. He did not use his flashlight. He kept close to hedges and trees when he could, and avoided high ground where he might be silhouetted against a sudden flash of moonlight. The sparse countryside was an abstract in black, grey and silver. The ground underfoot was a little soggy, as if there might be marshes nearby. A fox ran across a field in front of him, as fast as a greyhound, as graceful as a cat.

It was 11.30 p.m. when he came across the first indications of military activity – and very odd indications they were.

The moon came out and he saw, perhaps a quarter of a mile ahead, several rows of one-storey buildings laid out with the unmistakable precision of an Army barracks. He dropped to the ground immediately, but he was already doubting the reality of what he apparently saw; for there were no lights and no noise.

He lay still for ten minutes, to give explanations a chance to emerge, but nothing happened except that a badger lumbered into view, saw him, and made off.

Faber crawled forward.

As he got closer he realized that the barracks were

not just unoccupied, but unfinished. Most of them were little more than a roof supported by cornerposts. Some had one wall.

A sudden sound stopped him: a man's laugh. He lay still and watched. A match flared briefly and died, leaving two glowing red spots in one of the unfinished huts: guards.

Faber touched the stiletto in his sleeve, then began to crawl again, making for the side of the camp away from the sentries.

The half-built huts had no floors and no foundations. There were no construction vehicles around, no wheelbarrows, concrete mixers, shovels or piles of bricks. A mud track led away from the camp across the fields, but spring grass was growing in the ruts: it had not been used much lately.

It was as if someone had decided to billet ten thousand men here, then changed his mind a few weeks after building started.

Yet there was something about the place that did not quite fit that explanation.

Faber walked around softly, alert lest the sentries should take it into their heads to make a patrol. There was a group of military vehicles in the centre of the camp. They were old and rusting, and had been degutted – none had an engine or any interior components. But if one was going to cannibalize obsolete vehicles, why not take the shells for scrap?

Those huts which did have a wall were on the outermost rows, and their walls faced out. It was like a movie set, not a building site.

Faber decided he had learned all he could from this place. He walked to the east edge of the camp, then dropped to his hands and knees and crawled away until he was out of sight behind a hedge. Half a mile farther on, near the top of a rise, he looked back. Now it looked exactly like a barracks again.

The glimmer of an idea formed in his mind. He gave it time.

The land was still relatively flat, relieved only by gentle folds. There were patches of woodland and marshy scrub which Faber took advantage of. Once he had to detour around a lake, its surface a silver mirror under the moon. He heard the hoot of an owl, and looked in that direction to see a tumbledown barn in the distance.

Five miles on, he saw the airfield.

There were more planes here than he thought were possessed by the entire Royal Air Force. There were Pathfinders to drop flares, Lancasters and American B-17S for softening-up bombing, Hurricanes and Spitfires and Mosquitoes for reconnaissance and strafing: enough planes for an invasion.

Without exception their undercarriages had sunk into the soft earth, and they were up to their bellies in mud.

Once again there were no lights and no noise.

Faber followed the same procedure, crawling flat toward the planes until he located the guards. In the middle of the airfield was a small tent. The faint glow of a lamp shone through the canvas. Two men, perhaps three.

As Faber approached the planes they seemed to become flatter, as if they had all been squashed.

He reached the nearest and touched it in amazement. It was a piece of half-inch plywood, cut out in the outline of a Spitfire, painted with camouflage, and roped to the ground.

Every other plane was the same.

There were more than a thousand of them.

Faber got to his feet, watching the tent from the corner of his eye, ready to drop to the ground at the slightest sign of movement. He walked all around the phoney airfield, looking at the phoney fighters and bombers, connecting them with the movie-set barracks, reeling at the implications of what he had found.

He knew that if he continued to explore he would find more airfields like this, more half-built barracks. If he went to the Wash he would find a fleet of plywood destroyers and troop ships.

It was a vast, meticulous, costly, outrageous trick.

Of course, it could not possibly fool an onlooker for very long. But it was not designed to deceive observers on the ground.

It was meant to be seen from the air.

Even a low-flying reconnaissance plane equipped with the latest cameras and fast film would come back with pictures which indisputably showed an enormous concentration of men and machines.

No wonder the general staff were anticipating an invasion east of the Seine.

There would be other elements to the deception, he guessed. The British would refer to FUSAG in signals, using codes they knew to be broken. There would be phoney espionage reports channelled through the Spanish diplomatic bag to Hamburg. The possibilities were endless.

The British had had four years to arm themselves for this invasion. Most of the German army was fighting Russia. Once the Allies got a toehold on French soil, they would be unstoppable. The Germans' only chance was to catch them on the beaches and annihilate them as they came off the troop ships.

If they were waiting in the wrong place, they would lose that one chance.

The whole strategy was immediately clear. It was simple, and it was devastating.

Faber had to tell Hamburg.

He wondered whether they would believe him.

War strategy was rarely altered on the word of one man. His own standing was particularly high, but was it that high?

He needed to get proof, and then take it to Berlin.

He needed photographs.

He would take pictures of this gigantic dummy army, then he would go to Scotland and meet the U-boat, and he would deliver the pictures personally to the Führer. He could do no more.

For photography he needed light. He would have to wait until dawn. There had been a ruined barn a little way back: he could spend the rest of the night there.

He checked his compass and set off. The barn was farther than he thought, and the walk took him an hour. It was an old wooden building with holes in the roof. The rats had long ago deserted it for lack of food, but there were bats in the hayloft.

Faber lay down on some planks, but he could not sleep for the knowledge that he was now personally capable of altering the course of the greatest war in history.

Dawn was due at 05.21. At 04.20 Faber left the barn.

Although he had not slept, the two hours of immobility had rested his body and calmed his mind, and he was now in fine spirits. The cloud was clearing with a west wind, so although the moon had set there was starlight.

His timing was good. The sky was growing perceptibly brighter as he came in sight of the 'airfield'.

The sentries were still in their tent. With luck, they would be sleeping: Faber knew from his own experience of such duties that it was hardest to stay awake during the last few hours.

And if they did come out, he would just have to kill them.

He selected his position and loaded the Leica with a 36-frame roll of 35mm fast Agfa film. He hoped the film's light-sensitive chemicals had not spoiled, for it had been stored in his suitcase since before the war: you couldn't buy film in Britain nowadays. It should be all right, for he had kept it in a light-proof bag away from any heat.

When the red rim of the sun edged over the horizon he began shooting. He took a series of shots from different vantage points and various distances, finishing with a close-up of one dummy plane: the pictures would show both the illusion and the reality.

As he took the last he saw movement from the corner of his eye. He dropped flat and crawled under a plywood Mosquito. A soldier emerged from the tent, walked a few paces, and urinated on the ground. The man stretched and yawned, then lit a cigarette. He looked around the airfield, shivered, and returned to the tent.

Faber got up and ran.

A quarter of a mile away he looked back. The airfield was out of sight. He headed west, toward the barracks.

This would be more than an ordinary espionage coup. Hitler had had a life of being the only one in step. The man who brought the proof that, yet again, the Führer was right and all the experts were wrong, could look for more than a pat on the back. Faber knew that already Hitler rated him the Abwehr's best agent: this triumph would probably get him Canaris's job.

If he made it.

He increased his pace, jogging twenty yards, walking the next twenty, and jogging again, so that he reached the barracks by 06.30. It was bright daylight now, and he could not approach close, because these sentries were not in a tent, but in one of the wall-less huts, with a clear view all around them. He lay down by the hedge and took his pictures from a distance. Ordinary prints would just show a barracks, but big enlargements ought to reveal the details of the deception.

When he headed back toward the boat he had exposed thirty frames. Again he hurried, for he was now terribly conspicuous, a black-clad man carrying a canvas bag of equipment, jogging across the open fields of a restricted area.

He reached the fence an hour later, having seen nothing but wild geese. As he climbed over the wire, he felt a great release of tension. Inside the fence the balance of suspicion had been against him; outside it was in his favour. He could revert to his bird-watching, fishing, sailing role. The period of greatest risk was over.

He strolled through the belt of woodland, catching his breath and letting the strain of the night's work seep away. He would sail a few miles on, he decided, before mooring again to catch a few hours' sleep.

He reached the canal. It was over. The boat looked pretty in the morning sunshine. As soon as he was under way he would make some tea, then—

A man in uniform stepped out of the cabin of the boat and said: 'Well, well. And who might you be?'

Faber stood stock still, letting the icy calm and the old instincts come into play. The intruder wore the uniform of a captain in the Home Guard. He had some kind of handgun in a holster with a buttoned flap. He was tall and rangy, but he looked to be in his late fifties. White hair showed under his cap. He made no move to draw his gun. Faber took all this in as he said: 'You are on my boat, so I think it is I who should ask who you are.'

'Captain Stephen Langham, Home Guard.'

'James Baker.' Faber stayed on the bank. A captain did not patrol alone.

'And what are you doing?'

'I'm on holiday.'

'Where have you been?'

'Bird-watching.'

'Since before dawn? Cover him, Watson.'

A youngish man in denim uniform appeared on Faber's left, carrying a shotgun. Faber looked around. There was another man to his right and a fourth behind him.

The captain called: 'Which direction did he come from, Corporal?'

The reply came from the top of an oak tree. 'From the restricted area, sir.'

Faber was calculating odds. Four to one – until the corporal came down from the tree. They had only two guns: the shotgun and the captain's pistol. And they were amateurs. The boat would help, too.

He said: 'Restricted area? All I saw was a bit of fence. Look, do you mind pointing that blunderbuss away? It might go off.'

The captain said: 'Nobody goes bird-watching in the dark.'

'If you set up your hide under cover of darkness, you're concealed by the time the birds wake up. It's the accepted way to do it. Now look, the Home Guard is jolly patriotic and keen and all that, but let's not take it too far, what? Don't you just have to check my papers and file a report?'

The captain was looking a shade doubtful. 'What's in that canvas bag?'

'Binoculars, a camera, and a reference book.' Faber's hands went to the bag.

'No, you don't,' the captain said. 'Look inside it, Watson.'

There it was: the amateur's error.

Watson said: 'Hands up.'

Faber raised his hands above his head, his right hand close to the left sleeve of his jacket. Faber choreographed the next few seconds: there must be no gunfire.

Watson came up on Faber's left side, pointing the shotgun at him, and opened the flap of Faber's canvas bag. Faber drew the stiletto from his sleeve, moved inside Watson's guard, and plunged the knife downward into Watson's neck up to the hilt. Faber's other hand twisted the shotgun out of the young man's grasp.

The other two soldiers on the bank moved toward him, and the corporal began to crash down through the branches of the oak.

Faber tugged the stiletto out of Watson's neck as the man collapsed to the ground. The captain was fumbling at the flap of his holster. Faber leaped into the well of the boat. It rocked, sending the captain staggering. Faber struck at him with the knife, but the man was too far away for an accurate thrust. The point caught in the lapel of his uniform jacket, then jerked up, slashing his chin. His hand came away from the holster to clutch the wound.

Faber whipped around to face the bank. One of the soldiers jumped. Faber stepped forward and held his right arm out rigidly. The leaping soldier impaled himself on the eight-inch needle.

The impact knocked Faber off his feet, and he lost his grip on the stiletto. The soldier fell on top of the weapon. Faber got to his knees: there was no time to retrieve the stiletto, for the captain was opening his holster. Faber jumped at him, his hands going for the officer's face. The gun came out. Faber's thumbs gouged at the captain's eyes, and he screamed in pain and tried to push Faber's arms aside.

There was a thud as the fourth guardsman landed in the well of the boat. Faber turned from the captain, who would now be unable to see to fire his pistol even if he could get the safety off. The fourth man held a policeman's truncheon. He brought it down hard. Faber shifted to the right, so that the blow missed his head and caught his left shoulder. His left arm momentarily became paralysed. He chopped the man's neck with the side of his right hand, a powerful, accurate blow. Amazingly, the man survived it, and brought his truncheon up for a second swipe. Faber closed in. The feeling returned to his left arm, and it began to hurt mightily. He took the soldier's face in both his hands, pushed, twisted, and pushed again. There was a sharp crack as the man's neck broke. At the same instant the truncheon landed again, this time on Faber's head. He reeled away, dazed.

The captain bumped into him, still staggering. Faber pushed him. His cap went flying as he stumbled backward over the gunwale and fell into the canal with a huge splash.

The corporal jumped the last six feet from the oak tree on to the ground. Faber retrieved his stiletto from the impaled guard and leaped to the bank. Watson was still alive, but it would not be for long: blood was pumping out of the wound in his neck.

Faber and the corporal faced each other. The corporal had a gun.

He was utterly terrified. In the few seconds it had taken him to climb down the oak tree, this stranger had killed three of his mates and thrown the fourth into the canal. Horror shone from his eyes like torchlight.

Faber looked at the gun. It was *old* – it looked like a museum piece. If the corporal had any confidence in it, he would have fired it already.

The corporal took a step forward, and Faber noticed that he favoured his right leg – perhaps he had hurt it coming out of the tree. Faber stepped sideways, forcing the corporal to put his weight on the weak leg as he swung to keep his gun on target. Faber got the toe of his shoe under a stone and kicked upward. The corporal's eyes flicked to the stone, and Faber moved.

The corporal pulled the trigger, and nothing happened. The old gun had jammed. Even if it had fired, he would have missed Faber: his eyes were on the stone, he stumbled on the weak leg, and Faber had moved.

Faber killed him with the neck stab.

Only the captain was left.

Faber looked, to see the man clambering out of the water on the far bank. He found a stone and threw it.

It hit the captain's head, but the man heaved himself on to dry land and began to run.

Faber ran to the bank, dived in, swam a few strokes, and came up on the far side. The captain was a hundred yards away and running; but he was old. Faber gave chase. He gained steadily until he could hear the man's agonized, ragged breathing. The captain slowed, then collapsed into a bush.

Faber came up to him and turned him over.

The captain said: 'You're a . . . devil.'

'You saw my face,' Faber said, and killed him.

CHAPTER TWELVE

T HE JU-52 trimotor transport plane with swastikas on the wings bumped to a halt on the rain-
wet runway at Rastenburg in the East Prussian forest. A
small man with big features – a large nose, a wide
mouth, big ears – disembarked and walked quickly
across the tarmac to a waiting Mercedes car.

As the car drove through the gloomy, damp forest,
Field Marshal Erwin Rommel took off his cap and
rubbed a nervous hand along his receding hairline. In
a few weeks' time, he knew, another man would travel
this route with a bomb in his briefcase – a bomb
destined for the Führer himself. Meanwhile the fight
must go on, so that the new leader of Germany – who
might even be Rommel himself – could negotiate with
the Allies from a strong position.

At the end of a ten-mile drive the car arrived at the
Wolfsschanze, the Wolves' Lair, headquarters now for
Hitler and the increasingly tight, neurotic circle of
generals who surrounded him.

There was a steady drizzle, and raindrops dripped
from the tall conifers in the compound. At the gate to
Hitler's personal quarters, Rommel put on his cap and
got out of the car. Oberführer Rattenhuber, the chief

of the SS bodyguard, wordlessly held out his hand to receive Rommel's pistol.

The conference was to be held in the underground bunker, a cold, damp, airless shelter lined with concrete. Rommel went down the steps and entered. There were a dozen or so there already, waiting for the noon meeting: Himmler, Goering, von Ribbentrop, Keitel. Rommel nodded greetings and sat on a hard chair to wait.

They all stood when Hitler entered. He wore a grey tunic and black trousers, and he was becoming more and more stooped, Rommel observed. He walked straight to the far end of the bunker, where a large wall map of north-western Europe was tacked to the concrete. He looked tired and irritable. He spoke without preamble.

'There will be an Allied invasion of Europe. It will come this year. It will be launched from Britain, with English and American troops. They will land in France. We will destroy them at the high-water mark. On this there is no room for discussion.'

He looked around, as if daring his staff to contradict him. There was silence. Rommel shivered: the bunker was as cold as death.

'The question is: where will they land? Von Roenne – your report.'

Colonel Alexis von Roenne, who had taken over, effectively, from Canaris, got to his feet. A mere captain at the outbreak of war, he had distinguished himself with a superb report on the weaknesses of the French army – a report which had been called a decisive factor in the German victory. He had become chief of the army intelligence bureau in 1942, and that bureau had absorbed the Abwehr on the fall of Canaris. Rommel had heard that he was proud and outspoken, but able.

Roenne said: 'Our information is extensive, but by no means complete. The Allies' codename for the invasion is Overlord. Troop concentrations in Britain are as follows.' He picked up a pointer and crossed the room to the wall map. 'First: along the south coast. Second: here in the district known as East Anglia. Third: in Scotland. The East Anglian concentration is *by far* the greatest. We conclude that the invasion will be three-pronged. First: a diversionary attack on Normandy. Second: the main thrust, across the Straits of Dover to the Calais coast. Third: a flanking invasion from Scotland across the North Sea to Norway. All intelligence sources support this prognosis.' He sat down.

Hitler said: 'Comments?'

Rommel, who was Commander of Army Group B, which controlled the north coast of France, said: 'I can report one confirming sign: the Pas de Calais has received by far the greatest tonnage of bombs.'

Goering said: 'What intelligence sources support your prognosis, von Roenne?'

Roenne stood up again. 'There are three: air reconnaissance, monitoring of enemy wireless signals, and the reports of agents.' He sat down.

Hitler crossed his hands protectively in front of his genitals, a nervous habit which was a sign that he was about to make a speech. 'I shall now tell you,' he began, 'how I would be thinking if I were Winston Churchill. Two choices confront me: east of the Seine, or west of the Seine. East has one advantage: it is nearer. But in modern warfare there are only two distances – *within* fighter range and *outside* fighter range. *Both* of these choices are within fighter range. Therefore distance is not a consideration.

'West has a great port – Cherbourg – but east has none. And most important – east is more heavily fortified than west. The enemy too has air reconnaissance.

'So, I would choose west. And what would I do then? I would try to make the Germans think the opposite! I would send two bombers to the Pas de Calais for every one to Normandy. I would try to knock out every bridge over the Seine. I would put out misleading wireless signals, send false intelligence reports, dispose my troops in a misleading fashion. I would deceive fools like Rommel and von Roenne. I would hope to deceive the Führer himself!'

Goering spoke first after a lengthy silence. 'My Führer, I believe you flatter Churchill by crediting him with ingenuity equal to your own.'

There was a noticeable easing of tension in the uncomfortable bunker. Goering had said exactly the right thing, managing to voice his disagreement in the form of a compliment. The others followed him, each stating the case a little more strongly: the Allies would choose the shorter sea crossing for speed; the closer coast would allow the covering fighter aircraft to refuel and return in shorter time; the south-east was a better launch pad, with more estuaries and harbours; it was unlikely that all the intelligence reports would be unanimously wrong.

Hitler listened for half an hour, then held up his hand for silence. He picked up a yellowing sheaf of papers from the table and waved them. 'In 1941,' he said, 'I issued my directive *Construction of Coastal Defences*, in which I forecast that the decisive landing of the Allies would come at the protruding parts of Normandy and Brittany, where the excellent harbours would make ideal beachheads. That was what my intuition told me then, and that is what it tells me now!' A fleck of foam appeared on the Führer's lower lip.

Von Roenne spoke up. (He has more courage than I, Rommel thought.) 'My Führer, our investigations continue, quite naturally, and there is one particular line of inquiry which you should know about. I have in recent weeks sent an emissary to England to contact the agent known as Die Nadel.'

Hitler's eyes gleamed. 'Ah! I know the man. Carry on.'

'Die Nadel's orders are to assess the strength of the First United States Army Group under General Patton in East Anglia. If he finds that this has been exaggerated, we must surely reconsider our prognosis. If, however, he reports that the army is as strong as we presently believe, there can be little doubt that Calais is the target.'

Goering looked at von Roenne. 'Who is this Nadel?'

Hitler answered the question. 'The only decent agent Canaris ever recruited – because he recruited

him at my behest,' he said. 'I know his family – a pillar
of the Reich. Strong, loyal, upright Germans. And Die
Nadel – a brilliant man, brilliant! I see all his reports.
He has been in London since before the English started
the war. Earlier than that, in Russia—'

Von Roenne interrupted: 'My Führer—'

Hitler glared at him, but he seemed to realize that
the spy chief had been right to stop him. 'Well?'

Von Roenne said tentatively: 'Then you will accept
Die Nadel's report?'

Hitler nodded. 'That man will discover the truth.'

Part Three

CHAPTER THIRTEEN

F ABER LEANED against a tree, shivering, and threw up.

Then he considered whether he should bury the five dead men.

It would take between thirty and sixty minutes, he estimated, depending on how well he concealed the bodies. During that time he might be caught.

He had to weigh that risk against the precious hours he might gain by delaying the discovery of the deaths. The five men would be missed very soon: there would be a search under way by around nine o'clock. Assuming they were on a regular patrol, their route would be known. The searchers' first move would be to send a runner to cover the route. If the bodies were left as they were, he would see them and raise the alarm. Otherwise, he would report back and a full-scale search would be mounted, with bloodhounds and policemen beating the bushes. It might take them all day to discover the corpses. By that time Faber could be in London. It was important for him to be out of the area before they knew they were looking for a murderer. He decided to risk the additional hour.

He swam back across the canal with the elderly

captain across his shoulder. He dumped him uncer-
emoniously behind a bush. He retrieved the two bodies
from the well of the boat and piled them on top of the
captain. Then he added Watson and the corporal to
the heap.

He had no spade, and he needed a big grave. He
found a patch of loose earth a few yards into the wood.
The ground there was slightly hollowed, to give him an
advantage. He got a saucepan from the boat's tiny
galley and began to dig.

For a couple of feet there was just leaf-mould, and
the going was easy. Then he got down to clay, and
digging became extremely difficult. In half an hour he
had added only another eighteen inches of depth to
the hole. It would have to do.

He carried the bodies to the hole one by one and
threw them in. Then he took off his muddy, bloodstained clothes and dropped them on top. He covered
the grave with loose earth and a layer of foliage ripped
from nearby bushes and trees. It should be good
enough to pass that first, superficial inspection.

He kicked earth over the patch of ground near the
bank where the life-blood of Watson had poured out.
There was blood in the boat, too, where the impaled
soldier had lain. Faber found a rag and swabbed-down
the deck.

Then he put on clean clothes, made sail, and moved
off.

He did not fish or watch birds: this was no time for
pleasant embellishments to his cover. Instead he piled-
on the sail, putting as much distance as possible

between himself and the grave. He had to get off the water and into some faster transport as soon as possible. He reflected, as he sailed, on the relative merits of catching a train or stealing a car. A car was faster, if one could be found to steal; but the search for it might start quite soon, regardless of whether the theft was connected with the missing Home Guard patrol. Finding a railway station might take a long time, but it seemed safer: if he were careful he could escape suspicion for most of the day.

He wondered what to do about the boat. Ideally he would scuttle it, but he might be seen doing so. If he left it in a harbour somewhere, or simply moored at the canalside, the police would connect it with the murders that much sooner; and that would tell them in which direction he was moving. He postponed the decision.

Unfortunately, he was not sure where he was. His map of England's waterways gave every bridge, harbour and lock; but it did not show railway lines. He calculated he was within an hour or two's walk of half a dozen villages, but a village did not necessarily mean a station.

In the end luck solved two problems at once: the canal went under a railway bridge.

He took his compass, the film from the camera, his wallet and his stiletto. All his other possessions would go down with the boat.

The towpath on both sides was shaded with trees, and there were no roads nearby. He furled the sails, dismantled the base of the mast, and laid the pole on the deck. Then he removed the bung-hole stopper from the keel and stepped on to the bank, holding the rope.

Gradually filling with water, the boat drifted under the bridge. Faber hauled on the rope to hold the vessel in position directly under the brick arch as it sank. The after-deck went under first, the prow followed, and finally the water of the canal closed over the roof of the cabin. There were a few bubbles, then nothing. The outline of the boat was hidden from a casual glance by the shadow of the bridge. Faber threw the rope in.

The railway line ran north-east to south-west. Faber climbed the embankment and walked south-west, which was the direction in which London lay. It was a two-line track, probably a rural branch line. There would be few trains, but they would stop at all stations.

The sun grew stronger as he walked, and the exertion made him hot. When he had buried his blood-stained black clothes he had put on a double-breasted blazer and heavy flannel trousers. Now he took off the blazer and slung it over his shoulder.

After forty minutes he heard a distant chuff-chuff-chuff, and hid in a bush beside the line. An old steam engine went slowly by, heading north-west, puffing great clouds of smoke and hauling a train of coal trucks. If one came by in the opposite direction, he could jump it. Should he? It would save him a long walk. On the other hand, he would get conspicuously dirty, and he might have trouble disembarking without being seen. No, it was safer to walk.

The line ran straight as an arrow across the flat countryside. Faber passed a farmer, ploughing a field with a tractor. There was no way to avoid being seen.

The farmer waved to him without stopping in his work. He was too far away to get a good sight of Faber's face.

He had walked about ten miles when he saw a station ahead. It was half a mile away, and all he could see was the rise of the platforms and a cluster of signals. He left the line and cut across the fields, keeping close to borders of trees, until he met a road.

Within a few minutes he entered the village. There was nothing to tell him its name. Now that the threat of invasion was a memory, signposts and place-names were being re-erected, but this village had not got around to it.

There was a Post Office, a Corn Store, and a pub called The Bull. A woman with a pram gave him a friendly 'Good morning!' as he passed the War Memorial. The little station basked sleepily in the spring sunshine. Faber went in.

A timetable was pasted to a notice-board. Faber stood in front of it. From behind the little ticket window a voice said: 'I shouldn't take any notice of that, if I were you. It's the biggest work of fiction since *The Forsyte Saga*.'

Faber had known the timetable would be out-of-date, but he had needed to establish whether the trains went to London. They did. He said: 'Any idea what time the next train leaves for Liverpool Street?'

The clerk laughed sarcastically. 'Some time today, if you're lucky.'

'I'll buy a ticket anyway. Single, please.'

'Five-and-fourpence. They say the Italian trains run on time,' the clerk said.

'Not any more,' Faber remarked. 'Anyway, I'd rather have bad trains and our politics.'

The man shot him a nervous look. 'You're right, of course. Do you want to wait in The Bull? You'll hear the train – or, if not, I'll send for you.'

Faber did not want more people to see his face. 'No, thanks, I'd only spend money.' He took his ticket and went on to the platform.

The clerk followed him a few minutes later, and sat on the bench beside him in the sunshine. He said: 'You in a hurry?'

Faber shook his head. 'I've written today off. I got up late, I quarrelled with the boss, and the lorry that gave me a lift broke down.'

'One of those days. Ah, well.' The clerk looked at his watch. 'She went up on time this morning, and what goes up must come down, they say. You might be lucky.' He went back into his office.

Faber was lucky. The train came twenty minutes later. It was crowded with farmers, families, business-men and soldiers. Faber found a space on the floor close to a window. As the train lumbered away, he picked up a discarded two-day-old newspaper, bor-rowed a pencil, and started to do the crossword. He was proud of his ability to do crosswords in English: it was the acid test of fluency in a foreign language. After a while the motion of the train lulled him into a shallow sleep, and he dreamed.

*

It was a familiar dream, the dream of his arrival in London.

He had crossed from France, carrying a Belgian passport which said he was Jan van Gelder, a representative for Philips (which would explain his suitcase radio if the Customs opened it). His English then was fluent but not colloquial. The Customs had not bothered him: he was an ally. He had caught the train to London. In those days there had been plenty of empty seats in the carriages, and you could get a meal. Faber had dined on roast beef and Yorkshire pudding. It amused him. He had talked with a history student from Cardiff about the European political situation. The dream was like the reality until the train stopped at Waterloo. Then it turned into a nightmare.

The trouble started at the ticket barrier. Like all dreams it had its own weird illogicality. The document they queried was not his forged passport but his perfectly legitimate railway ticket. The collector said: 'This is an Abwehr ticket.'

'No, it is not,' said Faber, speaking with a ludicrously thick German accent. What had happened to his dainty English consonants? They would not come. 'I have it in Dover gekauft.' Damn, that did it.

But the ticket collector, who had turned into a London policeman complete with helmet, seemed to ignore the sudden lapse into German. He smiled politely and said: 'I'd better just check your Klamotte, sir.'

The station was crowded with people. Faber thought that if he could get into the crowd he might escape. He dropped the suitcase radio and fled, pushing his way through the crowd. Suddenly he realized he had left his trousers on the train, and there were swastikas on his socks. He would have to buy trousers at the very first shop, before people noticed the trouserless running man with Nazi hose – then someone in the crowd said: 'I've seen your face before,' and tripped him, and he fell with a bump and landed on the floor of the railway carriage where he had gone to sleep.

He blinked, yawned, and looked around him. He had a headache. For a moment he was filled with relief that it was all a dream, then he was amused by the ridiculousness of the symbolism – swastika socks, for God's sake!

A man in overalls beside him said: 'You had a good sleep.'

Faber looked up sharply. He was always afraid of talking in his sleep and giving himself away. He said: 'I had an unpleasant dream.' The man made no comment.

It was getting dark. He *had* slept for a long time. The carriage light came on suddenly, a single blue bulb, and someone drew the blinds. People's faces turned into pale, featureless ovals. The workman became talkative again. 'You missed the excitement,' he told Faber.

Faber frowned. 'What happened?' It was impossible he should have slept through some kind of police check.

'One of them Yank trains passed us. It was going about ten miles an hour, nigger driving it, ringing its bell, with a bloody great cow-catcher on the front! Talk about the Wild West.'

Faber smiled and thought back to the dream. In fact his arrival in London had been without incident. He had checked into an hotel at first, still using his Belgian cover. Within a week he had visited several country churchyards, taken the names of men his age from the gravestones, and applied for three duplicate birth certificates. Then he took lodgings and found humble work, using forged references from a non-existent Manchester firm. He had even got on to the electoral register in Highgate before the war. He voted Conservative. When rationing came in, the ration books were issued via householders to every person who had slept in the house on a particular night. Faber contrived to spend part of that night in each of three different houses, and so obtained papers for each of his personae. He burned the Belgian passport – in the unlikely event he should need a passport, he could get three British ones.

The train stopped, and from the noise outside the passengers guessed they had arrived. When Faber got out he realized how hungry and thirsty he was. His last meal had been sausage-meat, dry biscuits and bottled water, the day before. He went through the ticket barrier and found the station buffet. It was full of people, mostly soldiers, sleeping or trying to sleep at the tables. Faber asked for a cheese sandwich and a cup of tea.

'The food is reserved for servicemen,' said the woman behind the counter.

'Just the tea, then.'

'Got a cup?'

Faber was surprised. 'No, I haven't.'

'Neither have we, chum.'

Faber left in disgust. He contemplated going into the Great Eastern Hotel for dinner, but that would take time. He found a pub and drank two pints of weak beer, then bought a bag of chips at a fish-and-chip shop and ate them from the newspaper wrapping, standing on the pavement. They made him feel surprisingly full.

Now he had to find a chemist's shop and break in.

He wanted to develop his film, to make sure the pictures came out. He was not going to risk returning to Germany with a roll of spoiled, useless film. If the pictures were no good he would have to steal more film and go back. The thought was unbearable.

It would have to be a small independent shop, not a branch of a chain which would process film centrally. It must be in an area where the local people could afford cameras (or could have afforded them before the war). The part of East London in which Liverpool Street Station stood was no good. He decided to head toward Bloomsbury.

The moonlit streets were quiet. There had been no sirens so far tonight. Two Military Policemen stopped him in Chancery Lane and asked for his identity card. Faber pretended to be slightly drunk, and the MPs did not ask what he was doing out of doors.

He found the shop he was looking for at the north end of Southampton Row. There was a Kodak sign in the window. Surprisingly, the shop was open. He went in.

A stooped, irritable man with thinning hair and glasses stood behind the counter, wearing a white coat. He said: 'We're only open for doctors' prescriptions.'

'That's all right. I just want to ask whether you develop photographs.'

'Yes, if you come back tomorrow—'

'Do you do them on the premises?' Faber asked. 'I need them quickly, you see.'

'Yes, if you come back tomorrow—'

'Could I have the prints the same day? My brother's on leave, and he wants to take some back—'

'Twenty-four hours is the best we can do. Come back tomorrow.'

'Thank you, I will,' Faber lied. On his way out he noticed that the shop was due to close in ten minutes. He crossed the road and stood in the shadows, waiting.

Promptly at nine o'clock the pharmacist came out, locking the shop behind him, and walked off down the road. Faber went in the opposite direction and turned two corners.

There seemed to be no access to the back of the shop. That was something of a blow: Faber did not want to break in the front way, in case the unlocked door was noticed by a patrolling policeman while he was in there. He walked along the parallel street, looking for a way through. Apparently there was none. Yet there had to be a well of some kind at the back, for the two streets were too far apart for the buildings to be joined back-to-back.

Finally he came across a large old house with a nameplate marking it as a Hall of Residence for a nearby college. The front door was unlocked. Faber went in and walked quickly through to a communal kitchen. A lone girl sat at a table, drinking coffee and reading a book. Faber muttered: 'College blackout check.' She nodded and returned to her text. Faber went out of the back door.

He crossed a yard, bumping into a cluster of garbage cans on the way, and found a door to a lane. In seconds he was at the rear of the chemist's shop. This entrance was obviously never used. He clambered over some tyres and a discarded mattress, and threw his shoulder at the door. The rotten wood gave easily, and Faber was inside.

He found the darkroom and shut himself in. The light switch operated a dim red lamp in the ceiling. The place was quite well-equipped, with neatly labelled bottles of developing fluid, an enlarger, and even a dryer for prints.

Faber worked quickly but carefully, getting the temperature of the tanks exactly right, agitating the fluids to develop the film evenly, timing the processes by the hands of a large electric clock on the wall.

The negatives were perfect.

He let them dry, then fed them through the enlarger and made one complete set of ten-by-eight prints. He felt a sense of elation as he saw the images gradually appear in the bath of developer – God, he had done a good job!

There was now a major decision to be made.

The problem had been in his mind all day, and now that the pictures had come out he was forced to confront it.

What if he did not make it home?

The journey ahead of him was, to say the least, hazardous. He was confident of his own ability to make the rendezvous in spite of travel restrictions and coastal security; but he could not guarantee that the U-boat would be there; or that it would get back across the North Sea. Indeed, he might walk out of here and get run over by a bus.

The possibility that, having discovered the greatest secret of the war, he might die and his secret die with him, was too awful to contemplate.

He had to have a fall-back stratagem; a second method of ensuring that the evidence of the Allied deception reached the Abwehr. And that meant writing to Hamburg.

There was, of course, no postal service between England and Germany. Mail had to go via a neutral country. All such mail was sure to be censored. He could write in code, but there was no point: he had to send the pictures, for it was the evidence that counted.

There was a route, but it was an old one. At the Portuguese Embassy in London there was an official, sympathetic to Germany for political reasons and because he was well bribed, who would pass messages via the diplomatic bag to the German Embassy in Lisbon. The route had been opened early in 1939, and Faber had never used it except for one routine test communication Canaris had asked for.

It would have to do.

Faber felt irrationally angry. He *hated* to place his faith in others. This route might no longer be open, or it might be insecure; in which case the British could discover that he had found out their secret.

It was a fundamental rule of espionage that the opposition must not know which of their secrets you have found out; for if they do, the value of your discoveries is nullified. However, in this case that was not so; for what could the British do with their knowledge? They still had the problem of conquering France.

Faber's mind was clear. The balance of argument indisputably favoured entrusting his secret to the Portuguese Embassy contact.

Against all his instincts, he sat down to write a letter.

CHAPTER FOURTEEN

FREDERICK BLOGGS had spent an unpleasant afternoon in the countryside.

When five worried wives had contacted their local police station to say their husbands had not come home, a rural constable had exercised his limited powers of deduction and concluded that a whole patrol of the Home Guard had gone missing. He was fairly sure they had simply got lost – they were all deaf, daft or senile, otherwise they would have been in the Army – but all the same he notified his Constabulary head-quarters, just to cover himself. The operations-room sergeant who took the message realized at once that the missing men had been patrolling a particularly sensitive military area, and he notified his inspector, who notified Scotland Yard, who sent a Special Branch man down there and notified M15, who sent Bloggs.

The Special Branch man was Harris, who had been on the Stockwell murder. He and Bloggs met on the train, which was one of the Wild West locomotives lent to Britain by the Americans because of the shortage of trains. Harris repeated his invitation to Sunday dinner, and Bloggs told him again that he worked most Sundays.

When they got off the train they borrowed bicycles to ride along the canal towpath until they met up with the search party. Harris, ten years older than Bloggs and four stone heavier, found the ride a strain.

They met a section of the search party under a railway bridge. Harris welcomed the opportunity to get off the bicycle. 'What have you found?' he said. 'Bodies?'

'No, a boat,' said a policeman. 'Who are you?'

They introduced themselves. A constable stripped to his underwear was diving down to examine the vessel. He came up with a bung in his hand.

Bloggs looked at Harris. 'Deliberately scuttled?'

'Looks like it.' Harris turned to the diver. 'Notice anything else?'

'She hasn't been down there for long, she's in good condition, and the mast has been taken down, not broken.'

Harris said: 'That's a lot of information from a minute under water.'

'I'm a weekend sailor,' the diver said.

Harris and Bloggs mounted their cycles and moved on.

When they met up with the main party, the bodies had been found.

'Murdered, all five,' said the uniformed inspector in charge. 'Captain Langham, Corporal Lee, and Privates Watson, Dayton and Forbes. Dayton's neck was broken, the rest were killed with some kind of knife. Langham's body had been in the canal. All found together in a shallow grave. Bloody murder.' He was quite shaken.

Harris looked closely at the five bodies, laid out in a line. 'I've seen wounds like this before, Fred,' he said.

Bloggs looked closely. 'Jesus Christ, it's him.'

Harris nodded. 'Stiletto.'

The inspector said in astonishment: 'You know who did it?'

'We can guess,' Harris said. 'We think he's killed twice before. If it's the same man, we know *who* he is but not *where* he is.'

The inspector's eyes narrowed. 'What with the restricted area so close, and Special Branch and MI5 arriving on the scene so quick, is there anything else I need to know about this case?'

Harris answered: 'Just that you keep very quiet until your Chief Constable has talked to our people.'

''Nuff said.'

Bloggs asked. 'Anything else found, Inspector?'

'We're still combing the area, in ever-widening circles; but nothing so far. There were some clothes in the grave.' He pointed.

Bloggs touched them gingerly: black trousers, a black sweater, a short black leather jacket, RAF-style.

Harris said: 'Clothes for night work.'

'To fit a big man,' Bloggs added.

'How tall is your man?'

'Over six foot.'

The inspector said: 'Did you pass the men who found the sunken boat?'

'Yes.' Bloggs frowned. 'Where's the nearest lock?'

'Four miles upstream.'

'If our man was in a boat, the lock-keeper must have seen him, mustn't he?'

'Must have,' the inspector agreed.

Bloggs said: 'We'd better talk to him.' He returned to his cycle.

'Not another four miles,' Harris complained.

Bloggs said: 'Work off some of those Sunday dinners.'

The four-mile ride took them most of an hour, because the towpath was made for horses, not wheels, and it was uneven, muddy, and mined with loose boulders and tree roots. Harris was sweating and cursing by the time they reached the lock.

The lock-keeper was sitting outside his little house, smoking a pipe and enjoying the mild air of afternoon. He was a middle-aged man of slow speech and slower movements. He regarded the two cyclists with faint amusement.

Bloggs spoke, because Harris was out of breath. 'We're police officers,' he said.

'Is that so?' said the lock-keeper. 'What's the excitement?' He looked as excited as a cat in front of a fire.

Bloggs took the photograph of Die Nadel out of his wallet and gave it to the man. 'Have you ever seen him?'

The lock-keeper put the picture on his lap while he held a fresh match to his pipe. Then he studied the photograph for a while, and handed it back.

'Well?' Harris said.

'Aye.' The lock-keeper nodded slowly. 'He was here about this time yesterday. Came in for a cup of tea.

Nice enough chap. What's he done, shown a light after blackout?'

Bloggs sat down heavily. 'That clinches it,' he said.

Harris thought aloud. 'He moors the boat downstream from here, and goes into the restricted area after dark.' He spoke quietly, so that the lock-keeper should not hear. 'When he comes back, the Home Guard has his boat staked out. He deals with them, sails a bit farther to the railway, scuttles his boat and ... hops a train?'

Bloggs said to the lock-keeper: 'The railway line that crosses the canal a few miles downstream – where does it go?'

'London.'

Bloggs said: 'Oh, shit.'

Bloggs got back to the War Office in Whitehall at midnight. Godliman and Parkin were there, waiting for him. Bloggs said: 'It's him, all right,' and told them the story.

Parkin was excited, Godliman just looked tense. When Bloggs had finished, Godliman said: 'So now he's back in London, and we're looking for a needle in a haystack again.' He was playing with matches, forming a picture with them on his desk. 'Do you know, every time I look at that photograph I get the feeling I've actually *met* the damn fellow.'

'Well, think! 'Bloggs said. 'Where?'

Godliman shook his head in frustration. 'It must have been only once, and somewhere strange. It's like a face I've seen in a lecture audience, or in the background at a cocktail party. A fleeting glimpse, a casual encounter – when I remember it probably won't do us any good.'

Parkin said: 'What's in that area?'

'I don't know, which means it's probably highly important,' Godliman said.

There was a silence. Parkin lit a cigarette with one of Godliman's matches. Bloggs looked up. 'We could print a million copies of his picture – give one to every policeman, ARP warden, member of the Home Guard, serviceman, railway porter; paste them up on hoardings and publish them in the papers . . .'

Godliman shook his head. 'Too risky. What if he's already talked to Hamburg about whatever he's seen? If we make a public fuss about the man they'll know that his information is good. We'd only be lending credence to him.'

'We've got to do something.'

'Surely. We will circulate his picture to police officers. We'll give his description to the press, and say he's just a straightforward murderer. We can give the details of the Highgate and Stockwell murders, without saying that security is involved.'

Parkin said: 'What you're saying is, we can fight with one hand tied behind our back.'

'For now, anyway.'

'I'll start the ball rolling with the Yard,' Bloggs said. He picked up the phone.

Godliman looked at his watch. 'There's not much

more we can do tonight, but I don't feel like going home. I shan't sleep.'

Parkin stood up. 'In that case I'm going to find a kettle and make some tea.' He went out.

The matches on Godliman's desk made a picture of a horse and carriage. He took away one of the horse's legs and lit his pipe with it. 'Have you got a girl, Fred?' he asked conversationally.

'No.'

'Not since—?'

'No.'

Godliman puffed at his pipe. 'There has to be an end to grief, you know.'

Bloggs made no reply.

Godliman said: 'Look, perhaps I shouldn't talk to you like a Dutch uncle. But I know how you feel – I've been through it myself. The only difference was that I didn't have anyone to blame.'

'You didn't remarry,' Bloggs said, not looking at Godliman.

'No. And I don't want you to make the same mistake. When you reach middle age, living alone can be very depressing.'

'Did I ever tell you, they called her Fearless Bloggs.'

'Yes, you did.'

Bloggs looked at Godliman at last. 'Tell me, where in the world will I find another girl like that?'

'Does she have to be a hero?'

'After Christine – yes.'

'England is full of heroes, Fred.'

At that moment Colonel Terry walked in.

Godliman said: 'Ah, Uncle Andrew—'

Terry interrupted: 'Don't get up. This is important. Listen carefully, because I have to give it to you fast. Bloggs, you need to know this, too. Whoever killed those five Home Guard has learned our most vital secret.

'Number one: our invasion force for Europe will land at Normandy. Number two: the Germans believe it will land at Calais. Number three: one of the most vital aspects of the deception is a very large phoney army, called the First United States Army Group, located in the restricted area those men were patrolling. That area contains dummy barracks, cardboard aircraft, rubber tanks – a huge toy army which looks real to the observers in the reconnaissance planes we've been letting through.'

Bloggs said: 'How come you're so sure the spy found out?'

Terry went to the door. 'Come in, Rodriguez.'

A tall, handsome man with jet-black hair and a long nose entered the room and nodded politely to Godliman and Bloggs. Terry said: 'Senhor Rodriguez is our man at the Portuguese Embassy. Tell them what happened, Rodriguez.'

The man stood by the door, holding his hat. 'A taxi came to the Embassy at about eleven o'clock. The passenger did not get out, but the driver came to the door with an envelope addressed to Francisco. The doorman called me, as he has been instructed to do, and I took possession of the envelope. I was in time to take the number of the cab.'

'I'm having the cabbie traced,' Terry said. 'All right, Rodriguez, you'd better get back. And thank you.'

The tall Portuguese left the room. Terry handed to Godliman a large yellow envelope, addressed to Manuel Francisco. Godliman opened it – it had already been unsealed – and withdrew a second envelope marked with a meaningless series of letters: presumably a code.

Within the inner envelope were several sheets of paper covered with handwriting and a set of ten-by-eight photographs. Godliman examined the letter. 'It looks like a very basic code,' he said.

'You don't need to read it,' Terry said impatiently. 'Look at the photographs.'

Godliman did so. There were about thirty of them, and he looked at each one before speaking. He handed them to Bloggs and said: 'This is a catastrophe.'

Bloggs glanced through the pictures then put them down.

Godliman said: 'This is only his back-up. He's still got the negatives, *and he's going somewhere with them.*'

The three men sat still in the little office, like a tableau. The only illumination came from a spotlight on Godliman's desk. With the cream walls, the blacked-out window, the spare furniture and the worn Civil Service carpet, they might have been anywhere in the world.

Terry said: 'I'm going to have to tell Churchill.'

The phone rang, and the Colonel picked it up. 'Yes. Good. Bring him here right away, please – but before you do, ask him where he dropped the passenger. What? Really? Thank you, get here fast.' He hung up. 'The taxi dropped our man at University College Hospital.'

Bloggs said: 'Perhaps he was injured in the fight with the Home Guard.'

Terry said: 'Where is that hospital?'

'About five minutes' walk from Euston Station,' Godliman said. 'Trains from Euston go to Holyhead, Liverpool, Glasgow . . . all places from which you can catch a ferry to Ireland.'

'Liverpool to Belfast,' Bloggs said. 'Then a car to the border and across into Eire, and a U-boat on the Atlantic coast. He wouldn't risk Holyhead-to-Dublin because of the passport control, and there would be no point in going beyond Liverpool to Glasgow.'

Godliman said: 'Fred, you'd better go to the station and show the picture of Faber around, see if anyone noticed him getting on a train. I'll phone the station and warn them you're coming, and at the same time find out which trains have left since about ten-thirty.'

Bloggs picked up his hat and coat. 'I'm on my way.'

Godliman lifted the phone. 'Yes, we're on our way.'

There were still plenty of people at Euston Station. Although in normal times the station closed around midnight, wartime delays were such that the last train often had not left before the earliest milk train of the morning arrived. The station concourse was a mass of kitbags and sleeping bodies.

Bloggs showed the picture to three railway policemen. None of them recognized the face. He tried ten women porters: nothing. He went to every ticket barrier. One of the guards said: 'We look at tickets, not faces.' He tried half a dozen passengers without result. Finally he went into the ticket office and showed the picture to each of the clerks.

A very fat, bald clerk with ill-fitting false teeth recognized the face. 'I play a game,' he told Bloggs. 'I try to spot something about a passenger that tells me why he's catching a train. Like, he might have a black tie for a funeral, or muddy boots means he's a farmer going home, or there might be a college scarf, or a white mark on a woman's finger where she's took off her wedding ring ... know what I mean? This is a dull job – not that I'm complaining—'

'What did you notice about this chap?' Bloggs interrupted him.

'Nothing. That was it, see – I couldn't make him out at all. Almost like he was trying to be inconspicuous, know what I mean?'

'I know what you mean.' Bloggs paused. 'Now, I want you to think very carefully. Where was he going – can you remember?'

'Yes,' said the fat clerk. 'Inverness.'

'That doesn't mean he's going there,' said Godliman. 'He's a professional – he knows we can ask questions at railway stations. I expect he automatically buys a ticket for the wrong destination.' He looked at his watch. 'He must have caught the eleven forty-five. That train is now pulling into Stafford. I checked with the railway, they checked with the signalman,' he added by way of explanation. 'They're going to stop the train this side of Crewe. I've got a plane standing by to fly you two to Stoke-on-Trent.

'Parkin, you'll board the train where it's stopped, outside Crewe. You'll be dressed as a ticket inspector, and you'll look at every ticket – and every face – on that train. When you've spotted Faber, just stay close to him.

'Bloggs, you'll be waiting at the ticket barrier at Crewe, just in case Faber decides to hop off there. But he won't. You'll get on the train, and be first off at Liverpool, and waiting at the ticket barrier for Parkin and Faber to come off. Half the local constabulary will be there to back you up.'

'That's all very well if he doesn't recognize me,' Parkin said. 'What if he remembers my face from Highgate?'

Godliman opened a desk drawer, took out a pistol, and gave it to Parkin. 'If he recognizes you, shoot the bastard.'

Parkin pocketed the weapon without comment.

Godliman said: 'I want both of you to be quite clear on the importance of all this. If we don't catch this man, the invasion of Europe will have to be postponed – possibly for a year. In that year the balance of war could turn against us. The time may never be this right again.'

Bloggs said: 'Do we get told how long it is to D-Day?'

'All I know is that it's a matter of weeks.'

Parkin was thinking. 'It'll be June, then.'

Bloggs said: 'Shit.'

Godliman said: 'No comment.'

The phone rang and Godliman picked it up. After a moment he looked up. 'Your car's here.'

Bloggs and Parkin stood up.

Godliman said: 'Wait a minute.'

They stood by the door, looking at the professor. He was saying: 'Yes, sir. Certainly. I will. Goodbye, sir.'

Bloggs could not think of anyone Godliman called Sir. He said: 'Who was that?'

Godliman said: 'Churchill.'

'What did he have to say?' Parkin asked, awestruck.

Godliman said: 'He wishes you both good luck and Godspeed.'

CHAPTER FIFTEEN

THE CARRIAGE was pitch dark. Faber thought of the jokes people made: 'Take your hand off my knee. No, not you, you.' The British would make jokes out of anything. Their railways were now worse than ever, but nobody complained any more because it was in a good cause. Faber preferred the dark: it was anonymous.

There had been singing, earlier on. Three sailors in the corridor had started it, and the whole carriage had joined in. They had been through *Be Like The Kettle And Sing, There'll Always Be An England* (followed by *Glasgow Belongs To Me* and *Land Of My Fathers* for ethnic balance), and appropriately, *Don't Get Around Much Any More*.

There had been an air-raid warning, and the train slowed to thirty miles an hour. They were all supposed to lie on the floor, but of course there was no room. An anonymous female voice had said: 'Oh, God, I'm frightened,' and a male voice, equally anonymous except that it was Cockney, had said: 'You're in the safest place, girl – they can't 'it a movin' target.' Then everyone laughed and nobody was scared any more. Someone opened a suitcase and passed around a packet of dried-egg sandwiches.

One of the sailors wanted to play cards.

'How can we play cards in the dark?'

'Feel the edges. All Harry's cards are marked.'

The train stopped unaccountably at about 4 a.m. A cultured voice – the dried-egg sandwich supplier, Faber thought – said: 'My guess is we're outside Crewe.'

'Knowing the railways, we could be anywhere from Bolton to Bournemouth,' said the Cockney.

The train jerked and moved off, and everyone cheered. Where, Faber wondered, was the caricature Englishman, with his icy reserve and his stiff upper lip? Not here.

A few minutes later a voice in the corridor said: 'Tickets, please.' Faber noted the Yorkshire accent: they were in the north now. He fumbled in his pockets for his ticket.

He had the corner seat, near the door, so he could see into the corridor. The inspector was shining a torch on to the tickets. Faber saw the man's silhouette in the reflected light. It looked vaguely familiar.

He settled back in his seat to wait. He remembered the nightmare: 'This is an Abwehr ticket' – and smiled in the dark.

Then he frowned. The train stops unaccountably; shortly afterwards a ticket inspection begins; the inspector's face is vaguely familiar ... It might be nothing, but Faber stayed alive by worrying about things that *might* be nothing. He looked in the corridor again, but the man had entered a compartment.

The train stopped briefly – the station was Crewe, according to informed opinion in Faber's compartment – and moved off again.

Faber got another look at the inspector's face, and now he remembered. The boarding house in Highgate! The boy from Yorkshire who wanted to get into the Army!

Faber watched him carefully. His torch flashed across the face of every passenger. He was not just looking at the tickets.

No, Faber told himself, don't jump to conclusions. How could they possibly have got on to him? They could not have found out which train he was on, got hold of one of the few people in the world who knew what he looked like, and got the man on the train dressed as a ticket inspector in so short a time. It was unbelievable.

Parkin, that was his name. Billy Parkin. Somehow he looked a lot older now. He was coming closer.

It must be a look-alike – perhaps an elder brother. This had to be a coincidence.

Parkin entered the compartment next to Faber's. There was no time left.

Faber assumed the worst and prepared to deal with it.

He got up, left the compartment, and went along the corridor, picking his way over suitcases and kitbags and bodies, to the lavatory. It was vacant. He went in and locked the door.

He was only buying time – ticket inspectors did not fail to check the toilets. He sat on the seat and wondered how to get out of this. The train had speeded up, and was travelling too fast for him to jump off.

Besides, someone would see him go, and if they were really searching for him they would stop the train.

'All tickets, please.'

Parkin was getting close again.

Faber had an idea. The coupling between the carriages was a tiny space like an air-lock, enclosed by a bellows-like cover between the cars of the train, shut off at both ends by doors because of the noise and draughts. He left the lavatory, fought his way to the end of the carriage, opened the door, and stepped into the connecting passage. He closed the door behind him.

It was freezing cold, and the noise was terrific. Faber sat on the floor and curled up, pretending to sleep. Only a dead man could sleep here, but people did strange things on trains these days. He tried not to shiver.

The door opened behind him. 'Tickets, please.'

He ignored it. He heard the door close.

'Wake up, Sleeping Beauty.' The voice was unmistakable.

Faber pretended to stir, then got to his feet, keeping his back to Parkin. When he turned the stiletto was in his hand. He pushed Parkin up against the door, held the point of the knife at his throat, and said: 'Be still or I'll kill you.'

With his left hand he took Parkin's torch, and shone it into the young man's face. Parkin did not look as frightened as he ought to be.

Faber said: 'Well, well. Billy Parkin, who wanted to

join the Army, and ended up on the railways. Still, it's a uniform.'

Parkin said: 'You.'

'You know damn well it's me, little Billy Parkin. You were looking for me. Why?' He was doing his best to sound vicious.

'I don't know why I should be looking for you – I'm not a policeman.'

Faber jerked the knife melodramatically. 'Stop lying to me.'

'Honest, Mr Faber. Let me go – I promise I won't tell anyone I've seen you.'

Faber began to have doubts. Either Parkin was telling the truth, or he was overacting as much as Faber himself.

Parkin's body shifted, his right arm moving in the darkness. Faber grabbed the wrist in an iron grip. Parkin struggled for an instant, but Faber let the needle point of the stiletto sink a fraction of an inch into Parkin's throat, and the man was still. Faber found the pocket Parkin had been reaching for, and pulled out a gun.

'Ticket inspectors do not go armed,' he said. 'Who are you with, Parkin?'

'We all carry guns now – there's a lot of crime on trains because of the dark.'

Parkin was lying courageously and persistently. Faber decided that threats were not enough to loosen his tongue.

His movement was sudden, swift and accurate. The blade of the stiletto leaped in his fist. Its point entered a measured half-inch into Parkin's left eye and came out again.

Faber's hand covered Parkin's mouth. The muffled scream of agony was drowned by the noise of the train. Parkin's hands went to his ruined eye.

Faber pressed his advantage. 'Save yourself the other eye, Parkin. Who are you with?'

'Military Intelligence, oh God, please don't do it again.'

'Who? Menzies? Masterman?'

'Oh, God, it's Godliman, Percy Godliman.'

'Godliman!' Faber knew the name, but this was no time to search his memory for details. 'What have they got?'

'A picture – I picked you out from the files.'

'What picture? *What picture?*'

'A racing team – running – with a cup – the Army—'

Faber remembered. Christ, where had they got hold of that? It was his nightmare: *they had a picture.* People would know his face. His *face.*

He moved the knife closer to Parkin's right eye. 'How did you know where I was?'

'Don't do it, please – agent in the Portuguese Embassy intercepted your letter – took the cab's number – inquiries at Euston – please, not the other eye—' He covered both his eyes with his hands.

'What's the plan? Where is the trap?'

'Glasgow. They're waiting for you at Glasgow. The train will be emptied there.'

Faber lowered the knife to the level of Parkin's belly.

To distract him, he said: 'How many men?' Then he pushed hard, inward and upward to the heart.

Parkin's one eye stared in horror, and he did not die. It was the drawback to Faber's favoured method of killing. Normally the shock of the knife was enough to stop the heart. But if the heart was strong it did not always work – after all, surgeons sometimes stuck a hypodermic needle directly into the heart to inject adrenalin. If the heart continued to pump, the motion would work a hole around the blade, from which the blood would leak. It was just as fatal, but longer.

At last Parkin's body went limp. Faber held him against the wall for a moment, thinking. There had been something – a flicker of courage, the ghost of a smile – before the man died. It meant something. Such things always did.

He let the body fall to the floor, then arranged it in a sleeping position, with the wounds hidden from view. He kicked the railway cap into a corner. He cleaned his stiletto on Parkin's trousers, and wiped the ocular liquid from his hands. It had been a messy business.

He put the knife away in his sleeve and opened the door to the carriage. He made his way back to his compartment in the dark.

As he sat down the Cockney said: 'You took your time – is there a queue?'

Faber said: 'It must have been something I ate.'

'Probably a dried-egg sandwich.' The Cockney laughed.

Faber was thinking about Godliman. He knew the name – he could even put a vague face to it: a middle-aged, bespectacled face, with a pipe and an absent, professorial air. That was it – he was a professor.

It was coming back. In his first couple of years in London Faber had had little to do. The war had not yet started, and most people believed it would not come. (Faber was not among the optimists.) He had been able to do a little useful work – mostly checking and revising the Abwehr's out-of-date maps, plus general reports based on his own observations and his reading of the newspapers – but not much. To fill in time, to improve his English, and to flesh out his cover, he had gone sightseeing.

His purpose in visiting Canterbury Cathedral had been innocent, although he did buy an aerial view of the town and the cathedral which he sent back for the Luftwaffe – not that it did much good: they spent most of 1942 missing it. Faber had taken a whole day to see the building: reading the ancient initials carved in walls, distinguishing the different architectural styles, reading the guidebook line by line as he walked slowly around.

He had been in the south ambulatory of the choir, looking at the blind arcading, when he became conscious of another absorbed figure by his side; an older man. 'Fascinating, isn't it?' the man said; and Faber asked him what he meant.

'The one pointed arch in an arcade of round ones. No reason for it – that section obviously hasn't been rebuilt. For some reason, somebody just altered that one. I wonder why.'

Faber saw what he meant. The choir was Romanesque, the nave Gothic; yet here in the choir was a solitary Gothic arch. 'Perhaps,' he said, 'the monks demanded to see what the pointed arches would look like, and the architect did this to show them.'

The older man stared at him. 'What a splendid conjecture! Of course that's the reason. Are you an historian?'

Faber laughed. 'No, just a clerk and an occasional reader of history books.'

'People get doctorates for inspired guesses like that!'

'Are you? An historian, I mean.'

'Yes, for my sins.' He stuck out his hand. 'Percy Godliman.'

Was it possible, Faber thought as the train rattled on through Lancashire, that that unimpressive figure in a tweed suit could be the man who had discovered his identity? Spies generally claimed they were civil servants, or something equally vague; not historians – that lie could be too easily found out. Yet it was rumoured that Military Intelligence had been bolstered by a number of academics. Faber had imagined them to be young, fit, aggressive and bellicose as well as clever. Godliman was clever, but none of the rest. Unless he had changed.

Faber had seen him once again, although he had not spoken to him on the second occasion. After the brief encounter in the cathedral Faber had seen a notice advertising a public lecture on Henry II to be given by Professor Godliman at his college. He had gone along, out of curiosity. The talk had been erudite, lively and convincing. Godliman was still a faintly comic figure, prancing about behind the lectern, getting enthusiastic about his subject; but it was clear his mind was as sharp as a knife.

So that was the man who had discovered what Die Nadel looked like.

Jesus Christ, an *amateur*.

Well, he would make amateur mistakes. Sending Billy Parkin had been one: Faber had recognized the boy. Godliman should have sent someone Faber did not know. Parkin had a better chance of recognizing Faber, but no chance at all of surviving the encounter. A professional would have known that.

The train shuddered to a halt, and a muffled voice outside announced that this was Liverpool. Faber cursed under his breath: he should have been spending the time working out his next move, not remembering Percival Godliman.

They were waiting at Glasgow, Parkin had said before he died. Why Glasgow? Their inquiries at Euston would have told them he was going to Inverness. And if they suspected Inverness to be a red herring, they would have speculated that he was coming here, to Liverpool, for this was the nearest link point for an Irish ferry.

Faber hated snap decisions.

He had to get off the train, whatever.

He stood up, opened the door, stepped out, and headed for the ticket barrier.

He thought of something else. What was it that had flashed in Billy Parkin's eyes before he died? Not hatred, not fear, not pain – although all those had been present. It was more like . . . triumph.

Faber looked up, past the ticket collector, and understood.

Waiting on the other side, dressed in a hat and raincoat, was the blond young tail from Leicester Square.

Parkin, dying in agony and humiliation and betrayal, had deceived Faber at the last. The trap was here.

The man in the raincoat had not yet noticed Faber in the crowd. Faber turned and stepped back on to the train. Once inside, he pulled aside the blind and looked out. The tail was searching the faces in the crowd. He had not noticed the man who got back on the train.

Faber watched while the passengers filtered through the gate until the platform was empty. The blond man spoke urgently to the ticket collector, who shook his head in negation. The man seemed to insist. After a moment he waved to someone out of sight. A police officer emerged from the shadows and spoke to the collector. The platform guard joined the group, followed by a man in a civilian suit who was presumably a more senior railway official.

The engine driver and his fireman left the locomotive and went over to the barrier. There was more waving of arms and shaking of heads.

Finally the railwaymen shrugged, turned away, or rolled their eyes upward, all telegraphing surrender. The blond and the police officer summoned other policemen, and they moved determinedly on to the platform.

They were going to search the train.

All the railway officials, including the engine crew,

had disappeared in the opposite direction, no doubt to seek tea and sandwiches while the lunatics tried to search a jampacked train. That gave Faber an idea.

He opened the door and jumped out of the wrong side of the train, the side opposite the platform. Concealed from the police by the carriages, he ran along the tracks, stumbling on the sleepers and slipping on the gravel, toward the engine.

It had to be bad news, of course. From the moment he realized Billy Parkin was not going to saunter off that train, Frederick Bloggs knew that Die Nadel had slipped through their fingers again. As the uniformed police moved on to the train in pairs, two men to search each carriage, Bloggs thought of several possible explanations of Parkin's non-appearance; and all the explanations were depressing.

He turned up his coat collar and paced the draughty platform. He wanted very badly to catch Die Nadel: not just for the sake of the invasion – although that was reason enough, God knew – but for Percy Godliman, and for the five Home Guard, and for Christine.

He looked at his watch: four o'clock. Soon it would be day. Bloggs had been up all night, and he had not eaten since breakfast yesterday, but until now he had kept going on adrenalin. The failure of the trap – he was quite sure it *had* failed – drained him of energy. Hunger and fatigue caught up with him. He had to make a conscious effort not to daydream about hot food and a warm bed.

'Sir!' A policeman was leaning out of a carriage and waving at him. 'Sir!'

Bloggs walked toward him, then broke into a run. 'What have you found?'

'It might be your man Parkin.'

Bloggs climbed into the carriage. 'What do you mean, might be?'

'You'd better have a look.' The policeman opened the communicating door between the carriages and shone his torch inside.

It was Parkin; Bloggs could tell by the ticket-inspector's uniform. He was curled up on the floor. Bloggs took the policeman's torch, knelt down beside Parkin, and turned him over.

He saw Parkin's face, looked quickly away, and said: 'Oh, dear God.'

'I take it this is Parkin?' the policeman said.

Bloggs nodded. He got up, very slowly, without looking again at the body. 'We'll interview everybody in this carriage and the next,' he said. 'Anyone who saw or heard anything unusual will be detained for further questioning. Not that it will do us any good: the murderer must have jumped off the train before it got here.'

Bloggs went back out on to the platform. All the searchers had completed their tasks and were gathered in a group. He detailed six of them to help with the interviewing.

The police inspector said: 'Your villain's hopped it, then.'

'Almost certainly,' Bloggs agreed. 'You've looked in every toilet, and the guard's van?'

'Yes, and on top of the train and under it, and in the engine and the coal tender.'

A passenger got off the train and approached Bloggs and the inspector. He was a small man with a bad chest, and he wheezed badly. He said: 'Excuse me.'

'Yes, sir,' the inspector said.

The passenger said: 'I was wondering, are you looking for somebody?'

'Why do you ask?'

'Well, if you are, I was wondering, would he be a tall chap?'

The inspector said: 'Why do you ask?'

Bloggs interrupted impatiently. 'Yes, a tall man. Come on, spit it out.'

'Well, it's just that a tall chap got out the wrong side of the train.'

'When?'

'A minute or two after the train pulled into the station. He got on, like, then he got off, on the wrong side. Jumped down on to the track. Only he had no luggage, you see, which was another odd thing, and I just thought—'

The inspector said: 'Balls.'

'He must have spotted the trap,' Bloggs said. 'But how? He doesn't know my face, and your men were out of sight.'

'Something made him suspicious.'

'So he crossed the line to the next platform and went out that way. Wouldn't he have been seen?'

The inspector shrugged. 'Not too many people about, this late. And if he was seen he could just say he was too impatient to queue at the ticket barrier.'

'Didn't you have the other ticket barriers covered?'

'I didn't think of it.'

'Nor did I.'

'Well, we can search the surrounding area, and later on we can check various places in the city, and of course we'll watch the ferry—'

'Yes, please do,' Bloggs said.

But somehow he knew Faber would not be found.

It was more than an hour before the train started to move. Faber had cramp in his left calf and dust in his nose. He heard the footplatemen climb back into their cab, and caught snatches of conversation about a body being found on the train. There was a metallic rattle as the fireman shovelled coal, then the hiss of steam, a clanking of pistons, a jerk and a sigh of smoke as the train moved off. Gratefully, Faber shifted his position and indulged in a smothered sneeze. Then he felt better.

He was at the back of the coal tender, buried deep in the coal, where it would take a man with a shovel ten minutes' hard work to expose him. As he had hoped, the police search of the tender had consisted of one good long look and no more.

He wondered whether he could risk emerging now. It must be getting light: would he be visible from a bridge over the line? He thought not. His skin was now quite black, and in a moving train in the pale light of dawn he would just be a dark blur on a dark background. Yes, he would chance it. Slowly and carefully, he dug his way out of his grave of coal.

He breathed the cool air deeply. The coal was shovelled out of the tender via a small hole in the front end. Later, perhaps, the fireman would have to enter the tender, when the pile of fuel got lower. Faber was safe for now.

As the light strengthened he looked himself over. He was covered from head to toe in coal dust, like a miner coming up from the pit. Somehow he had to wash and change his clothes.

He chanced a peep over the side of the tender. The train was still in the suburbs, passing factories and warehouses and rows of grimy little houses. He had to think about his next move.

His original plan had been to get off the train at Glasgow and there catch another train to Dundee and up the east coast to Aberdeen. It was still possible for him to disembark at Glasgow. He could not get off at the station, of course, but he might jump off either just before or just after. However, there were risks in that. The train was sure to stop at intermediate stations between Liverpool and Glasgow, and at those stops Faber might be spotted. No, he had to get off the train soon and find other means of transport.

The ideal spot would be a lonely stretch of track just outside a city or village. It had to be lonely, for he must not be seen leaping from the coal tender; but it had to be fairly near houses so that he could steal clothes and a car. And it needed to be an uphill stretch of track, so that the train would be travelling slowly enough for him to jump.

Right now its speed was about forty miles an hour. Faber lay back on the coal to wait. He could not keep a permanent watch on the country through which he was passing, for fear of being seen. He decided he would look out whenever the train slowed down. Otherwise he would lie still.

After a few minutes he caught himself dropping off to sleep, despite the discomfort of his bed. He shifted his position and reclined on his elbows, so that if he did sleep he would fall and be wakened by the impact.

The train was gathering speed. Between London and Liverpool it had seemed to be stationary more than moving; now it steamed through the country at a fine pace. To complete his discomfort, it started to rain; a cold, steady drizzle that soaked right through his clothes and seemed to turn to ice on his skin. There was another reason for getting off the train: he could die of exposure before they reached Glasgow!

After half an hour at high speed he was contemplating killing the footplate crew and stopping the train himself. A signal box saved their lives. The train slowed suddenly as brakes were applied. It decelerated in stages: Faber guessed the track was marked with descending speed limits. He looked out. They were in the countryside again. He could see the reason for the slowdown – they were approaching a track junction, and the signals were against them.

Faber stayed in the tender while the train stood still. After five minutes it started up again. Faber scrambled up the side of the tender, perched on the edge for a moment, and jumped.

He landed on the embankment and lay, face down, in the overgrown weeds. When the train was out of earshot he got to his feet. The only sign of civilization nearby was the signal box, a two-storey wooden structure with large windows in the control room at the top, an outside staircase, and a door at ground-floor level. On the far side was a cinder track leading away.

Faber walked in a wide circle to approach the place from the back, where there were no windows. He entered a ground-floor door and found what he had been expecting: a toilet, a washbasin and a coat hanging on a peg.

He took off his soaking wet clothes, washed his hands and face, and rubbed himself vigorously all over with a grubby towel. The little cylindrical film can containing the negatives was still taped securely to his chest. He put his clothes back on, but substituted the signalman's overcoat for his own sopping wet jacket.

Now all he needed was transport. The signalman must have got here somehow. Faber went outside and found a bicycle padlocked to a rail on the other side of the little building. He snapped the little lock with the blade of his stiletto. Moving in a straight line away from the blank rear wall of the signal box, he wheeled the cycle until he was out of sight of the building. Then he cut across until he reached the cinder track, climbed on the cycle, and rode away.

CHAPTER SIXTEEN

PERCIVAL GODLIMAN had brought a little camp
bed from his home. He lay on it in his office,
dressed in trousers and shirt, trying in vain to sleep. He
had not suffered insomnia for almost forty years, since
he took his final exams at university. He would gladly
swap the anxieties of those days for the worries which
kept him awake now.

He had been a different man then, he knew; not just
younger, but also a lot less . . . abstracted. He had been
outgoing, aggressive, ambitious: he planned to go into
politics. He was not studious then – he had reason to
be anxious about the exams.

His two mismatched enthusiasms in those days had
been debating and ballroom dancing. He had spoken
with distinction at the Oxford Union and had been
pictured in *The Tatler* waltzing with debutantes. He was
no great womanizer: he wanted sex with a woman he
loved, not because he believed in any high-minded
principle to that effect, but because that was the way he
felt about it.

And so he had been a virgin until he met Eleanor,
who was not one of the debutantes, but a brilliant
graduate mathematician with grace and warmth and a

father dying of lung disease after forty years as a collier. The young Percival had taken her to meet his people. His father was Lord Lieutenant of the county, and the house had seemed a mansion to Eleanor, but she had been natural and charming and not in the least awe-struck; and when Percy's mother had been disgracefully condescending to her at one point she had reacted with merciless wit, for which he loved her all the more.

He had taken his master's degree, then after the Great War he taught in a public school and stood in three by-elections. They were both disappointed when they discovered they could not have children; but they loved each other totally, and they were happy, and her death was the most appalling tragedy Godliman ever knew. It had ended his interest in the real world, and he had retreated into the Middle Ages.

It had drawn him and Bloggs together, this common bereavement. The war had brought Godliman back to life; revived in him those characteristics of dash and aggression and fervour which had made him a great speaker and teacher and the hope of the Liberal Party. He wished for something in Bloggs's life to rescue him from an existence of bitterness and introversion.

While he was in Godliman's thoughts, Bloggs phoned from Liverpool to say that Die Nadel had slipped through the net, and Parkin had been killed.

Godliman, sitting on the edge of the camp bed to speak on the phone, closed his eyes in despair. 'I should have put you on the train,' he murmured.

'Thanks!' Bloggs said.

'Only because he doesn't know your face.'

'I think he may,' Bloggs argued. 'We suspect he spotted the trap, and mine was the only face visible to him as he got off the train.'

'But where could he have seen you? Oh! No, surely . . . not Leicester Square?'

'I don't see how, but then . . . we always seem to underestimate him.'

'I wish he were on our side,' Godliman muttered. 'Have you got the ferry covered?'

'Yes.'

'He won't use it, of course – too obvious. He's more likely to steal a boat. On the other hand, he may still be heading for Inverness.'

'I've alerted the police up there.'

'Good. But look, I don't think we can make any assumptions about his destination. Let's keep an open mind.'

'Agreed.'

Godliman stood, picked up the phone, and began to pace the carpet. 'Also, don't assume it was he who got off the train on the wrong side. Work on the premise that he got off before, at, or after Liverpool.' Godliman's brain was in gear again, sorting permutations and possibilities. 'Let me talk to the Chief Suprintendent.'

'He's here.'

There was a pause, then a new voice said: 'Chief Superintendent Anthony speaking.'

Godliman said: 'Do you agree with me that our man has got off this train somewhere in your area?'

'That seems likely, yes.'

'Good. Now the first thing he needs is transport – so I want you to get details of every car, boat, bicycle or donkey stolen within a hundred miles of Liverpool during the next twenty-four hours. Keep me informed, but give the information to Bloggs and work closely with him in following-up the leads.'

'Yes, sir.'

'Keep an eye on other crimes that might be committed by a fugitive – theft of food or clothing, unexplained assaults, identity card irregularities, and so on.'

'Right.'

'Now, Mr Anthony, you realize this man is more than just a mass murderer?'

'I assume so, sir, from the fact of your involvement. However, I don't know the details.'

'Nor shall you. Suffice it to say that this is a matter of national security so grave that the Prime Minister is in hourly contact with this office.'

'I understand. Uh, Mr Bloggs would like a word, sir.'

Bloggs came back on. 'Have you remembered how you know his face?'

'Oh, yes – but it's of no value, as I forecast. I met him by chance at Canterbury Cathedral, and we had a conversation about the architecture. All it tells us is that he's clever – he made some rather perceptive remarks, as I recall.'

'We knew he was clever.'

'Only too well.'

*

Chief Superintendent Anthony was a burly member of the middle class with a carefully softened Liverpool accent. He did not know whether to be peeved at the way MI5 ordered him about or thrilled at the chance to save England on his own manor.

Bloggs knew of the man's inner struggle – he met this sort of thing all the time when working with local police forces – and he knew how to tip the balance in his own favour. He said: 'I'm grateful for your helpfulness, Chief Superintendent. These things don't go unnoticed in Whitehall.'

'Only doing our duty,' Anthony said. He was not sure whether he was supposed to call Bloggs 'Sir'.

'Still, there's a big difference between reluctant assistance and willing help.'

'Yes. Well, it'll likely be a few hours before we pick up this man's scent again. Do you want to catch forty winks?'

'Yes,' Bloggs said gratefully. 'If you've got a chair in a corner somewhere . . .'

'Stay here,' Anthony said, indicating his office. 'I'll be down in the operations room. I'll wake you as soon as we've got something. Make yourself comfortable.'

Anthony went out, and Bloggs moved to an easy chair and sat back with his eyes closed. Immediately, he saw Godliman's face, as if projected on to the backs of his eyelids like a film, saying: 'There has to be an end to bereavement . . . I don't want you to make the same mistake.' Bloggs realized suddenly that he did not want the war to end, for that would make him face issues like the one Godliman had raised. The war made life simple, for he knew why he hated the enemy and he knew what he was supposed to do about it. Afterwards . . . the thought of another woman seemed disloyal, not just to Christine but, in some obscure way, to England.

He yawned and slumped farther into his seat, his thinking becoming woolly as sleep crept up on him. If Christine had died before the war, he would have felt very differently about remarrying. He had always been fond of her and respected her, of course; but after she took that ambulance job respect had turned to awe-struck admiration, and fondness turned to love. Then they had something special, something they knew other lovers did not share. Now, more than a year later, it would be easy for Bloggs to find another woman he could respect and be fond of, but he knew that would never be enough for him. An ordinary marriage, an ordinary woman, would always remind him that once he had possessed the ideal.

He stirred in his chair, trying to shake off imponder-ables so that he could sleep. England was full of heroes, Godliman had said. If Die Nadel got away England would be full of slaves. First things first . . .

Someone shook him. He was in a very deep sleep, dreaming that he was in a room with Die Nadel but could not pick him out because Die Nadel had blinded him with the stiletto. When he awoke he still thought he was blind because he could not see who was shaking him, until he realized he simply had his eyes closed. He opened them to see the large uniformed figure of Superintendent Anthony above him.

Bloggs raised himself to a more upright position and rubbed his eyes. 'Got something?' he asked.

'Lots of things,' Anthony said. 'Question is, which of 'em counts? Here's your breakfast.' He put a cup of tea and a biscuit on the desk and went to sit on the other side of it.

Bloggs left his easy chair and pulled a hard chair up to the desk. He sipped the tea. It was weak and very sweet. 'Let's get to it,' he said.

Anthony handed him a sheaf of five or six slips of paper.

Bloggs said: 'Don't tell me these are the only crimes in your area—'

'Of course not,' Anthony said. 'We're not interested in drunkenness, domestic disputes, blackout violations, traffic offences, or crimes for which arrests have already been made.'

'Sorry,' Bloggs said. 'I'm still waking up. Give me a chance to read these.'

There were three house burglaries. In two of them, valuables had been taken – jewellery in one case, furs in another. Bloggs said: 'He might steal valuables just to throw us off the scent. Mark these on the map, will you? They may show some pattern.' He handed the two slips back to Anthony. The third burglary had only just been reported, and no details were available. Anthony marked the location on the map.

A Food Office in Manchester had been robbed of

hundreds of ration books. Bloggs said: 'He doesn't need ration books – he needs food.' He set that one aside. There was a bicycle theft just outside Preston and a rape in Birkenhead. 'I don't think he's a rapist, but mark it anyway,' Bloggs told Anthony.

The bicycle theft and the third of the house burglaries were close together. Bloggs said: 'The signal box that the bike was stolen from – is that on the main line?'

'Yes, I think so,' Anthony said.

'Suppose Faber was hiding on that train and somehow we missed him. Would the signal box be the first place at which the train stopped after it left Liverpool?'

'It might be.'

Bloggs looked at the sheet of paper. 'An overcoat was stolen and a wet jacket left in its place.'

Anthony shrugged. 'Could mean anything.'

'No cars stolen?' Bloggs said sceptically.

'Nor boats, nor donkeys,' Anthony replied. 'We don't get many car thefts these days. Cars are easy to come by – it's petrol people steal.'

'I felt sure he'd steal a car in Liverpool,' Bloggs said. He thumped his knee in frustration. 'A bicycle isn't much use to him, surely.'

'I think we should follow it up, anyway,' Anthony pressed. 'It's our best lead.'

'All right. But meanwhile, double-check the burglaries to see whether food or clothing was pinched – the losers might not have noticed at first. Show Faber's picture to the rape victim, too. And keep checking all crimes. Can you fix me transport to Preston?'

'I'll get you a car,' Anthony said.

'How long will it take to get details of this third burglary?'

'They're probably interviewing at this minute,' Anthony said. 'By the time you reach the signal box I should have the complete picture.'

'Don't let them drag their feet.' Bloggs reached for his coat. 'I'll check with you the minute I get there.'

'Anthony? This is Bloggs. I'm at the signal box.'

'Don't waste any time there. The third burglary was your man.'

'Sure?'

'Unless there are two buggers running around threatening people with stiletto knives.'

'Who?'

'Two old ladies living alone in a little cottage.'

'Oh, God. Dead?'

'Not unless they died of excitement.'

'Eh?'

'Get over there. You'll see what I mean.'

'I'm on my way.'

It was the kind of cottage which is always inhabited by two elderly ladies living alone. It was small and square and old, and around the door grew a wild rose bush fertilized by thousands of pots of used tea leaves. Rows of vegetables sprouted tidily in a little front garden with a trimmed hedge. There were pink-and-white curtains at the leaded windows, and the gate creaked. The front door had been painted painstakingly by an amateur, and its knocker was made from a horse brass.

Bloggs's knock was answered by an octogenarian with a shotgun.

He said: 'Good morning. I'm from the police.'

'No, you're not,' she said. 'They've been already. Now get going before I blow your head off.'

Bloggs regarded her. She was less than five feet tall, with thick white hair in a bun and a pale, wrinkled face. Her hands were matchstick-thin, but her grasp on the shotgun was firm. The pocket of her apron was full of clothes-pegs. Bloggs looked down at her feet, and saw that she was wearing a man's working boots. He said: 'The police you saw this morning were local. I'm from Scotland Yard.'

'How do I know that?' she said.

Bloggs turned and called to his police driver. The constable got out of the car and came to the gate. Bloggs said to the old lady: 'Is the uniform enough to convince you?'

'All right,' she said, and stood aside for him to enter.

He stepped down into a low-ceilinged room with a tiled floor. The room was crammed with heavy, old furniture, and every surface was decorated with ornaments of china and glass. A small coal fire burned in the grate. The place smelled of lavender and cats.

A second old lady got out of a chair. She was like the first, but about twice as wide. Two cats spilled from her lap as she rose. She said: 'Hello, I'm Emma Parton, my sister is Jessie. Don't take any notice of that shotgun

215

– it's not loaded, thank God. Jessie loves drama. Will you sit down? You look so young to be a policeman. I'm surprised Scotland Yard is interested in our little robbery. Have you come from London this morning? Make the boy a cup of tea, Jessie.'

Bloggs sat down. 'If we're right about the identity of the burglar, he's a fugitive from justice,' he said.

'I told you!' Jessie said. 'We might have been done in – slaughtered, in cold blood!'

'Don't be silly,' Emma said. She turned to Bloggs. 'He was such a nice man.'

'Tell me what happened,' Bloggs said.

'Well, I'd gone out the back,' Emma began. 'I was in the hen coop, hoping for some eggs. Jessie was in the kitchen—'

'He surprised me,' Jessie interrupted. 'I didn't have time to go for me gun.'

'You see too many cowboy films,' Emma admonished her.

'They're better than your love films – all tears and kisses—'

Bloggs took the picture of Faber from his wallet. 'Is this the man?'

Jessie scrutinized it. 'That's him.'

'Aren't you clever?' Emma marvelled.

'If we were clever we'd have caught him by now,' Bloggs said. 'What did he do?'

Jessie said: 'He held a knife to my throat and said: "One false move and I'll slit your gizzard." And he meant it.'

'Oh, Jessie, you told me he said: "I won't harm you if you do as I say."'

'Words to that effect, Emma!'

Bloggs said: 'What did he want?'

'Food, a bath, dry clothes and a car. Well, we gave him the eggs, of course. We found some clothes that belonged to Jessie's late husband Norman—'

'Would you describe them?'

'Yes. A blue donkey jacket, blue overalls, a check shirt. And he took poor Norman's car. I don't know how we'll be able to go to the pictures without it. That's our only vice, you know – the pictures.'

'What sort of car?'

'A Morris. Norman bought it in 1924. It's served us well, that little car.'

Jessie said: 'He didn't get his hot bath, though!'

'Well,' Emma said, 'I had to explain to him that two ladies living alone can hardly have a man taking a bath in their kitchen . . .' She blushed.

Jessie said: 'You'd rather have your throat slit than see a man in his combinations, wouldn't you, you silly fool.'

Bloggs said: 'What did he say when you refused?'

'He laughed,' Emma said. 'But I think he understood our position.'

Bloggs could not help but smile. 'I think you're very brave,' he said.

'I don't know about that, I'm sure.'

'So he left here in a 1924 Morris, wearing overalls and a blue jacket. What time was that?'

'About half-past nine.'

Bloggs absently stroked a marmalade cat. It blinked and purred. 'Was there much petrol in the car?'

'A couple of gallons – but he took our coupons.'

A thought struck Bloggs. 'How do you ladies qualify for a petrol ration?'

'Agricultural purposes,' Emma said defensively. She blushed.

Jessie snorted. 'And we're isolated, and we're elderly. Of course we qualify.'

'We always go to the corn stores at the same time as the pictures,' Emma added. 'We don't waste petrol.'

Bloggs smiled and held up a hand. 'All right, don't worry – rationing isn't my department anyway. How fast does the car go?'

Emma said: 'We never exceed thirty miles per hour.'

Bloggs looked at his watch. 'Even at that speed he could be seventy-five miles away by now.' He stood up. 'I must phone the details to Liverpool. You don't have a telephone, do you?'

'No.'

'What kind of Morris is it?'

'A Cowley. Norman used to call it a Bullnose.'

'Colour?'

'Grey.'

'Registration number?'

'MLN 29.'

Bloggs wrote it all down.

Emma said: 'Will we ever get our car back, do you think?'

'I expect so – but it may not be in very good

condition. When someone is driving a stolen car he generally doesn't take good care of it.' He walked to the door.

'I hope you catch him,' Emma called.

Jessie saw him out. She was still clutching the shot-gun. At the door she caught Bloggs's sleeve and said in a stage whisper: 'Tell me – what is he? Escaped convict? Murderer? Rapist?'

Bloggs looked down at her. Her small green eyes were bright with excitement. She would believe anything he chose to tell her. He bent his head to speak quietly in her ear. 'Don't tell a soul,' he murmured, 'but he's a German spy.'

CHAPTER SEVENTEEN

FABER CROSSED the Sark Bridge and entered Scotland shortly after midday. He passed the Sark Toll Bar House, a low building with a signboard announcing that it was the first house in Scotland and a tablet above the door bearing some legend about marriages which he could not read. A quarter of a mile farther on he understood, when he entered the village of Gretna: he knew this was a place runaways came to get married.

The roads were still damp from the early rain, but the sun was drying them rapidly. Signposts and name-boards had been re-erected since the relaxation of invasion precautions, and Faber sped through a series of small lowland villages: Kirkpatrick, Kirtlebridge, Ecclefechan. The open countryside was pleasant, the green moors sparkling in the sunshine.

He had stopped for petrol in Carlisle. The pump attendant, a middle-aged woman in an oily apron, had not asked any awkward questions. Faber had filled the tank and the spare can fixed to the offside running-board.

He was very pleased with the little two-seater. It would still do fifty miles an hour, despite its age. The

four-cylinder, 1548cc side-valve engine worked smoothly
and tirelessly as he climbed and descended the Scottish
hills. The leather-upholstered bench seat was comfortable. He squeezed the bulb horn to warn a straying
sheep of his approach.

He went through the little market town of Lockerbie,
crossed the River Annan by the picturesque Johnstone
Bridge, and began the ascent to Beattock Summit. He
found himself using the three-speed gearbox more and
more.

He had decided not to take the most direct route to
Aberdeen, via Edinburgh and the coast road. Much of
Scotland's east coast, either side of the Firth of Forth,
was a restricted area. Visitors were prohibited from a
ten-mile-wide strip of land. Of course, the authorities
could not seriously police such a long border. Nevertheless, Faber was less likely to be stopped and questioned
while he stayed outside the security zone.

He would have to enter it eventually – later rather
than sooner – and he turned his mind to the story he
would tell if he were interrogated. Private motoring for
pleasure had virtually ceased in the last couple of years
because of the ever-stricter petrol rationing, and people
who had cars for essential journeys were liable to be
prosecuted for going a few yards off their necessary
route for personal reasons. Faber had read of a famous
impresario gaoled for using petrol supplied for agricultural purposes to take several actors from a theatre to
the Savoy Hotel. Endless propaganda told people that
a Lancaster bomber needed 2,000 gallons to get to the
Ruhr. Nothing would please Faber more than to waste

petrol which might otherwise be used to bomb his homeland, in normal circumstances; but to be stopped now, with the information he had taped to his chest, and arrested for a rationing violation would be an unbearable irony.

It was difficult. Most traffic was military, but he had no military papers. He could not claim to be delivering essential supplies because he had nothing in the car to deliver. He frowned. Who travelled, these days? Sailors on leave, officials, rare holidaymakers, skilled workmen . . . That was it. He would be an engineer, a specialist in some esoteric field like high-temperature gearbox oils, going to solve a manufacturing problem in a factory at Inverness. If he were asked which factory, he would say it was classified. (His fictitious destination had to be a long way from the real one so that he would never be questioned by someone who knew for certain there were no such factory.) He doubted whether consulting engineers ever wore overalls like the ones he had stolen from the elderly sisters – but anything was possible in wartime.

Having figured all that out, he felt he was reasonably safe from any random spot checks. The danger of being stopped by someone who was looking specifically for Henry Faber, fugitive spy, was another problem. They had that picture—

They knew his face. His face!

—and before long they would have a description of the car in which he was travelling. He did not think they would set up roadblocks, as they had no way of guessing where he was headed; but he was sure that every policeman in the land would be on the lookout for the grey Morris Cowley Bullnose, registration number MLN 29.

If he were spotted in the open country, he would not be captured immediately, for country policemen had bicycles, not cars. But the policeman would telephone his headquarters, and cars would be after Faber within minutes. If he saw a policeman, he decided, he would have to ditch this car, steal another, and divert from his planned route. However, in the sparsely populated Scottish lowlands there was a good chance he could get all the way to Aberdeen without passing a country policeman. The towns would be different. There, the danger of being chased by a police car was very great. He would be unlikely to escape: his car was old and relatively slow, and the police were generally good drivers. His best chance would be to get out of the vehicle and hope to lose himself in crowds or back streets. He contemplated ditching the car and stealing another each time he was forced to enter a major town. The problem there was that he would be leaving a trail a mile wide for MI5 to follow. Perhaps the best solution was a compromise: he would drive into the towns but try to use only the back streets. He looked at his watch. He would reach Glasgow around dusk, and thereafter he would benefit from the darkness.

Well, it was not satisfactory, but the only way to be totally safe was not to be a spy.

As he topped the one-thousand-feet-high Beattock Summit, it began to rain. Faber stopped the car and got out to raise the canvas roof. The air was oppressively warm. Faber looked up. The sky had clouded over very quickly. Thunder and lightning were promised.

As he drove on he discovered some of the little car's shortcomings. Wind and rain leaked in through several flaws in the canvas roof, and the small wiper sweeping the top half of the horizontally divided windscreen provided only a tunnel-like view of the road ahead. As the terrain became progressively more hilly, the engine note began to sound faintly ragged. It was hardly surprising: the twenty-year-old car was being pushed hard.

The shower ended. The threatened storm had not arrived, but the sky remained dark and the atmosphere forbidding.

Faber passed through Crawford, nestling in green hills; Abington, a church and a Post Office on the west bank of the River Clyde; and Lesmahagow, on the edge of a heathery moor.

Half an hour later he reached the outskirts of Glasgow. As soon as he entered the built-up area, he turned north off the main road, hoping to circumvent the city. He followed a succession of minor roads, crossing the major arteries into the city's east side, until he reached Cumbernauld Road, where he turned east again and sped out of the city.

It had been quicker than he expected. His luck was holding.

He was on the A80 road, passing factories, mines and farms. More Scots place-names drifted in and out of his consciousness: Millerston, Stepps, Muirhead, Mollinsburn, Condorrat.

His luck ran out between Cumbernauld and Stirling.

He was accelerating along a straight stretch of road, slightly downhill, with open fields on either side. As the speedometer needle touched forty-five there was a sudden, very loud noise from the engine; a heavy rattle, like the sound of a large chain pulling over a cog. He slowed to thirty, but the noise did not get perceptively quieter. Clearly some large and important piece of the mechanism had failed. Faber listened carefully. It was either a cracked ball-bearing in the transmission, or a hole in a big end. Certainly it was nothing so simple as a blocked carburettor or a dirty sparking-plug; nothing that could be repaired outside a workshop.

He pulled up and looked under the bonnet. There seemed to be a lot of oil everywhere, but otherwise he could see no clues. He got back behind the wheel and drove off. There was a definite loss of power, but the car would still go.

Three miles farther on, steam began to billow out of the radiator. Faber realized that the car would soon stop altogether. He looked for a place to dump it.

He found a mud track leading off the main road, presumably to a farm. One hundred yards from the road, the track curved behind a blackberry bush. Faber parked the car close to the bush and killed the engine. The hiss of escaping steam gradually subsided. He got out and locked the door. He felt a twinge of regret for Emma and Jessie, who would find it very difficult to get their car repaired before the end of the war.

He walked back to the main road. From there, the car could not be seen. It might be a day or even two before the abandoned vehicle aroused suspicion. By then, Faber thought, I may be in Berlin.

He began to walk. Sooner or later he would hit a town where he could steal another vehicle. He was doing well enough: it was less than twenty-four hours since he had left London, and he still had a whole day before the U-boat arrived at the rendezvous at six p.m. tomorrow.

The sun had set long ago, and now darkness fell suddenly. Faber could hardly see. Fortunately there was a painted white line down the middle of the road – a safety innovation made necessary by the blackout – and he was just about able to follow it. Because of the night silence he would hear an oncoming car in plenty of time.

In fact only one car passed him. He heard its deep-throated engine in the distance, and went off the road a few yards to lie out of sight until it had gone. It was a large car, a Vauxhall Ten, Faber guessed, and it was travelling at speed. He let it go by, then got up and resumed walking. Twenty minutes later he saw it again, parked by the roadside. He would have taken a detour across the field if he had noticed the car in time, but its light were off and its engine silent, and he almost bumped into it in the darkness.

Before he could consider what to do, a torch shone up toward him from under the car's bonnet, and a voice said: 'I say, is anybody there?'

Faber moved into the beam and said: 'Having trouble?'

'I'll say.'

The torch was pointed down, and as Faber moved closer he could see, by the reflected light, the moustached face of a middle-aged man in a double-breasted coat. In his other hand the man held, rather uncertainly, a large spanner; seeming unsure of what to do with it.

Faber looked at the engine. 'What's wrong?'

'Loss of power,' the man said, pronouncing it 'Lorse of par'. 'One moment she was going like a top, the next she started to hobble. I'm afraid I'm not much of a mechanic.' He shone the torch at Faber again. 'Are you?' he finished hopefully.

'Not exactly,' Faber said, 'but I know a disconnected lead when I see one.' He took the torch from the man, reached down into the engine, and plugged the stray lead back on to the cylinder head. 'Try her now.'

The man got into the car and started the engine. 'Perfect!' he shouted over the noise. 'You're a genius! Hop in.'

It crossed Faber's mind that this might be an elaborate MI5 trap, but he dismissed the thought: in the unlikely event they knew where he was, why should they tread softly? They could as easily send twenty policemen and a couple of armoured cars to pick him up.

He got in.

The driver pulled away and moved rapidly up through the gears until the car was travelling at a good speed. Faber made himself comfortable. The driver said: 'By the way, I'm Richard Porter.'

Faber thought quickly of the identity card in his wallet. 'James Baker.'

'How do you do. I must have passed you on the road back there – didn't see you.'

Faber realized the man was apologizing for not picking him up – everyone picked up hitch-hikers since the petrol shortage. 'It's okay,' Faber said. 'I was probably off the road, behind a bush, answering a call of nature. I did hear a car.'

'Have you come far?' Porter offered a cigar.

'It's good of you, but I don't smoke,' Faber said. 'Yes, I've come from London.'

'Hitch-hiked all the way?'

'No, my car broke down in Edinburgh. Apparently it requires a spare part which isn't in stock, so I had to leave it at the garage.'

'Hard luck. Well, I'm going to Aberdeen, so I can drop you anywhere along the way.'

Faber thought fast. This was a piece of good fortune. He closed his eyes and pictured the map of Scotland. 'That's marvellous,' he said. 'I'm going to Banff, so Aberdeen would be a great help. But I was planning to take the high road, because I didn't get myself a pass – is Aberdeen a Restricted Area?'

'Only the harbour,' Porter said. 'Anyway, you neen't worry about that sort of thing while you're in my car – I'm a JP and a member of the Watch Committee. How's that?'

Faber smiled in the darkness. It was his lucky day. 'Thank you,' he said. He decided to change the subject of the conversation. 'Is that a full-time job? Being a magistrate, I mean.'

Porter put a match to his cigar and puffed smoke.

'Not really. I'm semi-retired, y'know. Used to be a solicitor, until they discovered my weak heart.'

'Ah.' Faber tried to put some sympathy into his voice.

'Hope you don't mind the smoke?' Porter waved the fat cigar.

'Not a bit.'

'What takes you to Banff?'

'I'm an engineer. There's a problem in a factory . . . actually, the job is sort of classified.'

Porter held up his hand. 'Don't say another word. I understand.'

There was silence for a while. The car flashed through several towns. Porter obviously knew the road very well, to drive so fast in the blackout. The big car gobbled up the miles. Its smooth progress was soporific. Faber smothered a yawn.

'Damn, you must be tired,' Porter said. 'Silly of me. Don't be too polite to have a nap.'

'Thank you,' said Faber. 'I will.' He closed his eyes.

The motion of the car was like the rocking of a train, and Faber had his arrival nightmare again, only this time it was slightly different. Instead of dining on the train and talking politics with a fellow passenger, he was obliged for some unknown reason to travel in the coal tender, sitting on his suitcase radio with his back against the hard iron side of the truck. When the train arrived at Waterloo, everyone – including the disem-barking passengers – was carrying a little duplicated photograph of Faber in the running team; and they were all looking at each other and comparing the faces they saw with the face in the picture. At the ticket barrier the collector took his shoulder and said: 'You're the man in the photo, aren't you?' Faber found himself dumb. All he could do was stare at the photograph and remember the way he had run to win that cup. God, how he had run: he had peaked a shade too early, started his final burst a quarter of a mile sooner than he had planned, and for the last 500 metres he wanted to die – and now perhaps he would die, because of that photograph in the ticket collector's hand … The collector was saying: 'Wake up! Wake up!' and suddenly Faber was back in Richard Porter's Vauxhall Ten, and it was Porter who was telling him to wake up.

His right hand was half way to his left sleeve, where the stiletto was sheathed, in the split-second before he remembered that as far as Porter was concerned James Baker was an innocent hitch-hiker. Then his hand dropped and he relaxed.

'You wake up like a soldier,' Porter said with amusement. 'This is Aberdeen.'

Faber noted that 'soldier' had been pronounced 'sol-juh', and recalled that Porter was a magistrate and a member of the police authority. He looked at the man in the dull light of early day: Porter had a red face and a waxed moustache, and his camel-coloured overcoat looked expensive. He was wealthy and powerful in this town, Faber guessed. If he were to disappear he would be missed almost immediately. Faber decided not to kill him.

Faber said: 'Good morning.'

He looked out of the window at the granite city.

They were moving slowly along the main street with shops on either side. There were several early workers about, all moving purposefully in the same direction: fishermen, Faber reckoned. It seemed a cold, windy place.

Porter said: 'Would you like to have a shave and a bit of breakfast before you continue your journey? You're welcome to come to my place.'

'You're very kind—'

'Not at all. If it weren't for you I should still be on the A80 at Stirling, waiting for a garage to open.'

'—but I won't, thank you. I want to get on with the journey.'

Porter did not insist, and Faber suspected that he was relieved not to have his offer taken up. The man said: 'In that case, I'll drop you at George Street – that's the start of the A96, and it's a straight road to Banff.' A moment later he stopped the car at a corner. 'Here you are.'

Faber opened the door. 'Thanks for the lift.'

'A pleasure.' Porter offered a handshake. 'Good luck!'

Faber got out and closed the door, and the car pulled away. He had nothing to fear from Porter, he thought; the man would go home and sleep all day, and by the time he realized he had helped a fugitive, it would be too late to do anything about it.

He watched the Vauxhall out of sight, then crossed the road and entered the promisingly named Market Street. Shortly he found himself in the docks and, following his nose, arrived at the fish market. He felt safely anonymous in the bustling, noisy, smelly market, where everyone was dressed in working clothes as he was. Wet fish and cheerful profanities flew through the air. Faber found it hard to understand the clipped, guttural accents. At a stall he bought hot, strong tea in a chipped half-pint mug and a large bread roll with a doorstep of white cheese.

He sat on a barrel to eat and drink. This evening would be the time to steal a boat. It was galling, to have to wait all day; and it left him with the problem of concealing himself for the next twelve hours; but he was too close now to take risks, and stealing a boat in broad daylight was much more risky than at the twilit end of the day.

He finished his breakfast and stood up. It would be a couple of hours before the rest of the city came to life. He would use the time to pick out a good hiding-place.

He made a circuit of the docks and the tidal harbour. The security was perfunctory, and he spotted several places where he could slip past the checkpoints. He worked his way around to the sandy beach, and set off along the two-mile esplanade. At its far end, a couple of pleasure yachts were moored at the mouth of the River Don. They would have suited Faber's purpose very well, but they would have no fuel.

A thick ceiling of cloud hid the sunrise. The air became very warm and thundery again. A few determined holidaymakers emerged from the seafront hotels and sat stubbornly on the beach, waiting for sunshine. Faber doubted they would get it today.

The beach might be the place to hide. The police would check the railway station and the bus depot, but they would not mount a full-scale search of the city. They might check a few hotels and guest-houses. It was unlikely they would approach everyone on the beach. He decided to spend the day in a deck-chair.

He bought a newspaper from a stall and hired a chair. He removed his shirt and put it back on over his overalls. He left his jacket off.

He would see a policeman, if one came, well before he reached the spot where Faber sat. There would be plenty of time to leave the beach and vanish into the streets.

He began to read the paper. There was a new Allied offensive in Italy, the newspaper rejoiced. Faber was sceptical. Anzio had been a shambles. The paper was badly printed and there were no photographs. He read that the police were searching for one Henry Faber, who had murdered two people in London with a stiletto . . .

A woman in a bathing suit walked by, looking hard at Faber. His heart missed a beat. Then he realized she was being flirtatious. For an instant he was tempted to speak to her. It had been so long . . . He shook himself mentally. Patience, patience. Tomorrow he would be home.

She was a small fishing boat, fifty or sixty feet long and broad in the beam, with an inboard motor. The aerial told of a powerful radio. Most of the deck was taken up with hatches to the small hold below. The cabin was aft, and only large enough to hold two men, standing, plus the dashboard and controls. The hull was clinker-built and newly caulked, and the paintwork looked fresh.

Two other boats in the harbour would have done as well, but Faber had stood on the quay and watched the crew of this one tie her up and refuel before they left for their homes.

He gave them a few minutes to get well away, then walked around the edge of the harbour and jumped on to the boat. She was called *Marie II*.

He found the wheel chained up. He sat on the floor of the little cabin, out of sight, and spent ten minutes picking the lock. Darkness was coming early because of the cloud layer which still blanketed the sky.

When he had freed the wheel he raised the small anchor, then sprang back on to the quay and untied the ropes. He returned to the cabin, primed the diesel engine, and pulled the starter. The motor coughed and died. He tried again. This time it roared to life. He began to manoeuvre out of the mooring.

He got clear of the other craft at the quayside and found the main channel out of the harbour, marked by buoys. He guessed that only boats of much deeper draught really needed to stick to the channel, but he saw no harm in being overcautious.

Once outside the harbour, he felt a stiff breeze, and hoped it was not a sign that the weather was about to break. The sea was surprisingly rough, and the stout little boat lifted high on the waves. Faber opened the throttle wide, consulted the dashboard compass, and set a course. He found some charts in a locker below the wheel. They looked old and little-used: no doubt the boat's skipper knew the local waters too well to need charts. Faber checked the map reference he had memorized that night in Stockwell, set a more exact course, and engaged the wheel-clamp.

The cabin windows were obscured by water. Faber could not tell whether it was rain or spray. The wind was slicing off the tops of the waves now. He poked his head out of the cabin door for a moment, and got his face thoroughly wet.

He switched on the radio. It hummed for a moment, then crackled. He moved the frequency control, wandering the airwaves, and picked up a few garbled messages. The set was working perfectly. He tuned to the U-boat's frequency, then switched off – it was too soon to make contact.

The waves increased in size as he progressed into deeper waters. Now the boat reared up like a bucking horse with each wave, then teetered momentarily at the top before plunging sickeningly down into the next trough. Faber stared blindly out of the cabin windows. Night had fallen, and he could see nothing at all. He felt faintly seasick.

Each time he convinced himself that the waves could not possibly get bigger, a new monster taller than the rest lifted the vessel toward the sky. They started to come closer together, so that the boat was always lying with its stern pointed either up at the sky or down at the sea bed. In a particularly deep trough the little boat was suddenly illuminated, as clearly as if it were day, by a flash of lightning. Faber saw a grey-green mountain of water descend on the prow and wash over the deck and the cabin where he stood. He could not tell whether the terrible crack which sounded a second afterwards was the thunderclap or the noise of the timbers of the boat breaking up. Frantically he searched the little cabin for a life jacket. There was none.

The lightning came repeatedly then. Faber held the locked wheel and braced his back against the cabin wall to stay upright. There was no point in operating the controls now – the boat would go where the sea threw it.

He kept telling himself that the boat must be built to withstand such sudden summer gales. He could not convince himself. Experienced fishermen probably would have seen the signs of such a storm, and refrained from leaving shore, knowing their vessel could not survive such weather.

He had no idea where he was, now. He might be almost back in Aberdeen, or he might be at his rendez-vous. He sat on the cabin floor and switched on the radio. The wild rocking and shuddering made it difficult to operate the set. When it warmed up he experimented with the dials, and could pick up nothing. He turned the volume to maximum: still no sound.

The aerial must have been broken off its fixing on the cabin roof.

He switched to Transmit and repeated the simple message 'Come in, please,' several times; then left the set on Receive. He had little hope of his signal getting through.

He killed the engine to conserve fuel. He was going to have to ride out the storm – if he could – then find a way to repair or replace the aerial. He might need his fuel.

The boat slid terrifyingly sideways down the next big wave, and Faber realized he needed the engine power to ensure the vessel met waves head-on. He pulled the starter, but nothing happened. He tried several times, then gave up, cursing his foolishness for switching off.

The boat rolled so far on to its side that Faber fell and cracked his head on the wheel. He lay dazed on the cabin floor, expecting the vessel to turn turtle at any minute. Another wave crashed on the cabin, and this time the glass in the windows shattered. Suddenly Faber was under water. Certain the boat was sinking, he struggled to his feet, and broke surface. All the windows were out, but the vessel was still floating. He kicked open the cabin door, and the water gushed out. He clutched the wheel to prevent himself being washed into the sea.

Incredibly, the storm continued to get worse. One of Faber's last coherent thoughts was that these waters probably did not see such a storm more than once in a century. Then all his concentration and will were focused on the problem of keeping hold of the wheel. He should have tied himself to it, but now he did not dare to let go long enough to find a piece of rope. He lost all sense of up and down as the boat pitched and rolled on waves like cliffs. Gale force winds and thousands of gallons of water strained to pull him from his place. His feet slipped continually on the wet floor and walls, and the muscles of his arms burned with pain. He sucked air when he found his head above water, but otherwise held his breath. Many times he came close to blacking out. He vaguely realized that the flat roof of the cabin had disappeared.

He got brief, nightmarish glimpses of the sea whenever the lightning flashed. He was always surprised to see where the wave was: ahead, below, rearing up beside him, or completely out of sight. He discovered with a shock that he could not feel his hands, and looked down to see that they were still locked to the wheel, frozen in a grip like rigor mortis. There was a continuous roar in his ears, the wind indistinguishable from the thunder and the sea.

The power of intelligent thought slipped slowly away from him. In something that was less than a hallucination but more than a daydream, he saw the girl who had stared at him on the beach. She walked endlessly toward him over the bucking deck of the fishing boat, her swimsuit clinging to her body, always getting closer but never reaching him. He knew that, when she came within touching distance, he would take his dead hands from the wheel and reach for her, but he kept saying 'Not yet, not yet,' as she walked and smiled and swayed her hips. He was tempted to leave the wheel and close the gap himself, but something at the back of his mind told him that if he moved he would never reach her, so he waited and watched and smiled back at her from time to time, and even when he closed his eyes he could see her still.

He was slipping in and out of consciousness now.

His mind would drift away, the sea and the boat disappearing first, then the girl fading, until he would jerk awake to find that, incredibly, he was still standing, still holding the wheel, still alive; then for a while he would will himself to stay conscious, but eventually exhaustion would take over again.

In one of his last clear moments he noticed that the waves were moving in one direction, carrying the boat with them. Lightning flashed again, and he saw to one side a huge dark mass, an impossibly high wave – no, it was not a wave, it was a cliff . . . The realization that he was close to land was swamped by the fear of being hurled against the cliff and smashed. Stupidly, he pulled the starter, then hastily returned his hand to the wheel; but it would no longer grip.

A new wave lifted the boat and threw it down like a discarded toy. As he fell through the air, still clutching the wheel with one hand, Faber saw a pointed rock like a stiletto sticking up out of the trough of the wave. It seemed certain to impale the boat. But the hull of the little craft scraped the edge of the rock and was carried past.

The mountainous waves were breaking now. The next one was too much for the vessel's timbers. The boat hit the trough with a solid impact, and the sound of the hull splitting cracked the night like an explosion. Faber knew the boat was finished.

The water retreated, and Faber realized that the hull had broken because it had hit land. He stared in dumb astonishment as a new flash of lightning revealed a beach. The sea lifted the ruined boat off the sand as water crashed over the deck again, knocking Faber to the floor. But he had seen everything with daylight clarity in that moment. The beach was narrow, and the waves were breaking right up to the cliff. But there was a jetty, over to his right, and a bridge of some kind leading from the jetty to the cliff top. He knew that if he left the boat for the beach, the next wave would kill him with tons of water or break his head like an egg against the cliff. But if he could reach the jetty in between waves, he might scramble far enough up the bridge to be out of reach of the water.

He might survive yet.

The next wave split the deck open as if the seasoned wood were no stronger than a banana skin. The boat collapsed under Faber, and he found himself sucked backward by the receding surf. He scrambled upright, his legs like jelly beneath him, and broke into a run, splashing through the shallows toward the jetty. Running those few yards was the hardest thing he had ever done. He *wanted* to stumble, so that he could rest in the water and die; but he stayed upright, just as he had when he won the 5,000 metres race, until he crashed into one of the pillars of the jetty. He reached up and grabbed the boards with his hands, willing them to come back to life for a few seconds; and lifted himself until his chin was over the edge; then he swung his legs up and rolled over.

The wave came as he got to his knees. He threw himself forward. The wave carried him a few yards then flung him brutally against the wooden planking. He swallowed water and saw stars. When the weight lifted from his back he summoned the will to move. It would not come. He felt himself being dragged inexorably back. A sudden rage possessed him. He would not be beaten, not now! He screamed his hatred of the storm and the sea and the British and Percival Godliman, and suddenly he was on his feet and running, running, away from the sea and up the ramp, running with his eyes shut and his mouth open and madness in his heart, daring his lungs to burst and his bones to break; remembering, dimly, that he had called on this madness once before and almost died; running with no sense of destination, but knowing he would not stop until he lost his mind.

The ramp was long and steep. A strong man might have run all the way to the top, if he were in training and rested. An Olympic athlete, if he were tired, might have got half way. The average forty-year-old man would have managed a yard or two.

Faber made it to the top.

A yard from the end of the ramp he had a slight heart attack and lost consciousness, but his legs pumped twice more before he hit the sodden turf.

He never knew how long he lay there. When he opened his eyes the storm still raged, but day had broken, and he could see, a few yards away from him, a small cottage which looked inhabited.

He got to his knees and began the long crawl to the front door.

CHAPTER EIGHTEEN

THE *U-505* wheeled in a tedious circle, her powerful diesels chugging slowly as she nosed through the depths like a grey, toothless shark. Lieutenant-Commander Werner Heer, her master, was drinking ersatz coffee and trying not to smoke any more cigarettes. It had been a long day and a long night. He disliked his assignment, for he was a fighting man and there was no fighting to be done; and he disliked the quiet Abwehr officer with sly blue eyes who was an unwelcome guest aboard the submarine.

The Intelligence man, Major Wohl, sat opposite the captain. The man never looked tired, damn him. Those blue eyes looked around, taking things in, but the expression in them never changed. His uniform never got rumpled, despite the rigours of underwater life; and he lit a new cigarette every twenty minutes, on the dot, and smoked it to a quarter-inch stub. Heer would have stopped smoking, just so that he could enforce regulations and prevent Wohl from enjoying tobacco, but Heer himself was too much of an addict.

Heer never liked Intelligence people, because he always had the feeling they were gathering intelligence on him. Nor did he like working with Abwehr. His vessel was made for battle, not for skulking around the British coast waiting to pick up secret agents. It seemed to him plain madness to put at risk a costly piece of fighting machinery, not to mention its skilled crew, for the sake of one man who might even fail to appear.

He emptied his cup and made a face. 'Damn coffee,' he said. 'It tastes vile.'

Wohl's expressionless gaze rested on him for a moment then moved away. He said nothing.

Heer shifted restlessly in his seat. On the bridge of a ship he would have paced up and down, but men on submarines learn to avoid unnecessary movement. He said: 'Your man won't come in this weather, you know.'

Wohl looked at his watch. 'We will wait until six a.m.,' he said calmly.

It was not an order, for Wohl could not give orders to Heer; but the bald statement of fact was still an insult to a superior officer. Heer said: 'Damn you, I'm the master of this vessel!'

'We will both follow our orders,' Wohl said. 'As you know, they originate from a very high authority indeed.'

Heer controlled his anger. The young whipper-snapper was right, of course. Heer would follow his orders. When they returned to port he would report Wohl for insubordination. Not that it would do much good: fifteen years in the Navy had taught Heer that headquarters people were a law unto themselves.

He said: 'If your man is fool enough to venture out tonight, he is certainly not seaman enough to survive.'

Wohl's only reply was the same blank gaze.

Heer called to the radio operator. 'Weissman?'

'Nothing, sir.'

Wohl said: 'I have an unpleasant feeling that the murmurs we heard a few hours ago were from him.'

'If they were, he was a long way from the rendezvous, sir,' the radio operator volunteered. 'To me it sounded more like lightning.'

Heer added: 'If it was not him, it was not him. If it was him, he is now drowned.' His tone was smug.

'You don't know the man,' Wohl said, and this time there was a trace of emotion in his voice.

Heer subsided into silence. The engine note altered slightly, and he thought he could distinguish a faint rattle. If it increased on the journey home he would have it looked at in port. He might do that anyway, just to avoid another voyage with the unspeakable Major Wohl.

A seaman looked in. 'Coffee, sir?'

Heer shook his head. 'If I drink any more I'll be pissing coffee.'

Wohl said: 'I will, please.' He took out a cigarette.

That made Heer look at his watch. It was ten past six. The subtle Major Wohl had delayed his six o'clock cigarette to keep the U-boat there a few extra minutes. Heer said: 'Set a course for home.'

'One moment,' Wohl said. 'I think we should take a look on the surface before we leave.'

'Don't be a fool,' Heer said. He knew he was on safe ground now. 'Do you realize what kind of storm is raging up there? We would not be able to open the hatch, and the periscope will show us nothing that is more than a few yards away.'

'How can you tell what the storm is like from this depth?'

'Experience,' Heer told him.

'Then at least send a signal to base, telling them that our man has not made contact. They may order us to stay here.'

Heer gave an exasperated sigh. 'It's not possible to make radio contact from this depth, not with base,' he said.

Wohl's calm was shattered at last. 'Commander Heer, I strongly recommend you surface and radio home before leaving this rendezvous. The man we are to pick up has information vital to the future of the Reich. The Führer himself is waiting for his report!'

Heer looked at him. 'Thank you for letting me have your opinion, Major,' he said. He turned away. 'Full ahead both!' he barked.

The sound of the twin diesels rose to a roar, and the U-boat began to pick up speed.

Part Four

CHAPTER NINETEEN

WHEN LUCY woke up, the storm that had broken the evening before was still raging. She leaned over the edge of the bed, moving cautiously so that she would not disturb David, and picked up her wristwatch from the door. It was just after six. The wind was howling around the roof. David could sleep on: little work would be done today.

She wondered whether they had lost any slates off the roof during the night. She would need to check the loft. The job would have to wait until David was out, otherwise he would be angry that she had not asked him to do it.

She slipped out of bed. It was very cold. The warm weather of the last few days had been a phoney summer, the build-up to the storm. Now it was as cold as November. She pulled the flannel nightdress off over her head and quickly got into her underwear, trousers and sweater. David stirred. She looked at him: he turned over, but did not wake.

She crossed the tiny landing and looked into Jo's room. The three-year-old had graduated from a cot to a bed, and he often fell out during the night without waking. This morning he was on his bed, lying asleep on his back with his mouth wide open. Lucy smiled. He looked adorable when he was asleep.

She went quietly downstairs, wondering briefly why she had woken up so early. Perhaps Jo had made a noise, or maybe it was the storm.

She knelt in front of the fireplace, pushing back the sleeves of her sweater, and began to make the fire. As she swept out the grate she whistled a tune she had heard on the radio, *Is You Is Or Is You Ain't My Baby?* She raked the cold ashes, using the biggest lumps to form the base for today's fire. Dried bracken provided the tinder and wood and then coal went on top. Sometimes she just used wood, but coal was better in this weather. She held a page of newspaper across the fireplace for a few minutes to create an updraught in the chimney. When she removed it the wood was burning and the coal glowing red. She folded the paper and placed it under the coal scuttle for use tomorrow.

The blaze would soon warm the little house, but a hot cup of tea would help meanwhile. Lucy went into the kitchen and put the kettle on the electric cooker. She put two cups on a tray, then found David's cigarettes and an ashtray. She made the tea, filled the cups, and carried the tray through the hall to the stairs.

She had one foot on the lowest stair when she heard the tapping. She stopped, frowned, decided it was the wind rattling something, and took another step. The sound came again. It was like someone knocking on the front door.

That was ridiculous, of course. There was no one to

knock on the front door – only Tom, and he always came to the kitchen door and never knocked.

The tapping came again.

Just to assuage her curiosity, she came down the stairs and, balancing the tea tray on one hand, opened the front door.

She dropped the tray in shock. The man fell into the hall, knocking her over. Lucy screamed.

She was frightened only for a moment. The stranger lay prone beside her on the hall floor, plainly incapable of attacking anyone. His clothes were soaking wet, and his hands and face were stone-white with cold.

Lucy got to her feet. David slid down the stairs on his bottom, saying: 'What is it? What is it?'

'Him,' Lucy said, and pointed.

David arrived at the foot of the stairs, clad in pyjamas, and hauled himself into his wheelchair. 'I don't see what there is to scream about,' he said. He wheeled himself closer and peered at the man on the floor.

'I'm sorry. He startled me.' She bent over and, taking the man by his upper arms, dragged him into the living-room. David followed. Lucy laid the man in front of the fire.

David stared pensively at the unconscious body. 'Where the devil did he come from?' he wondered.

'He must be a shipwrecked sailor.'

'Of course.'

But he was wearing the clothes of a workman, not a sailor, Lucy noticed. She studied him. He was quite a big man, longer than the six-foot hearth-rug, and heavy around the neck and shoulders. His face was strong and fine-boned, with a high forehead and a long jaw. He might be handsome, she thought, if he were not such a ghastly colour.

The stranger stirred and opened his eyes. At first he looked terribly frightened, like a little boy waking in strange surroundings; but, very quickly, his expression became relaxed, and he looked about him sharply, his gaze resting briefly on Lucy, David, the window, the door, and the fire.

Lucy said: 'We must get him out of these clothes. Fetch a pair of pyjamas and a robe, David.'

David wheeled himself out, and Lucy knelt beside the stranger. She took off his boots and socks first. There almost seemed to be a hint of amusement in his eyes as he watched her. But when she reached for his jacket he crossed his arms protectively over his chest.

'You'll die of pneumonia if you keep these clothes on,' she said in her best bedside manner. 'Let me take them off.'

The stranger said: 'I really don't think we know each other well enough – after all, we haven't been introduced.'

It was the first time he had spoken. His voice was so confident, his words so formal, that the contrast with his terrible appearance made Lucy laugh out loud. 'You're shy?' she said.

'I just think a man should preserve an air of mystery.' He was grinning broadly, but his smile collapsed suddenly and his eyes closed in pain.

David came back in with clean nightclothes over his arm. 'You two seem to be getting on remarkably well already,' he said.

'You'll have to undress him,' Lucy said. 'He won't let me.'

David's look was unreadable.

The stranger said: 'I'll manage on my own, thanks – if it's not too awfully ungracious of me.'

'Suit yourself,' David said. He dumped the clothes on a chair and wheeled out.

'I'll make some more tea,' Lucy said as she followed. She closed the living-room door behind her.

In the kitchen, David was already filling the kettle, a lighted cigarette dangling from his lips. Lucy quickly cleared up the broken china in the hall then joined him.

David said: 'Five minutes ago I wasn't at all sure the chap was alive – and now he's dressing himself.'

Lucy busied herself with a teapot. 'Perhaps he was shamming.'

'The prospect of being undressed by you certainly brought about a rapid recovery.'

'I can't believe anyone could be that shy.'

'Your own deficiency in that area may lead you to underestimate its power in others.'

Lucy rattled cups. 'You don't usually get all bitter and twisted until after breakfast. Besides, how can an area be powerful?'

'Semantics is always your last line of defence.' David doused the butt of his cigarette in a pool of water in the sink.

Lucy poured boiling water into the teapot. 'Let's not quarrel today – we've got something more interesting to do, for a change.' She picked up the tray and walked into the living-room.

The stranger was buttoning his pyjama jacket. He turned his back to her as she walked in. She put the tray down and poured tea. When she turned back he was wearing David's robe.

'You're very kind,' he said. His gaze was direct.

He really didn't seem the shy type, Lucy thought. However, he was some years older than she – about forty, she guessed. That might account for it. He was looking less of a castaway every minute.

'Sit close to the fire,' she told him. She handed him a cup of tea.

'I'm not sure I can manage the saucer,' he said. 'My fingers aren't functioning.' He took the cup from her stiff-handed, holding it between both palms, and carried it carefully to his lips.

David came in and offered him a cigarette. He declined.

The stranger emptied the cup. 'Where am I?' he asked.

David said: 'This place is called Storm Island.'

The man showed a trace of relief. 'I thought I might have been blown back to the mainland.'

David spread his hands to the fire to warm his fingers. 'You were probably swept into the bay,' he said. 'Things usually are. That's how the beach was formed.'

Jo came in, bleary-eyed, trailing a one-armed panda

as big as himself. When he saw the stranger he ran to Lucy and hid his face.

'I've frightened your little girl,' the man smiled.

'He's a boy. I must cut his hair.' Lucy lifted Jo on to her lap.

'I'm sorry.' The stranger's eyes closed again, and he swayed in his seat.

Lucy stood up, dumping Jo on the sofa. 'We must put the poor man to bed, David.'

'Just a minute,' David said. He wheeled himself closer to the man. 'Might there be any other survivors?' he asked.

The man's face looked up. 'I was alone,' he muttered. He was very nearly all in.

'David—' Lucy began.

'One more question: Did you notify the coastguard of your route?'

'What does it matter?' Lucy said.

'It matters because, if he did, there may be men out there risking their lives looking for him, and we can let them know he's safe.'

The man said slowly: 'I . . . did . . . not.'

'That's enough,' Lucy told David. She knelt in front of the man. 'Can you make it upstairs?'

He nodded and got slowly to his feet.

Lucy looped his arm over her shoulders and began to walk him out. 'I'll put him in Jo's bed,' she said.

They took the stairs one at a time, pausing on each. When they reached the top, the little colour that the fire had restored to the man's face had drained away again. Lucy led him into the smaller bedroom. He collapsed on to the bed.

Lucy arranged the blankets over him, tucked him in, and left the room, closing the door quietly.

Relief washed over Faber in a tidal wave. For the last few minutes, the effort of self-control had been super-human. He felt limp, defeated and ill.

After the front door had opened, he had allowed himself to collapse for a while. The danger had come when the beautiful girl had started to undress him, and he had remembered the can of film taped to his chest. Dealing with that had restored his alertness for a while. He had also been afraid they might call for an ambu-lance, but that had not been mentioned: perhaps the island was too small to have a hospital. At least he was not on the mainland – there, it would have been impossible to prevent the reporting of the shipwreck. However, the trend of the husband's questions had indicated that no report would be made immediately.

Faber had no energy to speculate about perils farther in the future. He seemed to be safe for the time being, and that was as far as he could go. In the meantime he was warm and dry and alive, and the bed was soft.

He turned over, reconnoitring the room: door, window, chimney. The habit of caution survived every-thing but death itself. The walls were pink, as if the couple had hoped for a baby girl. There was a train set and a great many picture books on the floor. It was a safe, domestic place; a home. He was a wolf in a sheep fold, but a lame wolf.

He closed his eyes. Despite his exhaustion, he had to

force himself to relax, muscle by muscle. Gradually his head emptied of thought, and he slept.

Lucy tasted the porridge, and added another pinch of salt. They had got to like it the way Tom made it, the Scots way, without sugar. She would never go back to making sweet porridge, even when sugar became plentiful and unrationed again. It was funny how you got used to things when you had to: brown bread and margarine and salt porridge.

She ladled it out and the family sat down to breakfast. Jo had lots of milk to cool his. David ate vast quantities these days, without getting fat: it was the outdoor life. She looked at his hands, on the table. They were rough, and permanently brown, the hands of a manual worker. She had noticed the stranger's hands. His fingers were long, the skin white under the blood and the bruising. He was unused to the abrasive work of crewing a boat.

Lucy said: 'You won't get much done today. The storm looks like staying.'

'Makes no difference,' David grunted. 'Sheep still have to be cared for, whatever the weather.'

'Where will you be?'

'Tom's end. I'll go up there in the jeep.'

Jo said: 'Can I come?'

'Not today,' Lucy told him. 'It's too wet and cold.'

'But I don't like the man.'

Lucy smiled. 'Don't be silly. He won't do us any harm. He's almost too ill to move.'

'Who is he?'

'We don't know his name. He's been shipwrecked, and we have to look after him until he's well enough to go back to the mainland. He's a very nice man.'

'Is he my uncle?'

'Just a stranger, Jo. Eat up.'

Jo looked disappointed. He had met an uncle once. In his mind uncles were people who gave out candy, which he liked, and money, which he had no use for.

David finished his breakfast and put on his mackintosh. It was a tent-shaped garment, with sleeves and a hole for his head, and it covered most of his wheelchair as well as him. He put a sou'wester on his head and tied it under his chin. He kissed Jo and said goodbye to Lucy.

A minute or two later she heard the jeep start up. She went to the window to watch David drive off into the rain. The rear wheels of the vehicle slithered about in the mud. He would have to take care.

She turned to Jo. He said: 'This is a dog.' He was making a picture on the tablecloth with porridge and milk.

Lucy slapped his hand, saying: 'What a horrid mess!' The boy's face took on a grim, sulky look, and Lucy thought how much he resembled his father. They had the same dark skin and nearly black hair, and they both had a way of withdrawing when they were cross. But Jo laughed a lot – he had inherited something from Lucy's side of the family, thank God.

Jo mistook her contemplative stare for anger, and said: 'I'm sorry.'

She washed him at the kitchen sink, then cleared away the breakfast things, thinking about the stranger upstairs. Now that the immediate crisis was past, and she knew the man was not going to die, she was consumed with curiosity about him. Who was he? Where was he from? What had he been doing in the storm? Did he have a family? Why did he have workman's clothes, a clerk's hands, and a Home Counties accent? It was rather exciting.

It occurred to her that, if she had lived anywhere else, she would not have accepted his sudden appearance so readily. He might, she supposed, be a deserter, or a criminal, or even an escaped prisoner-of-war. But one forgot, living on the island, that other human beings could be threatening instead of companionable. It was so nice to see a new face that to harbour suspicions seemed ungrateful. Maybe – unpleasant thought – she more than most people was ready to welcome an attractive man ... She pushed the thought out of her mind.

Silly, silly. He was so tired and ill that he could not possibly threaten anyone. Even on the mainland, who could have refused to take him in, bedraggled and unconscious? When he felt better they could question him, and if his account of how he got here was less than plausible, they could radio the mainland from Tom's cottage.

When she had washed up she crept upstairs to peep at him. He slept facing the door, and when she looked in his eyes opened instantly. Again there was that initial, split-second flash of fear.

'It's all right,' Lucy whispered. 'Just making sure you're okay.'

He closed his eyes without speaking.

She went downstairs again. She dressed herself and Jo in oilskins and wellington boots, and they went out. The rain was still coming down in torrents and the wind was terrific. She glanced up at the roof: they had lost some slates. Leaning into the wind, she headed for the cliff top.

She held Jo's hand tightly – he might quite easily be blown away. Two minutes later she was wishing she had stayed indoors. Rain came in under her raincoat collar and over the tops of her boots, and she was soaked. Jo must be too, but now that they were wet they might as well stay wet for a few minutes more. Lucy wanted to go to the beach.

However, when they reached the top of the ramp she realized it was impossible. The narrow wooden walkway was slippery with rain, and in this wind she might lose her balance and fall off, to plunge sixty feet to the beach below. She had to content herself with looking.

It was quite a sight.

Vast waves, each the size of a small house, were rolling in rapidly, close on each other's heels. Crossing the beach the wave would rise even higher, its crest curling in a question mark, then throw itself against the foot of the cliff in a rage. Spray rose over the cliff top in sheets, causing Lucy to step back hurriedly and Jo to squeal with delight. Lucy could hear her son's laughter only because he had jumped into her arms, and his mouth was now close to her ear: the noise of the wind and the sea drowned more distant sounds.

There was something terribly thrilling in watching the elements spit and sway and roar in fury, in standing fractionally too close to the cliff edge, feeling threatened and safe at the same time, shivering with cold and yet perspiring in fear. It was thrilling, and there were few thrills in Lucy's life.

She was about to go back, mindful of Jo's health, when she saw the boat.

It was not a boat any more, of course; that was what was so shocking about it. All that was left were the huge timbers of the deck and the keel. They were scattered on the rocks below the cliffs like a dropped handful of matches. It had been a *big* boat, Lucy realized. One man might have piloted it alone, but not easily. And the damage the sea had wrought on man's craftsmanship was awesome. It was hard to spot two bits of wood still joined together.

How, in Heaven's name, had the stranger come out of it alive?

She shuddered when she thought of what those waves and those rocks might have done to a human body. Jo caught her sudden change of mood, and said into her ear: 'Go home, now.' She turned quickly away from the sea and hurried back along the muddy path to the cottage.

Back inside, they took off their wet coats, hats and boots, and hung them in the kitchen to dry. Lucy went upstairs and looked in on the stranger again. This time he did not open his eyes. He seemed to be sleeping very peacefully, yet she had a feeling that he had awakened and recognized her tread on the stairs, and closed his eyes again before she opened the door.

She ran a hot bath. She and the boy were soaked to the skin. She undressed Jo and put him in the tub, then – on impulse – took off her own clothes and got in with him. The heat was blissful. She closed her eyes and relaxed. This was good, too: to be in a house, feeling warm, while the storm beat impotently at the strong stone walls.

Life had turned interesting, all of a sudden. In one night there had come a storm, a shipwreck and a mystery man; this after three years of tedium. She hoped the stranger would wake up soon, so that she could find out all about him.

It was time she started cooking lunch for the men. She had some breast of lamb to make a stew. She got out of the bath and towelled herself gently. Jo was playing with his bath toy, a much-chewed rubber cat. Lucy looked at herself in the mirror, examining the stretch-marks on her belly left by pregnancy. They were fading, slowly, but they would never completely disappear. An all-over suntan would help, though. She smiled to herself, thinking: Fat chance of that! Besides, who was interested in her tummy? Nobody but herself.

Jo said: 'Can I stay in a minute more?' It was a phrase he used, 'a minute more', and it could mean anything up to half a day.

Lucy said: 'Just while I get dressed.' She hung the towel on a rail and moved toward the door.

The stranger stood in the doorway, looking at her.

They stared at each other. It was odd – Lucy thought later – that she felt not a bit afraid. It was the way he looked at her: there was no threat in his expression, no lewdness, no smirk, no lust. He was not looking at her pubis, or even her breasts, but at her face – into her eyes. She gazed back, a little shocked but not embarrassed, with just a tiny part of her mind wondering why she did not squeal, cover herself with her hands, and slam the door on him.

Something did come into his eyes, at last – perhaps she was imagining it, but she saw admiration, and a faint twinkle of honest humour, and a trace of sadness – and then the spell was broken, and he turned away and went back into his bedroom, closing the door. A moment later Lucy heard the springs creak as his weight settled on the bed.

And for no good reason at all she felt dreadfully guilty.

CHAPTER TWENTY

B Y THIS time Percival Godliman had pulled out
all the stops.

Every policeman in the UK had a copy of the
photograph of Faber, and about half of them were
engaged full-time in the search. In the cities they were
checking hotels and guest-houses, railway stations and
bus terminals, cafés and shopping centres; and the
bridges, arches, and bombed lots where the derelict
hang out. In the country they were looking in barns
and silos, empty cottages and ruined castles, thickets
and clearings and cornfields. They were showing the
photograph to ticket clerks, petrol station staff, ferry
hands and toll collectors. All the passenger ports and
airfields were covered, with the picture pinned behind
a board at every Passport Control desk.

The police thought they were looking for a straightforward murderer.

The cop on the street knew that the man in the
picture had killed two people with a knife in London.
Senior officers knew a bit more: that one of the murders
had been a sexual assault, another apparently motive-
less, and a third – which their men were not to know of
– was an unexplained but bloody attack on a soldier on

the Euston-to-Liverpool train. Only chief constables, and a few officers at Scotland Yard, realized that the soldier had been on temporary attachment to MI5 and that all the murders were connected with Security.

The newspapers, too, thought it was just an ordinary murder hunt. The day after Godliman had released details, most of the papers had carried the story in their later editions – the first editions, bound for Scotland, Ulster and North Wales, had missed it, so they had carried a shortened version a day later. The Stockwell victim had been identified as a labourer, and given a false name and a vague London background. Godliman's press release had connected that murder with the death of Mrs Una Garden in 1940, but had been vague about the nature of the link. The murder weapon was said to be a stiletto.

The two Liverpool newspapers heard very quickly of the body on the train, and both wondered whether the London knife murderer was responsible. Both made enquiries with the Liverpool police. The editors of both papers received phone calls from the Chief Constable. Neither paper carried the story.

A total of one hundred and fifty-seven tall dark men were arrested on suspicion of being Faber. All but twenty-nine of them were able to prove that they could not possibly have committed the murders. Interviewers from MI5 talked to the twenty-nine. Twenty-seven called in parents, relatives and neighbours who affirmed that they had been born in Britain and had been living there during the twenties, when Faber had been in Germany.

The last two were brought to London and interviewed again, this time by Godliman. Both were bachelors, living alone, with no surviving relatives, leading a transient existence.

The first was a well-dressed, confident man who claimed implausibly that his way of life was to travel the country taking odd jobs as a manual labourer. Godliman explained that he was looking for a German spy, and that he – unlike the police – had the power to incarcerate anyone for the duration of the war, and no questions asked. Furthermore, he went on, he was not in the least interested in capturing ordinary criminals, and any information given him here at the War Office was strictly confidential, and would go no further.

The prisoner promptly confessed to being a confidence trickster and gave the addresses of nineteen elderly ladies whom he had cheated out of their old jewellery during the past three weeks. Godliman turned him over to the police.

He felt no obligation to be honest with a professional liar.

The last suspect also cracked under Godliman's treatment. His secret was that he was not a bachelor at all, not by a long way. He had a wife in Brighton. And in Solihull, Birmingham. And in Colchester, Newbury and Exeter. All five were able to produce marriage certificates later that day. The bigamist went to gaol to await trial.

Godliman slept in his office while the hunt went on.

*

Bristol, Temple Meads, railway station:

'Good morning, Miss. Would you look at this, please?'

'Hey, girls – the bobby's going to show us his snaps!'

'Now, don't muck about, just tell me if you've seen him.'

'Ooh, ain't he handsome! I wish I had!'

'You wouldn't if you knew what he'd done. Would you all take a look, please?'

'Never seen him.'

'Me neither.'

'Not me.'

'No.'

'When you catch him, ask him if he wants to meet a nice young Bristol girl.'

'You girls – I don't know . . . Just because they give you a pair of trousers and a porter's job, you think you're supposed to act like men . . .'

The Woolwich Ferry:

'Filthy day, Constable.'

'Morning, Captain. I expect it's worse on the high seas.'

'Can I help you? Or are you just crossing the river?'

'I want you to look at a face, Captain.'

'Let me put my specs on. Oh, don't worry, I can see to guide the ship. It's close things I need the glasses for, Now then . . .'

'Ring any bells?'

'Sorry, Constable. Means nothing to me.'

'Well, let me know if you see him.'

'Certainly.'

'Bon voyage.'

Number thirty-five Leak Street, London E1:

'Sergeant Riley – what a nice surprise!'

'Never mind the lip, Mabel. Who've you got here?'

'All respectable guests, Sergeant; you know me.'

'I know you, all right. That's why I'm here. Would any of your nice respectable guests happen to be on the trot?'

'Since when have you been recruiting for the Army?'

'I'm not, Mabel, I'm looking for a villain, and if he's here, he's probably told you he's on the trot.'

'Look, Jack – if I tell you there's nobody here I don't know, will you go away and stop pestering me?'

'Why should I trust you?'

'Because of 1936.'

'You were better looking then, Mabel.'

'So were you, Jack.'

'You win … Take a butcher's at this. If chummy comes in here, send word, okay?'

'Promise.'

'Don't waste any time about it, either.'

'All right!'

'Mabel … he knifed a woman your age. I'm just marking your cards.'

'I know. Thanks.'

'Ta-ta.'
'Take care, Jacko.'

Bill's Café, on the A30 near Bagshot:

'Tea, please, Bill. Two sugars.'

'Good morning, Constable Pearson. Filthy day.'

'What's on that plate, Bill – pebbles from Portsmouth?'

'Buttered buns, as well you know.'

'Oh! I'll have two, then. Thanks . . . Now then, lads! Anyone who wants his lorry checked from top to bottom can leave right away . . . That's better. Take a look at this picture, please.'

'What are you after him for, Constable – cycling without lights?'

'Never mind the jokes, Harry – pass the picture round. Anybody given a lift to that bloke?'

'Not me.'

'No.'

'Sorry, Constable.'

'Never clapped eyes on him.'

'Thank you, lads. If you see him, report it. Cheerio.'

'Constable?'

'Yes, Bill?'

'You haven't paid for the buns.'

'I'm confiscating them as evidence. Cheerio.'

Smethwick's Garage, Carlisle:

'Morning, Missus. When you've got a minute . . .'

'Be right with you, officer. Just let me attend to this

gentleman . . . Twelve and sixpence, please, sir. Thank you. Goodbye . . .'

'How's business?'

'Terrible, as usual. What can I do for you?'

'Can we go in the office for a minute?'

'Aye, come on . . . Now, then.'

'Take a look at this picture and tell me whether you've served that man with petrol recently.'

'Well, it shouldn't be too difficult. It's not as if we get hordes of customers passing through . . . ooh! D'you know, I think I have served him!'

'When?'

'Day before yesterday, in the morning.'

'How sure are you?'

'Well . . . he was older than the picture, but I'm pretty sure.'

'What was he driving?'

'A grey car. I'm no good on makes, this is my husband's business really, but he's in the Navy now.'

'Well, what did it look like? Sports car? Limousine?'

'It was the old sort, with a canvas roof that comes up. A two-seater. Sporty. It had a spare petrol tank bolted to the running-board, and I filled that, too.'

'Do you remember what he was wearing?'

'Not really. Working clothes, I think.'

'A tall man?'

'Yes, taller than you.'

'By the heck, I think it's him! Have you got a telephone . . .?'

*

William Duncan was twenty-five years old, five-feet-ten, weighed a trim 150 pounds, and was in first-class health. His open-air life and total lack of interest in tobacco, drink, late nights and loose living kept him that way. Yet he was not in the Armed Services.

He had seemed to be a normal child, if a little backward, until the age of eight, when his mind simply stopped developing. There had been no trauma that anyone knew about, no physical damage to account for sudden breakdown. Indeed, it was some years before anyone noticed that there was anything wrong, for at the age of ten he was no more than a little backward, and at twelve he was just dim-witted; but by fifteen he was obviously simple, and by eighteen he was known as Daft Willie.

His parents both belonged to an obscure Fundamentalist religious group whose members were not allowed to marry outside the Church (which may or may not have had something to do with Willie's daftness). They prayed for him, of course; but they also took him to a specialist in Stirling. The doctor, an elderly man, did several tests and then told them, over the tops of his gold-rimmed half-glasses, that the boy had a mental age of eight and his mind would grow no older, ever. They continued to pray for him, but they suspected that the Lord had sent this to try them, so they made sure that Willie was Saved and looked forward to the day when they would meet him again in the Glory and he would be healed. Meanwhile, he needed a job.

An eight-year-old can herd cows, but herding cows is nevertheless a job, so Daft Willie became a cowherd.

And it was while herding cows that he saw the car for the first time.

He assumed there were lovers in it.

Willie knew about lovers. That is to say, he knew that lovers existed, and that they did unmentionable things to one another in dark places like copses and cinemas and cars; and that one did not speak of them. So he hurried the cows quickly past the bush beside which was parked the 1924 Morris Cowley Bullnose two-seater (he knew about cars, too, like any eight-year-old) and tried very hard not to look inside it in case he should behold sin.

He took his little herd into the cowshed for milking, went by a roundabout route to his home, ate supper, read a chapter from Leviticus to his father – aloud, painstakingly – then went to bed to dream about lovers.

The car was still there on the evening of the next day.

For all his innocence, Willie knew that lovers did not do whatever it was that they did to one another for twenty-four hours at a stretch.

This time he went right up to the car and looked inside. It was empty. The ground beneath the engine was black and sticky with oil. Willie devised a new explanation: the car had broken down and had been abandoned by its driver. It did not occur to him to wonder why it had been semi-concealed in a bush.

When he arrived at the cowshed he told the farmer what he had seen. 'There's a broken-down car on the path up by the main road.'

The farmer was a big man with heavy sand-coloured eyebrows which drew together when he was thinking. 'Was there nobody about?'

'No – and it was there yesterday.'

'Why did you not tell me yesterday, then?'

Willie blushed. 'I thought it was maybe . . . lovers.'

'Och! 'The farmer realized that Willie was not being coy, but was genuinely embarrassed. He patted the boy's shoulder. 'Well, away home and leave it to me to deal with.'

After the milking the farmer went to look for himself. It did occur to him to wonder why the car was semi-concealed. He had heard about the London stiletto murderer; and while he did not jump to the conclusion that the car had been abandoned by the killer, all the same he thought there might be a connection between the car and some crime or other. So after supper he sent his eldest son into the village on horseback to telephone the police in Stirling.

The police arrived before his son got back from the phone. There were at least a dozen of them, every one apparently a non-stop tea drinker. The farmer and his wife were up half the night looking after them.

Daft Willie was summoned to tell his story again, repeating that he had first seen the car the previous evening, blushing again when he explained that he had assumed it contained lovers.

All in all, it was the most exciting night of the war.

*

That evening Percival Godliman, facing his fourth consecutive night in the office, went home to bathe, change, and pack a suitcase.

He had a service flat in a block in Chelsea. It was small, though plenty big enough for a single man, and it was clean and tidy except for the study, which the cleaner was not allowed to enter and in consequence was littered with books and papers. The furniture was all pre-war, of course, but it was rather well-chosen, and the flat had a comfortable air. There were leather club chairs and a gramophone in the living-room, and the kitchen was full of hardly used labour-saving devices.

While his bath was filling he smoked a cigarette – he had taken to them lately, a pipe was so much fuss – and looked at his most valuable possession, a grimly fantastic medieval scene which was probably by Hieronymous Bosch. It was a family heirloom and Godliman had never sold it, even when he needed the money, because he liked it.

In the bath he thought about Barbara Dickens and her son, Peter. He had not told anyone about her, not even Bloggs, although he had been about to mention her during their conversation about remarrying, but Colonel Terry had interrupted. She was a widow: her husband had been killed in action at the very beginning of the war. Godliman did not know how old she was, but she looked about forty, which was young for the mother of a twenty-two-year-old boy. She worked on translations of intercepted enemy signals, and she was bright, amusing, and very attractive. She was also rich. Godliman had taken her to dinner, three times, before the present crisis blew up. He thought she was in love with him.

She had contrived a meeting between Godliman and her son Peter, who was a captain. Godliman liked the boy. But he knew something which neither Barbara nor her son was aware of: Peter was going to Normandy.

Which was all the more reason to catch Die Nadel.

He got out of the bath and took a long, careful shave, thinking: Am I in love with her? He was not sure what love ought to feel like in middle age. Not, surely, the burning passion of youth. Affection, admiration, tenderness, and a trace of uncertain lust? If they amounted to love, he loved her.

And he needed to share his life, now. For years he had wanted only solitude and his research. Now the camaraderie of Military Intelligence was sucking him in: the parties, the all-night sessions when something big broke, the spirit of dedicated amateurism, the frantic pleasure-seeking of people to whom death is always close and never predictable – all these had infected him. It would vanish after the war, he knew; but other things would remain: the need to talk to someone close about his disappointment and his triumphs, the need to touch someone else at night, the need to say: 'There! Look at that! Isn't it fine?'

War was gruelling and oppressive and frustrating and uncomfortable, but one had friends. If peace brought back loneliness, Godliman thought he would be unhappy.

Right now the feel of clean underwear and a crisply ironed shirt was the height of luxury. He put more fresh clothes in a case, then sat down to enjoy a glass of whisky before returning to the office. The military chauffeur in the commandeered Daimler outside could wait a little longer.

He was filling a pipe when the phone rang. He put down the pipe and lit a cigarette instead.

His phone was connected to the War Office switchboard. The telephonist told him that a Chief Superintendent Dalkeith was calling from Stirling.

He waited for the click of the connection, and said: 'Godliman speaking.'

'We've found your Morris Cowley,' Dalkeith said without preamble.

'Where?'

'On the A80 just south of Stirling.'

'Empty?'

'Aye, broken down. It's been there at least twenty-four hours. It was driven a few yards off the main road and hidden in a bush. A half-witted farm boy found it.'

'Is there a bus stop or railway station within walking distance of the spot?'

'No.'

Godliman grunted. 'So it's likely our man had to walk or hitch-hike after leaving the car.'

'Aye.'

'In that case, will you ask around—'

'We're already trying to find out whether anyone local saw him or gave him a lift.'

'Good. Let me know ... Meanwhile, I'll pass the news to the Yard. Thank you, Dalkeith.'

'We'll keep in touch. Goodbye, sir.'

Godliman put the phone on the hook and went into his study. He sat down with an atlas open to the road map of northern Britain. London, Liverpool, Carlisle, Stirling . . . Faber was heading for north-east Scotland.

Godliman wondered whether he should reconsider the theory that Faber was trying to get out. The best way out was west, via neutral Eire. Scotland's east coast, however, was the scene of military activity of various kinds. Was it possible that Faber had the nerve to continue his reconnaissance, knowing that MI5 was on his tail? It was possible, Godliman decided – he knew Faber had a lot of guts – but nevertheless unlikely. Nothing the man might discover in Scotland could be as important as the information he already had.

Therefore Faber was getting out via the east coast. Godliman ran over the methods of escape which were open to the spy: a light plane, landing on a lonely moor; a one-man voyage across the North Sea in a stolen vessel; a rendezvous with a U-boat off the coast; a passage in a merchant ship via a neutral country to the Baltic, disembarking in Sweden and crossing the border to occupied Norway . . . there were many ways.

The Yard must be told of the latest development. They would ask all Scots police forces to try to find someone who had picked up a hitch-hiker outside Stirling. Godliman returned to the living-room to phone, but the instrument rang before he got there. He picked it up.

'Godliman speaking.'

'A Mr Richard Porter is calling from Aberdeen.'

'Oh!' Godliman had been expecting Bloggs to check in from Carlisle. 'Put him on, please. Hello? Godliman speaking.'

'Ah, Richard Porter here. I'm on the local Watch Committee up here.'

'Yes, what can I do for you?'

'Well, actually, old boy, it's terribly embarrassing.'

Godliman controlled his impatience. 'Go on.'

'This chappie you're looking for – knife murders and so on. Well, I'm pretty sure I gave the bally fellow a lift in my own car.'

Godliman gripped the receiver more tightly. 'When?'

'Night before last. My car broke down on the A80 just outside Stirling. Middle of the bally night. Along comes this chappie, on foot, and mends it, just like that. So naturally—'

'Where did you drop him?'

'Right here in Aberdeen. Said he was going on to Banff. Thing is, I slept most of yesterday, so it wasn't until this afternoon—'

'Don't reproach yourself, Mr Porter. Thank you for calling.'

'Well, goodbye.'

Godliman jiggled the receiver and the War Office telephonist came back on the line.

Godliman said: 'Get Mr Bloggs for me, would you? He's in Carlisle.'

'He's holding on for you right now, sir.'

'Good!'

'Hello, Percy. What news?'

'We're on his trail again, Fred. He abandoned the Morris just outside Stirling and hitched a lift to Aberdeen.'

'Aberdeen!'

'He must be trying to get out through the east door.'

'When did he reach Aberdeen?'

'Probably early yesterday morning.'

'In that case he won't have had time to get out, unless he was very quick indeed. They're having the worst storm in living memory up here. It started last night and it's still going on. No ships are going out and it's certainly too rough to land a plane.'

'Good! Get up there as fast as you can. I'll start the local police moving in the meantime. Call me when you reach Aberdeen.'

'I'm on my way.'

'Fred?'

'Yes?'

'We'll catch the bastard yet.'

Fred was still laughing as Godliman hung up.

CHAPTER TWENTY-ONE

WHEN FABER woke up it was almost dark. Through the bedroom window he could see the last streaks of grey being inked out of the sky by the encroaching night. The storm had not eased: rain drummed on the roof and overflowed from a gutter, and the wind howled and gusted tirelessly.

He switched on the little lamp beside the bed. The effort tired him, and he slumped back on to the pillow. It frightened him, to be this weak. Those who believe that Might is Right must always be mighty, and Faber was sufficiently self-aware to know the implications of his own ethics. Fear was never far from the surface of his emotions: perhaps that was why he had survived so long. He was chronically incapable of feeling safe. He understood, in that vague way in which we understand the most fundamental things about ourselves, that his insecurity was the reason he chose the profession of spy: it was the only walk of life which permitted him instantly to kill anyone who posed him the slightest threat. The fear of being weak was part of the syndrome which included his obsessive independence, his insecurity, and his contempt for his military superiors.

He lay on the child's bed in the pink-walled bedroom

and inventoried his body. He seemed to be bruised just about everywhere, but apparently nothing was broken. He did not feel feverish: his constitution had withstood bronchial infection despite the night on the boat. There was just the weakness. He suspected it was more than exhaustion. He remembered a moment, as he had reached the top of the ramp, when he had thought he was going to die; and he wondered whether he had inflicted upon himself some permanent damage with that last mindbending uphill dash.

He checked his possessions, too. The can of photographic negatives was still taped to his chest, the stiletto was strapped to his left arm, and his papers and money were in the jacket pocket of his borrowed pyjamas.

He pushed the blankets aside and swung himself into a sitting position with his feet on the floor. A moment of dizziness came and went. He stood up. It was important not to permit oneself the psychological attitudes of the invalid. He put on the dressing-gown and went into the bathroom.

When he returned his own clothes were at the foot of the bed, clean and pressed: underwear, overalls, and shirt. Suddenly he remembered getting up some time during the morning and seeing the woman naked in the bathroom: it had been an odd scene, and he was not sure what it meant. She was very beautiful, he recalled.

He dressed slowly. He would have liked a shave, but he decided to ask his host's permission before borrowing the blade on the bathroom shelf: some men were as possessive of their razors as they were of their wives.

However, he did take the liberty of using the child's plastic comb he found in the top drawer of the chest.

He looked into the mirror without pride. He had no conceit. He knew that some women found him attractive, and others did not; and he assumed this was so for most men. Of course, he had had more women than most men, but he attributed this to his appetite, not to his looks. His reflection told him he was presentable, and that was all he needed to know.

Satisfied, he left the bedroom and went slowly down the stairs. Again he felt a wave of weakness; again he willed himself to overcome it, gripping the banister rail and placing one foot deliberately before the other until he reached the ground floor.

He paused outside the living-room door and, hearing no noise, went on to the kitchen. He knocked and went in. The young couple were at the table, finishing supper.

The woman stood up when he entered. 'You got up!' she said. 'Are you sure you should?'

Faber permitted himself to be led to a chair. 'Thank you,' he said. 'You really mustn't encourage me to pretend to be ill.'

'I don't think you realize what a terrible experience you've been through,' she said. 'Do you feel like food?'

'I'm imposing on you—'

'Not at all. Don't be silly. I kept some soup hot for you.'

Faber said: 'You're so kind, and I don't even know your names.'

'David and Lucy Rose.' She ladled soup into a bowl

and placed it on the table in front of him. 'Cut some bread, David, would you?'

'I'm Henry Baker.' Faber did not know why he had said that: he had no papers in that name. Henry Faber was the man the police were hunting, so he should have used his James Baker identity; but somehow he wanted this woman to call him Henry, the nearest English equivalent of his real name, Henrik. Perhaps it did not matter – he could always say his name was James but he had always been called Henry.

He took a sip of the soup, and suddenly he was ravenously hungry. He ate it all quickly, then the bread. When he had finished, Lucy laughed. She looked lovely when she laughed: her mouth opened wide, showing lots of even white teeth, and her eyes crinkled merrily at the corners.

'More?' she offered.

'Thank you very much.'

'I can see it doing you good. The colour is coming back to your cheeks.'

Faber realized he felt physically better. He ate his second helping more slowly, out of courtesy rather than repletion.

David said: 'How did you happen to be out in this storm?' It was the first time he had spoken.

Lucy said: 'Don't badger him, David.'

'It's all right,' Faber said. 'I was foolish, that's all. This is the first fishing holiday I've been able to have since before the war, and I just refused to let the weather spoil it. Are you a fisherman?'

David shook his head. 'Sheep farmer.'

'Do you have many employees?'

'Just one, old Tom.'

'I suppose there are other sheep farms on the island.'

'No. We live at this end, Tom lives at the other end, and in between there's nothing but sheep.'

Faber nodded slowly. This was good – very good. A woman, a cripple, a child and an old man could not constitute an obstacle. And he was feeling much stronger already.

Faber said: 'How do you contact the mainland?'

'There's a boat once a fortnight. It's due this Monday, but it won't come if the storm keeps up. There's a radio transmitter in Tom's cottage, but we can only use that in emergencies. If I thought people might be searching for you, or if you needed urgent medical help, I should use it. But as things are I don't feel it's necessary. There's little point: nobody can come to fetch you off the island until the storm clears, and when that happens the boat will come anyway.'

'Of course.' Faber concealed his delight. The problem of how to contact the U-boat on Monday had been nagging at the back of his mind. He had seen an ordinary wireless set in the Roses' living-room, and he would, in a pinch, have been able to rig up a transmitter from that. But the fact that Tom had a proper radio made everything so much easier.

Faber said: 'What does Tom need a transmitter for?'

'He's a member of the Royal Observer Corps. Aberdeen was bombed in July 1940. There was no air-raid warning. Consequently there were fifty casualties. That was when they recruited Tom. It's a good thing his hearing is better than his eyesight.'

'I suppose the bombers come from Norway.'

'I suppose so.'

Lucy stood up. 'Let's go into the other room.'

The two men followed her. Faber felt no weakness, no dizziness. He held the living-room door for David, who wheeled himself close to the fire. Lucy offered Faber brandy. He declined. She poured for her husband and herself.

Faber sat back and studied the couple. Lucy's looks were really quite striking: she had an oval face, wide-set eyes of an unusual, cat-like amber colour, and a lot of rich, dark-red hair. Under the mannish fisherman's sweater and baggy trousers there was the suggestion of a very fine, fullish figure. If she were to curl her hair and put on silk stockings and a cocktail dress she might be very glamorous. David was also good-looking – almost pretty, except for the shadow of a very dark beard. His hair was nearly black and his skin looked Mediterranean. He would have been tall, if he had had legs in proportion to his arms. Faber suspected that those arms might be powerful, muscled from years of pushing the wheels of the chair to get from A to B.

Yes, they were an attractive couple – but there was something badly wrong between them. Faber was no expert on marriage, but his training in interrogation techniques had taught him to read the silent language of the body – to know, from small gestures, when someone was frightened, confident, hiding something, or lying. Lucy and David rarely looked at one another, and never touched. They spoke to him more than to each other. They circled one another, like turkeys trying to keep in front of them a few square feet of vacant portable territory. The tension between them was enormous. They were like Churchill and Stalin, obliged temporarily to fight side by side, fiercely suppressing a deeper enmity. Faber wondered what awful trauma lay at the back of their hatred.

This cosy little house must be an emotional pressure-cooker, despite its rugs and its bright paintwork, its floral armchairs and blazing fires and framed water-colours. To live alone, with only an old man and a child for company, with this thing between them . . . it reminded him of a play he had seen in London, by an American called Tennessee something.

Abruptly, David swallowed his drink and said: 'I must turn in. My back's playing up.'

Faber got to his feet and said: 'I'm sorry – I've been keeping you up.'

David waved him down. 'Not at all. You've been asleep all day – you won't want to go back to bed right away. Besides, Lucy would like to chat, I'm sure. It's just that I mistreat my back – backs were designed to share the load with the legs, you know.'

Lucy said: 'You'd better take two pills tonight, then.' She took a bottle from the top shelf of the bookcase, shook out two tablets, and gave them to her husband.

He swallowed them dry. 'I'll say goodnight.' He wheeled himself out.

'Goodnight, David.'

'Goodnight, Mr Rose.'

After a moment Faber heard David dragging himself up the stairs, and wondered just how he did it.

Lucy spoke, as if to cover the sound of David. 'Where do you live, Mr Baker?'

'Please call me Henry. I live in London.'

'I haven't been to London for years. There's probably not much of it left.'

'It's changed, but not as much as you might think. When were you last there?'

'Nineteen-forty.' She poured herself another brandy. 'Since we came here, I've only been off the island once, and that was to have the baby. One can't travel much these days, can one?'

'What made you come here?'

'Um.' She sat down, sipped her drink, and looked into the fire.

'Perhaps I shouldn't—'

'It's all right. We had an accident the day we got married. That's how David lost his legs. He'd been training as a fighter pilot ... we both wanted to run away, I think. I believe it was a mistake, but it seemed like a good idea at the time.'

'It has allowed his resentment to incubate.'

She shot him a sharp look. 'You're a perceptive man.'

'It's obvious.' He spoke very quietly. 'You don't deserve such unhappiness.'

She blinked several times. 'You see too much.'

'It's not difficult. Why do you continue, if it's not working?'

'I don't know what to tell you. Do you want clichés? The vows of marriage, the child, the war . . . If there's another answer, I can't find words for it.'

'Guilt,' Faber said. 'But you're thinking of leaving him, aren't you?'

She stared at him, slowly shaking her head with incredulity. 'How do you know so much?'

'You've lost the art of dissembling in four years on this island. Besides, these things are so much simpler from the outside.'

'Have you ever been married?'

'No. That's what I mean.'

'Why not? I think you ought to be.'

It was Faber's turn to look pensively into the fire. Why not, indeed? His stock answer – to himself – was his profession. But he could not tell her that, and anyway it was too glib. He said suddenly: 'I don't trust myself to love anyone that much.' The words had come out without forethought, and he wondered whether they were true. A moment later he wondered how Lucy had got past his guard, when he had thought he was disarming her.

Neither of them spoke for a while. The fire was dying. A few stray raindrops found their way down the chimney and hissed in the cooling coals. The storm showed no sign of letting up. Faber found himself thinking of the last woman he had had. What was her name? Gertrude. It was seven years ago, but he could picture her now, in the flickering fire: a round German face, fair hair, green eyes, beautiful breasts, much-too-wide hips, fat legs, bad feet; the conversational style of an express train, a wild, inexhaustible enthusiasm for sex ... She had flattered him, admiring his mind (she said) and adoring his body (she had no need to tell him). She wrote lyrics for popular songs, and read them to him in a poor basement flat in Berlin: it was not a lucrative profession. He visualized her in that untidy bedroom, lying naked, urging him to do more bizarre and erotic things with her: to hurt her, to touch himself, to lie completely still while she made love to him ... He shook his head slightly to brush away the memories. He had not thought like that in all the years he had been celibate. Such visions were disturbing. He looked at Lucy.

'You were far away,' she said with a smile.

'Memories,' he said. 'This talk of love ...'

'I shouldn't burden you.'

'You're not.'

'Good memories?'

'Very good. And yours? You were thinking, too.'

She smiled again. 'I was in the future, not the past.'

'What do you see there?'

She seemed about to answer, then changed her mind. It happened twice. There were signs of tension about her eyes.

'I see you finding another man,' Faber said. As he spoke he was thinking: Why am I doing this? 'He is a weaker man than David, and less handsome; but it is for his weakness that you love him. He is clever, but not rich; compassionate without being sentimental; tender, caring, loving. He—'

The brandy glass in her hand shattered under the

pressure of her grip. The fragments fell into her lap and on to the carpet, and she ignored them. Faber crossed to her chair and knelt in front of her. Her thumb was bleeding. He took her hand.

'You've hurt yourself.'

She looked at him. She was crying.

'I'm sorry,' he said.

The cut was superficial. She took a handkerchief from her trousers pocket and staunched the blood. Faber released her hand and began to pick up the pieces of broken glass, wishing he had kissed her when he had the chance. He put the shards on the chimney-breast.

'I didn't mean to upset you,' he said.

She took away the handkerchief and looked at her thumb. It was still bleeding.

'A little bandage,' he suggested.

'In the kitchen.'

He found a roll of bandage, a pair of scissors, and a safety pin. He filled a small bowl with hot water and returned to the living-room.

In his absence she had somehow obliterated the evidence of tears on her face. She sat passively, limp, while he bathed her thumb in the hot water, dried it, and fixed a small strip of bandage over the cut. She looked all the time at his face, not at his hands; but her expression was unreadable.

He finished the job and stood back abruptly. This was silly: he had taken the thing too far. It was time to disengage. He said: 'I think I'd better go to bed.'

She nodded.

'I'm sorry—'

'Stop apologizing,' she told him. 'It doesn't suit you.'

Her tone was harsh. He guessed that she, too, felt the thing had got out of hand.

'Are you staying up?' he asked.

She shook her head.

'Well . . .' He walked to the door and held it for her.

She avoided his eyes as she passed him. He followed her through the hall and up the stairs. As he watched her climb, he could not help imagining her in other clothes, her hips swaying gently underneath some silky material, long legs clad in stockings instead of worsted grey trousers, high-heeled dress shoes instead of worn felt slippers.

At the top of the stairs, on the tiny landing, she turned and whispered: 'Goodnight.'

He said: 'Goodnight, Lucy.'

She looked at him for a moment. He reached for her hand, but she foresaw his intention and turned quickly away, entering her bedroom and closing the door without a backward look, leaving him standing there with his hand out and his mouth open, wondering what was in her mind and – more to the point – what was in his.

CHAPTER TWENTY-TWO

BLOGGS DROVE dangerously fast through the night in a commandeered Sunbeam Talbot with a souped-up engine. The hilly, winding Scottish roads were slick with rain and, in a few low places, two or three inches deep in water. The rain drove across the windscreen in sheets. On the more exposed hilltops the gale-force winds threatened to blow the car off the road and into the soggy turf alongside. For mile after mile, Bloggs sat forward in the seat, peering through the small area of glass that was cleared by the wiper, straining his eyes to make out the shape of the road in front as the headlights battled with the obscuring rain. Just north of Edinburgh he ran over three rabbits, feeling the sickening bump as the tyres squashed their small furry bodies. He did not slow the car, but for a while afterwards he wondered whether rabbits normally came out at night.

The strain gave him a headache, and his sitting position made his back hurt. He also felt hungry. He opened the window for a cold breeze to keep him awake, but so much water came in that he was forced to close it again immediately. He thought about Die Nadel, or Faber or whatever he was calling himself now:

a smiling young man in running-shorts holding a trophy. Well, Faber was winning this race. He was forty-eight hours ahead and he had the advantage that only he knew the route that had to be followed. Bloggs would have enjoyed a contest with that man, if the stakes had not been so high, so bloody high.

He wondered what he would do if he ever came face to face with the man. I'd shoot the bugger out of hand, he thought, before he killed me. Faber was a pro, and you couldn't mess with that type. Most spies were amateurs: frustrated revolutionaries of the left or right, people who wanted the imaginary glamour of espionage, greedy men or lovesick women, or blackmail victims. The few professionals were very dangerous indeed, because they knew that the professionals they were up against were not merciful men.

Dawn was still an hour or two away when Bloggs drove into Aberdeen. Never in his life had he been so grateful for street lights, dimmed and masked though they were. He had no idea where the police station was, and there was no one on the streets to give him directions, so he drove around the town until he saw the familiar blue lamp (also dimmed).

He parked the car and dashed through the rain into the building. He was expected. Godliman had been on the phone, and Godliman was now very senior indeed. Bloggs was shown into the office of Alan Kincaid, a Detective-Chief-Inspector in his middle fifties. There were three other officers in the room: Bloggs shook their hands and instantly forgot their names.

Kincaid said: 'You made bloody good time from Carlisle.'

'Nearly killed myself doing it,' Bloggs replied. He sat down. 'If you can rustle up a sandwich . . .'

'Of course.' Kincaid leaned his head out of the door and shouted something. 'It'll be here in two shakes,' he told Bloggs.

The office had off-white walls, a plank floor, and plain hard furniture: a desk, a few chairs and a filing cabinet. It was totally unrelieved: no pictures, no ornaments, no personal touches of any kind. There was a tray of dirty cups on the floor, and the air was thick with smoke. It smelled like somewhere men had been working all night.

Kincaid had a small moustache, thin grey hair, and spectacles. A big, intelligent-looking man in shirtsleeves and braces, he was the kind of policeman that – Bloggs thought – made up the backbone of the British police force. He spoke with a local accent, a sign that, like Bloggs, he had come up through the ranks – though from his age it was clear that his rise had been slower than Bloggs's.

Bloggs said: 'How much do you know of what this is all about?'

'Not much,' Kincaid said. 'But your governor, Godliman, did say that the London murders are the least of this man's crimes. We also know which department you're with, so we can put two and two together and conclude that Faber is a very dangerous spy.'

'That's about it,' Bloggs said.

Kincaid nodded.

'What have you done so far?' Bloggs asked.

Kincaid put his feet on his desk. 'He arrived here two days ago, yes?'

'Yes.'

'That was when we started looking for him. We had the pictures – I assume every force in the country got them.'

'Yes.'

'We checked the hotels and lodging houses, the station and the bus depot. We did it quite thoroughly, although at the time we didn't know he had come here. Needless to say, we had no results. We're checking again, of course; but my opinion is that he probably left Aberdeen immediately.'

A woman police constable came in with a cup of tea and a very thick cheese sandwich. Bloggs thanked her and set about the sandwich greedily.

Kincaid went on: 'We had a man at the railway station before the first train left in the morning. Ditto for the bus depot. So, if he left the town, either he stole a car or he hitched a ride. We've had no stolen cars reported.'

'Damn,' Bloggs said through a mouthful of wholemeal bread. He swallowed. 'That makes it about as difficult as it can be to trace him.'

'No doubt that's why he chose to hitch-hike.'

'He might have gone by sea.'

'Of the boats that left the harbour that day, none was big enough to stow away on. Since then, of course, nothing's gone out because of the storm.'

'Stolen boats?'

'None reported.'

Bloggs shrugged. 'If there's no prospect of going out, the owners might not come to the harbour – in which case the theft of a boat might go unnoticed until the storm ends.'

One of the officers in the room said: 'We missed that one, Chief.'

'We did,' Kincaid said.

Bloggs said: 'Perhaps the harbourmaster could look around all the regular moorings—'

'I'm with you,' Kincaid said. He was already dialling. After a moment he spoke into the phone. 'Captain Douglas? Kincaid. Aye, I know civilized people sleep at this hour. You haven't heard the worst – I want you to take a walk in the rain. Aye, you heard me right . . .'

The other policemen started to laugh.

Kincaid put his hand over the mouthpiece and said: 'You know what they say about seamen's language? It's true.' He spoke into the phone again. 'Go round all the regular moorings and make a note of any vessels not in their usual spot. Ignoring those you know to be legitimately out of port, give me the names and addresses – and phone numbers if you have them – of the owners. Aye. Aye, I know . . . I'll make it a double. All right, a bottle. And a good morning to you too, old friend.' He hung up.

Bloggs smiled. 'Salty?'

'If I did what he suggested I do with my truncheon, I'd never be able to sit down again.' Kincaid became serious. 'It'll take him about half an hour, then we'll need a couple of hours to check all the addresses.

It's worth doing, although I still think he hitched a ride.'

'So do I,' Bloggs said.

The door opened, and a middle-aged man in civilian clothes walked in. Kincaid and his officers stood up, and Bloggs followed suit.

Kincaid said: 'Good morning, sir. This is Mr Bloggs. Mr Bloggs, Richard Porter.'

They shook hands. Porter had a red face and a carefully cultivated moustache. He wore a double-breasted, camel-coloured overcoat. He said: 'How do you do. I'm the blighter that gave your chappie a lift to Aberdeen. Most embarrassing.' He had no local accent.

Bloggs said: 'How do you do.' On first acquaintance Porter seemed to be exactly the kind of silly ass who would give a spy a lift half across the country. However, Bloggs knew the type: the air of empty-headed heartiness might well mask a shrewd mind. He asked: 'What made you realize that the man you'd picked up was the . . . the stiletto murderer?'

'I heard about the abandoned Morris. I picked him up at that very spot.'

'You've seen the picture?'

'Yes. Of course, I didn't get a good look at the chappie, because it was dark for most of the journey. But I saw enough of him, in the light of the torch when we were under the bonnet, and afterwards when we entered Aberdeen – it was dawn by then. If I'd only seen the picture, I'd say it *could* have been him. Given the spot at which I picked him up, so near to where the Morris was found, I say it *was* him.'

'I agree,' Bloggs said. He thought for a moment, wondering what useful information he could get out of this man. 'How did Faber impress you?' he asked eventually.

Porter said promptly: 'He struck me as exhausted, nervous and determined, in that order. Also, he was no Scotsman.'

'How would you describe his accent?'

'Neutral. No trace of the Hun in his voice ... except perhaps in retrospect, and that might be my imagination. The accent – minor public school, Home Counties. Jarred with his clothes, if you know what I mean. He was wearing overalls. Another thing I didn't remark until afterwards.'

Kincaid interrupted to offer tea. Everyone accepted. The policeman went to the door.

Bloggs had decided that Porter was less foolish than he looked. 'What did you talk about?'

'Oh, nothing much.'

'But you were together for hours—'

'He slept most of the way. He mended the car – it was only a disconnected lead, but I'm afraid I'm hopeless with machines – then he told me his own car had broken down in Edinburgh, and he was going to Banff. Said he didn't really want to go through Aberdeen, as he didn't have a Restricted Area Pass. I'm afraid I ... I told him not to worry about that. Said I'd vouch for him if we were stopped. Makes one feel such a bloody fool, you know – but I felt I owed him a favour. He had got me out of a bit of a hole, y'know.'

Kincaid said: 'Nobody's blaming you, sir.'

Bloggs was, but he did not say so. Instead he said: 'There are very few people who have met Faber and can tell us what he's like. Can you think hard and tell me what kind of a man you took him to be?'

'He woke up like a soldier,' Porter said. 'He was courteous, and seemed intelligent. Firm handshake. I take notice of handshakes.'

'Anything else? Think very hard.'

'Something else about when he woke up . . .' Porter's florid face creased up in a frown. 'His right hand went to his left forearm, like this.' He demonstrated.

'That's something,' Bloggs said. 'That'll be where he keeps the knife. A sleeve-sheath.'

'Nothing else, I'm afraid.'

'And he said he was going to Banff. That means he's not.'

'Really?'

'Spies always lie, on principle. I'll bet you told him where you were going before he told you where he was going.'

'I believe I did.' Porter nodded thoughtfully. 'Well, well.'

'Either Aberdeen was his destination, or he went south after you dropped him. Since he said he was going north, he probably didn't go north.'

Kincaid said: 'That kind of second-guessing could get out of hand.'

'Sometimes it does,' Bloggs grinned. 'Did you tell him that you're a magistrate?'

'Yes.'

'That's why he didn't kill you.'

'What? Good Lord! What do you mean?'

'He knew you'd be missed.'

'Good Lord!' Porter repeated. He had gone slightly pale. The idea that he might actually have been killed clearly had not occurred to him.

The door opened again. The man who walked in said: 'I've got your information, and I hope it was fucken worth it.'

Bloggs grinned. This was, undoubtedly, the harbourmaster: a short man with cropped white hair, smoking a large pipe and wearing a blazer with brass buttons.

Kincaid said: 'Come in, Captain. How did you get so wet? You shouldn't go out in the rain.'

'Fuck off,' the Captain said. Bloggs was not sure how much of his anger was real: very little of it, to judge by the delighted expressions on the other faces in the room.

Porter said: 'Morning, Captain.'

'Good morning, Your Worship,' the Captain said.

Kincaid said: 'What have you got?'

The Captain took off his cap and shook drops of rain from its crown. 'The *Marie II* has gone missing,' he said. 'I saw her come in on the afternoon the storm began. I didn't see her go out, but I know she shouldn't have sailed again that day. However, it seems she did.'

'Who owns her?'

'Tam Halfpenny. I telephoned him. He left her in her mooring that day and hasn't seen her since.'

Bloggs said: 'What kind of vessel is she?'

'A small fishing boat, sixty feet and broad in the beam. Stout little craft. Inboard motor. No particular style – the fishermen round here don't follow the pattern book when they build boats.'

'Let me ask you a very important question,' Bloggs said. 'Could that boat have survived the storm?'

The Captain paused in the act of putting a match to his pipe. After a moment he said: 'With a very skilful sailor at the helm – maybe. Maybe not.'

'How far might he have got before the storm broke?'

'Not far – a few miles. The *Marie II* was not tied up until evening.'

Bloggs stood up, walked around his chair, and sat down again. 'So where is he now?'

'At the bottom of the sea, in all probability, the bloody fool.' The Captain's statement was not without relish.

Bloggs could take no satisfaction in the likelihood that Faber was dead. It was too inconclusive. The discontent spread to his body, and he felt restless, itchy, and frustrated. He scratched his chin: he needed a shave. 'I'll believe it when I see it,' he said.

'You won't.'

'Save your lugubrious guesswork,' Bloggs said sharply. 'I want information, not pessimism.' The other men in the room suddenly remembered that, despite his youth, he was the senior officer there. 'Let's rehearse the possibilities. One: he left Aberdeen by land and someone else stole the *Marie II*. In that case he has probably reached his destination by now, but he won't have left the country because of the storm. We already have all the other police forces looking for him, and that's all we can do about number one.

'Two: he's still in Aberdeen. Again, we have this possibility covered: we're still looking for him.

'Three: he left Aberdeen by sea. I think we're agreed this is the strongest option. Let's break it down. Three A: he transferred to another vessel – probably a U-boat – before the storm broke. We don't think he had time, but he might've. Three B: he found shelter somewhere, or was shipwrecked somewhere – mainland or island. Three C: he died.

'If he caught a U-boat, we've had it. We've lost. There's nothing more we can do. So let's forget that one. If he found shelter, or was shipwrecked, we'll find evidence sooner or later – either the *Marie II*, or bits of it. We can search the coastline right away and survey the sea as soon as the weather clears sufficiently for us to get a plane up. If he's gone to the bottom of the ocean we may still find bits of the boat floating.

'So we have three courses of action to take. We continue the searches already going on; we mount a new search of the coastline, working north and south from Aberdeen; and we prepare for an air-sea search the minute the weather improves.'

Bloggs had begun to pace up and down as he spoke, thinking on his feet. He stopped now, and looked around. 'Comments, queries and suggestions?'

The late hour had got to all of them. Bloggs's sudden access of energy jerked them out of a creeping lethargy. One leaned forward, rubbing his hands; another tied his shoelaces; a third put his jacket on. They wanted to go to work. There were no questions.

'All right,' said Bloggs. 'Let's win the war.'

CHAPTER TWENTY-THREE

FABER WAS awake. His body probably needed sleep, despite the fact that he had spent the day in bed; but his mind was hyperactive, turning over possibilities, sketching scenarios, thinking about women and about home.

Now that he was so close to getting out, his memories of home became quite painfully sweet. He thought of quite silly things, like sausages fat enough to eat in slices, and motor cars on the right-hand side of the road, and *really* tall trees, and most of all his own language – words with guts and precision, hard consonants and pure vowels and the verb at the end of the sentence where it ought to be, finality and meaning in the same climactic terminal.

Thoughts of climaxes brought Gertrude to mind again: her face beneath his, make-up washed away by his kisses, eyes closing tight in pleasure then opening again to look with delight into his, mouth stretched wide in a permanent gasp, saying '*Ja, Liebling, ja . . .*'

It was silly. He had led the life of a monk for seven years, but she had no reason to do the same. She would have had a dozen men since Faber. She might even be dead, bombed by the RAF or murdered by the maniacs because her nose was half an inch too long or run over by a motor car in the blackout. Anyway, she would hardly remember him. He would probably never see her again. But she was a symbol.

He did not normally permit himself the indulgence of sentiment. There was in his nature a very cold streak, and he cultivated it because it protected him. Now, however, he was within an inch of success, and he felt free, not to relax his vigilance, but to fantasize a little.

The storm was his safeguard while it continued. He would simply contact the U-boat with Tom's radio on Monday, and its captain would send a dinghy into the bay as soon as the weather cleared. However, if the storm ended before Monday, there was a slight complication: the supply boat. David and Lucy would naturally expect him to take the boat back to the mainland.

Lucy came into his thoughts in vivid, full-colour visions which he could not quite control. He saw her striking amber eyes watching him as he made a bandage for her thumb; her outline walking up the stairs in front of him clad in shapeless man's clothing; her heavy breasts, perfectly round, as she stood naked in the bathroom: and as the visions developed from memory into fantasy she leaned over the bandage and kissed his mouth, turned back on the stairs and took him in her arms, stepped out of the bathroom and placed his hands on her breasts.

He turned restlessly in the little bed, cursing the imagination which sent him dreams the like of which he had not suffered since his schooldays. At that time, before he had experienced the reality of sex, he had constructed elaborate sexual scenarios featuring the older women with whom he came into daily contact: the starchy Matron; Professor Nagel's dark, thin, intellectual wife; the shopkeeper in the village who wore red lipstick and talked to her husband with contempt. Sometimes he put all three of them into one orgiastic fantasy. When at the age of fifteen he had seduced a housemaid's daughter in the twilight of a West Prussian forest, he abandoned the imaginary orgies because they were so much better than the disappointing real thing. Young Henrik had been greatly puzzled by this: where was the blinding ecstasy, the sensation of soaring through the air like a bird, the mystical fusion of two bodies into one? The fantasies became painful, reminding him of his failure to make them real. Later, of course, the reality improved, and Henrik formed the view that ecstasy comes not from a man's pleasure in a woman, but from their pleasure in each other. He had voiced that opinion to his elder brother, who seemed to think it banal, a truism rather than a discovery; and before long Henrik saw it that way too.

He became a good lover, eventually. He found sex interesting, as well as physically pleasant. He was never a great seducer, for the thrill of conquest was not what he wanted. But he was expert at giving and receiving sexual gratification, without the expert's illusion that technique is all. For some women he was a highly desirable man, and the fact that he did not know this only served to make him even more attractive.

He tried to remember how many women he had had: Anna, Gretchen, Ingrid, the American girl, those two whores in Stuttgart ... he could not recall them all, but there could not have been more than about twenty.

None of them, he thought, had been quite as beautiful as Lucy. He gave an exasperated sigh: he had let this woman get to him, just because he was close to home and had been so careful for so long. He was annoyed with himself. It was undisciplined: one should not relax until the assignment was over, and this was not over, not quite.

There was the problem of the supply boat. Several solutions came to mind: perhaps the most promising was to incapacitate the island's inhabitants, meet the boat himself, and send the boatman away with a cock-and-bull story. He could say he was visiting them, had come out on another boat; that he was a relative, or a bird-watcher ... anything. It was too small a problem to engage his full attention at present. Later, when and if the weather improved, he would work something out.

He had no serious problems. A lonely island, miles off the coast, with four inhabitants – it was an ideal hideout. From now on, leaving Britain was going to be as easy as breaking out of a baby's playpen. When he thought of the situations he had already come through, the people he had killed – the five Home Guard men, the Yorkshire lad on the train, the Abwehr messenger – he considered himself now to be sitting pretty.

An old man, a cripple, a woman and a child ... Killing them would be so simple.

*

Lucy, too, lay awake. She was listening. There was a lot to hear. The weather was an orchestra, rain drumming on the roof, wind fluting in the eaves of the cottage, sea performing glissandi with the beach. The old house talked, too, creaking in its joints as it suffered the buffeting of the storm. Within the room there were more sounds: David's slow, regular breathing, threatening but never quite achieving a snore as he slept deeply under the influence of the double dose of soporific; and the quicker, shallow breaths of Jo, sprawled comfortably across a camp bed beside the far wall.

The noise is keeping me awake, Lucy thought; then immediately: Who am I trying to fool? Her wakefulness was caused by Henry, who had looked at her naked body, and had touched her hands gently as he bandaged her thumb, and who now lay in bed in the next room, probably fast asleep.

He had not told her much about himself, she realized: only that he was unmarried. She did not know where he had been born – his accent gave no clue. He had not even hinted at what he did for a living, though she imagined he must be a professional man, perhaps a dentist or a soldier. He was not dull enough to be a solicitor, too intelligent to be a journalist, and doctors could never keep their profession secret for longer than five minutes. He was not rich enough to be a barrister, too self-effacing to be an actor. She would bet on the Army.

Did he live alone, she wondered? Or with his mother? Or a woman? What did he wear when he wasn't fishing? She would like to see him in a dark blue suit, double-breasted, with a white handkerchief in the top pocket. Did he have a motor car? Yes, he would; something rather unusual, and quite new. He probably drove very fast.

That thought brought back memories of David's two-seater, and she closed her eyes tightly to shut out the nightmare images. Think of something else, think of something *else*.

She thought of Henry again, and realized an odd thing: she wanted to make love to him.

It was a peculiar wish; the kind of wish that, in her scheme of things, afflicted men but not women. A woman might meet a man briefly and find him attractive, want to get to know him better, even begin to fall in love with him; but she did not feel an immediate physical desire, not unless she was . . . abnormal.

She told herself that this was ridiculous; that what she needed was to make love with her husband, not to copulate with the first eligible man who came along. She told herself she was not that kind.

All the same, it was pleasant to speculate. David and Jo were fast asleep: there was nothing to stop her getting out of bed, crossing the landing, entering his room, sliding into bed next to him . . .

Nothing to stop her, except character, good breeding, and a respectable upbringing.

If she were going to do it with anybody, she would do it with someone like Henry. He would be kind, and gentle, and considerate; he would not despise her for offering herself like a Soho streetwalker.

She turned over in the bed, smiling at her own foolishness: for how could she possibly know whether he would despise her? She had known him only for a day, and he had spent most of that day asleep.

Still, it would be nice to have him look at her again, his expression of admiration tinged with some kind of amusement. It would be nice to feel his hands, to touch his body, to squeeze against the warmth of his skin.

She realized that her body was responding to the images in her mind. She felt the urge to touch herself, and resisted it, as she had done for four years. At least I haven't dried up, like an old crone, she thought.

She moved her legs, and sighed as a warm sensation spread through her loins. This was getting unreasonable. It was time to go to sleep. There was just no way she would make love to Henry, or to anyone else, tonight.

With that thought she got out of bed and went to the door.

Faber heard a footfall on the landing, and he reacted automatically.

His mind cleared instantly of the idle, lascivious thoughts with which it had been occupied. He swung his legs to the floor and slid out from under the bedclothes in a single, fluid movement; then silently crossed the room to stand beside the window in the darkest corner, the stiletto knife in his hand.

He heard the door open, heard the intruder step inside, heard the door close again. At that point he started to think, for an assassin would have left the door open for a quick getaway, and it occurred to him that there were a hundred reasons why it was impossible that an assassin should have found him here.

He ignored the thought, for he had survived this long by catering for the one-in-a-thousand chance. The wind dropped momentarily, and he heard an indrawn breath, a faint gasp, from beside his bed, enabling him to locate the intruder's exact position. He sprang.

He had her on the bed, face down, with his knife at her throat and his knee in the small of her back, before he realized that the intruder was a woman. A split-second later he guessed her identity. He eased his grip, reached out to the bedside table, and switched on the light.

Her face was pale in the dim glow of the lamp.

Faber sheathed the knife before she could see it. He took his weight off her body. 'I'm awfully sorry,' he said.

She turned on to her back and looked up at him as he straddled her. She began to giggle.

Faber added: 'I thought you were a burglar.'

'And where would a burglar come from?' she laughed. The colour rushed back to her cheeks in a blush.

She was wearing a very loose, old-fashioned flannel nightgown which covered her from her throat to her ankles. Her dark-red hair spread across Faber's pillow in disarray. Her eyes seemed very large, and her lips were moist.

'You are remarkably beautiful,' Faber said quietly.

She closed her eyes.

Faber bent over her and kissed her mouth. Her lips parted immediately, and she returned his kiss hungrily. With his fingertips he stroked her shoulders, her neck and her ears. She moved beneath him.

He wanted to kiss her for a long time, to explore her mouth and savour the intimacy; but he realized that she had no time for tenderness. She reached inside his pyjama trousers and squeezed. She moaned softly and began to breathe hard.

Still kissing her, Faber reached for the light and killed it. He pulled away from her and took off his pyjama jacket. Quickly, so that she would not wonder what he was doing, he tugged at the can stuck to his chest, ignoring the sting as the sticky tape was jerked away from his skin. He slid the photographs under the bed. He also unbuttoned the sheath on his left forearm and dropped that.

He pushed the skirt of her nightdress up to her waist. She wore nothing underneath.

'Quickly,' she said. 'Quickly.'

Faber lowered his body to hers.

Lucy did not feel the least bit guilty afterwards. She just felt content, satisfied, replete. She had had what she wanted, and she was glad. She lay still, eyes closed, stroking the bristly hair at the back of Henry's neck, enjoying the rough tickling sensation on her hands.

After a while she said: 'I was in such a rush . . .'

'It's not over yet,' he murmured.

She frowned in the dark. 'Didn't you . . . ?'

'No, I didn't. You hardly did.'

She smiled. 'I beg to differ.'

He turned on the light and looked at her. 'We'll see.'

He slipped down the bed, his torso between her thighs, and kissed her belly. His tongue flicked in and out of her navel. It was quite nice. Then his head went lower. Surely, she thought, he doesn't want to kiss me *there*. He did. And he did more than kiss. His lips pulled at the soft folds of her skin. She was paralysed by shock as his tongue began to probe in the crevices and then, as he parted her lips with his fingers, to thrust deep inside her.

Finally his restless tongue found a tiny, sensitive place, so small she had not known it existed, so sensitive that his touch was almost painful at first. She forgot her shock as she was overwhelmed by the most piercing sensation she had ever experienced. Unable to restrain herself, she moved her hips up and down, faster and faster, rubbing her slippery flesh over his mouth, his chin, his nose, his forehead; totally absorbed in her own pleasure. The thrill built and built, like feedback in a microphone, feeding upon itself, until she felt utterly possessed by joy and opened her mouth to scream, whereupon Henry clapped his hand over her face to quiet her; but she screamed in her throat as the climax went on and on, ending in something that felt like an explosion and left her so drained that she thought she would never get up.

Her mind seemed to go blank for a while. She knew

vaguely that Henry still lay between her legs, his bristly cheek against the soft inside of her thigh, his lips moving gently, affectionately.

Eventually she said: 'Now I *know* what Lawrence means.'

He lifted his head. 'I don't understand.'

She sighed. 'I didn't realize it could be like that. It was lovely.'

'*Was?*'

'Oh, God, I've no more energy . . .'

He changed position, kneeling astride her chest, and she realized what he wanted her to do, and for the second time she was frozen by shock: it was just too *big* . . . but suddenly she *wanted* to do it, she *needed* to take him into her mouth; so she lifted her head, and her lips closed around him, and he gave a soft groan.

He held her head in his hands, moving it to and fro, moaning quietly. She looked at his face. He was staring wild-eyed at her, drinking in the sight of what she was doing. She wondered what she would do when he . . . *came* . . . and she decided she didn't care, because everything else had been so good with him that she knew she would enjoy even that.

But it was not to be. When she thought he was on the point of losing control he stopped, moved away, lay on top of her, and entered her again. This time it was very slow and relaxed, like the rhythm of the sea on the beach; until he put his hands under her hips and grasped the globes of her bottom, and she looked at his face and knew that now, now he was ready to shed his self-control and lose himself in her. That excited her

313

more than anything, so that when at last he arched his back, his face screwed up into a mask of pain, and groaned deep in his chest, she wrapped her legs around his waist and abandoned herself to ecstasy; and then, after so long, she heard the trumpets and thunderstorms and the clash of cymbals that Lawrence had promised.

They were quiet for a long time. Lucy felt warm, as if she were glowing; she had never felt so warm in all her time on the island. When their breathing subsided she could hear the storm outside. Henry was heavy on top of her, but she did not want him to move: she liked his weight, and the faint tang of perspiration from his white skin. From time to time he moved his head to brush his lips against her cheek.

He was the perfect man to have an affair with. He knew more about her body than she did. His own body was very beautiful: broad and muscular at the shoulders, narrow at the waist and hips, with long, strong, hairy legs. She thought he had some scars: she was not sure. Strong, gentle and handsome: perfect. Yet she knew she would never fall in love with him, never want to run away with him and marry him. Deep inside him, she sensed, there was something very cold and hard, some part of him that was committed elsewhere, a readiness to abandon commonplace emotions for some higher duty. He would never belong to any woman, for he had some other ultimate loyalty – like a painter's art, a businessman's greed, a patriot's country, a socialist's revolution. She would have to hold him at arm's length, and use him cautiously, like an addictive drug.

Not that she would have time to get hooked: he would be gone in little more than a day.

She stirred at last, and immediately he rolled off her and on to his back. She lifted herself on one elbow and looked at his naked body. Yes, he did have scars: a long one on his chest, and a small mark like a star – it might have been a burn – on his hip. She rubbed his chest with the palm of her hand.

'It's not very ladylike,' she said, 'but I want to say thank you.'

He reached out to touch her cheek, and smiled. 'You're very ladylike.'

'You don't know what you've done. You've—'

He put a finger over her lips. 'I know what I've done.'

She bit his finger, then put his hand on her breast. He felt for her nipple. She said: 'Please do it again.'

'I don't think I can,' he said.

But he did.

She left him a couple of hours after dawn. There was a small noise from the other bedroom, and she seemed suddenly to remember that she had a husband and a son in the house. Faber wanted to tell her that it didn't matter, that neither he nor she had the least reason to care what the husband knew or thought; but he held his tongue and let her go. She kissed him once more, very wetly; then she stood up, smoothed her rumpled nightgown over her body, and tiptoed out. He watched her fondly.

She's quite something, he thought. He lay on his back and looked at the ceiling. She was quite naive, and very inexperienced, but all the same she had been very good. I could fall in love with her, he thought.

He got up and retrieved the film can and the knife in its sheath from under the bed. He wondered whether to keep them on his person. He might want to make love to her in the day . . . He decided to wear the knife – he would feel undressed without it – and leave the can somewhere. He put it on top of the chest-of-drawers and covered it with his papers and his wallet. He knew that he was breaking all the rules; but this was sure to be his last assignment, and he felt entitled to enjoy a woman. It would hardly matter if someone saw the pictures – what could they do?

He lay down on the bed, then got up again. Years of training would not let him take risks. He put the can and his papers into the pocket of his jacket. Now he could relax.

He heard the child's voice, then Lucy's tread as she went down the stairs, and then David dragging himself to the bathroom. He would have to get up and have breakfast with the household. He did not want to sleep now, anyway.

He stood at the rain-streaked window, watching the weather rage, until he heard the bathroom door open. Then he put on his pyjama jacket and went in to shave. He used David's razor, without permission.

It did not seem to matter now.

CHAPTER TWENTY-FOUR

ERWIN ROMMEL knew from the start that he was going to quarrel with Heinz Guderian.

General Guderian was exactly the kind of aristocratic Prussian officer Rommel hated. He had known him for some time. They had both, in their early days, commanded the Goslar Jaeger Battalion, and they had met again during the Polish campaign. When Rommel left Africa he had recommended Guderian to succeed him, knowing the battle was lost: the manoeuvre was a failure because at that time Guderian had been out of favour with Hitler and the recommendation was rejected out of hand.

The General was, Rommel felt, the kind of man who put a silk handkerchief on his knee to protect the crease in his trousers as he sat drinking in the Herrenklub. He was an officer because his father had been an officer and his grandfather had been rich. Rommel, the schoolteacher's son who had risen from Lieutenant-Colonel to Field Marshal in only four years, despised the military caste of which he had never been a member.

Now he stared across the table at the General, who was sipping brandy appropriated from the French

Rothschilds. Guderian and his sidekick, General von Geyr, had come to Rommel's headquarters at La Roche Guyon in Northern France to tell him how to deploy his troops. Rommel's reactions to such visits ranged from impatience to fury. In his view the General Staff were there to provide reliable intelligence and regular supplies, and he knew from his experience in Africa that they were incompetent at both tasks.

Guderian had a cropped, fair moustache, and the corners of his eyes were heavily wrinkled so that he always appeared to be grinning at you. He was tall and handsome, which did nothing to endear him to the short, ugly, balding Rommel. He seemed relaxed, and any German general who could relax at this stage of the war was surely a fool. The meal they had just finished – local veal and wine from farther south – was no excuse.

Rommel looked out of the window and watched the rain dripping from the lime trees into the courtyard while he waited for Guderian to begin the discussion. When eventually he spoke, it was clear the General had been thinking about the best way to make his point, and had decided to approach it sideways.

'In Turkey,' he began, 'the British 9th and 10th armies, with the Turkish army, are grouping at the border with Greece. In Yugoslavia, the partisans are also concentrating. The French in Algeria are preparing to invade the Riviera. The Russians appear to be mounting an amphibious invasion of Sweden. In Italy, the Allies are ready to march on Rome.

'There are smaller signals: a general kidnapped in

Crete; an Intelligence officer murdered at Lyon; a radar post attacked at Rhodes; an aircraft sabotaged with abrasive grease and destroyed at Athens; a commando raid on Sagvaag; an explosion in the oxygen factory at Boulogne-sur-Seine; a train derailed in the Ardennes; a petrol dump fired at Boussens . . . I could go on.

'The picture is clear. In occupied territories, there is ever-increasing sabotage and treachery; on our borders, everywhere we see preparations for invasion. None of us doubts that there will be a major Allied offensive this summer; and we can be equally sure that all this skirmishing is intended to confuse us about where the attack will come.'

The General paused. The lecture, delivered in schoolmaster style, was irritating Rommel, and he took the opportunity to interrupt. 'This is why we have a General Staff: to digest such information, produce appreciations of enemy activity, and forecast his future moves.'

Guderian smiled indulgently. 'We must also be aware of the limitations of such crystal-gazing. You have your ideas about where the attack will come, I'm sure: we all do. Our strategy must take into account the possibility that our guesses are wrong.'

Rommel now saw where the General's roundabout argument was leading, and he suppressed the urge to shout his disagreement before the conclusion was stated.

'You have four armoured divisions under your command,' Guderian continued. 'The 2nd Panzers at Amiens; the 116th at Rouen; the 21st at Caen; and the

2nd SS at Toulouse. General von Geyr has already proposed to you that these should be grouped well back from the coast, all together, ready for fast retaliation at any point. Indeed, this stratagem is a principle of OKW policy. Nevertheless, you have not only resisted von Geyr's suggestion, but have in fact moved the 21st right up to the Atlantic coast.'

'And the other three must be moved to the coast as soon as possible,' Rommel burst out. 'When will you people learn? *The Allies rule the air.* Once the invasion is launched there will be no further major movements of armour. Mobile operations are no longer possible. If your precious panzers are in Paris when the Allies land on the coast, they will *stay* in Paris – pinned down by the RAF – until the Allies march along the Boulevard St Michel. I *know* – they've done it to me. Twice!' He paused to draw breath. 'To group our armour as a mobile reserve is to render it useless. There will be no counter-attack. The invasion must be met on the beaches, when it is most vulnerable, and pushed back into the sea.'

The flush receded from his face as he began to expound his own defensive strategy. 'I have created underwater obstacles, strengthened the Atlantic Wall, laid minefields, and driven stakes into every meadow that might be used to land airplanes behind our lines. All my troops are engaged in digging defences whenever they're not actually training.

'My armoured divisions must be moved to the coast. The OKW reserve should be redeployed in France. The 9th and 10th SS divisions have to be brought back from the Eastern Front. Our whole strategy must be to prevent the Allies from securing a beachhead, for once they achieve that, the battle is lost . . . perhaps even the war.'

Guderian leaned forward, his eyes narrowing in that infuriating half-grin. 'You want us to defend the European coastline from Tromso in Norway all around the Iberian Peninsula to Rome. From where shall we get the armies?'

'That question should have been asked in 1938,' Rommel muttered.

There was an embarrassed silence after this remark, which was all the more shocking coming from the notoriously apolitical Rommel.

Von Geyr broke the spell. 'Where do *you* believe the attack will come, Field-Marshal?'

Rommel considered. 'Until recently I was convinced of the Pas de Calais theory. However, last time I was with the Führer I was impressed by his arguments in favour of Normandy. I am also impressed by his instinct, and its record of accuracy. Therefore I believe our panzers should be deployed primarily along the Normandy coast, with perhaps one division at the mouth of the Somme – this last supported by forces outside my group.'

Guderian shook his head solemnly. 'No, no, no. It's far too risky.'

'I'm prepared to take this argument to Hitler himself,' Rommel threatened.

'Then that's what you must do,' Guderian said resignedly, 'for I shan't assent to your plan, unless . . .'

'Well?' Rommel was surprised that the General's position might be qualified.

Guderian shifted in his seat, reluctant to give a concession to so obdurate an antagonist as Rommel. 'You may know that the Führer is waiting for a report from an unusually effective agent in England.'

'I remember,' Rommel nodded. 'Die Nadel.'

'Yes. He has been assigned to assess the strength of the First United States Army Group under Patton's command in the eastern part of England. If he finds – as I am certain he will – that that army is large, strong, and ready to move, then I shall continue to oppose you. However, if he finds that FUSAG is a bluff – a small army masquerading as an invasion force – then I shall concede that you are right, and you shall have your panzers. Will you accept that compromise?'

Rommel bowed his large head in assent. 'It all depends on Die Nadel, then.'

'It all depends on Die Nadel.'

Part Five

CHAPTER TWENTY-FIVE

T HE COTTAGE was terribly small, Lucy realized quite suddenly. As she went about her morning chores – lighting the stove, making porridge, tidying up, dressing Jo – the walls seemed to press in on her claustrophobically. After all, it was only four rooms, linked by a little passage with a staircase; you couldn't move without bumping into someone else. If you stood still and listened you could hear what everyone was doing: Henry running water into the wash-basin, David sliding down the stairs, Jo chastising his teddy-bear in the living-room. Lucy would have liked some time on her own before meeting people: time to let the events of the night settle into her memory, recede from the forefront of her thoughts, so that she could act normally without a conscious effort.

She guessed she was not going to be good at deception. It did not come naturally to her. She had no experience of it. She tried to think of another occasion in her life when she had deceived someone close to her, and she could not. It was not that she lived by very high principles – the *thought* of lying did not trouble her. It was just that she had never had reason for dishonesty. Does that mean, she wondered, that I've led a sheltered life?

David and Jo sat down at the kitchen table and began to eat. David was silent, Jo talked non-stop just for the pleasure of making words. Lucy did not want food.

'Aren't you eating?' David said casually.

'I've had some.' There – her first lie. It wasn't so bad.

The storm made the claustrophobia worse. The rain was so heavy that Lucy could hardly see the barn from the kitchen window. One felt even more shut-in when to open a door or window was a major operation. The low, steel-grey sky and the wisps of mist created a permanent twilight. In the garden, the rain ran in rivers between the rows of potato plants, and the herb patch was a shallow pond. The sparrow's nest under the outhouse roof had been washed away, and the birds flitted in and out of the eaves, panicking.

Lucy heard Henry coming down the stairs, and she felt better. For some reason, she was quite sure that he was very good at deception.

'Good morning!' Faber said heartily. David, sitting at the table in his wheelchair, looked up and smiled. Lucy busied herself at the stove. There was guilt written all over her face. Faber groaned inwardly, but David did not seem to notice her expression. Faber began to think that David was an oaf.

Lucy said: 'Sit down and have some breakfast, Henry.'

'Thank you very much.'

David said: 'Can't offer to take you to church, I'm

afraid. Hymn-singing on the wireless is the best we can do.'

Faber realized it was Sunday. 'Are you churchgoing people?'

'No,' David said. 'You?'

'No.'

'Sunday is much the same as any other day for farmers,' David continued. 'I'll be driving over to the other end of the island to see my shepherd. You could come, if you feel up to it.'

'I'd like to,' Faber told him. It would give him a chance to reconnoitre. He would need to know the way to the cottage with the transmitter. 'Would you like me to drive you?'

David looked at him sharply. 'I can manage quite well.' There was a strained moment of silence. 'In this weather, the road is just a memory. We'll be a lot safer with me at the wheel.'

'Of course.' Faber began to eat.

'It makes no difference to me,' David persisted. 'I don't want you to come if you think it would be too much—'

'Really, I'd be glad to.'

'Did you sleep all right? It didn't occur to me you might still be tired. I hope Lucy didn't keep you up late.'

Faber willed himself not to look at Lucy. Out of the corner of his eye he could see that she was blushing to the roots of her hair. 'I slept all day yesterday,' he said, trying to fix David's eyes with his own.

It was no use. David was looking at his wife. She

turned her back. The trace of a frown creased his forehead, and then just for a moment, his jaw dropped open in a classic expression of surprise.

Faber was mildly annoyed. David would be hostile now, and antagonism was half way to suspicion. It was not dangerous, but it might be tiresome.

The husband recovered his composure quickly. He pushed his chair away from the table and wheeled himself to the back door. 'I'll get the jeep out of the barn,' he muttered. He took an oilskin off a hook and put it over his head, then opened the door and rolled out.

In the few moments the door was open, the storm blew into the little kitchen, leaving the floor wet and the people cold. When it shut, Lucy shivered and began to mop the water from the tiles.

Faber reached out and touched her arm.

'Don't,' she said, jerking her head toward Jo in warning.

'You're being silly,' Faber told her.

'I think he knows,' she said.

'But, if you reflect for a minute, you don't really care whether he knows or not, do you?'

She considered. 'I'm not supposed to.'

Faber shrugged. The jeep's horn sounded impatiently outside. Lucy handed him an oilskin and a pair of wellington boots.

'Don't talk about me,' she said.

Faber put on the waterproof clothes and went to the front door. Lucy followed him, closing the kitchen door on Jo.

With his hand on the latch, Faber turned and kissed her.

She kissed him back, forcefully, then turned and went into the kitchen.

Faber dashed through the rain, across a sea of mud, and jumped into the jeep beside David. He pulled away immediately.

The vehicle had been specially adapted for the legless man to drive. It had a hand throttle, automatic gearshift, and a handle on the rim of the wheel to enable the driver to steer one-handed. The folded-up wheelchair slid into a special compartment behind the driver's seat. There was a shotgun in a rack above the windscreen.

David drove competently. He had been right about the road: it was no more than a strip of heath worn bare by the jeep's tyres. The rain pooled in the deep ruts. The car slithered about in the mud. David seemed to enjoy it. There was a cigarette between his lips, and he wore an incongruous air of bravado. Perhaps this was his substitute for flying.

'What do you do when you're not fishing?' he said around the cigarette.

'Civil servant,' Faber told him.

'What sort of work?'

'Finance. I'm just a cog in the machine.'

'Treasury, eh?'

'Mainly.'

Even that asinine answer did not stop David's questioning. 'Interesting work?' he persisted.

'Fairly.' Faber summoned up the energy to invent a

story. 'I know a bit about how much a given piece of engineering ought to cost, and I spend most of my time making sure the taxpayer isn't being overcharged.'

'Any particular sort of engineering?'

'Everything from paper clips to aircraft engines.'

'Ah, well. We all contribute to the war effort in our own way.'

It was a snide remark, and David would naturally have no idea why Faber did not resent it. 'I'm too old to fight,' Faber said mildly.

'Were you in the first lot?'

'Too young.'

'A lucky escape.'

'Doubtless.'

The track ran quite close to the cliff edge, but David did not slow down. It crossed Faber's mind that he might want to kill them both. He reached for a grab handle.

'Am I going too fast for you?' David asked.

'You seem to know the road,' Faber replied.

'You looked frightened,' David said.

Faber ignored that, and David slowed down a little, apparently satisfied that he had made some kind of point.

The island was fairly flat, and bare, Faber observed. The ground rose and fell slightly, but as yet he had seen no hills. The vegetation was mostly grass, with some ferns and bushes, but few trees: there was little protection from the weather. David Rose's sheep must be hardy, he thought.

'Are you married?' David asked suddenly.

'No.'

'Wise man.'

'Oh, I don't know.'

'I'll bet you put yourself about a bit up in London,' David leered.

Faber had never liked the nudging, contemptuous way some men talked about women. He said sharply: 'I should think you're extremely fortunate to have Lucy.'

'Oh, would you.'

'Yes.'

'Nothing like variety, though, eh?'

Faber thought: What the devil is he getting at? He said: 'I haven't had the chance to discover the merits of monogamy.'

'Quite.'

Faber thought: *He* doesn't know what he's getting at, either. He decided to say no more, since everything he said was fuel to the fire.

'I must say, you don't *look* like a Government account-ant. Where's the rolled umbrella and the bowler hat?'

Faber tried a thin smile.

'And you seem quite fit for a pen-pusher.'

'I ride a bicycle.'

'You must be quite tough, to have survived that wreck.'

'Thank you.'

'You don't *look* too old to be in the Army, either.'

Faber turned his gaze on David. 'What are you driving at, David?' he asked calmly.

'We're there,' David said.

Faber looked out of the windscreen and saw a

cottage very similar to Lucy's, with stone walls, a slate roof, and small windows. It stood at the top of a hill, the only hill Faber had seen on the island, and not much of a hill at that. The house had a squat, resilient look about it. Climbing up to it, the jeep skirted a small stand of pine and fir trees. Faber wondered why the cottage had not been built in the shelter of the trees.

Beside the house was a hawthorn tree in bedraggled blossom. David stopped the car. Faber watched him unfold the wheelchair and ease himself out of the driving seat into the chair: he would have resented an offer of help.

They entered the house by a plank door with no lock. They were greeted in the hall by a black-and-white collie, a small, broad-headed dog who wagged his tail but did not bark. The layout of the cottage was identical with that of Lucy's, but the atmosphere was different: this place was bare, cheerless, and none too clean.

David led the way into the kitchen. The shepherd sat by an old-fashioned wood-burning kitchen range, warming his hands. He stood up.

David said: 'Henry, this is Tom McAvity.'

'Pleased to meet you,' Tom said formally.

Faber shook his hand. He was a short man, and broad, with a face like an old tan suitcase. He was wearing a cloth cap and smoking a very large briar pipe with a lid. His grip was firm, and the skin of his hand felt like sandpaper. He had a very big nose. Faber had to concentrate hard to understand what he was saying: his Scots accent was very broad.

'I hope I'm not going to be in the way,' Faber said. 'I only came along for the ride.'

David wheeled himself up to the table. 'I don't suppose we'll do much this morning, Tom – just take a look around.'

'Aye. We'll have some tay before we go, though.'

Tom poured strong tea into three mugs, and added a shot of whisky to each. The three men sat and sipped it in silence, David smoking a cigarette and Tom drawing gently at his pipe, and Faber felt certain that the other two spent a great deal of time together in this way, smoking and warming their hands and saying nothing.

When they had finished their tea Tom put the mugs in the shallow stone sink and they went out in the jeep. Faber sat in the back. David drove slowly this time, and the dog, which was called Bob, loped alongside, keeping pace without apparent effort. It was obvious that David knew the terrain very well, for he steered confidently across the open grassland without once getting bogged down in swampy ground. The sheep looked very sorry for themselves. With their fleeces sopping wet, they huddled in hollows, or close to bramble bushes, or on the leeward slopes, too dispirited to graze. Even the lambs were subdued, hiding beneath their mothers.

Faber was watching the dog when it stopped, listened for a moment, and then raced off at a tangent.

Tom had been watching, too. 'Bob's found something,' he said.

The jeep followed the dog for a quarter of a mile. When they stopped Faber could hear the sea: they were close to the island's northern edge. The dog was standing at the brink of a small gully. When the men got out of the car they could hear what the dog had heard: the bleating of a sheep in distress. They went to the edge of the gully and looked down.

The animal lay on its side about twenty feet down, balanced precariously on the steeply sloping bank. It held one foreleg at an awkward angle. Tom went down to it, treading cautiously, and examined the leg.

'Mutton tonight,' he called.

David got the gun from the jeep and slid it down to him. Tom put the sheep out of its misery.

'Do you want to rope it up?' David called.

'Aye – unless Henry wants to come and give me a hand.'

'Surely,' Faber said. He picked his way down to where Tom stood. They took a leg each and dragged the dead animal back up the slope. Faber's oilskin caught on a thorny bush, and he almost fell before he tugged the material free with a loud ripping sound.

They threw the sheep into the jeep and drove on. Faber felt very wet, and he realized he had torn away most of the back of the oilskin. 'I'm afraid I've ruined this garment,' he said.

'All in a good cause,' Tom told him.

Soon they returned to Tom's cottage. Faber took off

the oilskin and his wet donkey jacket, and Tom put the jacket over the stove to dry. Then each went to the outhouse – Tom's cottage did not have the modern plumbing that had been added to Lucy's – and Tom made more tea.

'She's the first we've lost this year,' David said.

'Aye.'

'We'll fence the gully this summer.'

'Aye.'

Faber sensed a change in the atmosphere: it was not the same as it had been two or three hours earlier. They sat, drinking and smoking as before, but David seemed restless. Twice Faber caught the man staring at him, deep in thought.

Eventually David said: 'We'll leave you to butcher the ewe, Tom.'

'Aye.'

David and Faber left. Tom did not get up, but the dog saw them to the door.

Before starting the jeep David took the shotgun from its rack above the windscreen, reloaded it, and put it back.

On the way home he underwent another change of mood and became chatty. 'I used to fly Spitfires, you know. Lovely kites. Four guns in each wing – American Brownings, they were, firing one thousand two hundred and sixty rounds a minute. The Jerries prefer cannon, of course – their Me 109s only have two machine guns. A cannon does more damage, but our Brownings are faster, and more accurate.'

'Really?' Faber said politely.

'They put cannon in the Hurricanes later, but it was the Spitfire that won the Battle of Britain.'

Faber found his boastfulness irritating. He said: 'How many enemy aircraft did you shoot down?'

'I lost my legs while I was training,' David said.

Faber stole a glance at his face: it was a mask of repressed fury.

David said: 'No, I haven't killed a single German, yet.'

It was an unmistakable signal. Faber suddenly became very alert. He had no idea what David might have deduced or discovered, but there could be no doubt that the man knew something was up. Faber turned slightly sideways to face David, braced himself with his foot against the transmission tunnel on the floor, and rested his right hand lightly on his left forearm. He waited for David's next move.

'Are you interested in aircraft?' David asked.

'No.' Faber's voice was flat.

'It's become a national pastime, I gather – aircraft spotting. Like bird-watching. People buy books on aircraft identification. Spend whole afternoons on their backs, looking at the sky through telescopes. I thought you might be an enthusiast.'

'Why?'

'Pardon?'

'What made you think I might be an enthusiast?'

'Oh, I don't know.' David stopped the jeep to light a cigarette. They were at the island's mid-point, five miles from Tom's cottage with another five miles to go to

Lucy's. David dropped the match on the floor. 'Perhaps it was the photographs that fell out of your jacket pocket—'

As he spoke, he tossed the lighted cigarette at Faber's face, and reached for the gun above the windscreen.

CHAPTER TWENTY-SIX

S ID CRIPPS looked out of the window and cursed under his breath. The meadow was full of American tanks – at least eighty of them. He realized there was a war on, and all that, but if only they'd asked him he would have offered them another field, where the grass was not so lush. By now the caterpillar tracks would have chewed up his best grazing.

He pulled on his boots and went out. There were some Yank soldiers in the field, and he wondered whether they had noticed the bull. When he got to the stile he stopped and scratched his head. There was something very funny going on.

The tanks had *not* chewed up his grass. They had left no tracks. But the American soldiers were *making* tank tracks with a tool something like a harrow.

While Sid was trying to figure it all out, the bull noticed the tanks. It stared at them for a while, then pawed the ground and lumbered into a run. It was going to charge a tank.

'Daft bugger, you'll break your head,' Sid muttered.

The soldiers were watching the bull, too. They seemed to think it was funny.

The bull ran full-tilt into the tank, its horns piercing the armour-plated side of the vehicle. Sid hoped fervently that British tanks were stronger than the American ones.

There was a loud hissing noise as the bull worked its horns free. The tank collapsed like a deflated balloon. The American soldiers fell about laughing.

Sid Cripps scratched his head again. It was all very strange.

Percival Godliman walked quickly across Parliament Square, carrying an umbrella. He wore a dark striped suit under his raincoat, and his black shoes were highly polished – at least, they had been until he stepped out into the rain – for it was not every day, come to that it was not every year, that he had a private audience with Churchill.

A career soldier would have been nervous at going with such bad news to see the supreme commander of the nation's armed forces. Godliman was not nervous, for a distinguished historian has nothing to fear from soldiers and politicians, not unless his view of history is a good deal more radical than Godliman's was. Not nervous, then; but he was worried.

He was thinking about the effort, the forethought, the care, the money and the manpower that had gone into the creation of the totally phoney First United States Army Group stationed in East Anglia: the four hundred landing ships, made of canvas and scaffolding floated on oil drums, which thronged the harbours and estuaries; the carefully manufactured inflatable dummies of tanks, artillery, trucks, half-tracks and even ammunition dumps; the complaints planted in the correspondence columns of the local newspapers about the decline in moral standards since the arrival of thousands of American troops in the area; the phoney oil dock at Dover, designed by Britain's most distinguished architect and built – out of cardboard and old sewage pipes – by craftsmen borrowed from film studios; the carefully faked reports transmitted to Hamburg by German agents who had been 'turned' by the XX Committee; and the incessant radio chatter, broadcast solely for the benefit of the German listening posts, consisting of messages compiled by professional writers of fiction, and including such gems as 'I/5th Queen's Royal Regiment report a number of civilian women, presumably unauthorized, in the baggage train. What are we going to do with them – take them to Calais?'

A lot had been achieved. The signs were that the Germans had fallen for it. And now the whole elaborate deception had been placed in jeopardy because of one spy – a spy Godliman had failed to catch.

His short, birdlike paces measured the Westminster pavement to the small doorway at No 2, Great George Street. The armed guard standing beside the wall of sandbags examined his pass and waved him in. He crossed the lobby and went down the stairs to Churchill's underground headquarters.

It was like going below decks on a battleship. Protected from bombs by a four-foot-thick ceiling of reinforced concrete, the command post featured steel bulkhead doors and roof props of ancient timber. As

Godliman entered the map room a cluster of youngish people with solemn faces emerged from the conference room beyond. An aide followed them a moment later, and spotted Godliman.

'You're very punctual, sir,' the aide said. 'He's ready for you.'

Godliman stepped into the small, comfortable conference room. There were rugs on the floor and a portrait of the King on the wall. An electric fan stirred the tobacco smoke in the air. Churchill sat at the head of an old, mirror-smooth table in the centre of which was a statuette of a faun – the emblem of Churchill's own deception outfit, the London Controlling Section.

Godliman decided not to salute.

Churchill said: 'Sit down, Professor.'

Godliman suddenly realized that Churchill was not a big man – but he *sat* like a big man: shoulders hunched, elbows on the arms of his chair, chin lowered, legs apart. Instead of the famous siren suit he was wearing a solicitor's black-and-stripes – short black jacket and striped grey trousers – with a spotted blue bow tie and a brilliant-white shirt. Despite his stocky frame and his paunch, the hand holding the fountain pen was delicate, thin-fingered. His complexion was baby-pink. The other hand held a cigar, and on the table beside the papers stood a glass containing what looked like whisky.

He was making notes in the margin of a typewritten report, and as he scribbled he muttered occasionally. Godliman was not in the least awed by the great man. As a peacetime statesman Churchill had been, in Godliman's view, a disaster. However, the man had the qualities of a great warrior chieftain, and Godliman respected him for that. (Years later, Churchill modestly denied having been the British lion, saying that he had merely been privileged to give the roar: Godliman thought that assessment was just about right.)

He looked up abruptly and said: 'I suppose there's no doubt this damned spy has discovered what we're up to?'

'None whatsoever, sir,' Godliman said.

'You think he's got away?'

'We chased him to Aberdeen. It's almost certain that he left there two nights ago in a stolen boat – presumably for a rendezvous in the North Sea. However, he can't have been far out of port when the storm blew up. He may have met the U-boat before the storm hit, but it's unlikely. In all probability he drowned. I'm sorry we can't offer more definite information.'

'So am I,' Churchill said. Suddenly he seemed angry, though not with Godliman. He got out of his chair and went over to the clock on the wall, staring as if mesmerized at the inscription *Victoria RI, Ministry of Works, 1889.* Then, as if he had forgotten that Godliman was there, he began to pace up and down alongside the table, muttering to himself. Godliman was able to make out the words, and what he heard astonished him. The great man was mumbling: 'This stocky figure, with a slight stoop, striding up and down, suddenly unconscious of any presence beyond his own thoughts . . .' It was as if Churchill were acting out a Hollywood screenplay which he wrote as he went along.

The performance ended as abruptly as it had begun,

and if the man knew he had been behaving eccentrically, he gave no sign of it. He sat down, handed Godliman a sheet of paper, and said: 'This is the German order of battle as of last week.'

Godliman read:

Russian front:	122	*infantry divisions*
	25	*panzer divisions*
	17	*miscellaneous divisions*
Italy & Balkans:	37	*infantry divisions*
	9	*panzer divisions*
	4	*miscellaneous divisions*
Western front:	64	*infantry divisions*
	12	*panzer divisions*
	12	*miscellaneous divisions*
Germany:	3	*infantry divisions*
	1	*panzer division*
	4	*miscellaneous divisions*

Churchill said: 'Of those twelve panzer divisions in the west, only *one* is actually on the Normandy coast. The great SS divisions, *Das Reich* and *Adolf Hitler*, are at Toulouse and Brussels respectively and show no signs of moving. What does all this tell you, Professor?'

'Our deception and cover plans seem to have been successful,' Godliman answered.

'Totally!' Churchill barked. 'They are confused and uncertain, and their best guesses about our intentions are wildly wrong. And yet!' He paused for effect. 'And yet, despite all that, General Walter Bedell Smith – Ike's Chief of Staff – tells me that . . .' He picked up another piece of paper from the table and read it aloud. 'Our chances of holding the beachhead, particularly after the Germans get their buildup, are only fifty-fifty.'

He put his cigar down, and his voice became quite soft. 'It will be June the fifth – possibly the sixth or the seventh. The tides are right ... it has been decided. The build-up of troops in the West Country has already begun. The convoys are even now making their way along the country roads of England. It has taken the total military and industrial might of the whole English-speaking world – the greatest civilization since the Roman Empire – four years to win this fifty-fifty chance. If this spy gets out, we lose even that.'

He stared at Godliman for a moment, then he picked up his pen with a frail white hand. 'Don't bring me probabilities, Professor,' he said. 'Bring me the body of Die Nadel.'

He looked down and began to write. After a moment Percival Godliman got up and quietly left the room.

CHAPTER TWENTY-SEVEN

Cigarette tobacco burns at eight hundred degrees centigrade. However, the coal at the end of the cigarette is normally surrounded by a thin layer of ash. To cause a burn, the cigarette has to be pressed against the skin for the better part of a second: a glancing touch will hardly be felt. This applies even to the eyes, for blinking is the fastest involuntary reaction of the human body. Only amateurs throw cigarettes. Professionals – there are just a few people in the world for whom hand-to-hand fighting is a professional skill – ignore them.

Faber ignored the lighted cigarette that David Rose threw at him. He did right, for the cigarette glanced off his forehead and fell to the metal floor of the jeep. Then he made a grab for David's gun, and this was an error. He should have drawn his stiletto and stabbed David: for although David *might* have shot him first, he had never before pointed a gun at a human being, let alone killed somebody; so he would almost certainly have hesitated, and in that moment Faber could have killed him.

The mistake cost dear.

David had both hands on the midsection of the gun

– left hand on the barrel, right hand around the breech – and had pulled the weapon about six inches from its rack when Faber got a one-handed grip on the muzzle. David tugged the gun toward himself, but for a moment Faber's grasp held, and the gun pointed at the windscreen.

Faber was a strong man, but David was exceptionally strong. His shoulders, arms and wrists had moved his body and his wheelchair for four years, and the muscles had become abnormally developed. Furthermore, he had both hands on the gun in front of him, and Faber was holding on with one hand at an awkward angle. David tugged again, more determinedly this time, and the muzzle slipped from Faber's grasp.

At that instant, with the shotgun pointed at his belly and David's finger curling around the trigger, Faber felt very close to death.

He jerked upwards, catapulting himself out of his seat. His head hit the canvas roof of the jeep as the gun exploded with a crash that numbed the ears and produced a physical pain behind the eyes. The window by the passenger seat shattered into innumerable small pieces and the rain blew in through the empty frame. Faber twisted his body and fell back, not on to his own seat, but across David. He got both hands to David's throat and squeezed with his thumbs.

David tried to bring the gun around between their bodies to fire the other barrel, but the weapon was too big. Faber looked into his eyes, and saw . . . what was it? Exhilaration! Of course – at last the man had a chance to fight for his country. Then his expression changed as his body felt the lack of oxygen and he began to fight for breath.

David released his grip on the gun and brought both elbows back as far as he could, then punched Faber's lower ribs with a powerful double jab.

The pain was excruciating, and Faber screwed up his face in anguish, but he held his grip on David's throat. He knew he could withstand David's punches longer than David could hold his breath.

David must have had the same thought. He crossed his forearms between their bodies and pushed Faber away; then, when the gap was a few inches wide, he brought his hands up in an upward-and-outward blow against Faber's arms, breaking the stranglehold. He bunched his right fist and swung downwards with a mighty but unscientific punch which landed on Faber's cheekbone and brought water to his eyes.

Faber replied with a series of body jabs; David continued to bruise his face. They were too close together to do real damage to each other in a short time, but David's greater strength began to tell.

Grimly, Faber realized that David had shrewdly picked the time and place for the fight: he had had the advantages of surprise, the gun, and the confined space in which his muscle counted for much and Faber's better balance and greater manoeuvrability counted for little.

Faber shifted his weight slightly and his hip came into contact with the gearshift, throwing the transmission into forward. The engine was still running, and the car jerked, putting him off balance. David took the opportunity to release a long straight left which – more by luck than judgement – caught Faber full on the chin and threw him clear across the cab of the jeep. His head cracked against the A-post, he slumped with his shoulder on the door handle, the door opened, and he fell out of the car in a backward somersault to land on his face in the mud.

For a moment he was too dazed to move. When he opened his eyes he could see nothing but flashes of blue lightning against a misty red background. He heard the engine of the jeep racing. He shook his head, desperately trying to clear the fireworks from his vision, and struggled on to his hands and knees. The sound of the jeep receded and came closer again. He turned his head toward the noise, and as the colours in front of his eyes dissolved and disappeared, he saw the vehicle bearing down on him at high speed.

David was going to run him over.

With the front bumper less than a yard from his face he hurled himself sideways. He felt a blast of wind. A fender struck his outflung foot as the jeep roared past, its heavy-gauge tyres tearing up the spongy turf and spitting mud. He rolled over twice in the wet grass, then got to one knee. His foot hurt. He watched the jeep turn in a tight circle and come for him again.

He could see David's face through the windscreen. The young man was leaning forward, hunched over the steering wheel, his lips drawn back over his teeth in a savage, almost maniacal grin. He seemed to be imagining himself in the cockpit of a Spitfire, coming down out of the sun at an enemy plane with all eight Browning machine-guns blazing 1,260 rounds per minute.

Faber moved toward the cliff edge. The jeep gathered speed. Faber knew that, for a moment, he was incapable of running. He looked over the cliff: it was a rocky, almost vertical slope to the angry sea a hundred feet below. The jeep was coming straight down the cliff's edge toward him. Frantically, Faber looked up and down for a ledge, or even a foothold. There was none.

The jeep was four or five yards away, travelling at something like forty miles per hour. Its wheels were less than two feet from the cliff's edge. Faber dropped flat and swung his legs out into space, supporting his weight on his forearms as he hung on the brink.

The wheels passed him within inches. A few yards farther on, one tyre actually slipped over the edge. For a moment Faber thought the whole vehicle would slide over and fall into the sea below, but the other three wheels dragged the jeep to safety.

The ground under Faber's arms shifted. The vibration of the jeep's passing had loosened the earth. He felt himself slip a fraction. One hundred feet below, a raging sea boiled among the rocks. Faber stretched one arm to its farthest extent and dug his fingers deep into the soft ground. He felt a nail tear, and ignored it. He repeated the process with his other arm. With two hands anchored in the earth he pulled himself upward. It was agonizingly slow, but eventually his head drew level with his hands, his hips reached firm ground, and he was able to swivel around and roll away from the edge.

The jeep was turning again. Faber ran toward it. His foot was painful, but not broken. David accelerated for another pass. Faber turned and ran at right angles to the jeep's direction, forcing David to turn the wheel and consequently slow down.

Faber could not keep this up much longer. He was certain to tire before David. This had to be the last pass.

He ran faster. David steered an interception course, headed for a point in front of Faber. Faber doubled back, and the jeep zigzagged. It was now quite close. Faber broke into a sprint, his course compelling David to drive in a tight circle. The jeep was getting slower and Faber was getting closer. There were only a few yards between them when David realized what Faber was up to. He steered away, but it was too late. Faber raced to the jeep's side and threw himself upwards, landing face down on top of the canvas roof.

He lay there for a few seconds, catching his breath. His injured foot felt as if it was being held in a fire, and his lungs ached painfully.

The jeep was still moving. Faber drew the stiletto from its sheath under his sleeve and cut a long, jagged tear in the canvas roof. The material flapped downwards and Faber found himself staring at the back of David's head.

David looked up and back. A look of utter astonishment crossed his face. Faber drew back his arm for a knife thrust.

David jammed the throttle open and heaved the wheel around. The jeep leaped forward and lifted on two wheels as it screeched around in a tight curve. Faber struggled to stay on. The jeep, gathering speed still, crashed down on to four wheels then lifted again. It teetered precariously for a few yards, then the wheels slipped on the sodden ground and the vehicle toppled on to its side with a grinding crash.

Faber was thrown several yards and landed awkwardly. The breath was knocked out of him by the impact. It was several seconds before he could move.

The jeep's crazy course had taken it perilously close to the cliff once more.

Faber saw his knife in the grass a few yards away. He picked it up, then turned to the jeep.

Somehow, David had got himself and his wheelchair out through the ripped roof, and he was now sitting in the chair and pushing himself away along the cliff edge. Faber had to acknowledge his courage.

All the same, he had to die.

Faber ran after him. David must have heard the footsteps, for just before Faber caught up the chair stopped dead and spun around; and Faber glimpsed a heavy spanner in David's hand.

Faber crashed into the wheelchair, overturning it. His last thought was that both men and the chair might end up in the sea below – then the spanner hit the back of his head and he blacked out.

When he came to, the wheelchair lay beside him, but David was nowhere to be seen. He stood up and looked around in dazed puzzlement.

'Here!'

The voice came from over the cliff. David must have been flung from the chair and slid over the edge. Faber crawled to the cliff and looked over.

David had one hand around the stem of a bush which grew just under the lip of the cliff. The other hand was jammed into a small crevice in the rock. He hung suspended, just as Faber had a few minutes earlier. His bravado had gone, and there was naked terror in his eyes.

'Pull me up, for God's sake,' he shouted hoarsely.

Faber leaned closer. 'How did you know about the pictures?' he said.

'Help me, please!'

'Tell me about the pictures.'

'Oh, God.' David made a mighty effort to concentrate. 'When you went to Tom's outhouse you left your jacket drying in the kitchen. Tom went upstairs for more whisky, and I went through your pockets. I found the negatives.'

'And that was evidence enough for you to try to kill me?' Faber said wonderingly.

'That, and what you did with my wife in my house. No Englishman would behave like that.'

Faber could not help laughing. 'Where are the negatives now?'

'In my pocket.'

'Give them to me, and I'll pull you up.'

'You'll have to take them – I can't let go.'

Faber lay flat on his stomach and reached down, under David's oilskin, to the breast pocket of his jacket. He gave a sigh of satisfaction as his fingers touched the film can and withdrew it. He looked at the films: they all seemed to be there. He put the can in the pocket of his jacket, buttoned the flap, and reached down to David again.

He took hold of the bush David was clinging to and uprooted it with a savage jerk.

David screamed: 'No!' He scrabbled desperately for grip as his other hand slipped inexorably out of the crack in the rock.

'It's not fair!' he screamed. Then his hand came away from the crevice.

He seemed to hang in mid-air: then he dropped, faster and faster, bouncing twice against the cliff on his way down, until he hit the water with a huge splash.

Faber watched for a while to make sure he did not come up again. 'Not fair?' he murmured to himself. 'Not fair? Don't you know there's a war on?'

He looked down at the sea for some minutes. Once he thought he saw a flash of yellow oilskin on the surface, but it was gone before he could focus on it. There was just the sea and the rocks.

Suddenly he felt terribly tired. His injuries penetrated his consciousness one by one: the damaged foot, the bump on his head, the bruises all over his face. David Rose had been a fool, a braggart and a poor husband, and he had died screaming for mercy; but he had been a brave man too, and he had died for his country – he had got his wish.

Faber wondered whether his own death would be as good.

At last he turned away from the cliff edge and walked back toward the overturned jeep.

CHAPTER TWENTY-EIGHT

PERCIVAL GODLIMAN felt refreshed, determined, even inspired.

When he reflected on it, this made him uncomfortable. Pep-talks are for the rank-and-file, and intellectuals believe themselves immune from inspirational speeches. Yet, although he knew that the great man's performance had been carefully scripted, the crescendos and diminuendos of the speech predetermined like a symphony, nevertheless it had worked on him, as effectively as if he had been the captain of the school cricket team hearing last-minute exhortations from the games master.

He got back to his office itching to do *something*.

He dropped his brolly in the umbrella-stand, hung up his wet raincoat, and looked at himself in the mirror on the inside of the cupboard door. Without doubt something had happened to his face since he became one of England's spycatchers. The other day he had come across a photograph of himself taken in 1937, with a group of students at a seminar in Oxford. In those days he actually looked older than he did now: pale skin, wispy hair, the patchy shave and ill-fitting clothes of a retired man. The wispy hair had gone: he was now bald except for a monkish fringe. His clothes were those of a business executive, not a teacher. It seemed to him – he might, he supposed, have been imagining it – that the set of his jaw was firmer, his eyes were brighter, and he took more care shaving.

He sat down behind his desk and lit a cigarette. *That* innovation was not welcome: he had developed a cough, tried to give it up, and discovered that he had become addicted. But almost everybody smoked in wartime Britain, even some of the women. Well, they were doing men's jobs – they were entitled to masculine vices. The smoke caught in Godliman's throat, making him cough. He put the cigarette out in the tin-lid he used for an ashtray (crockery was scarce).

The trouble with being inspired to perform the impossible, he reflected, was that the inspiration gave you no clues to the practical means. He recalled his college thesis, about the travels of an obscure medieval monk called Thomas of the Tree. Godliman had set himself the minor but difficult task of plotting the monk's itinerary over a five-year period. There had been a baffling gap of eight months when he had been either in Paris or Canterbury, but Godliman had been unable to determine which, and this had threatened the value of the whole project. The records he was using simply did not contain the information. If the monk's stay had gone unrecorded, then there was no way to find out where he had been, and that was that. With the optimism of youth, young Godliman had refused to believe that the information was just not there, and he had worked on the assumption that *somewhere* there had to be a record of how Thomas had spent those months – despite the well-known fact that almost everything that happened in the Middle Ages went unrecorded. If Thomas was not in Paris or Canterbury he must have been in transit between the two, Godliman had argued; and then he had found shipping records in an Amsterdam museum which showed that Thomas had boarded a vessel bound for Dover which got blown off course and was eventually wrecked on the Irish coast. This model piece of historical research had got Godliman his professorship.

He might try applying that kind of thinking to the problem of what had happened to Faber.

It was most likely that Faber had drowned. If he had not, then he was probably in Germany by now. Neither of those possibilities presented any course of action that Godliman could follow, so they should be discounted. He must assume that Faber was alive and had reached land somewhere.

He left his office and went down one flight of stairs to the map room. His uncle, Colonel Terry, was there, standing in front of the map of Europe with a cigarette between his lips, thinking. Godliman realized that this was a familiar sight in the War Office these days: senior men gazing entranced at maps, silently making their own computations of whether the war would be won or lost. He guessed it was because all the plans had been made, the vast machine had been set in motion, and for those who made the big decisions there was nothing to do but wait and see if they had been right.

Terry saw him come in, and said: 'How did you get on with the great man?'

'He was drinking whisky,' Godliman said.

'He drinks all day, but it never seems to make any difference to him,' Terry said. 'What did he say?'

'He wants Die Nadel's head on a platter.' Godliman crossed the room to the wall map of Great Britain and put a finger on Aberdeen. 'If you were sending a U-boat in to pick up a fugitive spy, what would you think was the nearest the sub could safely come to the coast?'

Terry stood beside him and looked at the map. 'I wouldn't want to come closer than the three-mile limit. But for preference, I'd stop ten miles out.'

'Right.' Godliman drew two pencil lines parallel to the coast, three miles and ten miles out respectively. 'Now, if you were an amateur sailor setting out from Aberdeen in a smallish fishing boat, how far would you go before you began to get nervous?'

'You mean, what's a reasonable distance to travel in such a boat?'

'Indeed.'

Terry shrugged. 'Ask the Navy. I'd say fifteen or twenty miles.'

'I agree.' Godliman drew an arc of twenty miles radius with its centre on Aberdeen. 'Now: if Faber is alive, he's either back on the mainland or somewhere within this space.' He indicated the area bounded by the parallel lines and the arc.

'There's no land in that area.'

'Have we got a bigger map?'

Terry pulled open a drawer and got out a large-scale

map of Scotland. He spread it on top of the chest. Godliman copied the pencil marks from the smaller map on to the larger.

There was still no land within the area.

'But look,' Godliman said. Just to the east of the ten-mile limit was a long, narrow island.

Terry peered closer. 'Storm Island,' he read. 'How apt.'

Godliman snapped his fingers. 'I'll bet that's where he is.'

'Can you send someone there?'

'When the storm clears. Bloggs is up there: I'll get a plane laid on for him. He can take off the minute the weather improves.' He went to the door.

'Good luck!' Terry called after him.

Godliman ran up the stairs to the next floor and entered his office. He picked up the phone. 'Get Mr Bloggs in Aberdeen, please.'

While he waited he doodled on his blotter, drawing the island. It was shaped like the top half of a walking-stick, with the crook at the western end. It must have been about ten miles long, and perhaps a mile wide. He wondered what sort of place it was: was it a barren lump of rock, or a thriving community of crofters? If Faber was there he might still be able to contact his U-boat: Bloggs would have to get to the island before the submarine. It would be difficult.

'I have Mr Bloggs,' the switchboard girl said.

'Fred?'

'Hello, Percy.'

'I think he's on an island called Storm Island.'

'No, he's not,' Bloggs said. 'We've just arrested him.'

The stiletto was nine inches long, with an engraved handle and a stubby little crosspiece. Its needle-like point was extremely sharp. Bloggs thought it looked like a highly efficient killing instrument. It had recently been polished.

Bloggs and Detective-Chief-Inspector Kincaid stood looking at it, neither man wanting to touch it.

'He was trying to catch a bus to Edinburgh,' Kincaid said. 'A PC spotted him at the ticket office and asked for his identification. He dropped his suitcase and ran away. A woman bus-conductor hit him over the head with her ticket machine. He took ten minutes to come around.'

'Let's have a look at him,' Bloggs said.

They went down the corridor to the cells. 'This one,' Kincaid said.

Bloggs looked through the judas. The man sat on a stool in the far corner of the cell with his back against the wall. His legs were crossed, his eyes closed, his hands in his pockets. 'He's been in cells before,' Bloggs remarked. The man was tall, with a long, handsome face and dark hair. It could have been the man in the photograph, but it was hard to be certain.

'Want to go in?' Kincaid asked.

'In a minute. What was in his suitcase, apart from the stiletto?'

'The tools of a burglar's trade. Quite a lot of money

in small notes. A pistol and some ammunition. Black clothes and crepe-soled shoes. Two hundred Lucky Strike cigarettes.'

'No photographs?'

Kincaid shook his head.

'Balls,' Bloggs said feelingly.

'Papers identify him as Peter Fredericks, of Wembley, Middlesex. Says he's an unemployed toolmaker looking for work.'

'Toolmaker?' Bloggs said sceptically. 'There hasn't been an unemployed toolmaker in Britain in the last four years. You'd think a spy would know that. Still . . .'

Kincaid asked: 'Shall I start the questioning, or will you?'

'You.'

Kincaid opened the door and Bloggs followed him in. The man in the corner opened his eyes incuriously. He did not alter his position.

Kincaid sat at a small, plain table. Bloggs leaned against the wall.

Kincaid said: 'What's your real name?'

'Peter Fredericks.'

'What are you doing so far from home?'

'Looking for work.'

'Why aren't you in the Army?'

'Weak heart.'

'Where have you been for the last few days?'

'Here, in Aberdeen. Before that Dundee, before that Perth.'

'When did you arrive in Aberdeen?'

'The day before yesterday.'

Kincaid glanced at Bloggs, who nodded. Kincaid said: 'Your story is silly. Toolmakers don't need to look for work. The country hasn't got enough of them. You'd better tell the truth.'

'I'm telling the truth.'

Bloggs took all the loose change out of his pocket and tied it up in his handkerchief. He stood watching, saying nothing, swinging the little bundle in his right hand.

'Where are the photographs?' Kincaid said.

The man's expression did not change. 'I don't know what you're talking about.'

Kincaid shrugged, and looked at Bloggs.

Bloggs said: 'On your feet.'

'Pardon?' the man said.

'On your FEET!' Bloggs bawled.

The man stood up casually.

'Forward!'

He took two steps up to the table.

'Name?'

'Peter Fredericks.'

Bloggs came off the wall and hit the man with the weighted handkerchief. The blow caught him accurately on the bridge of the nose, and he cried out. His hands went to his face.

'Stand to attention!' Bloggs shouted. 'Name!'

The man stood upright, let his hands fall to his sides, and whispered: 'Peter Fredericks.'

Bloggs hit him again in exactly the same place. This time he went down on one knee, and his eyes watered.

'Where are the photographs?' Bloggs screamed.

The man shook his head dumbly.

Bloggs pulled him to his feet, kneed him in the groin, and punched his stomach. 'What did you do with the negatives?'

The man fell to the floor and threw up. Bloggs kicked his face. There was a sharp crack, as if something had broken. 'What about the U-boat? Where is the rendezvous? What is the signal?'

Kincaid grabbed Bloggs from behind. 'That's enough, Bloggs,' he said. 'This is my station, and I can only turn a blind eye for so long, you know.'

Bloggs rounded on him. 'We're not dealing with a case of petty housebreaking, Kincaid – this man is jeopardizing the whole war effort.' He wagged a finger under the detective's nose. 'Just remember: I'm MI5, and I'll do what I fucking well like in your station. If the prisoner dies, I'll take responsibility.' He turned back to the man on the floor.

The man was staring at Bloggs and Kincaid. His face, covered with blood, showed an expression of incredulity. 'What are you talking about?' he said weakly. 'What is this?'

Bloggs hauled him to his feet again. 'You are Henrik Rudolph Hans von Muller-Guder, born at Oln on 26 May 1900; also known as Henry Faber; a lieutenant-colonel in German Intelligence. Within three months you will be hanged for espionage, unless you turn out to be more useful to us dead than alive. You'd better start making yourself useful, Colonel Muller-Guder.'

'No,' the man said. 'No, no! I'm a thief, not a spy. Please!' He cowered away from Bloggs's upraised fist. 'I can prove it.'

Bloggs hit him again, and Kincaid intervened for the second time. 'Wait,' the detective said. 'All right, Fredericks – if that's your name – prove you're a thief.'

'I done three houses in Jubilee Crescent last week,' the man gasped. 'I took about five hundred quid from one and some jewellery from the next one – diamond rings and some pearls – and I never got nothing from the other one because of the dog ... you must know I'm telling the truth, they must have reported it, didn't they? Oh, Jesus—'

Kincaid looked at Bloggs. 'All those burglaries took place.'

'He could have read about them in the newspapers.'

'The third one wasn't reported.'

'Perhaps he did them – he could still be a spy. Spies can steal.'

'But this was last week – your man was in London, wasn't he?'

Bloggs was silent for a moment. Then he said: 'Well, fuck it,' and walked out.

Peter Fredericks looked up at Kincaid through a mask of blood. 'Who's he, the bleedin' Gestapo?' he said.

Kincaid stared at him thoughtfully. 'Be glad you're not really the man he's looking for.'

*

'Well?' Godliman said into the phone.

'False alarm.' Bloggs's voice was scratchy and distorted over the long-distance line. 'A small-time housebreaker who happens to carry a stiletto and look like Faber.'

'Back to square one,' Godliman said. 'Damn.'

'You said something about an island.'

'Yes. Storm Island – it's about ten miles off the coast, due east of Aberdeen. You'll find it on a large-scale map.'

'What makes you sure he's there?'

'I'm not sure; not at all. We still have to cover every other possibility – other towns, the coast, everything. But if he did steal that boat, the . . . ?'

'*Marie II.*'

'Yes. If he did steal it, his rendezvous was probably in the area of this island; and if I'm right about *that*, then he's either drowned or shipwrecked on the island.'

'Okay, that makes sense.'

'What's the weather like up there?'

'No change.'

'Could you reach the island in a big ship?'

Bloggs grunted. 'I suppose you can ride any storm if your ship's big enough. But this island won't have much of a dock, will it?'

'You'd better find out. However, I expect you're right. Now listen: there's an RAF fighter base near Edinburgh. By the time you get there, I'll have an amphibious plane standing by. You take off the minute the storm begins to clear. Have the local coastguard ready to move at a moment's notice, too – I'm not sure who'll get there first.'

'Mm.' Bloggs sounded dubious. 'If the U-boat is also waiting for the storm to clear, it will get there first.'

'You're right.' Godliman lit a cigarette, fumbling for inspiration. 'Well, we can get a Navy corvette to circle the island and listen for Faber's radio signal. When the storm clears it can land a boat on the island. Yes, that's a good idea.'

'What about some fighters?'

'Yes. Although like you, they'll have to wait until the weather breaks.'

'It can't go on much longer.'

'What do the Scottish meteorologists say?'

'Another day of it, at least.'

'Damn.'

'It doesn't make much difference,' Bloggs said. 'All the time we're grounded he's bottled up.'

'If he's there at all.'

'Yes.'

'All right,' Godliman said. 'We'll have a corvette, the coastguard, some fighters and an amphibian.'

'And me.'

'You'd better get on your way. Call me from Rosyth. Take care.'

'Cheerio.'

Godliman hung up. His cigarette, neglected in the ashtray, had burned down to a tiny stub. He lit another, then picked up the phone again and began organizing.

CHAPTER TWENTY-NINE

L YING ON its side, the jeep looked powerful but helpless, like a wounded elephant. The engine had stalled. Faber gave it a hefty push and it toppled majestically on to all four wheels. It had survived the fight relatively undamaged. The canvas roof was destroyed, of course: the rip Faber's knife had made had become a long tear running from one side to the other. The offside front wing, which had ploughed into the earth and stopped the vehicle, was crumpled. The headlight on that side had smashed. The window on the same side had been broken by the shot from the gun. The windscreen was miraculously intact.

Faber climbed into the driving seat, put the gearshift into neutral, and tried the starter. It kicked over and died. He tried again, and the engine fired. He sighed with relief: he could not have faced a long walk just then.

He sat in the car for a while, inventorying his wounds. He touched his right ankle gingerly: it was swelling massively. Perhaps he had cracked a bone. It was as well that the jeep was designed to be driven by a man with no legs, for Faber could not have pressed a brake pedal. The lump on the back of his head felt huge, the size of a golf ball; and when he touched it his hand came away sticky with blood. He examined his face in the driving mirror. It was a mass of small cuts and big bruises, like the face of the loser at the end of a boxing match.

He had abandoned his oilskin back at the cottage, so his jacket and overalls were soggy with rain and smeared with mud. He needed to get warm and dry very soon.

He gripped the steering wheel, and a burning pain shot through his hand: he had forgotten the torn fingernail. He looked at it. It was the nastiest of his injuries. He would have to drive one-handed.

He pulled away slowly and found what he guessed was the road. There was no danger of getting lost on this island – all he had to do was follow the cliff-edge until he came to Lucy's cottage.

He needed to invent a lie to explain to Lucy what had become of her husband. He might, of course, tell her the truth: there was nothing she could do about it. However, if she became awkward he might have to kill her; and there had grown within him an aversion to killing Lucy. Driving slowly along the cliff-top through the pouring rain and howling wind, he marvelled at this new thing inside him, this scruple. It was the first time he had ever felt reluctance to kill. It was not that he was amoral: quite the contrary. He had made up his mind that the killing he did was on the same moral level as death on the battlefield, and his emotions followed his intellect. He always had the physical reaction, the vomiting, after he killed, but that was some-thing incomprehensible which he ignored.

So why did he not want to kill Lucy?

The feeling was on a par with the affection which drove him to send the Luftwaffe erroneous directions to St Paul's Cathedral: a compulsion to protect a thing of beauty. She was a remarkable creation, as full of loveliness and subtlety as a work of art. Faber could live with himself as a killer, but not as an iconoclast. It was, he recognized as soon as the thought occurred to him, a peculiar way to be. But then, spies were peculiar people.

He thought of some of the spies who had been recruited by the Abwehr at the same time as he: Otto, the Nordic giant who made delicate paper sculptures in the Japanese fashion and hated women; Friedrich, the sly little mathematical genius who jumped at shadows and went into a five-day depression if he lost a game of chess; Helmut, who liked to read books about slavery in America and had soon joined the SS . . . all different, all peculiar. If they had anything more specific in common, he did not know what it was.

He seemed to be driving more and more slowly, and the rain and mist became more impenetrable. He began to worry about the cliff-edge on his left-hand side. He felt very hot, but suffered spasms of shivering. He realized he had been speaking aloud about Otto and Friedrich and Helmut; and he recognized the signs of delirium. He made an effort to think of nothing but the problem of keeping the jeep on a straight course.

The noise of the wind took on some kind of rhythm, becoming hypnotic. Once he found himself stationary, staring out over the sea, and had no idea how long he had stopped.

It seemed hours later that Lucy's cottage came into view. He steered toward it, thinking: I must remember to put the brake on before I hit the wall. There was a figure standing in the doorway, looking at him through the rain. He had to stay in control of himself long enough to tell her the lie. He had to remember, had to remember . . .

It was late afternoon by the time the jeep came back. Lucy was worried about what had happened to the men, and at the same time angry with them for not coming home for the lunch she had prepared. As the day waned she had spent more and more time at the windows, looking out for them.

When the jeep came down the slight slope to the cottage, it was clear something was wrong. It was moving terribly slowly, weaving all over the track, and there was only one person in it. It came closer, and she saw that the front was dented and the headlamp smashed.

'Oh, God,' she murmured.

The vehicle shuddered to a halt in front of the cottage, and she saw that the figure inside was Henry. He made no move to get out. Lucy ran out into the rain and opened the driver's door.

Henry sat there with his head back and his eyes half-closed. His hand was on the brake. His face was bloody and bruised.

Lucy said: 'What happened? *What happened?*'

Henry's hand slipped off the brake, and the jeep moved forward. Lucy leaned across him and slipped the gearshift into neutral.

Henry said: 'Left David at Tom's cottage . . . had crash on way back . . .' The words seemed to cost him a great effort.

Now that she knew what had happened, Lucy's panic subsided. 'Come inside,' she said sharply. The urgency in her voice got through to Henry. He turned toward her, put his foot on the running board to step down, and promptly fell to the ground. Lucy saw that his ankle was swollen like a balloon.

She got her hands under his shoulders and pulled him upright, saying: 'Put your weight on the other foot and lean on me.' She got his right arm around her neck and half-carried him inside.

Jo watched wide-eyed as she helped Henry into the living-room and got him on to the sofa. He lay back with his eyes shut. His clothes were soaked and muddy.

Lucy said: 'Jo, go upstairs and get your pyjamas on, please.'

'But I haven't had my story. Is *he* dead?'

'He's not dead, but he's had a car crash, and you can't have a story tonight. Go on.'

The child made a complaining sound, and Lucy looked threateningly at him. He went.

Lucy got the big scissors out of her sewing basket

and cut Henry's clothes away: first the jacket, then the overalls, then the shirt. She frowned in puzzlement when she saw the knife in its sheath strapped to his left forearm: she guessed it was a special implement for cleaning fish, or something. When she tried to take it off, Henry pushed her hand away. She shrugged, and turned her attention to his boots. The left one came off easily, and its sock; but he cried out in pain when she touched the right.

'It must come off,' she told him. 'You'll have to be brave.'

A funny kind of smile came over his face, then, and he nodded assent. She cut the laces, took the shoe gently but firmly in both hands, and pulled it off. This time he made no sound. She cut the elastic in the sock and pulled that off too.

Jo came in and said: 'He's in his pants!'

'His clothes are all wet.' She kissed the boy good-night. 'Put yourself to bed, darling. I'll tuck you up later.'

'Kiss teddy, then.'

'Goodnight, teddy.'

Jo went out. Lucy looked back to Henry. His eyes were open, and he was smiling. He said: 'Kiss Henry, then.'

She leaned over him and kissed his battered face. Then, carefully, she cut away his underpants.

The heat from the fire would quickly dry his naked skin. She went into the kitchen and filled a bowl with warm water and a little antiseptic to bathe his wounds.

She found a roll of cotton wool and returned to the living-room.

'This is the second time you've turned up on the doorstep half dead,' she said as she set about her task.

'The usual signal,' Henry said.

'What?'

'Waiting at Calais for a phantom army.'

'Henry, what are you talking about?'

'Every Friday and Monday.'

She realized he was delirious. 'Don't try to talk,' she said. She lifted his head slightly to clean away the dried blood from around the bump.

Suddenly he sat upright, looked fiercely at her, and said: 'What day is it? What day is it?'

'It's Sunday, relax.'

'Okay.'

He was quiet after that, and he let her remove the knife. She bathed his face, bandaged his finger where he had lost the nail, and put a dressing on his ankle. When she had finished she stood looking at him for a while. He seemed to be sleeping. She touched the long scar on his chest, and the star-shaped mark on his hip. The star was a birthmark, she decided.

She went through his pockets before throwing the lacerated clothes away. There wasn't much: some money, his papers, a leather wallet and a film can. She put them all in a little pile on the mantelpiece beside his fish knife. He would have to have some of David's clothes.

She left him and went upstairs to see Jo. The boy was

asleep, lying on his teddy bear, with his arms outflung. She kissed his soft cheek and tucked him in. She went outside and put the jeep in the barn.

She made herself a drink in the kitchen then sat watching Henry, wishing he would wake up and make love to her again.

It was almost midnight when he awoke. He opened his eyes, and his face showed the series of expressions which were now familiar to her: first the fear, then the wary survey of the room, then the relaxation. On impulse, she asked him: 'What are you afraid of, Henry?'

'I don't know what you mean.'

'You always look frightened when you wake up.'

'I don't know.' He shrugged, and the movement seemed to hurt. 'God, I'm battered.'

'Do you want to tell me what happened?'

'Yes, if you'll give me a small amount of brandy.'

She got the brandy out of the cupboard. 'You can have some of David's clothes.'

'In a minute . . . unless you're embarrassed.'

She handed him the glass, smiling. 'I'm afraid I'm enjoying it.'

'What happened to my clothes?'

'I had to cut them off you. I've thrown them away.'

'Not my papers, I hope.' He smiled, but there was some other emotion just below the surface.

'On the mantelpiece.' She pointed. 'I suppose that knife is for cleaning fish, or something.'

His right hand went to his left forearm, where the sheath had been. 'Something like that,' he said. He seemed uneasy for a moment, then relaxed with an effort and sipped his drink. 'That's good.'

After a moment she said: 'Well?'

'What?'

'How did you manage to lose my husband and crash my jeep?'

'David decided to stay over at Tom's for the night. Some of the sheep got into trouble in a place they called the Gully—'

'I know it.'

'—and six or seven of them were injured. They're all in Tom's kitchen, being bandaged up and making a frightful row. Anyway, David suggested I came back to tell you he would be staying. I don't really know how I managed to crash. The car is unfamiliar, there's no real road, I hit something and went into a skid, and the jeep ended up on its side. The details . . .' he shrugged.

'You must have been going quite fast – you were in an awful mess when you got here.'

'I suppose I rattled around inside the jeep a bit. Banged my head, twisted my ankle . . .'

'Lost a fingernail, bashed your face, and almost caught pneumonia. You must be accident-prone.'

He swung his legs to the floor, stood up, and went to the mantelpiece.

Lucy said: 'Your powers of recuperation are incredible.'

He was strapping the knife to his arm. 'We fishermen are very healthy. What about those clothes?'

She got up and stood close to him. 'What do you need clothes for? It's bedtime.'

He drew her to him, pressing her against his naked body, and kissed her hard. She stroked his thighs.

After a while he broke away from her. He picked up his things from the mantelpiece, took her hand, then, hobbling, he led her upstairs to bed.

CHAPTER THIRTY

THE WIDE, white autobahn snaked through the Bavarian valley up into the mountains. In the leather rear seat of the staff Mercedes, Field Marshal Gerd von Rundstedt was still and weary. Aged sixty-nine, he knew he was too fond of champagne and not fond enough of Hitler. His thin, lugubrious face reflected a career longer and more erratic than that of any of Hitler's other officers: he had been dismissed in disgrace more times than he could remember, but the Führer always asked him to come back.

As the car passed through the sixteenth-century village of Berchtesgaden, he wondered why he always returned to his command when Hitler forgave him. Money meant nothing to him: he had already achieved the highest possible rank; decorations were valueless in the Third Reich; and he believed that it was not possible to win honour in this war.

It was Rundstedt who had first called Hitler 'the Bohemian corporal'. The little man knew nothing of the German military tradition, nor – despite his flashes of inspiration – of military strategy. If he had, he would not have started this war, for it was unwinnable. Rundstedt was Germany's finest soldier, and he had proved it in Poland, France and Russia; but he had no hope of victory.

All the same, he would have nothing to do with the small group of generals who – he knew – were plotting to overthrow Hitler. He turned a blind eye to them, but the *Fahneneid*, the blood oath of the German warrior, was too strong within him to permit him to join the conspiracy. And that, he supposed, was why he continued to serve the Reich. Right or wrong, his country was in danger, and he had no option but to protect it. I'm like an old cavalry horse, he thought: if I stayed at home I should feel ashamed.

He commanded five armies on the Western front, now. A million and a half men were under him. They were not as strong as they might be – some divisions were little better than rest homes for invalids from the Russian front, there was a shortage of armour, and there were many non-German conscripts among the other ranks – but Rundstedt could still keep the Allies out of France if he deployed his forces shrewdly.

It was that deployment that he must now discuss with Hitler.

The car climbed the Kehlsteinstrasse until the road ended at a vast bronze door in the side of the Kehlstein Mountain. An SS guard touched a button, the door hummed open, and the car entered a long marble tunnel lit by bronze lanterns. At the far end of the tunnel the driver stopped the car, and Rundstedt walked to the elevator and sat in one of its leather seats for the four-hundred-foot ascent to the Adlerhorst, the Eagle's Nest.

In the anteroom Rattenhuber took his pistol and left him to wait. He stared unappreciatively at Hitler's porcelain and went over in his mind the words he would say.

A few moments later the blond bodyguard returned to usher him into the conference room.

The place made him think of an eighteenth-century palace. The walls were covered with oil paintings and tapestries, and there was a bust of Wagner and a huge clock with a bronze eagle on its top. The view from the side window was truly remarkable: one could see the hills of Salzburg and the peak of the Untersberg, the mountain where the body of the Emperor Frederick Barbarossa waited, according to legend, to rise from the grave and save the Fatherland. Inside the room, seated in the peculiarly rustic chairs, were Hitler and just three of his staff: Admiral Theodor Krancke, the naval commander in the west; General Alfred Jodl, chief of staff; and Admiral Karl Jesko von Puttkamer, Hitler's aide-de-camp.

Rundstedt saluted and was motioned to a chair. A footman brought a plate of caviar sandwiches and a glass of champagne. Hitler stood at the large window, looking out, with his hands clasped behind his back. Without turning, he said abruptly: 'Rundstedt has changed his mind. He now agrees with Rommel that the Allies will invade Normandy. This is what my instinct has all along told me. Krancke, however, still favours Calais. Rundstedt, tell Krancke how you arrived at your conclusion.'

Rundstedt swallowed a mouthful and coughed into

his hand. Damn, Hitler had no manners: didn't even give a chap a chance to catch his breath. 'There are two things: one new piece of information and one new line of reasoning,' Rundstedt began. 'First, the information. The latest summaries of Allied bombing in France show without doubt that their principal aim is to destroy every bridge across the River Seine. Now, if they land at Calais the Seine is irrelevant to the battle; but if they land in Normandy all our reserves have to cross the Seine to reach the zone of conflict.

'Second, the reasoning. I have given some thought to how I would invade France if I were commanding the Allied forces. My conclusion is that the first goal must be to establish a bridgehead through which men and supplies can be funnelled at speed. The initial thrust must therefore come in the region of a large and roomy harbour. The natural choice is Cherbourg.

'Both the bombing pattern and the strategic requirements point to Normandy,' he finished. He picked up his glass and emptied it, and the footman came forward to refill it.

Jodl said: 'All our intelligence points to Calais—'

'And we have just executed the head of the Abwehr as a traitor,' Hitler interrupted. 'Krancke, are you convinced?'

'My Führer, I am not,' the Admiral said. 'I, too, have considered how I would conduct the invasion if I were on the other side – but I have brought into the reasoning a number of factors of a nautical nature of which Rundstedt may not have been aware. I believe they will attack under cover of darkness, by moonlight, at full tide to sail over Rommel's underwater obstacles, and away from cliffs, rocky waters and strong currents. Normandy? Never.'

Hitler shook his head in disgusted disagreement. Jodl said: 'There is another small piece of information which I find significant. The Guards Armoured Division has been transferred from the north of England to Hove, on the south-east coast, to join the First United States Army Group under General Patton. We learned this from wireless surveillance – there was a baggage mix-up en route, one unit had another's silver cutlery, and the fools have been quarrelling about it over the radio. This is a crack British division, very blue-blooded, commanded by General Sir Allan Henry Shafto Adair. I feel sure they will not be far from the centre of the battle when it comes.'

Hitler's hands moved nervously, and his face twitched in an agony of indecision. 'Generals!' he barked at them. 'Either I get conflicting advice, or no advice at all! I have to tell you everything – everything!'

With characteristic boldness, Rundstedt plunged on. 'My Führer, you have four superb panzer divisions doing nothing here in Germany. If I am right, they will never get to Normandy in time to repel the invasion. I beg you, order them to France and put them under Rommel's command. If we are wrong, and the invasion begins at Calais, they will still be close enough to enter the battle at an early stage.'

'I don't know – I don't know!' Hitler's eyes widened, and Rundstedt wondered if he had pushed too hard – again.

Puttkamer spoke for the first time. 'My Führer, today is Sunday.'

'Well?'

'Tomorrow night the U-boat may pick up the spy, Die Nadel.'

'Ah, yes! Someone I can trust.'

'Of course, he can report by radio at any time. However, there may be some reason for him to avoid the radio; in which case he would bring his information personally. Given this possibility, you may like to consider postponing your decision for twenty-four hours, in case he does contact us, one way or the other, today or tomorrow.'

Rundstedt said: 'There isn't time to postpone decisions. Both air attacks and sabotage activities have increased dramatically. The invasion may come any day.'

'I disagree,' Krancke said. 'The weather conditions will not be right until early June.'

'That is not very far away!'

'Enough!' Hitler shouted. 'I have made up my mind. My panzers stay in Germany – for now. On Tuesday, when we have heard from Die Nadel, I will reconsider the disposition of these forces. If his information favours Normandy – as I believe it will – I will move the panzers.'

Rundstedt said softly: 'And if he does not report?'

'If he does not report, I shall reconsider just the same.'

Rundstedt bowed assent. 'With your permission, I shall return to my command.'

'Very well.'

Rundstedt got to his feet, saluted and went out. In the copper-lined elevator, falling four hundred feet to the underground garage, he felt his stomach turn over, and wondered whether the sensation was caused by the speed of descent or by the thought that the destiny of his country lay in the hands of a single, lonely spy.

Part Six

Part Six

CHAPTER THIRTY-ONE

LUCY WOKE up slowly. She rose gradually, languidly, from the warm void of deep sleep, up through layers of unconsciousness, perceiving the world piece by isolated piece: first the warm, hard male body beside her; then the strangeness of the little bed; the noise of the storm outside, as angry and tireless as yesterday and the day before; the faint smell of the man's skin; her arm across his chest, her leg thrown across his as if to keep him there, her breasts pressed against his side; the light of day beating against her eyelids; the regular, light breathing that blew softly across her face; and then, all at once like the solution to a puzzle, the realization that she was flagrantly and adulterously lying with a man she had met only forty-eight hours before, and that they were naked in bed in her husband's house.

She opened her eyes and saw Jo.

He was standing beside the bed in his rumpled pyjamas, hair tousled, a battered rag doll under his arm, sucking his thumb and staring wide-eyed at his mummy and the strange man cuddling each other in his, Jo's, bed. Lucy could not read his expression, for at this time of day he stared wide-eyed at most things, as if all the world was new and marvellous every morning. She stared back at him in silence, not knowing what to say.

Then Henry's deep voice said: 'Good morning.'

Jo took his thumb out of his mouth, said: 'Good morning,' turned around and went out of the bedroom.

Lucy said: 'Damn, damn, damn.'

Henry slid down in the bed until his face was level with hers, and kissed her. His hand went between her thighs and held her possessively.

She pushed him away. 'For God's sake, stop.'

'Why?'

'Jo's seen us!'

'So what?'

'He can talk, you know. Sooner or later he'll say something to David. What am I going to do?'

'Do nothing. So David finds out. Does it matter?'

'Of course it matters.'

'I don't see why. He has wronged you, and this is the consequence. You shouldn't feel guilty.'

Lucy suddenly realized that Henry simply had no conception of the complex tangle of loyalties and obligations that constituted a marriage. She said: 'It's not *that* simple.'

She got out of bed and crossed the landing to her own bedroom. She slipped into knickers, trousers and a sweater, then remembered she had destroyed all Henry's clothes and had to lend him some of David's. She found underwear and socks, a knitted shirt and a V-necked pullover, and finally – right at the bottom of a trunk – one pair of trousers that were not cut off at the knee and sewn up. All the while Jo watched her in silence.

She took the clothes into the other bedroom. Henry had gone into the bathroom to shave. She called through the door: 'Your clothes are on the bed.'

She went downstairs, lit the stove in the kitchen, and put a saucepan of water on to heat. She decided to have boiled eggs for breakfast. She washed Jo's face at the kitchen sink, combed his hair, and dressed him quickly. 'You're very quiet this morning,' she said brightly. He made no reply.

Henry came down and sat at the table, as naturally as if he had been doing it every morning for years. Lucy felt very weird, seeing him there in David's clothes, handing him a breakfast egg, putting a rack of toast on the table in front of him.

Jo said suddenly: 'Is my daddy dead?'

Henry gave the boy a queer look and said nothing.

Lucy said: 'Don't be silly. He's at Tom's house.'

Jo ignored her and spoke to Henry. 'You've got my daddy's clothes, *and* you've got my mummy. Are you going to be my daddy now?'

Lucy muttered: 'Out of the mouth of babes and sucklings . . .'

Henry said: 'Didn't you see my clothes last night?'

Jo nodded.

'Well, then, you know why I had to borrow some of your daddy's clothes. I'll give them back to him when I get some more of my own.'

'Will you give my mummy back?'

'Of course.'

Lucy said: 'Eat your egg, Jo.'

The child tucked into his breakfast, apparently satisfied. Lucy was gazing out of the kitchen window. 'The boat won't come today,' she said.

'Are you glad?' Henry asked her.

She looked at him. 'I don't know.'

Lucy did not feel hungry. She drank a cup of tea while Jo and Henry ate. Afterwards, Jo went upstairs to play and Henry cleared the table. As he stacked crockery in the sink he said: 'Are you afraid David will hurt you, physically?'

She shook her head in negation.

'You should forget him,' Henry went on. 'You were planning to leave him anyway. Why should it concern you whether he finds out or not?'

'He's my *husband*,' she said. 'That counts for something. The kind of husband he's been ... all that ... doesn't give me the right to humiliate him.'

'I think it gives you the right not to care whether he's humiliated or not.'

'It's not a question that can be settled logically. It's just the way I *feel*.'

He made a giving-up gesture with his arms. 'I'd better drive over to Tom's and find out whether your *husband* wants to come back. Where are my boots?'

'In the living-room. I'll get you a jacket.' She went upstairs and got David's old hacking jacket out of the wardrobe. It was a fine grey-green tweed, very elegant with a nipped-in waist and slanted pocket flaps. Lucy had put leather patches on the elbows to preserve it: you couldn't buy clothes like this any more. She took it down to the living-room, where Henry was putting his boots on. He had laced the left one, and was gingerly inserting his injured right foot into the other. Lucy knelt to help him.

'The swelling has gone down,' she said.

'The damn thing still hurts.'

They got the boot on, but left it untied and took the lace out. Henry stood up experimentally.

'It's okay,' he said.

Lucy helped him into the jacket. It was a little tight across the shoulders. 'We haven't got another oilskin,' she said.

'Then I'll get wet.' He pulled her to him and kissed her roughly. She put her arms around him and held tightly for a moment.

'Drive more carefully today,' she said.

He smiled and nodded, kissed her again – briefly this time – and went out. She watched him limp across to the barn, and stood at the window while he started the jeep and drove away, up the slight rise and out of sight. When he had gone she felt relieved, but somehow empty.

She began to put the house straight, making beds and washing dishes, cleaning and tidying; but she could summon up no enthusiasm for the task. She was restless. She worried at the problem of what to do with her life, following old arguments around in familiar circles, unable to put her mind to anything else. She found the cottage claustrophobic instead of snug. There was a big world out there somewhere, a world of war and heroism, full of colour and passion and people, millions of people; she wanted to be out there in the midst of it, to meet new minds and see cities and hear music. She turned on the radio: a futile gesture, for the news broadcast made her feel more isolated, not less. There was a battle report from Italy, the rationing regulations had been eased a little, the London stiletto murderer was still at large, Roosevelt had made a speech. Sandy Macpherson began to play a theatre organ, and Lucy switched off. None of it touched her, for she did not live in that world.

She wanted to scream.

She had to get out of the house, despite the weather. It would be only a symbolic escape, for the stone walls of the cottage were not what imprisoned her; but the symbol was better than nothing. She collected Jo from upstairs, separating him with some difficulty from a regiment of toy soldiers, and wrapped him up in waterproof clothing.

'Why are we going out?' he asked.

'To see if the boat comes.'

'You said it won't come today.'

'Just in case.'

They put bright yellow sou'westers on their heads, lacing them under their chins, and stepped outside the door.

The wind was like a physical blow, unbalancing Lucy so that she staggered. In seconds her face was as wet as if she had dipped it in a bowl, and the ends of hair protruding from under her hat lay limp and clinging on her cheeks and the shoulders of her oilskin. Jo screamed with delight and jumped in a puddle.

They walked along the cliff-top to the head of the bay, and looked down at the huge North Sea rollers hurling themselves to destruction against the cliffs and on the beach. The storm had uprooted underwater vegetation from God-only-knew what depth and flung it in heaps on the sand and rocks. Mother and son became absorbed in the ceaselessly shifting patterns of the waves. They had done this before: the sea had a hypnotic effect on both of them, and Lucy was never quite sure, afterwards, how long they had spent silently watching.

The spell was broken this time by something she saw. At first there was only a flash of colour in the trough of a wave, so fleeting that she was not certain what colour it had been, so small and far away that she immediately doubted whether she had seen it at all. She looked for it, but did not see it again, and her gaze drifted back to the bay and the little jetty, on which flotsam gathered in drifts only to be swept away by the next big wave. After the storm, on the first fine day, she and Jo would go beachcombing to see what treasures the sea had disgorged, and come back with oddly coloured rocks, bits of wood of mystifying origin, huge seashells and twisted fragments of rusted metal.

She saw the flash of colour again, much nearer, and this time it stayed within sight for a few seconds. It was bright yellow, the colour of all their oilskins. She peered at it through the sheets of rain, but could not identify its shape before it disappeared again. But the current was bringing it closer, as it brought everything to the bay, depositing its rubbish on the sand like a man emptying his trouser pockets on to a table.

It *was* an oilskin: she could see that when the sea lifted it on the crest of a wave and showed it to her for the third and final time. Henry had come back without his, yesterday, but how had it got into the sea? The wave broke over the jetty and flung the object on the wet wooden boards of the ramp, and Lucy realized it was not Henry's oilskin, for the owner was still inside it. Her gasp of horror was whipped away by the wind so that not even she could hear it. Who was he? Where had he come from? Another shipwreck?

It occurred to her that he might still be alive. She must go and see. She bent and shouted in Jo's ear: 'Stay here – keep still – don't move.' Then she ran down the ramp.

Half way down she heard footsteps behind her: Jo was following. The ramp was narrow and slippery, quite dangerous. She stopped, turned, and scooped the child up in her arms, saying: 'You naughty boy, I told you to wait!' She looked from the body below to the safety of the clifftop, dithered for a moment in painful indecision, discerned that the sea would wash the body away at any moment, and proceeded downward, carrying Jo.

A smaller wave covered the body, and when the water receded Lucy was close enough to see that it was a man, and that it had been in the sea long enough for the water to swell and distort the features. That meant he was dead. She could therefore do nothing for him, and she was not going to risk her life and her son's to preserve a corpse. She was about to turn back when something about the bloated face struck her as familiar. She stared at it, uncomprehending, trying to fit the features to something in her memory; and then, quite abruptly, she saw the face for what it was, and sheer, paralysing terror gripped her, and it seemed that her heart stopped, and she whispered: 'No, David, no!'

Oblivious now to the danger she walked forward. Another lesser wave broke around her knees, filling her wellington boots with foamy salt water, but she did not notice. Jo twisted in her arms to face forward, but she screamed 'Don't look!' in his ear and pushed his face into her shoulder. He began to cry.

She knelt beside the body and touched the horrible face with her hand. It was David. There was no doubt. He was dead, and had been for some time. Moved by some deep instinct to make absolutely certain, she lifted the skirt of the oilskin and looked at the stumps of his legs.

It was impossible to take in the fact of the death. She had, in a way, been wishing him dead; but her feelings about him were confused by guilt and the fear of being found out in infidelity. Grief, horror, liberation, relief: they fluttered in her mind like birds, none of them willing to settle.

She would have stayed there, motionless, but the next wave was a big one. Its force knocked her flying, and she took a great gulp of sea water. Somehow she managed to keep Jo in her grasp and stay on the ramp;

and when the surf settled she got to her feet and ran up out of the greedy reach of the ocean.

She walked all the way to the cliff-top without looking back. When she came within sight of the cottage, she saw the jeep standing outside. Henry was back.

Still carrying Jo, she broke into a stumbling run, desperate to share her hurt with Henry, to feel his arms around her and have him comfort her. Her breath came in ragged sobs, and tears mixed invisibly with the rain on her face. She went to the back of the cottage, burst into the kitchen, and dumped Jo urgently on the floor.

Henry said: 'David decided to stay over at Tom's another day.'

She stared at him, her mind an incredulous blank; and then, in a flash of intuition, she understood everything.

Henry had killed David.

The conclusion came first, like a punch in the stomach, winding her; the reasons followed a split-second later. The shipwreck, the odd-shaped knife he was so attached to, the crashed jeep, the news bulletin about the London stiletto murderer: suddenly everything fitted together, a box of jigsaw pieces thrown in the air and landing, improbably, fully assembled.

'Don't look so surprised,' Henry said with a smile. 'They've got a lot of work to do over there, and I didn't encourage him to come back.'

Tom. She had to go to Tom. He would know what to do; he would protect her and Jo until the police came; he had a dog and a gun.

Her fear was interrupted by a shaft of sadness, of sorrow for the Henry she had believed in, had almost loved; for clearly he did not exist – she had imagined him. Instead of a warm, strong, affectionate man, she saw in front of her a monster who sat and smiled and calmly gave her invented messages from the husband he had murdered.

She suppressed a shudder. Taking Jo's hand, she walked out of the kitchen, along the hall, and out of the front door. She got into the jeep, sat Jo beside her, and started the engine.

But Henry was there, resting his foot casually on the running-board, and holding David's shotgun, saying: 'Where are you going?'

Her heart sank. If she drove away now he might shoot – what instinct had warned him to take the gun into the house this time? – and while she herself might chance it, she could not endanger Jo. She said: 'Just putting the jeep away.'

'You need Jo's help for that?'

'He likes the ride. Don't cross-examine me!'

Henry shrugged, and stepped back.

She looked at him for a moment, wearing David's hacking jacket and holding David's gun so casually, and wondered whether he really would shoot her if she simply drove away. Then she recalled the vein of ice she had sensed within him right from the start, and knew that that ultimate commitment, that ruthlessness, would permit him to do anything.

With an awful feeling of weariness, she surrendered. She threw the jeep into reverse and backed into the barn. She switched off, got out, and walked with Jo back into the cottage. She had no idea what she would say to Henry, what she would do in his presence, how she would hide her knowledge – if, indeed she had not already betrayed it.

She had no plans.

But she had left the barn door open.

CHAPTER THIRTY-TWO

'T HAT'S THE place, Number One,' the captain said, and lowered his telescope.

The first lieutenant peered out through the rain and the spray. 'Not quite the ideal holiday resort, what, sir? Jolly stark, I should say.'

'Indeed.' The captain was an old-fashioned naval officer with a grizzled beard who had been at sea during the first war with Germany. However, he had learned to overlook his first lieutenant's foppish conversational style, for the boy had turned out – against all expectations – to be a perfectly good sailor.

The 'boy', who was past thirty and an old salt by this war's standards, had no idea of the magnanimity from which he benefited. He held on to a rail and braced himself as the corvette mounted the steep side of a wave, righted itself at the crest, and dived into the trough 'Now that we're here, sir, what do we do?'

'Circle the island.'

'Very good, sir.'

'And keep our eyes open for a U-boat.'

'We're not likely to get one anywhere near the surface in this weather – and if we did, we couldn't see it unless it came within spitting distance.'

'The storm will blow itself out tonight – tomorrow at the latest.' The captain began stuffing tobacco into a pipe.

'Do you think so?'

'I'm sure.'

'Nautical instinct, I suppose?'

The captain grunted. 'That, and the weather forecast.'

The corvette rounded a headland, and they saw a small bay with a jetty. Above it, on the cliff top, was a little cottage standing small and square, hunched against the wind.

The captain pointed. 'We'll land a party there as soon as we can.'

The first lieutenant nodded. 'All the same . . .'

'Well?'

'Each circuit of the island will take us about an hour, I should say.'

'So?'

'So, unless we're jolly lucky and happen to be in exactly the right place at exactly the right time . . .'

'The U-boat will surface, take on its passenger, and submerge again without us even seeing the ripples,' the captain finished.

'Yes.'

The captain lit his pipe with an expertise which spoke of long experience of lighting pipes in heavy seas. He puffed a few times, then inhaled a lungful of smoke. 'Ours not to reason why,' he said, and blew smoke through his nostrils.

'A rather unfortunate quotation, sir.'

'Why?'

'It refers to the notorious charge of the Light Brigade.'

'Good God! I never knew that.' The captain puffed contentedly. 'What it must be to be educated.'

There was another little cottage at the eastern end of the island. The captain scrutinized it through his telescope, and observed that it had a large, professional-looking radio aerial. 'Sparks!' he called. 'See if you can raise that cottage. Try the Royal Observer Corps's frequency.'

'Aye, aye, sir.'

When the cottage had passed out of sight, the radio operator called: 'No response, sir.'

'All right, Sparks,' the captain said. 'It wasn't important.'

The crew of the coastguard cutter sat below decks in Aberdeen Harbour, playing pontoon for halfpennies and musing on the feeble-mindedness which seemed invariably to accompany high rank.

'Twist,' said Jack Smith, who was more Scots than his name.

Albert 'Slim' Parish, a fat Londoner far from home, dealt him a jack.

'Bust,' Smith said.

Slim raked in his stake. 'A penny-ha'penny,' he said in mock wonder. 'I only hope I live to spend it.'

Smith rubbed condensation off the inside of a port-hole and peered out at the boats bobbing up and down in the harbour. 'The way the skipper's panicking,' he observed, 'you'd think we were going to bloody Berlin, not Storm Island.'

'Didn't you know? We're the spearhead of the Allied invasion.' Slim turned over a ten, dealt himself a king, and said: 'Pay twenty-ones.'

Smith said: 'What is this guy, anyway – a deserter? If you ask me, it's a job for the military police, not us.'

Slim shuffled the pack. 'I'll tell you what he is: an escaped prisoner-of-war.'

There was a chorus of disbelieving jeers.

'All right, don't listen to me. But when we pick him up, just take note of his accent.' He put the cards down. 'Listen: what boats go to Storm Island?'

'Only the grocer,' someone said.

'So, if he's a deserter, the only way he can get back to the mainland is on the grocer's boat. So, the Military Police just have to wait for Charlie's regular trip to the island, and pick the deserter up when he steps off the boat at this end. There's no reason for us to be sitting here, waiting to weigh anchor and shoot over there at the speed of light the minute the weather clears, unless . . .' He paused melodramatically. 'Unless he's got some other means of getting off the island.'

'Like what?'

'A U-boat.'

'Bollocks,' Smith said contemptuously. The others merely laughed.

Slim dealt another hand. Smith won this time, but everyone else lost. 'I'm a shilling up,' Slim said. 'I think

I'll retire to that nice little cottage in Devon. We won't catch him, of course.'

'The deserter?'

'The prisoner-of-war.'

'Why not?'

Slim tapped his head. 'Use your noddle. When the storm clears, we'll be here and the U-boat will be at the bottom of the bay in the island. So who'll get there first? The Jerries.'

'So why are we doing it?' Smith said.

'Because the people who are giving the orders are not as sharp as yours truly, Albert Parish. You may laugh!' He dealt another hand. 'Place your bets. You'll see I'm right. What's that, Smithie, a penny? Gorblimey, don't go mad. I tell you what, I'll give odds of five to one we come back from Storm Island empty-handed. Any takers? What if I say ten to one? Eh? Ten to one?'

'No takers,' said Smith. 'Deal the cards.'

Slim dealt the cards.

Squadron-Leader Peterkin Blenkinsop (he had tried to shorten Peterkin to Peter, but somehow the men always found out) stood ramrod-straight in front of the map and addressed the room. 'We fly in formations of three,' he began. 'The first three will take off as soon as weather permits. Our target—' he touched the map with a pointer. '—is here. Storm Island. On arrival, we will circle for twenty minutes at low altitudes, looking for U-boats. After twenty minutes, we return to base.'

He paused. 'Those of you with a logical turn of mind will by now have deduced that, to achieve continuous cover, the second formation of three aircraft must take off precisely twenty minutes after the first, and so on. Any questions?'

Flying-Officer Longman said: 'Sir?'

'Longman?'

'What do we do if we see this U-boat?'

'Strafe it, of course. Drop a few grenades. Cause trouble.'

'But we're flying fighters, sir – there's not much we can do to stop a U-boat. That's a job for battleships, isn't it?'

Blenkinsop sighed. 'As usual, those of you who can think of better ways to win the war are invited to write directly to Mr Winston Churchill, number ten Downing Street, London South-West-One. Now, are there any questions, as opposed to fat-headed criticisms?'

There were no questions.

The later years of the war had produced a different kind of RAF officer, Bloggs mused. He sat on a soft chair in the scramble room, close to the fire, listening to the rain drumming on the tin roof, and intermittently dozing. The Battle of Britain pilots had seemed incorrigibly cheerful, with their undergraduate slang, their perpetual drinking, their tirelessness, and their cavalier disregard of the flaming death they faced every day. That schoolboy heroism had not been enough to carry them through subsequent years, as the war dragged on in places far from home, and the emphasis shifted from the dashing individuality of aerial dogfighting to the mechanical drudgery of bombing missions. They still drank and talked in jargon, but they appeared older, harder, more cynical: there was nothing in them now of *Tom Brown's Schooldays*. Bloggs recalled what he had done to that poor common-or-garden housebreaker in the police cells at Aberdeen, and he thought: It's happened to us all.

They were very quiet. They sat all around him: some dozing, like himself; others reading books or playing board games. A bespectacled navigator in a corner was learning Russian.

As Bloggs surveyed the room with half-closed eyes, another pilot came in, and he thought immediately that this one had not been aged by the war. He had a wide grin and a fresh face that looked as if it hardly needed shaving more than once a week. He wore his jacket open and carried his helmet. He made a beeline for Bloggs.

'Detective-Inspector Bloggs?'

'That's me.'

'Jolly good show. I'm your pilot. Charles Calder.'

'Fine.' Bloggs shook hands.

'The kite's all ready, and the engine's as sweet as a bird. She's an amphibian, I suppose you know.'

'Yes.'

'Jolly good show. We'll land on the sea, taxi in to about ten yards from the shore, and put you off in a dinghy.'

'Then you wait for me to come back.'

'Indeed. Well, all we need now is the weather.'

'Yes. Look, Charles, I've been chasing this bloke all over the country for six days and nights, so I'm catching up on my sleep while I've got the chance. You won't mind.'

'Of course not!' The pilot sat down and produced a thick book from under his jacket. 'Catching up on my education,' he said. '*War and Peace*.'

Bloggs said: 'Jolly good show,' and closed his eyes.

Percival Godliman and his uncle, Colonel Terry, sat side by side in the map room, drinking coffee and tapping the ash of their cigarettes into a fire bucket on the floor between them. Godliman was repeating himself.

'I can't think of anything more we can do,' he said.

'So you said.'

'The corvette is already there, and the fighters are only a few minutes away, so the sub will come under fire as soon as she shows herself above the surface.'

'If she's seen.'

'The corvette will land a party as soon as possible. Bloggs will be there soon after that, and the coastguard will bring up the rear.'

'And none of them can be sure to get there in time.'

'I know,' Godliman said wearily. 'We've done all we can, but is it enough?'

Terry lit another cigarette. 'What about the inhabitants of the island?'

'Oh, yes. There are only two houses there. There's a

sheep farmer and his wife in one – they have a young child – and an old shepherd lives in the other. The shepherd's got a radio – Royal Observer Corps – but we can't raise him: he probably keeps the set switched to Transmit. He's old.'

'The farmer sounds promising,' Terry said. 'If he's a bright fellow he might stop your spy.'

Godliman shook his head. 'The poor chap's in a wheelchair.'

'Dear God, we don't get any luck, do we?'

'No,' said Godliman. 'Die Nadel gets all the luck there is.'

CHAPTER THIRTY-THREE

Lucy was becoming quite calm. The feeling crept over her gradually, like the icy spread of an anaesthetic, deadening her emotions and sharpening her wits. The times when she was momentarily paralysed by the thought that she was sharing a house with a murderer became fewer, and she was possessed by a cool-headed watchfulness that surprised her.

As she went about the household chores, sweeping around Henry as he sat in the living-room reading a novel, she wondered how much he had noticed of the change in her feelings. He was very observant: he did not miss much, and there had been a definite wariness, if not outright suspicion, in that confrontation over the jeep. He must have known she was shaken by something. On the other hand, she had been upset before he left, because Jo had discovered them in bed together: he might think that that was all that had been wrong.

She had the strangest feeling that he knew exactly what was in her mind, but he preferred to pretend that everything was all right.

She hung her laundry on a clothes-horse in the kitchen to dry. 'I'm sorry about this,' she said, 'but I can't wait forever for the rain to stop.'

He looked uninterestedly at the clothes and said: 'That's all right.' He went back into the living-room.

Scattered among the wet garments was a complete set of clean, dry clothes for Lucy.

For lunch she made a vegetable pie using an austerity recipe. She called Jo and Henry to the table and served up.

David's gun was propped in a corner of the kitchen. Lucy said: 'I don't like having a loaded gun in the house, Henry.'

'I'll take it outside after lunch,' he said. 'The pie is good.'

'I don't like it,' Jo said.

Lucy picked up the gun and put it on top of the Welsh dresser. 'I suppose it's all right as long as it's out of Jo's reach.'

Jo said: 'When I grow up I'm going to shoot Germans.'

'This afternoon I want you to have a sleep,' Lucy told him. She went into the living-room and took one of David's sleeping pills from the bottle in the cupboard. Two of the pills were a heavy dose for a 160-pound man, she reasoned, therefore one quarter of one pill should be just enough to make a 50-pound boy sleep in the afternoon. She put the pill on her chopping-block and halved it, then halved it again. She put a quarter on a spoon, crushed it with the back of another spoon, and stirred the powder into a small glass of milk. She gave the glass to Jo and said: 'I want you to drink every last drop.'

Henry watched the whole thing without comment.

After lunch she settled Jo on the sofa with a pile of books. He could not read, of course; but he had heard the stories read aloud so many times that he knew them by heart, and he could turn the pages of the books, looking at the pictures and reciting from memory the words on the page.

'Would you like some coffee?' she asked Henry.

'Real coffee?' he said, surprised.

'I've got a little hoard.'

'Yes, please!'

He watched her making it. She wondered if he was afraid she might try to give him sleeping pills, too. She could hear Jo's voice from the next room:

'What I said was, "Is anybody at home?"' called out Pooh very loudly.

'No!' said a voice . . .

– and he laughed heartily, as he always did at that joke. Oh, God, Lucy thought: don't let Jo be hurt.

She poured the coffee and sat opposite Henry. He reached across the table and held her hand. They sat in silence, sipping coffee and listening to the rain and Jo's voice.

'How long does getting thin take?' asked Pooh anxiously.

'About a week, I should think.'

'But I can't stay here for a week!'

He began to sound sleepy, and then he stopped. Lucy went and covered him with a blanket. She picked up the book, which had slipped from his fingers to the floor. It had been hers when she was a child, and she, too, knew the stories by heart. The flyleaf was inscribed in her mother's copperplate: 'To Lucy, aged four, with love from Mother and Father.' She put the book on the sideboard.

She went back into the kitchen. 'He's asleep.'

'And . . . ?'

She held out her hand. Henry took it. She tugged gently. He stood up. She led him upstairs and into the bedroom. She closed the door, then pulled her sweater off over her head.

For a moment he stood still, looking at her breasts. Then he began to undress.

As she got into the bed, she thought: Give me strength. This was the part that she dreaded, the part she was not sure she could manage: pretending to enjoy his body, when really all she could feel was fear, loathing, and guilt.

He got into bed and embraced her.

In a little while she found she did not have to pretend after all.

For a few seconds she lay in the crook of his arm, wondering how it was that a man could kill so coldly and love so warmly.

But what she said was: 'Would you like a cup of tea?'

He grinned. 'No, thank you.'

'Well, I would.' She extricated herself and got up. When he moved, she put her hand on his flat belly and said: 'No, you stay there. I'll bring the tea up. I haven't finished with you.'

He grinned again. 'You're really making up for your four wasted years.'

As soon as she was outside the room the smile dropped from her face like a mask. Her heart pounded in her chest as she went quickly, naked, down the stairs. In the kitchen she banged the kettle on the stove and rattled some china for realism. Then she began to put on the clothes she had left hidden in the wet laundry. Her hands were shaking so much that she could hardly button the trousers.

She heard the bed creak upstairs, and she stood frozen to the spot, listening, thinking: Stay there! Stay there! But he was only shifting his position.

She was ready. She went into the living-room. Jo was in a deep sleep, grinding his teeth. Dear God, don't let him wake up, Lucy prayed. She picked him up. He muttered in his sleep, something about Christopher Robin, and Lucy closed her eyes tightly and *willed* him to be quiet.

She wrapped the blanket around him securely. She went back into the kitchen and reached up to the top of the Welsh dresser for the gun. It slipped from her grasp and fell to the shelf, smashing a plate and two cups. The crash was deafening. She stood rooted to the spot.

'What happened?' Henry called from upstairs.

'I dropped a cup,' she shouted. She could not suppress the tremor in her voice.

The bed creaked again, and there was a footfall on the floor above her. But it was now too late for her to turn back. She picked up the gun, opened the back door, and, clutching Jo to her, ran across to the barn.

On the way she had a moment of panic: had she left the keys in the jeep? Surely she had: she always did.

She slipped in the wet mud and fell to her knees. She burst into tears. For a second she was tempted to stay there, and let him catch her and kill her as he had killed her husband; then she remembered the child in her arms, and she got up and ran on.

She entered the barn and opened the passenger door of the jeep. She put Jo on the seat. He slipped sideways. Lucy sobbed: 'Oh, God!' She pulled Jo upright, and this time he stayed that way. She ran around to the other side of the jeep and got in, dropping the gun on to the floor between her legs.

She turned the starter.

It coughed and died.

'Please, *please*!'

She turned it again.

The engine roared into life.

Henry came out of the back door at a run.

Lucy raced the engine and threw the gearshift into forward. The jeep leaped out of the barn. She rammed the throttle open.

The wheels spun in the mud for a second, then bit again. The jeep gathered speed with agonizing languor. She steered away from Henry. He chased the vehicle, barefoot in the mud.

She realized he was gaining on her.

She pushed the hand-throttle with all her might, almost snapping the thin lever. She wanted to scream with frustration. Henry was only a yard or so away, almost level with her, running like an athlete, his arms going like pistons, his bare feet pounding the turf, his cheeks blowing, his naked chest heaving.

The engine screamed, and there was a jerk as the automatic transmission changed up, then a new surge of power.

Lucy looked sideways again. Henry seemed to see that he had almost lost her. He flung himself forward through the air in a dive. He got a grip on the door handle with his left hand, and brought the right hand across. Pulled by the jeep, he ran alongside for a few paces, his feet hardly touching the ground. Lucy stared at his face, so close to hers: it was red with effort, twisted in pain; the cords of his powerful neck bulged with the strain.

Suddenly she knew what she had to do.

She took her hand off the wheel, reached through the open window, and poked him viciously in the eye with a long-nailed forefinger.

He let go and fell away, his hands covering his face.

The distance between him and the jeep increased rapidly.

Lucy realized she was crying like a baby.

Two miles from her cottage she saw the wheelchair.

It stood on the cliff top like a memorial, its metal frame and big rubber tyres impervious to the incessant rain. Lucy approached it from a slight dip, and saw its black outline framed by the slate-grey sky and the boiling sea. It had a wounded look, like the hole left by an uprooted tree or a house with broken windows; as if its passenger had been wrenched from it.

She recalled the first time she had seen it, in the hospital. It had stood beside David's bed, new and shiny, and he had swung himself into it expertly and swished up and down the ward, showing off. 'She's light as a feather – made of aircraft alloy,' he had said with brittle enthusiasm, and sped off between the rows of beds. He had stopped at the far end of the ward with his back to her, and after a minute she went up behind him and saw that he was weeping. She had knelt in front of him and held his hands, saying nothing.

It was the last time she had been able to comfort him.

There on the cliff-top, the rain and the salt wind would soon blemish the alloy, and eventually it would rust and crumble, its rubber perished, its leather seat rotted away.

Lucy drove past without slowing.

Three miles farther on, when she was half way between the two cottages, she ran out of petrol.

She fought down the panic and tried to think rationally as the jeep shuddered to a halt.

People walked at four miles an hour, she remembered reading somewhere. Henry was athletic, but he had hurt his ankle, and even though it seemed to have healed rapidly, the running he had done after the jeep must have hurt it. Therefore she must be a good hour ahead of him.

(She had no doubt he *would* come after her: he knew as well as she did that there was a wireless transmitter in Tom's cottage.)

Shc had plenty of time. In the back of the jeep was a half-gallon can of fuel for just such occasions as this. She got out of the car, fumbled the can out of the back, and opened the petrol cap.

Then she thought again, and the inspiration that came to her surprised her by its fiendishness.

She replaced the petrol cap and went to the front of the car. She checked that the ignition was off and opened the bonnet. She was no mechanic, but she could identify the distributor cap and trace the leads to the engine. She lodged the petrol can securely beside the wheel arch and took off its cap.

There was a plug spanner in the tool kit. She took out a plug, checked again that the ignition was off, and put the plug in the mouth of the petrol can, securing it there with tape. Then she closed the bonnet.

When Henry came along he was certain to try to start the jeep. He would switch on, the starter motor would turn, the plug would spark and the half-gallon of petrol would explode.

She was not sure how much damage it would do, but she could be certain it would be no help.

An hour later she was regretting her cleverness.

Trudging through the mud, soaked to the skin, with the sleeping child a dead weight over her shoulder, she wanted nothing more than to lie down and die. The booby-trap seemed, on reflection, dubious and risky: petrol would burn, not explode; if there was not enough air in the mouth of the can it might not even ignite; worst of all, Henry might suspect a trap, look under the bonnet, dismantle the bomb, pour the petrol into the tank and drive after her.

She contemplated stopping for a rest, but decided that if she sat down she might never get up again.

She should have been in sight of Tom's house by now. She could not possibly have got lost – even if she had not walked this path a dozen times before, the whole island just was not big enough to get lost on.

She recognized a thicket where she and Jo had once seen a fox. She must be about a mile from the shepherd's home. She could have seen it, but for the rain.

She shifted Jo to the other shoulder, switched the shotgun from one hand to the other, and forced herself to continue putting one foot in front of the other.

When at last the cottage became visible through the sheeting rain she could have cried with relief. She was nearer than she thought – perhaps a quarter of a mile.

Suddenly Jo seemed lighter, and although the last stretch was uphill – the only hill on the island – she seemed to cover it in no time at all.

'Tom!' she called as she approached the front door, 'Tom, oh, Tom!'

She heard the answering bark of Bob.

She went in by the front door. 'Tom, quickly!' Bob dodged excitedly about her ankles, barking furiously. Tom could not be far away – he was probably in the outhouse. Lucy went upstairs and laid Jo on Tom's bed.

The wireless was in the bedroom, a complex-looking construction of wires and dials and knobs. There was something that looked like a Morse key: she touched it experimentally, and it gave a beep. A thought came to her from the depths of her memory – something from a schoolgirl thriller – the Morse code for SOS. She touched the key again: three short, three long, three short.

Where was Tom?

She heard a noise, and rushed to the window.

The jeep was making its way up the hill to the house.

Henry had found the booby-trap, and used the petrol to fill the tank.

Where was Tom?

She rushed out of the bedroom, intending to go and bang on the outhouse door. At the head of the stairs she paused. Bob was standing in the open doorway of the other bedroom, the empty one.

'Come here, Bob,' she said. The dog stood his ground, barking. She went to him and bent to pick him up.

Then she saw Tom.

He lay on his back, on the bare floorboards of the vacant bedroom, his eyes staring sightlessly at the ceiling, his cap upside-down on the floor behind his head. His jacket was open, and there was a small spot of blood on the shirt underneath. Close to his hand was a crate of whisky, and Lucy found herself thinking wildly, irrelevantly: I didn't know he drank that much.

She felt his pulse.

He was dead.

Think, *think*!

Yesterday Henry had returned to Lucy's cottage

battered, as if he had been in a fight. That must have been when he killed David. Today he had come here, to Tom's cottage, 'to fetch David' he had said. But he had known David was not there. So why had he made the journey?

Obviously, to kill Tom.

What drove him? What purpose burned inside him so fiercely that he would get in a car, drive ten miles, stick a knife into an old man, and drive back as calm and quiet and composed as if he had been out to take the air? Lucy shuddered.

Now she was on her own.

She took hold of the dog by its collar and dragged it away from the body of its master. On impulse, she returned and buttoned the jacket over the small stiletto wound which had killed the shepherd. Then she closed the door on the corpse. She said to the dog: 'He's dead, but I need you.'

She returned to the front bedroom and looked out of the window.

The jeep drew up in front of the house and stopped; and Henry got out.

CHAPTER THIRTY-FOUR

Lucy's distress call was heard by the corvette. 'Captain, sir,' said Sparks, 'I just picked up an SOS from the island.'

The captain frowned. 'Nothing we can do until we can land a boat,' he said. 'Did they say anything else?'

'Not a thing, sir. It wasn't even repeated.'

The captain thought a little more. 'Nothing we can do,' he said again. 'Send a signal to the mainland, reporting it. And keep listening.'

'Aye, aye, sir.'

It was also picked up by an M18 listening post on top of a Scottish mountain. The R/T operator, a young man with abdominal wounds who had been invalided out of the RAF and had only six months to live, was trying to pick up German Navy signals from Norway, and he ignored the SOS. However, he went off duty five minutes later, and he mentioned it casually to his Commanding Officer.

'It was only broadcast once,' he said. 'Probably a

fishing vessel off the Scottish coast – there might well be the odd small ship in trouble, in this weather.'

'Leave it with me,' the CO said. 'I'll give the Navy a buzz. And I suppose I'd better inform Whitehall. Protocol, y'know.'

'Thank you, sir.'

At the Royal Observer Corps station there was something of a panic. Of course, SOS was not the signal an observer was *supposed* to give when he sighted enemy aircraft, but they knew that Tom was old, and who could say what he might send if he got excited? So the air-raid sirens were sounded, and all other posts were alerted, and anti-aircraft guns were rolled out all over the east coast of Scotland, and the radio operator tried frantically to raise Tom.

No German bombers came, of course; and the War Office wanted to know why a full alert had been sounded when there was nothing in the sky but a few bedraggled geese?

So they were told.

The Coastguard heard it, too.

They would have responded to it, if it had been on the correct frequency, and if they had been able to establish the position of the transmitter, and if that position had been within reasonable distance of the coast.

As it was they guessed, from the fact that the signal

came over on the Observer Corps frequency, that it originated from Old Tom; and they were already doing all they could about *that* situation, whatever the hell that situation was.

When the news reached the below-deck card game on the cutter in the harbour at Aberdeen, Slim dealt another hand of pontoon and said: 'I'll tell you what's happened. Old Tom's caught the prisoner-of-war and he's sitting on his head waiting for the Army to arrive and take the bugger away.'

'Bollocks,' said Smith, and there was general agreement with that sentiment.

And the *U-505* heard it.

She was still more than thirty nautical miles away from Storm Island, but Weissman was roaming the dial to see what he could pick up – and hoping, improbably, to hear Glenn Miller records from the American Forces Network in Britain – and his tuner happened to be on the right wavelength at the right time. He passed the information to Lieutenant-Commander Heer, adding: 'It was not on our man's frequency.'

Major Wohl, who was still around and as irritating as ever, said: 'Then it means nothing.'

Heer did not miss the opportunity to correct him. 'It means *something*,' he said. 'It means that there may be some activity on the surface when we go up.'

'But this is unlikely to trouble us.'

'Most unlikely,' Heer agreed.

'Then it is meaningless.'

'It is *probably* meaningless.'

They argued about it all the way to the island.

So it was that within the space of five minutes the Navy, the Royal Observer Corps, M18 and the Coastguard all phoned Godliman to tell him about the SOS. And Godliman phoned Bloggs.

Bloggs had finally fallen into a deep sleep in front of the fire in the scramble room. The shrill ring of the telephone startled him, and he leaped to his feet, thinking that the planes were about to take off.

A pilot picked it up, said 'Yes' into it twice, and handed it to Bloggs. 'A Mr Godliman for you.'

Bloggs said: 'Hello, Percy.'

'Fred, somebody on the island just broadcast an SOS.'

Bloggs shook his head to clear the last remaining clouds of sleep. 'Who?'

'We don't know. There was just the one signal, not repeated, and they don't seem to be receiving at all.'

'Still, there's not much doubt now.'

'No. Everything ready up there?'

'All except the weather.'

'Good luck.'

'Thanks.'

Bloggs hung up and turned to the young pilot who was still reading *War and Peace*. 'Good news,' he told him. 'The bastard's definitely on the island.'

'Jolly good show,' said the pilot.

CHAPTER THIRTY-FIVE

HENRY CLOSED the door of the jeep and began walking quite slowly toward the house. He was wearing David's hacking jacket again. There was mud all over his trousers, where he had fallen, and his hair was plastered wetly against his skull. He was limping slightly on his right foot.

Lucy backed away from the window and ran out of the bedroom and down the stairs. The shotgun was on the floor in the hall, where she had dropped it. She picked it up. Suddenly it felt very heavy. She had never actually fired a gun, and she had no idea how to check whether this one was loaded. She could figure it out, given time; but there was no time.

She took a deep breath and flung open the front door. 'Stop!' she shouted. Her voice was pitched higher than she had intended, and it sounded shrill and hysterical.

Henry smiled pleasantly and kept on walking.

Lucy pointed the gun at him, holding the barrel with her left hand and the breech with her right. Her finger was on the trigger. 'I'll kill you!' she yelled.

'Don't be silly, Lucy,' he said mildly. 'How could you hurt me? After all the things we've done together? Haven't we loved each other, a little . . . ?'

It was true. She had told herself she could not fall in love with him, and that was true too; but she *had* felt *something* for him, and if it was not love, it was something very like.

'You knew about me this afternoon,' he said, and now he was thirty yards away, 'but it made no difference to you then, did it?'

That was true. For a moment, she saw in her mind's eye a vivid picture of herself sitting astride him, holding his sensitive hands to her breasts, and then she realized what he was doing—

'We can work something out, Lucy, we can still have each other—'

– and she pulled the trigger.

There was an ear-splitting crash, and the weapon jumped in her hands like a live thing, its butt bruising her hip with the recoil. She almost dropped it in shock. She had never imagined that firing a gun would feel like that. She was quite deaf for a moment.

The shot went high over Henry's head, but all the same he ducked, turned, and ran zig-zagging back to the jeep. Lucy was tempted to fire again, but she stopped herself just in time, realizing that if he knew both barrels had been emptied there would be nothing to stop him turning and coming back.

He flung open the door of the jeep, leaped in, and shot off down the hill.

Lucy knew he would be back.

Suddenly she felt happy, almost gay. She had won the first round – she had driven him off – and she was a woman!

425

But he would be back.

Still, she had the upper hand. She was indoors, and she had the gun. And she had time to prepare.

Prepare. She must be ready for him. Next time he would be more subtle. He would surely try to creep up on her.

She hoped he would wait until dark, for that would give her time.

First she had to reload the gun.

She went into the kitchen. Tom kept everything in his kitchen – food, coal, tools, stores – and he had a gun like David's. She knew the two firearms were the same, for David had examined Tom's then sent away for one exactly like it. The two men had enjoyed long discussions about weaponry.

She found Tom's gun and a box of ammunition. She put the two guns and the box on the kitchen table.

Machines were simple, she was convinced: it was apprehension, not stupidity, which made women fumble when faced with a piece of engineering.

She fiddled with David's gun, keeping the barrel pointed away from herself, until it came open at the breech. Then she worked out what she had done to open it, and practised doing it again a couple of times.

It was incredibly simple.

She loaded both guns. Then, to make sure she had done everything correctly, she pointed Tom's gun at the kitchen wall and pulled the trigger.

There was a shower of plaster, Bob barked like a maniac, and she bruised her hip and deafened herself again. But she was armed.

She must remember to pull the triggers gently so as not to jerk the gun and spoil her aim. Men probably got taught that kind of thing in the Army.

What to do next? She should make it difficult for Henry to get into the house.

Neither of the doors had locks, of course: if a house was burgled on this island, one would know that the culprit lived in the other house. Lucy rummaged in Tom's tool box and found a shiny, sharp-bladed axe. She stood on the stairs and began to hack away at the bannister.

The work made her arms ache, but in five minutes she had six short lengths of stout, seasoned oak. She found a hammer and some nails, and fixed the oak bars across the front and back doors, three bars to each door, four nails to each bar. When it was done her wrists were agony and the hammer felt as heavy as lead, but she was not finished.

She got another handful of the shiny, four-inch nails, and went around every window in the house, nailing them shut. She realized, with a sense of discovery, why men always put nails in their mouths: it was because you needed both hands for the work and if you put them in your pocket they stuck into your skin.

By the time she had finished it was dark. She left the lights off.

He could still get into the house, of course; but he could not get in quietly. He would have to break something and give himself away – and then she would be ready with the guns.

She went upstairs, carrying both guns, to check on

Jo. He was still asleep, wrapped in his blanket, on Tom's bed. Lucy struck a match to look at his face. The sleeping pill must have really knocked him out, but he was an average sort of colour, his temperature seemed normal, and he was breathing easily. 'Just stay that way, little boy,' Lucy whispered. The sudden access of tenderness left her feeling more savage toward Henry.

She patrolled the house restlessly for a while, peering through the windows into the darkness, the dog following her everywhere. She took to carrying just one of the guns, leaving the other at the head of the stairs; but she hooked the axe into the belt of her trousers.

She remembered the radio, and tapped out her SOS several more times. She had no idea whether anybody was listening, or even whether the radio was working. She knew no more Morse, so she could not broadcast anything else.

It occurred to her that Tom probably did not know Morse code. Surely he must have a book somewhere? If only she could tell someone what was happening here! She searched the house, using dozens of matches, feeling terrified every time she lit one within sight of a downstairs window; but she found nothing.

All right, perhaps he *did* know Morse.

On the other hand, why should he need it? He only had to tell the mainland that there were enemy aircraft approaching, and there was no reason why that information shouldn't go over the air . . . what was the phrase David had used? . . . *en clair.*

She went back to the bedroom and looked again at

the wireless set. To one side of the main cabinet, hidden from her previous cursory glance, was a microphone.

If she could talk to them, they could talk to her.

The sound of another human voice – a normal, sane, mainland voice – suddenly seemed the most desirable thing in the world.

She picked up the microphone and began to experiment with the switches.

Bob growled softly.

She put the mike down and reached out her hand toward the dog in the darkness. 'What is it, Bob?'

He growled again. She could feel his ears standing stiffly upright. She was terribly afraid: the confidence won by confronting Henry with the gun, by learning how to reload, by barricading the doors and nailing down the windows . . . all evaporated at one growl from an alert dog.

'Downstairs,' she whispered. 'Quietly.'

She held his collar and let him lead her down the stairs. In the darkness she felt for the bannister, forgetting that she had chopped it up for barricades, and she almost overbalanced. She regained her equilibrium and sucked at a splinter in her finger.

The dog hesitated in the hall, then growled more loudly and tugged her toward the kitchen. She picked him up and held his muzzle shut to silence him. Then she crept through the doorway.

She looked in the direction of the window, but there was nothing in front of her eyes other than velvet blackness.

She listened. The window creaked: at first almost inaudibly, then louder. He was trying to get in. Bob rumbled threateningly, deep in his throat, but seemed to understand the sudden squeeze she gave his muzzle.

The night became quieter. Lucy realized the storm was easing, almost imperceptibly. Henry seemed to have given up on the kitchen window. She moved to the living-room.

She heard the same creak of old wood resisting pressure. Now Henry seemed more determined: there were three muffled bumps, as if he were tapping the window-frame with the cushioned heel of his hand.

Lucy put the dog down and hefted the shotgun. It might almost have been imagination, but she could just make out the window as a square of grey in the blank darkness. If he got the window open, she would fire immediately.

There was a much harder bang. Bob lost control and gave a loud bark. She heard a scuffling noise outside.

Then came the voice.

'Lucy?'

She bit her lip.

'Lucy?'

He was using the voice he used in bed: deep, soft, and intimate.

'Lucy, can you hear me? Don't be afraid. I don't want to hurt you. Talk to me, please.'

She had to fight the urge to pull both triggers there and then, just to silence that awful sound and repress the memories it brought to her unwilling consciousness.

'Lucy, my darling ...' She thought she heard a muffled sob. 'Lucy, he attacked me – I had to kill him ... I killed for my country, you shouldn't hate me for that.'

She could not understand that. It sounded mad. Could he be insane, and have hidden it for two intimate days? He had seemed saner than most people – and yet he had murdered before ... unless he was a victim of injustice ... Damn. She was softening up, and that must be exactly what he wanted.

She had an idea.

'Lucy, just speak to me ...'

His voice faded as she tip-toed into the kitchen. Bob would warn her if Henry did anything more than talk. She fumbled in Tom's tool-box and found a pair of pliers. She went to the kitchen window and found with her fingertips the heads of the three nails she had hammered there. Carefully, as quietly as possible, she drew them out. The job demanded all her strength.

When they were out she went back into the living-room to listen.

' ... don't obstruct me, and I'll leave you ...'

As silently as she could she lifted the kitchen window open. She crept into the living-room, picked the dog up, and returned yet again to the kitchen.

' ... hurt you, last thing in the world ...'

She stroked the dog once or twice, and murmured: 'I wouldn't do this if I didn't have to, boy.' Then she pushed him out of the window.

She closed it rapidly, found a nail, and hammered it in at a new spot with three sharp blows.

She dropped the hammer, picked up the gun, and ran into the front room to stand close to the window, pressing herself up against the wall.

' . . . give you one last chance – ah!'

There was a rush of small feet; a blood-curdling bark Lucy had never heard from a sheepdog before; a scuffling sound; and the noise of a big man falling. She could hear Henry's breathing, gasping, grunting; then another flurry of canine paws; a shout of pain; a curse in a foreign language; another bark. She wished she could see what was happening.

The noises became muffled and more distant, then suddenly ceased. Lucy waited, pressed against the wall next to the window, straining her ears. She wanted to go and check on Jo, wanted to try the radio again, wanted to cough; but she did not dare to move. Bloodthirsty visions of what Bob might have done to Henry passed in and out of her mind, and she yearned to hear the dog snuffling at the door.

She looked at the window. Then she *realized* she was looking at the window: she could see, not just a square patch of faintly lighter grey, but the wooden crosspiece of the frame. It was still night, but only just: she knew that if she looked outside the sky would be faintly diffused with a just-perceptible light, instead of being impenetrably black. Dawn would come at any minute. Then she would be able to see the furniture in the room, and Henry would no longer be able to surprise her in the darkness—

There was a crash of breaking glass inches away from her face. She jumped. She felt a small sharp pain in her cheek, touched the spot, and knew that she had been cut by a flying shard. She hefted the shotgun, waiting for Henry to come through the window; but nothing happened. It was not until a minute or two had passed that she wondered what had broken the window.

She peered at the floor. Among the pieces of broken glass was a large dark shape. She found she could see it better if she looked to one side of it rather than directly at it. When she did that, she was able to make out the familiar shape of the dog.

She closed her eyes, then looked away. She was unable to feel any emotion at all at the death of the faithful sheepdog. Her heart had been numbed by all the danger and death that had gone before: first David, then Tom, then the endless screaming tension of the all-night siege . . . All she felt was hunger. All day yesterday she had been too nervous to eat, which meant it was thirty-six hours since her last meal. Now, incongruously, ridiculously, she found herself longing for a cheese sandwich.

Something else was coming through the window.

She saw it out of the corner of her eye, then turned her head to look directly at it.

It was Henry's hand.

She stared at it, mesmerized: a long-fingered hand, without rings, white under the dirt, with cared-for nails and a band-aid around the tip of the index finger; a hand that had touched her intimately, had played her body like a harp, and thrust a knife into the heart of an old shepherd.

The hand broke away a piece of glass, then another,

enlarging the hole in the pane. Then it reached right through, up to the elbow, and fumbled along the windowsill, searching for a catch to unfasten.

Trying to be utterly silent, with painful slowness, Lucy shifted the gun to her left hand, and with her right took the axe from her belt, lifted it high above her head, and brought it down with all her might on Henry's hand.

He must have sensed it, or heard the rush of wind, or seen a blur of ghostly movement behind the window; for he moved sharply a split-second before the blow landed.

The axe thudded into the wood of the windowsill, sticking there. For a fraction of an instant Lucy thought she had missed: then, from outside, there came a scream of pain and loss, and she saw beside the axe blade, lying on the varnished wood like caterpillars, two severed fingers.

She heard the sound of feet running away.

Lucy threw up.

The exhaustion hit her then, closely followed by a surge of self-pity. She had suffered enough, surely to God, had she not? There were policemen and soldiers in the world to deal with situations like this – nobody could expect an ordinary housewife and mother to keep a killer at bay indefinitely. Who could blame her if she gave up now? Who could honestly say they would have done better, lasted longer, stayed brave and resolute and resourceful for another minute?

She was finished. *They* would have to take over: the outside world, the policemen and soldiers, whoever was at the other end of that radio link. She could do no more.

She tore her eyes away from the grotesque objects on the windowsill and went wearily up the stairs. She picked up the second gun and took both weapons into the bedroom with her.

Jo was still asleep, bless him. He had hardly moved all night, utterly oblivious to the apocalypse going on around him. She could tell, somehow, that he was not sleeping so deeply now: something about the look on his face and the way he breathed let her know that he would wake soon and want his breakfast.

She longed for that simple life, now: getting up in the morning, making breakfast, dressing Jo, doing simple, tedious, *safe* household chores like washing and cleaning and cutting herbs from the garden and making pots of tea. It seemed incredible that she had been so dissatisfied with David's lovelessness, the long boring evenings, the endless bleak landscape of turf and heather and rain.

It would never come back, that life.

She had wanted excitement, cities, music, people, ideas. Now the desire for those things had left her, and she could not understand how she had ever wanted them. Peace was all a human being ought to ask for, it seemed to her.

She sat in front of the radio and studied its switches and dials. She would do this one thing, then she would rest. She made a tremendous effort and forced herself to think analytically for a little longer. There were not *so* many possible combinations of switch and dial. She found a knob with two settings, turned it, and tapped the Morse key. There was no sound. Perhaps that meant the microphone was now in circuit.

She pulled it to her and spoke into it. 'Hello, hello, is there anybody there? Hello?'

There was a switch which had 'Transmit' above it and 'Receive' below. It was turned to 'Transmit'. If the world was to talk back to her, obviously she had to throw the switch to 'Receive'.

She said: 'Hello, is anybody listening?' and threw the switch to 'Receive'.

Nothing.

Then: 'Come in, Storm Island, receiving you loud and clear.'

It was a man's voice. He sounded young and strong, capable and confident and reassuring and alive and *normal.*

'Come in, Storm Island, we've been trying to raise you all night . . . where the devil have you *been?*'

Lucy switched to 'Transmit', tried to speak, and burst into tears.

CHAPTER THIRTY-SIX

Percival Godliman had a headache from too many cigarettes and too little sleep. He had taken a little whisky to help him through the long, worried night in his office, and that had been a mistake. Everything oppressed him: the weather, his office, his job, the war. For the first time since he had become a spycatcher he found himself longing for dusty libraries, illegible manuscripts, and medieval Latin.

Colonel Terry walked in with two cups of tea on a tray. 'Nobody around here sleeps,' he said cheerfully. He sat down. 'Ship's biscuit?' He offered Godliman a plate.

Godliman refused the biscuit and drank the tea. It gave him a temporary lift.

'I just had a call from the man with the fat cigar,' Terry said. 'He's keeping the night vigil with us.'

'I can't imagine why,' Godliman said sourly.

'He's worried.'

The phone rang.

'Godliman.'

'I have the Royal Observer Corps in Aberdeen for you, sir.'

'Yes.'

A new voice came on, the voice of a young man. 'Royal Observer Corps, Aberdeen, here, sir.'

'Yes.'

'Is that Mr Godliman?'

'*Yes.*' Dear God, these military types took their time.

'We've raised Storm Island at last, sir.'

'Thank God!'

'It's not our regular observer. In fact it's a woman.'

'What did she say?'

'Nothing, yet, sir.'

'What do you *mean*?' Godliman fought down the angry impatience that rose inside him.

'She's just . . . well, crying, sir.'

'Oh.' Godliman hesitated. 'Can you connect me to her?'

'Yes. Hold on.' There was a pause punctuated by several clicks and a hum. Then Godliman heard the sound of a woman weeping.

He said: 'Hello, can you hear me?'

The weeping went on.

The young man came back on the line to say: 'She won't be able to hear you until she switches to "Receive", sir – ah, she's done it. Go ahead.'

Godliman said: 'Hello, young lady. When I've finished speaking I'll say "Over", then you switch to "Transmit" to speak to me and *you* say "Over" when *you* have finished. Do you understand? Over.'

The woman's voice came on. 'Oh, thank God for somebody sane. Yes, I understand. Over.'

'Now, then,' Godliman said gently, 'tell me what's been happening there. Over.'

'A man was shipwrecked here two – no, three days ago. I think he's the stiletto murderer from London. He killed my husband and our shepherd, and now he's outside the house, and I've got my little boy here ... I've nailed the windows shut, and fired at him with a shotgun, and barred the doors, and set the dog on him but he killed the dog, and I hit him with the axe when he tried to get in through the window and *I can't do it any more so please come and save me* ... Over.'

Godliman put his hand over the phone. His face was white. 'You poor woman,' he breathed. But when he spoke to her, he was brisk. 'You must hold on a little longer,' he began. 'There are sailors and coastguards and policemen and all sorts of people on their way to you, but they can't land until the storm ends. Now, there's something I want you to do, and I can't tell you why you must do it because the wrong people may be listening to us, but I can tell you that it is *absolutely essential.* Are you hearing me clearly? Over.'

'Yes, go on. Over.'

'You must destroy your radio. Over.'

'Oh, no, please ... must I?'

'Yes,' Godliman said, then he realized she was still transmitting.

'I don't ... I can't ...' Then there was a scream.

Godliman said: 'Hello, Aberdeen, what's happening?'

The young man came on. 'The set's still transmitting, sir, but she's not speaking. We can't hear anything.'

'She screamed.'

'Yes, we got that.'

'Damn.' Godliman thought for a minute. 'What's the weather like up there?'

'It's raining, sir.' The young man sounded puzzled.

'I'm not making conversation, lad,' Godliman snapped. 'Is there any sign of the storm letting up?'

'It has eased a little in the last few minutes, sir.'

'Good. Get back to me the instant that woman comes back on air.'

'Very good, sir.'

Godliman said to Terry: 'God only knows what that girl's going through up there.' He jiggled the cradle of the phone.

The Colonel crossed his legs. 'If only she would smash up the radio, then . . .'

'Then we don't care if he kills her?'

'You said it.'

Godliman spoke into the phone. 'Get me Bloggs at Rosyth.'

Bloggs woke up with a start, and listened. Outside, it was dawn. Everyone in the scramble hut was listening, too. They could hear nothing. That was what they were listening to: the silence.

The rain had stopped drumming on the tin roof.

Bloggs went to the window. The sky was grey with a band of white on the eastern horizon. The wind had dropped suddenly, and the rain had become a light drizzle.

The pilots started putting on jackets and helmets, lacing boots, lighting last cigarettes.

A klaxon sounded, and a voice boomed out over the airfield: 'Scramble! Scramble!'

The phone rang. The pilots ignored it and piled out through the door. Bloggs picked it up. 'Yes?'

'Percy here, Fred. We just contacted the island. He's killed the two men. The woman's holding him off at the moment, but she won't last much longer.'

Bloggs said: 'The rain has stopped. We're taking off now.'

'Make it fast, Fred. Goodbye.'

Bloggs hung up and looked around for his pilot. Charles Calder had fallen asleep over *War and Peace*. Bloggs shook him roughly. 'Wake up, you dozy bastard, wake up!'

He opened his eyes.

Bloggs could have hit him. 'Wake up, come on, we're going, the storm's ended!'

The pilot jumped to his feet. 'Jolly good show,' he said.

He ran out of the door and Bloggs followed him.

The lifeboat dropped into the water with a crack like a pistol and a wide, V-shaped splash. The sea was far from calm, but here in the partial shelter of the bay there was no risk to a stout boat in the hands of experienced sailors.

The captain said: 'Carry on, Number One.'

The first lieutenant was standing at the rail with three ratings. He wore a pistol in a waterproof holster. He said: 'Let's go, chaps.'

The four men scrambled down the ladders and into the boat. The first mate sat in the stern and the three sailors broke out the oars and began to row.

For a few moments the captain watched their steady progress toward the jetty. Then he returned to the bridge and gave orders for the corvette to continue circling the island.

The shrill ringing of a bell broke up the card game on the cutter.

Slim said: 'I thought something was different. We aren't going up and down so much. Almost motionless, really. Makes me quite seasick.'

Nobody was listening: the crew were hurrying to their stations, some of them fastening life-jackets as they went.

The engines fired with a roar, and the vessel began to tremble faintly but perceptibly.

Up on deck, Smith stood in the prow, enjoying the fresh air and the spray on his face after a day and a night below.

As the cutter left the harbour Slim joined him.

'Here we go again,' Slim said.

'I knew the bell was going to ring then,' Smith said. 'You know why?'

'Tell me.'

'Know what I had in my hand? Ace and a king.'

'Banker's pontoon,' said Slim. 'Well I never.'

*

442

Lieutenant-Commander Werner Heer looked at his watch and said: 'Thirty minutes.'

Major Wohl nodded impassively. 'What is the weather like?' he asked.

'The storm has ended,' Heer said reluctantly. He would have preferred to keep that information to himself.

'Then we should surface.'

'If your man were there, he would send us a signal.'

'The war is not won by hypothesis, Captain,' said Wohl. 'I firmly suggest that we surface.'

There had been a blazing row, while the U-boat was in dock, between Heer's superior officer and Wohl's; and Wohl's had won. Heer was still captain of the ship, but he had been told in no uncertain terms that he had better have a damned good reason next time he ignored one of Major Wohl's firm suggestions.

'We will surface at six o'clock exactly,' he said.

Wohl nodded again and looked away.

CHAPTER THIRTY-SEVEN

T HE SOUND of breaking glass, then an explosion like an incendiary bomb:

Whooomph!

Lucy dropped the microphone. Something was happening downstairs. She picked up a shotgun and ran down.

The living-room was ablaze. The fire centred on a broken jar on the floor. Henry had made some kind of bomb with the petrol from the jeep. The flames were spreading hungrily across Tom's threadbare carpet and licking up over the loose covers of his ancient three-piece suite. A feather-filled cushion caught, and the fire reached up toward the ceiling.

Lucy picked up the cushion and flung it through the broken window, singeing her hand. She tore her coat off and threw it on the carpet, stamping on it. She picked it up again and draped it over the floral settee. She was winning—

There was another crash of glass.

It came from upstairs.

Lucy screamed: 'Jo!'

She dropped the coat and raced up the stairs and into the front bedroom.

Henry was sitting on the bed with Jo on his lap. The child was awake, sucking his thumb, wearing his wide-eyed morning look. Henry was stroking his tousled hair.

Henry said: 'Throw the gun on the bed, Lucy.'

Her shoulders sagged in defeat, and she did as he said. 'You climbed the wall and got through the window,' she said dully.

Henry dumped Jo off his lap. 'Go to Mummy.'

Jo ran to her and she lifted him up.

Henry picked up both guns and went to the radio. He was holding his right hand under his left armpit, and there was a great red bloodstain on his jacket. He sat down. 'You hurt me,' he said. Then he turned his attention to the transmitter.

Suddenly it spoke. 'Come in, Storm Island.'

Henry picked up the microphone. 'Hello?'

'Just a minute.'

There was a pause, then another voice came on. Lucy recognized it as the man in London who had told her to destroy the radio. He would be disappointed in her. It said: 'Hello, this is Godliman again. Can you hear me? Over.'

Henry said: 'Yes, I can hear you, Professor. Seen any good cathedrals lately?'

'Is that . . .'

'Yes.' Henry smiled. 'How do you do.' Then the smile left his face abruptly, as if playtime was over, and he turned the frequency dial of the radio.

Lucy turned and left the room. It was over, and she had lost. She walked listlessly down the stairs and into the kitchen. There was nothing for her to do but wait for him to kill her. She could not run away – she did not have the energy, and he obviously knew it.

She looked out of the window. The storm had ended. The howling gale had dropped to a stiff breeze, there was no rain, and the eastern sky was bright with the promise of sunshine. The sea—

She frowned, and looked again.

Yes, it *was* a submarine.

Destroy the radio, the Professor had said.

Last night Henry had cursed in a foreign language.

'*I did it for my country*,' he had said.

And, in his delirium: *Waiting at Calais for a phantom army*.

Destroy the radio.

Why would a man take a wallet of photographic negatives on a fishing trip?

She had known all along he was not insane.

The submarine was a German U-boat, Henry was an enemy agent, and he was at this very second trying to contact the vessel by radio.

Destroy the radio.

She knew what she had to do. She had no right to give up, now that she understood; for it was not only her life that was at stake. She had to do this one last thing for David and for all the other young men who had died in the war.

She knew what she had to do. She was not afraid of the pain – it would be *very* painful, she knew, and might well kill her – but she had known the pain of childbirth, and it could not be worse than that.

She knew what she had to do. She would have liked to put Jo somewhere else, where he could not see it; but there was no time for that, for Henry would find his frequency at any second, and then it might be too late.

She knew what she had to do. She had to destroy the radio, but the radio was upstairs with Henry, and he had both the guns and he *would* kill her.

She knew what she had to do.

She placed one of Tom's kitchen chairs in the centre of the room, stood on it, reached up and unscrewed the light bulb.

She got off the chair, went to the door, and threw the switch.

'Are you changing the bulb?' Jo said.

Lucy climbed on the chair, hesitated for a moment, then thrust three fingers into the live socket.

There was a bang, an instant of agony, and then unconsciousness.

Faber heard the bang. He had found the right frequency on the transmitter, had thrown the switch to 'Transmit', and had picked up the microphone. He was about to speak when the noise came. Immediately afterwards the lights on the dials of the wireless set went out.

His face suffused with anger. She had short-circuited the electricity supply to the whole house. He had not credited her with that much ingenuity.

He should have killed her before. What the hell was wrong with him? He had never hesitated, not ever, until he met this woman.

He picked up one of the guns and went downstairs.

The child was crying. Lucy lay in the kitchen doorway, out cold. Faber took in the empty light socket with the chair beneath it. He frowned in amazement.

She had done it with her *hand*.

Faber said: 'Jesus Christ Almighty.'

Lucy's eyes opened. She hurt all over.

Henry was standing over her with the gun in his hands. He said: 'Why did you use your hand? Why not a screwdriver?'

She said: 'I didn't know you could do it with a screwdriver.'

He shook his head in incredulity. 'You are a truly astonishing woman,' he said. He lifted the gun, aimed it at her, and lowered it again. '*Damn* you!'

His gaze went to the window, and he started.

'You saw it,' he said.

She nodded.

He stood tense for a moment, then he went to the door. Finding it nailed shut, he smashed the window with the butt of his gun and climbed out.

Lucy got to her feet. Jo threw his arms around her legs. She did not feel strong enough to pick him up. She staggered to the window and looked out.

Henry was running toward the cliff. The U-boat was still there, perhaps half a mile offshore. Henry reached the cliff edge and crawled over. He was going to try to swim to the submarine.

Lucy had to stop him.

Dear God, no more, she prayed.

She climbed through the window, blotting out the cries of her son, and ran after Henry.

When she reached the cliff edge she lay down and looked over. He was about half way between her and the sea. He looked up and saw her, froze for a moment, and then began to move faster, dangerously fast.

Her first thought was to climb down after him. But what would she do then? Even if she caught him, she could not stop him.

The ground beneath her shifted slightly. She scrambled back, afraid it would give way and throw her down the cliff.

That gave her an idea.

She thumped on the rocky ground with both fists. It seemed to shake a little more, and a crack appeared. She got one hand over the edge and thrust the other into the crack. A piece of earthy chalk the size of a watermelon came away in her hands.

She looked over the edge and sighted Henry.

She took careful aim and dropped the stone.

It seemed to fall very slowly. He saw it coming, and covered his head with his arm. It looked as if it would miss him.

The rock passed within a couple of inches of his head, and hit his left shoulder. He was holding on with his left hand. He seemed to loosen his grip. He balanced precariously for a moment. The right hand, the injured one, scrabbled for a hold. Then he appeared to lean out, away from the face of the rock, arms windmilling, until his feet slipped from their narrow ledge and he was suddenly in mid-air, suspended; and finally he dropped like a stone to the rocks below.

He made no sound.

He landed on a flat rock that jutted above the surface of the water. The noise his body made hitting the rock was sickening. He lay there on his back like a broken doll, arms outflung, head at an impossible angle.

Something vile seeped out from inside him on to the stone, and Lucy turned away.

She had killed him.

Everything happened at once, then.

There was a roaring sound from the sky and three aircraft with RAF circles on their wings flew out of the clouds and dipped low over the U-boat, their guns blazing.

Four sailors came up the hill toward the house at a jog-trot, one of them shouting 'Left-right-left-right-left-right.'

Another plane landed on the sea, a dinghy emerged, and a man in a life-jacket began to row toward the cliff.

A small ship came around the headland and steamed aggressively toward the U-boat.

The U-boat submerged.

The dinghy bumped into the rocks at the foot of the cliff, and the man got out and examined the body of Henry.

A boat she recognized as the coastguard cutter appeared.

One of the sailors came up to her and said: 'Are you all right, love? Only there's a little girl in the cottage crying for her mummy.'

'It's a boy,' Lucy said. 'I must cut his hair.' And for no reason at all she smiled.

Bloggs steered the dinghy toward the body at the foot of the cliff. The boat bumped against the rock, and he scrambled out and on to the flat surface.

It was Die Nadel.

He was very dead. His skull had smashed like a glass goblet when he hit the rock. Looking more closely, Bloggs could see that the man had been somewhat battered even before the fall: his right hand was mutilated and there was something wrong with his ankle.

Bloggs searched the body. The stiletto was where he had guessed it might be: in a sheath strapped to the left forearm. In the inside pocket of the expensive-looking, bloodstained jacket, Bloggs found a wallet, papers, money, and a little film can containing twenty-four 35mm photographic negatives. He held them up to the strengthening light: they were the negatives of the prints found in the envelopes Faber had sent to the Portuguese Embassy.

The sailors on the cliff top threw down a rope. Bloggs put Faber's possessions into his own pockets, then tied the rope around the corpse. They hauled it up, then sent the rope down for Bloggs.

When he got to the top one of the sailors said: 'You left his brains on the rock, but never mind.'

The sub-lieutenant introduced himself, and they walked across to the little cottage on top of the hill.

'We haven't touched anything, for fear of destroying evidence,' the senior sailor said.

'Don't worry too much,' Bloggs told him. 'There won't be a prosecution.'

They had to enter the house through the broken kitchen window. The woman was sitting at a table, with the child on her lap. Bloggs smiled at her. He could not think of anything to say.

He looked quickly around the little cottage. It was a battlefield. He saw the nailed-up windows, the barred doors, the remains of the fire, the dog with its throat cut, the shotguns, the broken bannister, and the axe embedded in the windowsill beside two severed fingers.

He thought: What kind of woman is she?

He set the sailors to work: one to tidy the house and unbar the doors and windows; another to mend the blown fuse; a third to make tea.

He sat down in front of the woman and looked at her. She was dressed in ill-fitting, mannish clothes; her hair was wet; her face was dirty. Despite all that she was remarkably beautiful, with lovely amber eyes in an oval face.

Bloggs smiled at the child and spoke very gently to the woman. 'What you've done is enormously important to the war,' he said. 'One of these days I'll explain just how important it is. But for now, I have to ask you two questions. Is that, okay?'

Her eyes focused on him, and after a moment she nodded.

'Did the man Faber succeed in contacting the U-boat by radio?'

The woman just looked blank.

Bloggs found a toffee in his trousers pocket. 'Can I give the boy a sweet?' he asked. 'He looks hungry.'

'Thank you,' she said.

'Now: did Faber contact the U-boat?'

'His name was Henry Baker,' she said.

'Ah. Well, did he?'

'No. I short-circuited the electricity.'

'That was smart,' Bloggs said. 'How did you do it?' She pointed at the empty light socket above them.

'Screwdriver, eh?'

'No.' She smiled thinly. 'I wasn't that smart. Fingers.'

He gave her a look of horror. The thought of deliberately . . . He shook himself. It was ghastly. He put it out of his mind. 'Right. Do you think anyone on the U-boat could have seen him coming down the cliff?'

The effort of concentration showed on her face. 'Nobody came out of the hatch,' she said. 'Could they have seen him through their periscope?'

'No,' he said confidently. 'This is good news. It means they don't know he's been captured and . . . neutralized. Anyway . . .' He changed the subject hastily. 'You've been through as much as men on the front line are expected to suffer. We're going to get you and the boy to a hospital on the mainland.'

'Yes,' she said.

Bloggs addressed the senior sailor. 'Is there any form of transport around?'

'Yes – a jeep down in that little stand of trees.'

'Good. Will you drive these two over to the jetty and get them on to your boat?'

'Surely.'

'Treat them gently.'

'Of course.'

Bloggs turned to the woman again. He felt an overwhelming surge of affection and admiration for her. She looked frail and helpless, now: but he knew she was brave and strong as well as beautiful. Impulsively, he took her hand. 'When you've been in hospital a day or two, you'll begin to feel terribly depressed. That's a sign you're getting better. I won't be far away, and the doctors will tell me. I'll want to talk to you some more. But not before you feel like it. Okay?'

At last she smiled at him, and it felt like the warmth of a fire. 'You're kind,' she said.

She stood up and carried her child out of the house.

'Kind?' Bloggs muttered to himself. 'God's truth, what a woman.'

He went upstairs to the radio and tuned it to the Royal Observer Corps frequency.

'Storm Island calling, over.'

'Come in, Storm Island.'

'Patch me through to London.'

'Hold on.' There was a long pause, then a familiar voice. 'Godliman.'

'Percy. We caught the . . . smuggler. He's dead.'

'Marvellous, marvellous.' There was triumph in Godliman's voice. 'Did he manage to contact his partner?'

'Almost certainly not.'

'Well done, well done!'

'Don't congratulate me,' Bloggs said. 'By the time I got here it was all over bar the tidying up.'

'Who killed him, then?'

'The woman.'

'Well, I'm damned. What's she like?'

Bloggs grinned. 'She's a hero, Percy.'

Godliman laughed aloud. 'I think I know what you mean.'

CHAPTER THIRTY-EIGHT

HITLER STOOD at the panoramic window, looking out at the mountains. He wore his dovegrey uniform, and he looked tired and depressed. He had called his physician during the night.

Admiral Puttkamer saluted and said: 'Good morning, my Führer.'

Hitler turned and peered closely at his aide-de-camp. Those beady eyes never failed to unnerve Puttkamer. Hitler said: 'Was Die Nadel picked up?'

'No.' There was some trouble at the rendezvous – the English police were chasing smugglers. It appears Die Nadel was not there, anyway. He sent a wireless message a few minutes ago.' He proffered a sheet of paper.

Hitler took it from him, put on his spectacles, and began to read:

YOUR RENDEZVOUS INSECURE YOU CUNTS I AM
WOUNDED AND TRANSMITTING LEFT HANDED
FIRST UNITED STATES ARMY GROUP ASSEMBLED
EAST ANGLIA UNDER PATTON ORDER OF BATTLE
AS FOLLOWS TWENTYONE INFANTRY DIVISIONS
FIVE ARMOURED DIVISIONS APPROXIMATELY FIVE
THOUSAND AIRCRAFT PLUS REQUISITE TROOP

SHIPS IN THE WASH FUSAG WILL ATTACK CALAIS
JUNE FIFTEENTH REGARDS TO WILLI

Hitler handed the message back to Puttkamer and sighed. 'So it's Calais after all.'

'Can we be sure of this man?' the aide asked.

'Absolutely.' Hitler turned and walked across the room to a chair. His movements were stiff, and he seemed in pain. 'He is a loyal German. I know his family.'

'But your instinct . . .'

'Ach . . . I said I would trust this man's report, and so I shall.' He made a gesture of dismissal. 'Tell Rommel and Rundstedt they can't have their panzers. And send in that damned doctor.'

Puttkamer saluted again and went out to relay the orders.

Epilogue

CHAPTER THIRTY-NINE

WHEN GERMANY defeated England in the quarter-final of the 1970 World Cup soccer tournament Grandpa was furious.

He sat in front of the colour television set and muttered through his beard at the screen. 'Cunning!' he told the assorted experts who were now dissecting the game. 'Cunning and stealth! That's the way to defeat the Hun!'

He would not be mollified until his grandchildren arrived. Jo's white Jaguar drew up on the drive of the modest three-bedroom house, and little David rushed in to sit on Grandpa's lap and pull his beard. The rest of the family followed more sedately: Rebecca, David's little sister; then Jo's wife Ann; then Jo himself, prosperous-looking in a suede jacket. Grandma came out of the kitchen to greet them.

Jo said: 'Did you watch the football, Pop?'

'Terrible,' Grandpa said. 'We were rubbish.' Since he retired from the Force and had more leisure time, he had taken an interest in sport.

Jo scratched his moustache. 'The Germans were better,' he said. 'They play good football. We can't win it every time.'

'Don't talk to me about bloody Germans,' Grandpa said.

Jo grinned. 'I do a lot of business with Germany.'

Grandma's voice came from the kitchen. 'Don't start him off, Jo!' She pretended to be going deaf, but there was not much she missed.

'I know,' Grandpa said. 'Forgive and forget, and drive round in a bloody Audi.'

'Good cars.'

'Cunning and stealth, that's the way to defeat the Hun,' Grandpa repeated. He addressed the grandson on his lap, who was not really his grandson, since Jo was not his son. 'That's the way we beat them in the war, Davy – we tricked them.'

'How did you trick them?' David asked, with the child's assumption that his forebears did everything in history.

'Well, see, we made them think—' Grandpa's voice became low and conspiratorial, and the child giggled in anticipation. 'We made them think we were going to attack Calais—'

'That's in France, not Germany.'

'Yes, but the Germans were all over France, then. The Froggies didn't defend themselves as well as we did.'

Jo said: 'Nothing to do with the fact that we're an island, of course.'

Ann shushed him. 'Let Grandpa tell his war stories.'

'Anyway,' Grandpa continued, 'we made them think we were going to attack Calais, so they put all their tanks and soldiers there.' He used a cushion to repre-

LIE DOWN WITH LIONS

to Barbara

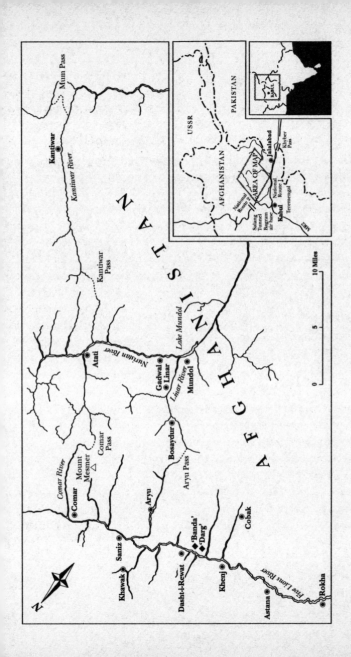

Part One
1981

Part One
1981

CHAPTER ONE

T HE MEN who wanted to kill Ahmet Yilmaz were
serious people. They were exiled Turkish students living in Paris, and they had already murdered an
attaché at the Turkish Embassy and firebombed the
home of a senior executive of Turkish Airlines. They
chose Yilmaz as their next target because he was a
wealthy supporter of the military dictatorship and
because he lived, conveniently, in Paris.

His home and office were well guarded and his
Mercedes limousine was armoured, but every man has
a weakness, the students believed, and that weakness is
usually sex. In the case of Yilmaz they were right. A
couple of weeks of casual surveillance revealed that
Yilmaz would leave his house, on two or three evenings
each week, driving the Renault station wagon his servants used for shopping, and go to a side street in the
Fifteenth District to visit a beautiful young Turkish
woman who was in love with him.

The students decided to put a bomb in the Renault
while Yilmaz was getting laid.

They knew where to get the explosives: from Pepe
Gozzi one of the many sons of the Corsican godfather
Mémé Gozzi. Pepe was a weapons dealer. He would sell

to anyone, but he preferred political customers, for – as he cheerfully admitted – 'Idealists pay higher prices.' He had helped the Turkish students with both their previous outrages.

There was a snag in the car-bomb plan. Usually Yilmaz would leave the girl's place alone in the Renault – but not always. Sometimes he took her out to dinner. Often she went off in the car and returned half an hour later laden with bread, fruit, cheese and wine, evidently for a cosy feast. Occasionally Yilmaz would go home in a taxi, and the girl would borrow the car for a day or two. The students were romantic, like all terrorists, and they were reluctant to risk killing a beautiful woman whose only crime was the readily pardonable one of loving a man unworthy of her.

They discussed this problem in a democratic fashion. They made all decisions by vote and acknowledged no leaders; but all the same there was one among them whose strength of personality made him dominant. His name was Rahmi Coskun, and he was a handsome, passionate young man with a bushy moustache and a certain bound-for-glory light in his eyes. It was his energy and determination which had pushed through the previous two projects despite the problems and the risks. Rahmi proposed consulting a bomb expert.

At first the others did not like this idea. Whom could they trust? they asked. Rahmi suggested Ellis Thaler. An American who called himself a poet but in fact made a living giving English lessons, he had learned about explosives as a conscript in Vietnam. Rahmi had known him for a year or so: they had both worked on a

4

short-lived revolutionary newspaper called *Chaos,* and together they had organised a poetry reading to raise funds for the Palestine Liberation Organisation. He seemed to understand Rahmi's rage at what was being done to Turkey and his hatred of the barbarians who were doing it. Some of the other students also knew Ellis slightly: he had been seen on several demonstrations, and they had assumed he was a graduate student or a young professor. Still they were reluctant to bring in a non-Turk; but Rahmi was insistent and in the end they consented.

Ellis came up with the solution to their problem immediately. The bomb should have a radio-controlled arming device, he said. Rahmi would sit at a window opposite the girl's apartment, or in a parked car along the street, watching the Renault. In his hand he would have a small radio transmitter the size of a pack of cigarettes – the kind of thing used to open automatic garage doors. If Yilmaz got into the car alone, as he most often did, then Rahmi would press the button on the transmitter, and a radio signal would activate a switch in the bomb, which would then be armed and would explode as soon as Yilmaz started the engine. But if it should be the girl who got into the car, Rahmi would not press the button, and she could drive away in blissful ignorance. The bomb would be quite safe until it was armed. 'No button, no bang,' said Ellis.

Rahmi liked the idea and asked Ellis if he would collaborate with Pepe Gozzi on making the bomb.

'Sure,' said Ellis.

Then there was one more snag.

'I've got a friend,' Rahmi said, 'who wants to meet you both, Ellis and Pepe. To tell the truth, he *must* meet you, otherwise the whole deal is off; for this is the friend who gives us the money for explosives and cars and bribes and guns and everything.'

'Why does he want to meet us?' Ellis and Pepe wanted to know.

'He needs to be sure that the bomb will work, and he wants to feel that he can trust you,' Rahmi said apologetically. 'All you have to do is bring the bomb to him and explain to him how it will work and shake his hand and let him look you in the eye, is that so much to ask, for the man who is making the whole thing possible?'

'It's all right with me,' said Ellis.

Pepe hesitated. He wanted the money he would make on the deal – he always wanted money, as a pig always wants the trough – but he hated to meet new people.

Ellis reasoned with him. 'Listen,' he said, 'these student groups bloom and die like mimosa in the spring, and Rahmi is sure to be blown away before long; but if you know his "friend" then you will be able to continue to do business after Rahmi is gone.'

'You're right,' said Pepe, who was no genius but could grasp business principles if they were explained simply.

Ellis told Rahmi that Pepe had agreed, and Rahmi set up a rendezvous for the three of them on the following Sunday.

*

That morning Ellis woke up in Jane's bed. He came awake suddenly, feeling frightened, as if he had had a nightmare. A moment later he remembered the reason why he was so tense.

He glanced at the clock. He was early. In his mind he ran over his plan. If all went well, today would be the triumphant conclusion to more than a year of patient, careful work. And he would be able to share that triumph with Jane, if he was still alive at the end of the day.

He turned his head to look at her, moving carefully to avoid waking her. His heart leaped, as it did every time he saw her face. She lay flat on her back, with her turned-up nose pointing at the ceiling and her dark hair spread across the pillow like a bird's unfolded wing. He looked at her wide mouth, the full lips that kissed him so often and so lusciously. Spring sunlight revealed the dense blonde down on her cheeks – her beard, he called it, when he wanted to tease her.

It was a rare delight to see her like this, in repose, her face relaxed and expressionless. Normally she was animated – laughing, frowning, grimacing, registering surprise or scepticism or compassion. Her commonest expression was a wicked grin, like that of a mischievous small boy who had just perpetrated a particularly fiendish practical joke. Only when she was sleeping or thinking very hard was she like this; yet this was how he loved her most, for now, when she was unguarded and unselfconscious, her appearance hinted at the languid sensuality that burned just beneath her surface like a

7

slow, hot, underground fire. When he saw her like this his hands almost itched to touch her.

This had surprised him. When he first met her, soon after he came to Paris, she had struck him as typical of the kind of busybody always found among the young and the radical in capital cities, chairing committees and organising campaigns against apartheid and for nuclear disarmament, leading protest marches about El Salvador and water pollution, raising money for starving people in Chad and trying to promote a talented young film-maker. People were drawn to her by her striking good looks, captivated by her charm, and energised by her enthusiasm. He had dated her a couple of times, just for the pleasure of watching a pretty girl demolish a steak; and then – he could never remember exactly how it happened – he had discovered that inside this excitable girl there lived a passionate woman, and he had fallen in love.

His gaze wandered around her little studio flat. He noted with pleasure the familiar personal possessions that marked the place as hers: a pretty lamp made of a small Chinese vase; a shelf of books on economics and world poverty; a big soft sofa you could drown in; a photograph of her father, a handsome man in a double-breasted coat, probably taken in the early sixties; a small silver cup won by her on her pony Dandelion and dated 1971, ten years ago. She was thirteen, Ellis thought, and I was twenty-three; and while she was winning pony trials in Hampshire I was in Laos, laying anti-personnel mines along the Ho Chi Minh Trail.

When he had first seen the flat, almost a year ago,

she had just moved here from the suburbs, and it had been rather bare: just a little attic room with a kitchen in an alcove, a shower in a closet, and a toilet down the hall. Gradually she had transformed it from a grimy garret into a cheerful nest. She earned a good salary as an interpreter, translating French and Russian into English, but her rent was also high – the apartment was near the Boulevard St Michel – so she had bought carefully, saving her money for just the right mahogany table, antique bedstead and Tabriz rug. She was what Ellis's father would call a classy dame. You're going to like her, Dad, thought Ellis. You're going to be just crazy about her.

He rolled on to his side, facing her, and the movement woke her, as he had known it would. Her large blue eyes stared at the ceiling for a fraction of a second, then she looked at him, smiled, and rolled over into his arms. 'Hello,' she whispered, and he kissed her.

He got hard immediately. They lay together for a while, half asleep, kissing now and again; then she draped one leg across his hips and they began to make love languorously, without speaking.

When they had first become lovers, and they had started to make love morning and night and often midafternoon too, Ellis had assumed that such horniness would not last, and that after a few days, or maybe a couple of weeks, the novelty would wear off and they would revert to the statistical average of two-and-a-half times a week, or whatever it was. He had been wrong. A year later they were still screwing like honeymooners.

She rolled on top of him, letting her full weight rest

on his body. Her damp skin clung to his. He wrapped his arms around her small body and hugged her as he thrust deep inside her. She sensed that his climax was coming, and she lifted her head and looked down at him, then kissed him with her mouth open while he was coming inside her. Immediately afterwards she gave a soft, low-pitched moan, and he felt her come with a long, gentle, wavy Sunday-morning orgasm. She stayed on top of him, half asleep still. He stroked her hair.

After a while she stirred. 'Do you know what day it is?' she mumbled.

'Sunday.'

'It's your Sunday to make lunch.'

'I hadn't forgotten.'

'Good.' There was a pause. 'What are you going to give me?'

'Steak, potatoes, snow peas, goat's cheese, strawberries and chantilly cream.'

She lifted her head, laughing. 'That's what you always make!'

'It is not. Last time we had French beans.'

'And the time before that you had forgotten, so we ate out. How about some variety in your cooking?'

'Hey, wait a minute. The deal was, each of us would make lunch on alternate Sundays. Nobody said anything about making a *different* lunch each time.'

She slumped on him again, feigning defeat.

His day's work had been at the back of his mind all along. He was going to need her unconscious help, and this was the moment to ask her. 'I have to see Rahmi this morning,' he began.

10

'All right. I'll meet you at your place later.'

'There's something you could do for me, if you wouldn't mind getting there a little early.'

'What?'

'Cook the lunch. No! No! Just kidding. I want you to help me with a little conspiracy.'

'Go on,' she said.

'Today is Rahmi's birthday, and his brother Mustafa is in town, but Rahmi doesn't know.' If this works out, Ellis thought, I'll never lie to you again. 'I want Mustafa to turn up at Rahmi's lunch party as a surprise. But I need an accomplice.'

'I'm game,' she said. She rolled off him and sat upright, crossing her legs. Her breasts were like apples, smooth and round and hard. The ends of her hair teased her nipples. 'What do I have to do?'

'The problem is simple. I have to tell Mustafa where to go, but Rahmi hasn't yet made up his mind where he wants to eat. So I have to get the message to Mustafa at the last minute. And Rahmi will probably be beside me when I make the call.'

'And the solution?'

'I'll call *you*. I'll talk nonsense. Ignore everything except the address. Call Mustafa, give him the address and tell him how to get there.' All this had sounded okay when Ellis dreamed it up, but now it seemed wildly implausible.

However, Jane did not seem suspicious. 'It sounds simple enough,' she said.

'Good,' Ellis said briskly, concealing his relief.

'And after you call, how soon will you be home?'

11

'Less than an hour. I want to wait and see the surprise, but I'll get out of having lunch there.'

Jane looked thoughtful. 'They invited you but not me.'

Ellis shrugged. 'I presume it's a masculine celebration.' He reached for the notepad on the bedside table and wrote *Mustafa* and the phone number.

Jane got off the bed and crossed the room to the shower closet. She opened the door and turned on the tap. Her mood had changed. She was not smiling. Ellis said: 'What are you mad about?'

'I'm not mad,' she said. 'Sometimes I dislike the way your friends treat me.'

'But you know how the Turks are about girls.'

'Exactly – *girls*. They don't mind respectable women, but I'm a *girl*.'

Ellis sighed. 'It's not like you to get needled by the prehistoric attitudes of a few chauvinists. What are you *really* trying to tell me?'

She considered for a moment, standing naked beside the shower, and she was so lovely that Ellis wanted to make love again. She said: 'I suppose I'm saying that I don't like my status. I'm committed to you, everyone knows that – I don't sleep with anyone else, don't even go out with other men – but you're not committed to me. We don't live together, I don't know where you go or what you do a lot of the time, we've never met one another's parents . . . and people know all this, so they treat me like a tart.'

'I think you're exaggerating.'

'You always say that.' She stepped into the shower

and banged the door. Ellis took his razor from the drawer where he kept his overnight kit and began to shave at the kitchen sink. They had had this argument before, at much greater length, and he knew what was at the bottom of it: Jane wanted them to live together.

He wanted it too, of course; he wanted to marry her and live with her for the rest of his life. But he had to wait until this assignment was over; and he could not tell her that, so he said things such as *I'm not ready* and *All I need is time*, and these vague evasions infuriated her. It seemed to her that a year was a long time to love a man without getting any kind of commitment from him. She was right, of course. But if all went well today he could make everything right.

He finished shaving, wrapped his razor in a towel and put it in his drawer. Jane got out of the shower and he took her place. We're not talking, he thought; this is silly.

While he was in the shower she made coffee. He dressed quickly in faded denim jeans and a black T-shirt and sat opposite her at the little mahogany table. She poured his coffee and said: 'I want to have a serious talk with you.'

'Okay,' he said quickly, 'let's do it at lunchtime.'

'Why not now?'

'I don't have time.'

'Is Rahmi's birthday more important than our relationship?'

'Of course not.' Ellis heard irritation in his tone, and a warning voice told him *Be gentle, you could lose her*. 'But I promised, and it's important that I keep my promises;

13

whereas it doesn't seem very important whether we have this conversation now or later.'

Jane's face took on a set, stubborn look that he knew: she wore it when she had made a decision and someone tried to deflect her from her path. 'It's important to *me* that we talk *now*.'

For a moment he was tempted to tell her the whole truth right away. But this was not the way he had planned it. He was short of time, his mind was on something else, and he was not prepared. It would be much better later, when they were both relaxed, and he would be able to tell her that his job in Paris was done. So he said: 'I think you're being silly, and I won't be bullied. Please let's talk later. I have to go now.' He stood up.

As he walked to the door she said: 'Jean-Pierre has asked me to go to Afghanistan with him.'

This was so completely unexpected that Ellis had to think for a moment before he could take it in. 'Are you *serious?*' he said incredulously.

'I'm serious.'

Ellis knew Jean-Pierre was in love with Jane. So were half a dozen other men: that kind of thing was inevitable with such a woman. None of the men were serious rivals, though; at least, he had thought not, until this moment. He began to recover his composure. He said: 'Why would you want to visit a war zone with a wimp?'

'It's not a joking matter!' she said fiercely. 'I'm talking about my *life.*'

He shook his head in disbelief. 'You can't go to Afghanistan.'

'Why not?'

'Because you love me.'

'That doesn't put me at your disposal.'

At least she had not said *No I don't.* He looked at his watch. This was ridiculous: in a few hours' time he was going to tell her everything she wanted to hear. 'I'm not willing to do this,' he said. 'We're talking about our future, and it's a discussion that can't be rushed.'

'I won't wait forever,' she said.

'I'm not asking you to wait forever, I'm asking you to wait a few hours.' He touched her cheek. 'Let's not fight about a few hours.'

She stood up and kissed his mouth hard.

He said: 'You won't go to Afghanistan, will you?'

'I don't know,' she said levelly.

He tried a grin. 'At least, not before lunch.'

She smiled back and nodded. 'Not before lunch.'

He looked at her for a moment longer, then he went out.

The broad boulevards of the Champs Elysées were thronged with tourists and Parisians out for a morning stroll, milling about like sheep in a fold under the warm spring sun, and all the pavement cafés were full. Ellis stood near the appointed place, carrying a backpack he had bought in a cheap luggage store. He looked like an American on a hitch-hiking tour of Europe.

He wished Jane had not chosen this morning for a confrontation: she would be brooding now, and would be in a jagged mood by the time he arrived.

15

Well, he would just have to smooth her ruffled feathers for a while.

He put Jane out of his mind and concentrated on the task ahead of him.

There were two possibilities as to the identity of Rahmi's 'friend', the one who financed the little terrorist group. The first was that he was a wealthy freedom-loving Turk who had decided, for political or personal reasons, that violence was justified against the military dictatorship and its supporters. If this was the case then Ellis would be disappointed.

The second possibility was that he was Boris.

'Boris' was a legendary figure in the circle within which Ellis moved – among the revolutionary students, the exiled Palestinians, the part-time politics lecturers, the editors of badly-printed extremist newspapers, the anarchists and the Maoists and the Armenians and the militant vegetarians. He was said to be a Russian, a KGB man willing to fund any leftist act of violence in the West. Many people doubted his existence, especially those who had tried and failed to get funds out of the Russians. But Ellis had noticed, from time to time, that a group who for months had done nothing but complain that they could not afford a duplicating machine would suddenly stop talking about money and become very security-conscious; and then, a little later, there would be a kidnapping or a shooting or a bomb.

It was certain, Ellis thought, that the Russians gave money to such groups as the Turkish dissidents: they could hardly resist such a cheap and low-risk way of causing trouble. Besides, the US financed kidnappers

16

and murderers in Central America, and he could not imagine that the Soviet Union would be more scrupulous than his own country. And since in this line of work money was not kept in bank accounts or moved around by telex, somebody had to hand over the actual banknotes, so it followed that there had to be a Boris figure.

Ellis wanted very badly to meet him.

Rahmi walked by at exactly ten-thirty, wearing a pink Lacoste shirt and immaculately pressed tan trousers, looking edgy. He threw one burning glance at Ellis then turned his head away.

Ellis followed him, staying ten or fifteen yards behind, as they had previously arranged.

At the next pavement café sat the muscular, overweight form of Pepe Gozzi, in a black silk suit as if he had been to Mass, which he probably had. He held a large briefcase in his lap. He got up and fell in more or less alongside Ellis, in such a way that a casual observer would have been unsure whether they were together or not.

Rahmi headed up the hill towards the Arc de Triomphe.

Ellis watched Pepe out of the corner of his eye. The Corsican had an animal's instinct for self-preservation: unobtrusively, he checked whether he was being followed – once when he crossed the road, and could quite naturally glance back along the boulevard while he stood waiting for the lights to change, and again passing a corner shop where he could see the people behind him reflected in the diagonal window.

Ellis liked Rahmi but not Pepe. Rahmi was sincere and high-principled, and the people he killed probably deserved to die. Pepe was completely different. He did this for money, and because he was too coarse and stupid to survive in the world of legitimate business.

Three blocks east of the Arc de Triomphe, Rahmi turned into a side street. Ellis and Pepe followed. Rahmi led them across the road and turned into the Hotel Lancaster.

So this was the rendezvous. Ellis hoped the meeting was to take place in a bar or restaurant in the hotel: he would feel safer in a public room.

The marbled entrance hall was cool after the heat of the street. Ellis shivered. A waiter in a tuxedo looked askance at his jeans. Rahmi was getting into a tiny elevator at the far end of the L-shaped lobby. It was to be a hotel room, then. So be it. Ellis followed Rahmi into the elevator and Pepe squeezed in behind. Ellis's nerves were drawn wire-tight as they went up. They got off at the fourth floor and Rahmi led them to Room 41 and knocked.

Ellis tried to make his face calm and impassive.

The door opened slowly.

It was Boris. Ellis knew it as soon as he set eyes on the man, and he felt a thrill of triumph and at the same time a cold shiver of fear. Moscow was written all over the man, from his cheap haircut to his solidly practical shoes, and there was the unmistakable style of the KGB in his hard-eyed look of appraisal and the brutal set of his mouth. This man was not like Rahmi or Pepe; he was neither a hotheaded idealist nor a swinish mafioso.

18

Boris was a stone-hearted professional terrorist who would not hesitate to blow the head off any or all of the three men who now stood before him.

I've been looking for you for a long time, thought Ellis.

Boris held the door half open for a moment, partly shielding his body while he studied them, then he stepped back and said in French: 'Come in.'

They walked into the sitting-room of a suite. It was rather exquisitely decorated, and furnished with chairs, occasional tables and a cupboard which appeared to be eighteenth-century antiques. A carton of Marlboro cigarettes and a duty-free litre of brandy stood on a delicate bow-legged side table. In the far corner a half-opened door led to a bedroom.

Rahmi's introductions were nervously perfunctory. 'Pepe. Ellis. My friend.'

Boris was a broad-shouldered man wearing a white shirt with the sleeves rolled to show meaty, hair-covered forearms. His blue serge trousers were too heavy for this weather. Over the back of a chair was slung a black-and-tan check jacket which would look wrong with the blue trousers.

Ellis put his backpack on the rug and sat down.

Boris gestured at the brandy bottle. 'A drink?'

Ellis did not want brandy at eleven o'clock in the morning. He said: 'Yes, please – coffee.'

Boris gave him a hard, hostile look, then said: 'We'll all have coffee,' and went to the phone. He's used to everyone being afraid of him, Ellis thought; he doesn't like it that I treat him as an equal.

Rahmi was plainly in awe of Boris, and fidgeted anxiously, fastening and unfastening the top button of his pink polo shirt while the Russian called room service.

Boris hung up the phone and addressed Pepe. 'I'm glad to meet you,' he said in French. 'I think we can help each other.'

Pepe nodded without speaking. He sat forward in the velvet chair, his powerful bulk in the black suit looking oddly vulnerable against the pretty furniture, as if *it* might break *him*. Pepe has a lot in common with Boris, thought Ellis: they're both strong, cruel men without decency or compassion. If Pepe were Russian, he would be in the KGB; and if Boris were French he'd be in the Mafia.

'Show me the bomb,' said Boris.

Pepe opened his briefcase. It was packed with blocks, about a foot long and a couple of inches square, of a yellowish substance. Boris knelt on the rug beside the case and poked one of the blocks with a forefinger. The substance yielded like putty. Boris sniffed it. 'I presume this is C3,' he said to Pepe.

Pepe nodded.

'Where is the mechanism?'

Rahmi said: 'Ellis has it in his backpack.'

Ellis said: 'No, I don't.'

The room went very quiet for a moment. A look of panic came over Rahmi's handsome young face. 'What do you mean?' he said agitatedly. His frightened eyes switched from Ellis to Boris and back again. 'You said . . . I told him you would—'

'Shut up,' Boris said harshly. Rahmi fell silent. Boris looked expectantly at Ellis.

Ellis spoke with a casual indifference that he did not feel. 'I was afraid this might be a trap, so I left the mechanism at home. It can be here in a few minutes. I just have to call my girl.'

Boris stared at him for several seconds. Ellis returned his look as coolly as he could. Finally Boris said: 'Why did you think this might be a trap?'

Ellis decided that to try to justify himself would appear defensive. It was a dumb question, anyway. He shot an arrogant look at Boris, then shrugged and said nothing.

Boris continued to look searchingly at him. Finally the Russian said: 'I shall make the call.'

A protest rose to Ellis's lips and he choked it back. This was a development he had not expected. He carefully maintained his I-don't-give-a-damn pose while thinking furiously. How would Jane react to the voice of a stranger? And what if she were not there, what if she had decided to break her promise? He regretted using her as a cut-out. But it was too late now.

'You're a careful man,' he said to Boris.

'You, too. What is your phone number?'

Ellis told him. Boris wrote the number on the message pad by the phone then began to dial.

The others waited in silence.

Boris said: 'Hello? I am calling on behalf of Ellis.'

Perhaps the unknown voice would not throw her, Ellis thought: she had been expecting a somewhat wacky call anyway. *Ignore everything except the address*, he had told her.

'What?' Boris said irritably, and Ellis thought: Oh, shit, what is she saying now? 'Yes, I am, but never mind that,' Boris said. 'Ellis wants you to bring the mechanism to Room 41 at the Hotel Lancaster in the rue de Berri.'

There was another pause.

Play the game, Jane, thought Ellis.

'Yes, it's a very nice hotel.'

Stop kidding around! Just tell the man you'll do it – please!

'Thank you,' Boris said, and he added sarcastically: 'You are most kind.' Then he hung up.

Ellis tried to look as if he had expected all along there would be no problem.

Boris said: 'She knew I was Russian. How did she find out?'

Ellis was puzzled for a moment, then realised. 'She's a linguist,' he said. 'She knows accents.'

Pepe spoke for the first time. 'While we're waiting for this cunt to arrive, let's see the money.'

'All right.' Boris went into the bedroom.

While he was out, Rahmi spoke to Ellis in a low hiss. 'I didn't know you were going to pull that trick!'

'Of course you didn't,' said Ellis in a feigned tone of boredom. 'If you had known what I was going to do, it wouldn't have worked as a safeguard, would it?'

Boris came back in with a large brown envelope and handed it to Pepe. Pepe opened it and began counting 100-franc notes.

Boris unwrapped the carton of Marlboro and lit a cigarette.

Ellis thought: I hope Jane doesn't *wait* before making the call to 'Mustafa'. I should have told her it was important to pass the message on immediately.

After a while Pepe said: 'It's all there.' He put the money back into the envelope, licked the flap, sealed it, and put it on a side table.

The four men sat in silence for several minutes.

Boris asked Ellis: 'How far away is your place?'

'Fifteen minutes on a motor scooter.'

There was a knock at the door. Ellis tensed.

'She drove fast,' Boris said. He opened the door. 'Coffee,' he said disgustedly, and returned to his seat.

Two white-jacketed waiters wheeled a trolley into the room. They straightened up and turned around, each holding in his hand a Model 'D' M.A.B. pistol, standard issue for French detectives. One of them said: 'Nobody move.'

Ellis felt Boris gather himself to spring. Why were there only two detectives? If Rahmi were to do something foolish, and get himself shot, it would create enough of a diversion for Pepe and Boris together to overpower the armed men—

The bedroom door flew open, and two more men in waiters' uniforms stood there, armed like their colleagues.

Boris relaxed, and a look of resignation came over his face.

Ellis realised he had been holding his breath. He let it out in a long sigh.

23

It was all over.

A uniformed police officer walked into the room.

'A trap!' Rahmi burst out. 'This *is* a trap!'

'Shut up,' said Boris, and once again his harsh voice silenced Rahmi. He addressed the police officer. 'I object most strongly to this outrage,' he began. 'Please take note that—'

The policeman punched him in the mouth with a leather-gloved fist.

Boris touched his lips then looked at the smear of blood on his hand. His manner changed completely as he realised this was far too serious for him to bluff his way out. 'Remember my face,' he told the police officer in a voice as cold as the grave. 'You will see it again.'

'But who is the traitor?' cried Rahmi. 'Who betrayed us?'

'Him,' said Boris, pointing at Ellis.

'Ellis?' Rahmi said incredulously.

'The phone call,' said Boris. 'The address.'

Rahmi stared at Ellis. He looked wounded to the quick.

Several more uniformed policemen came in. The officer pointed at Pepe. 'That's Gozzi,' he said. Two policemen handcuffed Pepe and led him away. The officer looked at Boris. 'Who are you?'

Boris looked bored. 'My name is Jan Hocht,' he said. 'I am a citizen of Argentina—'

'Don't bother,' said the officer disgustedly. 'Take him away.' He turned to Rahmi. 'Well?'

'I have nothing to say!' Rahmi said, managing to make it sound heroic.

The officer gave a jerk of his head and Rahmi, too, was handcuffed. He glared at Ellis until he was led out.

The prisoners were taken down in the elevator one at a time. Pepe's briefcase and the envelope full of 100-franc notes were shrouded in polythene. A police photographer came in and set up his tripod.

The officer said to Ellis: 'There is a black Citroën DS parked outside the hotel.' Hesitantly he added: 'Sir.'

I'm back on the side of the law, Ellis thought. A pity Rahmi is so much more attractive a man than this cop.

He went down in the elevator. In the hotel lobby the manager, in black coat and striped trousers, stood with a pained expression frozen to his face as more policemen marched in.

Ellis went out into the sunshine. The black Citroën was on the other side of the street. There was a driver in the front and a passenger in the back. Ellis got into the back. The car pulled away fast.

The passenger turned to Ellis and said: 'Hello, John.'

Ellis smiled. The use of his real name was strange after more than a year. He said: 'How are you, Bill?'

'Relieved!' said Bill. 'For thirteen months we hear nothing from you but demands for money. Then we get a peremptory phone call telling us we've got twenty-four hours to arrange a local arrest squad. Imagine what we had to do to persuade the French to do that without telling them why! The squad had to be ready in the vicinity of the Champs Elysées, but to get the exact address we had to wait for a phone call from an unknown woman asking for Mustafa. And that's all we know!'

'It was the only way,' Ellis said apologetically.

'Well, it took some doing – and I now owe some big favours in this town – but we did it. So tell me whether it was worth it. Who have we got in the bag?'

'The Russian is Boris,' said Ellis.

Bill's face broke into a broad grin. 'I'll be a son of a bitch,' he said. 'You brought in Boris. No kidding.'

'No kidding.'

'Jesus, I better get him back from the French before they figure out who he is.'

Ellis shrugged. 'Nobody's going to get much information out of him anyway. He's the dedicated type. The important thing is that we've taken him out of circulation. It will take them a couple of years to break in a replacement and for the new Boris to build his contacts. Meanwhile we've really slowed their operation down.'

'You just bet we have. This is sensational.'

'The Corsican is Pepe Gozzi, a weapons dealer,' Ellis went on. 'He supplied the hardware for just about every terrorist action in France in the last couple of years, and a lot more in other countries. He's the one to interrogate. Send a French detective to talk to his father, Mémé Gozzi, in Marseilles. I predict you'll find the old man never did like the idea of the family getting involved in political crimes. Offer him a deal: immunity for Pepe if Pepe will testify against all the political people he sold stuff to – none of the ordinary criminals. Mémé will go for that, because it won't count as betrayal of friends. And if Mémé goes for it, Pepe will do it. The French can prosecute for years.'

'Incredible.' Bill looked dazed. 'In one day you've

nailed probably the two biggest instigators of terrorism in the world.'

'One day?' Ellis smiled. 'It took a year.'

'It was worth it.'

'The young guy is Rahmi Coskun,' Ellis said. He was hurrying on because there was someone else to whom he wanted to tell all this. 'Rahmi and his group did the Turkish Airlines firebomb a couple of months ago and killed an Embassy attaché before that. If you round up the whole group you're sure to find some forensic evidence.'

'Or the French police will persuade them to confess.'

'Yes. Give me a pencil and I'll write down the names and addresses.'

'Save it,' said Bill. 'I'm going to debrief you completely back at the Embassy.'

'I'm not going back to the Embassy.'

'John, don't fight the programme.'

'I'll give you these names, then you'll have all the really essential information, even if I get run down by a mad French cab driver this afternoon. If I survive, I'll meet you tomorrow morning and give you the detail stuff.'

'Why wait?'

'I have a lunch date.'

Bill rolled his eyes up. 'I suppose we owe you this,' he said reluctantly.

'That's what I figured.'

'Who's your date?'

'Jane Lambert. Hers was one of the names you gave me when you originally briefed me.'

'I remember. I told you that if you wormed your way into her affections she would introduce you to every mad leftist, Arab terrorist, Bader-Meinhof hanger-on and avant-garde poet in Paris.'

'That's how it worked, except I fell in love with her.'

Bill looked like a Connecticut banker being told that his son is going to marry the daughter of a black millionaire: he did not know whether to be thrilled or appalled. 'Uh, what's she really like?'

'She's not crazy, although she has some crazy friends. What can I tell you? She's as pretty as a picture, bright as a pin, and horny as a jackass. She's wonderful. She's the woman I've been looking for all my life.'

'Well, I can see why you'd rather celebrate with her than with me. What are you going to do?'

Ellis smiled. 'I'm going to open a bottle of wine, fry a couple of steaks, tell her I catch terrorists for a living and ask her to marry me.'

CHAPTER TWO

JEAN-PIERRE LEANED forward across the canteen table and fixed the brunette with a compassionate gaze. 'I think I know how you feel,' he said warmly. 'I remember being very depressed towards the end of my first year in medical school. It seems as if you've been given more information than one brain can absorb and you just don't know how you're going to master it in time for the exams.'

'That's *exactly* it,' she said, nodding vigorously. She was almost in tears.

'It's a good sign,' he reassured her. 'It means you're on top of the course. The people who aren't worried are the ones who will flunk.'

Her brown eyes were moist with gratitude. 'Do you really think so?'

'I'm sure of it.'

She looked adoringly at him. You'd rather eat me than your lunch, wouldn't you? he thought. She shifted slightly, and the neck of her sweater gaped open, showing the lacy trimming of her bra. Jean-Pierre was momentarily tempted. In the east wing of the hospital there was a linen store that was never used after about nine-thirty in the morning. Jean-Pierre had taken advantage of it more than once. You could lock the door from the inside and lie down on a soft pile of clean sheets . . .

The brunette sighed and forked a piece of steak into her mouth, and as she began to chew, Jean-Pierre lost interest. He hated to watch people eat. Anyway, he had only been flexing his muscles, to prove he could still do it: he did not really want to seduce her. She was very pretty, with curly hair and warm Mediterranean colouring, and she had a lovely body, but lately Jean-Pierre had no enthusiasm for casual conquests. The only girl who could fascinate him for more than a few minutes was Jane Lambert – and she would not even kiss him.

He looked away from the brunette and his gaze roamed restlessly around the hospital canteen. He saw no one he knew. The place was almost empty: he was having lunch early because he was working the early shift.

It was six months now since he had first seen Jane's stunningly pretty face across a crowded room at a cocktail party to launch a new book on feminist gynae-cology. He had suggested to her that there was no such thing as feminist medicine, there was just good medi-cine and bad medicine. She had replied that there was no such thing as Christian mathematics, but still it took a heretic such as Galileo to prove that the earth goes around the sun. Jean-Pierre had exclaimed: 'You are right!' in his most disarming manner and they had become friends.

Yet she was resistant to his charms, if not quite impervious. She liked him, but she seemed to be committed to the American, even though Ellis was a good deal older than she. Somehow that made her even more desirable to Jean-Pierre. If only Ellis would drop out of the picture – get run over by a bus, or something. . . . Lately Jane's resistance had seemed to be weakening – or was that wishful thinking?

The brunette said: 'Is it true you're going to Afghanistan for two years?'

'That's right.'

'Why?'

'Because I believe in freedom, I suppose. And because I didn't go through all this training just to do coronary by-passes for fat businessmen.' The lies came automatically to his lips.

'But why two years? People who do this usually go for three to six months, a year at the most. Two years seems like forever.'

'Does it?' Jean-Pierre gave a wry smile. 'It's difficult, you see, to achieve anything of real value in a shorter period. The idea of sending doctors there for a brief visit is highly inefficient. What the rebels need is some kind of permanent medical set-up, a hospital that stays in the same place and has at least some of the same staff from one year to the next. As things are, half the people don't know where to take their sick and wounded, they don't follow the doctor's orders because they never get to know him well enough to trust him, and nobody has any time for health education. And the cost of transporting the volunteers to the country and bringing them back makes their "free" services rather expensive.' Jean-Pierre put so much effort into this speech that he almost believed it himself, and he had to remind himself of his true motive for going to Afghanistan, and of the real reason he had to stay for two years.

A voice behind him said: 'Who's going to give their services free?'

He turned around to see another couple carrying trays of food: Valérie, who was an intern like him; and her boyfriend, a radiologist. They sat down with Jean-Pierre and the brunette.

The brunette answered Valérie's question. 'Jean-Pierre is going to Afghanistan to work for the rebels.'

'Really?' Valérie was surprised. 'I heard you had been offered a marvellous job in Houston.'

'I turned it down.'

She was impressed. 'But why?'

'I consider it worthwhile to save the lives of freedom fighters; but a few Texan millionaires more or less won't make any difference to anything.'

The radiologist was not as fascinated by Jean-Pierre as his girlfriend was. He swallowed a mouthful of potatoes and said: 'No sweat. After you come back, you'll have no trouble getting that same job offer again – you'll be a hero as well as a doctor.'

'Do you think so?' said Jean-Pierre coolly. He did not like the turn the conversation was taking.

'Two people from this hospital went to Afghanistan last year,' the radiologist went on. 'They both got great jobs when they came back.'

Jean-Pierre gave a tolerant smile. 'It's nice to know that I'll be employable if I survive.'

'I should hope so!' said the brunette indignantly. 'After such a sacrifice!'

'What do your parents think of the idea?' wondered Valérie.

'My mother approves,' said Jean-Pierre. Of course she approved: she loved a hero. Jean-Pierre could imagine what his father would say about idealistic young doctors who went to work for the Afghan rebels. *Socialism doesn't mean everyone can do what they want!* he would say, his voice hoarse and urgent, his face reddening a little. *What do you think those rebels are? They're bandits, preying on the law-abiding peasants. Feudal institutions have to be wiped out before socialism can come in.* He would hammer the table with one great fist. *To make a soufflé you have to break eggs – to make socialism, you have to break heads!* Don't worry, Papa, I know all that. 'My father is dead,' Jean-Pierre said. 'But he was a freedom fighter himself. He fought in the Resistance during the war.'

'What did he do?' said the sceptical radiologist, but Jean-Pierre never answered him, because he had seen, coming across the canteen, Raoul Clermont, the editor of *La Révolte*, sweating in his Sunday suit. What the devil was the fat journalist doing in the hospital canteen?

'I need to have a word with you,' said Raoul without preamble. He was out of breath.

Jean-Pierre gestured to a chair. 'Raoul—'

'It's urgent,' Raoul cut in, almost as if he did not want the others to hear his name.

'Why don't you join us for lunch? Then we could talk at leisure.'

'I regret I cannot.'

Jean-Pierre heard a note of panic in the fat man's voice. Looking into his eyes, he saw that they were pleading with him to stop fooling around. Surprised, he stood up. 'Okay,' he said. To cover the suddenness of it all he said playfully to the others: 'Don't eat my lunch – I'll be back.' He took Raoul's arm and they walked out of the canteen.

Jean-Pierre had intended to stop and talk outside the door, but Raoul kept on walking along the corridor. 'Monsieur Leblond sent me,' he said.

'I was beginning to think he must be behind this,' said Jean-Pierre. It was a month ago that Raoul had taken him to meet Leblond, who had asked him to go to Afghanistan, ostensibly to help the rebels as many young French doctors did, but actually to spy for the Russians. Jean-Pierre had felt proud, apprehensive, and most of all thrilled at the opportunity to do something really spectacular for the cause. His only fear had been that the organisations which sent doctors to Afghanistan would turn him down because he was a communist. They had no way of knowing he was actually a Party member, and he certainly would not tell them – but they might know he was a communist sympathiser. However, there were plenty of French communists who were opposed to the invasion of Afghanistan. There was nevertheless a remote possibility that a cautious organisation might suggest that Jean-Pierre would be happier working for some other group of freedom fighters – they also sent people to help the rebels in El

Salvador, for example. In the end it had not happened: Jean-Pierre had been accepted immediately by *Médecins pour la Liberté*. He had told Raoul the good news, and Raoul had said there would be another meeting with Leblond. Perhaps this was to do with that. 'But why the panic?'

'He wants to see you now.'

'*Now?*' Jean-Pierre was annoyed. 'I'm on duty. I have patients—'

'Surely someone else will take care of them.'

'But what is the urgency? I don't leave for another two months.'

'It's not about Afghanistan.'

'Well, what *is* it about?'

'I don't know.'

Then what has frightened you? wondered Jean-Pierre. 'Have you no idea at all?'

'I know that Rahmi Coskun has been arrested.'

'The Turkish student?'

'Yes.'

'What for?'

'I don't know.'

'And what is it to do with me? I hardly know him.'

'Monsieur Leblond will explain.'

Jean-Pierre threw up his hands. 'I can't just walk out of here.'

'What would happen if you were taken ill?' said Raoul.

'I would tell the Nursing Officer, and she would call in a replacement. But—'

35

'So call her.' They had reached the entrance of the hospital, and there was a bank of internal phones on the wall.

This may be a test, thought Jean-Pierre; a loyalty test, to see whether I am serious enough to be given this mission. He decided to risk the wrath of the hospital authorities. He picked up the phone.

'I have been called away by a sudden family emergency,' he said when he got through. 'You must get in touch with Doctor Roche immediately.'

'Yes, Doctor,' the nurse replied calmly. 'I hope you have not received sad news.'

'I'll tell you later,' he said hastily. 'Goodbye. Oh – just a minute.' He had a postoperative patient who had been haemorrhaging during the night. 'How is Madame Ferier?'

'Fine. The bleeding has not recommenced.'

'Good. Keep a close watch on her.'

'Yes, Doctor.'

Jean-Pierre hung up. 'All right,' he said to Raoul. 'Let's go.'

They walked to the car park and got into Raoul's Renault 5. The inside of the car was hot from the midday sun. Raoul drove fast through back streets. Jean-Pierre felt nervous. He did not know *exactly* who Leblond was, but he assumed the man was *something* in the KGB. Jean-Pierre found himself wondering whether he had done anything to offend that much-feared organisation; and, if so, what the punishment might be.

Surely they could not have found out about Jane.

His asking her to go to Afghanistan with him was no

business of theirs. There were sure to be others in the party anyway, perhaps a nurse to help Jean-Pierre at his destination, perhaps other doctors headed for various parts of the country: why shouldn't Jane be among them? She was not a nurse, but she could take a crash course, and her great advantage was that she could speak some Farsi, the Persian language, a form of which was spoken in the area where Jean-Pierre was going.

He hoped she would go with him out of idealism and a sense of adventure. He hoped she would forget about Ellis while she was there, and would fall in love with the nearest European, who would of course be Jean-Pierre.

He had also hoped the Party would never know that he had encouraged her to go for his own reasons. There was no need for them to know, no way they would find out, normally – or so he had thought. Perhaps he had been wrong. Perhaps they were angry.

This is foolish, he told himself. I've done nothing wrong, really; and if I had there would be no punishment. This is the real KGB, not the mythical institution that strikes fear into the hearts of subscribers to the *Reader's Digest.*

Raoul parked the car. They had stopped outside an expensive apartment building in the rue de l'Université. It was the place where Jean-Pierre had met Leblond the last time. They left the car and went inside.

The lobby was gloomy. They climbed the curving staircase to the first floor and rang a bell. How much my life has changed, thought Jean-Pierre, since the last time I waited at this door!

Monsieur Leblond opened it. He was a short, slight, balding man with spectacles, and in his charcoal-grey suit and silver tie he looked like a butler. He led them to the room at the back of the building where Jean-Pierre had been interviewed. The tall windows and the elaborate mouldings indicated that it had once been an elegant drawing-room, but now it had a nylon carpet, a cheap office desk and some moulded-plastic chairs, orange in colour.

'Wait here for a moment,' said Leblond. His voice was quiet, clipped, and as dry as dust. A slight but unmistakable accent suggested that his name was not Leblond. He went out through a different door.

Jean-Pierre sat on one of the plastic chairs. Raoul remained standing. In this room, thought Jean-Pierre, that dry voice said to me *You have been a quietly loyal member of the Party since childhood. Your character and your family background suggest that you would serve the Party well in a covert role.*

I hope I haven't ruined everything because of Jane, he thought.

Leblond came back in with another man. The two of them stood in the doorway, and Leblond pointed at Jean-Pierre. The second man looked hard at Jean-Pierre, as if committing his face to memory. Jean-Pierre returned his gaze. The man was very big, with broad shoulders like a football player. His hair was long at the sides but thinning on top, and he had a droopy moustache. He wore a green corduroy jacket with a rip in the sleeve. After a few seconds he nodded and went out.

Leblond closed the door behind him and sat behind the desk. 'There has been a disaster,' he said.

It's not about Jane, thought Jean-Pierre. Thank God.

Leblond said: 'There is a CIA agent among your circle of friends.'

'My God!' said Jean-Pierre.

'That is not the disaster,' Leblond said irritably. 'It is hardly surprising that there should be an American spy among your friends. No doubt there are Israeli and South African and French spies too. What would these people have to do if they did not infiltrate groups of young political activists? And we also have one, of course.'

'Who?'

'You.'

'Oh!' Jean-Pierre was taken aback: he had not thought of himself as a *spy*, exactly. But what else did it mean to *serve the Party in a covert role*? 'Who is the CIA agent?' he asked, intensely curious.

'Someone called Ellis Thaler.'

Jean-Pierre was so shocked that he stood up. '*Ellis?*'

'You *do* know him. Good.'

'Ellis is a CIA spy?'

'Sit down,' Leblond said levelly. 'Our problem is not who he is, but what he has done.'

Jean-Pierre was thinking: If Jane finds out about this she will drop Ellis like a hot brick. Will they let me tell her? If not, will she find out some other way? Will she believe it? Will Ellis deny it?

Leblond was speaking. Jean-Pierre forced himself to concentrate on what was being said. 'The disaster is that Ellis set a trap, and in it he has caught someone rather important to us.'

Jean-Pierre remembered Raoul saying that Rahmi Coskun had been arrested. 'Rahmi is important to us?'

'Not Rahmi.'

'Who, then?'

'You don't need to know.'

'Then why have you brought me here?'

'Shut up and listen,' Leblond snapped, and for the first time Jean-Pierre was afraid of him. 'I have never met your friend Ellis, of course. Unhappily, Raoul has not either. Therefore neither of us knows what he looks like. But you do. That is why I have brought you here. Do you also know where Ellis lives?'

'Yes. He has a room above a restaurant in the rue de l'Ancienne Comédie.'

'Does the room overlook the street?'

Jean-Pierre frowned. He had been there only once: Ellis did not invite people home much. 'I think it does.'

'You're not sure?'

'Let me think.' He had gone there late one night, with Jane and a bunch of other people, after a film show at the Sorbonne. Ellis had given them coffee. It was a small room. Jane had sat on the floor by the window . . . 'Yes. The window faces the street. Why is it important?'

'It means you can signal.'

'Me? Why? To whom?'

Leblond shot a dangerous look at him.

'Sorry,' said Jean-Pierre.

Leblond hesitated. When he spoke again, his voice

was just a shade softer, although his expression remained blank. 'You're suffering a baptism of fire. I regret having to use you in an . . . *action* . . . such as this when you have never done anything for us before. But you know Ellis, and you are here, and right now we don't have anybody else who knows him; and what we want to do will lose its impact if it is not done immediately. So. Listen carefully, for this is important. You are to go to his room. If he is there, you will go inside – think of some pretext. Go to the window, lean out, and make sure you are seen by Raoul, who will be waiting in the street.'

Raoul fidgeted like a dog that hears people mention its name in conversation.

Jean-Pierre asked: 'And if Ellis is not there?'

'Speak to his neighbours. Try to find out where he has gone and when he will be back. If it seems he has left only for a few minutes, or even an hour or so, wait for him. When he returns, proceed as before: go inside, go to the window, and make sure you are seen by Raoul. Your appearance at the window is the sign that Ellis is inside – so, whatever you do, don't go to the window if he is not there. Have you understood?'

'I know what you want me to do,' said Jean-Pierre. 'I don't understand the purpose of all this.'

'To identify Ellis.'

'And when I have identified him?'

Leblond gave the answer Jean-Pierre had hardly dared to hope for, and it thrilled him to the core: 'We are going to kill him, of course.'

CHAPTER THREE

J ANE SPREAD a patched white cloth on Ellis's tiny
table and laid two places with an assortment of
battered cutlery. She found a bottle of Fleurie in
the cupboard under the sink, and opened it. She was
tempted to taste it, then decided to wait for Ellis. She
put out glasses, salt and pepper, mustard, and paper
napkins. She wondered whether to start cooking. No, it
was better to leave it to him.

She did not like Ellis's room. It was bare, cramped
and impersonal. She had been quite shocked when she
first saw it. She had been dating this warm, relaxed,
mature man, and she expected him to live in a place
that expressed his personality, an attractive, comfortable apartment containing mementoes of a past rich in
experience. But you would never guess that the man
who lived here had been married, had fought in a war,
had taken LSD, had captained his school football team.
The cold white walls were decorated with a few hastily-
chosen posters. The china came from junk shops and
the cooking pots were cheap tinware. There were no
inscriptions in the paperback volumes of poetry on the
bookshelf. He kept his jeans and sweaters in a plastic
suitcase under the creaky bed. Where were his old

school reports, the photographs of his nephews and nieces, his treasured copy of *Heartbreak Hotel*, his souvenir penknife from Boulogne or Niagara Falls, the teak salad bowl everybody gets from their parents sooner or later? The room contained nothing really important, none of those things one keeps not for what they are but for what they represent, no part of his soul.

It was the room of a withdrawn man, a secretive man, a man who would never share his innermost thoughts with anyone. Gradually, and with terrible sadness, Jane had come to realise that Ellis *was* like that, like his room, cold and secretive.

It was incredible. He was such a self-confident man. He walked with his head high, as if he had never been afraid of anyone in his life. In bed he was utterly uninhibited, totally at ease with his sexuality. He would do anything and say anything, without anxiety or hesitation or shame. Jane had never known a man like this. But there had been too many times – in bed, or in restaurants, or just walking on the street – when she had been laughing with him, or listening to him talk, or watching the skin around his eyes crinkle as he thought hard, or hugging his warm body, only to find that he had suddenly turned off. In those switched-off moods he was no longer loving, no longer amusing, no longer thoughtful or considerate or gentlemanly or compassionate. He made her feel excluded, a stranger, an intruder into his private world. It was like the sun going behind a cloud.

She knew she was going to have to leave him. She loved him to distraction, but it seemed he could not love her the same way. He was thirty-three years old, and if he had not learned the art of intimacy by now he never would.

She sat on the sofa and began to read *The Observer*, which she had bought from an international newsstand in the Boulevard Raspail on her way over. There was a report from Afghanistan on the front page. It sounded like a good place to go to forget Ellis.

The idea had appealed to her immediately. Although she loved Paris, and her job was at least varied, she wanted more: experience, adventure, and a chance to strike a blow for freedom. She was not afraid. Jean-Pierre said the doctors were considered too valuable to be sent into the combat zone. There was a risk of being hit by a stray bomb or caught in a skirmish, but it was probably no worse than the danger of being run down by a Parisian motorist. She was intensely curious about the lifestyle of the Afghan rebels. 'What do they eat there?' she had asked Jean-Pierre. 'What do they wear? Do they live in tents? Do they have toilets?'

'No toilets,' he had replied. 'No electricity. No roads. No wine. No cars. No central heating. No dentists. No postmen. No phones. No restaurants. No advertisements. No Coca-Cola. No weather forecasts, no stock market reports, no decorators, no social workers, no lipstick, no tampax, no fashions, no dinner parties, no taxi ranks, no bus queues—'

'Stop!' she had interrupted him: he could go on like that for hours. 'They must have buses and taxis.'

'Not in the countryside. I'm going to a region called Five Lions Valley, a rebel stronghold in the foothills of the Himalayas. It was primitive even before the Russians bombed it.'

Jane was quite sure she could live happily without plumbing or lipstick or weather forecasts. She suspected he was underestimating the danger, even outside the combat zone; but somehow that did not deter her. Her mother would have hysterics, of course. Her father, if he were still alive, would have said: 'Good luck, Janey.' He had understood the importance of doing something *worthwhile* with one's life. Although he had been a good doctor, he had never made any money, because wherever they lived – Nassau, Cairo, Singapore, but mostly Rhodesia – he would always treat poor people free, so they had come to him in crowds, and had driven away the fee-paying customers.

Her reverie was disturbed by a footfall on the stair. She had not read more than a few lines of the newspaper, she realised. She cocked her head, listening. It did not sound like Ellis's step. Nevertheless there was a tap at the door.

Jane put down her paper and opened the door. There stood Jean-Pierre. He was almost as surprised as she was. They stared at one another in silence for a moment. Jane said: 'You look guilty. Do I?'

'Yes,' he said, and he grinned.

'I was just thinking about you. Come in.'

He stepped inside and glanced around. 'Ellis not here?'

'I'm expecting him soon. Have a seat.'

Jean-Pierre lowered his long body into the sofa. Jane thought, not for the first time, that he was probably the most beautiful man she had ever met. His face was perfectly regular, with high forehead, a strong, rather aristocratic nose, liquid brown eyes, and a sensual mouth partly hidden by a full, dark-brown beard with stray flashes of auburn in the moustache. His clothes were cheap but carefully chosen, and he wore them with a nonchalant elegance that Jane herself envied.

She liked him a lot. His great fault was that he thought too well of himself; but in this he was so naive as to be disarming, like a boastful child. She liked his idealism and his dedication to medicine. He had enormous charm. He also had a manic imagination which could sometimes be very funny: sparked by some absurdity, perhaps just a slip of the tongue, he would launch into a fanciful monologue which could go on for ten or fifteen minutes. When someone had quoted a remark made by Jean-Paul Sartre about soccer, Jean-Pierre had spontaneously given a commentary on a football match as it might have been described by an existentialist philosopher. Jane had laughed until it hurt. People said that his gaiety had its reverse side, in moods of black depression, but Jane had never seen any evidence of that.

'Have some of Ellis's wine,' she said, picking up the bottle from the table.

'No, thanks.'

'Are you rehearsing for life in a Muslim country?'

'Not especially.'

He was looking very solemn. 'What's the matter?' she asked.

'I need to have a serious talk with you,' he said.

'We had it, three days ago, don't you remember?'
she said flippantly. 'You asked me to leave my boyfriend
and go to Afghanistan with you – an offer few girls
could resist.'

'Be serious.'

'All right. I still haven't made up my mind.'

'Jane. I've discovered something terrible about Ellis.'

She looked at him speculatively. What was coming?
Would he invent a story, tell a lie, in order to persuade
her to go with him? She thought not. 'Okay, what?'

'He's not what he pretends to be,' said Jean-Pierre.

He was being terribly melodramatic. 'There's no
need to speak in a voice like an undertaker. What do
you mean?'

'He's not a penniless poet. He works for the American government.'

Jane frowned. 'For the American government?' Her
first thought was that Jean-Pierre had got the wrong
end of the stick. 'He gives English lessons to some
French people who work for the US government—'

'I don't mean that. He spies on radical groups. He's
an agent. He works for the CIA.'

Jane burst out laughing. 'You're absurd! Did you
think you could make me leave him by telling me that?'

'It's true, Jane.'

'It's not true. Ellis couldn't be a spy. Don't you think
I'd know? I've been practically living with him for a
year.'

'But you haven't, though, have you?'

'It makes no difference. I *know* him.' Even while she
spoke Jane was thinking: it could explain a lot. She did

not *really* know Ellis. But she knew him well enough to be sure that he was not base, mean, treacherous and just plain *evil.*

'It's all over town,' Jean-Pierre was saying. 'Rahmi Coskun was arrested this morning and everyone says Ellis was responsible.'

'Why was Rahmi arrested?'

Jean-Pierre shrugged. 'Subversion, no doubt. Anyway, Raoul Clermont is running around town trying to find Ellis and *somebody* wants revenge.'

'Oh, Jean-Pierre, it's laughable,' said Jane. She suddenly felt very warm. She went to the window and threw it open. As she glanced down to the street she saw Ellis's blond head ducking into the front door. 'Well,' she said to Jean-Pierre, 'here he comes. Now you're going to have to repeat this ludicrous story in front of him.' She heard Ellis's step on the stairs.

'I intend to,' said Jean-Pierre. 'Why do you think I am here? I came to warn him that they're after him.'

Jane realised that Jean-Pierre was actually sincere: he really believed this story. Well, Ellis would soon set him straight.

The door opened and Ellis walked in.

He looked very happy, as if he were bursting with good news, and when she saw his round, smiling face with its broken nose and penetrating blue eyes, Jane's heart leapt with guilt to think she had been flirting with Jean-Pierre.

Ellis stopped in the doorway, surprised to see Jean-Pierre. His smile faded a little. 'Hello, you two,' he said.

He closed the door behind him and locked it, as was his habit. Jane had always thought that an eccentricity but now it occurred to her that it was what a spy would do. She pushed the thought out of her mind.

Jean-Pierre spoke first. 'They're on to you, Ellis. They know. They're coming after you.'

Jane looked from one to the other. Jean-Pierre was taller than Ellis, but Ellis was broad-shouldered and deep-chested. They stood looking at one another like two cats sizing each other up.

Jane put her arms around Ellis, kissed him guiltily, and said: 'Jean-Pierre has been told some absurd story about you being a CIA spy.'

Jean-Pierre was leaning out of the window, scanning the street below. Now he turned back to face them. 'Tell her, Ellis.'

'Where did you get this idea?' Ellis asked him.

'It's all around town.'

'And who, exactly, did *you* hear it from?' asked Ellis in a steely voice.

'Raoul Clermont.'

Ellis nodded. Switching into English, he said: 'Jane, would you sit down?'

'I don't want to sit down,' she said irritably.

'I have something to tell you,' he said.

It couldn't be true, it *couldn't*. Jane felt panic rise in her throat. 'Then tell me,' she said, 'and stop asking me to sit down!'

Ellis glanced at Jean-Pierre. 'Would you leave us?' he said in French.

Jane began to feel angry. 'What are you going to tell me? Why won't you simply say that Jean-Pierre is wrong? Tell me you're not a spy, Ellis, before I go crazy!'

'It's not that simple,' said Ellis.

'It is simple!' She could no longer keep the hysterical note out of her voice. 'He says that you're a spy, that you work for the American government, and that you've been lying to me, continuously and shamelessly and treacherously, ever since I met you. Is that true? Is that true or not? Well?'

Ellis sighed. 'I guess it's true.'

Jane felt she would explode. 'You bastard!' she screamed. 'You fucking bastard!'

Ellis's face was set like stone. 'I was going to tell you today,' he said.

There was a knock at the door. They both ignored it. 'You've been spying on me and all my friends!' Jane yelled. 'I feel so *ashamed.*'

'My work here is finished,' Ellis said. 'I don't need to lie to you any more.'

'You won't get the chance. I never want to see you again.'

The knocking came again, and Jean-Pierre said in French: 'There's someone at the door.'

Ellis said: 'You don't mean that – that you don't want to see me again.'

'You just don't understand what you've done to me, do you?' she said.

Jean-Pierre said: 'Open the damn door, for God's sake!'

Jane muttered: 'Jesus *Christ*,' and stepped to the

door. She unlocked it and opened it. There stood a big, broad-shouldered man in a green corduroy jacket with a rip in the sleeve. Jane had never seen him before. She said: 'What the hell do you want?' Then she saw that he had a gun in his hand.

The next few seconds seemed to pass very slowly.

Jane realised, in a flash, that if Jean-Pierre had been right about Ellis being a spy then probably he was also right about somebody wanting revenge; and that in the world Ellis secretly inhabited, 'revenge' really could mean a knock at the door and a man with a gun.

She opened her mouth to scream.

The man hesitated for a fraction of a second. He looked surprised, as if he had not expected to see a woman. His eyes went from Jane to Jean-Pierre and back: he knew that Jean-Pierre was not his target. But he was confused because he could not see Ellis, who was hidden by the half-open door.

Instead of screaming, Jane tried to slam the door.

As she swung it towards the gunman, he saw what she was doing and stuck his foot in the way. The door hit his shoe and bounced back. But in the act of stepping forward he had spread his arms, for balance, and now his gun was pointing up into the corner of the ceiling.

He's going to kill Ellis, Jane thought. He's going to kill Ellis.

She threw herself at the gunman, beating his face with her fists, for suddenly, although she hated Ellis, she did not want him to die.

The man was distracted only for a fraction of a

second. With one strong arm he hurled Jane aside. She fell heavily, landing in a sitting position, bruising the base of her spine.

She saw what happened next with terrible clarity.

The arm that had shoved her aside came back and flung the door wide. As the man swung his gun hand around, Ellis came at him with the bottle of wine raised high above his head. The gun went off as the bottle came down, and the shot coincided with the sound of glass breaking.

Jane stared, horrified, at the two men.

Then the gunman slumped, and Ellis remained standing, and she realised that the shot had missed.

Ellis bent down and snatched the gun from the man's hand.

Jane got to her feet with an effort.

'Are you all right?' Ellis asked her.

'Alive,' she said.

He turned to Jean-Pierre. 'How many on the street?'

Jean-Pierre glanced out of the window. 'None.'

Ellis looked surprised. 'They must be concealed.' He pocketed the gun and went to his bookcase. 'Stand back,' he said, and hurled it to the floor.

Behind it was a door.

Ellis opened the door.

He looked at Jane for a long moment, as if he had something to say but could not find the words. Then he stepped through the door and was gone.

After a moment, Jane walked slowly over to the secret door and looked through. There was another studio flat, sparsely furnished and dreadfully dusty, as if it had not been occupied for a year. There was an open door and, beyond it, a staircase.

She turned back and looked into Ellis's room. The gunman lay on the floor, out cold in a puddle of wine. He had tried to kill Ellis, right here in this room: already it seemed unreal. It all seemed unreal: Ellis being a spy; Jean-Pierre knowing about it; Rahmi being arrested; and Ellis's escape route.

He had gone. *I never want to see you again,* she had said to him just a few seconds ago. It seemed that her wish would be granted.

She heard footsteps on the stair.

She raised her gaze from the gunman and looked at Jean-Pierre. He, too, seemed stunned. After a moment he crossed the room to her and put his arms around her. She slumped on his shoulder and burst into tears.

Part Two
1982

Part Two

1987

CHAPTER FOUR

THE RIVER came down from the ice line, cold and clear and always in a rush, and it filled the Valley with its noise as it boiled through the ravines and flashed past the wheat fields in a headlong dash for the faraway lowlands. For almost a year that sound had been constantly in Jane's ears: sometimes loud, when she went to bathe or when she took the winding cliffside paths between villages; and sometimes soft, as now, when she was high on the hillside and the Five Lions River was just a glint and a murmur in the distance. When eventually she left the Valley she would find the silence unnerving, she thought, like city dwellers on holiday in the countryside who cannot sleep because it is too quiet. Listening, she heard something else, and she realised that the sound had made her aware of the old. Swelling over the river's chorus came the baritone of a propeller-driven aircraft.

Jane opened her eyes. It was an Antonov, the predatory slow-moving reconnaissance plane whose incessant growl was the usual herald of faster, noisier jet aircraft on a bombing run. She sat up and looked anxiously across the Valley.

She was in her secret refuge, a broad, flat shelf half

way up a cliff. Above her, the overhang hid her from view without blocking the sun, and would dissuade anyone but a mountaineer from climbing down. Below, the approach to her refuge was steep and stony and bare of vegetation: no one could climb it without being heard and seen by Jane. There was no reason for anyone to come here, anyway. Jane had only found the place by wandering from the path and getting lost. The privacy of the place was important because she came here to take off her clothes and lie in the sun, and the Afghans were as modest as nuns: if she were seen naked she would be lynched.

To her right the dusty hillside fell away rapidly. Towards its foot, where the slope began to level out near the river, was the village of Banda, fifty or sixty houses clinging to a patch of uneven, rocky ground that no one could farm. The houses were made of grey stones and mud bricks, and each one had a flat roof of pressed earth laid over mats. Next to the little mosque was a small group of wretched houses: one of the Russian bombers had scored a direct hit a couple of months back. Jane could see the village clearly, although it was a twenty-minute scramble away. She scanned the roofs and walled courtyards and mud footpaths, looking for stray children, but happily there were none – Banda was deserted under the hot blue sky.

To her left, the Valley broadened out. The small stony fields were dotted with bomb craters, and, on the lower slopes of the mountainside, several of the ancient terrace walls had collapsed. The wheat was ripe, but no one was reaping.

Beyond the fields, at the foot of the cliff wall that formed the far side of the Valley, ran the Five Lions River: deep in places, shallow in others; now broad, now narrow; always fast and always rocky. Jane scrutinized its length. There were no women bathing or washing clothes, no children playing in the shallows, no men leading horses or donkeys across the ford.

Jane contemplated throwing on her clothes and leaving her refuge to climb farther up the mountainside to the caves. That was where the villagers were, the men sleeping after a night working in their fields, the women cooking and trying to stop the children wandering, the cows penned and the goats tethered and the dogs fighting over scraps. She was probably quite safe here, for the Russians bombed the villages, not the bare hillsides; but there was always the chance of a stray bomb, and a cave would protect her from everything but a direct hit.

Before she had made up her mind she heard the roar of the jets. She squinted into the sun to look at them. Their noise filled the Valley, swamping the rush of the river, as they passed over her, heading northeast, high but descending, one, two, three, four silver killers, the summit of mankind's ingenuity deployed to maim illiterate farmers and knock down mud-brick houses and return to base at seven hundred miles per hour.

In a minute they were gone. Banda was to be spared, for today. Slowly, Jane relaxed. The jets terrified her. Banda had escaped bombing completely last summer, and the whole of the Valley got a respite during the winter; but it had started again in earnest this spring, and Banda had been hit several times, once in the centre of the village. Since then Jane had hated the jets.

The courage of the villagers was amazing. Each family had made a second home up there in the caves, and they climbed the hill every morning to spend the day there, returning at dusk, for there was no bombing at night. Since it was unsafe to work in the fields by day, the men did it at night – or rather, the older ones did, for the young men were away most of the time, shooting at Russians down at the southern end of the Valley or farther afield. This summer the bombing was more intensive than ever in *all* the rebel areas, according to what Jean-Pierre heard from the guerrillas. If Afghans in other parts of the country were like these here in the Valley, they were able to adapt and survive: salvaging a few precious possessions from the rubble of a bombed house, tirelessly replanting a ruined vegetable garden, nursing the wounded and burying the dead and sending ever-younger teenage boys to join the guerrilla leaders. The Russians could never defeat these people, Jane felt, unless they turned the whole country into a radioactive desert.

As to whether the rebels could ever defeat the Russians – that was another question. They were brave and irrepressible, and they controlled the countryside, but rival tribes hated one another almost as much as they hated the invaders, and their rifles were useless against jet bombers and armoured helicopters.

She pushed thoughts of war out of her mind. This

was the heat of the day, the siesta time, when she liked to be alone and relax. She put her hand into a goatskin bag of clarified butter and began to oil the taut skin of her enormous belly, wondering how she could possibly have been so foolish as to get pregnant in Afghanistan.

She had arrived with a two-years' supply of contraceptive pills, a diaphragm, and a whole carton of spermicidal jelly; and yet, just a few weeks later, she had forgotten to re-start the pills after her period and then forgotten to put in the diaphragm – several times. 'How could you make such a mistake?' Jean-Pierre had yelled, and she had had no answer.

But now, lying in the sun, cheerfully pregnant with lovely swollen breasts and a permanent backache, she could see that it had been a deliberate mistake, a kind of professional foul perpetrated by her unconscious mind. She had wanted a baby, and she knew Jean-Pierre did not, so she had started one by accident.

Why did I want a baby so badly? she asked herself, and the answer came to her out of nowhere: because I was lonely.

'Is that true?' she said aloud. It would be ironic. She had never felt lonely in Paris, living on her own and shopping for one and talking to herself in the mirror; but when she was married, and spent every evening and every night with her husband and worked alongside him most of every day, then she felt isolated, frightened and alone.

They had married in Paris just before coming here. It had seemed a natural part of the adventure, somehow: another challenge, another risk, another thrill.

Everyone had said how happy and beautiful and brave and in love they were, and it had been true.

No doubt she had expected too much. She had looked forward to ever-growing love and intimacy with Jean-Pierre. She had thought she would learn about his childhood sweetheart and what he was *really* frightened of and whether it was true that men shook the drops off after peeing; and in turn she would tell him that her father had been an alcoholic and that she had a fantasy about being raped by a black man and that she sometimes sucked her thumb when she was anxious. But Jean-Pierre seemed to think their relationship after marriage should be just what it had been before. He treated her courteously, made her laugh in his manic moods, fell helpless into her arms when he was depressed, discussed politics and the war, made love to her expertly once a week with his lean young body and his strong, sensitive surgeon's hands, and behaved in every way like a boyfriend rather than a husband. She still felt unable to talk to him about silly, embarrassing things such as whether a hat made her nose look longer and how angry she still was about having been spanked for spilling red ink on the drawing-room rug when in fact her sister Pauline had done it. She wanted to ask someone *Is this how it's supposed to be, or will it get better?* but her friends and family were all far away and the Afghan women would have found her expectations outrageous. She had resisted the temptation to confront Jean-Pierre with her disappointment, partly because her complaint was so vague, and partly because she was frightened of what his answer might be.

Looking back, she could see that the idea of a baby had been creeping up on her even earlier, when she was seeing Ellis Thaler. That year she had flown from Paris to London for the christening of her sister Pauline's third child, something she would not normally have done, for she disliked formal family occasions. She had also started babysitting for a couple in her building, a hysterical antique dealer and his aristocratic wife, and she had enjoyed it most when the baby had cried and she had had to pick him up and comfort him.

And then, here in the Valley, where her duty was to encourage the women to space out their babies for the sake of healthier children, she had found herself sharing the joy with which each new pregnancy was greeted even in the poorest and most overcrowded households. Thus loneliness and the maternal instinct had conspired against common sense.

Had there been a time – even just a fleeting instant – when she realised that her unconscious mind was trying to get her pregnant? Had she thought *I might have a baby* at the moment when Jean-Pierre penetrated her, gliding in slowly and gracefully like a ship into a dock, while she tightened her arms about his body; or in the second of hesitation, immediately before his climax, when he shut his eyes tightly and seemed to retreat from her deep into himself, a spaceship falling into the heart of the sun; or afterwards, as she was drifting blissfully into sleep with his seed hot inside her? 'Did I realise?' she said aloud; but thinking about making love had turned her on, and she began to caress herself luxuriously with her butter-slippery hands, forgetting the question and letting her mind fill with vague swirling images of passion.

The scream of jets jerked her back to the real world. She stared, frightened, as another four bombers streaked up the Valley and disappeared. When the noise died away she started to touch herself again, but her mood had been spoiled. She lay still in the sun and thought about her baby.

Jean-Pierre had reacted to her pregnancy as if it had been premeditated. So furious had he been that he had wanted to perform an abortion himself, immediately. Jane had found that wish of his dreadfully macabre, and he had suddenly seemed a stranger. But hardest to bear was the feeling of having been rejected. The thought that her husband did not want her baby had made her utterly desolate. He had made matters worse by refusing to touch her. She had never been so miserable in her life. For the first time she understood why people sometimes kill themselves. The withdrawal of physical contact was the worst torture of all – she genuinely wished Jean-Pierre would beat her instead, so badly did she need to be touched. When she remembered those days she still felt angry with him, even though she knew she had brought it on herself.

Then, one morning, he had put his arm around her and apologised for his behaviour; and although part of her had wanted to say 'Being *sorry* isn't enough, you bastard,' the rest of her was desperate for his love, and she had forgiven him immediately. He had explained that he was already afraid of losing her; and that if she were to be the mother of his son he would be absolutely terrified, for then he would lose them both. This confession had moved her to tears, and she had realised that in getting pregnant she had made the ultimate commitment to Jean-Pierre, and she made up her mind that she would make this marriage work, come what may.

He had been warmer to her after that. He had taken an interest in the growing baby, and had become anxious about Jane's health and safety, the way expectant fathers were supposed to. Their marriage would be an imperfect but happy union, Jane thought, and she envisaged an ideal future, with Jean-Pierre as the French Minister of Health in a Socialist administration, herself a Member of the European Parliament, and three brilliant children, one at the Sorbonne, one at the London School of Economics, and one at the New York School for the Performing Arts.

In this fantasy, the eldest and most brilliant child was a girl. Jane touched her tummy, pressing gently with her fingertips, feeling the shape of the baby: according to Rabia Gul, the old village midwife, it would be a girl, for it could be felt on the left side, whereas boys grew on the right side. Rabia had accordingly prescribed a diet of vegetables. For a boy she would have recommended plenty of meat. In Afghanistan the males were better fed even before they were born.

Jane's thoughts were interrupted by a loud bang. For a moment she was confused, associating the explosion with the jets which had passed overhead several minutes before on their way to bomb some other village; then she heard, quite close by, the high continuous scream of a child in pain and panicking.

She realised instantly what had happened. The Russians, using tactics they had learned from the Americans in Vietnam, had littered the countryside with anti-personnel mines. Their ostensible aim was to block guerrilla supply lines; but since the 'guerrilla supply lines' were the mountain pathways used daily by old men, women, children and animals, the real purpose was straightforward terror. That scream meant a child had detonated a mine.

Jane jumped to her feet. The sound seemed to be coming from somewhere near the mullah's house, which was about half a mile outside the village on the hillside footpath. Jane could just see it, away to her left and a little lower down. She stepped into her shoes, grabbed her clothes, and ran that way. The first long scream ended and became a series of short, terrified yells: it sounded to Jane as if the child had seen the damage the mine had done to its body and was screaming with fright now. Rushing through the coarse undergrowth, Jane realised that she herself was panicking, so peremptory was the summons of a child in distress. 'Calm down,' she said breathlessly to herself. If she were to fall badly there would be two people in trouble and no one to help; and anyway the worst thing for a frightened child was a frightened adult.

She was near now. The child would be hidden in the bushes, not on the footpath, for all the paths were cleared by the menfolk each time they were mined, but it was impossible to sweep the entire mountainside.

She stopped, listening. Her panting was so loud that she had to hold her breath. The screams were coming from a clump of camelgrass and juniper bushes. She pushed through the shrubbery and glimpsed part of a bright blue coat. The child must be Mousa, the nine-year-old son of Mohammed Khan, one of the leading guerrillas. A moment later she was beside him.

He was kneeling on the dusty ground. He had evidently tried to pick up the mine, for it had blown off his hand, and now he was staring wild-eyed at the bloody stump and screaming in terror.

Jane had seen a lot of wounds in the past year but still this one moved her to pity. 'Oh, dear God,' she said. 'You poor child.' She knelt in front of him, hugged him, and murmured soothing noises. After a minute he stopped screaming. She hoped he would begin to cry instead, but he was too shocked, and lapsed into silence. As she held him she searched for and found the pressure point in his armpit, and stopped the gush of blood.

She was going to need his help. She must make him speak. 'Mousa, what was it?' she said in Dari.

He made no reply. She asked him again.

'I thought . . .' His eyes opened wide as he remembered, and his voice rose to a scream as he said: 'I thought it was A BALL!'

'Hush, hush,' she murmured. 'Tell me what you did.'

'I PICKED IT UP! I PICKED IT UP!'

She held him tight, soothing him. 'And what happened?'

His voice was shaky but no longer hysterical. 'It went bang,' he said. He was rapidly becoming calmer.

She took his right hand and put it under his left arm. 'Press where I'm pressing,' she said. She guided his fingertips to the point then withdrew her own. The blood started to flow from the wound again. 'Push hard,' she told him. He did as she said. The flow stopped. She kissed his forehead. It was damp and cold.

She had dropped her bundle of clothing on the ground beside Mousa. Her clothes were what the Afghan women wore: a sack-shaped dress over cotton trousers. She picked up the dress and tore the thin material into several strips, then began to make a tourniquet. Mousa watched her, wide-eyed and silent. She snapped a dry twig from a juniper bush and used it to finish the tourniquet.

Now he needed a dressing, a sedative, an antibiotic to prevent infection, and his mother to prevent trauma.

Jane pulled on her trousers and tied the drawstring. She wished she had been less hasty about tearing up her dress, for she might have preserved enough of it to cover her upper half. Now she would just have to hope she did not meet any men on the way to the caves.

And how would she get Mousa there? She did not want to try to make him walk. She could not carry him on her back, for he could not hold on. She sighed: she would just have to take him in her arms. She crouched down, put one arm around his shoulders and the other under his thighs, and picked him up, lifting with her knees rather than with her back, the way she had learned at her feminist fitness class. Cradling the child to her bosom with his back lying on the rise of her belly, she began to walk slowly up the hill. She could manage it only because he was half starved: a nine-year-old European child would have been too heavy.

She soon emerged from the bushes and found the footpath. But after forty or fifty yards she became exhausted. In the last few weeks she had found herself tiring very quickly, and it infuriated her, but she had learned not to fight it. She set Mousa down and stood with him, hugging him gently, while she rested, leaning against the cliff wall that ran along one side of the mountain path. He had lapsed into a frozen silence which she found more worrying than his screams. As soon as she felt better she picked him up and started again.

She was resting near the top of the hill, fifteen minutes later, when a man appeared on the path ahead. Jane recognised him. 'Oh, no,' she said in English. 'Of all people – Abdullah.'

He was a short man of about fifty-five and he was rather tubby despite the local shortage of food. With his tan turban and billowing black trousers he wore an Argyle sweater and a blue double-breasted pin-striped jacket that looked as if it had once been worn by a London stockbroker. His luxuriant beard was red: he was Banda's mullah.

Abdullah mistrusted foreigners, despised women,

and hated all practitioners of foreign medicine. Jane, being all three, had never had the chance of winning his affection. To make matters worse, many people in the Valley had realised that taking Jane's antibiotics was a more effective treatment for infections than inhaling the smoke from a burning slip of paper on which Abdullah had written with saffron ink, and consequently the mullah was losing money. His reaction was to refer to Jane as 'the Western whore', but it was difficult for him to do more, for she and Jean-Pierre were under the protection of Ahmed Shah Masud, the guerrilla leader, and even a mullah hesitated to cross swords with such a great hero.

When he saw her he stopped dead in his tracks, an expression of utter incredulity transforming his normally solemn face into a comic mask. He was the worst possible person to meet. Any other of the village men would have been embarrassed, and perhaps offended, to see her half-naked; but Abdullah would be enraged.

Jane decided to brazen it out. She said in Dari: 'Peace be with you.' This was the beginning of a formal exchange of greetings which could sometimes go on for several minutes. But Abdullah did not respond with the usual *And with you.* Instead, he opened his mouth and began in a high pitched shout to abuse her with a stream of imprecations which included the Dari words for *prostitute, pervert* and *seducer of children.* His face empurpled with fury, he walked towards her and raised his stick.

This was going too far. She pointed at Mousa, who stood silent by her side, dazed by pain and weak from loss of blood. 'Look!' she yelled at Abdullah. 'Can't you see—'

But he was blinded by rage. Before she could finish what she was trying to say he brought down his stick on her head with a whack. Jane cried out with pain and anger: she was surprised at how *much* it hurt and *furious* that he should do this.

He still had not noticed Mousa's wound. The mullah's staring eyes were focused on Jane's chest, and she realised, in a flash, that for him to see, in broad daylight, the naked breasts of a pregnant white Western woman was a sight so overloaded with different kinds of sexual anxiety that he was bound to blow his top. He was not planning to chastise her with a blow or two, as he might chastise his wife for disobedience. There was murder in his heart.

Suddenly Jane was very frightened – for herself, for Mousa, and for her unborn child. She stumbled backwards, out of range, but he stepped towards her and raised his stick again. Suddenly inspired, she leaped at him and poked her fingers into his eyes.

He roared like a wounded bull. He was not hurt, so much as indignant that a woman he was beating should have the temerity to fight back. While he was blinded, Jane grabbed his beard with both hands and tugged. He stumbled forward, and tripped, and fell. He rolled a couple of yards downhill and came to rest in a dwarf willow bush.

Jane thought: Oh, God, what have I done?

Looking at the pompous, malevolent priest in his humiliation, Jane knew he would never forget what she had done. He might complain to the 'whitebeards' – the village elders. He might go to Masud and demand that the foreign doctors be sent home. He might even try to inflame the menfolk of Banda into stoning Jane. But almost as soon as she had had this thought, it struck her that, in order to make any kind of complaint, he would have to tell his story in all its ignominious details, and the villagers would ridicule him for ever afterwards – the Afghans were nothing if not cruel. So perhaps she would get away with it.

She turned around. She had something more important to worry about. Mousa was standing where she had set him down, silent and expressionless, too shocked to understand what had been going on. Jane took a deep breath, picked him up, and walked on.

She reached the crest of the hill after a few paces, and she was able to walk faster as the ground levelled out. She crossed the stony plateau. She was tired and her back hurt but she was almost there: the caves were just below the brow of the mountain. She reached the far side of the ridge and heard children's voices as she began to descend. A moment later she saw a group of six-year-olds playing Heaven-and-Hell, a game which involved holding your toes while two other children carried you to Heaven – if you succeeded in keeping hold of your toes – or Hell, usually a rubbish dump or a latrine, if you let go. She realised that Mousa would never play that game again, and she was suddenly overwhelmed by a sense of tragedy. The children noticed her then, and as she passed them they stopped playing and stared. One of them whispered: 'Mousa.'

Another repeated the name, then the spell was broken and they all ran ahead of Jane, shouting the news.

The daytime hideout of the villagers of Banda looked like the desert encampment of a tribe of nomads: the dusty ground, the blazing midday sun, the remains of cooking fires, the hooded women, the dirty children. Jane crossed the small square of level ground in front of the caves. The women were already converging on the largest cave, which Jane and Jean-Pierre had made their clinic. Jean-Pierre heard the commotion and came out. Gratefully, Jane handed Mousa to him, saying in French: 'It was a mine. He's lost his hand. Give me your shirt.'

Jean-Pierre took Mousa inside and laid him down on the rug which served as an examination table. Before attending to the child he stripped off his bleached-khaki shirt and gave it to Jane. She put it on.

She felt a little light-headed. She thought she would sit down and rest in the cool rear of the cave, but after taking a couple of steps in that direction she changed her mind and sat down immediately. Jean-Pierre said: 'Get me some swabs.' She ignored him. Mousa's mother, Halima, came running into the cave and began screaming when she saw her son. I should calm her, Jane thought, so that she can comfort the child: why can't I get up? I think I'll close my eyes. Just for a minute.

By nightfall Jane knew her baby was coming.

When she came round after fainting in the cave she

had what she thought was a backache – caused, she assumed, by carrying Mousa. Jean-Pierre agreed with her diagnosis, gave her an aspirin, and told her to lie still. Rabia, the midwife, came into the cave to see Mousa, and gave Jane a hard look, but at the time Jane did not understand its significance. Jean-Pierre cleaned and dressed Mousa's stump, gave him penicillin, and injected him against tetanus. The child would not die of infection, as almost certainly he would have without Western medicines; but all the same Jane wondered whether his life would be worth living – survival here was hard even for the fittest, and crippled children generally died young.

Late in the afternoon Jean-Pierre prepared to leave. He was scheduled to hold a clinic tomorrow in a village several miles away, and – for some reason Jane had never quite understood – he never missed such appointments, even though he knew that no Afghan would have been surprised if he had been a day or even a week late.

By the time he kissed Jane goodbye she was beginning to wonder whether her backache might be the beginning of labour, brought on early by her ordeal with Mousa, but as she had never had a baby before, she could not tell, and it seemed unlikely. She asked Jean-Pierre. 'Don't worry,' he said briskly. 'You've got another six weeks to wait.' She asked him whether he ought perhaps to stay, just in case, but he thought it quite unnecessary, and she began to feel foolish; so she let him go, with his medical supplies loaded on a scrawny pony, to reach his destination before dark so that he could begin work first thing in the morning.

When the sun began to set behind the western cliff wall, and the valley was brim-full of shadow, Jane walked with the women and children down the mountainside to the darkening village, and the men headed for their fields, to reap their crops while the bombers slept.

The house in which Jane and Jean-Pierre lived actually belonged to the village shopkeeper, who had given up hope of making money in wartime – there was almost nothing to sell – and had decamped, with his family, to Pakistan. The front room, formerly the shop, had been Jean-Pierre's clinic until the intensity of the summer bombing had driven the villagers to the caves during the day. The house had two back rooms: one would have been for the men and their guests, the other for women and children. Jane and Jean-Pierre used them as bedroom and living-room. At the side of the house was a mud-walled courtyard containing the cooking-fire and a small pool for washing clothes, dishes and children. The shopkeeper had left behind some home-made wooden furniture, and the villagers had loaned Jane several beautiful rugs for the floors. Jane and Jean-Pierre slept on a mattress, like the Afghans, but they had a down sleeping bag instead of blankets. Like the Afghans, they rolled the mattress up during the day or put it on the flat roof to air in fine weather. In the summer everyone slept on the roofs.

Walking from the cave to the house had a peculiar

effect on Jane. Her backache got much worse, and when she reached home she was ready to collapse with pain and exhaustion. She had a desperate urge to pee, but she was too tired to go outside to the latrine, so she used the emergency pot behind the screen in the bedroom. It was then that she noticed a small blood-streaked stain in the crotch of her cotton trousers.

She did not have the energy to climb up the outside ladder on to the roof to fetch the mattress, so she lay on a rug in the bedroom. The 'backache' came in waves. She put her hands on her tummy during the next wave, and felt the bulge shift, sticking farther out as the pain increased then flattening again as it eased. Now she was in no doubt that she was having contractions.

She was frightened. She recalled talking to her sister Pauline about childbirth. After Pauline's first, Jane had visited her, taking a bottle of champagne and a little marijuana. When they were both extremely relaxed Jane had asked what it was really like, and Pauline had replied: 'Like shitting a melon.' They had giggled for what seemed like hours.

But Pauline had given birth at University College Hospital in the heart of London, not in a mud-brick house in the Five Lions Valley.

Jane thought: What am I going to *do?*

I mustn't panic. I must wash myself with warm water and soap; find a sharp scissors and put it in boiling water for fifteen minutes; get clean sheets to lie on; sip liquids; and relax.

But before she could do anything another contraction began, and this one *really* hurt. She closed her eyes and tried to take slow, deep, regular breaths, as Jean-Pierre had explained, but it was difficult to be so controlled when all she wanted to do was cry out in fear and pain.

The spasm left her drained. She lay still, recovering. She realized she could not do any of the things she had listed: she could not manage on her own. As soon as she felt strong enough she would get up and go to the nearest house and ask the women to fetch the midwife.

The next contraction came sooner than she had expected, after what seemed like only a minute or two. As the tension reached its peak Jane said aloud: 'Why don't they *tell* you how much it *hurts*?'

As soon as it passed its peak she forced herself to get up. The terror of giving birth all alone gave her strength. She hobbled from the bedroom into the living-room. She felt a little stronger with each step. She made it out into the courtyard, then suddenly there was a gush of warm fluid between her thighs, and her trousers were instantly drenched: the waters had broken. 'Oh, no,' she groaned. She leaned against the doorpost. She was not sure she could walk even a few yards with her trousers falling down like this. She felt humiliated. 'I must,' she said; but a new contraction began, and she sank to the ground, thinking: I'm going to have to do this alone.

Next time she opened her eyes there was a man's face close to her own. He looked like an Arab sheik: he had dark brown skin, black eyes, and a black moustache, and his features were aristocratic – high cheekbones, a Roman nose, white teeth and a long jaw. It was Mohammed Khan, the father of Mousa.

'Thank God,' Jane muttered thickly.

'I came to thank you for saving the life of my son,' Mohammed said in Dari. 'Are you sick?'

'I'm having a baby.'

'Now?' he said, startled.

'Soon. Help me into the house.'

He hesitated – childbirth, like all things uniquely feminine, was considered unclean – but to his credit the hesitation was only momentary. He lifted her to her feet and supported her as she walked through the living-room and into the bedroom. She lay down on the rug again. 'Get help,' she told him.

He frowned, unsure what to do, looking very boyish and handsome. 'Where is Jean-Pierre?'

'Gone to Khawak. I need Rabia.'

'Yes,' he said. 'I'll send my wife.'

'Before you go . . .'

'Yes?'

'Please give me some water.'

He looked shocked. It was unheard-of for a man to serve a woman, even with a simple drink of water.

Jane added: 'From the special jug.' She kept handy a jug of filtered boiled water for drinking: this was the only way to avoid the numerous intestinal parasites from which almost all the local people suffered all their lives.

Mohammed decided to flout convention. 'Of course,' he said. He went into the next room and returned a moment later with a cup of water. Jane thanked him and sipped gratefully.

'I'll send Halima to fetch the midwife,' he said.

Halima was his wife. 'Thank you,' said Jane. 'Tell her to hurry.'

Mohammed left. Jane was lucky it was he and not one of the other men. The others would have refused to touch a sick woman, but Mohammed was different. He was one of the most important guerrillas, and in practice was the local representative of the rebel leader, Masud. Mohammed was only twenty-four, but in this country that was not too young to be a guerrilla leader nor to have a nine-year-old son. He had studied in Kabul, he spoke a little French, and he knew that the customs of the Valley were not the only forms of polite behaviour in the world. His main responsibility was to organise the convoys to and from Pakistan with their vital supplies of arms and ammunition for the rebels. It was one such convoy that had brought Jane and Jean-Pierre to the Valley.

Waiting for the next contraction, Jane recalled that awful journey. She had thought of herself as a healthy, active and strong person, easily capable of walking all day; but she had not anticipated the shortage of food, the steep climbs, the rough stony paths and the incapacitating diarrhoea. For parts of the trip they had moved only at night, for fear of Russian helicopters. They had also to contend with hostile villagers in places: fearing that the convoy would attract a Russian attack, the locals would refuse to sell food to the guerrillas, or hide behind barred doors, or direct the convoy to meadow or orchard a few miles away, a perfect camping spot which turned out not to exist.

Because of the Russian attacks Mohammed changed his routes constantly. Jean-Pierre had got hold of American maps of Afghanistan in Paris, and they were better than anything the rebels had, so Mohammed often came to the house to look at them before sending a new convoy off.

In fact Mohammed came oftener than was really necessary. He also addressed Jane more than Afghan men usually did, and made eye contact with her a little too much, and stole too many glances at her body. She thought he was in love with her, or at least he had been until her pregnancy became visible.

She in turn had been drawn to him at the time when she was miserable about Jean-Pierre. Mohammed was lean and brown and strong and powerful, and for the first time in her life Jane had been attracted to a dyed-in-the-wool male chauvinist pig.

She could have had an affair with him. He was a devout Muslim, as were all the guerrillas, but she doubted whether that would have made any difference. She believed what her father had used to say: 'Religious conviction may thwart a timid desire but nothing can stand against genuine lust.' That particular line had enraged Mummy. No, there was as much adultery in this puritan peasant community as there was anywhere else, as Jane had realised listening to the riverside gossip among the women as they fetched water or bathed. Jane knew how it was managed, too.

Mohammed had told her. 'You can see the fish jump at dusk under the waterfall beyond the last water-mill,' he had said one day. 'I go there some nights to catch them.' At dusk the women were all cooking and the men were sitting in the courtyard of the mosque, talking and smoking: lovers would not be discovered so far from the village, and neither Jane nor Mohammed would have been missed.

The idea of making love by a waterfall with this handsome, primitive tribesman tempted Jane; but then she had got pregnant, and Jean-Pierre had confessed how frightened he was of losing her, and she had decided to devote all her energies to making her marriage work, come what may; and so she never went to the waterfall, and after her pregnancy began to show Mohammed did not look at her body.

Perhaps it was their latent intimacy that had emboldened Mohammed to come in and to help her, when other men would have refused and might even have turned away at the door. Or perhaps it was Mousa. Mohammed had only one son – and three daughters – and he probably now felt unbearably indebted to Jane. I made a friend and an enemy today, she thought: Mohammed and Abdullah.

The pain began again, and she realised she had enjoyed a longer-than-usual respite. Were the contractions becoming irregular? Why? Jean-Pierre had said nothing about that. But he had forgotten much of the gynaecology he had studied three or four years ago.

This one was the worst so far, and it left her feeling shivery and nauseous. What had happened to the midwife? Mohammed *must* have sent his wife to fetch her – he would not forget, or change his mind. But would she obey her husband? Of course – Afghan women always did. But she might walk slowly, gossiping on the way, or even stop off at some other house to drink tea. If there was adultery in the Five Lions Valley there would be jealousy too, and Halima was sure to know or at least guess at her husband's feelings for Jane – wives always did. She might now resent being asked to rush to the aid of her rival, the exotic white-skinned educated foreigner who so fascinated her husband. Suddenly Jane felt very angry with Mohammed and with Halima too. I've done nothing wrong, she thought. Why have they all deserted me? Why isn't my husband here?

When another contraction began, she burst into tears. It was just too much. 'I can't go on,' she said aloud. She was shaking uncontrollably. She wanted to die before the pain could get worse. 'Mummy, help me, Mummy,' she sobbed.

Suddenly there was a strong arm around her shoulders and a woman's voice in her ear murmuring something incomprensible but soothing in Dari. Without opening her eyes, she held on to the other woman, weeping and crying out as the contraction grew more intense; until at length it began to fade, too slowly, but with a feeling of finality, as if it might be the last, or perhaps the last bad one.

She looked up and saw the serene brown eyes and nutshell cheeks of old Rabia, the midwife.

'May God be with you, Jane Debout.'

Jane felt relief like the lifting of a crushing burden. 'And with you, Rabia Gul,' she whispered gratefully.

'Are the pains coming fast?'

'Every minute or two.'

Another woman's voice said: 'The baby is coming early.'

Jane turned her head and saw Zahara Gul, Rabia's daughter-in-law, a voluptuous girl of Jane's age with wavy near-black hair and a wide, laughing mouth. Of all the women in the village, Zahara was the one to whom Jane felt close. 'I'm glad you're here,' she said.

Rabia said: 'The birth has been brought on by carrying Mousa up the hillside.'

'Is that all?' said Jane.

'It is plenty.'

So they don't know about the fight with Abdullah, Jane thought. He has decided to keep it to himself.

Rabia said: 'Shall I make everything ready for the baby?'

'Yes, please.' Goodness knows what kind of primitive gynaecology I'm letting myself in for, Jane thought; but I can't do this alone, I just can't.

'Would you like Zahara to make some tea?' Rabia asked.

'Yes, please.' There was nothing superstitious about that, at least.

The two women got busy. Just having them there made Jane feel better. It was nice, she thought, that Rabia had asked permission to help – a Western doctor would have walked in and taken charge as if he owned the place. Rabia washed her hands ritually, calling on

83

the prophets to make her red-faced – which meant successful – and then washed them again, thoroughly with soap and lots of water. Zahara brought in a jar of wild rue, and Rabia lit a handful of the small dark seeds with some charcoal. Jane recalled that evil spirits were said to be frightened off by the smell of burning rue. She consoled herself with the thought that the acrid smoke would serve to keep flies out of the room.

Rabia was a little more than a midwife. Delivering babies was her main work, but she also had herbal and magical treatments to increase the fertility of women who were having difficulty getting pregnant. She had methods of preventing conception and bringing on abortion, too, but there was much less demand for these: Afghan women generally wanted lots of children. Rabia would also be consulted about any 'feminine' illness. And she was usually asked to wash the dead – a task which, like delivering babies, was considered unclean.

Jane watched her move around the room. She was probably the oldest woman in the village, being some-where around sixty. She was short – not much more than five feet tall – and very thin, like most of the people here. Her wrinkled brown face was surrounded by white hair. She moved quietly, her bony old hands precise and efficient.

Jane's relationship with her had begun in mistrust and hostility. When Jane had asked whom Rabia called upon in case of difficult deliveries, Rabia had snapped: 'May the devil be deaf, I've never had a difficult birth and I've never lost a mother or a child.' But later, when village women came to Jane with minor menstrual problems or routine pregnancies, Jane would send them to Rabia instead of prescribing placebos; and this was the beginning of a working relationship. Rabia had consulted Jane about a recently-delivered mother who had a vaginal infection. Jane had given Rabia a supply of penicillin and had explained how to prescribe it. Rabia's prestige had rocketed when it became known that she had been entrusted with Western medicine; and Jane had been able to tell her, without giving offence, that Rabia herself had probably caused the infection by her practice of manually lubricating the birth canal during delivery.

From then on Rabia began to turn up at the clinic once or twice a week to talk to Jane and watch her work. Jane took these opportunities to explain, rather casually, such things as why she washed her hands so often, why she put all her instruments in boiling water after using them, and why she gave lots of fluids to infants with diarrhoea.

In turn, Rabia told Jane some of her secrets. Jane was interested to learn what was in the potions Rabia made, and she could guess how some of them might work: medicines to promote pregnancy contained rabbit brains or cat spleen which might provide hormones missing from the patient's metabolism; and the mint and catnip in many preparations probably helped to clear up infections which hindered conception. Rabia also had a physic for wives to give to impotent husbands, and there was no doubt about how that worked: it contained opium.

Mistrust had given way to wary mutual respect, but Jane had not consulted Rabia about her own pregnancy. It was one thing to allow that Rabia's mixture of folklore and witchcraft might work on Afghan women, and quite another to subject oneself to it. Besides, Jane had expected Jean-Pierre to deliver her baby. So, when Rabia had asked about the position of the baby, and had prescribed a vegetable diet for a girl, Jane had made it clear that this pregnancy was going to be a Western one. Rabia had looked hurt, but had accepted the ruling with dignity. And now Jean-Pierre was in Khawak and Rabia was right here, and Jane was glad to have the help of an old woman who had delivered hundreds of babies and had herself given birth to eleven.

There had been no pain for a while, but in the last few minutes, as she watched Rabia move quietly around the room, Jane had been feeling new sensations in her abdomen: a distinct feeling of pressure accompanied by a growing urge to *push*. The urge became irresistible, and as she pushed, she groaned, not because she was in pain, but just with the sheer effort of pushing.

She heard Rabia's voice, as if from a distance, saying: 'It begins. This is good.'

After a while the urge went away. Zahara brought a cup of green tea. Jane sat upright and sipped gratefully. It was warm and very sweet. Zahara is the same age as me, Jane thought, and she's had four children already, not counting miscarriages and stillborn babies. But she was one of those women who seemed to be full of vitality, like a healthy young lioness. She would probably have several more children. She had greeted Jane with open curiosity, when most of the women had been suspicious and hostile, in the early days; and Jane had discovered that Zahara was impatient of the sillier customs and traditions of the Valley and eager to learn what she could of foreign ideas on health, child care and nutrition. Consequently Zahara had become not just Jane's friend but the spearhead of her health education programme.

Today, however, Jane was learning about Afghan methods. She watched Rabia spread a plastic sheet on the floor (what did they use in the days before there was all this waste plastic around?) and cover it with a layer of sandy earth which Zahara brought from outside in a bucket. Rabia had laid out a few things on a cloth on the floor, and Jane was pleased to see clean cotton rags and a new razor blade still in its wrapping.

The need to push came again, and Jane closed her eyes to concentrate. It did not *hurt*, exactly; it was more like being incredibly, impossibly constipated. She found it helpful to groan as she strained, and she wanted to explain to Rabia that this was not a groan of agony; but she was too busy pushing to talk.

In the next pause, Rabia knelt down and untied the drawstring of Jane's trousers then eased them off. 'Do you want to make water before I wash you?' she said.

'Yes.'

She helped Jane get up and walk behind the screen, then held her shoulders while she sat on the pot.

Zahara brought a bowl of warm water and took the pot away. Rabia washed Jane's tummy, thighs, and private parts, assuming for the first time a rather brisk air as she did so. Then Jane lay down again. Rabia washed her own hands and dried them. She showed Jane a small jar of blue powder – copper sulphate, Jane guessed – and said: 'This colour frightens the evil spirits.'

'What do you want to do?'

'Put a little on your brow.'

'All right,' said Jane, then she added: 'Thank you.'

Rabia smeared a little of the powder on Jane's forehead. I don't mind magic when it's harmless, Jane thought, but what will she do if there is a real medical problem? And just exactly how many weeks premature is this baby?

She was still worrying when the next contraction began, so that she was not concentrating on riding the wave of pressure, and in consequence it was very painful. I mustn't worry, she thought; I must make myself relax.

Afterwards she felt exhausted and rather sleepy. She closed her eyes. She felt Rabia unbutton her shirt – the one she had borrowed from Jean-Pierre that afternoon, a hundred years ago. Rabia began to massage Jane's tummy with some kind of lubricant, probably clarified butter. She dug her fingers in. Jane opened her eyes and said: 'Don't try to move the baby.'

Rabia nodded but continued to probe, one hand on the top of Jane's bulge and the other at the bottom. 'The head is down,' she said finally. 'All is well. But the baby will come very soon. You should get up now.'

Zahara and Rabia helped Jane stand and take two

steps forward on to the earth-covered plastic sheet.
Rabia got behind her and said: 'Stand on my feet.'

Jane did as she was told, although she was not sure
of the logic of this. Rabia eased her into a squat,
crouching behind her. So this was the local birthing
position. 'Sit on me,' said Rabia. 'I can hold you.' Jane
let her weight settle on the old woman's thighs. The
position was surprisingly comfortable and reassuring.

Jane felt her muscles begin to tighten again. She
gritted her teeth and bore down, groaning. Zahara
squatted in front of her. For a while there was nothing
in Jane's mind but the pressure. At last it eased, and
she slumped, exhausted and half asleep, letting Rabia
take her weight.

When it started again there was a new pain a sharp
burning sensation in her crotch. Zahara suddenly said:
'It comes.'

'Don't push, now,' said Rabia. 'Let the baby swim
out.'

The pressure eased. Rabia and Zahara changed
places, and Rabia now squatted between Jane's legs,
watching intently. The pressure began again. Jane
gritted her teeth. Rabia said: 'Don't push. Be calm.'
Jane tried to relax. Rabia looked at her and reached up
to touch her face, saying: 'Don't bite down. Make your
mouth loose.' Jane let her jaw sag, and found that it
helped her to relax.

The burning sensation came again, worse than ever,
and Jane knew the baby was almost born: she could feel
its head pushing through, stretching her opening
impossibly wide. She cried out with the pain – and

suddenly it eased, and for a moment she could feel nothing. She looked down. Rabia reached between her thighs, calling out the names of the prophets. Through a haze of tears Jane saw something round and dark in the midwife's hands.

'Don't pull,' Jane said. 'Don't pull the head.'

'No,' said Rabia.

Jane felt the pressure again. At that moment Rabia said: 'A small push for the shoulder.' Jane closed her eyes and squeezed gently.

A few moments later Rabia said: 'Now the other shoulder.'

Jane squeezed again, and then there was an enormous relief of tension, and she knew that the baby was born. She looked down and saw its tiny form cradled on Rabia's arm. Its skin was wrinkled and wet, and its head was covered with damp dark hair. The umbilical cord looked weird, a thick blue rope pulsing like a vein.

'Is it all right?' Jane asked.

Rabia did not reply. She pursed her lips and blew on the baby's squashed, immobile face.

Oh, God, it's dead, thought Jane.

'Is it all right?' she repeated.

Rabia blew again, and the baby opened its tiny mouth and cried.

Jane said: 'Oh, thank God – it's alive.'

Rabia picked up a clean cotton rag and wiped the baby's face.

'Is it normal?' asked Jane.

At last Rabia spoke. She looked into Jane's eyes, smiled, and said: 'Yes. She is normal.'

She's normal, Jane thought. She. I made a little girl. A girl.

Suddenly she felt utterly drained. She could not remain upright a moment longer. 'I want to lie down,' she said.

Zahara helped her step back to the mattress and put cushions behind her so that she was sitting up, while Rabia held the baby, still attached to Jane by the cord. When Jane was settled Rabia began to pat the baby dry with cotton rags.

Jane saw the cord stop pulsing, shrivel, and turn white. 'You can cut the cord,' she said to Rabia.

'We always wait for the afterbirth,' Rabia said.

'Do it now, please.'

Rabia looked dubious, but complied. She took a piece of white string from her table and tied it around the cord a few inches from the baby's navel. It should have been closer, Jane thought; but it doesn't matter.

Rabia unwrapped the new razor blade. 'In the name of Allah,' she said, and cut the cord.

'Give her to me,' said Jane.

Rabia handed the baby to her, saying: 'Don't let her suckle.'

Jane knew Rabia was wrong about this. 'It helps the afterbirth,' she said.

Rabia shrugged.

Jane put the baby's face to her breast. Her nipples were enlarged and felt deliciously sensitive, like when Jean-Pierre kissed them. As her nipple touched the baby's cheek, the child turned her head reflexively and opened her little mouth. As soon as the nipple went in she began to suck. Jane was astonished to find that it felt sexy. For a moment she was shocked and embarrassed, then she thought: what the hell.

She sensed further movements in her abdomen. She obeyed an urge to push, and then felt the placenta come out, a slippery small birth. Rabia wrapped it carefully in a rag.

The baby stopped sucking and seemed to fall asleep.

Zahara handed Jane a cup of water. She drank it in one gulp. It tasted wonderful. She asked for more.

She was sore, exhausted and blissfully happy. She looked down at the little girl sleeping peacefully at her breast. She felt ready to sleep herself.

Rabia said: 'We should wrap the little one.'

Jane lifted the baby – she was as light as a doll – and handed her to the old woman. 'Chantal,' she said as Rabia took her. 'Her name is Chantal.' Then she closed her eyes.

CHAPTER FIVE

ELLIS THALER took the Eastern Airlines shuttle from Washington to New York. At La Guardia airport he got a cab to the Plaza Hotel in New York City. The cab dropped him at the Fifth Avenue entrance to the hotel. Ellis went inside. In the lobby he turned left and went to the 58th Street elevators. A man in a business suit and a woman carrying a Saks shopping bag got in with him. The man got out at the seventh floor. Ellis got out at the eighth, the woman went on up. Ellis walked along the cavernous hotel corridor, all alone, until he came to the 59th Street elevators. He went down to the ground floor and left the hotel by the 59th Street entrance.

Satisfied that no one was following him, he hailed a cab on Central Park South, went to Penn Station, and took the train to Douglaston, Queens.

Some lines from Auden's *Lullaby* were repeating in his head as he rode the train:

> *Time and fevers burn away*
> *Individual beauty from*
> *Thoughtful children, and the grave*
> *Proves the child ephemeral.*

It was more than a year since he had posed as an aspiring American poet in Paris, but he had not lost the taste for verse.

He continued to check for a tail, for this was one assignation his enemies must never learn about. He got off the train at Flushing and waited on the platform for the next train. No one waited with him.

Because of his elaborate precautions it was five o'clock when he reached Douglaston. From the station he walked briskly for half an hour, running over in his mind the approach he was about to make, the words he would use, the various possible reactions he might expect.

He reached a suburban street within sight of Long Island Sound and stopped outside a small, neat house with mock-Tudor gables and a stained-glass window in one wall. There was a small Japanese car in the driveway. As he walked up the path, the front door was opened by a blonde girl of thirteen years.

Ellis said: 'Hello, Petal.'

'Hi, Daddy,' she replied.

He bent down to kiss her, feeling as always a glow of pride simultaneously with a stab of guilt.

He looked her up and down. Underneath her Michael Jackson T-shirt she was wearing a bra. He was pretty sure that was new. She's turning into a woman, he thought. I'll be damned.

'Would you like to come inside for a moment?' she said politely.

'Sure.'

He followed her into the house. From behind she

looked even more womanly. He was reminded of his first girlfriend. He had been fifteen and she had been not much older than Petal ... No, wait, he thought; she was *younger*, she was *twelve*. And I used to put my hand up her sweater. Lord protect my daughter from fifteen-year-old boys.

They went into a small, neat living-room. 'Won't you sit down?' said Petal.

Ellis sat down.

'Can I get you something?' she asked.

'Relax,' Ellis told her. 'You don't have to be so polite. I'm your Daddy.'

She looked puzzled and uncertain, as if she had been rebuked for something she did not know to be wrong. After a moment she said: 'I have to brush my hair. Then we can go. Excuse me.'

'Sure,' said Ellis. She went out. He found her courtesy painful. It was a sign that he was still a stranger. He had not yet succeeded in becoming a normal member of her family.

He had been seeing her at least once a month for the past year, ever since he came back from Paris. Sometimes they would spend a day together, but more often he would just take her out to dinner, as he was going to today. To be with her for that hour, he had to make a five-hour trip with maximum security, but of course she did not know that. His aim was a modest one: without any fuss or drama he wanted to take a small but permanent place in his daughter's life.

It had meant changing the type of work he did. He had given up field work. His superiors had been highly displeased: there were too few good undercover agents (and hundreds of bad ones). He, too, had been reluctant, feeling that he had a duty to use his talent. But he could not win his daughter's affection if he had to disappear every year or so to some remote corner of the world, unable to tell her where he was going or why or even for how long. And he could not risk getting himself killed when she was learning to love him.

He missed the excitement, the danger, the thrill of the chase and the feeling that he was doing an important job that nobody else could do quite as well. But for too long his only emotional attachments had been fleeting ones, and after he lost Jane he felt the need of at least one person whose love was permanent.

While he was waiting, Gill came into the room. Ellis stood up. His ex-wife was cool and composed in a white summer dress. He kissed her proffered cheek. 'How are you?' she said.

'The same as ever. You?'

'I'm *incredibly* busy.' She started to tell him, in some detail, how much she had to do, and, as always, Ellis tuned out. He was fond of her, although she bored him to death. It was odd to think he had once been married to her. But she was the prettiest girl in the English Department, and he was the cleverest boy, and it was 1967, when everyone was stoned and anything could happen, especially in California. They were married in white robes, at the end of their first year, and someone played the Wedding March on a sitar. Then Ellis flunked his exams and got thrown out of college and was therefore drafted, and instead of going to Canada or Sweden he went to the draft office like a lamb to the slaughter, surprising the hell out of everyone except Gill, who knew by then that the marriage was not going to work and was just waiting to see how Ellis would make his escape.

He was in the hospital in Saigon with a bullet wound in his calf – the helicopter pilot's commonest injury, because his seat is armoured but the floor is not – when the divorce became final. Someone dumped the notification on his bed while he was in the john, and he found it when he got back, along with another Oak Leaf Cluster, his twenty-fifth (they were passing out medals kind of fast in those days). *I just got divorced,* he had said, and the soldier in the next bed had replied *No shit. Want to play a little cards?*

She had not told him about the baby. He found out, a few years later, when he became a spy and tracked Gill down as an exercise, and learned that she had a child with the unmistakably late-sixties name of Petal, and a husband called Bernard who was seeing a fertility specialist. Not telling him about Petal was the only truly mean thing Gill had ever done to him, he thought, although she still maintained it had been for his own good.

He had insisted on seeing Petal from time to time, and he had stopped her calling Bernard 'Daddy'. But he had not sought to become part of their family life, not until last year.

'Do you want to take my car?' Gill was saying.

'If it's all right.'

'Sure it is.'

'Thanks.' It was embarrassing, having to borrow Gill's car, but the drive from Washington was too long, and Ellis did not want to rent cars frequently in this area, for then one day his enemies would find out, through the records of the rental agencies or the credit card companies, and then they would be on the way to finding out about Petal. The alternative would have been to use a different identity every time he rented a car, but identities were expensive and the Agency would not provide them for a desk man. So he used Gill's Honda, or hired the local taxi.

Petal came back in, with her blonde hair wafting about her shoulders. Ellis stood up. Gill said: 'The keys are in the car.'

Ellis said to Petal: 'Jump in the car. I'll be right there.' Petal went out. He said to Gill: 'I'd like to invite her to Washington for a weekend.'

Gill was kind but firm. 'If she wants to go, she certainly can, but if she doesn't, I won't make her.'

Ellis nodded. 'That's fair. See you later.'

He drove Petal to a Chinese restaurant in Little Neck. She liked Chinese food. She relaxed a little once she was away from the house. She thanked Ellis for sending her a poem on her birthday. 'Nobody I know has ever had a poem for their birthday,' she said.

He was not sure whether that was good or bad. 'Better than a birthday card with a picture of a cute kitten on the front, I hope.'

'Yeah.' She laughed. 'All my friends think you're so romantic. My English teacher asked me if you had ever had anything published.'

'I've never written anything good enough,' he said. 'Are you still enjoying English?'

'I like it a *lot* better than maths. I'm *terrible* at maths.'

'What do you study? Any plays?'

'No, but we have poems sometimes.'

'Any you like?'

She thought for a moment. 'I like the one about the daffodils.'

Ellis nodded. 'I do, too.'

'I forgot who wrote it.'

'William Wordsworth.'

'Oh, right.'

'Any others?'

'Not really. I'm more into music. Do you like Michael Jackson?'

'I don't know. I'm not sure I've heard his records.'

'He's really cute.' She giggled. 'All my friends are crazy about him.'

It was the second time she had mentioned *all my friends*. Right now her peer group was the most important thing in her life. 'I'd like to meet some of your friends, some time,' he said.

'Oh, *daddy*,' she chided him. 'You wouldn't like that – they're just *girls*.'

Feeling mildly rebuffed, Ellis concentrated on his food for a while. He drank a glass of white wine with it: French habits had stayed with him.

When he had finished he said: 'Listen, I've been thinking. Why don't you come to Washington and stay at my place one weekend. It's only an hour on the plane, and we could have a good time.'

She was quite surprised. 'What's in Washington?'

'Well, we could take a tour of the White House, where the President lives. And Washington has some of the best museums in the whole world. And you've never even seen my apartment. I have a spare bedroom . . .' He tailed off. He could see she was not interested.

'Oh, Daddy, I don't know,' she said. 'I have so much to do on weekends – homework, and parties, and shopping, and dance lessons and everything . . .'

Ellis hid his disappointment. 'Don't worry,' he said. 'Maybe some time when you're not so busy you could come.'

'Yes, okay,' she said, visibly relieved.

'I could fix up the spare bedroom so you could come any time you like.'

'Okay.'

'What colour shall I paint it?'

'I don't know.'

'What's your favourite colour?'

'Pink, I guess.'

'Pink it is.' Ellis forced a smile. 'Let's go.'

In the car on the way home she asked him whether he would mind if she had her ears pierced.

'I don't know,' he said guardedly. 'How does Mommy feel about it?'

'She said it's okay with her if it's okay with you.'

Was Gill thoughtfully including him in the decision or just passing the buck? 'I don't think I like the idea,' Ellis said. 'You may be a little young to begin making holes in yourself for decoration.'

'Do you think I'm too young to have a boyfriend?'

Ellis wanted to say Yes. She seemed far too young. But he couldn't stop her growing up. 'You're old enough to date, but not to go steady,' he said. He glanced at her to catch her reaction. She looked amused. Maybe they don't talk about going steady any more, he thought.

When they reached the house, Bernard's Ford was parked in the driveway. Ellis pulled the Honda in behind it and went in with Petal. Bernard was in the living-room. A small man with very short hair, he was good-natured and utterly without imagination. Petal greeted him enthusiastically, hugging and kissing him. He seemed a little embarrassed. He shook Ellis's hand firmly, saying: 'Government still ticking over okay, back in Washington?'

'Same as always,' Ellis said. They thought that he worked for the State Department and that his job was to read French newspapers and magazines and prepare a daily digest for the French Desk.

'How about a beer?'

Ellis did not really want one but he accepted just to be friendly. Bernard went into the kitchen to get it. He was credit manager for a department store in New York City. Petal seemed to like and respect him, and he was gently affectionate with her. He and Gill had no other children: that fertility specialist had done him no good.

He came back with two glasses of beer and handed one to Ellis. 'Go and do your homework, now,' he said to Petal. 'Daddy will say goodbye before he leaves.'

She kissed him again and ran off. When she was out of earshot he said: 'She isn't normally so affectionate.

She seems to overdo it when you're around. I don't understand it.'

Ellis understood it only too well, but he did not want to think about it yet. 'Don't worry about it,' he said. 'How's business?'

'Not bad. High interest rates haven't hit us as badly as we feared they might. It seems that people are still willing to borrow money to buy things – in New York, at least.' He sat down and sipped his beer.

Ellis always felt that Bernard was physically frightened of him. It showed in the way the man walked around, like a pet dog that is not really allowed indoors, careful to stay an inch or two out of kicking distance.

They talked about the economy for a few minutes and Ellis drank his beer as fast as he could, then got up to leave. He went to the foot of the staircase and called: 'Bye, Petal.'

She came to the top of the stairs. 'What about having my ears pierced?'

'Can I think about it?' he said.

'Sure. Bye.'

Gill came down the stairs. 'I'll drive you to the airport,' she said.

Ellis was surprised. 'Okay. Thanks.'

When they were on the road Gill said: 'She told me she didn't want to spend a weekend with you.'

'Right.'

'You're upset, aren't you?'

'Does it show?'

'To me it does. I used to be married to you.' She paused. 'I'm sorry, John.'

'It's my fault. I didn't think it through. Before I came along, she had a Mommy and a Daddy and a home – all any child wants. I'm not *just* superfluous, though. By being around I threaten her happiness. I'm an intruder, a destabilising factor. That's why she hugs Bernard in front of me. She doesn't mean to hurt me. She does it because she's afraid of losing *him*. And it's me who makes her afraid.'

'She'll get over it,' Gill said. 'America is full of kids with two Daddies.'

'That's no excuse. I fucked up, and I should face it.'

She surprised him again by patting his knee. 'Don't be too hard on yourself,' she said. 'You just weren't made for this. I knew that within a month of marrying you. You don't want a house, a job, the suburbs, children. You're a little weird. That's why I fell in love with you, and that's why I let you go so readily. I loved you because you were different, crazy, original, exciting. You would do *anything*. But you're no family man.'

He sat in silence, thinking about what she had said, while she drove. It was meant kindly, and for that he was warmly grateful; but was it true? He thought not. I don't want a house in the suburbs, he thought, but I'd like a home: maybe a villa in Morocco or a loft in Greenwich Village or a penthouse in Rome. I don't want a wife to be my housekeeper, cooking and cleaning and shopping and taking the minutes at the PTA; but I'd like a companion, someone to share books and movies and poetry with, someone to talk to at night. I'd even like to have kids, and raise them to know about something more than Michael Jackson.

He did not say any of this to Gill.

She stopped the car and he realised they were outside the Eastern terminal. He looked at his watch: eight-fifty. If he hurried he would get on the nine o'clock shuttle. 'Thanks for the ride,' he said.

'What you need is a woman like you, one of your kind,' Gill said.

Ellis thought of Jane. 'I met one, once.'

'What happened?'

'She married a handsome doctor.'

'Is the doctor crazy like you?'

'I don't think so.'

'Then it won't last. When did she get married?'

'About a year ago.'

'Ah.' Gill was probably figuring that that was when Ellis had come back into Petal's life in a big way; but she had the grace not to say so. 'Take my advice,' she said. 'Check her out.'

Ellis got out of the car. 'Talk to you soon.'

'Bye.'

He slammed the door and she drove off.

Ellis hurried into the building. He made the flight with a minute or two to spare. As the plane took off he found a news magazine in the seat pocket in front of him and looked for a report from Afghanistan.

He had been following the war closely since he had heard, from Bill in Paris, that Jane had carried out her intention of going there with Jean-Pierre. The war was no longer front-page news. Often a week or two would go by with no reports about it at all. But now the winter lull was over and there was something in the press at least once a week.

This magazine had an analysis of the Russian situation in Afghanistan. Ellis began it mistrustfully, for he knew that many such articles in news magazines emanated from the CIA: a reporter would get an exclusive briefing on the CIA's intelligence appraisal of some situation, but in fact he would be the unconscious channel for a piece of disinformation aimed at another country's intelligence service, and the report he wrote would have no more relation to the truth than an article in *Pravda*.

However, this article seemed straight. There was a build-up of Russian troops and arms going on, it said, in preparation for a major summer offensive. This was seen by Moscow as a make-or-break summer: they *had* to crush the resistance this year or they would be forced to reach an accommodation of some kind with the rebels. This made sense to Ellis: he would check to see what the CIA's people in Moscow were saying, but he had a feeling it would tally.

Among the crucial target areas, the article listed the Panisher Valley.

Ellis remembered Jean-Pierre talking about the Five Lions Valley. The article also mentioned Masud, the rebel leader: Ellis recalled Jean-Pierre speaking of him, too.

He looked out of the window, watching the sun set. There was no doubt, he thought with a pang of dread, that Jane was going to be in grave danger this summer.

But it was none of his business. She was married to someone else, now. Anyway, there was nothing Ellis could do about it.

He looked down at his magazine, turned the page, and started reading about El Salvador. The plane roared on towards Washington. In the west, the sun went down, and darkness fell.

Allen Winderman took Ellis Thaler to lunch at a seafood restaurant overlooking the Potomac river. Winderman arrived half an hour late. He was a typical Washington operator: dark-grey suit, white shirt, striped tie; as smooth as a shark. As the White House was paying, Ellis ordered lobster and a glass of white wine. Winderman asked for Perrier and a salad. Everything about Winderman was too tight: his tie, his shoes, his schedule and his self-control.

Ellis was on his guard. He could not refuse such an invitation from a Presidential aide, but he did not like discreet, unofficial lunches, and he did not like Allen Winderman.

Winderman got right down to business. 'I want your advice,' he began.

Ellis stopped him. 'First of all, I need to know whether you told the Agency about our meeting.' If the White House wanted to plan covert action without telling the CIA, Ellis would have nothing to do with it.

'Of course,' Winderman said. 'What do you know about Afghanistan?'

Ellis felt suddenly cold. Sooner or later, this is going

106

to involve Jane, he thought. They know about her, of course: I made no secret of it. I told Bill in Paris I was going to ask her to marry me. I called Bill subsequently to find out whether she really did go to Afghanistan. All that went down on my file. Now this bastard knows about her, and he's going to use his knowledge. 'I know a little about it,' he said cautiously, and then he recalled a verse of Kipling, and recited it:

> When you're wounded an' left on Afghanistan's plains,
> An' the women come out to cut up your remains,
> Just roll to your rifle an' blow out your brains,
> An' go to your Gawd like a soldier.

Winderman looked ill-at-ease, for the first time. 'After two years of posing as a poet you must know a lot of that stuff.'

'So do the Afghans,' said Ellis. 'They're all poets, the way all Frenchmen are gourmets and all Welshmen are singers.'

'Is that so?'

'It's because they can't read or write. Poetry is a spoken art form.' Winderman was getting visibly impatient: his schedule did not allow for poetry. Ellis went on: 'The Afghans are wild, ragged, fierce mountain tribesmen, hardly out of the middle ages. They're said to be elaborately polite, brave as lions, and pitilessly cruel. Their country is harsh and arid and barren. What do *you* know about them?'

'There's no such thing as an Afghan,' Winderman said. 'There are six million Pushtuns in the south, three million Tajiks in the west, a million Uzbaks in the north, and another dozen or so nationalities with fewer than a million. Modern borders mean little to them: there are Tajiks in the Soviet Union and Pushtuns in Pakistan. Some of them are divided into tribes. They're like the Red Indians, who never thought of themselves as American, but Apache or Crow or Sioux. And they would just as soon fight one another as fight the Russians. Our problem is to get the Apache and the Sioux to unite against the palefaces.'

'I see.' Ellis nodded. He was wondering: when does Jane come into all this? He said: 'So the main question is: who will be the Big Chief?'

'That's easy. The most promising of the guerrilla leaders, by far, is Ahmed Shah Masud, in the Panisher Valley.'

The Five Lions Valley. What are you up to, you slimy bastard? Ellis studied Winderman's smooth-shaven face. The man was imperturbable. Ellis asked: 'What makes Masud so special?'

'Most of the rebel leaders are content to control their tribes, collect taxes, and deny the government access to their territory. Masud does more than that. He comes out of his mountain stronghold and attacks. He's within striking distance of the three strategic targets: the capital city, Kabul; the Salang tunnel, on the only highway from Kabul to the Soviet Union; and Bagram, the principal military air base. He's in a position to inflict major damage, and he does. He has studied the art of guerrilla warfare, he's read Mao. He's easily the best military brain in the country. And he has finance. Emeralds are mined in his valley and sold in Pakistan: Masud takes a ten per cent tax on all sales and uses the money to fund his army. He's twenty-eight years old, and charismatic – the people worship him. Finally, he's a Tajik. The largest group is the Pushtuns, and all the others hate *them*, so the leader can't be a Pushtun. Tajiks are the next biggest nation. There's a chance they might unite under a Tajik.'

'And we want to facilitate this?'

'That's right. The stronger the rebels are, the more damage they do to the Russians. Furthermore, a triumph for the US intelligence community would be very useful this year.'

It was of no consequence to Winderman and his kind that the Afghans were fighting for their freedom against a brutal invader, Ellis thought. Morality was out of fashion in Washington: the power game was all that mattered. If Winderman had been born in Leningrad instead of Los Angeles he would have been just as happy, just as successful and just as powerful, and he would have used just the same tactics fighting for the other side. 'What do you want from me?' Ellis asked him.

'I want to pick your brains. Is there any way an undercover agent could promote an alliance between the different Afghan tribes?'

'I expect so,' said Ellis. The food came, interrupting him and giving him a few moments to think. When the waiter had gone away he said: 'It should be possible, provided there is something *they* want from *us* – and I imagine that would be weapons.'

'Right.' Winderman started to eat, hesitantly, like a

man who has an ulcer. Between small mouthfuls he said: 'At the moment they buy their weapons across the border in Pakistan. All they can get there is copies of Victorian British rifles – or, if not copies, the genuine damned article, a hundred years old and still firing. They also steal Kalashnikovs from dead Russian soldiers. But they're desperate for small artillery – anti-aircraft guns and hand-launched ground-to-air missiles – so they can shoot down planes and helicopters.'

'Are we willing to give them these weapons?'

'Yes. Not directly – we would want to conceal our involvement by sending them through intermediaries. But that's no problem. We could use the Saudis.'

'Okay.' Ellis swallowed some lobster. It was good. 'Let me say what I think is the first step. In each guerrilla group you need a nucleus of men who know, understand and trust Masud. That nucleus then becomes the liaison group for communication with Masud. They build their role gradually: exchange of information first, then mutual co-operation, and finally co-ordinated battle plans.'

'Sounds good,' said Winderman. 'How might that be set up?'

'I'd have Masud run a training scheme in the Five Lions Valley. Each rebel group would send a few young men to fight alongside Masud for a while and learn the methods that make him so successful. They would also learn to respect him and trust him, if he is as good a leader as you say.'

Winderman nodded thoughtfully. 'That's the kind of proposal that might be acceptable to tribal leaders who would reject any plan that committed them to take orders from Masud.'

'Is there one rival leader in particular whose co-operation is essential to any alliance?'

'Yes. In fact there are two: Jahan Kamil and Amal Azizi, both Pushtuns.'

'Then I would send in an undercover agent with the objective of getting the two of them around a table with Masud. When he came back with all three signatures on a piece of paper we would send the first load of rocket launchers. Further consignments would depend on how well the training programme was going.'

Winderman put down his fork and lit a cigarette. He definitely has an ulcer, Ellis thought. Winderman said: 'This is exactly the kind of thing I had in mind.' Ellis could see he was already figuring out how to take the credit for the idea. By tomorrow he would be saying *We cooked up a scheme over lunch* and his written report would read *Covert action specialists assessed my scheme as viable.* 'What's the downside risk?'

Ellis considered. 'If the Russians caught the agent, they could get considerable propaganda value out of the whole thing. At the moment they have what the White House would call "an image problem" in Afghanistan. Their allies in the Third World don't enjoy watching them overrun a small primitive country. Their Muslim friends, in particular, tend to sympathise with the rebels. Now, the Russians' line is that the so-called rebels are just bandits, financed and armed by the CIA. They would just love to be able to prove it by catching a real live CIA spook right there in the country and putting him on trial. In terms of global politics, I imagine that could do us a lot a damage.'

'What are the chances that the Russians would catch our man?'

'Slender. If they can't catch Masud, why would they be able to catch an undercover agent sent to meet Masud?'

'Good.' Winderman stubbed out his cigarette. 'I want you to be that agent.'

Ellis was taken by surprise. He should have seen this coming, he realised, but he had been engrossed in the problem. 'I don't do that stuff any more,' he said, but his voice sounded thick and he could not help thinking: I would see Jane. I would see Jane!

'I talked to your boss on the phone,' Winderman said. 'His opinion was that an assignment in Afghanistan might tempt you back into the field work.'

So it was a set-up. The White House wanted to achieve something dramatic in Afghanistan, so they asked the CIA to loan them an agent. The CIA wanted Ellis to work in the field again, so they told the White House to offer him this assignment, knowing or suspecting that the prospect of meeting up with Jane again was almost irresistible.

Ellis hated to be manipulated.

But he wanted to go to the Five Lions Valley.

There had been a long silence. Winderman said impatiently: 'Will you do it?'

'I'll think about it,' Ellis replied.

*

Ellis's father belched quietly, begged pardon, and said: 'That was good.'

Ellis pushed away his dish of cherry pie and whipped cream. He was having to watch his weight for the first time in his life. 'Real good, Mom, but I can't eat any more,' he said apologetically.

'Nobody eats like they used to,' she said. She stood up and began clearing away. 'It's because they go everywhere in cars.'

His father pushed back his chair. 'I've got some figures to look over.'

'You *still* don't have an accountant?' Ellis said.

'Nobody takes care of your money as well as you do,' his father said. 'You'll find that out if you ever make any.' He left the room, heading for his den.

Ellis helped his mother clear away. The family had moved into this four-bedroom house in Tea Neck, New Jersey, when Ellis was thirteen; but he could remember the move as if it were yesterday. It had been anticipated for literally years. His father had built the house, on his own at first, later using employees of his growing construction business, but always doing the work in slack periods and leaving it when business was good. When they moved in it was not really finished: the heating did not work, there were no cupboards in the kitchen, and nothing had been painted. They got hot water the following day only because Mom threatened divorce otherwise. But it got finished eventually, and Ellis and his brothers and sisters all had room to grow up in it. It was bigger than Mom and Dad needed, now, but he hoped they would keep it. It had a good feel about it.

When they had loaded the dishwasher he said: 'Mom, do you remember that suitcase I left here when I came back from Asia?'

'Sure. It's in the closet in the small bedroom.'

'Thanks. I want to look through it.'

'Go on, then. I'll finish up here.'

Ellis climbed the stairs and went to the little bedroom at the top of the house. It was rarely used, and the single bed was crowded around with a couple of broken chairs, an old sofa, and four or five cardboard boxes containing children's books and toys. Ellis opened the cupboard and took out a small black plastic suitcase. He laid it on the bed, turned the combination locks and lifted the lid. There was a musty smell: it had not been opened for a decade. Everything was there: the medals; both the bullets they had taken out of him; Army Field Manual FM 5–31, entitled *Boobytraps*; a picture of Ellis standing beside a helicopter, his first Huey, grinning, looking young and (*oh shit,*) thin; a note from Frankie Amalfi which said *To the bastard that stole my leg* – a brave joke, for Ellis had gently untied Frankie's lace then tugged at his boot and pulled away his foot and half his leg, severed at the knee by a wildly flexing rotor blade; Jimmy Jones's watch, stopped forever at half past five – *You keep it, son,* Jimmy's father had said to Ellis through an alcoholic haze, *'cause you were his frien', and that's more than I ever wuz*; and the diary.

He leafed through the pages. He only had to read a few words to recall a whole day, a week, a battle. The journal began cheerfully, with a sense of adventure, and

very self-consciously; and it got progressively disen-
chanted, sombre, bleak, despairing, and eventually sui-
cidal. The grim phrases brought vivid scenes to his
mind: *goddam Arvins wouldn't get out of the helicopter, if
they're so keen to be rescued from Communism how come they
don't fight?* and then *Capt. Johnson always was an A. hole I
guess but what a way to die, grenaded by one of his own men,*
and later *The women have rifles up their skirts and the kids
have grenades in their shirts so what the fuck are we supposed
to do, surrender?* The last entry read *What is wrong with
this war is that we are on the wrong side. We are the bad guys.
That is why the kids dodge the draft; that is why the Vietnamese
won't fight, that is why we kill women and children; that is
why the generals lie to the politicians, and the politicians lie to
the reporters, and the newspapers lie to the public.* After that
his thoughts had become too seditious to be committed
to paper, his guilt too great to be expiated by mere
words. It seemed to him that he would have to spend
the rest of his life righting the wrongs he had done in
that war. After all these years it still seemed that way.
When he added up the murderers he had jailed since
then, the kidnappers and the hijackers and the bombers
he had arrested, they were as nothing when balanced
against the tons of explosives he had dropped and the
thousands of rounds of ammunition he had fired in
Vietnam, Laos and Cambodia.

It was irrational, he knew. He had realized that when
he came back from Paris and reflected for a while on
how his job had ruined his life. He had decided to stop
trying to redeem the sins of America. But this ... this
was different. Here was a chance to fight for the little

guy, to fight against the lying generals and the power brokers and the blinkered journalists; a chance not just to fight, not just to pay a small contribution, but to make a real difference, to change the course of a war, to alter the fate of a country, and to strike a blow for freedom on a big scale.

And then there was Jane.

The mere possibility of seeing her again had rekindled his passion. Just a few days ago he had been able to think of her and the danger she was in, and put the thought out of his mind and turn the page of the magazine. Now he could hardly stop thinking about her. He wondered whether her hair was long or short, was she fatter or thinner, did she feel good about what she was doing with her life, did the Afghans like her, and – most of all – did she still love Jean-Pierre. *Take my advice,* Gill had said; *check her out.* Clever Gill.

Finally he thought about Petal. I tried, he said to himself; I really tried, and I don't think I handled it too badly – I think it was a doomed project. Gill and Bernard give her all she needs. There is no room for me in her life. She's happy without me.

He closed the diary and returned it to the case. Next he took out a small, cheap jeweller's box. Inside were a small pair of gold earrings, each with a pearl in the centre. The woman they had been intended for, a slant-eyed girl with small breasts who had taught him that nothing is taboo, had died – killed by a drunken soldier in a Saigon bar – before he gave them to her. He had not loved her: he just liked her and felt grateful to her. The earrings were to have been a farewell gift.

He took a plain card and a pen from his shirt pocket. He thought for a minute, then wrote:

To Petal –
  Yes, you can have them pierced.
    With love from Daddy.

CHAPTER SIX

THE FIVE Lions River was never warm, but it seemed a little less cold now, in the balmy evening air at the end of a dusty day, when the women came down to their own exclusive stretch of the bank to bathe. Jane gritted her teeth against the chill and waded into the water with the others, lifting her dress inch by inch as it got deeper, until it was up to her waist, then she began to wash: after long practice she had mastered the peculiar Afghan skill of getting clean all over without undressing.

When she had finished she came out of the river, shivering, and stood near Zahara, who was washing her hair in a pool with much splashing and spluttering, and at the same time carrying on a boisterous conversation. Zahara dipped her head in the water one more time then reached for her towel. She scrabbled around in a hollow in the sandy earth, but the towel was not there. 'Where's my towel?' she yelled. 'I put it in this hole. Who stole it?'

Jane picked up the towel from behind Zahara and said: 'Here it is. You put it in the wrong hole.'

'That's what the Mullah's wife said!' Zahara shouted, and the others shrieked with laughter.

Jane was now accepted by the village women as one of them. The last vestiges of reserve or wariness had vanished after the birth of Chantal, which seemed to have confirmed that Jane was a woman like any other. The talk at the riverside was surprisingly frank – perhaps because the children were left behind in the care of older sisters and grandmothers, but more probably because of Zahara. Her loud voice, her flashing eyes and her rich, throaty laughter dominated the scene. No doubt she was all the more extrovert here for having to repress her personality for the rest of the day. She had a vulgar sense of humour, which Jane had not come across in any other Afghan, male or female, and Zahara's ribald remarks and double-meaning jokes often opened up the way for serious discussion. Consequently Jane was sometimes able to turn the evening bathing session into an impromptu health education class. Birth control was the most popular topic, although the women of Banda were more interested in how to ensure pregnancy than how to prevent it. However, there was some sympathy for the idea, which Jane was trying to promote, that a woman was better able to feed and care for her children if they were born two years apart rather than every twelve or fifteen months. Yesterday they had talked about the menstrual cycle, and it had transpired that Afghan women thought the fertile time was just before and just after the period. Jane had told them that it was from the twelfth day to the sixteenth, and they had appeared to accept this, but she had a disconcerting suspicion that they thought *she* was wrong and were too polite to say so.

Today there was an air of excitement. The latest Pakistan convoy was due back. The men would bring small luxuries – a shawl, some oranges, plastic bangles – as well as the all-important guns, ammunition and explosives for the war.

Zahara's husband Ahmed Gul, one of the sons of the midwife Rabia, was leader of the convoy, and Zahara was visibly excited at the prospect of seeing him again. When they were together they were like all Afghan couples: she silent and subservient, he casually imperious. But Jane could tell, by the way they looked at one another, that they were in love; and it was clear from the way Zahara talked that their love was highly physical. Today she was almost beside herself with desire, rubbing her hair dry with fierce, frantic energy. Jane sympathised: she had felt that way herself sometimes. No doubt she and Zahara had become friends because each recognised a kindred spirit in the other.

Jane's skin dried almost immediately in the warm, dusty air. It was now the height of summer, and every day was long, dry and hot. The good weather would last a month or two longer, and then the rest of the year it would be bitterly cold.

Zahara was still interested in yesterday's topic of conversation. She stopped rubbing her hair for a moment to say: 'Whatever anyone says, the way to get pregnant is to Do It every day.'

There was agreement from Halima, the sullen, dark-eyed wife of Mohammed Khan. 'And the only way *not* to get pregnant is *never* to Do It.' She had four children, but only one of them – Mousa – was a boy, and she had been disappointed to learn that Jane knew no way to improve one's chances of having a boy.

Zahara said: 'But then, what do you say to your husband when he comes home after six weeks with a convoy?'

Jane said: 'Be like the Mullah's wife, and put it in the wrong hole.'

Zahara roared with laughter. Jane smiled. That was a birth control technique which had not been mentioned in her crash courses in Paris, but it was clear that modern methods would not arrive in the Five Lions Valley for many years yet, so traditional means would have to serve – helped, perhaps, by a little education.

The talk turned to the harvest. The Valley was a sea of golden wheat and bearded barley, but much of it would rot in the fields, for the young men were away fighting most of the time and the older ones found it slow work reaping by moonlight. Towards the end of the summer all the families would add up their sacks of flour and baskets of dried fruit, look at their chickens and goats, and count their pennies; and they would contemplate the coming shortages of eggs and meat, and hazard a guess at this winter's prices for rice and yoghurt; and some of them would pack a few precious possessions and make the long trek across the mountains to set up new homes in the refugee camps of Pakistan, as the shopkeeper had, along with millions of other Afghans.

Jane feared that the Russians would make this evacuation their policy – that, unable to defeat the guerrillas, they would try to destroy the communities within which the guerrillas lived, as the Americans had in Vietnam, by carpet-bombing whole areas of the countryside, so that the Five Lions Valley would become an uninhabited wasteland, and Mohammed and Zahara and Rabia would join the homeless, stateless, aimless occupants of the camps. The rebels could not begin to resist an all-out blitzkrieg, for they had virtually no anti-aircraft weapons.

It was getting dark. The women began to drift back to the village. Jane walked with Zahara, half-listening to the talk and thinking about Chantal. Her feelings about the baby had gone through several stages. Immediately after the birth she had felt exhilarated by relief, triumph and joy at having produced a living, perfect baby. When the reaction set in she had felt utterly miserable. She had not known how to look after a baby, and contrary to what people said she had no instinctive knowledge at all. She had been frightened of the baby. There had been no gush of maternal love. Instead she had suffered weird and terrifying dreams and fantasies in which the baby died – dropped in the river, or killed by a bomb, or stolen away in the night by the snow tiger. She still had not told Jean-Pierre about these thoughts in case he should think her mad.

There had been conflicts with the midwife, Rabia Gull. She said women should not breast-feed for the first three days, because what came out was not milk. Jane decided it was ludicrous to believe that nature would make women's breasts produce something that was bad for new-born babies, and she ignored the old woman's advice. Rabia also said the baby should not be washed for forty days, but Chantal was bathed every day like any other Western baby. Then Jane had caught Rabia giving Chantal butter mixed with sugar, feeding the stuff to the child on the end of her wrinkled old finger; and Jane had got cross. The next day Rabia went to attend another birth, and sent one of her many granddaughters, a thirteen-year-old called Fara, to help Jane. This was a great improvement. Fara had no preconceptions about child care and simply did as she was told. She required no pay: she worked for her food – which was better at Jane's house than at Fara's parents' – and for the privilege of learning about babies in preparation for her own marriage, which would probably take place within a year or two. Jane also thought Rabia might be grooming Fara as a future midwife, in which case the girl would gain kudos from having helped the Western nurse care for her baby.

With Rabia out of the way, Jean-Pierre had come into his own. He was gentle yet confident with Chantal, and considerate and loving with Jane. It was he who had suggested, rather firmly, that Chantal could be given boiled goat's milk when she woke in the night, and he had improvised a feeding bottle from his medical supplies so that he could be the one to get up. Of course Jane always woke when Chantal cried, and stayed awake while Jean-Pierre fed her; but this was much less tiring, and at last she got rid of that feeling of utter, despairing exhaustion which had been so depressing.

Finally, although she was still anxious and unselfconfident, she had found within herself a degree of patience that she had never previously possessed; and this, though it was not the deep instinctive knowledge and assurance she had been hoping for, nevertheless enabled her to confront the daily crises with equanimity. Even now, she realised, she had been away from Chantal for almost an hour without worrying.

The group of women reached the cluster of houses which formed the nucleus of the village, and one by one they disappeared behind the mud walls of their courtyards. Jane scared off a flurry of chickens and shoved aside a scrawny cow to get into her own house. Inside, she found Fara singing to Chantal in the lamplight. The baby was alert and wide-eyed, apparently fascinated by the sound of the girl's singing. It was a lullaby with simple words and a complex, Oriental-sounding tune. She's such a *pretty* baby, Jane thought, with her fat cheeks and her tiny nose and her blue, blue eyes.

She sent Fara to make tea. The girl was terribly shy and had arrived in fear and trembling to work for the foreigners; but her nervousness was easing, and her initial awe of Jane was gradually turning into something more like adoring loyalty.

A few minutes later Jean-Pierre came in. His baggy cotton trousers and shirt were grimy and bloodstained, and there was dust in his long brown hair and his dark beard. He looked tired. He had been to Khenj, a village ten miles down the valley, to treat the survivors of a bombing raid. Jane stood on tiptoe to kiss him. 'How was it?' she said in French.

'Bad.' He gave her a squeeze, then went to lean over Chantal. 'Hello, little one.' He smiled, and Chantal gurgled.

'What happened?' Jane asked.

'It was a family whose house was some distance from the rest of the village, so they thought they were safe.' Jean-Pierre shrugged. 'Then some wounded guerrillas were brought in from a skirmish farther south. That's why I'm so late.' He sat down on a pile of cushions. 'Is there any tea?'

'It's coming,' Jane said. 'What kind of skirmish?'

He closed his eyes. 'Usual thing. The Army came in helicopters and occupied a village for reasons known only to themselves. The villagers fled. The menfolk regrouped, got reinforcements, and started to harry the Russians from the hillsides. Casualties on both sides. The guerrillas finally ran out of ammunition and withdrew.'

Jane nodded. She felt sorry for Jean-Pierre: it was a depressing task to tend the victims of a pointless battle. Banda had never been raided, but she lived in constant fear of it – she had a nightmare vision of herself running, running, with Chantal clutched to her, while the helicopters beat the air above and the machine-gun bullets thudded into the dusty ground at her feet.

Fara came in with hot green tea, some of the flat bread they called *nan*, and a stone jar of new butter. Jane and Jean-Pierre began to eat. The butter was a rare treat. Their evening *nan* was usually dipped in yoghurt, curds or oil. At midday they normally ate rice with a meat-flavoured sauce that might or might not have meat in it. Once a week they had chicken or goat. Jane, eating for two still, indulged in the luxury of an egg every day. At this time of year there was plenty of fresh fruit – apricots, plums, apples, and mulberries by the sackful – for dessert. Jane felt very healthy on this diet, although most English people would have considered it starvation rations, and some Frenchmen would have thought it reason for suicide. She smiled at her husband. 'A little more Béarnaise sauce with your steak?'

'No, thank you.' He held out his cup. 'Perhaps another drop of the Château Cheval Blanc.' Jane gave him more tea, and he pretended to taste it as if it were wine, chewing and gargling. 'The nineteen sixty-two is an underrated vintage, following as it did the unforgettable sixty-one, but I have always felt that its relative amiability and impeccable good manners give almost as much pleasure as the perfection of elegance which is the austere mark of its highbrow predecessor.'

Jane grinned. He was beginning to feel himself again.

Chantal cried, and Jane felt an immediate answering twinge in her breasts. She picked up the baby and began to feed her. Jean-Pierre carried on eating. Jane said: 'Leave some butter for Fara.'

'Okay.' He took the remains of their supper outside, and returned with a bowl of mulberries. Jane ate while Chantal suckled. Soon the baby fell asleep, but Jane knew she would wake again in a few minutes and want more.

Jean-Pierre pushed away the bowl and said: 'I got another complaint about you today.'

'From whom?' Jane said sharply.

Jean-Pierre looked defensive but stubborn. 'Mohammed Khan.'

'But he wasn't speaking for himself.'

'Perhaps not.'

'What did he say?'

'That you have been teaching the village women to be barren.'

Jane sighed. It was not just the stupidity of the village menfolk that annoyed her, but also Jean-Pierre's accommodating attitude to their complaints. She wanted him to defend her, not defer to her accusers. 'Abdullah Karim is behind it, of course,' she said. The mullah's wife was often at the riverside, and no doubt she reported to her husband everything she heard.

'You may have to stop,' said Jean-Pierre.

'Stop what?' Jane could hear the dangerous tone in her own voice.

'Telling them how to avoid pregnancy.'

That was not a fair description of what Jane taught the women, but she was not willing to defend herself or apologise. 'Why should I stop?' she said.

'It's creating difficulties,' said Jean-Pierre with a patient air that irritated Jane. 'If we offend the mullah grievously we may have to leave Afghanistan. More importantly, it would give the *Médecins pour la Liberté* organisation a bad name, and the rebels might refuse other doctors. This is a holy war, you know – spiritual health is more important than the physical kind. They could decide to do without us.'

There were other organisations sending idealistic young French doctors to Afghanistan, but Jane did not say that. Instead she said flatly: 'We'll just have to take that risk.'

'Shall we?' he said, and she could see that he was getting angry. 'And why should we?'

'Because there is really only one thing of permanent value that we can give these people, and that is *information*. It's all very well to patch their wounds and give them drugs to kill germs, but they will never have enough surgeons or enough drugs. We can improve their health *permanently* by teaching them basic nutrition, hygiene and health care. Better to offend Abdullah than to stop doing that.'

'Still, I wish you hadn't made an enemy of that man.'

'He hit me with a stick!' Jane shouted furiously. Chantal began to cry. Jane forced herself to be calm. She rocked Chantal for a moment, then began to feed her. Why couldn't Jean-Pierre see how cowardly his attitude was? How could he be intimidated by the threat of expulsion from this godforsaken country? Jane sighed. Chantal turned her face away from Jane's breast and made discontented noises. Before the argument could continue they heard distant shouting.

Jean-Pierre frowned, listening, then got up. A man's voice came from their courtyard. Jean-Pierre picked up a shawl and draped it over Jane's shoulders. She pulled it together in the front. This was a compromise: it was not really sufficient covering, by Afghan standards, but she refused point-blank to scuttle out of the room like a second-class citizen if a man walked into her house while she was feeding her baby; and anyone who objected, she had announced, had better not come to see the doctor.

Jean-Pierre called out in Dari: 'Come in.'

It was Mohammed Khan. Jane was in a mood to tell him just what she thought of him and the rest of the village men, but she hesitated when she saw the strain on his handsome face. For once he hardly looked at her. 'The convoy was ambushed,' he said without preamble. 'We lost twenty-seven men – and all the supplies.'

Jane closed her eyes in pain. She had travelled with such a convoy when she first came to the Five Lions Valley, and she could not help but picture the ambush: the moonlit line of brown-skinned men and scrawny horses stretched out unevenly along a stony trail through a narrow, shadowy valley; the beat of the rotor blades in a sudden crescendo; the flares, the grenades, the machine-gun fire; the panic as the men tried to take cover on the bare hillside; the hopeless shots fired at the invulnerable helicopters; and then at last the shouts of the wounded and the screams of the dying.

She thought suddenly of Zahara: her husband had been with the convoy. 'What – what about Ahmed Gul?'

'He came back.'

'Oh, thank God,' Jane breathed.

'But he's wounded.'

'Who from this village died?'

129

'None. Banda was lucky. My brother Matullah is all right, and so is Alishan Karim, the brother of the mullah. There are three other survivors – two of them wounded.'

Jean-Pierre said: 'I'll come right away.' He stepped into the front room of the house, the room that had once been the shop, and then the clinic, and was now the medical storeroom.

Jane put Chantal down in her makeshift cradle in the corner and hastily tidied herself up. Jean-Pierre would need her help, and if he did not then Zahara could use some sympathy.

Mohammed said: 'We have almost no ammunition.'

Jane felt little regret about that. She was revolted by the war, and she would shed no tears if the rebels were obliged for a while to stop killing poor miserable homesick seventeen-year-old Russian soldier boys.

Mohammed went on: 'We have lost four convoys in a year. Only three got through.'

'How are the Russians able to find them?' asked Jane.

Jean-Pierre, who was listening in the next room, spoke through the open doorway. 'They must have intensified their surveillance of the passes by low-flying helicopters – or perhaps even by satellite photography.'

Mohammed shook his head. 'The Pushtuns betray us.'

Jane thought this was possible. In the villages through which they passed, the convoys were sometimes seen as a magnet for Russian raids, and it was conceivable that some villagers might buy their safety by telling the Russians where the convoys were – although it was not clear to Jane just how they would pass the information to the Russians.

She thought of what she had been hoping for from the ambushed convoy. She had asked for more antibiotics, some hypodermic needles, and a lot of sterile dressings. Jean-Pierre had written out a long list of drugs. The organisation *Médecins pour la Liberté* had a liaison man in Peshawar, the city in north-west Pakistan where the guerrillas bought their weapons. He might have got the basic supplies locally, but he would have had the drugs flown from Western Europe. What a waste. It might be months before replacements arrived. In Jane's view that was a far greater loss than the ammunition.

Jean-Pierre came back in, carrying his bag. The three of them went out into the courtyard. It was dark. Jane paused to give instructions to Fara about changing Chantal, then hurried after the two men.

She caught up with them as they approached the mosque. It was not an impressive building. It had none of the gorgeous colours or exquisite decoration familiar from coffee-table books about Islamic art. It was an open-sided building, its mat roof supported by stone columns, and Jane thought it looked like a glorified bus shelter, or perhaps the verandah of a ruined Colonial mansion. An archway through the middle of the building led to a walled yard. The villagers treated it with small reverence. They prayed there, but they also used it as a meeting hall, market place, schoolroom and guest house. And tonight it would be a hospital.

Oil lamps suspended from hooks in the stone columns now lit the verandah-like mosque building. The villagers formed a crowd to the left of the archway. They were subdued: several women were sobbing quietly, and the voices of two men could be heard, one asking questions and the other answering. The crowd parted to admit Jean-Pierre, Mohammed and Jane.

The six survivors of the ambush were huddled in a group on the beaten-earth floor. The three uninjured ones squatted on their haunches, still wearing their round Chitrali caps, looking dirty, dispirited, and exhausted. Jane recognised Matullah Khan, a younger version of his brother Mohammed; and Alishan Karim, thinner than his brother the mullah but just as mean-looking. Two of the wounded men sat on the floor with their backs to the wall, one with a filthy, bloodstained bandage around his head and the other with his arm in an improvised sling. Jane did not know either of them. She automatically assessed their wounds: at first glance they appeared slight.

The third injured man, Ahmed Gul, was lying flat on a stretcher made from two sticks and a blanket. His eyes were closed and his skin was grey. His wife, Zahara, squatted behind him, cradling his head in her lap, stroking his hair, and weeping silently. Jane could not see his wounds, but she could tell they must be serious.

Jean-Pierre called for a table, hot water, and towels, then got down on his knees beside Ahmed. After a few seconds he looked up at the other guerrillas and said in Dari: 'Was he in an explosion?'

'The helicopters had rockets,' said one of the unin-jured. 'One went off beside him.'

Jean-Pierre reverted to French and spoke to Jane. 'He's in a bad way. It's a miracle he survived the journey.'

Jane could see bloodstains on Ahmed's chin: he had been coughing blood, a sign that he had internal injuries.

Zahara looked pleadingly at Jane. 'How is he?' she said in Dari.

'I'm sorry, my friend,' said Jane as gently as she could. 'He's bad.'

Zahara nodded resignedly: she had known it, but the confirmation brought fresh tears to her handsome face.

Jean-Pierre said to Jane: 'Check the others for me – I don't want to lose a minute here.'

Jane examined the other two wounded men. 'The head wound is just a scratch,' she said after a moment.

'Deal with it,' said Jean-Pierre. He was supervising the lifting of Ahmed on to a table.

She looked at the man with his arm in a sling. He was more seriously hurt: it looked as if a bullet had smashed a bone. 'This must have hurt,' she said to the guerrilla in Dari. He grinned and nodded. These men were made of cast iron. 'The bullet broke the bone,' she said to Jean-Pierre.

Jean-Pierre did not look up from Ahmed. 'Give him a local anaesthetic, clean the wound, take out the bits, and give him a clean sling. We'll set the bone later.'

She began to prepare the injection. When Jean-

Pierre needed her assistance he would call. It looked as if it might be a long night.

Ahmed died a few minutes after midnight, and Jean-Pierre felt like crying – not with sadness, for he hardly knew Ahmed, but with sheer frustration, for he knew he could have saved the man's life, if only he had had an anaesthetist and electricity and an operating theatre.

He covered the dead man's face, then looked at the wife, who had been standing motionless, watching, for hours. 'I'm sorry,' he said to her. She nodded. He was glad she was calm. Sometimes they accused him of not trying everything: they seemed to think he knew so much that there was nothing he couldn't cure, and he wanted to scream *I am not God* at them; but this one seemed to understand.

He turned away from the corpse. He was weary to his bones. He had been working on mangled bodies all day, but this was the first patient he had lost. The people who had been watching him, mostly relatives of the dead man, came forward now to deal with the body. The widow began to wail, and Jane led her away.

Jean-Pierre felt a hand on his shoulder. He turned to see Mohammed, the guerrilla who organised the convoys. He felt a stab of guilt.

Mohammed said: 'It's the will of Allah.'

Jean-Pierre nodded. Mohammed took out a pack of Pakistani cigarettes and lit one. Jean-Pierre began to gather up his instruments and put them into his bag.

Without looking at Mohammed he said: 'What will you do now?'

'Send another convoy immediately,' Mohammed said. 'We must have ammunition.'

Jean-Pierre was suddenly alert, despite his fatigue. 'Do you want to look at the maps?'

'Yes.'

Jean-Pierre closed his bag, and the two men walked away from the mosque. The stars illuminated their way through the village to the shopkeeper's house. In the living-room, Fara was asleep on a rug beside Chantal's cradle. She awoke instantly and stood up. 'You can go home now,' Jean-Pierre told her. She left without speaking.

Jean-Pierre put his bag down on the floor, then picked up the cradle gently and carried it into the bedroom. Chantal stayed asleep until he put the cradle down, then she began to cry. 'Now, what is it?' he murmured to her. He looked at his wristwatch and realised she probably wanted feeding. 'Mama's coming soon,' he told her. This had no effect. He lifted her out of the cradle and began to rock her. She became quiet. He carried her back into the living-room.

Mohammed was standing waiting. Jean-Pierre said: 'You know where they are.'

Mohammed nodded and opened a painted wooden chest. He took out a thick bundle of folded maps, selected several, and spread them on the floor. Jean-Pierre rocked Chantal and looked over Mohammed's shoulder. 'Where was the ambush?' he asked.

Mohammed pointed to a spot near the city of Jalalabad.

The trails followed by Mohammed's convoys were not shown on these or any other maps. However, Jean-Pierre's maps showed some of the valleys, plateaus and seasonal streams where there *might* be trails. Sometimes Mohammed knew from memory what was there. Sometimes he had to guess, and he would discuss with Jean-Pierre the precise interpretation of contour lines or the more obscure terrain features such as moraines.

Jean-Pierre suggested: 'You could swing more to the north around Jalalabad.' Above the plain in which the city stood, there was a maze of valleys like a cobweb stretched between the Konar and Nuristan rivers.

Mohammed lit another cigarette – like most of the guerrillas he was a heavy smoker – and shook his head dubiously as he exhaled. 'There have been too many ambushes in that area,' he said. 'If they are not betraying us already they soon will. No; the next convoy will swing *south* of Jalalabad.'

Jean-Pierre frowned. 'I don't see how that's possible. To the south, there's nothing but open country all the way from the Khyber Pass. You'd be spotted.'

'We won't use the Khyber Pass,' said Mohammed. He put his finger on the map, then traced the Afghanistan-Pakistan border southward. 'We will cross the border at Teremengal.' His finger reached the town he had named, then traced a route from there to the Five Lions Valley.

Jean-Pierre nodded, hiding his jubilation. 'It makes a lot of sense. When will the new convoy leave here?'

Mohammed began to fold up the charts. 'The day after tomorrow. There is no time to lose.' He replaced the maps in the painted chest then went to the door.

Jane came in just as he was leaving. He said 'Good-night' to her in an absent-minded way. Jean-Pierre was glad the handsome guerrilla no longer had the hots for Jane since her pregnancy. She was definitely oversexed, in Jean-Pierre's opinion, and quite capable of letting herself be seduced; and for her to have an affair with an Afghan would have caused endless trouble.

Jean-Pierre's medical bag was on the floor where he had left it, and Jane bent down to pick it up. His heart missed a beat. He took the bag from her quickly. She gave him a mildly surprised look. 'I'll put this away,' he said. 'You see to Chantal. She needs feeding.' He gave the baby to her.

He carried the bag and a map into the front room as Jane settled down to feed Chantal. Cartons of medical supplies were stacked on the dirt floor. Already-opened boxes were arranged on the shopkeeper's crude wooden shelves. Jean-Pierre put his medical bag on the blue-tiled counter and took out a black plastic object about the size and shape of a portable telephone. This he put in his pocket.

He emptied his bag, putting the instruments for sterilization to one side and stowing the unused items on the shelves.

He returned to the living-room. 'I'm going down to the river to bathe,' he said to Jane. 'I'm too dirty to go to bed.'

She gave him the dreamy, contented smile she often wore when feeding the baby. 'Be quick,' she said.

He went out.

The village was going to sleep, at last. Lamps still burned in a few houses, and he heard from one window the sound of a woman weeping bitterly, but most places were quiet and dark. Passing the last house in the village he heard a woman's voice raised in a high, mournful song of bereavement, and for a moment he felt the crushing weight of the deaths he had caused; then he put the thought out of his mind.

He followed a stony path between two barley fields, looking around constantly and listening carefully: the men of the village would now be at work. In one field he heard the hiss of scythes, and on a narrow terrace he saw two men weeding by lamplight. He did not speak to them.

He reached the river, crossed the ford, and climbed the winding path up the opposite cliff. He knew he was quite safe, yet he felt increasingly tense as he ascended the steep path in the faint light.

After ten minutes he reached the high point he was seeking. He took the radio from his trousers pocket and extended its telescopic antenna. It was the latest and most sophisticated small transmitter the KGB had, but even so, the terrain here was so inimical to radio transmission that the Russians had built a special relay station, on a hilltop just inside the territory they controlled, to pick up his signals and pass them on.

He pressed the talk button and spoke in English and in code. 'This is Simplex. Come in, please.'

He waited, then called again.

After the third try he got a crackly, accented reply. '*Here is Butler. Go ahead, Simplex.*'

'Your party was a big success.'

'*I repeat: The party was a big success,*' came the reply.

'Twenty-seven people attended and one more came later.'

'*I repeat: Twenty-seven attended and one came later.*'

'In preparation for the next one, I need three camels.' In the code, that meant 'Meet me three days from today.'

'*I repeat: You need three camels.*'

'I will see you at the mosque.' That, too, was code: 'the mosque' was a place some miles away where three valleys met.

'*I repeat: At the mosque.*'

'Today is Sunday.' That was not code: it was a precaution against the possibility that the dullard who was taking all this down might not realise it was after midnight, with the consequence that Jean-Pierre's contact would arrive a day early at the rendezvous.

'*I repeat: Today is Sunday.*'

'Over and out.'

Jean-Pierre collapsed the antenna and returned the radio to his trousers pocket, then he made his way down the cliff to the riverside.

He stripped off his clothes quickly. From the pocket of the shirt he took a nail-brush and a small piece of soap. Soap was a scarce commodity but he as doctor had priority.

He stepped gingerly into the Five Lions River, knelt

down, and splashed icy water all over himself. He soaped his skin and his hair, then picked up the brush and began to scrub himself: his legs, his belly, his chest, his face, his arms and his hands. He worked especially hard on his hands, soaping them again and again. Kneeling in the shallows, naked and shivering beneath the stars, he scrubbed and scrubbed as if he would never stop.

CHAPTER SEVEN

'T HE CHILD has measles, gastro-enteritis and ringworm,' said Jean-Pierre. 'It is also dirty and undernourished.'

'Aren't they all,' said Jane.

They were speaking French, as they normally did together, and the child's mother looked from one to the other of them as they spoke, wondering what they were saying. Jean-Pierre observed her anxiety and spoke to her in Dari, saying simply: 'Your son will get well.'

He crossed to the other side of the cave and opened his drugs case. All children brought to the clinic were automatically vaccinated against tuberculosis. As he prepared the BCG injection he watched Jane out of the corner of his eye. She was giving the boy small sips of rehydration drink – a mixture of glucose, salt, baking soda and potassium chloride dissolved in clean water – and, between sips, was gently washing his grimy face. Her movements were quick and graceful, like those of a craftsman – a potter moulding clay, perhaps, or a bricklayer wielding a trowel. He observed her narrow hands as she touched the frightened child with light, reassuring caresses. He liked her hands.

He turned away as he took the needle out, so that

the child should not see it, then he held it concealed by his sleeve and turned again, waiting for Jane. He studied her face as she cleaned the skin of the boy's right shoulder and swabbed a patch with alcohol. It was an impish face, with big eyes, a turned-up nose, and a wide mouth that smiled more often than not. Now her expression was serious, and she was moving her jaw from side to side, as if grinding her teeth – a sign that she was concentrating. Jean-Pierre knew all of her expressions and none of her thoughts.

He speculated often – almost continually – about what she was thinking, but he was afraid to ask her, for such conversations could so easily wander into forbidden territory. He had to be constantly on his guard, like an unfaithful husband, for fear that something he said – or even the expression on his face – might betray him. Any talk of truth and dishonesty, or trust and betrayal, or freedom and tyranny, was taboo; and so were any subjects which might lead to these, such as love, war and politics. He was wary even when talking of quite innocent topics. Consequently there was a peculiar lack of intimacy in their marriage. Making love was weird. He found that he could not reach a climax unless he closed his eyes and pretended he was somewhere else. It was a relief to him that he had not had to perform for the last few weeks because of the birth of Chantal.

'Ready when you are,' Jane said, and he realised she was smiling at him.

He took the child's arm and said in Dari: 'How old are you?'

'Five.'

As the boy spoke, Jean-Pierre stuck the needle in. The child immediately began to wail. The sound of its voice made Jean-Pierre think of himself at the age of five, riding his first bicycle and falling off and crying just like that, a sharp howl of protest at an unexpected pain. He stared at the screwed-up face of his five-year-old patient, remembering how much it had hurt and how angry he had felt, and he found himself thinking: How did I get *here* from *there*?

He released the child and it went to its mother. He counted out thirty 250-gram capsules of griseofulvin and handed them to the woman. 'Make him take one every day until they are all gone,' he said in simple Dari. 'Don't give them to anyone else – he needs them all.' That would deal with the ringworm. The measles and the gastro-enteritis would take their own course. 'Keep him in bed until the spots disappear, and make sure he drinks a lot.'

The woman nodded.

'Does he have any brothers and sisters?' Jean-Pierre asked.

'Five brothers and two sisters,' the woman said proudly.

'He should sleep alone, or they will get sick too.' The woman looked dubious: she probably had only one bed for all her children. There was nothing Jean-Pierre could do about that. He went on: 'If he is not better when the tablets are finished, bring him back to me.' What the child really needed was the one thing neither Jean-Pierre nor its mother could provide – plenty of good, nutritious food.

The two of them left the cave, the thin, sick child and the frail, weary mother. They had probably come several miles, she carrying the boy most of the way, and now they would walk back. The boy might die anyway. But not of tuberculosis.

There was one more patient: the *malang*. He was Banda's holy man. Half mad, and often more-than-half naked, he wandered the Five Lions Valley from Comar, twenty-five miles upstream of Banda, to Charikar in the Russian-controlled plain sixty miles to the south-west. He spoke gibberish and saw visions. The Afghans believed *malangs* to be lucky, and not only tolerated their behaviour but gave them food and drink and clothing.

He came in, wearing rags around his loins and a Russian officer's cap. He clutched his middle, miming pain. Jean-Pierre shook out a handful of diamorphine pills and gave them to him. The madman ran off, clutching his synthetic heroin tablets.

'He must be addicted to that stuff by now,' Jane said. There was a distinct note of disapproval in her voice.

'He is,' Jean-Pierre admitted.

'Why do you give it to him?'

'The man has an ulcer. What else should I do – operate?'

'You're the doctor.'

Jean-Pierre began to pack his bag. In the morning he had to hold a clinic in Cobak, six or seven miles away across the mountains – and he had a rendezvous to keep on the way.

144

The crying of the five-year-old had brought an air of the past into the cave, like a smell of old toys, or a strange light that makes you rub your eyes. Jean-Pierre felt faintly disoriented by it. He kept seeing people from his childhood, their faces superimposed on the things around him, like scenes from a film cast by a misaligned projector on to the backs of the audience instead of the screen. He saw his first teacher, the steel-rimmed Mademoiselle Médecin; Jacques Lafontaine who had given him a bloody nose for calling him *con*; his mother, thin and ill-dressed and always distraught; and most of all his father, a big, beefy, angry man on the other side of a barred partition.

He made an effort to concentrate on the equipment and drugs he might need at Cobak. He filled a flask with purified water for himself to drink while he was away. He would be fed by the villagers there.

He took his bags outside and loaded them on to the bad-tempered old mare he used for such trips. This animal would walk all day in a straight line but was highly reluctant to turn corners, on account of which Jane had named it Maggie, after the British Prime Minister Margaret Thatcher.

Jean-Pierre was ready. He went back into the cave and kissed Jane's soft mouth. As he turned to leave, Fara came in with Chantal. The baby was crying. Jane unbuttoned her shirt and put Chantal to her breast immediately. Jean-Pierre touched his daughter's pink cheek and said: 'Bon appetit.' Then he went out.

He led Maggie down the mountain to the deserted

village and headed south-west, following the river bank. He walked quickly and tirelessly under the hot sun: he was used to it.

As he left his doctor persona behind and thought ahead to his rendezvous, he began to feel anxious. Would Anatoly be there? He might have been delayed. He might even have been captured. If captured, had he talked? Had he betrayed Jean-Pierre under torture? Would there be a party of guerrillas waiting for Jean-Pierre, merciless and sadistic and bent on revenge?

For all their poetry and their piety they were barbarians, these Afghans. Their national sport was *buzkashi*, a dangerous and bloody game: the headless body of a calf was placed in the centre of a field, and the two opposing teams lined up on horseback, then, at the rifle shot, they all charged towards the carcase. The aim was to pick it up, carry it to a predetermined turning-point about a mile away, and bring it back to the circle without allowing any of the opposing players to wrench it from your grasp. When the grisly object got ripped apart, as often happened, a referee was there to decide which team had control of the larger remnant; Jean-Pierre had come across a game in progress last winter, just outside the town of Rokha down the valley, and he had watched it for a few minutes before realizing that they were not using a calf, but a man, *and the man was still alive.* Sickened, he had tried to stop the game, but someone had told him the man was a Russian officer, as if that were all the explanation anyone could possibly want. The players just ignored Jean-Pierre then, and there was nothing he could do to get the attention of fifty highly excited riders intent on their savage game. He had not stayed to watch the man die, but perhaps he should have, for the image that remained in his mind, and returned to him every time he worried about being found out, was of that Russian, helpless and bleeding, being torn to pieces alive.

The sense of the past was still with him, and as he looked at the khaki-coloured rock walls of the gully through which he was striding he saw scenes from his childhood alternating with nightmares about being caught by the guerrillas. His earliest memory was of the trial, and of the overwhelming sense of outrage and injustice he had felt when they had sent his Papa to jail. He could hardly read, but he could make out his father's name in the newspaper headlines. At that age – he must have been four – he did not know what it meant to be a hero of the Resistance. He knew his father was a Communist, as were his father's friends, the priest and the cobbler and the man behind the counter in the village post office; but he thought they called him Red Roland because of his ruddy complexion. When his father was convicted of treason and sentenced to five years in jail, they had told Jean-Pierre that it had to do with Uncle Abdul, a frightened brown-skinned man who had stayed in the house for several weeks, and who was from the FLN, but Jean-Pierre did not know what the FLN was and thought they meant the elephant in the zoo. The only thing he understood clearly and always believed was that the police were cruel and the judges were dishonest and the people were fooled by the newspapers.

As the years went by he understood more and suffered more and his sense of outrage grew. When he went to school the other boys said his father was a traitor. He told them that, on the contrary, his father had fought bravely and risked his life in the war, but they did not believe him. He and his mother went to live in another village for a while, but somehow the neighbours found out who they were and told their children not to play with Jean-Pierre. But the worst part was visiting the prison. His father changed visibly, becoming thin, pale and sickly; but worse than that was to see him confined, dressed in a drab uniform, cowed, and frightened, saying 'Sir' to strutting bullies with truncheons. After a while the smell of the prison began to make Jean-Pierre nauseous, and he would throw up as soon as he entered its doors; and his mother stopped taking him.

It was not until Papa came out of prison that Jean-Pierre talked to him at length and finally understood it all, and saw that the injustice of what had happened was even more gross than he had thought. After the Germans invaded France the French Communists, being already organised in cells, had played a leading role in the Resistance. When the war was over his father had carried on the fight against right-wing tyranny. At that time Algeria had been a French colony. Its people were oppressed and exploited, but struggling courageously for their freedom. Young Frenchmen were conscripted into the army and forced to fight against the Algerians in a cruel war in which the atrocities committed by the French Army reminded many people of the work of the Nazis. The FLN, which for Jean-Pierre would always be associated with an image of a mangy old elephant in a provincial zoo, was the *Front de Libération Nationale*, the National Liberation Front of the Algerian people.

Jean-Pierre's father was one of 121 well-known people who signed a petition in favour of freedom for the Algerians. France was at war, and the petition was called seditious, for it might be construed as encouraging French soldiers to desert. But Papa had done worse than that: he had taken a suitcase full of money collected from French people for the FLN and had carried it across the border into Switzerland, where he had put it into a bank; and he had sheltered Uncle Abdul, who was not an uncle at all, but an Algerian wanted by the DST, the secret police.

These were the kind of things he had done in the war against the Nazis, he had explained to Jean-Pierre. He was still fighting the same fight. The enemy had never been the Germans, just as the enemy now was not the French people: it was the capitalists, the owners of property, the rich and privileged, the ruling class who would use any means, no matter how vicious, to protect their position. They were so powerful they controlled half the world – but nevertheless there was hope for the poor, the powerless and the oppressed, for in Moscow the people ruled, and throughout the rest of the world the working class looked to the Soviet Union for help, guidance and inspiration in the battle for freedom.

As Jean-Pierre grew older the picture became tarnished, and he found out that the Soviet Union was not a workers' paradise; but he learned nothing to change his basic conviction that the Communist movement, guided from Moscow, was the only hope for the oppressed people of the world, and the only means of destroying the judges and the police and the newspapers who had so brutally betrayed his Papa.

The father had succeeded in handing the torch on to the son. And, as if he knew this, Papa had gone into a decline. He never regained his red face. He no longer went on demonstrations, organised fund-raising dances, or wrote letters to the local newspapers. He held a series of undemanding clerical jobs. He belonged to the Party, of course, and to a trade union, but he did not resume the chairmanship of committees, the taking of minutes, the preparation of agendas. He still played chess and drank anisette with the priest and the cobbler and the man who ran the village post office, but their political discussions, which had once been passionate, were now lacklustre, as if the revolution for which they had worked so hard had been indefinitely postponed. Within a few years Papa died. It was only then that Jean-Pierre discovered he had contracted tuberculosis in jail, and had never recovered. They took away his freedom, they broke his spirit, and they ruined his health. But the worst thing they did to him was to brand him a traitor. He was a hero who had risked life for his fellow men, but he died convicted of treason.

They'd regret it now, Papa, if they knew what revenge I'm taking, Jean-Pierre thought as he led his bony mare up an Afghan mountainside. Because of the intelligence I have provided, the Communists here have been able to strangle Masud's supply lines. Last winter, he was unable to stockpile weapons and ammunition. This summer, instead of launching attacks on the air base and the power stations and the supply trucks on the highway, he is struggling to defend himself against government raids on *his* territory. Single-handedly, Papa, I have almost destroyed the effectiveness of this barbarian who wants to take his country back to the dark ages of savagery, underdevelopment and Islamic superstition.

Of course, strangling Masud's supply lines was not enough. The man was already a figure of national stature. Furthermore, he had the brains and the strength of character to graduate from rebel leader to legitimate president. He was a Tito, a de Gaulle, a Mugabe. He had to be not just neutralised, but destroyed – taken by the Russians, dead or alive.

The difficulty was that Masud moved about quickly and silently, like a deer in a forest, suddenly emerging from the undergrowth and then disappearing again just as abruptly. But Jean-Pierre was patient, and so were the Russians: there would come a time, sooner or later, when Jean-Pierre would know for certain exactly where Masud was going to be for the next twenty-four hours – perhaps if he were wounded, or planning to attend a funeral – and then Jean-Pierre would use his radio to transmit a special code, and the hawk would strike.

He wished that he could tell Jane what he was really doing here. He might even convince her that it was right. He would point out that their medical work was useless, for helping the rebels served only to perpetuate the misery of poverty and ignorance in which the people lived, and to delay the moment when the Soviet Union would be able to grab this country by the scruff of the neck, as it were, and drag it kicking and screaming into the twentieth century. She might well understand that. However, he knew instinctively that she would not forgive him for deceiving her as he had. In fact she would be enraged. He could imagine her, remorseless, implacable, proud. She would leave him immediately, the way she had left Ellis Thaler. She would be doubly furious at having been deceived in exactly the same way by two successive men.

So, in his terror of losing her, he continued to deceive her, like a man on a precipice paralysed by fright.

She knew *something* was wrong, of course; he could tell by the way she looked at him sometimes. But she felt it was a problem in their relationship, he was sure – it did not occur to her that his whole life was a monumental pretence.

Complete safety was not possible, but he took every precaution against discovery by her or by anyone else. When using the radio he spoke in code, not because the rebels might be listening in – they had no radios – but because the Afghan Army might, and it was so riddled with traitors that it had no secrets from Masud. Jean-Pierre's radio was small enough to be concealed in the false bottom of his medical bag, or in the pocket of his shirt or waistcoat when he was not carrying the bag. Its disadvantage was that it was powerful enough only for very short conversation. It would have taken a long broadcast to dictate full details of the routes and timing of the convoys – especially in code – and would have required a radio and battery pack a great deal larger. Jean-Pierre and Monsieur Leblond had decided against that. In consequence, Jean-Pierre had to meet with his contact to pass on his information.

He breasted a rise and looked down. He was at the head of a small valley. The trail he was on led down to another valley, running at right angles to this one and bifurcated by a tumbling mountain stream that glittered in the afternoon sun. On the far side of the stream another valley led on up into the mountains towards Cobak, his ultimate destination. Where the three valleys met, on the near side of the river, was a little stone hut. The region was dotted with such primitive buildings. Jean-Pierre imagined they had been put up by the nomads and travelling merchants who used them at night.

He set off down the hill, leading Maggie. Anatoly was probably there already. Jean-Pierre did not know his real name or rank, but assumed he was in the KGB and guessed, from something he had once said about Generals, that he was a Colonel. Whatever his rank, he was no desk man. Between here and Bagram was fifty miles of mountain country, and Anatoly walked it, alone, taking a day and a half. He was an Oriental Russian with high cheekbones and yellow skin, and in Afghan clothes he passed as an Uzbak, a member of the Mongoloid ethnic group of north Afghanistan. This explained his hesitant Dari – the Uzbaks had their own language. Anatoly was brave: he did not speak the Uzbak tongue, of course, so there was a chance he might be unmasked; and he, too, knew that the guerrillas played *buzkashi* with captured Russian officers.

The risk to Jean-Pierre of these meetings was a little less. His constant travelling to outlying villages to hold clinics was only mildly odd. However, suspicion might be aroused if anyone noticed that he happened to bump into the same wandering Uzbak more than once or twice. And, of course, if somehow an Afghan who spoke French should overhear the doctor's conversation with that wandering Uzbak, Jean-Pierre could only hope to die fast.

His sandals made no noise on the footpath, and Maggie's hooves sank silently into the dusty earth, so as he neared the hut he whistled a tune, in case anyone other than Anatoly should be inside: he was careful not to startle Afghans, who were all armed and jumpy. He ducked his head and entered. To his surprise the cool interior of the hut was empty. He sat down with his back to the stone wall and settled to wait. After a few minutes he closed his eyes. He was tired, but too tense to sleep. This was the worst part of what he was doing: the combination of fear and boredom which overcame him during these long waits. He had learned to accept delays, in this country without wristwatches, but he had never acquired the imperturbable patience of the Afghans. He could not help but imagine the various disasters which might have overtaken Anatoly. How ironic it would be if Anatoly had trodden on a Russian anti-personnel mine and blown his foot off. Those mines actually injured more livestock than humans, but they were no less effective for that: the loss of a cow could kill an Afghan family as surely as if their house had been bombed with them all inside. Jean-Pierre no longer laughed when he saw a cow or a goat with a rough-hewn wooden leg.

In his reverie he sensed the presence of someone else, and opened his eyes to see Anatoly's Oriental face inches from his own.

'I could have robbed you,' said Anatoly in fluent French.

'I wasn't asleep.'

Anatoly sat down, cross-legged, on the dirt floor. He was a squat, muscular figure in baggy cotton shirt and trousers with a turban, a check scarf and a mud-coloured woollen blanket, called a *pattu*, around his shoulders. He let the scarf drop from his face and smiled, showing tobacco-stained teeth. 'How are you, my friend?'

'Well.'

'And your wife?'

There was something sinister in the way Anatoly always asked about Jane. The Russians had been dead against the idea of his bringing Jane to Afghanistan, arguing that she would interfere with his work. Jean-Pierre had pointed out that he had to take a nurse with him anyway – it was the policy of *Médecins pour la Liberté* always to send pairs – and that he would probably sleep with whoever accompanied him, unless she looked like King Kong. In the end the Russians had agreed, but reluctantly. 'Jane is fine,' he said. 'She had the baby six weeks ago. A girl.'

'Congratulations!' Anatoly seemed genuinely pleased. 'But wasn't it a little early?'

'Yes. Fortunately there were no complications. In fact the village midwife delivered the baby.'

'Not you?'

'I wasn't there. I was with you.'

'My God.' Anatoly looked horrified. 'That I should have kept you away on such an important day . . .'

Jean-Pierre was pleased by Anatoly's concern, but he did not show it. 'It couldn't be anticipated,' he said. 'Besides, it was worth it: you hit the convoy I told you of.'

'Yes. Your information is very good. Congratulations again.'

Jean-Pierre felt a glow of pride, but he tried to appear matter-of-fact. 'Our system seems to be working very well,' he said modestly.

Anatoly nodded. 'What was their reaction to the ambush?'

'Increasing desperation.' It occurred to Jean-Pierre, as he spoke, that another advantage of meeting his contact in person was that he could give this kind of background information, feelings and impressions, stuff which was not concrete enough to be sent by radio in code. 'They're constantly running out of ammunition now.'

'And the next convoy – when will it depart?'

'It left yesterday.'

'They *are* desperate. Good.' Anatoly reached inside

his shirt and brought out a map. He unfolded it on the floor. It showed the area between the Five Lions Valley and the Pakistan border.

Jean-Pierre concentrated hard, recalling the details he had memorized during his conversation with Mohammed, and began to trace for Anatoly the route the convoy would follow on its way back from Pakistan. He did not know exactly when they would return, for Mohammed did not know how long they would spend in Peshawar buying what they needed. However, Anatoly had people in Peshawar who would let him know when the Five Lions convoy departed, and from that he would be able to work out their timetable.

Anatoly made no notes, but memorised every word Jean-Pierre said. When they had finished they went over the whole thing again, with Anatoly repeating it to Jean-Pierre as a check.

The Russian folded the map and put it back inside his shirt. 'And what of Masud?' he said quietly.

'We haven't seen him since last I spoke to you,' said Jean-Pierre. 'I've only seen Mohammed – and he is never quite sure where Masud is or when he will appear.'

'Masud is a fox,' said Anatoly with a rare flash of emotion.

'We will catch him,' said Jean-Pierre.

'Oh, we will catch him. He knows the hunt is in full cry, so he covers his tracks. But the hounds have his scent, and he cannot elude us for ever – we are so many, and so strong, and our blood is up.' He suddenly became conscious that he was revealing his feelings. He smiled and became practical again. 'Batteries,' he said, and he brought a battery pack out of his shirt.

Jean-Pierre took the little radio transceiver from the concealed compartment in the bottom of his medical bag, extracted the old batteries, and exchanged them for new ones. They did this every time they met to be sure that Jean-Pierre should not lose contact simply by running out of power. Anatoly would carry the old ones all the way back to Bagram, for there was no point in taking the risk of throwing away Russian-made batteries here in the Five Lions Valley where there were no electrical appliances.

As Jean-Pierre was putting the radio back into his medical bag, Anatoly said: 'Have you got anything in there for blisters? My feet – ' then he stopped suddenly, frowned, and cocked his head, listening.

Jean-Pierre tensed. So far they had never been observed together. It was bound to happen sooner or later, they knew, and they had planned what they would do, how they would act like strangers sharing a resting-place and continue their conversation when the intruder had left – or, if the intruder showed signs of staying long, they would leave together, as if by chance they happened to be heading in the same direction. All that had been previously agreed, but nevertheless Jean-Pierre now felt as if his guilt must be written all over his face.

In the next instant he heard a footfall outside, and the sound of someone breathing hard; and then a shadow darkened the sunlit entrance, and Jane walked in.

'Jane!' he said.

Both men sprang to their feet.

Jean-Pierre said: 'What is it? Why are you here?'

'Thank God I caught up with you,' she said breathlessly.

Out of the corner of his eye, Jean-Pierre saw Anatoly turn away, as an Afghan would turn away from a brazen woman. The gesture helped Jean-Pierre recover from the shock of seeing Jane. He looked around quickly. Anatoly had put the maps away several minutes earlier, fortunately. But the radio – the radio was sticking out an inch or two from the medical bag. However, Jane had not seen it – yet.

'Sit down,' said Jean-Pierre. 'Catch your breath.' He sat down at the same time and used the movement as an excuse to shift his bag so that the radio poked out from the side facing him and away from Jane. 'What's the matter?' he said.

'A medical problem I can't solve.'

Jean-Pierre's tension eased a fraction: he had been afraid she might have followed him because she suspected something. 'Have some water,' he said. He reached into his bag with one hand, and with the other pushed the radio in while he rummaged. When the radio was concealed he drew out his flask of purified water and handed it to her. His heartbeat began to return to normal. He was recovering his presence of mind. The evidence was now out of sight. What else was there to make her suspicious? She might have heard Anatoly speaking French – but that was not uncommon: if an Afghan had a second language it was often French

159

and an Uzbak might speak French better than he spoke Dari. What had Anatoly been saying when she walked in? Jean-Pierre remembered: he had been asking for blister ointment. That was perfect. Afghans always asked for medicine when they met a doctor, even if they were in perfect health.

Jane drank from the flask and began to speak. 'A few minutes after you left, they brought in a boy of eighteen with a very bad thigh wound.' She took another sip. She was ignoring Anatoly and Jean-Pierre realised she was so concerned about the medical emergency that she had hardly noticed the other man. 'He was hurt in the fighting near Rokha, and his father had carried him all the way up the Valley – it took him two days. The wound was badly gangrenous by the time they arrived. I gave him six hundred milligrams of crystalline penicillin, injected into the buttock, then I cleaned out the wound.'

'Exactly correct,' said Jean-Pierre.

'A few minutes later he broke out in a cold sweat and became confused. I took his pulse: it was rapid but weak.'

'Did he go pale or grey, and have difficulty breathing?'

'Yes.'

'What did you do?'

'I treated him for shock – raised his feet, covered him with a blanket, and gave him tea – then I came after you.' She was close to tears. 'His father carried him for two days – I can't let him die.'

'He needn't,' said Jean-Pierre. 'Allergic shock is a

rare, but quite well known, reaction to penicillin injections. The treatment is half a millilitre of adrenalin, injected into a muscle, followed by an antihistamine – say six millilitres of diphenhydramine. Would you like me to come back with you?' As he made that offer he glanced at Anatoly, but the Russian showed no reaction.

Jane sighed. 'No,' she said. 'There will be someone else dying on the far side of the hill. You go to Cobak.'

'If you're sure.'

'Yes.'

A match flared as Anatoly lit a cigarette. Jane glanced at him then looked at Jean-Pierre again. 'Half a millilitre of adrenalin and then six millilitres of diphenhydramine.' She stood up.

'Yes.' Jean-Pierre stood up with her and kissed her. 'Are you sure you can manage?'

'Of course.'

'You must hurry.'

'Yes.'

'Would you like to take Maggie?'

Jane considered. 'I don't think so. On that path, walking is faster.'

'Whatever you think best.'

'Goodbye.

'Goodbye, Jane.'

Jean-Pierre watched her go out. He stood still for a while. Neither he nor Anatoly said anything. After a minute or two he went to the doorway and looked out. He could see Jane, two or three hundred yards away, a small, slight figure in a thin cotton dress, striding determinedly up the valley, alone in the dusty brown landscape. He watched her until she disappeared into a fold in the hills.

He came back inside and sat down with his back to the wall. He and Anatoly looked at one another. 'Jesus Christ Almighty,' said Jean-Pierre. 'That was close.'

CHAPTER EIGHT

THE BOY died.

He had been dead almost an hour when Jane arrived, hot and dusty and exhausted to the point of collapse. The father was waiting for her at the mouth of the cave, looking numb and reproachful. She could tell from his resigned posture and his calm brown eyes that it was all over. He said nothing. She went into the cave and looked at the boy. Too tired to feel angry, she was overwhelmed by disappointment. Jean-Pierre was away and Zahara was deep in mourning, so she had no one with whom to share her grief.

She wept later, as she lay in her bed on the roof of the shopkeeper's house, with Chantal on a tiny mattress beside her, murmuring from time to time in a sleep of contented ignorance. She wept for the father as much as for the dead boy. Like her, he had driven himself beyond ordinary exhaustion in trying to save the boy. How much greater his sadness would be. Her tears blurred the stars before she fell asleep.

She dreamed that Mohammed came to her bed and made love to her while the whole village looked on; then he told her that Jean-Pierre was having an affair with Simone, the wife of the fat journalist Raoul

Clermont, and that the two lovers met in Cobak when Jean-Pierre was supposed to be holding a clinic.

Next day she ached all over, as a result of having to run most of the way to the little stone hut. It was fortunate, she reflected as she went about her routine chores, that Jean-Pierre had stopped – to rest, presumably – at the little stone hut, giving her a chance to catch up with him. She had been so relieved to see Maggie tethered outside, and to find Jean-Pierre in the hut with that funny little Uzbak man. The two of them had jumped out of their skins when she walked in. It had been almost comical. It was the first time she had ever seen an Afghan stand up when a woman came in.

She walked up the mountainside with her medicine case and opened the cave clinic. As she dealt with the usual cases of malnutrition, malaria, infected wounds and intestinal parasites, she thought over yesterday's crisis. She had never heard of allergic shock before. No doubt people who had to give penicillin injections were normally taught what to do about it, but her training had been so rushed that a lot of things had been left out. In fact the medical details had been almost entirely skimped, on the grounds that Jean-Pierre was a fully qualified doctor and would be around to tell her what to do.

What an anxious time that had been, sitting in classrooms, sometimes with trainee nurses, sometimes on her own, trying to absorb the rules and procedures of medicine and health education, wondering what awaited her in Afghanistan. Some of her lessons had been the opposite of reassuring. Her first task, she had been told, would be to build an earth closet for herself. Why? Because the fastest way of improving the health of people in underdeveloped countries was to stop them using the rivers and streams as toilets, and this could be impressed upon them by setting an example. Her teacher, Stephanie, a bespectacled fortyish earth-mother-type in dungarees and sandals, had also emphasised the dangers of prescribing medicines too generously. Most illnesses and minor injuries would get better without medical help, but primitive (and not-so-primitive) people always wanted pills and potions. Jane recalled that the little Uzbak man had been asking Jean-Pierre for blister ointment. He must have been walking long distances all his life, yet because he met a doctor he said his feet hurt. The snag about over-prescribing – apart from the waste of medicines – was that a drug given for a trivial ailment might cause the patient to develop tolerance, so that when he was seriously ill the treatment would not cure him. Stephanie had also advised Jane to try to work with, rather than against, traditional healers in the community. She had been successful with Rabia, the midwife, but not with Abdullah the mullah.

Learning the language had been the easiest part. In Paris, before she ever thought of coming to Afghanistan, she had been studying Farsi, the Persian language, with the object of improving her usefulness as an interpreter. Farsi and Dari were dialects of the same language. The other main language in Afghanistan was Pashto, the tongue of the Pushtuns, but Dari was the language of the Tajiks, and the Five Lions Valley was in

Tajik territory. Those few Afghans who travelled – the nomads, for example – usually spoke both Pashto and Dari. If they had a European language it was English or French. The Uzbak man in the stone hut had been speaking French to Jean-Pierre. It was the first time Jane had heard French spoken with an Uzbak accent. It sounded the same as a Russian accent.

Her mind kept returning to the Uzbak during the day. The thought of him nagged her. It was a feeling she sometimes got when she knew there was something important she was supposed to do but she could not remember what it was. There had been something odd about him, perhaps.

At noon, she closed the clinic, fed and changed Chantal, then cooked a lunch of rice and meat sauce and shared it with Fara. The girl had become utterly devoted to Jane, eager to do anything to please her, reluctant to go home at night. Jane was trying to treat her more as an equal, but this seemed to serve only to increase her adoration.

In the heat of the day Jane left Chantal with Fara and went down to her secret place, the sunny ledge hidden below an overhang on the mountainside. There she did her post-natal exercises, determined to get her figure back. As she clenched her pelvic floor muscles she kept visualizing the Uzbak man, rising to his feet in the little stone hut, and the expression of astonishment on his Oriental face. For some reason she felt a sense of impending tragedy.

When she realized the truth it did not come in a sudden flash of insight, but was more like an avalanche, starting small but growing inexorably until it swamped everything.

No Afghan would complain of blisters on his feet, even in pretence, for they had no knowledge of such things: it was as unlikely as a Gloucestershire farmer saying he had beri-beri. And no Afghan, no matter how surprised, would react by standing up when a woman walked in. If he was not Afghan, what then was he? His accent told her, though few people would have recognized it: it was only because she was a linguist, speaking both Russian and French, that she was able to recognize that he had been speaking French with a Russian accent.

So Jean-Pierre had met a Russian disguised as an Uzbak in a stone hut at a deserted location.

Was it an accident? That was possible, barely, but she could picture her husband's face when she had walked in, and now she could read the expression which at the time she had not noticed: a look of guilt.

No, it was no accidental encounter – it was a rendezvous. Perhaps it was not the first. Jean-Pierre was constantly travelling to outlying villages to hold clinics – indeed, he was unnecessarily scrupulous about keeping to his schedule of visits, a foolish insistence in a country without calendars and diaries – but not so foolish if there was another schedule, a clandestine series of secret meetings.

And *why* did he meet with the Russian? That, too, was obvious, and hot tears welled up in Jane's eyes as she realized that his purpose must be treachery. He gave them information, of course. He told them about the convoys. He always knew the routes because Mohammed used his maps. He knew the approximate timing because he saw the men leaving, from Banda and from other villages in the Five Lions Valley. He gave this information to the Russians, obviously; and that was why the Russians had become so successful at ambushing convoys in the last year; that was why there were so many grieving widows and sad orphans in the valley now.

What's wrong with me? she thought in a sudden fit of self-pity, and fresh tears rolled down her cheeks. First Ellis, then Jean-Pierre – why do I pick these bastards? Is there something about a secretive man that appeals to me? Is it the challenge of breaking down his defences? Am I that crazy?

She remembered Jean-Pierre arguing that the Soviet invasion of Afghanistan was justified. At some point he had changed his mind, and she thought she had convinced him that he was wrong. Obviously the change had been faked. When he decided to come to Afghanistan to spy for the Russians he had adopted an anti-Soviet point of view as part of his cover.

Was his love also faked?

The question alone was heartbreaking. She buried her face in her hands. It was almost unthinkable. She had fallen in love with him, married him, kissed his sour-faced mother, got used to his way of making love, survived their first row, struggled to make their partnership work, and given birth to his child in fear and pain – had she done all that for an illusion, a cardboard cut-out of a husband, a man who cared for her not at all?

It was like walking and running so many miles to ask how to cure the eighteen-year-old boy and then returning to find him already dead. It was worse than that. It was, she imagined, how the father had felt, having carried his son for two days only to see him die.

There was a sensation of fullness in her breasts, and she realized it must be time for Chantal's feed. She put her clothes on, wiped her face in her sleeve, and headed back up the mountain. As her immediate grief receded and she began to think more clearly, it seemed to her that she had felt a vague dissatisfaction throughout their year of marriage, and now she could understand. In a way she had all along *sensed* Jean-Pierre's deceit. Because of that barrier between them they had failed to become intimate.

When she reached the cave Chantal was grizzling and Fara was rocking her. Jane took the baby and held her to her breast. Chantal began to suck. Jane felt the initial discomfort, like a cramp, in her tummy, and then a sensation in her breast which was pleasant and rather erotic.

She wanted to be alone. She told Fara to go and take her siesta in her mother's cave.

Feeding Chantal was soothing. Jean-Pierre's treachery came to seem less than cataclysmic. She felt sure his love for her was not faked. What would be the point? Why should he have brought her here? She was of no use to him in his spying. It must have been because he loved her.

And if he loved her, all other problems could be solved. He would have to stop working for the Russians, of course. For the moment she could not quite see herself confronting him – would she say 'All is revealed!' for example? No. But the words would come to her when she needed them. Then he would have to take her and Chantal back to Europe—

Back to Europe. When she realized they would have to go home she was flooded by a sense of relief. It took her by surprise. If anyone had asked her how she liked Afghanistan, she would have said that what she was doing was fascinating and worthwhile and she was coping very well indeed and even enjoying it. But now that the prospect of returning to civilization was in front of her, her resilience crumbled, and she admitted to herself that the harsh landscape, the bitter winter weather, the alien people, the bombing and the endless stream of maimed and mangled men and boys had strained her nerves to breaking-point.

The truth is, she thought, that it's *awful* here.

Chantal stopped sucking and dropped off to sleep. Jane put her down, changed her, and moved her to her mattress, all without waking her. The baby's unshakable equanimity was a great blessing. She slept through all kinds of crisis – no amount of noise or movement would wake her if she was full and comfortable. However, she was sensitive to Jane's moods, and often woke when Jane was distressed, even when there was not much noise.

Jane sat cross-legged on her mattress, watching her sleeping baby, thinking about Jean-Pierre. She wished he were here now so she could talk to him right away. She wondered why she was not more angry – not to say outraged – that he had been betraying the guerrillas to the Russians. Was it because she was reconciled to the knowledge that all men were liars? Had she come to believe that the only innocent people in this war were the mothers, the wives and the daughters on both sides? Was it that being a wife and a mother had altered her personality, so that such a betrayal no longer outraged her? Or was it just that she loved Jean-Pierre? She did not know.

Anyway, it was time to think about the future, not the past. They would go back to Paris, where there were postmen and bookshops and tap water. Chantal would have pretty clothes, and a pram, and disposable diapers. The three of them would live in a small apartment in an interesting neighbourhood where the only real danger to life would be the taxi drivers. Jane and Jean-Pierre would start again, and this time they would really get to know one another. The two of them would work to make the world a better place by gradual and legitimate means, without intrigue or treachery. Their experience in Afghanistan would help them to get jobs in Third World development, perhaps with the World Health Organisation. Married life would be as she had imagined it, with the three of them doing good and being happy and feeling safe.

Fara came in. Siesta time was over. She greeted Jane respectfully, looked at Chantal, then, seeing that the baby was asleep, sat cross-legged on the ground, waiting for instructions. She was the daughter of Rabia's eldest son, Ismael Gul, who was away at present, with the convoy—

Jane gasped. Fara looked enquiringly at her. Jane made a deprecatory motion with her hand, and Fara looked away.

Her father is with the convoy, Jane thought.

Jean-Pierre had betrayed that convoy to the Russians. Fara's father would die in the ambush – unless Jane could do something to prevent it. But what? A runner could be sent to meet the convoy at the Khyber Pass and divert it on to a new route. Mohammed could arrange that. But Jane would have to tell him how she knew that the convoy was due to be ambushed – and then Mohammed would undoubtedly kill Jean-Pierre, probably with his bare hands.

If one of them has to die, let it be Ismael rather than Jean-Pierre, thought Jane.

Then she thought of the other thirty or so men from the Valley who were with the convoy, and the thought struck her: shall they *all* die to save my husband – Kahmir Khan with the wispy beard, and scarred old Shahazai Gul, and Yussuf Gul who sings so beautifully, and Sher Kador the goat-boy and Abdur Mohammed with no front teeth and Ali Ghanim who has fourteen children?

There had to be another way.

She went to the mouth of the cave and stood looking out. Now that the siesta was over, the children had come out of the caves and resumed their games among the rocks and thorny bushes. There was nine-year-old Mousa, the only son of Mohammed – even more spoilt now that he had one hand – swaggering with the new knife that his doting father had given him. She saw

Fara's mother toiling up the hill with a bundle of firewood on her head. There was the mullah's wife, washing out Abdullah's shirt. She did not see Mohammed or his wife Halima. She knew he was here in Banda, for she had seen him in the morning. He would have eaten with his wife and children in their cave – most families had a cave to themselves. He would be there now, but Jane was reluctant to seek him out openly, for that would scandalize the community, and she needed to be discreet.

What shall I tell him? she thought.

She considered a straightforward appeal: *Do this for me, because I ask it.* It would have worked on any Western man who had fallen in love with her, but Muslim men did not seem to have a romantic idea of love – what Mohammed felt for her was more like a rather tender kind of lust. It certainly did not put him at her disposal. And she wasn't sure he still felt it, anyway. What, then? He did not owe her anything. She had never treated him or his wife. But she had treated Mousa – she had saved the boy's life. Mohammed owed her a debt of honour.

Do this for me, because I saved your son. It might work.

But Mohammed would ask why.

More women were appearing, fetching water and sweeping out their caves, tending to animals and preparing food. Jane knew she would see Mohammed shortly.

What shall I say to him?

The Russians know the route of the convoy.

How did they find out?

I don't know, Mohammed.

Then what makes you so sure?

I can't tell you. I overheard a conversation. I got a message from the British Secret Service. I have a hunch. I saw it in the cards. I had a dream.

That was it: a dream.

She saw him. He stepped from his cave, tall and handsome, wearing travelling clothes: the round Chitrali cap, like Masud's, the type most of the guerrillas sported; the mud-coloured *pattu* which served as cloak, towel, blanket and camouflage; and the calf-length leather boots he had taken from the corpse of a Russian soldier. He walked across the clearing with the stride of one who has a long way to go before sundown. He took the footpath down the mountainside, towards the deserted village.

Jane watched his tall figure disappear. It's now or never, she thought; and she followed him. At first she walked slowly and casually, so that it would not be obvious she was going after Mohammed; then, when she was out of sight of the caves, she broke into a run. She slithered and stumbled down the dusty trail, thinking: I wonder what all this running is doing to my insides. When she saw Mohammed ahead of her she called out to him. He stopped, turned, and waited for her.

'God be with you, Mohammed Khan,' she said when she caught up with him.

'And with you, Jane Debout,' he said politely.

She paused, catching her breath. He watched her,

wearing an expression of amused tolerance. 'How is Mousa?' she said.

'He is well and happy, and learning to use his left hand. He will kill Russians with it one day.'

This was a little joke: the left hand was traditionally used for 'dirty' jobs, the right for eating. Jane smiled in acknowledgement of his wit, then said: 'I'm so glad we were able to save his life.'

If he thought her ungracious he did not show it. 'I am forever in your debt,' he said.

That was what she had been angling for. 'There is something you could do for me,' she said.

His expression was unreadable. 'If it is within my power . . .'

She looked around for somewhere to sit. They were standing near a bombed house. Stones and earth from the front wall had spilled across the pathway, and they could see inside the building, where the only furnishings left were a cracked pot and, absurdly, a colour picture of a Cadillac pinned to a wall. Jane sat on the rubble and, after a moment's hesitation, Mohammed sat beside her.

'It is within your power,' she said. 'But it will cause you some small trouble.'

'What is it?'

'You may think it the whim of a foolish woman.'

'Perhaps.'

'You'll be tempted to deceive me, by agreeing to my request and then "forgetting" to carry it out.'

'No.'

'I ask you to deal truthfully with me, whether you refuse or not.'

'I shall.'

Enough of that, she thought. 'I want you to send a runner to the convoy and order them to change their homeward route.'

He was quite taken aback – he had probably been expecting some trivial, domestic request. 'But why?' he said.

'Do you believe in dreams, Mohammed Khan?'

He shrugged. 'Dreams are dreams,' he said evasively.

Perhaps that was the wrong approach, she thought; a vision might be better. 'While I lay alone in my cave, in the heat of the day, I thought I saw a white pigeon.'

He was suddenly attentive, and she knew she had said the right thing: Afghans believed that white pigeons were sometimes inhabited by spirits.

Jane went on: 'But I must have been dreaming, for the bird tried to speak to me.'

'Ah!'

He took that as a sign that she had had a vision, not a dream, Jane thought. She went on: 'I couldn't understand what it was saying, although I listened as hard as I could. I think it was speaking Pashto.'

Mohammed was wide-eyed. 'A messenger from Pushtun territory . . .'

'Then I saw Ismael Gul, the son of Rabia, the father of Fara, standing behind the pigeon.' She put her hand on Mohammed's arm and looked into his eyes, thinking: I could turn you on like an electric light, you vain, foolish man. 'There was a knife in his heart, and he was weeping tears of blood. He pointed to the handle of the knife, as if he wanted me to pull it out of his chest. The handle was encrusted with jewels.' Somewhere in the back of her mind she was thinking: Where did I *get* this stuff? 'I got up from my bed and walked to him. I was afraid, but I had to save his life. Then, as I reached out to grasp the knife . . .'

'What?'

'He vanished. I think I woke up.'

Mohammed closed his wide-open mouth, recovered his poise, and frowned importantly, as if carefully considering the interpretation of the dream. Now, Jane thought, it is time to pander to him a little bit.

'It may be all foolishness,' she said, arranging her face into a little-girl expression, all ready to defer to his superior masculine judgement. 'That's why I ask you to do this *for me*, for the person who saved your son's life; to give me peace of mind.'

He immediately looked a little haughty. 'There is no need to invoke a debt of honour.'

'Does that mean you'll do it?'

He answered with a question. 'What kind of jewels were in the handle of the knife?'

Oh, God, she thought, what is the correct answer supposed to be? She thought to say 'emeralds,' but they were associated with the Five Lions Valley, so it might imply that Ismael had been killed by a traitor in the Valley. 'Rubies,' she said.

He nodded slowly. 'Did Ismael not speak to you?'

'He seemed to be trying to speak, but unable to.'

He nodded again, and Jane thought: Come *on*, make

177

up your bloody mind. At last he said: 'The omen is clear. The convoy must be diverted.'

Thank God for that, thought Jane. 'I'm so relieved,' she said truthfully. 'I didn't know what to do. Now I can be sure Ahmed will be saved.' She wondered what she could do to nail Mohammed down and make it impossible for him to change his mind. She could not make him swear an oath. She wondered whether to shake his hand. Finally she decided to seal his promise with an even older gesture: she leaned forward and kissed his mouth, quickly but softly, not giving him a chance either to refuse or to respond. 'Thank you!' she said. 'I know you are a man of your word.' She stood up. Leaving him seated, looking a little dazed, she turned and ran up the path towards the caves.

At the top of the rise she stopped and looked back. Mohammed was striding down the hill, already some distance from the bombed cottage, his head high and his arms swinging He got a big charge from that kiss, Jane thought. I should be ashamed. I played on his superstition, his vanity and his sexuality. As a feminist I ought not to exploit his preconceptions – psychic woman, submissive woman, coquettish woman – to manipulate him. But it worked. It worked!

She walked on. Next she had to deal with Jean-Pierre. He would be home around dusk: he would have waited until mid-afternoon, when the sun was a little less hot, before starting on his journey, just as Mohammed had. She felt that Jean-Pierre would be easier to handle than Mohammed had been. For one thing, she could tell the truth with Jean-Pierre. For another, he was in the wrong.

She reached the caves. The little encampment was busy now. A flight of Russian jets roared across the sky. Everyone stopped work to watch them, although they were too high and too far away for bombing. When they had gone the small boys stuck out their arms like wings and ran around making jet-engine sounds. In their imaginary flights, Jane wondered, who were they bombing?

She went into the cave, checked on Chantal, smiled at Fara, and took out the journal. Both she and Jean-Pierre wrote in it almost every day. It was primarily a medical record, and they would take it back to Europe with them for the benefit of others who would follow them to Afghanistan. They had been encouraged to record personal feelings and problems, too, so that others would know what to expect; and Jane had written quite full notes on her pregnancy and the birth of Chantal; but it was a highly censored account of her emotional life that had been logged.

She sat with her back to the cave wall and the book on her knee, and wrote the story of the eighteen-year-old boy who had died of allergic shock. It made her feel sad, but not depressed – a healthy reaction, she told herself.

She added brief details of today's minor cases, then, idly, she leafed backward through the volume. The entries in Jean-Pierre's slapdash, spidery handwriting were highly abbreviated, consisting almost entirely of symptoms, diagnoses, treatments and results: *Worms*, he would write, or *Malaria*; then *Cured* or *Stable* or sometimes *Died*. Jane tended to write sentences such as *She felt better this morning* or *The mother has tuberculosis*. She read about the early days of her pregnancy, sore nipples and thickening thighs and nausea in the morning. She was interested to see that almost a year ago she had written *I'm frightened of Abdullah*. She had forgotten that.

She put the journal away. She and Fara spent the next couple of hours cleaning and tidying up the cave clinic; then it was time to go down into the village and prepare for the night. As she walked down the mountainside and then busied herself in the shopkeeper's house, Jane considered how to handle her confrontation with Jean-Pierre. She knew what to do – she would take him for a walk, she thought – but she was not sure exactly what to say.

She still had not made up her mind when he arrived a few minutes later. She wiped the dust from his face with a damp towel and gave him green tea in a china cup. He was pleasantly tired, rather than exhausted, she knew: he was capable of walking much longer distances. She sat with him while he drank his tea, trying not to stare at him, thinking *You lied to me*. When he had rested for a little while she said: 'Let's go out, like we used to.'

He was a little surprised. 'Where do you want to go?'

'Anywhere. Don't you remember, last summer, how we used to go out just to enjoy the evening?'

He smiled. 'Yes, I do.' She loved him when he smiled like that. He said: 'Will we take Chantal?'

'No.' Jane did not want to be distracted. 'She'll be fine with Fara.'

'All right,' he said, faintly bemused.

Jane told Fara to prepare their evening meal – tea, bread and yoghurt – then she and Jean-Pierre left the house. The daylight was fading and the evening air was mild and fragrant. This was the best time of day in summer. As they strolled through the fields to the river, she recalled how she had felt on this same pathway last summer: anxious, confused, excited, and determined to succeed. She was proud that she had coped so well, but glad the adventure was about to end.

She began to feel tense as the moment of confrontation drew nearer, even though she kept telling herself that she had nothing to hide, nothing to feel guilty about, and nothing to fear. They waded across the river at a place where it spread wide and shallow over a rock shelf, then they climbed a steep, winding path up the face of the cliff on the other side. At the top they sat on the ground and dangled their legs over the precipice. A hundred feet below them the Five Lions River hurried along, jostling boulders and foaming angrily through the rapids. Jane looked over the Valley. The cultivated ground was criss-crossed with irrigation channels and stone walls. The bright green and gold colours of ripening crops made the fields look like shards of coloured glass from a smashed toy. Here and there the picture was blemished by bomb damage – fallen walls, blocked ditches, and craters of mud amid the waving grain. The occasional round cap or dark turban showed that some of the men were already at work, bringing in their crops as the Russians parked their jets and put away their bombs for the night. Scarved heads or smaller figures were women and older children who would help while the light lasted. On the far side of the Valley the farmland struggled to climb the lower slopes of the mountain, but soon surrendered to the dusty rock. From the cluster of houses off to the left the smoke of a few cooking fires rose in pencil-straight lines until the light breeze untidied it. The same breeze brought unintelligible snatches of conversation from the women bathing beyond a bend in the river upstream. Their voices were subdued, and Zahara's hearty laugh was no longer heard, for she was in mourning. And all because of Jean-Pierre . . .

The thought gave Jane courage. 'I want you to take me home,' she said abruptly.

At first he misunderstood her. 'We've only just got here,' he said irritably; then he looked at her and his frown cleared. 'Oh,' he said.

There was a note of imperturbability in his voice which Jane found ominous, and she realized that she might not get her way without a struggle. 'Yes,' she said firmly. 'Home.'

He put his arm around her. 'This country gets one down at times,' he said. He was not looking at her but at the rushing river far below their feet. 'You're especially vulnerable to depression at the moment, just after the birth. In a few weeks' time, you'll find—'

'Don't patronize me!' she snapped. She was not going to let him get away with that kind of nonsense. 'Save your bedside manner for your patients.'

'All right.' He took his arm away. 'We decided, before we came, that we would stay here for two years. Short tours are inefficient, we agreed, because of the time and money wasted in training, travelling and settling down, We were determined to make a real impact, so we *committed* ourselves to a two-year stint—'

'And then we had a baby.'

'It wasn't my idea!'

'Anyway, I've changed my mind.'

'You're not *entitled* to change your mind.'

'You don't own me!' she said angrily.

'It's out of the question. Let us stop discussing it.'

'We've only just begun,' she said. His attitude infuriated her. The conversation had turned into an argument about her rights as an individual, and somehow she did not want to win by telling him that she knew about his spying, not yet, anyway; she wanted him to admit that she was free to make her own decisions. 'You have no right to ignore me or override my wishes,' she said. 'I want to leave this summer.'

'The answer is No.'

She decided to try reasoning with him. 'We've been here a year. We *have* made an impact. We've also made considerable sacrifices, more than we anticipated. Haven't we done enough?'

'We agreed on two years,' he said stubbornly.

'That was a long time ago, and before we had Chantal.'

'Then the two of you should go, and leave me here.'

For a moment Jane considered that. To travel on a convoy to Pakistan carrying a baby was difficult and dangerous. Without a husband it would be a nightmare. But it was not impossible. However, it would mean leaving Jean-Pierre behind. He would be able to continue betraying the convoys, and every few weeks more husbands and sons from the Valley would die. And there was another reason why she could not leave him behind: it would destroy their marriage. 'No,' she said. 'I can't go alone. You must come too.'

'I will not,' he said angrily. 'I will not!'

Now she *had* to confront him with what she knew. She took a deep breath. 'You'll just have to,' she began.

'I don't have to,' he interrupted. He pointed his forefinger at her, and she looked into his eyes and saw something there that frightened her. 'You can't force me to. Don't try.'

'But I *can*—'

'I advise you not to,' he said, and his voice was terribly cold.

Suddenly he seemed a stranger to her, a man she did not know. She was silent for a moment, thinking. She watched a pigeon rise up from the village and fly towards her. It homed in on the cliff face a little way below her feet. I don't know this man! she thought in a panic. After a whole year I still don't know who he is! 'Do you love me?' she asked him.

'Loving you doesn't mean I have to do everything you want.'

'Is that a Yes?'

He stared at her. She met his gaze unflinchingly. Slowly, the hard, manic light went out of his eyes, and he relaxed. At last he smiled. 'It's a Yes,' he said. She leaned towards him, and he put his arm around her again. 'Yes, I love you,' he said softly. He kissed the top of her head.

She rested her cheek on his chest and looked down. The pigeon she had watched flew off again. It was a white pigeon, like the one in her invented vision. It floated away, gliding effortlessly down towards the far bank of the river. Jane thought: Oh, God, what do I do now?

It was Mohammed's son Mousa – now known as Left-hand – who was the first to spot the convoy when it returned. He came racing into the clearing in front of the caves, yelling at the top of his voice: 'They're back! They're back!' Nobody needed to ask who *they* were.

It was mid-morning, and Jane and Jean-Pierre were in the cave clinic. Jane looked at Jean-Pierre. The faintest hint of a puzzled frown crossed his face: he was wondering why the Russians had not acted on his intelligence and ambushed the convoy. Jane turned away from him so that he should not see the triumph she felt. She had saved their lives! Yussuf would sing tonight, and Sher Kador would count his goats, and Ali Ghanim would kiss each of his fourteen children. Yussuf was one of Rabia's sons: saving his life repaid Rabia for helping to bring Chantal into the world. All the mothers and daughters who would have been in mourning would now rejoice.

She wondered how Jean-Pierre felt. Was he angry, or frustrated, or disappointed? It was hard to imagine someone being disappointed because people had not been killed. She stole a glance at him, but his face was blank. I wish I knew what's going on in his mind, she thought.

Their patients melted away within minutes: everybody was going down to the village to welcome the travellers home. 'Shall we go down?' Jane said.

'You go,' Jean-Pierre said. 'I'll finish up here, then follow you.'

'All right,' said Jane. He wanted some time to compose himself, she guessed, so that he could pretend to be delighted at their safe return when he saw them.

She picked up Chantal and took the steep footpath towards the village. She could feel the heat of the rock through the thin soles of her sandals.

She still had not confronted Jean-Pierre. However, this could not go on indefinitely. Sooner or later he would learn that Mohammed had sent a runner to divert the convoy from its prearranged route. Naturally, he would then ask Mohammed why this had been done, and Mohammed would tell him about Jane's 'vision'. But Jean-Pierre knew Jane did not believe in visions . . .

Why am I afraid? she asked herself. I'm not the guilty one – he is. Yet I feel as if his secret is something I must be ashamed of. I should have spoken to him about it immediately, that evening we walked up to the top of the cliff. By nursing it to myself for so long, I too have become a deceiver. Perhaps that's it. Or perhaps it's the peculiar look in his eyes sometimes . . .

She had not given up her determination to go home, but so far she had failed to think of a way to persuade

Jean-Pierre to go. She had dreamed up a dozen bizarre schemes, from faking a message to say that his mother was dying, to poisoning his yoghurt with something that would give him symptoms of an illness which would force him to return to Europe for treatment. The simplest, and least far-fetched, of her ideas was to threaten to tell Mohammed that Jean-Pierre was a spy. She would never do it, of course, for to unmask him would be as good as killing him. But would Jean-Pierre *think* she might carry out the threat? Probably not. It would take a hard, pitiless, stone-hearted man to believe her capable of virtually killing her husband – and if Jean-Pierre were that hard and pitiless and stone-hearted he might kill Jane.

She shivered despite the heat. This talk of killing was grotesque. When two people take such a delight in one another's bodies as we do, she thought, how can they possibly do each other violence?

As she reached the village she began to hear the random, exuberant gunfire that signified an Afghan celebration. She made her way to the mosque – everything happened at the mosque. The convoy was in the courtyard, men and horses and baggage surrounded by smiling women and squealing children. Jane stood at the edge of the crowd, watching. It was worth it, she thought. It was worth the worry and the fear, and it was worth manipulating Mohammed in that undignified way, in order to see this, the men safely reunited with their wives and mothers and sons and daughters.

What happened next was probably the greatest shock of her life.

There in the crowd, among the caps and turbans, appeared a head of curly blond hair. At first she did not recognize it, even though its familiarity tugged at her heartstrings. Then it emerged from the crowd and she saw, hiding behind an incredibly bushy blond beard, the face of Ellis Thaler.

Jane's knees suddenly felt weak. Ellis? Here? It was impossible.

He walked towards her. He was wearing the loose pyjama-like cotton clothes of the Afghans, and a dirty blanket around his broad shoulders. The little of his face that was still visible above the beard was deeply tanned, so that his sky-blue eyes were even more striking than usual, like cornflowers in a field of ripe wheat.

Jane was struck dumb.

Ellis stood in front of her, his face solemn. 'Hello, Jane.'

She realized she no longer hated him. A month ago she would have cursed him for deceiving her and spying on her friends; but now her anger had gone. She would never like him, but she could tolerate him. And it was nice to hear English spoken for the first time in more than a year.

'Ellis,' she said weakly. 'What in heaven's name are you doing here?'

'The same as you,' he said.

What did that mean? Spying? No, Ellis did not know what Jean-Pierre was.

Ellis saw Jane's confused expression and said: 'I mean I'm here to help the rebels.'

Would he find out about Jean-Pierre? Jane was suddenly afraid for her husband. Ellis might kill him—

'Who does the baby belong to?' Ellis said.

'Me. And Jean-Pierre. Her name is Chantal.' Jane saw that Ellis suddenly looked terribly sad. She realized he had been hoping to find her unhappy with her husband. Oh, God, I think he's still in love with me, she thought. She tried to change the subject. 'But how will you help the rebels?'

He hefted his bag. It was a large, sausage-shaped thing of khaki canvas, like an old-fashioned soldier's kitbag. 'I'm going to teach them how to blow up roads and bridges,' he said. 'So, you see, in this war I'm on the same side as you.'

But not the same side as Jean-Pierre, she thought. What will happen now? The Afghans did not for one moment suspect Jean-Pierre, but Ellis was trained in ways of deception. Sooner or later he would guess what was going on. 'How long are you going to be here?' she asked him. If it was a short stay he might not have time to develop suspicions.

'For the summer,' he said imprecisely.

Perhaps he would not spend much time around Jean-Pierre. 'Where will you live?' she asked him.

'In this village.'

'Oh.'

He heard the disappointment in her voice and gave a wry smile. 'I guess I shouldn't have expected you to be *glad* to see me . . .'

Jane's mind was racing ahead. If she could make Jean-Pierre quit, he would be in no further danger.

Suddenly she felt able to confront him. Why is that? she
wondered. It's because I'm not afraid of him any more.
Why am I not afraid of him? Because Ellis is here.

I hadn't realized I was afraid of my husband.

'On the contrary,' she said to Ellis, thinking *How cool
I am!* 'I'm happy you're here.'

There was a silence. Ellis clearly did not know what
to make of Jane's reaction. After a moment he said:
'Uh, I have a lot of explosives and stuff somewhere in
this zoo. I'd better get to it.'

Jane nodded. 'Okay.'

Ellis turned away and disappeared into the mêlée.
Jane walked slowly out of the courtyard, feeling a little
stunned. Ellis was *here*, in the Five Lions Valley, and
apparently still in love with her.

As she reached the shopkeeper's house, Jean-Pierre
came out. He had stopped there on his way to the
mosque, probably to put away his medical bag. Jane was
not sure what to say to him. 'The convoy brought
someone you know,' she began.

'A European?'

'Yes.'

'Well, who?'

'Go and see. You'll be surprised.'

He hurried off. Jane went inside. What would Jean-
Pierre do about Ellis? she wondered. Well, he would
want to tell the Russians. And the Russians would want
to kill Ellis.

The thought made her angry. 'There is to be no
more killing!' she said aloud. 'I will not permit it!' Her

voice made Chantal cry. Jane rocked her and she became quiet.

What am I going to do about it? thought Jane.

I have to stop him getting in touch with the Russians. How?

His contact can't meet him here in the village. So all I have to do is keep Jean-Pierre here.

I'll say to him: You must promise not to leave the village. If you refuse I'll tell Ellis that you're a spy and *he* will make sure you don't leave the village.

Suppose Jean-Pierre makes the promise then breaks it?

Well, I would *know* he had gone out of the village, and I would *know* he was meeting his contact, and I could then warn Ellis.

Has he any other way of communicating with the Russians?

He must have some means of getting in touch with them in an emergency.

But there are no phones here, no post, no courier service, no carrier pigeons—

He must have a radio.

If he has a radio there's no way I can stop him.

The more she thought about it, the more convinced she was that he had a radio. He needed to arrange those meetings in stone huts. In theory they might have all been scheduled before he left Paris, but in practice that was almost impossible: what would happen when he had to break an appointment, or when he was late, or when he needed to meet his contact urgently?

He *must* have a radio.

What can I do if he has a radio?

I can take it away from him.

She put Chantal down in her cradle and looked around the house. She went into the front room. There on the tiled counter in the middle of what had been the shop was Jean-Pierre's medical bag.

It was the obvious place. No one was allowed to open the bag except Jane, and she never had any reason to.

She undid the clasp and went through the contents, taking them out one by one.

There was no radio.

It was not going to be that easy.

He *must* have one, she thought, and I *must* find it: if I don't, either Ellis will kill him or he will kill Ellis.

She decided to search the house.

She checked through the medical supplies on the shopkeeper's shelves, looking in all the boxes and packets whose seals had been broken, hurrying for fear that he should come back before she was finished. She found nothing.

She went into the bedroom. She rummaged through his clothes, then in the winter bedding which was stored in a corner. Nothing. Moving faster, she went into the living-room and looked around frantically for possible hiding-places. The map chest! She opened it. Only the maps were there. She closed the lid with a bang. Chantal stirred but did not cry, even though it was almost time for her feed. You're a good baby, thought Jane; thank God! She looked behind the food cupboard and lifted the rug in case there was a concealed hole in the floor.

Nothing.

It had to be here somewhere. She could not imagine that he would take the risk of hiding it *outside* the house, for there would be a terrible danger of its being found by accident.

She went back into the shop. If only she could find his radio everything would be all right – he would have no option but to give in.

His bag was so much the obvious place, for he took it with him wherever he went. She picked it up. It was heavy. She felt around inside it yet again. It had a thick base.

Suddenly she was inspired.

The bag could have a false bottom.

She probed the base with her fingers. It must be here, she thought; it *must*.

She pushed her fingers down beside the base and lifted.

The false bottom came up easily.

With her heart in her mouth, she looked inside.

There, in the hidden compartment, was a black plastic box. She took it out.

That's it, she thought; he calls them on this little radio.

Why does he meet them as well?

Perhaps he cannot tell them secrets over the radio for fear that someone is listening. Perhaps the radio is only for arranging meetings, and for emergencies.

Like when he can't leave the village.

She heard the back door open. Terrified, she dropped the radio to the floor and spun around, looking into the living-room. It was only Fara with a broom. 'Oh, Christ,' she said aloud. She turned back, her heart racing.

She had got to get rid of the radio before Jean-Pierre returned.

But how? She could not throw it away – it would be found.

She had to smash it.

With what?

She did not have a hammer.

A stone, then.

She hurried through the living-room and into the courtyard. The courtyard wall was made of rough stones held together with sandy mortar. She reached up and wiggled one of the top row of stones. It seemed firm. She tried the next, and the next. The fourth stone seemed a little loose. She reached up and tugged at it. It moved a little. 'Come on, come *on*,' she cried. She pulled hard. The rough stone cut into the skin of her hands. She gave a mighty heave and the stone came loose. She jumped back as it fell to the ground. It was about the size of a can of beans: just right. She picked it up in both hands and hurried back into the house.

She went into the front room. She picked up the black plastic radio transmitter from the floor and placed it on the tiled counter. Then she lifted the stone above her head and brought it down with all her might on the radio.

The plastic casing cracked.

She would have to hit it harder.

She lifted the stone and brought it down again. This time the casing broke, revealing the innards of the instrument: she saw a printed circuit, a loudspeaker cone and pair of batteries with Russian script on them. She took out the batteries and threw them on the floor, then started to smash the mechanism.

She was grabbed from behind suddenly, and Jean-Pierre's voice shouted: 'What are you doing?'

She struggled against his grip, got free for a moment, and struck another blow at the little radio.

He grasped her shoulders and hurled her aside. She stumbled and fell to the floor. She landed awkwardly, twisting her wrist.

He stared at the radio. 'It's ruined!' he said. 'It's irreparable!' He grabbed her by the shirt and hauled her to her feet. 'You don't know what you've done!' he screamed. There was despair and hot rage in his eyes.

'Let me go!' she shouted at him. He had no right to act like this when it was *he* who had lied to *her*. 'How *dare* you manhandle me!'

'How *dare* I?' He let go of her shirt, drew back his arm and punched her hard. The blow landed in the middle of her abdomen. For a split-second she was simply paralysed with shock; then the pain came, deep inside where she was still sore from having Chantal, and she cried out and bent over with her hands clutching her middle.

Her eyes were shut tight, so she did not see the second blow coming.

His punch landed full on her mouth. She screamed. She could hardly believe he was doing this to her. She opened her eyes and looked at him, terrified that he would hit her again.

'How *dare* I?' he screamed. 'How *dare* I?'

She fell to her knees on the dirt floor and began to sob with shock and pain and misery. Her mouth hurt so much she could hardly speak. 'Please don't hit me,' she managed. 'Don't hit me again.' She held a hand in front of her face defensively.

He knelt down, shoved her hand aside, and thrust his face into hers. 'How long have you known?' he hissed.

She licked her lips. They were swelling already. She dabbed at them with her sleeve, and it came away bloody. She said: 'Since I saw you in the stone hut . . . on the way to Cobak.'

'But you didn't see anything!'

'He spoke with a Russian accent, and said he had blisters. I figured it out from there.'

There was a pause while that sank in. 'Why now?' he said. 'Why didn't you break the radio before?'

'I didn't dare to.'

'And now?'

'Ellis is here.'

'So?'

Jane summoned up what little courage she had left. 'If you don't stop this . . . spying . . . I'll tell Ellis, and he will stop you.'

He took her by the throat. 'And what if I strangle you, you bitch.'

'If any harm comes to me . . . Ellis will want to know why. He's still in love with me.'

She stared at him. Hatred burned in his eyes. 'Now I'll never get him!' he said. She wondered who he meant. Ellis? No. Masud? Could it be that Jean-Pierre's ultimate purpose was to kill Masud? His hands were still around her throat. She felt his grip tighten. She watched his face fearfully.

Then Chantal cried.

Jean-Pierre's expression changed dramatically. The hostility went from his eyes, and the fixed, taut look of anger crumpled; and finally, to Jane's amazement, he put his hands over his eyes and began to cry.

She gazed at him with incredulity. She found herself feeling pity for him, and thought: Don't be a fool, the bastard just beat you up. But despite herself she was touched by his tears. 'Don't cry,' she said quietly. Her voice was surprisingly gentle. She touched his cheek.

'I'm sorry,' he said. 'I'm sorry for what I did to you. My life's work . . . all for nothing.'

She realized with astonishment and a trace of self-disgust that she was no longer angry with him, despite her swollen lips and the continuing pain in her tummy. She gave in to the sentiment, and put her arms around him, patting his back as if comforting a child.

'Just because of Anatoly's accent,' he mumbled. 'Just because of that.'

'Forget Anatoly,' she said. 'We'll leave Afghanistan and go back to Europe. We'll go with the next convoy.'

He took his hands from his face and looked at her. 'When we get back to Paris . . .'

'Yes?'

'When we're home . . . I still want us to be together. Can you forgive me? I love you – truly, I always loved you. And we're married. And there's Chantal. Please, Jane – please don't leave me. Please?'

To her surprise she felt no hesitation. Here was the man she loved, her husband, the father of her child; and he was in trouble and appealing for help. 'I'm not going anywhere,' she replied.

'Promise,' he said. 'Promise you won't leave me.'

She smiled at him with her bleeding mouth. 'I love you,' she said. 'I promise I won't leave you.'

CHAPTER NINE

ELLIS WAS frustrated, impatient and angry. He was frustrated because he had been in the Five Lions Valley for seven days and still had not seen Masud. He was impatient because it was a daily purgatory for him to see Jane and Jean-Pierre living together and working together and sharing the pleasure of their happy little baby girl. And he was angry because he and nobody else had got himself into this wretched situation.

They had said he would meet Masud today, but the great man had not shown up so far. Ellis had walked all day yesterday to get here. He was at the south-western end of the Five Lions Valley, in Russian territory. He had left Banda accompanied by three guerrillas – Ali Ghanim, Matullah Khan and Yussuf Gul – but they had accumulated two or three more at each village and now they were thirty altogether. They sat in a circle, underneath a fig tree near the top of a hill, eating figs and waiting.

At the foot of the hill on which they sat, a flattish plain began and stretched south – all the way to Kabul, in fact, although that was fifty miles away and they could not see it. In the same direction, but much closer, was Bagram air base, just ten miles away: its buildings were not visible but they could see the occasional jet rising into the air. The plain was a fertile mosaic of fields and orchards, criss-crossed with streams all feeding into the Five Lions River as it ran, wider and deeper now but just as fast, towards the capital city. A rough road ran past the foot of the hill and went up the Valley as far as the town of Rokha, which was the northernmost limit of Russian territory here. There was not much traffic on the road: a few peasant carts and the occasional armoured car. Where the road crossed the river there was a new Russian-built bridge.

Ellis was going to blow up the bridge.

The lessons in explosives, which he was giving in order to mask for as long as possible his real mission, were hugely popular, and he had been obliged to limit the numbers attending. This was despite his hesitant Dari. He remembered a little Farsi from Teheran, and he had picked up a lot of Dari on his way here with the convoy, so that he could talk about the landscape, food, horses and weapons, but he still could not say such things as *The indentation in the explosive material has the effect of focusing the blast.* Nevertheless the idea of blowing things up appealed so much to the Afghan machismo that he always had an attentive audience. He could not teach them the formulas for calculating the amount of TNT required for a job, or even show them how to use his idiot-proof US Army computing tape, for none of them had done elementary-school maths and most of them could not read. Nevertheless he was able to show them how to destroy things more decisively

200

and at the same time use less material – which was very important to them, for all ordnance was in short supply. He had also tried to get them to adopt basic safety precautions, but in this he had failed: to them caution was cowardly.

Meanwhile, he was tortured by Jane.

He was jealous when he saw her touch Jean-Pierre; he was envious when he saw the two of them in the cave clinic, working so efficiently and harmoniously together; and he was consumed by lust when he caught a glimpse of Jane's swollen breast as she fed her baby. He would lie awake at night, under his sleeping bag in the house of Ismael Gul, where he was staying, and he would turn constantly, sometimes sweating and sometimes shivering, unable to get comfortable on the floor of packed earth, trying not to hear the muffled sounds of Ismael and his wife making love a few yards away in the next room; and the palms of his hands seemed to itch to touch Jane.

He had nobody to blame but himself for all this. He had volunteered for the mission in the foolish hope that he might win Jane back. It was unprofessional, as well as immature. All he could do was get out of here as quickly as possible.

And he could do nothing until he met Masud.

He stood up and walked around restlessly, careful nonetheless to stay in the shade of the tree so that he would not be visible from the road. A few yards away there was a mass of twisted metal where a helicopter had crashed. He saw a thin piece of steel about the size and shape of a dinner plate, and that gave him an idea.

He had been wondering how to demonstrate the effect of shaped charges and now he saw a way.

He took from his kitbag a small flat piece of TNT and a pocket knife. The guerrillas clustered closer around him. Among them was Ali Ghanim, a small, misshapen man – twisted nose, deformed teeth, and a slightly hunched back – who was said to have fourteen children. Ellis carved the name *Ali* into the TNT in Persian script. He showed it to them. Ali recognized his name. 'Ali,' he said, grinning and showing his hideous teeth.

Ellis placed the explosive, carved side down, on the piece of steel. 'I hope this works,' he said with a smile, and they all smiled back, although none of them spoke English. He took a coil of blasting fuse from his capacious bag and cut off a four-foot length. He got out his cap box, took a blasting cap, and inserted the end of the fuse into the cylindrical cap. He taped the cap to the TNT.

He looked down the hill to the road. He could see no traffic. He carried his little bomb across the hillside and put it down about fifty yards away. He lit the fuse with a match and then walked back to the fig tree.

The fuse was slow-burning. Ellis wondered, while he waited, whether Masud was having him watched and weighed up by the other guerrillas. Was the leader waiting for assurance that Ellis was a serious person whom the guerrillas could respect? Protocol was always important in an army, even a revolutionary one. But Ellis could not pussyfoot around much longer. If Masud did not show today, Ellis would have to drop all this explosives nonsense, confess to being an envoy from the White House, and demand a meeting with the rebel leader immediately.

There was an unimpressive bang and a small cloud of dust. The guerrillas looked disappointed at such a feeble blast. Ellis retrieved the piece of metal, using his scarf to hold it in case it was hot. The name *Ali* was cut through it in ragged-edged letters of Persian script. He showed it to the guerrillas, and they burst into excited chatter. Ellis was pleased: it was a vivid demonstration of the point that the explosive was *more* powerful where it was indented, contrary to what common sense would suggest.

The guerrillas went suddenly quiet. Ellis looked around and saw another group of seven or eight men approaching over the hill. Their rifles and round Chitrali caps marked them as guerrillas. As they came nearer, Ali stiffened, almost as if he were about to salute. Ellis said: 'Who is it?'

'Masud,' Ali replied.

'Which one is he?'

'The one in the middle.'

Ellis looked hard at the central figure in the group. Masud looked just like the others at first: a thin man of average height, dressed in khaki clothes and Russian boots. Ellis scrutinized his face. He was light-skinned, with a sparse moustache and the wispy beard of a teenager. He had a long nose with a hooked point. His alert dark eyes were surrounded by heavy lines which made him look at least five years older than his reputed age of twenty-eight. It was not a handsome face, but there was in it an air of lively intelligence and calm authority that distinguished him from the men around him.

He came directly to Ellis with his hand outstretched. 'I am Masud.'

'Ellis Thaler.' Ellis shook his hand.

'We're going to blow up this bridge,' Masud said in French.

'You want to get started?'

'Yes.'

Ellis packed his equipment into his kitbag while Masud went around the group of guerrillas, shaking hands with some, nodding to others, embracing one or two, speaking a few words to each.

When they were ready they went down the hill in a straggle, hoping – Ellis presumed – that if they were seen they would be taken for a group of peasants rather than a unit of the rebel army. When they reached the foot of the hill they were no longer visible from the road, although anyone overhead in a helicopter would have noticed them: Ellis presumed they would take cover if they heard a chopper. They headed for the river, following a footpath through the cultivated fields. They passed small houses and were seen by the people working in the fields, some of whom ignored them studiously while others waved and called out greetings. The guerrillas reached the river and walked along its bank, gaining what cover they could from the boulders and sparse vegetation at the water's edge. When they were about three hundred yards from the bridge a small convoy of army lorries began to cross it, and they all hid while the vehicles rumbled by, heading for Rokha. Ellis lay beneath a willow tree and found Masud beside him. 'If we destroy the bridge,' Masud said, 'we will cut off their supply line to Rokha.'

After the lorries had gone they waited a few minutes then walked the rest of the way to the bridge and clustered beneath it, invisible from the road.

At its mid-point the bridge was twenty feet above the river, which seemed to be about ten feet deep here. Ellis saw that it was a simple stringer bridge – two long steel girders, or stringers, supporting a flat slab of concrete road, and stretching from one bank to the other without intermediate support. The concrete was dead load – the girders took the strain. Break them and the bridge was ruined.

Ellis set about his preparations. His TNT was in one-pound yellow blocks. He made a stack of ten blocks and taped them together. Then he made three more identical stacks, using all his explosive. He was using TNT because that was the explosive most often found in bombs, shells, mines and hand grenades, and the guerrillas got most of their supplies from unexploded Russian ordnance. Plastic explosive would have been more suitable for their needs, for it could be stuffed into holes, wrapped around girders, and generally moulded into any shape required – but they had to work with the materials they could find and steal. They could occasionally get a little *plastique* from the Russian engineers by trading it for marijuana grown in the Valley, but the transaction – which involved intermediaries in the Afghan regular army – was risky and supplies were limited. All this Ellis had been told by the CIA's man in Peshawar, and it had turned out to be right.

The girders above him were I-beams spaced about eight feet apart. Ellis said in Dari: 'Somebody find me a stick this long,' indicating the space between the beams. One of the guerrillas walked along the river bank and uprooted a young tree. 'I need another one just the same,' Ellis said.

He put a stack of TNT on the lower lip of one of the I-beams and asked a guerrilla to hold it in place. He put another stack on the other I-beam in a similar position; then he forced the young tree between the two stacks so that it kept them both where they were.

He waded through the river and did exactly the same at the other end of the bridge.

He described everything he was doing in a mixture of Dari, French and English, letting them pick up what they could – the most important thing was for them to see what he was doing, and its results. He fused the charges with Primacord, the high-explosive detonating cord that burned at 21,000 feet per second, and he connected the four stacks so that they would explode simultaneously. He then made a ring main by looping the Primacord back on itself. The effect, he explained to Masud in French, would be that the cord would burn down to the TNT from both ends, so that if somehow the cable was severed in one place the bomb would still go off. He recommended this as a routine precaution.

He felt oddly happy as he worked. There was something soothing about mechanical tasks and the dispassionate calculation of poundage of explosive. And now that Masud had shown up at last he could get on with his mission.

He trailed the Primacord through the water, so that it was less visible – it would burn perfectly well under water – and brought it out on to the river bank. He attached a blasting cap to the end of the Primacord, then added a four-minute length of ordinary, slow-burning blasting fuse.

'Ready?' he said to Masud.

Masud said: 'Yes.'

Ellis lit the fuse.

They all walked briskly away, heading upstream along the river bank. Ellis felt a certain secret boyish glee about the enormous bang he was about to create. The others seemed excited, too, and he wondered whether he was as bad at concealing his enthusiasm as they were. It was while he was looking at them in this way that their expressions altered dramatically, and they all became alert suddenly, like birds listening for worms in the ground; and then Ellis heard it – the distant rumble of tank tracks.

The road was not visible from where they were, but one of the guerrillas quickly shinned up a tree. 'Two,' he reported.

Masud took Ellis's arm. 'Can you destroy the bridge while the tanks are on it?' he said.

Oh, shit, thought Ellis; this is a test. 'Yes,' he said rashly.

Masud nodded, smiling faintly. 'Good.'

Ellis scrambled up the tree alongside the guerrilla

and looked across the fields. There were two black tanks trundling heavily along the narrow stony road from Kabul. He felt very tense: this was his first sight of the enemy. With their armour plating and their enormous guns they looked invulnerable, especially by contrast with the ragged guerrillas and their rifles; and yet the Valley was littered with the remains of tanks the guerrillas had destroyed with home-made mines, well-placed grenades, and stolen rockets.

There were no other vehicles with the tanks. It was not a patrol, then, nor a raiding party; the tanks were probably being delivered to Rokha after being repaired at Bagram, or perhaps they had just arrived from the Soviet Union.

He began calculating.

The tanks were going at about ten miles per hour, so they would reach the bridge in a minute and a half. The fuse had been burning for less than a minute: it had at least three minutes to go. At present the tanks would be across the bridge and a safe distance away before the explosion.

He dropped from the tree and started to run, thinking: how the hell many years is it since the last time I was in a combat zone?

He heard footsteps behind him and glanced back. Ali was running right behind him, grinning horribly, and two more men were close on his heels. The others were taking cover along the river bank.

A moment later he reached the bridge and dropped to one knee beside his slow-burning fuse, slipping his kitbag off his shoulder as he did so. He continued to calculate while he fumbled the bag open and rooted around for his pocket knife. The tanks were now a minute away, he thought. Blasting fuse burned at the rate of a foot every thirty to forty-five seconds. Was this particular reel slow, average or fast? He seemed to recall that it was fast. Say a foot, then, for a thirty-second delay. In thirty seconds he could run about a hundred and fifty yards – enough for safety, just barely.

He opened the pocket knife and handed it to Ali, who had knelt down beside him. Ellis grabbed the fuse wire at a point a foot from where it was joined to the blasting cap, and held it with both hands for Ali to cut. He held the severed end in his left hand and the burning fuse in his right. He was not sure whether it was yet time to re-light the severed end. He had to see how far away the tanks were.

He scrambled up the embankment, still holding both pieces of fuse wire. Behind him, the Primacord trailed in the river. He poked his head up over the parapet of the bridge. The great black tanks rolled steadily closer. How soon? He was guessing wildly. He counted seconds, measuring their progress; and then, not calculating but hoping for the best, he put the burning end of the disconnected blasting fuse to the cut end that was still connected with the bombs.

He put the burning fuse down carefully on the ground and started to run.

Ali and the other two guerrillas followed him.

At first they were hidden from the tanks by the river

bank, but as the tanks came closer the four running men were clearly visible. Ellis was counting slow seconds as the rumble of the tanks turned into a roar.

The gunners in the tanks hesitated only momentarily: Afghans running away could be presumed to be guerrillas, and therefore suitable for target practice. There was a double *boom* and two shells flew over Ellis's head. He changed direction, running off to the side, away from the river, thinking: The gunner adjusts his range ... now he swings the barrel towards me ... he aims ... *now*. He dodged again, veering back towards the river, and a second later heard another boom. The shell landed close enough to spatter him with earth and stones. The next one will hit me, he thought, unless the damn bomb goes off first. Shit. Why did I have to show Masud how fucking macho I am? Then he heard a machine-gun open up. It's hard to aim straight from a moving tank, he thought; but perhaps they will stop. He visualized the spray of machine-gun bullets waving towards him, and he began to bob and weave. He realized all of a sudden that he could guess exactly what the Russians would do: they would stop the tanks where they got the clearest view of the fleeing guerrillas, and that would be on the bridge. But would the bomb go off before the machine-gunners hit their targets? He ran harder, his heart pounding and his breath coming in great gulps. I don't want to die, even if she loves him, he thought. He saw bullets chip a boulder almost in his path. He swerved suddenly, but the stream of fire followed him. It seemed hopeless: he was an easy target. He heard one of the guerrillas behind him cry out, then he was hit, twice in succession: he felt a burning pain across his hip, then an impact, like a heavy blow, in his right buttock. The second slug paralysed his leg momentarily, and he stumbled and fell, bruising his chest, then rolled over on to his back. He sat up, ignoring the pain, and tried to move. The two tanks had stopped on the bridge. Ali, who had been right behind him, now put his hands under Ellis's armpits and tried to lift him. The pair of them were sitting ducks: the gunners in the tanks could not miss.

Then the bomb went off.

It was beautiful.

The four simultaneous explosions sheared the bridge at both ends, leaving the midsection – with two tanks on it – totally unsupported. At first it fell slowly, its broken ends grinding; then it came free and dropped, spectacularly, into the rushing river, landing flat with a monster splash. The waters parted majestically, leaving the river bed visible for a moment, then came together again with a sound like a thunderclap.

When the noise died away, Ellis heard the guerrillas cheering.

Some of them emerged from cover and ran towards the half-submerged tanks. Ali lifted Ellis to his feet. The feeling returned to his legs in a rush, and he realized that he was hurting. 'I'm not sure I can walk,' he said to Ali in Dari. He took a step, and would have fallen if Ali had not been holding him. 'Oh, shit,' Ellis said in English, 'I think I've got a bullet in my ass.'

He heard shots. Looking up, he saw the surviving Russians trying to escape from the tanks, and the guerrillas picking them off as they emerged. They were cold-blooded bastards, these Afghans. Looking down, he saw that the right leg of his trousers was soaked with blood. That would be from the surface wound, he surmised: he felt that the bullet was still plugging the other wound.

Masud came up to him, smiling broadly. 'That was well done, the bridge,' he said in his heavily-accented French. 'Magnificent!'

'Thanks,' said Ellis. 'But I didn't come here to blow up bridges.' He felt weak and a little dizzy, but now was the time to state his business. 'I came to make a deal.'

Masud looked at him curiously. 'Where are you from?'

'Washington. The White House. I represent the President of the United States.'

Masud nodded, unsurprised. 'Good. I'm glad.'

It was at that moment that Ellis fainted.

He made his pitch to Masud that night.

The guerrillas rigged up a stretcher and carried him up the valley to Astana, where they stopped at dusk. Masud had already sent a runner on to Banda to fetch Jean-Pierre, who would arrive some time tomorrow to take the bullet out of Ellis's backside. Meanwhile they all settled down in the courtyard of a farmhouse. Ellis's pain had dulled but the journey had made him weaker. The guerrillas had put primitive dressings on his wounds.

An hour or so after arrival he was given hot, sweet

green tea, which revived him somewhat, and a little later they all had mulberries and yoghurt for supper. It was usually like that with the guerrillas, Ellis had observed, while travelling with the convoy from Pakistan to the Valley: an hour or two after they arrived somewhere, food would appear. Ellis did not know whether they bought it, commandeered it, or received it as a gift, but he guessed that it was given to them free, sometimes willingly and sometimes reluctantly.

When they had eaten, Masud sat near Ellis, and in the next few minutes most of the other guerrillas casually moved off, leaving Masud and two of his lieutenants alone with Ellis. Ellis knew he had to talk to Masud now, for there might not be another chance for another week. Yet he felt too feeble and exhausted for this subtle and difficult task.

Masud said: 'Many years ago, a foreign country asked the King of Afghanistan for five hundred warriors to help in a war. The Afghan King sent five men from our Valley, with a message saying that it is better to have five lions than five hundred foxes. This is how our Valley came to be called the Valley of the Five Lions.' He smiled. 'You were a lion today.'

Ellis said: 'I heard a legend saying there used to be five great warriors, known as the Five Lions, each of whom guarded one of the five ways into the Valley. And I heard that this is why they call you the Sixth Lion.'

'Enough of legends,' Masud said with a smile. 'What do you have to tell me?'

Ellis had rehearsed this conversation, and in his script it did not begin so abruptly. Clearly, Oriental indirection was not Masud's style. Ellis said: 'I have first to ask for your assessment of the war.'

Masud nodded, thought for a few seconds, and said: 'The Russians have twelve thousand troops in the town of Rokha, the gateway to the Valley. Their dispositions are as always: first minefields, then Afghan troops, then Russian troops to stop the Afghans running away. They are expecting another twelve hundred men as reinforcements. They plan to launch a major offensive up the Valley within two weeks. Their aim is to destroy our forces.'

Ellis wondered how Masud got such precise intelligence, but he was not so tactless as to ask. Instead he said: 'And will the offensive succeed?'

'No,' said Masud with quiet confidence. 'When they attack we melt into the hills, so there is no one here for them to fight. When they stop, we harass them from the high ground and cut their lines of communication. Gradually we wear them down. They find themselves spending vast resources to hold territory which gives them no military advantage. Finally they retreat. It is always so.'

It was a textbook account of guerrilla war, Ellis reflected. There was no question that Masud could teach the other tribal leaders a lot. 'How long do you think the Russians can go on making such futile attacks?'

Masud shrugged. 'It is in God's hands.'

'Will you ever be able to drive them out of your country?'

'The Vietnamese drove the Americans out,' Masud said with a smile.

'I know – I was there,' said Ellis. 'Do you know *how* they did it?'

'One important factor, in my opinion, is that the Vietnamese were receiving from the Russians supplies of the most modern weapons, especially portable surface-to-air-missiles. This is the only way guerrilla forces can fight back against aircraft and helicopters.'

'I agree,' said Ellis. 'More importantly, the United States government agrees. We would like to help you get hold of better weapons. But we would need to see you make real progress against your enemy with those weapons. The American people like to see what they're getting for their money. How soon do you think the Afghan resistance will be able to launch unified, countrywide assaults on the Russians, the way the Vietnamese did towards the end of the war?'

Masud shook his head dubiously. 'The unification of the resistance is at a very early stage.'

'What are the main obstacles?' Ellis held his breath, praying that Masud would give the expected answer.

'Mistrust between different fighting groups is the main obstacle.'

Ellis breathed a clandestine sigh of relief.

Masud went on: 'We are different tribes, different nations, and we have different commanders. Other guerrilla groups ambush my convoys and steal my supplies.'

'Mistrust,' Ellis repeated. 'What else?'

'Communication. We need a regular network of messengers. Eventually we must have radio contact, but that is far in the future.'

'Mistrust, and inadequate communications.' This was what Ellis had hoped to hear. 'Let's talk about something else.' He felt terribly tired: he had lost quite a lot of blood. He fought off a powerful desire to close his eyes. 'You here in the Valley have developed the art of guerrilla warfare more successfully than they have anywhere else in Afghanistan. Other leaders still waste their resources defending lowland territory and attacking strong positions. We would like you to train men from other parts of the country in modern guerrilla tactics. Would you consider that?'

'Yes – and I think I see where you're heading,' said Masud. 'After a year or so there would be in each zone of the Resistance a small cadre of men who had been trained in the Five Lions Valley. They could form a communications net. They would understand one another, they would trust me . . .' His voice tailed off, but Ellis could see from his face that he was still unwinding the implications in his head.

'All right,' said Ellis. He had run out of energy, but he was almost done. 'Here's the deal. If you can get the agreement of other commanders and set up that training programme, the US will supply you with RPG–7 rocket launchers, ground-to-air missiles and radio equipment. But there are two other commanders in particular who *must* be part of the agreement. They are Jahan Kamil, in the Pich Valley, and Amal Azizi, the commander of Faizabad.'

Masud grinned ruefully. 'You picked the toughest.'

'I know,' said Ellis. 'Can you do it?'

'Let me think about it,' said Masud.

'All right.' Exhausted, Ellis lay back on the cold ground and shut his eyes. A moment later he was asleep.

CHAPTER TEN

JEAN-PIERRE walked aimlessly through the moonlit fields in the depths of a black depression. A week ago he had been fulfilled and happy, master of the situation, doing useful work while he waited for his big chance. Now it was all over, and he felt worthless, a failure, a might-have-been.

There was no way out. He ran over the possibilities again and again, but he always ended up with the same conclusion: he had to leave Afghanistan.

His usefulness as a spy was over. He had no means of contacting Anatoly; and, even if Jane had not smashed the radio, he was unable to leave the village to meet Anatoly, for Jane would immediately know what he was doing, and would tell Eilis. He might have been able to silence Jane, somehow (*Don't think about it, don't even think about it*) but if anything happened to her Ellis would want to know why. It all came down to Ellis. I'd like to kill Ellis, he thought, if I had the nerve. But how? I have no gun. What would I do, cut his throat with a scalpel? He's much stronger than I am – I could never overcome him.

He thought about how it had gone wrong. He and Anatoly had become careless. They should have met in

218

a place from which they had a good view of the approaches all around, so that they could have been forewarned of any approach. But who would have thought that Jane might follow him? He was the victim of the most appallingly bad luck: that the wounded boy was allergic to penicillin; that Jane had heard Anatoly speak; that she was able to recognize a Russian accent; and that Ellis had turned up to give her courage. It *was* bad luck. But the history books do not remember the men who *almost* achieved greatness. I did my best, Papa, he thought; and he could almost hear his father's reply: I'm not interested in whether you did your best, I want to know whether you succeeded or failed.

He was approaching the village. He decided to turn in. He was sleeping badly, but he had nothing else to do but go to bed. He headed for home.

Somehow the fact that he still had Jane was not much consolation. Her discovery of his secret seemed to have made them less intimate, not more. A new distance had grown up between them, even though they were planning their return home and even talking about their new life back in Europe.

At least they still hugged one another in bed at night. That was something.

He went into the shopkeeper's house. He had expected Jane to be in bed already, but to his surprise she was still up. She spoke as soon as he walked in. 'A runner came for you from Masud. You have to go to Astana. Ellis is wounded.'

Ellis wounded. Jean-Pierre's heart beat faster. 'How?'

'Nothing serious. I gather he's got a bullet in his bum.'

'I'll go first thing in the morning.'

Jane nodded. 'The runner will go with you. You can be back by nightfall.'

'I see.' Jane was making sure he had no opportunity of meeting with Anatoly. Her caution was unnecessary: Jean-Pierre had no way of arranging such a meeting. Besides, Jane was guarding against a minor peril and overlooking a major one. Ellis was *wounded*. That made him *vulnerable*. Which changed everything.

Now Jean-Pierre could kill him.

Jean-Pierre was awake all night, thinking about it. He imagined Ellis, lying on a mattress under a fig tree, gritting his teeth against the pain of a smashed bone, or perhaps pale and weak from loss of blood. He saw himself preparing an injection. 'This is an antibiotic to prevent infection of the wound,' he would say, then he would inject him with an overdose of digitalis, which would give him a heart attack.

A natural heart attack was unlikely, but by no means impossible, in a man of thirty-four years, especially one who had been exercising strenuously after a long period of relatively sedentary work. Anyway, there would be no inquest, no post-mortem, and no suspicions: in the West they would not doubt that Ellis had been wounded in action and had died of his wounds. Here in the Valley, everyone would accept Jean-Pierre's diagnosis. He was trusted as much as any of Masud's closest lieutenants – quite naturally, for he had sacrificed as much as any of them for the cause, it must seem to them. No, the only doubter would be Jane. And what could she do?

He was not sure. Jane was a formidable opponent when she was backed up by Ellis; but Jane alone was not. Jean-Pierre might be able to persuade Jane to stay in the Valley for another year: he could promise not to betray the convoys, then find a way to re-establish contact with Anatoly and just wait for his chance to pinpoint Masud for the Russians.

He gave Chantal her bottle at two a.m. then went back to bed. He did not even try to sleep. He was too anxious, too excited, and too frightened. As he lay there waiting for the sun to rise he thought of all the things that could go wrong: Ellis might refuse treatment, Jean-Pierre might get the dosage wrong, Ellis might have suffered a mere scratch and be walking around normally, Ellis and Masud might even have left Astana already.

Jane's sleep was troubled by dreams. She tossed and turned beside him, occasionally muttering incomprehensible syllables. Only Chantal slept well.

Just before dawn Jean-Pierre got up, lit the fire, and went to the river to bathe. When he came back the runner was in his courtyard, drinking tea made by Fara and eating yesterday's left-over bread. Jean-Pierre took some tea but could not eat anything.

Jane was feeding Chantal on the roof. Jean-Pierre went up and kissed them both goodbye. Every time he touched Jane he remembered how he had punched her, and he felt as if his whole being shuddered with shame. She seemed to have forgiven him, but he could not forgive himself.

He led his old mare through the village and down to the riverside, then, with the runner at his side, he headed downstream. Between here and Astana there was a road, or what passed for a road in Five Lions: a strip of rocky earth, eight or ten feet wide and more or less flat, suitable for wooden carts or army jeeps although it would destroy an ordinary car within minutes. The Valley was a series of narrow rocky gorges broadening out at intervals to form small cultivated plains, a mile or two long and less than a mile wide, where the villagers scraped a living from the unwilling soil by hard work and clever irrigation. The road was good enough for Jean-Pierre to ride on the downhill stretches. (The horse was not good enough for him to ride uphill.)

The Valley must have been an idyllic place, once upon a time, he thought as he rode south in the bright morning sunshine. Watered by the Five Lions River, made secure by its high valley walls, organized according to ancient traditions, and undisturbed except by a few butter-carriers from Nuristan and the occasional ribbon salesman from Kabul, it must have been a throwback to the Middle Ages. Now the twentieth century had overtaken it with a vengeance. Almost every village had suffered some bomb damage: a watermill ruined, a meadow pitted with craters, an ancient wooden aqueduct smashed to splinters, a rubble-and-mortar bridge reduced to a few stepping-stones in the fast-moving river. The effect of all this on the economic life of the Valley was evident to Jean-Pierre's careful scrutiny. This house was a butcher's shop, but the wooden slab out front was bare of meat. This patch of weeds had once been a vegetable garden, but its owner had fled to Pakistan. There was an orchard, with fruit rotting on the ground when it should have been drying on a roof ready to be stored for the long, cold winter: the woman and children who had used to tend the orchard were dead, and the husband was a full-time guerrilla. That heap of mud and stones had been a mosque, and the villagers had decided not to rebuild it because it would probably get bombed again. All this waste and destruction happened because men such as Masud tried to resist the tide of history, and bamboozled the ignorant peasants into supporting them. With Masud out of the way, all this would end.

And with Ellis out of the way, Jean-Pierre could deal with Masud.

He wondered, as they approached Astana towards noon, whether he would find it difficult to stick the needle in. The idea of killing a patient was so grotesque that he did not know how to react. He had seen patients die, of course; but even then he was consumed by regret that he could not save them. When he had Ellis helpless before him, and the needle in his hand, would he be tortured by doubt, like Macbeth, or vacillate, like Raskolnikov in *Crime and Punishment*?

They went through Sangana, with its cemetery and sandy beach, then followed the road around a bend in the river. There was a stretch of farmland in front of them and a cluster of houses up on the hillside. A minute or two later a boy of eleven or twelve approached them across the fields and led them not to the village on the hill but to a large house at the edge of the farmland.

Still Jean-Pierre felt no doubts, no hesitation; just a kind of anxious apprehension, like the hour before an important exam.

He took his medical bag off the horse, gave the reins to the boy, and went into the courtyard of the farmhouse.

Twenty or more guerrillas were scattered around, squatting on their haunches and staring into space, waiting with aboriginal patience. Masud was not there, Jean-Pierre noticed on looking around, but two of his closest aides were. Ellis was in a shady corner, lying on a blanket.

Jean-Pierre knelt down beside him. Ellis was evidently in some pain from the bullet. He was lying on his front. His face was taut, his teeth gritted. His skin was pale and there was perspiration on his forehead. His breathing sounded harsh.

'It hurts, eh?' said Jean-Pierre in English.

'Fuckin'-A well told,' said Ellis through his teeth.

Jean-Pierre pulled the sheet off him. The guerrillas had cut away his clothes and had put a makeshift dressing on the wound. Jean-Pierre removed the dressing. He could see immediately that the injury was not grave. Ellis had bled a lot, and the bullet still lodged in his muscle obviously hurt like hell, but it was well away from any bones or major blood vessels – it would heal fast.

No, it won't, Jean-Pierre reminded himself. It won't heal at all.

'First I'll give you something to ease the pain,' he said.

'I'd appreciate that,' Ellis said fervently.

Jean-Pierre pulled the blanket up. Ellis had a huge scar, shaped like a cross, on his back. Jean-Pierre wondered how he had got it.

I'll never know, he thought.

He opened his medical bag. Now I'm going to kill Ellis, he thought. I've never killed anyone, not even by accident. What is it like to be a murderer? People do it every day, all over the world: men kill their wives, women kill their children, assassins kill politicians, burglars kill householders, public executioners kill murderers. He took a large syringe and began to fill it with digitoxin: the drug came in small vials and he had to empty four of them to get a lethal dose.

What would it be like to watch Ellis die? The first effect of the drug would be to increase Ellis's heart rate. He would feel this, and it would make him anxious and uncomfortable. Then, as the poison affected the timing mechanism of his heart, he would get extra heartbeats, one small one after each normal beat. Now he would feel terribly sick. Finally the heartbeats would become totally irregular, the upper and lower chambers of the heart would beat independently, and Ellis would die in agony and terror. What will I do,

Jean-Pierre thought, when he cries out in pain, asking me, the doctor, to help him? Will I let him know that I want him to die? Will he guess that I have poisoned him? Will I speak soothing words, in my best bedside manner, and try to ease his passing? *Just relax, this is a normal side-effect of the pain-killer, everything is going to be all right.*

The injection was ready.

I can do it, Jean-Pierre realised. I can kill him. I just don't know what will happen to me afterwards.

He bared Ellis's upper arm and, from sheer force of habit, swabbed a patch with alcohol.

At that moment Masud arrived.

Jean-Pierre had not heard him approach, so he seemed to come from nowhere, making Jean-Pierre jump. Masud put a hand on his arm. 'I startled you, *Monsieur le docteur,*' he said. He knelt down at Ellis's head. 'I have considered the proposal of the American government,' he said in French to Ellis.

Jean-Pierre knelt there, frozen in position with the syringe in his right hand. What proposal? What the hell was this? Masud was talking openly, as if Jean-Pierre was just another of his comrades – which he was, in a way – but Ellis . . . Ellis might suggest they talk in private.

Ellis raised himself on to one elbow with an effort. Jean-Pierre held his breath. But all Ellis said was: 'Go on.'

He's too exhausted, thought Jean-Pierre, and he's in too much pain, to think of elaborate security precautions; and besides, he has no more reason to suspect me than does Masud.

'It is good,' Masud was saying. 'But I have been

asking myself how I am going to fulfil my part of the bargain.'

Of course! thought Jean-Pierre. The Americans have not sent a top CIA agent here just to teach a few guerrillas how to blow up bridges and tunnels. Ellis is here to make a deal!

Masud went on: 'This plan to train cadres from other zones must be explained to the other commanders. This will be difficult. They will be suspicious – especially if I present the proposal. I think *you* must put it to them, and tell them what your government is offering them.'

Jean-Pierre was riveted. A plan to train cadres from other zones! What the hell was the idea?

Ellis spoke with some difficulty. 'I'd be glad to do that. You would have to bring them all together.'

'Yes.' Masud smiled. 'I shall call a conference of all the Resistance leaders, to be held here in the Five Lions Valley, in the village of Darg, in eight days' time. I will send runners today, with the message that a represent-ative of the United States government is here to discuss arms supplies.'

A conference! Arms supplies! The shape of the deal was becoming clear to Jean-Pierre. But what should he do about it?

'Will they come?' Ellis asked.

'Many will,' Masud replied. 'Our comrades from the western deserts will not – it's too far, and they don't know us.'

'What about the two we particularly want – Kamil and Azizi?'

Masud shrugged. 'It is in God's hands.'

Jean-Pierre was trembling with excitement. This would be the most important event in the history of the Afghan Resistance.

Ellis was fumbling in his kitbag, which was on the floor near his head. 'I may be able to help you persuade Kamil and Azizi,' he was saying. He drew from the bag two small packages and opened one. It contained a flat rectangular piece of yellow metal. 'Gold,' said Ellis. 'Each of these is worth about five thousand dollars.'

It was a fortune: five thousand dollars was more than two years' income for the average Afghan.

Masud took the piece of gold and hefted it in his hand. 'What's that?' he said, pointing to an indented figure in the middle of the rectangle.

'The seal of the President of the United States,' said Ellis.

Clever, thought Jean-Pierre. Just the thing to impress tribal leaders and at the same time make them irresistibly curious to meet Ellis.

'Will that help to persuade Kamil and Azizi?' said Ellis.

Masud nodded. 'I think they will come.'

You bet your *life* they'll come, thought Jean-Pierre.

And suddenly he knew exactly what he had to do. Masud, Kamil and Azizi, the three great leaders of the Resistance, would be together in the village of Darg in eight days' time.

He had to tell Anatoly.

Then Anatoly could kill them all.

This is it, thought Jean-Pierre; this is the moment I've been waiting for ever since I came to the Valley. I've got Masud where I want him – and two other rebel leaders too.

But how can I tell Anatoly?

There *must* be a way.

'A summit meeting,' Masud was saying. He smiled rather proudly. 'It will be a good start to the new unity of the Resistance, will it not?'

Either that, Jean-Pierre thought, or the beginning of the end. He lowered his hand, pointing the needle at the ground, and depressed the plunger, emptying the syringe. He watched the poison soak into the dusty earth. A new start, or the beginning of the end.

Jean-Pierre gave Ellis an anaesthetic, took out the bullet, cleaned the wound, put a new dressing on it, and injected him with antibiotics to prevent infection. He then dealt with two guerrillas who also had minor wounds from the skirmish. By that time word had got around the village that the doctor was here, and a little cluster of patients gathered in the courtyard of the farmhouse. Jean-Pierre dealt with a bronchitic baby, three minor infections, and a mullah with worms. Then he had lunch. Around mid-afternoon he packed his bag and climbed on to Maggie for the journey home.

He left Ellis behind. Ellis would be much better off staying where he was for a few days – the wound would heal faster if he lay still and quiet. Jean-Pierre was now paradoxically anxious that Ellis should remain in good health, for if he were to die the conference would be cancelled.

As he rode the old horse up the valley, he racked his brains for a means of getting in touch with Anatoly. Of course, he could simply turn around and ride down the Valley to Rokha, and there give himself up to the Russians. Provided they did not shoot him on sight, he would be in Anatoly's presence in no time. But then Jane would know where he had gone and what he had done, and she would tell Ellis, and Ellis would change the time and place of the conference.

Somehow he had to send a letter to Anatoly. But who would deliver it?

There was a constant trickle of people passing through the Valley on the way to Charikar, the Russian-occupied town sixty or seventy miles away in the plain, or to Kabul, the capital city, a hundred miles away. There were dairy farmers from Nuristan with their butter and cheese; travelling merchants selling pots and pans; shepherds bringing small flocks of fat-tailed sheep to market; and families of nomads going about their mysterious nomadic business. Any of them might be bribed to take a letter to a post office, or even just to thrust it into the hands of a Russian soldier. Kabul was three days' journey, Charikar two. Rokha, where there were Russian soldiers but no post office, was only a day away. Jean-Pierre was fairly sure he could find someone to accept the commission. There was a danger, of course, that the letter would be opened and read, and Jean-Pierre would be found out, and tortured and killed. He might have been prepared to take that risk. But there was another snag. When the messenger had taken the money, would he deliver the letter? There was nothing to stop him 'losing' it on the way. Jean-Pierre might never know what had happened. The whole scheme was just too *uncertain*.

He had not resolved the problem when he reached Banda at dusk. Jane was on the roof of the shopkeeper's house, catching the evening breeze, with Chantal on her knee. Jean-Pierre waved to them then went inside the house and put his medical bag on the tiled counter in the storeroom. It was when he was emptying the bag, at the moment when he saw the diamorphine pills, that he realized there was one person he could trust with the letter to Anatoly.

He found a pencil in his bag. He took the paper wrapping from a package of cotton-wool swabs and tore a neat rectangle out of it – there was no writing-paper in the Valley. He wrote in French:

To Colonel Anatoly of the KGB—

It sounded oddly melodramatic, but he did not know how else to begin. He did not know Anatoly's full name and he did not have an address.

He went on:

Masud has called a council of leaders of the Rebellion. They meet eight days from today, on Thursday 27th August, at Darg, which is the next village to the south of Banda. They will probably all sleep in the mosque that

night and stay together all day Friday which is a holy day.
The conference has been called for them to talk with a CIA
agent known to me as Ellis Thaler who arrived in the
Valley a week ago.

 This is our chance!

He added the date and signed it 'Simplex'.

He did not have an envelope – he had not seen one
of those since he left Europe. He wondered just what
was the best way to enclose the letter. As he looked
around his eye fell on a carton of plastic containers for
dispensing tablets. They came with self-adhesive labels
which Jean-Pierre never used because he could not
write the Persian script. He rolled his letter into a
cylinder and put it in one of the containers.

He wondered how to mark it. At some point in its
journey the package would find its way into the hands
of a lowly Russian soldier. Jean-Pierre imagined a
bespectacled, anxious clerk in a cold office, or perhaps
a stupid ox of a man on sentry duty outside a barbed-
wire fence. No doubt the art of buck-passing was as well
developed in the Russian army as it had been in the
French when Jean-Pierre did his military service. He
considered how he might make the thing look important enough to be handed to a superior officer. There
was no point in writing 'Important' or 'KGB' or anything at all in French or English or even Dari because
the soldier would not be able to read the European or
Persian letters. Jean-Pierre did not know any Russian
script. It was ironic that the woman on the roof, whose
voice he could now hear singing a lullaby, was a fluent

speaker of Russian and could have told him how to write anything at all, had she been willing. In the end he wrote 'Anatoly – KGB' in European letters and stuck the label on the container, then put the container into an empty drugs box which was marked *Poison!* in fifteen languages and three international symbols. He tied up the box with string.

Moving quickly, he put everything back in his medical bag and replaced the items he had used at Astana. He took a handful of diamorphine tablets and put them in his shirt pocket. Finally he wrapped the *Poison!* box in a threadbare towel.

He left the house. 'I'm going to the river to wash,' he called up to Jane.

'Okay.'

He walked quickly through the village, nodding curtly to one or two people, and headed out through the fields. He was full of optimism. All sorts of risks attended his plans but he could once again hope for a great triumph. He skirted a clover field that belonged to the mullah and climbed down a series of terraces. A mile or so from the village, on a rocky outcrop of the mountain, was a solitary cottage that had been bombed. It was getting dark when Jean-Pierre came within sight of it. He walked slowly towards it, picking his way gingerly across the uneven ground, regretting that he had not brought a lamp.

He stopped at the pile of rubble that had once been the front of the house. He thought of going in, but the smell as well as the darkness dissuaded him. He called out: 'Hey!'

A shapeless form rose from the ground at his feet and scared him. He jumped back, cursing.

The *malang* stood up.

Jean-Pierre peered at the skeletal face and matted beard of the mad fellow. Recovering his composure, he said in Dari: 'God be with you, holy man.'

'And with you, Doctor.'

Jean-Pierre had caught him in a coherent phase. Good. 'How is your belly?'

The man mimed a stomach-ache: as always, he wanted drugs. Jean-Pierre gave him one diamorphine pill, letting him see the others then putting them back in his pocket. The *malang* ate his heroin and said: 'I want more.'

'You can have more,' Jean-Pierre told him. 'A lot more.'

He held out his hand.

'But you have to do something for me,' said Jean-Pierre.

He nodded eagerly.

'You have to go to Charikar and give this to a Russian soldier.' Jean-Pierre had decided on Charikar, despite the extra day's journey it involved, because he feared Rokha, being a rebel town temporarily occupied by the Russians, might be in a state of confusion, and the package could get lost; whereas Charikar was permanently in Russian territory. And he had decided on a soldier, rather than a post office, as the destination because the *malang* might not be able to deal with the business of buying a stamp and mailing something.

He looked carefully at the man's unwashed face. He

had been wondering whether the fellow would comprehend even these simple instructions, but the look of fear on his face at the mention of a Russian soldier indicated that he had understood perfectly.

Now, was there any way Jean-Pierre could ensure that the *malang* actually followed these orders? He, too, could throw the package away and come back swearing that he had carried out the task, for if he was intelligent enough to understand what he had to do he might be capable of lying about it.

Jean-Pierre was inspired with an idea. 'And buy a pack of Russian cigarettes,' he said.

The *malang* held out empty hands. 'No money.'

Jean-Pierre knew he had no money. He gave him 100 afghanis. That should ensure that he actually went to Charikar. Was there a way to compel him to deliver the package?

Jean-Pierre said: 'If you do this, I'll give you all the pills you want. But do not cheat me – for if you do, I shall know, and I will never give you pills again, and your bellyache will grow worse and worse and you will swell up and then your guts will burst like a grenade and you will die in agony. Do you understand?'

'Yes.'

Jean-Pierre stared at him in the faint light. The whites of his mad eyes gleamed back. He seemed terrified. Jean-Pierre gave him the rest of the diamorphine pills. 'Eat one every morning until you come back to Banda.'

He nodded vigorously.

'Go now, and do not try to cheat me.'

The man turned away and began to run along the rough path with his odd, animal-like gait. Watching him disappear into the gathering darkness, Jean-Pierre thought: The future of this country is in your filthy hands, you poor mad wretch. May God go with you.

A week later the *malang* had not returned.

By Wednesday, the day before the conference, Jean-Pierre was distraught. Every hour, he told himself the man could be here within the next hour. At the end of each day, he said he would come tomorrow.

Aircraft activity in the Valley had increased, as if to add to Jean-Pierre's worries. All week the jets had been howling overhead to bomb the villages. Banda had been lucky: only one bomb had landed, and it had merely made a big hole in Abdullah's clover field; but the constant noise and danger made everyone irritable. The tension produced, in Jean-Pierre's clinic, a predictable crop of patients with stress symptoms: miscarriages, domestic accidents, unexplained vomiting, and headaches. It was the children who got the headaches. In Europe, Jean-Pierre would have recommended psychiatry. Here, he sent them to the mullah. Neither psychiatry nor Islam would do much good, for what was wrong with the children was the war.

He went through the morning's patients mechanically, asking his routine questions in Dari, announcing his diagnosis to Jane in French, dressing wounds and giving injections and handing out plastic containers of tablets and glass bottles of coloured medicine. It should

have taken the *malang* two days to walk to Charikar.
Allow him a day to work up the nerve to approach a
Russian soldier and a night to get over it. Setting off
the next morning, he had another two days' journey.
He should have got back the day before yesterday.
What had happened? Had he lost the package, and
stayed away in fear and trembling? Had he taken all the
pills at once and made himself ill? Had he fallen in the
damn river and drowned? Had the Russians used him
for target practice?

Jean-Pierre looked at his wristwatch. It was ten-thirty.
Any minute now the *malang* might arrive, bearing a
pack of Russian cigarettes as proof that he had been to
Charikar. Jean-Pierre wondered briefly how he would
explain the cigarettes to Jane, for he did not smoke. He
decided that no explanation was necessary for the acts
of a lunatic.

He was bandaging a small boy from the next valley
who had burned his hand on a cooking fire when there
came from outside the flurry of footsteps and greetings
which meant someone had arrived. Jean-Pierre contained his eagerness and continued wrapping the boy's
hand. When he heard Jane speak he looked around,
and to his intense disappointment saw that it was not
the *malang* but two strangers.

The first of them said: 'God be with you, Doctor.'

'And with you,' said Jean-Pierre. In order to pre-
empt a lengthy exchange of civilities he said: 'What is
the matter?'

'There has been a terrible bombing at Skabun. Many
people are dead and many wounded.'

Jean-Pierre looked at Jane. He still could not leave Banda without her permission, for she was afraid he would get in touch with the Russians somehow. But clearly he could not have contrived this summons. 'Shall I go?' he said to her in French. 'Or will you?' He really did not want to go, for it would mean an overnight stay in all probability, and he was desperate to see the *malang*.

Jane hesitated. Jean-Pierre knew she was thinking that if she went she would have to take Chantal. Besides, she knew she could not deal with major traumatic wounds.

'It's up to you,' Jean-Pierre said.

'You go,' she said.

'All right.' Skabun was a couple of hours away. If he worked quickly, and if there were not too many wounded, he might just get away at dusk, Jean-Pierre thought. He said: 'I'll try to get back tonight.'

She came over and kissed his cheek. 'Thank you,' she said.

He checked his bag quickly: morphine for the pain, penicillin to prevent wound infections, needles and surgical thread, plenty of dressings. He put a cap on his head and a blanket over his shoulders.

'I won't take Maggie,' he said to Jane. 'Skabun is not far and the trail is very bad.' He kissed her again, then turned to the two messengers. 'Let's go,' he said.

They walked down to the village then forded the river and climbed the steep steps on the far side. Jean-Pierre was thinking about kissing Jane. If he succeeded in his plan, and the Russians killed Masud, how would she react? She would know he had been behind it. But she would not betray him, he was sure. Would she still love him? He wanted her. Since they had been together he had suffered less and less from the black depressions which had used to assault him regularly. Just by loving him she made him feel that he was all right. He wanted that. But he also wanted to succeed in this mission. He thought: I suppose I must want success more than happiness, and that is why I'm prepared to risk losing her for the sake of killing Masud.

The three of them walked south-west along the cliff-top footpath with the rushing river loud in their ears. Jean-Pierre said: 'How many people dead?'

'Many people,' said one of the messengers.

Jean-Pierre was used to this sort of thing. Patiently he said: 'Five? Ten? Twenty? Forty?'

'A hundred.'

Jean-Pierre did not believe him: there were not a hundred inhabitants in Skabun. 'How many wounded?'

'Two hundred.'

That was ludicrous. Did the man not know, Jean-Pierre wondered? Or was he exaggerating for fear that if he gave small numbers the doctor would turn around and go back? Perhaps it was just that he could not count beyond ten. 'What kind of wounds?' Jean-Pierre asked him.

'Holes and cuts and bleeding.'

Those sounded more like battle injuries. Bombing produced concussion, burns, and compression damage from falling buildings. This man was obviously a poor witness. There was no point in questioning him further.

A couple of miles outside Banda they turned off the cliff path and headed north on a path unfamiliar to Jean-Pierre. 'Is this the way to Skabun?' he asked.

'Yes.'

It was obviously a short cut he had never discovered. They were certainly heading in the right general direction.

A few minutes later they saw one of the little stone huts in which travellers would rest or spend the night. To Jean-Pierre's surprise, the messengers headed for its doorless entrance. 'We haven't time to rest,' he told them irritably. 'Sick people are waiting for me.'

Then Anatoly stepped out of the hut.

Jean-Pierre was dumbfounded. He did not know whether to be exultant because now he could tell Anatoly about the conference, or terrified that the Afghans would kill Anatoly.

'Don't worry,' Anatoly said, reading his expression. 'They're soldiers of the Afghan regular army. I sent them to fetch you.'

'My God!' It was brilliant. There had been no bombing at Skabun – that had been a ruse, dreamed up by Anatoly, for getting Jean-Pierre to come. 'Tomorrow,' Jean-Pierre said excitedly, 'tomorrow something terribly important is happening—'

'I know, I know – I got your message. That's why I'm here.'

'So you will get Masud . . .?'

Anatoly smiled mirthlessly, showing his tobacco-stained teeth. 'We will get Masud. Calm down.'

Jean-Pierre realized he was behaving like an excited

child at Christmas time. He suppressed his enthusiasm with an effort. 'When the *malang* failed to come back, I thought . . .'

'He arrived in Charikar yesterday,' said Anatoly. 'God knows what happened to him on the way. Why didn't you use your radio?'

'It broke,' said Jean-Pierre. He did not want to explain about Jane right now. 'The *malang* will do anything for me because I supply him with heroin, to which he is addicted.'

Anatoly looked hard at Jean-Pierre for a moment, and in his eyes there was something like admiration. 'I'm glad you're on my side,' he said.

Jean-Pierre smiled.

'I want to know more,' said Anatoly. He put an arm around Jean-Pierre's shoulders and led him into the hut. They sat on the earth floor and Anatoly lit a cigarette. 'How do you know about this conference?' he began.

Jean-Pierre told him about Ellis, about the bullet wound, about Masud talking to Ellis when Jean-Pierre was about to inject him, about the bars of gold and the training scheme and the promised weapons.

'This is fantastic,' said Anatoly. 'Where is Masud now?'

'I don't know. But he will arrive in Darg today, probably. Tomorrow at the latest.'

'How do you know?'

'He called the meeting – how can he fail to come?'

Anatoly nodded. 'Describe the CIA man.'

'Well, five foot ten, a hundred and fifty pounds,

blond hair and blue eyes, age thirty-four but looks a little older, college-educated.'

'I'll put all that through the computer.' Anatoly stood up. He went outside and Jean-Pierre followed him.

Anatoly took from his pocket a small radio transmitter. He extended its telescopic aerial, pressed a button, and muttered into it in Russian. Then he turned back to Jean-Pierre. 'My friend, you have succeeded in your mission,' he said.

It's true, Jean-Pierre thought. I succeeded.

He said: 'When will you strike?'

'Tomorrow, of course.'

Tomorrow. Jean-Pierre felt a wave of savage glee. Tomorrow.

The others were looking up. He followed their gaze and saw a helicopter descending: Anatoly had presumably summoned it with his transmitter. The Russian was throwing caution to the wind, now: the game was almost over, this was the last hand, and stealth and disguise were to be replaced by boldness and speed. The machine came down and landed, with difficulty, on a small patch of level ground a hundred yards away.

Jean-Pierre walked over to the helicopter with the other three men. He wondered where to go when they had departed. There was nothing for him to do at Skabun, but he could not return to Banda immediately without revealing that there had been no bombing victims for him to take care of. He decided he had better sit in the stone hut for a few hours then return home.

He held out his hand to shake with Anatoly. 'Au revoir.'

Anatoly did not take his hand. 'Get in.'

'What?'

'Get in the helicopter.'

Jean-Pierre was flabbergasted. 'Why?'

'You're coming with us.'

'Where? To Bagram? To Russian territory?'

'Yes.'

'But I can't—'

'Stop blustering and listen,' Anatoly said patiently. 'Firstly, your work is done. Your assignment in Afghanistan is over. You have achieved your goal. Tomorrow we will capture Masud. You can go home. Secondly, you are now a security risk. You know what we plan to do tomorrow. So for the sake of secrecy you cannot remain in rebel territory.'

'But I wouldn't tell anyone!'

'Suppose they tortured you? Suppose they tortured your wife in front of your eyes? Suppose they were to tear your baby daughter limb from limb in front of your wife?'

'But what will happen to them if I go with you?'

'Tomorrow, in the raid, we will capture them and bring them to you.'

'I can't believe this.' Jean-Pierre knew that Anatoly was right, but the idea of not returning to Banda was so unexpected that it disoriented him. Would Jane and Chantal be safe? Would the Russians really pick them up? Would Anatoly let the three of them go back to Paris? How soon could they leave?

'Get in,' Anatoly repeated.

The two Afghan messengers were standing either side of Jean-Pierre, and he realized that he had no choice: if he refused to get in they would pick him up and put him in.

He climbed into the helicopter.

Anatoly and the Afghans jumped in after him, and the chopper lifted. Nobody closed the door.

As the helicopter rose, Jean-Pierre got his first aerial view of the Five Lions Valley. The white river zig-zagging through the dun-coloured land reminded him of the scar of an old knife wound on the brown forehead of Shahazai Gul, the brother of the midwife. He could see the village of Banda with its yellow-and-green patchwork fields. He looked hard at the hilltop where the caves were but he saw no signs of occupation: the villagers had chosen their hiding-place well. The helicopter went higher and turned, and he could no longer see Banda. He looked for other landmarks. I spent a year of my life there, he thought, and now I'll never see it again. He identified the village of Darg, with its doomed mosque. This Valley was the stronghold of the Resistance, he thought. By tomorrow it will be a memorial to a failed rebellion. And all because of me.

Suddenly the helicopter veered south and crossed the mountain, and within seconds the Valley was lost from view.

CHAPTER ELEVEN

WHEN FARA learned that Jane and Jean-Pierre would be leaving with the next convoy, she cried for a whole day. She had developed a strong attachment to Jane and a great fondness for Chantal. Jane was pleased, but embarrassed: sometimes it seemed as if Fara preferred Jane to her own mother. However, Fara seemed to get used to the idea that Jane was leaving, and the next day she was her usual self, devoted as ever but no longer heartbroken.

Jane herself became anxious about the journey home. From the Valley to the Khyber Pass was a 150-mile trek. Coming in, it had taken fourteen days. She had suffered from blisters and diarrhoea as well as the inevitable aches and pains. Now she had to do the return journey carrying a two-month-old baby. There would be horses, but for much of the way it would not be safe to ride them, for the convoys travelled by the smallest and steepest of mountain paths, often at night.

She made a sort of hammock of cotton, to be slung around her neck, for carrying Chantal. Jean-Pierre would have to carry whatever supplies they needed during the day, for – as Jane had learned on the journey in – horses and men walked at different speeds, the horses going faster than the men uphill and slower down, so that the people got separated from the baggage for long periods.

Deciding *what* supplies to take was the problem that occupied her this afternoon, while Jean-Pierre was at Skabun. There would be a basic medical kit – antibiotics, wound dressings, morphine – which Jean-Pierre would put together. They would have to take some food. Coming in, they had had a lot of high-energy Western rations, chocolate and packet soups and the perennial explorers' favourite, Kendal Mint Cake. Going out, they would have only what they could find in the Valley: rice, dried fruit, cheese, hard bread, and anything they could buy on the road. It was a good thing they did not have to worry about food for Chantal.

However, there were other difficulties with the baby. Mothers here did not use diapers, but left the baby's lower half uncovered, and washed the towel on which it lay. Jane thought it was a much healthier arrangement than the Western system, but it was no good for travelling. Jane had made three diapers out of towels, and had improvised a pair of waterproof underpants for Chantal out of the polythene wrappings from Jean-Pierre's medical supplies. She would have to wash a diaper every evening – in cold water, of course – and try to dry it overnight. If it did not dry, there was a spare one; and if both were damp, Chantal would get sore. No baby ever died of diaper rash, she told herself. The convoy certainly would not stop for a baby to sleep or be fed and changed, so Chantal would have to feed and doze in motion and be changed whenever the opportunity arose.

In some ways Jane was tougher than she had been a year ago. The skin of her feet was hard and her stomach was resistant to the commoner local bacteria. Her legs, which had hurt so badly on the incoming journey, were now used to walking many miles. But the pregnancy seemed to have made her prone to backache, and she was worried about carrying a baby all day. Her body seemed to have recovered from the trauma of child-birth. She felt she would be able to make love, although she had not told Jean-Pierre this – she was not sure why.

She had taken a lot of photographs, when she first arrived, with her Polaroid camera. She would leave the camera behind – it was a cheap one – but of course she wanted to take most of the photographs. She looked through them, wondering which to throw away. She had pictures of most of the villagers. Here were the guerrillas, Mohammed and Alishan and Kahmir and Matullah, striking ludicrously heroic poses and looking fierce. Here were the women, the voluptuous Zahara, wrinkled old Rabia, and dark-eyed Halima, all giggling like schoolgirls. Here were the children: Mohammed's three girls; his boy Mousa; Zahara's toddlers aged two, three, four and five; and the mullah's four children. She could not throw away any: she would have to take them all with her.

She was packing clothes into a bag while Fara swept the floor and Chantal slept in the next room. They had

247

come down from the caves early to get the work done. However, there was not much to pack: apart from Chantal's diapers, just one clean pair of knickers for herself and one for Jean-Pierre and a spare pair of socks for each of them. None of them would have a change of outer clothing. Chantal had no clothes anyway – she lived in a shawl, or nothing at all. For Jane and Jean-Pierre, one pair of trousers, a shirt, a scarf and a *pattu*-type blanket would suffice for the whole trip and would probably be burned in a hotel in Peshawar in celebration of their return to civilisation.

That thought would give her strength for the journey. She vaguely remembered thinking that Dean's Hotel in Peshawar was primitive, but it was difficult to recall what had been wrong with it. Was it *possible* she had complained that the air-conditioner was noisy? The place had *showers*, for God's sake!

'Civilisation,' she said aloud, and Fara looked at her enquiringly. Jane smiled and said in Dari: 'I'm happy because I'm going back to the big town.'

'I like the big town,' Fara said. 'I went to Rokha once.' She carried on sweeping. 'My brother has gone to Jalalabad,' she added in a tone of envy.

'When will he be back?' Jane asked, but Fara had become dumb and embarrassed, and after a moment Jane realized why: the sound of whistling and a man's footsteps came from the courtyard, there was a tap at the door, and Ellis Thaler's voice said: 'Anyone at home?'

'Come in,' Jane called. He walked in, limping. Although she was no longer romantically interested in him she had been concerned about his injury. He had remained in Astana to recover. He must have come back today. 'How do you feel?' she asked him.

'Foolish,' he said with a rueful grin. 'It's an embarrassing place to get shot in.'

'If embarrassed is all you feel, it must be getting better.'

He nodded. 'Is the doctor in?'

'He's gone to Skabun,' Jane said. 'There was a bad bombing raid and they sent for him. Anything I can do?'

'I just wanted to tell him that my convalescence is over.'

'He'll be back tonight or tomorrow morning.' She was observing Ellis's appearance: with his mane of blond hair and curly golden beard he looked like a lion. 'Why don't you cut your hair?'

'The guerrillas told me to grow it, and not to shave.'

'They always say that. The object of the exercise is to make Westerners less conspicuous. In your case it has the opposite effect.'

'I'm going to look conspicuous in this country regardless of my haircut.'

'That's true.' It occurred to Jane that this was the first time she and Ellis had been together without Jean-Pierre. They had slipped very easily into their old conversational style. It was hard to remember how terribly angry she had been with him.

He was looking curiously at her packing. 'What's that for?'

'For the journey home.'

'How will you travel?'

'With a convoy, as we came.'

'The Russians have taken a lot of territory during the last few days,' he said. 'Didn't you know?'

Jane felt a chill of apprehension. 'What are you telling me?'

'The Russians have launched their summer offensive. They've advanced over big stretches of country through which the convoys ordinarily pass.'

'Are you saying the route to Pakistan is closed?'

'The *regular* route is closed. You can't get from here to the Khyber Pass. There may be other routes—'

Jane saw her dream of returning home fade. 'Nobody *told* me!' she said angrily.

'I guess Jean-Pierre didn't know. I've been with Masud a lot so I'm right up to date.'

'Yes,' Jane said, not looking at him. Perhaps Jean-Pierre really did not know this. Or perhaps he knew but had not told her about it because he did not want to go back to Europe anyway. Whichever it was, she was not going to accept the situation. First, she would find out for certain whether Ellis was right. Then she would look at ways of solving the problem.

She went to Jean-Pierre's chest and took out his American maps of Afghanistan. They were rolled into a cylinder and fastened with an elastic band. Impatiently, she snapped the band and dropped the maps on the floor. Somewhere in the back of her mind a voice said: That may have been the only rubber band within a one-hundred-mile radius.

Calm down, she told herself.

She knelt on the floor and began to shuffle through the maps. They were on a very large scale, so she had to put several of them together to show all of the territory between the Valley and the Khyber Pass. Ellis looked over her shoulder. 'These are good maps!' he said. 'Where did you get them?'

'Jean-Pierre brought them from Paris.'

'They're better than what Masud has.'

'I know. Mohammed always uses these to plan the convoys. Right. Show me how far the Russians have advanced.'

Ellis knelt on the rug beside her and traced a line across the map with his finger.

Jane felt a surge of hope. 'It doesn't look to me as if the Khyber Pass is cut off,' she said. 'Why can't we go this way?' She drew an imaginary line across the map a little to the north of the Russian front.

'I don't know whether that's a route,' Ellis said. 'It may be impassable – you'd have to ask the guerrillas. But the other thing is that Masud's information is at least a day or two old, and the Russians are still advancing. A valley or pass might be open one day and closed the next.'

'Damn!' She was *not* going to be defeated. She leaned over the map and peered closely at the border zone. 'Look, the Khyber Pass isn't the only way across.'

'A river valley runs all along the border, with mountains on the Afghan side. It may be that you can only reach those other passes from the south – which means from Russian-occupied territory.'

'There's no point in speculating,' Jane said. She put

the maps together and rolled them up. 'Someone must *know.*'

'I guess so.'

She stood up. 'There's got to be more than one way out of this bloody country,' she said. She tucked the maps under her arm and went out, leaving Ellis kneeling on the rug.

The women and children had returned from the caves and the village had come to life. The smoke of cooking fires drifted over courtyard walls. In front of the mosque, five children were sitting in a circle playing a game called (for no apparent reason) 'Melon'. It was a storytelling game, in which the teller stopped before the end and the next child had to carry on. Jane spotted Mousa, the son of Mohammed, sitting in the circle, wearing at his belt the rather wicked-looking knife his father had given him after the accident with the mine. Mousa was telling the story. Jane heard: '. . . and the bear tried to bite the boy's hand off, but the boy drew his knife . . .'

She headed for Mohammed's house. Mohammed himself might not be there – she had not seen him for a long time – but he lived with his brothers, in the usual Afghan extended family, and they too were guerrillas – all the fit young men were – so if they were there they might be able to give her some information.

She hesitated outside the house. By custom she should stop in the courtyard and speak to the women, who would be there preparing the evening meal; and then, after an exchange of courtesies, the most senior woman might have gone into the house to enquire whether the menfolk would condescend to speak to Jane. She heard her mother's voice say: 'Don't make an exhibition of yourself!' Jane said aloud: 'Go to hell, Mother.' She walked in, ignoring the women in the courtyard, and marched straight into the front room of the house – the men's parlour.

There were three men there: Mohammed's eighteen-year-old brother Kahmir Khan, with a handsome face and a wispy beard; his brother-in-law, Matullah; and Mohammed himself. It was unusual to have so many guerrillas at home. They all looked up at her, startled.

'God be with you, Mohammed Khan,' Jane said. Without pausing to let him reply she went on: 'When did you get back?'

'Today,' he replied automatically.

She squatted on her haunches like them. They were too astonished to say anything. She spread out her maps on the floor. The three men leaned forward reflexively to look at them: already they were forgetting Jane's breach of etiquette. 'Look,' she said. 'The Russians have advanced this far – am I right?' She retraced the line Ellis had shown her.

Mohammed nodded agreement.

'So the regular convoy route is blocked.'

Mohammed nodded again.

'What is the best way out now?'

They all looked dubious and shook their heads. This was normal: when talking of difficulties, they liked to make a meal of it. Jane thought it was because their local knowledge was the only power they had over foreigners such as she. Usually she was tolerant, but today she had no patience. 'Why not this way?' she asked peremptorily, drawing a line parallel with the Russian front.

'Too close to the Russians,' said Mohammed.

'Here, then.' She traced a more careful route, following the contours of the land.

'No,' he said again.

'Why not?'

'Here—' He pointed to a place on the map, between the heads of two valleys, where Jane had blithely run her finger over a mountain range. 'Here there is no saddle.' A saddle was a pass.

Jane outlined a more northerly route. 'This way?'

'Worse still.'

'There *must* be another way out!' Jane cried. She had a feeling they were enjoying her frustration. She decided to say something mildly offensive, to liven them up a bit. 'Is this country a house with one door, cut off from the rest of the world just because you cannot get to the Khyber Pass?' The phrase *the house with one door* was a euphemism for the privy.

'Of course not,' said Mohammed stiffly. 'In summer there is the Butter Trail.'

'Show me.'

Mohammed's finger traced a complex route which began by going due east of the Valley, through a series of high passes and dried-up rivers, then turned north into the Himalayas, and finally crossed the border near the entrance to the uninhabited Waikhan Corridor before swinging south-east to the Pakistani town of

Chitral. 'This is how the people of Nuristan take their butter and yoghurt and cheese to market in Pakistan.' He smiled and touched his round cap. 'That is where we get the hats.' Jane recalled that they were called Chitrali caps.

'Good,' said Jane. 'We will go home that way.'

Mohammed shook his head. 'You cannot.'

'And why not?'

Kahmir and Matullah gave knowing smiles. Jane ignored them. After a moment Mohammed said: 'The first problem is the altitude. This route goes above the ice line. That means the snow never melts, and there is no running water, even in summer. Second is the landscape. The hills are very steep and the paths are narrow and treacherous. It is hard to find your way: even local guides get lost. But the worst problem of all is the people. That region is called Nuristan, but it used to be called Kafiristan, because the people were unbelievers, and drank wine. Now they are true believers, but still they cheat, rob and sometimes murder travellers. This route is no good for Europeans, impossible for women. Only the youngest and strongest men can use it – and even then, many travellers are killed.'

'Will you send convoys that way?'

'No. We will wait until the southerly route is reopened.'

She studied his handsome face. He was not exaggerating, she could tell: he was being drily factual. She stood up and began to shuffle her maps together. She was bitterly disappointed. Her return home was postponed indefinitely. The strain of life in the Valley suddenly seemed insupportable, and she felt like crying.

She rolled her maps into a cylinder and forced herself to be polite. 'You were away a long time,' she said to Mohammed.

'I went to Faizabad.'

'A long trip.' Faizabad was a large town in the far north. The Resistance was very strong there: the army had mutinied and the Russians had never regained control. 'Aren't you tired?'

It was a formal question, like *How do you do?* in English, and Mohammed gave the formal reply: 'I'm still alive!'

She tucked her roll of maps under her arm and went out.

The women in the courtyard looked at her fearfully as she passed them. She nodded at Halima, Mohammed's dark-eyed wife, and got a nervous half-smile in return.

The guerrillas were doing a lot of travelling lately. Mohammed had been to Faizabad, Fara's brother had gone to Jalalabad . . . Jane recalled that one of her patients, a woman from Dasht i-Rewat, had said that her husband had been sent to Pagman, near Kabul. And Zahara's brother-in-law Yussuf Gul, the brother of her dead husband, had been sent to the Logar Valley, on the far side of Kabul. All four places were rebel strongholds.

Something was going on.

Jane forgot her disappointment for a while as she tried to figure out what was happening. Masud had sent messengers to many – perhaps all – of the other Resistance commanders. Was it a coincidence that this happened so soon after Ellis's arrival in the Valley? If not, what could Ellis be up to? Perhaps the US was collaborating with Masud in organizing a concerted offensive. If all the rebels acted together they could really achieve something – they could probably take Kabul temporarily.

Jane went into her house and dropped the maps in the chest. Chantal was still asleep. Fara was preparing food for supper: bread, yoghurt and apples. Jane said: 'Why did your brother go to Jalalabad?'

'He was sent,' said Fara with the air of one who states the obvious.

'Who sent him?'

'Masud.'

'What for?'

'I don't know.' Fara looked surprised that Jane should ask such a question: who could be so foolish as to think that a man would tell his sister his reason for a journey?

'Did he have something to do there, or did he take a message, or what?'

'I don't know,' Fara repeated. She was beginning to look anxious.

'Never mind,' Jane said with a smile. Of all the women in the village, Fara was probably the least likely to know what was going on. Who was the most likely? Zahara, of course.

Jane picked up a towel and headed for the river.

Zahara was no longer in mourning for her husband,

although she was a good deal less boisterous than she used to be. Jane wondered how soon she would marry again. Zahara and Ahmed had been the only Afghan couple Jane had come across who actually seemed to be in love. However, Zahara was a powerfully sensual woman who would have trouble living without a man for very long. Ahmed's younger brother Yussuf, the singer, lived in the same house as Zahara, and was still unmarried at the age of eighteen: there was speculation among the village women that Yussuf might marry Zahara.

Brothers lived together, here; sisters were always separated. A bride routinely went to live with her husband in the home of the husband's parents. It was just one more way in which the men of this country oppressed their women.

Jane strode quickly along the footpath through the fields. A few men were working in the evening light. The harvest was coming to an end. It would soon be too late to take the Butter Trail anyway, Jane thought: Mohammed had said it was a summer-only route.

She reached the women's beach. Eight or ten village women were bathing in the river or in pools at the water's edge. Zahara was out in mid-stream, splashing a lot as usual but not laughing and joking.

Jane dropped her towel and waded into the water. She decided to be a little less direct with Zahara than she had been with Fara. She would not be able to fool Zahara, of course, but she would try to give the impression that she was gossiping rather than interrogating. She did not approach Zahara immediately.

When the other women got out of the water, Jane followed a minute or two later, and dried herself with her towel in silence. It was not until Zahara and a few other women began to drift back towards the village that Jane spoke. 'How soon will Yussuf be back?' she asked Zahara in Dari.

'Today or tomorrow. He went to the Logar Valley.'

'I know. Did he go alone?'

'Yes – but he said he may bring someone home with him.'

'Who?'

Zahara shrugged. 'A wife, perhaps.'

Jane was momentarily diverted. Zahara was too coolly indifferent. That meant she was worried: she did not want Yussuf to bring home a wife. It looked as if the village rumours were true. Jane hoped so. Zahara needed a man. 'I don't think he has gone to get a wife,' Jane said.

'Why?'

'Something important is happening. Masud has sent out many messengers. They can't all be after wives.'

Zahara continued to try to look indifferent, but Jane could tell she was pleased. Was there any significance, Jane wondered, in the possibility that Yussuf might have gone to the Logar Valley to fetch someone?

Night was falling as they approached the village. From the mosque came a low chant: the eerie sound of the most bloodthirsty men in the world at prayer. It always reminded Jane of Josef, a young Russian soldier who had survived a helicopter crash just over the mountain from Banda. Some women had brought him

259

to the shopkeeper's house – this was in the winter, before they moved the clinic to the cave – and Jean-Pierre and Jane had tended his wounds while a message was sent to Masud asking what should be done. Jane had learned what Masud's reply had been one evening when Alishan Karim walked into the front room of the shopkeeper's house, where Josef lay in bandages, and put the muzzle of his rifle to the boy's ear and blew his head off. It had been about this time of day, and the sound of the men praying had been in the air while Jane washed the blood off the wall and scooped up the boy's brains off the floor.

The women climbed the last stretch of the footpath up from the river and paused in front of the mosque, finishing their conversations before going to their separate homes. Jane glanced into the mosque. The men were praying on their knees, with Abdullah the mullah leading them. Their weapons, the usual mixture of ancient rifles and modern submachine guns, were piled in a corner. The prayers were just finishing. As the men stood up, Jane saw that there were a number of strangers among them. She said to Zahara: 'Who are they?'

'By their turbans, they must be from the Pich Valley and Jalalabad,' Zahara replied. 'They are Pushtuns – normally they are our enemies. Why are they here?' As she was speaking, a very tall man with an eye patch emerged from the crowd. 'That must be Jahan Kamil – Masud's great enemy!'

'But there is Masud, talking to him,' said Jane, and she added in English: 'Just fancy that!'

Zahara imitated her. 'Jass fencey hat!'

It was the first joke Zahara had made since her husband died. That was a good sign: Zahara was recovering.

The men began to come out, and the women scuttled away to their homes, all except Jane. She thought she was beginning to understand what was happening; and she wanted confirmation. When Mohammed came out, she approached him and spoke to him in French. 'I forgot to ask whether your trip to Faizabad was successful.'

'It was,' he said without pausing in his stride: he did not want his comrades or the Pushtuns to see him answering a woman's questions.

Jane hurried alongside him as he headed for his house. 'So the Commander of Faizabad is here?'

'Yes.'

Jane had guessed right: Masud had invited all the rebel commanders here. 'What do you think of this idea?' she asked him. She was still fishing for details.

Mohammed looked thoughtful, and dropped his hauteur, as he always did when he got interested in the conversation. 'Everything depends on what Ellis does tomorrow,' he said. 'If he impresses them as a man of honour, and wins their respect, I think they will agree to his plan.'

'And you think his plan is good?'

'Obviously it will be a good thing if the Resistance is united and gets weapons from the United States.'

So that was it! American weapons for the rebels, on

condition they fought together against the Russians instead of fighting one another half the time.

They reached Mohammed's house, and Jane turned away with a wave. Her breasts felt full: it was time for Chantal to be fed. The right breast felt a little heavier, because at the last feed she had started with the left, and Chantal always emptied the first one more thoroughly.

Jane reached the house and went into the bedroom. Chantal lay naked on a folded towel inside her cradle, which was actually a cardboard box cut in half. She had no need of clothes in the warm air of the Afghan summer. At night she would be covered with a sheet, that was all. The rebels and the war, Ellis and Mohammed and Masud all receded into the background as Jane looked at her baby. She had always thought small babies ugly, but Chantal seemed very pretty to her. As Jane watched, Chantal stirred, opened her mouth, and cried. Jane's right breast immediately leaked milk in response, and a warm damp patch spread on her shirt. She undid the buttons and picked up Chantal.

Jean-Pierre said she should wash her breasts with surgical spirit before feeding, but she never did because she knew Chantal would not like the taste. She sat on a rug with her back to the wall and cradled Chantal in her right arm. The baby waved her fat little arms and moved her head from side to side, frantically seeking with her open mouth. Jane guided her to the nipple. The toothless gums clamped hard and the baby sucked fiercely. Jane winced at the first hard pull, then at the second. The third suck was gentler. A small plump hand reached up and touched the round side of Jane's swollen breast, pressing it with a blind, clumsy caress. Jane relaxed.

Feeding her baby made her feel terribly tender and protective. Also, to her surprise, it was erotic. At first she had felt guilty about being turned on by it, but she soon decided that if it was natural it could not be bad, and settled down to enjoy it.

She was looking forward to showing Chantal off if they ever got back to Europe. Jean-Pierre's mother would tell her she was doing everything wrong, no doubt, and her own mother would want to have the baby christened, but her father would adore Chantal through an alcoholic haze, and her sister would be proud and enthusiastic. Who else? Jean-Pierre's father was dead . . .

A voice came from the courtyard. 'Anybody at home?'

It was Ellis. 'Come in,' Jane called. She did not feel she needed to cover herself: Ellis was not an Afghan, and anyway he had once been her lover.

He came in, saw her feeding the baby, and did a double-take. 'Shall I leave?'

She shook her head. 'You've seen my tits before.'

'I don't think so,' he said. 'You must have changed them.'

She laughed. 'Pregnancy gives you great tits.' Ellis had been married once, she knew, and had a child, although he gave the impression he no longer saw either the child or its mother. That was one of the things he would never talk about very much. 'Don't you remember from when your wife was pregnant?'

'I missed it,' he said, in that curt tone he used when he wanted you to shut up. 'I was away.'

She was too relaxed to respond in like manner. In fact she felt sorry for him. He had made a mess of his life, but it was not all his own fault; and he had certainly been punished for his sins – not least by her.

'Jean-Pierre didn't come back,' Ellis said.

'No.' The sucking eased as Jane's breast emptied. She gently pulled her nipple from Chantal's mouth and lifted the baby to her shoulder, patting the narrow back to make her burp.

'Masud would like to borrow his maps,' Ellis said.

'Of course. You know where they are.' Chantal belched loudly. 'Good girl,' Jane said. She put the baby to her left breast. Hungry again after burping, Chantal began to suck. Giving in to an impulse, Jane said: 'Why don't you see your child?'

He took the maps from the chest, closed its lid, and straightened up. 'I do,' he said. 'But not often.'

Jane was shocked. I almost lived with him for six months, she thought, and I never really knew him. 'A boy or a girl?'

'Girl.'

'She must be . . .'

'Thirteen.'

'My God.' That was practically grown up. Jane was suddenly intensely curious. Why had she never questioned him about all this? Perhaps she had not been interested before she had a child of her own. 'Where does she live?'

He hesitated.

'Don't tell me,' she said. She could read his face. 'You were about to lie to me.'

'You're right,' he said. 'But do you understand *why* I have to lie about it?'

She thought for a moment. 'Are you afraid that your enemies will attack you through the child?'

'Yes.'

'That's a good reason.'

'Thank you. And thanks for these.' He waved the maps at her, then went out.

Chantal had gone to sleep with Jane's nipple in her mouth. Jane disengaged her gently and lifted her to shoulder level. She burped without waking. The child could sleep through anything.

Jane wished Jean-Pierre had come back. She was sure he could do no harm, but all the same she would have felt easier if he had been under her eye. He could not contact the Russians because she had smashed his radio. There was no other means of communication between Banda and Russian territory. Masud could send messengers by runner, of course; but Jean-Pierre had no runners, and anyway if he sent someone the whole village would know about it. The only thing he could possibly do was to walk all the way to Rokha, and he had not had time for that.

As well as being anxious, she hated to sleep alone. In Europe she had not minded, but here she was frightened of the brutal, unpredictable tribesmen who thought it as normal for a man to beat his wife as for a mother to smack her child. And Jane was no ordinary woman in their eyes: with her liberated views and her direct gaze and her says-who attitude she was a symbol of forbidden sexual delights. She had not followed the conventions of sexual behaviour, and the only other women they knew like that were whores.

When Jean-Pierre was there she always reached out to touch him just before falling asleep. He always slept curled up facing away from her, and although he moved a lot in his sleep he never reached out for her. The only other man she had shared a bed with for a long period was Ellis, and he had been just the opposite: all night long he was touching her, hugging her and kissing her; sometimes half awake and sometimes when he was fast asleep. Twice or three times he had tried to make love to her, roughly, in his sleep: she would giggle and try to accommodate him, but after a few seconds he would roll off and start snoring, and in the morning he had no recollection of what he had done. How different he was from Jean-Pierre. Ellis touched her with clumsy affection, like a child playing with a beloved pet; Jean-Pierre touched her the way a violinist might handle a Stradivarius. They had loved her differently, but they had betrayed her the same way.

Chantal gurgled. She was awake. Jane laid her in her lap, supporting her head so that they could look directly at one another, and began to talk to her, partly in nonsense syllables and partly in real words. Chantal liked this. After a while Jane ran out of small talk and began to sing. She was in the middle of *Daddy's gone to London in a puffer train* when she was interrupted by a voice from outside. 'Come in,' she called. She said to Chantal: 'We have visitors all the time, don't we? It's like living in the National Gallery, isn't it?' She pulled the front of her shirt together to hide her cleavage.

Mohammed walked in and said: 'Where is Jean-Pierre?' in Dari.

'Gone to Skabun. Anything I can do?'

'When will he be back?'

'In the morning, I expect. Do you want to tell me what the problem is, or do you plan to continue talking like a Kabul policeman?'

He grinned at her. When she spoke disrespectfully to him he found her sexy, which was not the effect she intended. He said: 'Alishan has arrived with Masud. He wants more pills.'

'Ah, yes.' Alishan Karim was the brother of the mullah, and he suffered from angina. Of course he would not give up his guerrilla activities, so Jean-Pierre gave him trinitrin to take immediately before battle or other exertion. 'I'll give you some pills,' she said. She stood up and handed Chantal to Mohammed.

Mohammed took the baby automatically and then looked embarrassed. Jane grinned at him and went into the front room. She found the tablets on a shelf beneath the shopkeeper's counter. She poured about a hundred into a container and returned to the living-room. Chantal was staring, fascinated, at Mohammed. Jane took the baby and handed over the pills. 'Tell Alishan to rest more,' she said.

Mohammed shook his head. 'He's not frightened of me,' he said. 'You tell him.'

Jane laughed. Coming from an Afghan, that joke was almost feminist.

Mohammed said: 'Why did Jean-Pierre go to Skabun?'

'There was a bombing there this morning.'

'No, there wasn't.'

'Of course there wa—' Jane stopped suddenly.

Mohammed shrugged. 'I was there all day with Masud. You must be mistaken.'

She tried to keep her face composed. 'Yes. I must have misheard.'

'Thank you for the pills.' He went out.

Jane sat down heavily on a stool. There had been no bombing at Skabun. Jean-Pierre had gone to meet Anatoly. She did not see quite how he had arranged it but she had no doubt whatsoever.

What was she to do?

If Jean-Pierre knew about the gathering tomorrow, and could tell the Russians about it, then the Russians would be able to attack—

They could wipe out the entire leadership of the Afghan Resistance in a single day.

She had to see Ellis.

She wrapped a shawl around Chantal – the air would be a little cooler, now – and left the house, heading for the mosque. Ellis was in the courtyard with the rest of the men, poring over Jean-Pierre's maps with Masud and Mohammed and the man with the eye patch. Some guerrillas were passing a hookah around, others were eating. They stared in surprise as she walked in with her baby on her hip. 'Ellis,' she said. He looked up. 'I need to talk to you. Would you come outside?'

He got up and they went out through the arch and stood in front of the mosque.

'What is it?' he said.

'Does Jean-Pierre know about this gathering you have arranged, of all the Resistance leaders?'

'Yes – when Masud and I first talked about it, he was right there, taking the slug out of my ass. Why?'

Jane's heart sank. Her last hope had been that Jean-Pierre might not know. Now she had no choice. She looked around. There was no one else within earshot; and anyway they were speaking English 'I have something to tell you,' she said, 'but I want your promise that no harm will come to him.'

He stared at her for a moment. 'Oh, *shit*,' he said fervently. 'Oh fuck, oh shit. He works for them. Of course! Why didn't I guess? In Paris, he must have led those motherfuckers to my apartment! He's been telling them about the convoys – that's why they've been losing so many! The *bastard*—' He stopped suddenly, and spoke more gently. 'It must have been terrible for you.'

'Yes,' she said. Irresistibly her face crumpled, tears rushed to her eyes, and she began to sob. She felt weak and foolish and ashamed of herself for crying, but she also felt as if a huge weight had been lifted from her.

Ellis put his arms around her and Chantal. 'You poor thing,' he said.

'Yes,' she sobbed 'It was awful.'

'How long have you known?'

'A few weeks.'

'You didn't know when you married him.'

'No.'

'Both of us,' he said. 'We both did it to you.'

'Yes.'

'You mixed with the wrong crowd.'

'Yes.'

She buried her face in his shirt and cried without restraint, for all the lies and betrayals and spent time and wasted love. Chantal cried too. Ellis held her close and stroked her hair until eventually she stopped shaking and began to calm down and wiped her nose on her sleeve. 'I broke his radio, you see,' she said, 'and then I thought he had no way of getting in touch with them; but today he was called to Skabun to see to the bomb wounded, but there was no bombing at Skabun today . . .'

Mohammed came out of the mosque. Ellis let go of Jane and looked embarrassed. 'What's happening?' he said to Mohammed in French.

'They're arguing,' he said. 'Some say this is a good plan and it will help us defeat the Russians. Others ask why Masud is considered the only good commander, and who is Ellis Thaler, that he should judge Afghan leaders? You must come back and talk to them some more.'

'Wait,' Ellis said. 'There's been a new development.'

Jane thought: Oh, God, Mohammed will kill somebody when he hears this—

'There has been a leak.'

'What do you mean?' Mohammed said dangerously.

Ellis hesitated, as if reluctant to spill the beans; and then he seemed to decide that he had no alternative. 'The Russians may know about the conference—'

'Who?' Mohammed demanded. 'Who is the traitor?'

'Possibly the doctor, but—'

Mohammed rounded on Jane. 'How long have you known this?'

'You'll speak to me politely or not at all,' she snapped back.

'Hold it,' said Ellis.

Jane was not going to let Mohammed get away with his accusatory tone of voice. 'I warned you, didn't I?' she said. 'I told you to change the route of the convoy. I saved your damned life, so don't point your finger at *me*.'

Mohammed's anger evaporated, and he looked a little sheepish.

Ellis said: 'So that's why the route was changed.' He looked at Jane with something like admiration.

Mohammed said: 'Where is he now?'

'We're not sure,' Ellis replied.

'When he comes back he must be killed.'

'No!' said Jane.

Ellis put a restraining hand on her shoulder and said to Mohammed: 'Would you kill a man who has saved the lives of so many of your comrades?'

'He must face justice,' Mohammed insisted.

Mohammed had talked about *if* he comes back, and

Jane realized she had been assuming that he would return. Surely he would not abandon her and their baby?

Ellis was saying: 'If he is a traitor, and if he has succeeded in contacting the Russians, then he has told them about tomorrow's meeting. They will surely attack and try to take Masud.'

'This is very bad,' said Mohammed. 'Masud must leave immediately. The conference will have to be called off—'

'Not necessarily,' Ellis said. 'Think. We could turn this to advantage.'

'How?'

Ellis said: 'In fact, the more I think about it, the more I like it. This may turn out to have been the best thing that could possibly happen . . .'

CHAPTER TWELVE

THEY EVACUATED the village of Darg at dawn. Masud's men went from house to house, gently waking the occupants and telling them that their village was to be attacked by the Russians today and they must go up the Valley to Banda, taking with them their more precious possessions. By sunrise there was a ragged crocodile of women, children, old people and livestock wending its way out of the village along the dirt road that ran beside the river.

Darg was different in shape from Banda. At Banda, the houses were clustered at the eastern end of the plain, where the Valley narrowed and the ground was rocky. In Darg all the houses were crammed together on a thin shelf between the foot of the cliff and the bank of the river. There was a bridge just in front of the mosque, and the fields were on the other side of the river.

It was a good place for an ambush.

Masud had devised his plan during the night, and now Mohammed and Alishan made the dispositions. They moved around with quiet efficiency, Mohammed tall and handsome and gracious, Alishan short and mean-looking, both of them giving instructions in soft voices, imitating their leader's low-key style.

Ellis wondered, as he laid his charges, whether the Russians would come. Jean-Pierre had not reappeared, so it seemed certain that he had succeeded in contacting his masters; and it was almost inconceivable that they should resist the temptation to capture or kill Masud. But that was all circumstantial. And if they did not come, Ellis would look foolish, having caused Masud to set an elaborate trap for a no-show victim. The guerrillas would not make a pact with a fool. But if the Russians do come, Ellis thought, and if the ambush works, the boost to my prestige and Masud's might be enough to clinch the whole deal.

He was trying not to think about Jane. When he had put his arms around her and her baby, and she had wet his shirt with her tears, his passion for her had flared up anew. It was like throwing petrol on a bonfire. He had wanted to stand there forever, with her narrow shoulders shaking under his arm and her head against his chest. Poor Jane. She was so honest, and her men were so treacherous.

He trailed his detonating cord in the river and brought its end out at his position, which was in a tiny wooden house on the river bank a couple of hundred yards upstream of the mosque. He used his crimper to attach a blasting cap to the cord, then finished the assembly with a simple army-issue pull-ring firing device.

He approved of Masud's plan. Ellis had taught ambush and counter-ambush at Fort Bragg for a year in between his two tours in Asia, and he would have given Masud's set-up nine out of ten. The lost mark was due to Masud's failure to provide an exit route for his troops in case the fight should go against them. Of course, Masud might not consider that a mistake.

By nine o'clock everything was ready, and the guerrillas made breakfast. Even that was part of the ambush: they could all get into position in minutes, if not seconds, and then the village seen from the air would look more natural, as if the villagers had all rushed to hide from the helicopters, leaving behind their bowls and rugs and cooking fires; so that the commander of the Russian force would have no reason to suspect a trap.

Ellis ate some bread and drank several cups of green tea, then settled down to wait as the sun rose high over the Valley. There was always a lot of waiting. He remembered it in Asia. In those days he had often been high, on marijuana or speed or cocaine, and then the waiting hardly seemed to matter because he enjoyed it. It was funny, he thought, how he had lost interest in drugs after the war.

Ellis expected the attack either this afternoon or at dawn tomorrow. If he were the Russian commander he would reason that the rebel leaders would have assembled yesterday and would leave tomorrow, and he would want to attack late enough to catch any latecomers, but not so late that some of them might have left already.

At around mid-morning the heavy weapons arrived, a pair of Dashoka's, 12.7mm anti-aircraft machine-guns,

each pulled along the road on its two-wheeled mounting by a guerrilla. A donkey followed, loaded down with
cases of 5–0 Chinese armour-piercing bullets.

Masud announced that one of the guns would be
manned by Yussuf, the singer, who, according to village
rumour, was likely to marry Jane's friend Zahara; the
other by a guerrilla from the Pich Valley, one Abdur,
whom Ellis did not know. Yussuf had already shot down
three helicopters with his Kalashnikov, it was said. Ellis
was sceptical about this: he had flown helicopters in
Asia and he knew it was close to impossible to shoot
one down with a rifle. However, Yussuf explained with
a grin that the trick was to get above the target and fire
down at it from a mountainside, a tactic that was not
possible in Vietnam because the landscape was
different.

Although Yussuf had a much bigger weapon today,
he was going to use the same technique. The guns were
dismounted then taken, each carried by two men, up
the steep steps cut into the cliffside that towered over
the village. The mounts and the ammunition followed.

Ellis watched from below as they reassembled the
guns. At the top of the cliff was a shelf ten or fifteen
feet wide, then the mountainside continued up at a
gentler slope. The guerrillas set up the guns about ten
yards apart on the shelf and camouflaged them. The
helicopter pilots would soon find out where the guns
were, of course, but they would find it very difficult to
knock them out in that position.

When that was done, Ellis went back to his position

in the little wooden house by the riverside. His mind kept returning to the sixties.

He had begun the decade as a schoolboy and ended a soldier. He had gone to Berkeley in 1967 confident that he knew what the future held for him: he wanted to be a producer of television documentaries, and since he was bright and creative, and this was California where anybody could be anything if he worked hard, there had been no reason that he could see why he should not achieve his ambition. Then he had been overtaken by peace and flower power, anti-war marches and love-ins, the Doors and bell-bottom jeans and LSD; and once again he had thought he knew what the future held: he was going to change the world. That dream had also been short-lived, and soon he was overtaken once again, this time by the mindless brutality of the army and the drugged horror of Vietnam. Whenever he looked back like this, he could see that it was the times in which he felt confident and settled when life would hit him with the really big changes.

Midday passed without lunch. That would be because the guerrillas did not have any food. Ellis found it hard to get used to the essentially rather simple idea that when there was no food then nobody could have lunch. It occurred to him that this might be why nearly all the guerrillas were heavy smokers: tobacco deadened the appetite.

It was hot even in the shade. He sat in the doorway of the little wooden house, trying to catch what little breeze there was. He could see the fields, the river with its arched rubble-and-mortar bridge, the village with its mosque, and the overhanging cliff. Most of the guerrillas were in their positions, which provided them with shelter from the sun as well as cover. The majority of them were in houses close to the cliff, where it would be difficult for helicopters to strafe them; but inevitably some were in the more vulnerable forward positions, nearer the river. The rough stone façade of the mosque was pierced by three arched doorways, and one guerrilla sat cross-legged under each arch. They made Ellis think of guardsmen in sentry-boxes. Ellis knew all three of them: there was Mohammed in the farthest arch; his brother Kahmir, with the wispy beard, in the middle; and in the nearest arch Ali Ghanim, the ugly man with the twisted spine and the family of fourteen children, the man who had been wounded with Ellis down in the plain. Each of the three had a Kalashnikov across his knees and a cigarette between his lips. Ellis wondered which of them would be alive tomorrow.

The first essay he had written in college had been about the wait before battle as handled by Shakespeare. He had contrasted two pre-combat speeches: the inspirational one in *Henry V* in which the King says: 'Once more unto the breach, dear friends, once more; or seal the wall up with our English dead;' and Falstaff's cynical soliloquy on honour in *I Henry IV*: 'Can honour set to a leg? No. Or an arm? No. Honour hath no skill in surgery, then? No . . . Who hath it? He that died o' Wednesday.' The nineteen-year-old Ellis had got an A for that – his first, and his last, for afterwards he was too busy arguing that Shakespeare and indeed the entire English course were 'irrelevant'.

His reverie was interrupted by a series of shouts. He did not understand the Dari words used but he had no need to: he knew, from the urgency of tone, that the sentries on surrounding hillsides had spotted distant helicopters, and had signalled to Yussuf on the cliff top, who had spread the word. There was a flurry of movement throughout the sun-baked village as guerrillas manned their posts, retreated farther into their cover, checked their weapons, and lit fresh cigarettes. The three men in the archways of the mosque melted into its shadowy interior. Now the village seen from the air would appear deserted, as it normally would during the hottest part of the day, when most people rested.

Ellis listened hard and heard the menacing throb of approaching helicopter rotors. His bowels felt watery: nerves. This is how the slants felt, he thought, hiding in the dripping jungle, when they heard my helicopter gunship coming towards them through the rainclouds. You reap what you sow, baby.

He loosened the safety pins in the firing device.

The helicopters roared closer, but still he could not see them. He wondered how many there were: he could not tell from the noise. He saw something out of the corner of his eye, and turned to see a guerrilla dive into the river from the far bank and begin to swim across towards him. When the figure emerged near Ellis he could see that it was scarred old Shahazai Gul, the brother of the midwife. Shahazai's speciality was mines. He dashed past Ellis and took cover in a house.

For a few moments the village was still and there was nothing but the heartstopping throb of rotor blades, and Ellis was thinking *Jesus, how the hell many of them have they sent?* and then the first one flashed into view over the cliff, going *fast*, and wheeled down towards the village. It hesitated over the bridge like a giant humming-bird.

It was an Mi-24, known in the West as a Hind (the Russians called them Hunchbacks, because of the bulky twin turboshaft engines mounted on top of the passenger cabin). The gunner sat low in the nose with the pilot behind and above him, like children playing piggyback; and the windows all around the flight deck looked like the multifaceted eye of a monstrous insect. The helicopter had a three-wheeled undercarriage and short, stubby wings with underslung rocket pods.

How the hell could a few ragged tribesmen fight against machinery like that?

Five more Hinds followed in rapid succession. They overflew the village and the ground all around it, scouting, Ellis presumed, for enemy positions. This was a routine precaution – the Russians had no reason to expect heavy resistance, for they believed their attack would be a surprise.

A second type of helicopter began to appear, and Ellis recognized the Mi-8, known as the Hip. Larger than the Hind but less fearsome, it could carry twenty or thirty men, and its purpose was troop transport rather than assault. The first one hesitated over the village then dropped suddenly sideways and came down in the barley field. It was followed by five more. A hundred and fifty men, Ellis thought. As the Hips landed the troops jumped out and lay flat, pointing their guns towards the village but not shooting.

To take the village they had to cross the river, and to cross the river they had to take the bridge. But they did not know that. They were just being cautious: they expected the element of surprise to enable them to prevail easily.

Ellis worried that the village might appear *too* deserted. By now, a couple of minutes after the first helicopter appeared, there would normally be a few people visible, running away. He strained his hearing for the first shot. He was no longer scared. He was concentrating too hard on too many things to feel fear. From the back of his mind came the thought: It's always like this once it starts.

Shahazai had laid mines in the barley field, Ellis recalled. Why had none of them exploded yet? A moment later he had the answer. One of the soldiers stood up – an officer, presumably – and shouted an order. Twenty or thirty men scrambled to their feet and ran towards the bridge. Suddenly there was a deafening bang, loud even over the whirlwind of helicopter noise, then another and another as the ground seemed to explode under the soldiers' running feet – Ellis thought *Shahazai pepped up his mines with extra TNT* – and clouds of brown earth and golden barley obscured them, all but one man who was thrown high in the air and fell slowly, turning over and over like an acrobat until he hit the ground crumpled in a heap. As the echoes died there was another sound, a deep, stomach-thudding drumbeat that came from the cliff top as Yussuf and Abdur opened fire. The Russians retreated in disarray as the guerrillas in the village started firing their Kalashnikovs across the river.

Surprise had given the guerrillas a tremendous initial advantage, but it would not last for ever: the Russian commander would rally his troops. But before he could achieve anything he had to clear the approach to the bridge.

One of the Hips in the barley field blew apart, and Ellis realized that Yussuf and Abdur must have hit it. He was impressed: although the Dashoka had a range of a mile, and the helicopters were less than half a mile away, it took good shooting to destroy one at this distance.

The Hinds – the humpbacked gunships – were still in the air, circling above the village. Now the Russian commander brought them into action. One of them swooped low over the river and shelled Shahazai's minefield. Yussuf and Abdur fired at it but missed. Shahazai's mines exploded harmlessly, one after another. Ellis thought anxiously: I wish the mines had knocked out more of the enemy – twenty or so men out of a hundred and fifty isn't much. The Hind rose again, driven off by Yussuf; but another one descended and strafed the minefield again. Yussuf and Abdur poured a constant stream of fire at it. Suddenly it lurched, part of a wing fell off, and it nose-dived into the river; and Ellis thought: nice shooting, Yussuf! But the approach to the bridge was clear, and the Russians still had more than a hundred men and ten helicopters, and Ellis realized with a chill of fear that the guerrillas could lose this battle.

The Russians took heart, then, and most of them – eighty or more men, Ellis estimated – began moving towards the bridge on their bellies, firing constantly. They can't be as dispirited or undisciplined as the American newspapers say, Ellis thought, unless this is an elite outfit. Then he realized that the soldiers all seemed white-skinned. There were no Afghans in this force. It was just like Vietnam, where the Arvins were always kept out of anything really important.

Suddenly there was a lull. The Russians in the barley field and the guerrillas in the village exchanged fire across the river in a desultory fashion, the Russians shooting more or less at random, the guerrillas using their ammunition sparingly. Ellis looked up. The Hinds in the air were going after Yussuf and Abdur on the cliff. The Russian commander had correctly identified the heavy machine-guns as his main target.

As a Hind swooped towards the cliff-top gunners, Ellis had a moment of admiration for the pilot, for flying directly at the guns: he knew how much nerve that took. The aircraft veered away: they had missed one another.

Their chances were roughly equal, Ellis thought: it was easier for Yussuf to aim accurately, because he was stationary whereas the aircraft was moving; but by the same token he was the easier target because he was still. Ellis recalled that in the Hind the wing-mounted rockets were fired by the pilot, while the gunner operated the machine-gun in the nose. It would be hard for a pilot to aim accurately in such terrifying circumstances, Ellis thought; and since the Dashoka had a greater range than the helicopter's four-barrel Gatling-type gun, perhaps Yussuf and Abdur had a slight edge.

I hope so, for the sake of all of us, Ellis thought.

Another Hind descended towards the cliff like a hawk falling on a rabbit, but the guns drummed and the helicopter exploded in mid-air. Ellis felt like cheering – which was ironic, for he knew so well the terror and barely-controlled panic of the helicopter crew under fire.

Another Hind swooped. The gunners were a fraction wide this time, but they shot off the helicopter's tail, and it went out of control and crashed into the face of the cliff, and Ellis thought: Jesus Christ, we may yet get them all! But the note of the guns had changed, and after a moment Ellis realized that only one was firing. The other had been knocked out. Ellis peered through the dust and saw a Chitrali cap moving up there. Yussuf was still alive. Abdur had been hit.

The three remaining Hinds circled and re-positioned. One climbed high above the battle: the Russian commander must be in that one, Ellis thought. The other two descended on Yussuf in a pincer move-ment. That was smart thinking, Ellis thought anxiously, for Yussuf could not shoot at both of them at once. Ellis watched them come down. When Yussuf aimed at one, the other swooped lower. Ellis noticed that the Russians flew with their doors open, just as the Americans had in Vietnam.

The Hinds pounced. One dived at Yussuf and veered away, but he scored a direct hit and it burst into flames; then the second was swooping, rocket pods and guns blazing away, and Ellis thought *Yussuf doesn't stand a chance!* and then the second Hind seemed to hesitate in mid-air. Had it been hit? It fell suddenly, going twenty or thirty feet straight down – *When your engine cuts out,* the instructor in flight school had said, *your helicopter will glide like a grand piano* – and crashed on the ledge just a few yards from Yussuf; but then its engine seemed to catch again, and to Ellis's surprise it began to lift. It's tougher than a goddam Huey, he thought; helicopters have improved in the last ten years. Its gunner had been blazing away all the time, but now he stopped. Ellis saw why, and his heart sank. A Dashoka came tumbling over the edge of the cliff in a welter of camouflage, bushes and branches; and it was followed immediately by a limp mud-coloured bundle that was Yussuf. As he fell down the face of the cliff he bounced off a jagged outcrop half way, and his round Chitrali cap came off. A moment later he disappeared from Ellis's view. He had almost won the battle single-handed: there would be no medal for him, but his story would be told beside campfires in the cold Afghan mountains for a hundred years.

The Russians had lost four of their six Hinds, one Hip, and about twenty-five men; but the guerrillas had lost both their heavy guns, and now they had no defence as the two remaining Hinds began to strafe the village. Ellis huddled inside his hut, wishing it were not made of wood. The strafing was a softening-up tactic: after a minute or two, as if at a signal, the Russians in the barley field rose from the ground and rushed the bridge.

This is it, Ellis thought; this is the end, one way or another.

The guerrillas in the village fired on the charging troops, but they were inhibited by the air cover and few Russians fell. Almost all the Russians were on their feet now, eighty or ninety men, firing blindly across the river as they ran. They were yelling enthusiastically, encouraged by the thinness of the defence. The guerrillas' shooting became a little more accurate as the Russians reached the bridge, and several more fell, but not enough to halt the charge. Seconds later the first of them had crossed the river and were diving for cover among the houses of the village.

There were about sixty men on or near the bridge when Ellis pulled the handle of the firing device.

The ancient stonework of the bridge blew up like a volcano.

Ellis had laid his charges to kill, not for a neat demolition, and the explosion sprayed lethal chunks of masonry like a burst from a giant machine-gun, taking out all the men on the bridge and many still in the barley field. Ellis ducked back into his hut as rubble rained on the village When it stopped he looked back out again.

Where the bridge had been, there was just a low pile

of stones and bodies in a grisly mélange. Part of the mosque and two village houses had also collapsed. And the Russians were in full retreat.

As he watched, the twenty or thirty men still left alive scrambled into the open doors of the Hips. Ellis did not blame them. If they stayed in the barley field, with no cover, they would be wiped out slowly by the guerrillas in good positions in the village; and if they tried to cross the river they would be picked off in the water like fish in a barrel.

Seconds later, the three surviving Hips took off from the field to join the two Hinds in the air, and then, without a parting shot, the aircraft soared away over the cliff top and disappeared.

As the beat of their rotors faded, he heard another noise. After a moment he realized that it was the sound of men cheering. We won, he realized. Hell, we won. And he started cheering too.

CHAPTER THIRTEEN

'A ND WHERE have all the guerrillas gone?' Jane asked.

'They scattered,' Ellis replied. 'This is Masud's technique. He melts away into the hills before the Russians can catch their breath. They may come back with reinforcements – they could even be at Darg now but they will find nobody to fight. The guerrillas have gone, all but these few.'

There were seven wounded men in Jane's clinic. None of them would die. Twelve more had been treated for minor wounds and sent on their way. Only two men had died in the battle, but by a heartbreaking stroke of bad luck one of them was Yussuf. Zahara would be in mourning again – and again it was because of Jean-Pierre.

Jane felt depressed, despite Ellis's euphoria. I must stop brooding, she thought. Jean-Pierre has gone, and he isn't coming back, and there's no point in grieving. I should think positively. I should take an interest in other people's lives.

'What about your conference?' she asked Ellis. 'If all the guerrillas have gone away . . .'

'They all agreed,' Ellis said. 'They were so euphoric,

288

after the success of the ambush, that they were ready to say yes to anything. In a way the ambush proved what some of them had doubted: that Masud is a brilliant leader and that by uniting under him they can achieve great victories. It also established my macho credentials, which helped.'

'So you've succeeded.'

'Yes. I even have a treaty, signed by all the rebel leaders and witnessed by the mullah.'

'You must be proud.' She reached out and squeezed his arm, then withdrew her hand quickly. She was so glad he was here to keep her from being alone that she felt guilty about having been angry with him for such a long time. But she was afraid she might accidentally give him the mistaken impression that she still cared for him in the old way, which would be awkward.

She turned away from him and looked around the cave. The bandages and syringes were in their boxes and the drugs were in her bag. The wounded guerrillas were comfortable on rugs or blankets. They would stay in the cave all night: it was too difficult to move them all down the hill. They had water and a little bread, and two or three of them were well enough to get up and make tea. Mousa, the one-handed son of Mohammed, was squatting in the mouth of the cave, playing a mysterious game in the dust with the knife his father had given him: he would stay with the wounded men, and in the unlikely event that one of them should need medical attention during the night, the boy would run down the hill and fetch Jane.

Everything was in order. She wished them good

night, patted Mousa on the head, and went outside. Ellis followed. Jane felt a hint of cold in the evening breeze. It was the first sign of the end of summer. She looked up at the distant mountain tops of the Hindu Kush, from where the winter would come. The snowy peaks were pink with the reflection of the setting sun. This was a beautiful country: that was too easy to forget, especially on busy days. I'm glad I've seen it, she thought, even though I can't wait to go home.

She walked down the hill with Ellis at her side. She glanced at him now and again. The sunset made his face appear bronzed and craggy. She realized that he probably had not slept much the night before. 'You look tired,' she said.

'It's a long time since I was in a real war,' he replied. 'Peace makes you soft.'

He was very matter-of-fact about it. At least he did not relish the slaughter, as the Afghan men did. He had told her the bare fact that he had blown up the bridge at Darg, but one of the wounded guerrillas had given her the details, explaining how the timing of the explosion had turned the tide of the battle and graphically describing the carnage.

Down in the village of Banda, there was an air of celebration. Men and women stood talking animatedly in groups, instead of retiring to their courtyards. The children were playing noisy war games, ambushing imaginary Russians in imitation of their older brothers. Somewhere a man was singing to the beat of a drum. The thought of spending the evening alone suddenly seemed unbearably dreary to Jane, and on impulse she said to Ellis: 'Come and have tea with me – if you don't mind my feeding Chantal.'

'I'd like that,' he said.

The baby was crying as they entered the house, and as always Jane's body responded: one of her breasts sprang a sudden leak. She said hurriedly: 'Sit down, and Fara will bring you some tea,' then she darted into the other room before Ellis could see the embarrassing stain on her shirt.

She undid her buttons quickly and picked up the baby. There was the usual moment of blind panic as Chantal sought the nipple, then she began to suck, painfully hard at first and then more gently. Jane felt awkward about going back into the other room. Don't be silly, she told herself; you asked him, and he said it was okay, and in any case you spent practically every night in his bed at one time . . . All the same, she felt herself flush slightly as she walked through the door.

Ellis was looking at Jean-Pierre's maps. 'This was the cleverest thing,' he said. 'He knew all the routes because Mohammed always used his maps.' He looked up at her, saw her expression, and said hastily: 'But let's not talk about that. What will you do now?'

She sat on the cushion with her back against the wall, her favourite position for nursing. Ellis did not seem embarrassed by her exposed breast and she began to feel more comfortable. 'I have to wait,' she said. 'As soon as the route to Pakistan is open and the convoys begin again, I'll go home. What about you?'

'The same. My work here is over. The agreement will have to be supervised, of course, but the Agency has people in Pakistan who can do that.'

Fara brought the tea. Jane wondered what Ellis's next job would be: plotting a coup in Nicaragua, or blackmailing a Soviet diplomat in Washington, or perhaps assassinating an African Communist? She had questioned him, when they were lovers, about going to Vietnam, and he had told her that everybody had expected him to dodge the draft but he was a contrary son of a bitch and so he did the opposite. She was not sure she believed that, but even if it were true it did not explain why he had remained in this violent line of work even after he got out of the army. 'So what will you do when you get home?' she asked. 'Go back to devising cute ways of killing Castro?'

'The Agency is not supposed to do assassinations,' he said.

'But it does.'

'There's a lunatic element that gives us a bad name. Unfortunately, Presidents can't resist the temptation to play secret-agent games, and that encourages the nut-case faction.'

'Why don't you turn your back on them all and join the human race?'

'Look. America is full of people who believe that other countries as well as their own have a right to be free – but they're the type of people who "turn their backs and join the human race". In consequence, the Agency employs too many psychopaths and too few decent, compassionate citizens. Then, when the Agency brings down a foreign government at the whim of a President, they all ask how this kind of thing can possibly happen. The answer is because they let it. My country is a democracy, so there's nobody to blame but me when things are wrong; and if things are to be put right, I have to do it, because it's my responsibility.'

Jane was unconvinced. 'Would you say that the way to reform the KGB is to join it?'

'No, because the KGB is not ultimately controlled by the people. The Agency is.'

'Control isn't that simple,' said Jane. 'The CIA tells lies to the people. You can't control them if you have no way of knowing what they're doing.'

'But in the end it's our Agency and our responsibility.'

'You could work to abolish it instead of joining it.'

'But we need a central intelligence agency. We live in a hostile world and we need information about our enemies.'

Jane sighed. 'But look what it leads to,' she said. 'You're planning to send more and bigger guns to Masud so that he can kill more people faster. And that's what you people *always* end up doing.'

'It's *not* just so that he can kill more people faster,' Ellis protested. 'The Afghans are fighting for their freedom – and they're fighting *against* a bunch of murderers—'

'They're *all* fighting for their freedom,' Jane interrupted. 'The PLO, the Cuban exiles, the Weathermen, the IRA, the white South Africans and the Free Wales Army.'

'Some are right and some aren't.'

'And the CIA knows the difference?'

'It ought to—'

'But it doesn't. Whose freedom is Masud fighting for?'

'The freedom of all Afghans.'

'Bullshit,' Jane said fiercely. 'He's a Muslim fundamentalist, and if he ever takes power the first thing he'll do is clamp down on women. He will never give them the vote – he wants to take away what few rights they have. And how do you think he will treat his political opponents, given that his political hero is the Ayatollah Khomeini? Will scientists and teachers have academic freedom? Will gay men and women have sexual freedom? What will happen to the Hindus, the Buddhists, the atheists and the Plymouth Brethren?'

Ellis said: 'Do you *seriously* think Masud's regime would be worse than that of the Russians?'

Jane thought for a moment. 'I don't know. The only thing that's certain is that Masud's regime will be an Afghan tyranny instead of a Russian tyranny. And it's not worth killing people to exchange a local dictator for a foreigner.'

'The Afghans seem to think it is.'

'Most of them have never been asked.'

'I think it's obvious. However, I don't normally do this sort of work anyway. Usually I'm more of a detective type.'

This was something about which Jane had been curious for a year. 'What exactly was your mission in Paris?'

'When I spied on all our friends?' he smiled thinly. 'Didn't Jean-Pierre tell you?'

'He said he didn't really know.'

'Perhaps he didn't. I was hunting terrorists.'

'Among our friends?'

'That's where they are usually to be found – among dissidents, dropouts and criminals.'

'Was Rahmi Coskun a terrorist?' Jean-Pierre had said that Rahmi got arrested because of Ellis.

'Yes. He was responsible for the Turkish Airlines firebombing in the Avenue Felix Faure.'

'Rahmi? How do you know?'

'He told me. And when I had him arrested he was planning another bombing.'

'He told you that, too?'

'He asked me to help him with the bomb.'

'My God.' Handsome Rahmi, with the smouldering eyes and passionate hatred of his wretched country's government . . .

Ellis had not finished. 'Remember Pepe Gozzi?'

Jane frowned. 'Do you mean the funny little Corsican who had a Rolls-Royce?'

'Yes. He supplied guns and explosives to every nutcase in Paris. He'd sell to anyone who could afford his prices, but he specialized in "political" customers.'

Jane was flabbergasted. She had assumed that Pepe was somewhat disreputable, purely on the grounds that he was both rich and Corsican; but she had supposed that at worst he was involved in some everyday crime such as smuggling or dope dealing. To think that he sold guns to murderers! Jane was beginning to feel as if she had been living in a dream, while intrigue and violence went on in the real world all around her. Am I so naive? she thought.

Ellis ploughed on. 'I also pulled in a Russian who had financed a lot of assassinations and kidnappings. Then Pepe was interrogated and spilled the beans on half the terrorists in Europe.'

'That's what you were doing, all the time we were lovers,' Jane said dreamily. She recalled the parties, the rock concerts, the demonstrations, the political arguments in cafés, the endless bottles of *vin rouge ordinaire* in attic studios... Since their break-up she had assumed vaguely that he had been writing little reports on all the radicals, saying who was influential, who was extreme, who had money, who had the largest following among students, who had Communist Party connections, and so on. It was hard now to accept the idea that he had been after real criminals, and that he had actually found some among their friends. 'I can't believe it,' she said in amazement.

'It was a great triumph, if you want to know the truth.'

'You probably shouldn't be telling me.'

'I shouldn't. But when I've lied to you in the past, I have regretted doing so – to put it mildly.'

Jane felt awkward and did not know what to say. She shifted Chantal to her left breast then, catching Ellis's eye, covered her right breast with her shirt. The conversation was becoming uncomfortably personal, but she was intensely curious to know more. She could see now how he justified himself – although she did not agree with his reasoning – but still she wondered about his motivation. If I don't find out now, she thought, I may never get another chance. She said: 'I don't understand what makes a man decide to spend his life doing this sort of thing.'

He glanced away. 'I'm good at it and it's worth doing and the pay's terrific.'

'And I expect you liked the pension plan and the canteen menu. It's all right – you don't have to explain yourself to me if you don't want to.'

He gave her a hard look, as if he were trying to read her thoughts. 'I do want to tell you,' he said. 'Are you sure you want to hear it?'

'Yes. Please.'

'It's to do with the war,' he began, and suddenly Jane knew he was about to say something he had never told to anyone else. 'One of the terrible things about flying in Vietnam was that it was so hard to differentiate between Vietcong and civilians. Whenever we gave air support to ground troops, say, or mined a jungle trail, or declared a free-fire zone, we knew that we would kill more women and children and old men than guerrillas. We used to say they had been sheltering the enemy, but who knows? And who cares? We killed them. *We were the terrorists then.* And I'm not talking about isolated cases – although I saw atrocities too – I'm talking about our regular everyday tactics. And there was no justification, you see; that was the kicker. We did all those terrible things in a cause that turned out to be all lies and corruption and self-deceit. We were on the wrong side.' His face was drawn, as if he were in pain from some persistent internal injury. In the relentless lamp-light his skin was shadowed and sallow. 'There's no excuse, you see; no forgiveness.'

Gently, Jane encouraged him to say more. 'So why did you stay?' she asked him. 'Why volunteer for a second tour?'

'Because I didn't see all of that so clearly then; because I was fighting for my country and you can't walk away from a war; because I was a good officer, and if I had gone home my job might have been taken over by some jerk and my men would have got killed: and none of these reasons is good enough, of course, so at some point I asked myself "What are you going to do about it?" I wanted . . . I didn't realize it at the time, but I wanted to do something to redeem myself. In the sixties we would have called it a guilt trip.'

'Yes, but . . .' He looked so uncertain and vulnerable that she found it hard to ask him direct questions, but he needed to talk and she wanted to hear it, so she ploughed on. 'But why *this*?'

'I was in Intelligence, towards the end, and they offered me the chance to continue in the same line of work in the civilian world. They said I would be able to work under cover because I was familiar with that milieu. They knew about my radical past, you see. It seemed to me that by catching terrorists I might be able to undo some of the things I had done. So I became a counter-terrorist expert. It sounds simplistic when I put it into words – but I've been successful, you know. The Agency doesn't like me because I sometimes refuse a mission, such as the time they killed the

President of Chile, and agents aren't supposed to refuse missions; but I've been responsible for incarcerating some very nasty people, and I'm proud of myself.'

Chantal was asleep. Jane laid her in the box that was her cradle. She said to Ellis: 'I suppose I ought to say that . . . that I seem to have misjudged you.'

He smiled. 'Thank God for that.'

For a moment she was seized by nostalgia as she thought of the time – was it only a year and a half ago? – when she and Ellis had been happy and none of *this* had happened: no CIA, no Jean-Pierre, no Afghanistan. 'You can't wipe it out, though, can you,' she said. 'Everything that has happened – your lies, my anger.'

'No.' He was sitting on the stool, looking up at her as she stood in front of him, studying her intently. He held out his arms, hesitated, then rested his hands on her hips in a gesture which might have been brotherly affection or something more. Then Chantal said: 'Mumumumummmm . . .' Jane turned around and looked at her, and Ellis let his hands fall. Chantal was wide awake, waving her arms and legs in the air. Jane picked her up, and she burped immediately.

Jane turned back to face Ellis. He had folded his arms across his chest and was watching her, smiling. Suddenly she did not want him to leave. On impulse, she said: 'Why don't you have supper with me. It's only bread and curds, though.'

'All right.'

She held Chantal out to him. 'Let me go and tell Fara.' He took the baby and she went out into the courtyard. Fara was heating water for Chantal's bath.

Jane tested the temperature with her elbow and found it just right. 'Make bread for two people, please,' she said in Dari. Fara's eyes widened, and Jane realized it was shocking for a woman alone to invite a man to supper. To hell with all that, she thought. She picked up the pot of water and carried it back into the house.

Ellis was sitting on the big cushion under the oil lamp, dangling Chantal on his knee, saying a rhyme in a low voice. His big hairy hands encircled her tiny pink body. She was looking up at him, gurgling happily and kicking her fat feet. Jane stopped in the doorway, transfixed by the scene, and a thought came unbidden into her mind: Ellis should have been Chantal's father.

Is that true? she asked herself as she looked at them. Do I really wish it? Ellis finished the rhyme and looked up at her and smiled a little sheepishly, and she thought: yes, I really do.

They walked up the mountainside at midnight, Jane leading the way, Ellis following with his big down sleeping bag under his arm. They had bathed Chantal, eaten their meagre supper of bread and curds, fed Chantal again, and settled the baby down for the night on the roof, where she was now fast asleep beside Fara, who would protect her with her life. Ellis had wanted to take Jane away from the house where she had been someone else's wife, and Jane had felt the same, so she had said: 'I know a place where we can go.'

Now she turned off the mountain path and led Ellis

across the sloping, stony ground to her secret retreat, the concealed ledge where she had sunbathed naked and oiled her tummy before Chantal was born. She found it easily in the moonlight. She looked down into the village, where the embers of cooking fires glowed in the courtyards and a few lamps still flickered behind glassless windows. She could just make out the shape of her house. In a few hours, as soon as day began to break, she would be able to see the sleeping forms of Chantal and Fara on the roof. She would be glad: this was the first time she had left Chantal at night.

She turned around. Ellis had completely unzipped the sleeping bag and was spreading it on the ground like a blanket. Jane felt awkward and uncomfortable. The surge of warmth and lust which had overcome her in the house, when she watched him saying a nursery rhyme to her baby, had gone. All her old feelings had returned, momentarily: the urge to touch him, her love of the way he smiled when he felt selfconscious, the need to feel his big hands on her skin, the obsessive wish to see him naked. A few weeks before Chantal was born she had lost her desire for sex, and it had not come back until that moment. But the mood had been dissipated, bit by bit, in the succeeding hours, as they had made clumsy practical arrangements to be alone, for all the world like a pair of teenagers trying to get away from their parents for a petting session.

'Come and sit down,' Ellis said.

She sat beside him on the sleeping bag. They both looked down to the darkened village. They were not touching. There was a moment of strained silence. 'Nobody else has ever been here,' Jane remarked, just for something to say.

'What did you use it for?'

'Oh, I just used to lie in the sun and think about nothing,' she said, then she thought *Oh, what the hell*, and she said: 'No, that's not quite true, I used to masturbate.'

He laughed, then put his arm around her and hugged her. 'I'm glad you still haven't learned to mince your words,' he said.

She turned her face to him. He kissed her mouth softly. He likes me for my faults, she thought: my tactlessness and my quick temper and my cursing, my wilfulness and my being opinionated. 'You don't want to change me,' she said.

'Oh, Jane, I've missed you.' He closed his eyes and spoke in a murmur. 'Most of the time I didn't even realize that I was missing you.' He lay back, pulling her with him, so that she ended up leaning over him. She kissed his face lightly. The awkward feeling was going rapidly. She thought: Last time I kissed him he had no beard. She felt his hands move: he was unbuttoning her shirt. She was not wearing a bra – she did not have one big enough – and her breasts felt very naked. She slipped her hand inside his shirt and touched the long hairs around his nipple. She had almost forgotten what men felt like. For months her life had been full of the soft voices and smooth faces of women and babies: now suddenly she wanted to feel rough skin and hard thighs and bristly cheeks. She twined her fingers in his beard and pushed his mouth open with her tongue. His hands found her swollen breasts, she felt a pang of pleasure – and then she knew what was going to happen and was powerless to stop it, for even as she pulled abruptly away from him she felt both her nipples spurt warm milk over his hands, and she flushed with shame and said: 'Oh, God, I'm sorry, how disgusting, I can't help it—'

He silenced her with a finger over her lips. 'It's all right,' he said. He caressed her breasts as he spoke, and they became slippery all over. 'It's normal. It always happens. It's sexy.'

It *can't* be sexy, she thought, but he shifted his position and brought his face to her chest and started to kiss her breasts and stroke them at the same time, and gradually she relaxed and started to enjoy the sensation. Eventually she felt another sharp pang of pleasure as she leaked again, but this time she did not mind. Ellis said 'Aaah,' and the rough surface of his tongue touched her tender nipple, and she thought *If he sucks them I'll come.*

It was as if he had read her mind. He closed his lips around one long nipple, pulled it into his mouth and sucked it while holding the other between finger and thumb, squeezing gently and rhythmically. Helplessly Jane yielded to the sensation, and as her breasts squirted milk, one into his hand and the other into his mouth, the feeling was so exquisite that she shuddered uncontrollably and moaned 'Oh God oh God oh God' until it died away and she slumped on top of him.

For a while there was nothing in her mind but what

she could feel: his warm breath on her wet breasts, his beard scratching her skin, the cool night air wafting over her heated cheeks, the nylon sleeping bag and the hard ground beneath. After a while his muffled voice said: 'I'm suffocating.'

She rolled off him. 'Are we weird?' she said.

'Yes.'

She giggled. 'Have you ever done that before?'

He hesitated, then said: 'Yes.'

'What . . .' She still felt faintly embarrassed. 'What does it taste like?'

'Warm and sweet. Like canned milk. Did you come?'

'Didn't you notice?'

'I wasn't sure. It's hard to tell with girls, sometimes.'

She kissed him. 'I came. A little one, but unmistakable. A boob-inal orgasm.'

'I almost came.'

'Really?' she ran her hand down his body. He had on the thin cotton pyjama-like shirt and trousers that Afghans all wore. She could feel his ribs and his hipbone: he had lost the soft under-skin fat which all but the thinnest Westerners had. Her hand encountered his prick, standing upright inside the trousers, and she said 'Ahhh,' and grasped it. 'It feels good,' she said.

'Also at this end.'

She wanted to give him as much pleasure as he had given her. She sat upright, untied the drawstring of his trousers, and took out his prick. Stroking it gently, she bent over and kissed the end. Then the imp of mischief seized her, and she said: 'How many girls have you had since me?'

304

'Just keep doing that and I'll tell you.'

'Okay.' She resumed stroking and kissing. He was silent. 'Okay,' she said after a minute, 'how many?'

'Wait, I'm still counting.'

'Bastard!' she said, and bit his prick.

'Ouch! Not many, really . . . I swear!'

'What do you do when you haven't got a girl?'

'Take three guesses.'

She was not to be put off. 'Do you do it with your hand?'

'Aw, shucks, Miz Janey, I'se bashful.'

'You do,' she said triumphantly. 'What do you think about while you're doing it?'

'Would you believe Princess Diana?'

'No.'

'Now I *am* embarrassed.'

Jane was consumed with curiosity. 'You have to tell the truth.'

'Pam Ewing.'

'Who the hell is she?'

'You *have* been out of touch. She's Bobby Ewing's wife, in *Dallas.*'

Jane remembered the television show and the actress, and she was astonished. 'You can't be serious.'

'You asked for the truth.'

'But she's made of plastic!'

'We're talking *fantasy* here.'

'Can't you fantasize a liberated woman?'

'Fantasy is no place for politics.'

'I'm shocked.' She hesitated. 'How do you do it?'

'What?'

'What you do. With your hand.'

'Kind of like what you're doing, but harder.'

'Show me.'

'I'm not just embarrassed, now,' he said. 'I'm mortified.'

'Please. Please show me. I've always wanted to see a man do that. I've never had the nerve to ask before – if you turn me down I may never know.' She took his hand and placed it where hers had been.

After a moment he started to move his hand slowly. He made several half-hearted strokes, then he sighed, closed his eyes, and started to rub it in earnest.

'You're so rough with it!' she exclaimed.

He stopped. 'I can't do this . . . unless you do it too.'

'It's a deal,' she said eagerly. Quickly she slipped off her trousers and panties. She knelt beside him and started to stroke herself.

'Come closer,' he said. His voice sounded a little hoarse. 'I can't see you.'

He was lying flat on his back. She shuffled closer until she was kneeling upright beside his head, with the moonlight silvering her nipples and her pubic hair. He started to rub his prick again, faster this time, and he stared at her hand as if transfixed as she caressed herself.

'Oh, Jane,' he said.

She began to enjoy the familiar darts of pleasure spreading from her fingertips. She saw Ellis's hips start to move up and down in rhythm with his hand. 'I want you to come,' she said. 'I want to see it shoot out.' Part of her was shocked at herself but that part was swamped by excitement and desire.

He groaned. She looked at his face. His mouth was open and he was breathing hard. His eyes were fixed on her cunt. She stroked the lips with her middle finger. 'Put your finger in,' he breathed. 'I want to see your finger go inside.'

That was something she did not normally do. She pushed her fingertip inside. It felt smooth and slippery. She put it all the way in. He gasped, and because he was so excited by what she was doing, she got turned on too. She turned her gaze back to his prick. His hips jerked faster as he fucked his hand. She moved her finger in and out of her cunt with mounting pleasure. Suddenly he arched his back, thrusting his pelvis high in the air and groaning, and a streak of white semen shot out from him. Involuntarily Jane cried 'Oh, my God!' then as she gazed, fascinated, at the tiny hole in the end of his organ there was another jet, and another, and a fourth, spurting up into the air, gleaming in the moonlight, and landing on his chest and her arm and in her hair; and then when he collapsed she herself was racked by spasms of pleasure fired by her fast-moving finger until she, too, was exhausted.

She slumped, lying beside him on the sleeping bag with her head on his thigh. His prick was still stiff. She leaned over weakly and kissed it. She could taste a trace of salty semen on the end. She felt his face nuzzle between her thighs in response.

For a while they were quiet. The only sounds were

their breathing and the rushing river on the far side of the Valley. Jane looked at the stars. They were very bright, and there were no clouds. The night air was becoming cooler. We'll have to get inside this sleeping bag before too long, she thought. She looked forward to falling asleep close to him.

'Are we weird?' said Ellis.

'Oh, yes,' she said.

His prick had fallen sideways and lay on his belly. She teased the red-gold hair of his groin with her fingertips. She had almost forgotten what it was like to make love to Ellis. He was so different to Jean-Pierre. Jean-Pierre liked a lot of preparation; bath oil, scent, candlelight, wine, violins. He was a fastidious lover. He liked her to wash before making love, and he always hurried to the bathroom afterwards. He would never touch her while she had her period, and he certainly would not have sucked her breasts and swallowed the milk as Ellis had. Ellis would do *anything*, she thought, and the more unhygienic the better. She grinned in the dark. It occurred to her that she had never been completely convinced that Jean-Pierre actually *liked* performing oral sex, good at it though he was. With Ellis there was no doubt.

The thought made her want him to do it. She opened her thighs invitingly. She felt him kiss her, his lips brushing the wiry hair, then his tongue started to probe lasciviously between the folds of her lips. After a while he rolled her on to her back, knelt between her thighs, and lifted her legs over his shoulders. She felt utterly naked, terribly open and vulnerable and yet greatly cherished. His tongue moved in a long, slow curve, starting at the base of her spine – *Oh, God*, she thought, *I remember how he does this* – licking along the cleft of her buttocks, pausing to push deep into her vagina, then lifting to tease the sensitive skin where the lips met and the tingling clitoris between them. After seven or eight long licks she held his head over her clitoris, making him concentrate on that, and she began to lift and lower her hips, telling him by the pressure of her fingertips on his temples to lick harder or more lightly, higher or lower, left or right. She felt his hand on her cunt, pushing into the moist interior, and guessed what he was going to do: a moment later he withdrew his hand, and then pushed a wet finger slowly into her anus. She remembered how shocked she had been the first time he did that, and how quickly she had grown to like it. Jean-Pierre would never do that in a million years. As the muscles of her body began to tense for the climax, the thought came into her mind that she had missed Ellis more than she had ever admitted, even to herself; indeed, that the reason she had been so angry with him for so long was that she had continued to love him all along, and she loved him still; and as she admitted that, a terrible weight lifted from her mind and she started to come, shaking like a tree in a gale, and Ellis, knowing what she liked, thrust his tongue deep inside her while she ground her sex frantically against his face.

It seemed it would go on for ever. Each time the sensations eased he would thrust his finger deeper into her ass, or lick her clitoris, or bite the lips of her cunt, and it would start all over again; until, out of sheer exhaustion, she pleaded: 'Stop, stop, I've no energy left, it will kill me,' and at last he lifted his face from her cunt and lowered her legs to the ground.

He leaned over her, resting his weight on his hands, and kissed her mouth. The smell of her cunt was in his beard. She lay prone, too tired to open her eyes, too tired even to kiss him back. She felt his hand on her cunt, opening it, then his prick nosing in, and she thought *He got hard again quickly* and then *It's been so long oh God it feels good.*

He began to move in and out, slowly at first and then faster. She opened her eyes. His face was above hers and he was gazing at her. Then he bent his neck and looked down to where their bodies were joined. His eyes widened and his mouth opened as he watched his prick going in and out of her cunt, and the sight so inflamed him that she wished she could see it too. Suddenly he slowed his pace, thrusting deeper, and she remembered that he did this before the climax. He looked into her eyes. 'Kiss me while I come,' he said, and he lowered his cunt-smelling lips to hers. She thrust her tongue into his mouth. She loved it when he came. His back arched and his head lifted, and he gave a cry like a wild animal, and she felt him spurt inside her.

When it was over he lowered his head to her shoulder and moved his lips gently against the soft skin of her neck, whispering words which she could not make out. After a minute or two he gave a deep sigh of contentment, kissed her mouth, then raised himself to his knees and kissed each of her breasts in turn. Finally he kissed her cunt. Her body responded instantly, and she moved her hips to push against his lips. Knowing that she was getting turned on yet again, he began to lick; and, as always, the thought of him licking her cunt while it was still dripping with his semen almost drove her mad, and she came immediately, crying his name until the spasm passed.

He slumped beside her at last. Automatically they moved into the position they had always lain in after making love: his arm around her, her head on his shoulder, her thigh lying across his hips. He yawned hugely, and she giggled at him. They touched one another lethargically, she reaching down to toy with his limp penis, he moving his fingers in and out of her sopping cunt. She licked his chest and tasted salt perspiration on his skin. She looked at his neck. The moon highlighted the lines and furrows, betraying his age: He's ten years older than me, Jane thought. Maybe that's why he's such a great fuck, because he's older. 'Why are you such a great fuck?' she said aloud. He did not reply; he was asleep. So she said: 'I love you, dear, sleep well,' and then she closed her eyes.

After a year in the Valley, Jean-Pierre found the city of Kabul bewildering and frightening. The buildings were too tall, the cars went too fast, and there were too many people. He had to cover his ears as enormous Russian trucks roared by in convoy. Everything assaulted him with the shock of the new: apartment blocks, schoolgirls in uniform, street lights, elevators, tablecloths, and the taste of wine. After twenty-four hours he was still jumpy. It was ironic: he was a Parisian!

He had been given a room in the unmarried officers' quarters. They had promised him that he would get an apartment as soon as Jane arrived with Chantal. Meanwhile he felt as if he were living in a cheap hotel. The building probably had been a hotel before the Russians came. If Jane were to arrive now – she was due at any time – the three of them would have to make the best of it here for the rest of the night. I can't complain, thought Jean-Pierre; I'm not a hero – yet.

He stood at his window, looking over Kabul at night. For a couple of hours the power had been out all over the city, due presumably to the urban counterparts of Masud and his guerrillas, but a few minutes ago it had come back on again, and there was a faint glow over the city centre, which had street lighting. The only noise was the howl of engines as army cars, trucks and tanks hurtled through the city hurrying to their mysterious destinations. What was so urgent, at midnight in Kabul? Jean-Pierre had done military service, and he thought that if the Russian army was anything like the French, the kind of task done at the double in the middle of the night was something like moving five hundred chairs from a barracks to a hall on the other side of town in preparation for a concert which was to take place in two weeks' time and would probably get cancelled.

He could not smell the night air, for his window was nailed shut. His door was not locked, but there was a Russian sergeant with a pistol sitting blank-faced on a straight-backed chair at the end of the corridor, next to the toilet, and Jean-Pierre felt that if he wanted to leave the sergeant would probably prevent him.

Where was Jane? The raid on Darg must have been over by nightfall. For a helicopter to go from Darg to Banda and pick up Jane and Chantal would be the work of a few minutes. The helicopter could get from Banda to Kabul in under an hour. But perhaps the attacking force was returning to Bagram, the air base near the mouth of the Valley, in which case Jane might have had to come from Bagram to Kabul by road, no doubt accompanied by Anatoly.

She would be so glad to see her husband that she would be ready to forgive his deceit, see his point of view about Masud, and let bygones be bygones, Jean-Pierre thought. For a moment he wondered whether that was wishful thinking. No, he decided; he knew her quite well, and she was basically under his thumb.

And she would *know*. Only a few people would share the secret and comprehend the magnitude of what he had achieved: he was glad she would be one of them.

He hoped Masud had been captured, rather than killed. If he had been captured, the Russians could put him on trial, so that all the rebels would know for sure he was finished. Death was almost as good provided they had the body. If there were no body, or an unrecognizable corpse, the rebels' propagandists in Peshawar would put out press releases claiming that Masud was still alive. Of course it would become clear in the end that he was dead, but the impact would be a little softened. Jean-Pierre hoped they had the body.

He heard footsteps in the corridor. Would it be Anatoly, or Jane – or both? It sounded like a masculine tread. He opened the door and saw two rather large Russian soldiers and a third, smaller man in an officer's uniform. No doubt they had come to take him to wherever Anatoly and Jane were. He was disappointed. He looked enquiringly at the officer, who made a gesture with his hand. The two soldiers stepped through the door rudely. Jean-Pierre went back a pace with a protest rising to his lips, but before he could speak the nearer of the two grabbed him by the shirt and smashed a huge fist into his face.

Jean-Pierre let out a howl of pain and fear. The other soldier kicked him in the groin with a heavy boot: the pain was excruciating, and Jean-Pierre sank to his knees knowing that the most terrible moment of his life had arrived.

The two soldiers pulled him upright and held him standing, one at each arm, and the officer came in. Through a haze of tears Jean-Pierre saw a short, thick-set young man with some kind of deformity which made one side of his face appear flushed and swollen and gave him a permanent sneer. He carried a truncheon in his gloved hand.

For the next five minutes the two soldiers held Jean-Pierre's squirming, shuddering body while the officer smashed the wooden truncheon repeatedly into his face, his shoulders, his knees, his shins, his belly and his groin – always his groin. Every blow was carefully placed and viciously delivered, and there was always a pause between blows, so that the agony of the last could fade just enough to allow Jean-Pierre to dread the next for a second before it came. Every blow made him scream in pain, and every pause made him scream in anticipation of the next blow. At last there was a longer pause, and Jean-Pierre began to babble, not knowing whether they could understand him or not: 'Oh, please, don't hit me, please, don't hit me again, sir, I'll do anything, what is it you want, please don't hit me no don't hit me—'

'Enough!' said a voice in French.

Jean-Pierre opened his eyes and tried to peer through the blood streaming down his face at this saviour who had said *Enough*. It was Anatoly.

The two soldiers slowly let Jean-Pierre sink to the ground. His body felt as if it was on fire. Every move was agony. Every bone felt broken, his balls felt crushed, his face seemed to have swollen enormously. He opened his mouth, and blood came out. He swallowed, and spoke through smashed lips. 'Why ... why have they done this?'

'You know why,' said Anatoly.

Jean-Pierre shook his head from side to side slowly and tried to keep from descending into utter madness. 'I risked my life for you ... I gave everything ... why?'

'You set a trap,' Anatoly said. 'Eighty-one men died today because of you.'

The raid must have gone wrong, Jean-Pierre realized, and somehow he was being blamed. 'No,' he said, 'not I—'

'You expected to be miles away when the trap was sprung,' Anatoly went on. 'But I surprised you by making you get into the helicopter and come with me. So you are here to take your punishment – which will be painful and very, very prolonged.' He turned away.

'No,' said Jean-Pierre. 'Wait!'

Anatoly turned back.

Jean-Pierre fought to think despite the pain. 'I came here ... I risked my life ... I gave you information on the convoys ... you attacked the convoys ... did far more damage than the loss of eighty men ... not logical, it's not logical.' He gathered his strength for one coherent sentence. 'If I had known of a trap I could have warned you yesterday and begged for mercy.'

'Then how did they know we would attack the village?' Anatoly demanded.

'They must have guessed ...'

'How?'

Jean-Pierre racked his confused brains. 'Was Skabun bombed?'

'I think not.'

That was it, Jean-Pierre realized; someone had found out that there had been no bombing at Skabun. 'You should have bombed it,' he said.

Anatoly looked thoughtful. 'Somebody there is very good at making connections.'

It was Jane, thought Jean-Pierre, and for a second he hated her.

Anatoly said: 'Has Ellis Thaler got any distinguishing marks?'

Jean-Pierre wanted to pass out but he was afraid they

would hit him again. 'Yes,' he said miserably. 'A big scar on his back shaped like a cross.'

'Then it *is* him,' said Anatoly in a near-whisper.

'Who?'

'John Michael Raleigh, age thirty-four, born in New Jersey, eldest son of a builder. He was a dropout from the University of California at Berkeley and a Captain in the U.S. Marines. He has been a CIA agent since 1972. Marital status: divorced once, one child, whereabouts of the family a closely guarded secret.' He waved his hand as if to brush such details aside. 'There's no doubt it was he who out-guessed me at Darg today. He's brilliant and very dangerous. If I could have my pick of all the agents of the Western imperialist nations I would choose to catch him. In the last ten years he has done us irreparable damage on at least three occasions. Last year in Paris he destroyed a network that had taken seven or eight years of patient work to develop. The year before that he found an agent we had planted in the Secret Service in *nineteen sixty-five* – a man who could have assassinated a President one day. And now – now we have him here.'

Jean-Pierre, kneeling on the floor and hugging his battered body, let his head fall forward and closed his eyes in despair: he had all along been far out of his depth, blithely pitting himself against the grand masters of this merciless game, a naked child in a den of lions.

He had had such high hopes. Working alone, he was to have dealt the Afghan Resistance a blow from which it would never recover. He would have changed the course of history in this area of the globe. And he would have taken his revenge on the smug rulers of the West; he would have deceived and dismayed the establishment that had betrayed and killed his father. But instead of that triumph, he had been defeated. It had all been snatched from him at the last moment – by Ellis.

He heard Anatoly's voice like a background murmur. 'We can be sure he achieved what he wanted with the rebels. We don't know the details, but the outline is enough: a unity pact among the bandit leaders in exchange for American arms. That kind of thing could keep the rebellion going for years. We've got to stop it before it gets started.'

Jean-Pierre opened his eyes and looked up. 'How?'

'We have to catch this man before he can return to the United States. That way nobody will know that he agreed the treaty, the rebels will never get their arms, and the whole thing will fizzle out.'

Jean-Pierre listened, fascinated despite the pain: could it be that there was still a chance of wreaking his revenge?

'Catching him would almost make up for losing Masud,' Anatoly went on, and Jean-Pierre's heart leaped with new hope. 'Not only would we have neutralized the single most dangerous agent the imperialists have. Think of it: a real live CIA man caught here in Afghanistan ... For three years the American propaganda machine has been saying that the Afghan bandits are freedom fighters waging a heroic David-

318

and-Goliath struggle against the might of the Soviet Union. Now we have *proof* of what we have been saying all along – that Masud and the others are mere lackeys of American imperialism. We can put Ellis on trial . . .'

'But the Western newspapers will deny everything,' said Jean-Pierre. 'The capitalist press—'

'Who cares about the West? It is the non-aligned countries, the Third World waverers, and the Muslim nations in particular whom we want to impress.'

It *was* possible, Jean-Pierre realized, to turn this into a triumph; and it would still be a triumph for him personally, because it was he who had alerted the Russians to the presence of a CIA agent in the Five Lions Valley.

'Now,' said Anatoly, '*where* is Ellis tonight?'

'He moves around with Masud,' said Jean-Pierre. Catching Ellis was easier said than done: it had taken Jean-Pierre a whole year to pin Masud down.

'I don't see why he should continue to be with Masud,' said Anatoly. 'Did he have a base?'

'Yes – he lived with a family in Banda, theoretically. But he was rarely there.'

'Nevertheless, that is obviously the place to begin.'

Yes, of course, thought Jean-Pierre. If Ellis is not at Banda, somebody there may know where he has gone . . . Somebody like Jane. If Anatoly went to Banda looking for Ellis, he might at the same time find Jane. Jean-Pierre's pain seemed to ease as he realized that he might get his revenge on the establishment, capture Ellis who had stolen his triumph, *and* get Jane and Chantal back. 'Will I go with you to Banda?' he asked.

Anatoly considered. 'I think so. You know the village and the people – it may be useful to have you on hand.'

Jean-Pierre struggled to his feet, gritting his teeth against the agony in his groin. 'When do we go?'

'Now,' said Anatoly.

CHAPTER FOURTEEN

ELLIS WAS hurrying to catch a train, and he was panicking even though he knew he was dreaming. First he could not park his car – he was driving Gill's Honda – then he could not find the ticket window. Having decided to get on the train without a ticket, he found himself pushing through a dense crowd of people in the vast concourse of Grand Central Station. At that point he remembered that he had dreamed this dream before, several times, and quite recently; and he never caught the train. The dreams always left him with an unbearable feeling that all happiness had passed him by, permanently, and now he was terrified that the same thing would happen again. He shoved through the crowd with increasing violence, and at last reached the gate. This was where he had previously stood watching the rear end of the train disappearing into the distance, but today it was in the station. Ellis ran along the platform and jumped aboard just as it started to move.

He was so delighted to have caught the train that he felt almost high. He sat in a first-class carriage, and it did not seem at all strange that he was in a sleeping bag with Jane. Outside the window dawn was breaking over the Five Lions Valley.

There was no sharp division between sleep and wakefulness. The train gradually faded until all that was left was the sleeping bag and the Valley and Jane and the sense of delight. At some point during the short night they had zipped up the bag, and now they lay very close together, hardly able to move. He could feel her warm breath on his neck, and her enlarged breasts were squashed against his ribs. Her bones prodded him, her hip and her knee, her elbow and her foot, but he liked it. They had always slept close together, he remembered. The antique bed in her Paris apartment had been too small for anything else, anyway. His own bed had been bigger but even there they had slept entangled. She always claimed that he molested her during the night, but he never remembered it in the morning.

It was a long time since he had slept all night with a woman. He tried to recall who was the last one, and realized it was Jane: the girls he had taken to his apartment in Washington had never stayed to breakfast.

Jane was the last and the *only* person with whom he had had such uninhibited sex. He ran over in his mind the things they had done last night, and he began to get an erection. There seemed to be no limit to the number of times he could get hard with her. In Paris they had sometimes stayed in bed all day, getting up only to raid the fridge or open some wine, and he would come five or six times, while she just lost count of her orgasms. He had never thought of himself as a sexual athlete, and subsequent experience proved that he was not one, except with her. She freed something that was imprisoned, when he was with other women, by fear or guilt or something. No one else had done that to him, although one woman had come close: a Vietnamese with whom he had had a brief, doomed affair in 1970.

It was obvious now that he had never stopped loving Jane. For the past year he had done his work, dated women, visited Petal and gone to the supermarket like an actor playing a part, pretending for the sake of verisimilitude that this was the real him, but knowing in his heart of hearts that it was not. He would have mourned her forever if he had not come to Afghanistan.

It seemed to him that he was often blind to the most important facts about himself. He had not realized, back in 1968, that he wanted to fight for his country; he had not realized that he did not want to marry Gill; in Vietnam he had not realized that he was against the war. Each of these revelations had astonished him and overturned his whole life. Self-deceit was not necessarily a bad thing, he believed: he could not have survived the war without it, and what would he have done if he had never come to Afghanistan, other than tell himself he did not want Jane?

Do I have her now? he wondered. She had not said much, except *I love you dear, sleep well* just as he was falling asleep. He thought that was the most delightful thing he had ever heard.

'What are you smiling about?'

He opened his eyes and looked at her. 'I thought you were asleep,' he replied.

'I've been watching you. You looked so happy.'

'Yes.' He took a deep breath of the cool morning air and raised himself on his elbow to look across the Valley. The fields were almost colourless in the dawn light, and the sky was pearl-grey. He was on the point of telling her what he was happy about when he heard a buzzing noise. He cocked his head to listen.

'What is it?' she said.

He put a finger to her lips. A moment later she heard it. In a few seconds the noise swelled until it was unmistakably the sound of helicopters. Ellis had a sense of impending disaster. 'Oh, shit,' he said feelingly.

The aircraft came into view over their heads, emerging from behind the mountain: three hunchbacked Hinds bristling with armament and one big troop-carrying Hip.

'Get your head in,' Ellis snapped at Jane. The sleeping bag was brown and dusty, like the ground all around them: if they could stay under it they might be invisible from the air. The guerrillas employed the same principle in hiding from aircraft – they covered themselves with the mud-coloured blankets, called *pattus*, that they all carried.

Jane burrowed down into the sleeping bag. The bag had a flap at its open end to hold a pillow, although there was no pillow in it at the moment. If they got that above them it would cover their heads. Ellis held Jane tight and rolled over, and the pillowcase flopped over. Now they were practically invisible.

They lay on their stomachs, he half on top of her, and looked down at the village. The helicopters seemed to be descending.

Jane said: 'They aren't going to land *here*, surely?'

Ellis said slowly: 'I think they are . . .'

Jane started to get up, saying: 'I've got to go down—'

'No!' Ellis held her shoulders, using his weight to force her down. 'Wait – just a few seconds and see what will happen—'

'But Chantal—'

'Wait!'

She gave up the struggle but he continued to hold her tightly. On the roofs of the houses sleepy people were sitting up, rubbing their eyes and staring dazedly at the huge machines beating the air like giant birds above them. Ellis located Jane's house. He could see Fara, standing up and wrapping a sheet around herself. There beside her was the tiny mattress on which Chantal lay hidden by bedding.

The helicopters circled cautiously. They're aiming to land here, Ellis thought, but they're wary after the ambush at Darg.

The villagers were galvanized. Some were running out of their houses and others were running into their houses. Children and livestock were rounded up and herded indoors. Several people tried to flee, but one of the Hinds flew low over the pathways out of the village and forced them back.

The scene convinced the Russian commander that there was no ambush here. The troop-carrying Hip and one of the three Hinds made their ungainly descent and landed in a field. Seconds later, soldiers emerged from the Hip, jumping out of its huge belly like insects.

'It's no good,' Jane cried. 'I'll have to go down now.'

'Listen!' said Ellis. 'She's in no danger – whatever the Russians want, they're not after babies. But they might be after *you*.'

'I must be with her—'

'Stop panicking,' he shouted. 'If you're with her she *will* be in danger. If you stay here she's safe. Don't you see? Rushing to her is the worst thing you could possibly do.'

'Ellis, I *can't*—'

'You *must*.'

'Oh, God!' She closed her eyes. 'Hold me tight.'

He gripped her shoulders and squeezed.

The troops encircled the little village. Only one house was outside their net: the home of the mullah, which was four or five hundred yards from the other houses, on the footpath that led up the mountainside. As Ellis noticed this a man came scurrying out of the house. He was close enough for Ellis to see his red-dyed beard: it was Abdullah. Three children of different sizes and a woman carrying a baby followed him out of the house and ran behind him up the mountain path.

The Russians saw him almost immediately. Ellis and Jane pulled the sleeping bag farther over their heads as the airborne helicopter veered away from the village and came to hover over the path. There was a burst from the machine-guns low in the nose of the helicopter, and dust exploded in a neatly-stitched line at

Abdullah's feet. He stopped short, looking almost comical as he nearly fell over, then he turned around and ran back, waving his hands and yelling at his family to return. When they approached the house another warning burst from the machine-gun prevented them from entering, and after a moment the whole family headed downhill towards the village.

Occasional shots could be heard through the oppressive heat of the rotor blades, but the soldiers appeared to be firing into the air to subdue the villagers. They were entering houses and driving out the occupants in their nightshirts and underwear. The Hind that had rounded up the mullah and his family now began to circle the village, very low, as if looking for more strays.

'What are they going to do?' said Jane in an unsteady voice.

'I'm not sure.'

'Is this a . . . reprisal?'

'God forbid.'

'What, then?' she persisted.

Ellis felt like saying *How the fuck should I know?* but instead he said: 'They may be having another try at capturing Masud.'

'But he never stays near the scene of a battle.'

'They may hope he's getting careless, or lazy; or that he might be wounded . . .' In truth Ellis did not know what was happening but he feared a My-Lai-style massacre.

The villagers were being herded into the courtyard of the mosque by soldiers who seemed to be treating them roughly but not brutally.

Suddenly Jane cried: 'Fara!'

'What is it?'

'What's she doing?'

Ellis located the roof of Jane's house. Fara was kneeling beside Chantal's tiny mattress, and Ellis could just see a tiny pink head peeping out. Chantal appeared still to be asleep. She would have been given a bottle at some time in the middle of the night by Fara, but although she was not yet hungry the noise of the helicopters might have been expected to wake her. Ellis hoped she would stay asleep.

He saw Fara place a cushion beside Chantal's head, then pull the sheet up over the baby's face.

'She's hiding her,' said Jane. 'The cushion props open the cover to let air in.'

'She's a clever girl.'

'I wish I was *there*.'

Fara rumpled the sheet then draped another sheet untidily over Chantal's body. She paused for a moment, studying the effect. From a distance the baby looked exactly like a hastily-abandoned pile of bedding. Fara seemed satisfied with the illusion, for she went to the edge of the roof and descended the steps into the courtyard.

'She's leaving her,' said Jane.

'Chantal is as safe as she could possibly be in the circumstances—'

'I know, I know!'

Fara was pushed into the mosque with the others. She was one of the last to go in. 'All the babies are with their mothers,' said Jane. 'I think Fara should have taken Chantal . . .'

'No,' said Ellis. 'Wait. You'll see.' He still did not know what would happen but if there was going to be a massacre Chantal was safest where she was.

When everyone seemed to be within the walls of the mosque, the soldiers began to search the village again, running into and out of the houses, firing into the air. *They* were not short of ammunition, Ellis thought. The helicopter that had stayed in the air flew low and scanned the outskirts of the village in ever-increasing circles, as if searching.

One of the soldiers went into the courtyard of Jane's house.

Ellis felt her go rigid. 'It'll be all right,' he said into her ear.

The soldier entered the building. Ellis and Jane stared fixedly at the door. A few seconds later he came out and quickly ran up the outside staircase.

'Oh, God save her,' whispered Jane.

He stood on the roof, glanced at the rumpled bedding, looked around at the other nearby roofs, and returned his attention to Jane's. Fara's mattress was nearest to him: Chantal was just beyond it. He poked Fara's mattress with his toe.

Suddenly he turned away and ran down the stairs.

Ellis breathed again and looked at Jane. She was ghastly white. 'I told you it would be all right,' he said. She began to shake.

Ellis returned his attention to the mosque. He could

see only a part of the courtyard inside. The villagers appeared to be sitting down in rows, but there was some movement to and fro. He tried to guess what was going on in there. Were they being interrogated about Masud and his whereabouts? There were only three people down there who might know, three guerrillas who were from Banda and who had not melted into the hills with Masud yesterday: Shahazai Gul, the one with the scar; Alishan Karim, the brother of Abdullah the mullah; and Sher Kador, the goat boy. Shahazai and Alishan were both in their forties, and could easily play the part of cowed old men. Sher Kador was only fourteen. All three could plausibly say they knew nothing of Masud. It was fortunate that Mohammed was not here: the Russians would not have believed in his innocence so readily. Their weapons were skilfully hidden in places where the Russians would not look: in the roof of a privy, among the leaves of a mulberry tree, deep in a hole in the river bank.

'Oh, look!' Jane gasped. 'The man in front of the mosque!'

Ellis looked. 'The Russian officer in the peaked hat?'

'Yes. I know who that is – I've seen him before. It's the man who was in the stone hut with Jean-Pierre, it's Anatoly.'

'His contact,' Ellis breathed. He looked hard, trying to make out the man's features: at this distance he seemed somewhat Oriental. What was he like? He had ventured alone into rebel territory to meet with Jean-Pierre, so he must be brave. Today he was certainly angry, for he had led the Russians into a trap at Darg.

He would want to strike back fast, to recover the initiative—

Ellis's speculations were abruptly cut off as another figure emerged from the mosque, a bearded man in an open-neck white shirt and dark Western-style trousers. 'Jesus Christ Almighty,' Ellis said. 'It's Jean-Pierre.'

'Oh!' Jane cried out.

'Now what the hell is going on?' muttered Ellis.

'I thought I'd never see him again,' said Jane. Ellis looked at her. Her face wore an odd expression. After a moment he realized it was a look of remorse.

He returned his attention to the scene in the village. Jean-Pierre was speaking to the Russian officer and gesticulating, pointing up the mountainside.

'He's standing oddly,' said Jane. 'I think he's hurt himself.'

'Is he pointing towards us?' Ellis asked.

'He doesn't know about this place – nobody does. Can he see us?'

'No.'

'We can see him,' she said dubiously.

'But he's standing upright against a plain background. We're lying flat, peeping out from under a blanket, against a mottled hillside. He couldn't spot us unless he knew where to look.'

'Then he must be pointing towards the caves.'

'Yes.'

'He must be telling the Russians to look there.'

'Yes.'

'But that's *awful*. How could he . . .' Her voice tailed off, and after a pause she said: 'But of course that's

331

what he's been doing ever since he got here – betraying people to the Russians.'

Ellis noticed that Anatoly appeared to be speaking into a walkie-talkie. A moment later one of the circling Hinds roared over the hooded heads of Ellis and Jane to land, audible but out of sight, on the hilltop.

Jean-Pierre and Anatoly were walking away from the mosque.

Jean-Pierre was limping. 'He *is* hurt,' said Ellis.

'I wonder what happened?'

It looked to Ellis as if Jean-Pierre had been beaten up, but he did not say so. He was wondering what was going on in Jane's mind. There was her husband, walking with a KGB officer – a Colonel, Ellis thought from the uniform. Here she was, in a makeshift bed with another man. Did she feel guilty? Ashamed? Disloyal? Or unrepentant? Did she hate Jean-Pierre, or was she merely disappointed in him? She had been in love with him: was there any love left? He said: 'How do you *feel* about him?'

She gave Ellis a long, hard look, and for a moment he thought she was going to get mad, but it was only that she was taking his question very seriously. Finally she said: 'Sad.' She turned her gaze back to the village.

Jean-Pierre and Anatoly were heading for Jane's house, where Chantal lay concealed on the roof.

Jane said: 'I think they're looking for me.'

Her expression was drawn and scared as she stared at the two men down below. Ellis did not think the Russians had come all this way with so many men and machines just for Jane, but he did not say so.

332

Jean-Pierre and Anatoly walked through the courtyard of the shopkeeper's house and entered the
building.

'Don't cry, little girl,' whispered Jane.

It was a miracle the baby was still asleep, Ellis
thought. Perhaps she was not: perhaps she was awake
and crying, but her cries were drowned by the noise
of the helicopters. Perhaps the soldiers had not heard
her because there had been a chopper directly overhead at that moment. Perhaps the more sensitive ears
of her father would hear sounds which had failed to
catch the attention of a disinterested stranger.
Perhaps—

The two men came out of the house.

They stood in the courtyard for a moment, talking
intently. Jean-Pierre limped across to the wooden staircase which led to the roof. He mounted the first step
with evident difficulty, then got down again. There was
another short exchange of words, and the Russian
mounted the stairs.

Ellis held his breath.

Anatoly reached the top of the stair and stepped on
to the roof. Like the soldier before him, he glanced at
the scattered bedding, looked around at other houses,
and then returned his attention to this one. Like the
soldier, he poked at Fara's mattress with the toe of his
boot. Then he knelt down beside Chantal.

Gently, he drew back the sheet.

Jane gave an inarticulate cry as Chantal's pink face
came into view.

If they're after Jane, Ellis thought, they will take

Chantal, for they know she would give herself up in order to be reunited with her baby.

Anatoly stared at the tiny bundle for several seconds.

'Oh, God, I can't stand this, I can't stand it,' Jane groaned.

Ellis held her tight and said: 'Wait, wait and see.'

He strained his eyes to make out the expression on the baby's face, but the distance was too great.

The Russian appeared to be thinking.

Suddenly he seemed to make up his mind.

He dropped the sheet, tucked it in around the baby, stood up, and walked away.

Jane burst into tears.

From the roof, Anatoly spoke to Jean-Pierre, shaking his head in negation. Then he descended into the courtyard.

'Now why did he do that?' Ellis mused, thinking aloud. The shake of the head meant that Anatoly was lying to Jean-Pierre, saying: 'There is nobody on the roof.' The implication was that Jean-Pierre would have wanted to take the baby, but Anatoly did not. That meant that Jean-Pierre wanted to find Jane, but the Russian was not interested in her.

So what *was* he interested in?

It was obvious. He was after Ellis.

'I believe I may have fucked up,' Ellis said, mainly to himself. Jean-Pierre wanted Jane and Chantal, but Anatoly was looking for Ellis. He wanted revenge for yesterday's humiliation; he wanted to prevent Ellis returning to the West with the treaty the rebel commanders had signed; and he wanted to put Ellis on trial to prove to the world that the CIA was behind the Afghan rebellion. I should have thought of all this yesterday, Ellis reflected bitterly, but I was flushed with success and thinking only about Jane. Besides, Anatoly could not *know* I was here – I might have been in Darg, or Astana, or hiding out in the hills with Masud – so it must have been a long shot. But it had almost worked. Anatoly had good instincts. He was a formidable opponent – and the battle was not yet over.

Jane was weeping. Ellis stroked her hair and made soothing noises while he watched Jean-Pierre and Anatoly walk back towards the helicopters which were still standing in the fields with their rotors churning the air.

The Hind that had landed on the hilltop near the caves took off again and rose over the heads of Ellis and Jane. Ellis wondered whether the seven wounded guerrillas in the cave clinic had been interrogated or taken prisoner or both.

It ended very quickly. The soldiers came out of the mosque at the double and piled into the Hip as fast as they had emerged. Jean-Pierre and Anatoly boarded one of the Hinds. The ugly aircraft took off one by one, lifting giddily until they were higher than the hill and then speeding southward in a straight line.

Ellis, knowing what was in Jane's mind, said: 'Just wait a few more seconds, until all the choppers have gone – don't spoil everything now.'

She nodded tearful acquiescence.

The villagers began to trickle out of the mosque, looking scared. The last helicopter took off and headed south. Jane scrambled out of the sleeping bag, pulled on her trousers, shrugged into her shirt, and ran off down the hillside, slipping and stumbling and buttoning her shirt as she went. Ellis watched her go, feeling that somehow she had spurned him, knowing that the feeling was irrational, unable nevertheless to shake it. He would not follow her yet, he decided. He would leave her alone for her reunion with Chantal.

She went out of sight beyond the mullah's house. Ellis looked down at the village. It was beginning to return to normal. He could hear voices raised in excited cries. The children were running around playing helicopters or pointing imaginary guns and herding chickens into courtyards to be interrogated. Most of the adults were walking slowly back to their homes, looking cowed.

Ellis remembered the seven wounded guerrillas and the boy with one hand in the cave clinic. He decided he would check on them. He pulled on his clothes, rolled up his sleeping bag, and set off up the mountain path.

He remembered Allen Winderman, in his grey suit and his striped tie, picking over a salad in a Washington restaurant and saying: 'What are the chances that the Russians would catch our man?' *Slender*, Ellis had said. *If they can't catch Masud, why would they be able to catch an undercover agent sent to meet Masud?* Now he knew the answer to that question: because of Jean-Pierre. 'God damn Jean-Pierre,' said Ellis aloud.

He reached the clearing. There was no noise coming from the cave clinic. He hoped the Russians had not

taken the child, Mousa, as well as the wounde
las – Mohammed would be inconsolable.

He went into the cave. The sun was up now a
could see quite clearly. They were all there, lying
and quiet. 'Are you all right?' Ellis asked in Dari.

There was no reply. None of them moved.

'Oh, God,' Ellis whispered.

He knelt beside the nearest guerrilla and touched
the bearded face. The man was lying in a pool of blood.
He had been shot in the head at point-blank range.

Moving quickly, Ellis checked each of them.

They were all dead.

And so was the child.

CHAPTER FIFTEEN

JANE DASHED through the village in a blind panic, pushing people aside, cannoning into walls, stumbling and falling and getting up again, sobbing and panting and moaning all at the same time. 'She must be all right,' she told herself, repeating it like a litany; but just the same her brain kept asking *Why didn't Chantal wake up?* and *What did Anatoly do?* and *Is my baby hurt?*

She stumbled into the courtyard of the shopkeeper's house and climbed the steps two at a time to the roof. She fell on her knees and pulled the sheet off the little mattress. Chantal's eyes were closed. Jane thought: is she breathing? Is she breathing? Then the baby's eyes opened, she looked at her mother, and – for the first time ever – she smiled.

Jane snatched her up and hugged her fiercely, feeling as if her heart would burst. Chantal cried at the sudden squeeze, and Jane cried too, awash with joy and relief because her little girl was still here, still alive and warm and squalling, and because she had just smiled her first smile.

After a while Jane calmed down, and Chantal, sensing the change, became quiet. Jane rocked her, patting

her back rhythmically and kissing the top of her soft bald head. Eventually Jane remembered that there were other people in the world, and she wondered what had happened to the villagers in the mosque, and whether they were all right. She went down into her courtyard, and there she met Fara.

Jane looked at the girl for a moment; silent, anxious Fara, timid and so easily shocked: where had she found the courage and presence of mind and sheer nerve to conceal Chantal under a rumpled sheet while the Russians were landing their helicopters and firing their rifles a few yards away? 'You saved her,' Jane said.

Fara looked frightened, as if it had been an accusation.

Jane shifted Chantal to her left hip and put her right arm around Fara, hugging her. 'You saved my baby!' she said. 'Thank you! Thank you!'

Fara beamed with pleasure for a moment, then burst into tears.

Jane soothed her, patting her back as she had patted Chantal's. As soon as Fara was quiet Jane said: 'What happened in the mosque? What did they do? Is anyone hurt?'

'Yes,' said Fara dazedly.

Jane smiled: you couldn't ask Fara three questions one after another and expect a sensible answer. 'What happened when you went into the mosque?'

'They asked where the American was.'

'Whom did they ask?'

'Everyone. But nobody knew. The doctor asked me where you and the baby were, and I said I didn't know.

Then they picked out three of the men: first my uncle Shahazai, then the mullah, then Alishan Karim the mullah's brother. They asked them again, but it was no use, for the men did not know where the American had gone. So they beat them.'

'Are they badly hurt?'

'Just beaten.'

'I'll take a look at them.' Alishan had a heart condition, Jane recalled anxiously. 'Where are they now?'

'Still in the mosque.'

'Come with me.' Jane went into the house and Fara followed. In the front room Jane found her nursing bag on the shopkeeper's counter. She added some nitroglycerin pills to her regular kit and went out again. As she headed for the mosque, clutching Chantal tightly still, she said to Fara:

'Did they hurt you?'

'No. The doctor seemed very angry, but they didn't beat me.'

Jane wondered whether Jean-Pierre had been angry because he guessed that she was spending the night with Ellis. It occurred to her that the whole village was guessing the same thing. She wondered how they would react. This might be the final proof that she was the Whore of Babylon.

Still, they would not shun her yet, not while there were injured people to be attended to. She reached the mosque and entered the courtyard. Abdullah's wife saw her, bustled over importantly, and led her to where he lay on the ground. At first glance he looked all right, and Jane was worried about Alishan's heart, so she left the mullah – ignoring his wife's indignant protests – and went to Alishan, who was lying nearby.

He was grey-faced and breathing with difficulty, and he had one hand on his chest: as Jane had feared, the beating had brought on an attack of angina. She gave him a tablet, saying: 'Chew, don't swallow it.'

She handed Chantal to Fara and examined Alishan quickly. He was badly bruised, but no bones were broken. 'How did they beat you?' she asked him.

'With their rifles,' he answered hoarsely.

She nodded. He was lucky: the only real damage they had done was to subject him to the stress that was so bad for his heart, and he was already recovering from that. She dabbed iodine on his cuts and told him to lie where he was for an hour.

She returned to Abdullah. However, when the mullah saw her approach he waved her away with an angry roar. She knew what had infuriated him: he thought he was entitled to priority treatment, and he was insulted that she had seen Alishan first. Jane was not going to make excuses. She had told him before that she treated people in order of urgency, not status. Now she turned away. There was no point in insisting on examining the old fool. If he was well enough to yell at her he would live.

She went to Shahazai, the scarred old fighter. He had already been examined by his sister Rabia, the midwife, who was bathing his cuts. Rabia's herbal ointments were not quite as antiseptic as they should be but Jane thought they probably did more good than harm on balance, so she contented herself with making him wiggle his fingers and toes. He was all right.

We were lucky, Jane thought. The Russians came, but we escaped with minor injuries. Thank God. Perhaps now we can hope they will leave us alone for a while – maybe until the route to the Khyber Pass is open again . . .

'Is the doctor a Russian?' Rabia asked abruptly.

'No.' For the first time, Jane wondered just exactly what had been in Jean-Pierre's mind. If he had found me, she thought, what would he have said to me? 'No, Rabia, he's not a Russian. But he seems to have joined their side.'

'So he is a traitor.'

'Yes, I suppose he is.' Now Jane wondered what was in old Rabia's mind.

'Can a Christian divorce her husband for being a traitor?'

In Europe she can divorce him for a good deal less, thought Jane, so she said: 'Yes.'

'Is this why you have now married the American?'

Jane saw how Rabia was thinking. Spending the night on the mountainside with Ellis had, indeed, confirmed Abdullah's accusation that she was a Western whore. Rabia, who had long been Jane's leading supporter in the village, was planning to counter that accusation with an alternative interpretation, according to which Jane had been rapidly divorced from the traitor under strange Christian laws unknown to True Believers and was now married to Ellis under those same laws. So be it, Jane thought. 'Yes,' she said, 'that is why I have married the American.'

Rabia nodded, satisfied.

Jane almost felt as if there were an element of truth in the mullah's epithet. She had, after all, moved from one man's bed to another's with indecent rapidity. She felt a little ashamed, then caught herself: she had never let her behaviour be ruled by other people's expectations. Let them think what they like, she said to herself.

She did not consider herself married to Ellis. Do I feel divorced from Jean-Pierre? she asked herself. The answer was No. However, she *did* feel that her obligations to him had ended. After what he's done, she thought, I don't owe him anything. It should have come as some kind of relief to her, but in fact she just felt sad.

Her musings were interrupted. There was a flurry of activity over at the mosque entrance, and Jane turned around to see Ellis walk in carrying something in his arms. As he came nearer she could see that his face was a mask of rage, and it flashed through her mind that she had seen him like that once before: when a careless taxi driver had made a sudden U-turn and knocked down a young man on a motorcycle, injuring him quite badly. Ellis and Jane had witnessed the whole thing and called the ambulance – in those days she had known nothing of medicine – and Ellis had said over and over again: 'So unnecessary, it was so unnecessary.'

She made out the shape of the bundle in his arms: it was a child, and she realized that his expression meant that the child was dead. Her first, shameful reaction was to think *Thank God it's not my baby*; then, when she looked closely, she saw that it was the one child in the village who sometimes seemed like her own – one-handed Mousa, the boy whose life she had saved. She felt the dreadful sense of disappointment and loss that came when a patient died after she and Jean-Pierre had fought long and hard for his life. But his was especially painful, for Mousa had been brave and determined in coping with his disability; and his father was proud of him. Why him? thought Jane as the tears came to her eyes. Why him?

The villagers clustered around Ellis, but he looked at Jane.

'They are all dead,' he said, speaking Dari so that the others could understand. Some of the village women began to weep.

'How?' Jane asked.

'Shot by the Russians, each one.'

'Oh, my God.' Only last night she had said *None of them will die* – of their wounds, she had meant, but nonetheless she had foreseen each of them getting better, quickly or slowly, and returning to full health and strength under her care. Now – all dead. 'But why did they kill the child?' she cried.

'I think he annoyed them.'

Jane frowned, puzzled.

Ellis shifted his burden slightly so that Mousa's hand came into view. The small fingers were rigidly grasping the handle of the knife his father had given him. There was blood on the blade.

Suddenly a great wail was heard, and Halima pushed through the crowd. She took the body of her son from Ellis and sank to the ground with the dead child in her arms, screaming his name. The women gathered around her. Jane turned away.

Beckoning Fara to follow her with Chantal, Jane left the mosque and walked slowly home. Just a few minutes ago she had been thinking that the village had had a lucky escape. Now seven men and a boy were dead. Jane had no tears left, for she had cried too much: she just felt weak with grief.

She went into the house and sat down to feed Chantal. 'How patient you have been, little one,' she said as she put the baby to her breast.

A minute or two later Ellis came in. He leaned over her and kissed her. He looked at her for a moment, then said: 'You seem angry with me.'

Jane realised that she was. 'Men are so bloody,' she said bitterly. 'That child obviously tried to attack armed Russian troops with his hunting knife – who taught him to be foolhardy? Who told him it was his role in life to kill Russians? When he threw himself at the man with the Kalashnikov, who was his role model? Not his mother. It's his father; it's Mohammed's fault that he died; Mohammed's fault and yours.'

Ellis looked astonished. 'Why mine?'

She knew she was being harsh but she could not stop. 'They beat Abdullah, Alishan and Shahazai in an attempt to make them tell where you were,' she said. 'They were looking for you. That was the object of the exercise.'

'I know. Does that make it my fault that they shot the little boy?'

'It happened because you're here, where you don't belong.'

'Perhaps. Anyway, I have the solution to *that* problem. I'm leaving. My presence brings violence and bloodshed, as you are so quick to point out. If I stay, not only am I liable to get caught – for we were very lucky last night – but my fragile little scheme to start these tribes working together against their common enemy will fall apart. It's worse than that, in fact. The Russians would put me on public trial for the maximum propaganda. "See how the CIA attempts to exploit the internal problems of a Third World country." That sort of thing.'

'You really are big cheese, aren't you?' It seemed odd that what happened here in the Valley, among this small group of peoples should have such great global consequences. 'But you can't go. The route to the Khyber Pass is blocked.'

'There's another way: the Butter Trail.'

'Oh, Ellis . . . it's very hard – and dangerous.' She thought of him climbing those high passes in the bitter winds. He might lose his way and freeze to death in the snow, or be robbed and murdered by the bandits. 'Please don't do that.'

'If I had another choice I'd take it.'

So she would lose him again, and she would be alone. The thought made her miserable. That was surprising. She had only spent one night with him. What had she expected? She was not sure. More, anyway, than this abrupt parting. 'I didn't think I'd lose you again so soon,' she said. She moved Chantal to the other breast.

He knelt in front of her and took her hand. 'You haven't thought this situation through,' he said. 'Think about Jean-Pierre. Don't you know he wants you back?'

Jane considered that. Ellis was right, she realized. Jean-Pierre would now be feeling humiliated and emasculated: the only thing that would heal his wounds would be to have her back, in his bed and in his power. 'But what would he do with me?' she said.

'He will want you and Chantal to live out the rest of your lives in some mining town in Siberia, while he spies in Europe and visits you every two or three years for a holiday between assignments.'

'What could he do if I were to refuse?'

'He could make you. Or he could kill you.'

Jane remembered Jean-Pierre punching her. She felt a little nauseous. 'Will the Russians help him to find me?' she said.

'Yes.'

'But why? Why should they care about me?'

'First because they owe him. Second because they figure you will keep him happy. Third because you know too much. You know Jean-Pierre intimately and you've seen Anatoly: you could provide good descriptions of both of them for the CIA's computer, if you were able to get back to Europe.'

So there would be more bloodshed, Jane thought; the Russians would raid villages, interrogate people, and beat and torture them to find out where she was.

'That Russian officer . . . Anatoly, his name is. He saw Chantal.' Jane hugged her baby tighter for a moment as she remembered those dreadful seconds. 'I thought he was going to pick her up. Didn't he realise that, if he had taken her, I would have given myself up just to be with her?'

Ellis nodded. 'That puzzled me at the time. But I'm more important to them than you are; and I think he decided that, while he wants eventually to capture you, in the meantime he has another use for you.'

'What use? What could they want me to do?'

'Slow me down.'

'By making you stay here?'

'No, by coming with me.'

As soon as he said it she realized he was right, and a sense of doom settled over her like a shroud. She had to go with him, she and her baby; there was no alternative. If we die, we die, she thought fatalistically. So be it. 'I suppose I have a better chance of escaping from here with you than escaping from Siberia alone,' she said.

Ellis nodded. 'That's about it.'

'I'll start packing,' said Jane. There was no time to lose. 'We'd better leave first thing tomorrow morning.'

Ellis shook his head. 'I want to be out of here in an hour.'

Jane panicked. She had been planning to leave, of course, but not so suddenly; and now she felt she did not have time to *think*. She began to rush around the little house, throwing clothes and food and medical

348

supplies indiscriminately into an assortment of bags, terrified that she would forget something crucial but too rushed to pack sensibly.

Ellis understood her mood and stopped her. He held her shoulders, kissed her forehead, and spoke calmly to her. 'Tell me something,' he said. 'Do you happen to know what the highest mountain in Britain is?'

She wondered if he was crazy. 'Ben Nevis,' she said. 'It's in Scotland.'

'How high is it?'

'Over four thousand feet.'

'Some of the passes we're going to climb are sixteen and seventeen thousand feet high – that's *four times* as high as the highest mountain in Britain. Although the distance is only a hundred and fifty miles, it's going to take us at least two weeks. So stop; think; and plan. If you take a little more than an hour to pack, too bad – it's better than going without the antibiotics.'

She nodded, took a deep breath, and started again.

She had two saddlebags that could double as back-packs. Into one she put clothes: Chantal's diapers, a change of underwear for all of them, Ellis's quilted down coat from New York, and the fur-lined raincoat, complete with hood, that she had brought from Paris. She used the other bag for medical supplies and food – iron rations for emergencies. There was no Kendal Mint cake, of course, but Jane had found a local substitute, a cake made of dried mulberries and wal-nuts, almost indigestible but packed with concentrated energy. They also had a lot of rice and a lump of hard cheese. The only souvenir Jane took was her collection of Polaroid photographs of the villagers. They also took their sleeping bags, a saucepan, and Ellis's military kitbag, which contained some explosives and blasting equipment – their only weapon. Ellis lashed all the baggage to Maggie, the unidirectional mare.

Their hurried leave-taking was tearful. Jane was embraced by Zahara, old Rabia the midwife, and even Halima, Mohammed's wife. A sour note was introduced by Abdullah, who passed by just before they left and spat on the ground, hurrying his family along; but a few seconds later his wife came back, looking frightened but determined, and pressed into Jane's hand a present for Chantal, a primitive rag doll with a miniature shawl and veil.

Jane hugged and kissed Fara, who was inconsolable. The girl was thirteen: soon she would have a husband to adore. In a year or two she would marry and move into the home of her husband's parents. She would have eight or ten children, of whom perhaps half would live past the age of five. Her daughters would marry and leave home. Those of her sons who survived the fighting would get married and bring their wives home. Eventually, when the family grew too large, the sons and the daughters-in-law and the grandchildren would begin to move out to start new extended families of their own. Then Fara would become a midwife, like her grandmother Rabia. I hope, Jane thought, that she'll remember a few of the lessons I taught her.

Ellis was embraced by Alishan and Shahazai, and then they left, to cries of 'God go with you!' The village children accompanied them to the bend in the river. Jane paused there and looked back for a moment at the little huddle of mud-coloured houses that had been her home for a year. She knew she would never come back; but she had a feeling that, if she survived, she would be telling stories of Banda to her grandchildren.

They walked briskly along the river bank. Jane found herself straining her hearing for the sound of helicopters. How soon would the Russians start looking for them? Would they send a few helicopters to hunt more or less at random or would they take the time to organize a really thorough search? Jane did not know which to hope for.

It took them less than an hour to reach Dasht-i-Riwat, 'The Plain with a Fort', a pleasant village where the cottages with their shaded courtyards were dotted along the northern bank of the river. Here it was that the cart track – the pitted, snaking, now-you-see-it-now-you-don't dirt path that passed for a road in the Five Lions Valley – came to an end. Any wheeled vehicles robust enough to survive the road had to stop here, so the village did a little business horse trading. The fort mentioned in the name was up a side valley, and was now a prison, run by the guerrillas, housing a few captured government troops, a Russian or two, and the occasional thief. Jane had visited it once, to treat a miserable nomad from the western desert who had been conscripted into the regular army, had contracted pneumonia in the cold Kabul winter, and had deserted. He was being 're-educated' before being allowed to join the guerrillas.

It was midday but neither of them wanted to stop and eat. They hoped to reach Saniz, ten miles away at the head of the Valley, by nightfall; and although ten miles was no great distance on level ground, in this landscape it could take many hours.

The last stretch of the road wound in and out of the houses on the north bank. The south bank was a cliff two hundred feet high. Ellis led the horse and Jane carried Chantal in the sling she had devised, which enabled her to feed Chantal without stopping. The village ended at a water mill close to the mouth of the side valley called the Riwat, which led to the prison. After they had passed that point they were not able to walk so fast. The ground began to slope up, gradually at first and then more steeply. They climbed steadily under the hot sun. Jane covered her head with her *pattu*, the brown blanket all travellers carried. Chantal was shaded by the sling. Ellis wore his Chitrali cap, a gift from Mohammed.

When they reached the summit of the pass she noted, with some satisfaction, that she was not even breathing hard. She had never been this fit in her life – and she probably never would be so again. Ellis was not only panting but perspiring, she observed. He was in quite good shape but he was not as hardened to hours of walking as she was. It made her feel rather smug, until she remembered he had suffered two bullet wounds just nine days ago.

Beyond the pass, the track ran along the mountain-side, high above the Five Lions River. Here, unusually, the river was sluggish. Where it was deep and still the

water appeared bright green, the colour of the emeralds which were found all around Dasht-i-Riwat and
taken to Pakistan to be sold. Jane had a fright when her
hypersensitised ears picked up the sound of distant
aircraft: there was nowhere to hide on the bare cliff
top, and she was seized by a sudden desire to jump off
the cliff into the river a hundred feet below. But it was
only a flight of jets, too high to see anyone on the
ground. Nevertheless, from then on Jane scanned the
terrain constantly for trees, bushes and hollows in
which they might hide. A devil inside her said *You don't
have to do this, you could go back, you could give yourself up
and be reunited with your husband,* but somehow it seemed
an academic question, a technicality.

The path was still climbing, but more gently, so they
made better speed. They were delayed, every mile or
two, by the tributaries which came rushing in from the
side valleys to join the main river: the track would dive
down to a log bridge or a ford. Ellis would have to drag
the unwilling Maggie into the water, with Jane yelling
and throwing stones at her from behind.

An irrigation channel ran the full length of the
gorge, on the cliffside high above the river. Its purpose
was to enlarge the cultivable area in the plain. Jane
wondered how long ago it was that the Valley had had
time and men and peace enough to carry out such a
big engineering project: hundreds of years, perhaps.

The gorge narrowed and the river below was littered
with granite boulders. There were caves in the lime-
stone cliffs: Jane noted them as possible hiding places.
The landscape became bleak and a cold wind blew

down the Valley, making Jane shiver for a moment despite the sunshine. The rocky terrain and the sheer cliffs suited birds: there were scores of Asian magpies.

At last the gorge gave way to another plain. Far to the east, Jane could see a range of hills; and above the hills were visible the white mountains of Nuristan. Oh, my God, that's where we're going, Jane thought; and she was afraid.

·In the plain stood a small cluster of poor houses. 'I guess this is it,' said Ellis. 'Welcome to Saniz.'

They walked into the plain, looking for a mosque or one of those stone huts for travellers. As they drew level with the first of the houses, a figure stepped out of it, and Jane recognised the handsome face of Mohammed. He was as surprised as she. Her surprise gave way to horror when she realised she was going to have to tell him that his son had been killed.

Ellis gave her time to collect her thoughts by saying in Dari: 'Why are you here?'

'Masud is here,' Mohammed replied. Jane realised that this must be a guerrilla hideout. Mohammed went on: 'Why are *you* here?'

'We're going to Pakistan.'

'This way?' Mohammed's face became grave. 'What happened?'

Jane knew she had to be the one to tell him, for she had known him longer. 'We bring bad news, my friend Mohammed. The Russians came to Banda. They killed seven men – and a child . . .' He guessed, then, what she was going to say, and the look of pain on his face made Jane want to cry. 'Mousa was the child,' she finished.

Mohammed composed himself rigidly. 'How did my son die?'

'Ellis found him,' said Jane.

Ellis, struggling to find the Dari words he needed, said: 'He died . . . knife in hand, blood on knife.'

Mohammed's eyes widened. 'Tell me everything.'

Jane took over, because she could speak the language better. 'The Russians came at dawn,' she began. 'They were looking for Ellis and for me. We were up on the mountainside, so they didn't find us. They beat Alishan and Shahazai and Abdullah, but they didn't kill them. Then they found the cave. The seven wounded mujahideen were there, and Mousa was with them, to run to the village if they needed help in the night. When the Russians had gone, Ellis went to the cave. All the men had been killed, and so had Mousa—'

'How?' Mohammed interrupted. 'How was he killed?'

Jane looked at Ellis. Ellis said: 'Kalashnikov,' using a word that needed no translation. He pointed to his heart to show where the bullet had struck.

Jane added: 'He must have tried to defend the wounded men, for there was blood on the point of his knife.'

Mohammed swelled with pride even as the tears came to his eyes. 'He attacked them – grown men, armed with guns – he went for them with his knife! The

355

knife his father gave him! The one-handed boy is now surely in the warrior's heaven.'

To die in a holy war was the greatest possible honour for a Muslim, Jane recalled. Little Mousa would probably become a minor saint. She was glad that Mohammed had that comfort, but she could not help thinking cynically: This is how warlike men assuage their consciences – by talk of glory.

Ellis embraced Mohammed solemnly, saying nothing.

Jane suddenly remembered her photographs. She had several of Mousa. Afghans loved photos anyway, and Mohammed would be overjoyed to have one of his son. She opened one of the bags on Maggie's back and rummaged through the medical supplies until she found the cardboard box of Polaroids. She located a picture of Mousa, took it out, and repacked the bag. Then she handed the picture to Mohammed.

She had never seen an Afghan man so profoundly moved. He was unable to speak. For a moment it seemed that he would weep. He turned away, trying to control himself. When he turned back, his face was composed, but wet with tears. 'Come with me,' he said.

They followed him through the little village to the edge of the river, where a group of fifteen or twenty guerrillas were squatting around a cooking fire. Mohammed strode into the group and without preamble began to tell the story of Mousa's death, with tears and gesticulations.

Jane turned away. She had seen too much grief.

She looked around her anxiously. Where will we run to, if the Russians come? she wondered. There was nothing but the fields, the river and the few hovels. But Masud seemed to think it was safe. Perhaps the village was just too small to attract the attention of the army.

She did not have the energy to worry any more. She sat on the ground with her back to a tree, grateful to rest her legs, and began to feed Chantal. Ellis tethered Maggie and unloaded the bags, and the horse began to graze the rich greenery beside the river. It's been a long day, Jane thought; and a terrible day. And I didn't get much sleep last night. She smiled a secret smile as she remembered the night.

Ellis got Jean-Pierre's maps out and sat beside Jane to study them in the rapidly-fading evening light. Jane looked over his shoulder. Their planned route continued up the valley to a village called Comar, where they would turn south-east into a side valley which led to Nuristan. The valley was also called Comar, and so was the first high pass they would encounter. 'Fifteen thousand feet,' said Ellis, pointing to the pass. 'This is where it gets cold.'

Jane shivered.

When Chantal had drunk her fill, Jane changed her diaper and washed the old one in the river. She returned to find Ellis deep in conversation with Masud. She squatted beside them.

'You have made the right decision,' Masud was saying. 'You must get out of Afghanistan, with our treaty in your pocket. If the Russians catch you, all is lost.'

Ellis nodded agreement. Jane thought: I've never seen Ellis like this before – he treats Masud with deference.

Masud went on: 'However, it is a journey of extra-ordinary difficulty. Much of the trail is above the ice line. Sometimes the path is hard to find in the snow, and if you get lost there, you die.'

Jane wondered where all this was leading. It seemed to her ominous that Masud was carefully addressing Ellis, not her.

'I can help you,' Masud went on. 'But, like you, I want to make a deal.'

'Go on,' said Ellis.

'I will give you Mohammed as a guide, to take you through Nuristan and into Pakistan.'

Jane's heart leaped. Mohammed as a guide! It would make a world of difference to the journey.

'What is my part of the bargain?' Ellis asked.

'You go alone. The doctor's wife and the child stay here.'

It was heartbreakingly clear to Jane that she must agree to this. It was foolhardy for the two of them to try to make it alone – they would probably both die. This way she could at least save Ellis's life. 'You *must* say Yes,' she told him.

Ellis smiled at her and looked at Masud. 'It's out of the question,' he said.

Masud stood up, visibly offended, and walked back to the circle of guerrillas.

Jane said: 'Oh, Ellis, was that wise?'

'No,' he said. He held out his hand. 'But I'm not going to let you go that easily.'

She squeezed his hand. 'I ... I've made you no promises.'

'I know,' he said. 'When we get back to civilization, you're free to do whatever you like – live with Jean-Pierre, if that's what you want, and if you can find him. I'll settle for the next two weeks, if that's all I can get. Anyway, we may not live that long.'

That was true. Why agonise over the future, she thought, when we probably don't have a future anyway?

Masud came back, smiling again. 'I'm not a good negotiator,' he said. 'I'll give you Mohammed anyway.'

CHAPTER SIXTEEN

T HEY TOOK off half an hour before dawn. One by one, the helicopters lifted from the concrete apron and disappeared into the night sky beyond the range of the floodlights. In its turn, the Hind Jean-Pierre and Anatoly were in struggled into the air like an ungainly bird and joined the convoy. Soon the lights of the air base were lost from view, and once again Jean-Pierre and Anatoly were flying over the mountain-tops towards the Five Lions Valley.

Anatoly had worked a miracle. In less than twenty-four hours he had mounted what was probably the largest operation in the history of the Afghan war – and he was in command of it.

He had spent most of yesterday on the phone to Moscow. He had had to galvanise the slumbering bureaucracy of the Soviet army by explaining, first to his superiors in the KGB and then to a series of military bigwigs, just how important it was to catch Ellis Thaler. Jean-Pierre had listened, not understanding the words but admiring the precise combination of authority, calm, and urgency in Anatoly's tone of voice.

Formal permission was given late in the afternoon, and then Anatoly had faced the challenge of putting it into practice. To get the number of helicopters he wanted he had begged favours, called in old debts, and scattered threats and promises from Jalalabad to Moscow. When a general in Kabul had refused to release his machines without a written order, Anatoly had called the KGB in Moscow and persuaded an old friend to sneak a look at the general's private file, then called the general and threatened to cut off his supply of child pornography from Germany.

The Soviets had six hundred helicopters in Afghanistan: by three a.m. five hundred of them were on the tarmac at Bagram, under Anatoly's command.

Jean-Pierre and Anatoly had spent the last hour bent over maps, deciding where each helicopter should go and giving the appropriate orders to a stream of officers. The deployments were precise, thanks to Anatoly's compulsive attention to detail and Jean-Pierre's intimate knowledge of the terrain.

Although Ellis and Jane had not been in the village yesterday when Jean-Pierre and Anatoly went to find them, nevertheless it was almost certain they had heard about the raid and had now gone into hiding. They would not be in Banda. They might be living in a mosque in another village – short-term visitors normally slept in the mosques – or, if they felt the villages were unsafe, they might move into one of the little one-room stone huts for travellers which dotted the countryside. They could be anywhere in the Valley, or they could be in one of the many little side valleys.

Anatoly had all these possibilities covered.

Helicopters would land at every village in the Valley

and every hamlet in every side valley. The pilots would overfly all the trails and footpaths. The troops – more than a thousand of them – were instructed to search every building and look under large trees and inside caves. Anatoly was determined not to fail again. Today they would *find* Ellis.

And Jane.

The interior of the Hind was cramped and bare. There was nothing in the passenger cabin but a bench fixed to the fuselage opposite the door. Jean-Pierre shared it with Anatoly. They could see the flight deck. The pilot's seat was raised two or three feet off the floor, with a step beside it for access. All the money had been spent on machinery – the armament, speed and manoeuvrability of the aircraft – and none on comfort.

As they flew north, Jean-Pierre brooded. Ellis had pretended to be his friend, while working all the time for the Americans. Using that friendship, he had ruined Jean-Pierre's scheme for catching Masud, thereby destroying a year's painstaking work. And finally, Jean-Pierre thought, he seduced my wife.

His mind went in circles, always returning to that seduction. He stared out into the darkness, watching the lights of the other helicopters, and imagined the two lovers as they must have been the night before, lying on a blanket under the stars in some field, playing with one another's bodies and whispering endearments. He wondered whether Ellis was good in bed. He had asked Jane which of them was the better lover, but she said neither was better, they were just different. Was that what she said to Ellis? Or did she murmur

You're the best, baby, the very best? Jean-Pierre was beginning to hate her as well. How *could* she go back to a man who was nine years older than she, a crass American, and a CIA spook?

Jean-Pierre looked at Anatoly. The Russian sat still and blank-faced, like a stone statue of a Chinese mandarin. He had got very little sleep during the previous forty-eight hours, but he did not look tired, just dogged. Jean-Pierre was seeing a new side to the man. In their meetings over the past year Anatoly had been relaxed and affable, but now he was taut, unemotional, and tireless, driving himself and his colleagues relentlessly. He was calmly obsessed.

When dawn broke they could see the other helicopters. It was an awesome sight: they were like a vast cloud of giant bees swarming over the mountains. The noise of their buzzing must have been deafening on the ground.

As they approached the Valley, they began to divide into smaller groups. Jean-Pierre and Anatoly were with the flight going to Comar, the northernmost village of the Valley. For the last stretch of the journey they followed the river. The rapidly-brightening morning light revealed tidy ranks of sheaves in the wheat fields: the bombing had not completely disrupted farming here in the upper Valley.

The sun was in their eyes as they descended to Comar. The village was a cluster of houses peeping over a heavy wall on the hillside: it reminded Jean-Pierre of perched hill-villages in the South of France, and he felt a pang of homesickness. Wouldn't it be good to go home, and hear French spoken properly, and eat fresh bread and tasty food, or get into a taxi and go to the cinema!

He shifted his weight in the hard seat. Right now it would be good just to get out of the helicopter. He had been in pain more or less constantly since the beating. But worse than the pain was the memory of the humiliation, the way he had screamed and wept and begged for mercy: each time he thought of that he flinched, physically, and wished he could hide. He wanted revenge for that. He felt he would never sleep peacefully until he had evened that score. And there was only one way that would satisfy him. He wanted to see Ellis beaten, in the same way, by the same brute soldiers, until he sobbed and screamed and pleaded for mercy, but with one extra refinement: Jane would be watching.

By the middle of the afternoon failure stared them in the face yet again.

They had searched the village of Comar, all the hamlets around it, all the side valleys in the area, and each of the single farmhouses in the almost-barren land to the north of the village. Anatoly was in constant touch with the commanders of the other squads by radio. They had conducted equally thorough searches throughout the entire Valley. They had found arms caches in a few caves and houses; they had fought skirmishes with several groups of men, presumably guerrillas, especially in the hills around Saniz, but the skirmishes had been notable only for greater-than-normal Russian casualties due to the guerrillas' new expertise with explosives; they had looked at the naked faces of all veiled women and examined the skin colour of every tiny baby; and still they had not found Ellis or Jane or Chantal.

Jean-Pierre and Anatoly finished up at a horse station in the hills above Comar. The place had no name: it was a handful of bare stone houses and a dusty meadow where malnourished nags grazed the sparse grass. The only male inhabitant seemed to be the horse coper, a barefoot old man wearing a long nightshirt with a voluminous hood to keep flies off. There were also a couple of young women and a huddle of frightened children. Clearly the young men were guerrillas, and were away somewhere with Masud. The hamlet did not take long to search. When they had done, Anatoly sat in the dust with his back to a stone wall, looking thoughtful. Jean-Pierre sat down beside him.

Across the hills they could see the distant white peak of Mesmer, almost twenty thousand feet high, which had attracted climbers from Europe in the old days. Anatoly said: 'See if you can get some tea.'

Jean-Pierre looked around and saw the old man in the hood lurking nearby. 'Make tea,' he shouted at him in Dari. The man scurried away. A moment later Jean-Pierre heard him shouting at the women. 'Tea is coming,' he said to Anatoly in French.

Anatoly's men, seeing that they were to stay here a while, killed the engines of their helicopters and sat around in the dust, waiting patiently.

Anatoly stared into the distance. Weariness showed on his flat face. 'We are in trouble,' he said.

Jean-Pierre found it ominous that he said *we*.

Anatoly went on: 'In our profession, it is wise to minimise the importance of a mission until one is certain of success, at which point one begins to exaggerate it. In this case I could not follow that pattern. In order to secure the use of two hundred helicopters and a thousand men I had to persuade my superiors of the overwhelming importance of catching Ellis Thaler. I had to make it very clear to them the dangers that face us if he escapes. I succeeded. And their anger at me for *not* catching him will now be all the greater. Your future, of course, is tied to mine.'

Jean-Pierre had not previously thought of it that way. 'What will they do?'

'My career will simply stop. My salary will stay the same but I will lose all privileges. No more Scotch whisky, no more Rive Gauche for my wife, no more family holidays on the Black Sea, no more denim jeans and Rolling Stones records for my children . . . but I could live without those things. What I couldn't stand would be the sheer boredom of the kind of job given to failures in my profession. They would send me to a small town in the Far East where there is really no security work to do. I know how our men spend their time and justify their existence in such places. You have to ingratiate yourself with mildly discontented people, get them to trust you and talk to you, encourage them to make remarks critical of the government and the Party, then arrest them for subversion. It's such a waste of time . . .' He seemed to realise he was rambling, and tailed off.

'And me?' said Jean-Pierre. 'What will happen to me?'

'You'll become a nobody,' said Anatoly. 'You won't work for us any more. They might let you stay in Moscow, but most likely they would send you back.'

'If Ellis gets away, I can never go back to France – they would kill me.'

'You have committed no crime in France.'

'Nor had my father, but they killed him.'

'Maybe you could go to some neutral country – Nicaragua, say, or Eygpt.'

'Shit.'

'But let us not give up hope,' Anatoly said a little more brightly. 'People cannot vanish into thin air. Our fugitives are *somewhere*.'

'If we can't find them with a thousand men, I don't suppose we can find them with ten thousand,' said Jean-Pierre gloomily.

'We shan't have a thousand, let alone ten thousand,' said Anatoly. 'From now on we have to use our brains, and minimal resources. All our credit is used up. Let's try a different approach. Think: somebody must have helped them hide. That means that somebody knows where they are.'

Jean-Pierre considered. 'If they had help it was probably from the guerrillas – the people least likely to tell.'

'Others may *know* about it.'

'Perhaps. But will they tell?'

'Our fugitives must have *some* enemies,' Anatoly persisted.

Jean-Pierre shook his head. 'Ellis hasn't been here long enough to make enemies, and Jane is a heroine – they treat her like Joan of Arc. Nobody dislikes her – oh!' Even as he was speaking he realised it was not true.

'Well?'

'The mullah.'

'Aaah.'

'Somehow she irritated him beyond reason. It was partly that her cures were more effective than his, but not only that, for mine were too but he never disliked me particularly.'

'He probably called her a Western whore.'

'How did you guess?'

'They always do. Where does this mullah live?'

'Abdullah lives in Banda, in a house about half a kilometre outside the village.'

'Will he talk?'

'He probably hates Jane enough to give her away to us,' said Jean-Pierre reflectively. 'But he couldn't be *seen* to do it. We can't just land in the village and pick him up – everyone would know what had happened and he would clam up. I'd have to meet him in secret somehow...' Jean-Pierre wondered what kind of danger he might put himself in if he continued thinking along this line. Then he thought of the humiliation he had suffered: revenge was worth any risk. 'If you drop me near the village I can make my way to the path between the village and his house and hide there until he comes along.'

'What if he doesn't "come along" all day?'

'Yes . . .'

'We'll just have to make sure he does.' Anatoly frowned. 'We'll round up all the villagers in the mosque, as we did before – then just let them go. Abdullah will almost certainly go back to his house.'

'But will he be alone?'

'Hmmm. Suppose we let the women go first, and order them to return to their homes. Then, when the men are released they will all want to check on their wives. Does anyone else live near Abdullah?'

'No.'

'Then he *should* hurry along that footpath all alone. You step out from behind a bush—'

'And he slits my throat from ear to ear.'

'He carries a knife?'

'Did you ever meet an Afghan who didn't?'

Anatoly shrugged. 'You can take my pistol.'

Jean-Pierre was pleased, and a little surprised, to be trusted that much, even though he did not know how to use a gun. 'I suppose it may serve as a threat,' he said anxiously. 'I'll need some native clothes, just in case I'm seen by someone other than Abdullah. What if I meet someone who knows me? I'll have to cover my face with a scarf or something . . .'

'That's easy,' said Anatoly. He shouted something in Russian, and three of the soldiers jumped to their feet. They disappeared into the houses and emerged a few seconds later with the old horse coper. 'You can take his clothes,' said Anatoly.

'Good,' said Jean-Pierre. 'The hood will hide my face.' He switched to Dari and shouted at the old man: 'Take off your clothes.'

The man began to protest: nakedness was terribly shameful to Afghans. Anatoly shouted an abrupt command in Russian and the soldiers threw the man on the ground and pulled off his nightshirt. They all laughed uproariously to see his stick-thin legs poking out of his ragged undershorts. They let him go and he scuttled away with his hands over his genitals, which made them laugh all the more.

Jean-Pierre was too nervous to find it funny. He took off his European-style shirt and trousers and donned the old man's hooded nightshirt.

'You smell of horse piss,' said Anatoly.

'It's even worse from the inside,' Jean-Pierre replied.

They climbed into their helicopter. Anatoly took the pilot's headset and spoke into the radio microphone at length in Russian. Jean-Pierre was very uneasy about what he was about to do. Suppose three guerrillas were to come over the mountain and catch him threatening Abdullah with the gun? He was known by literally everyone in the Valley. The news that he had visited Banda with the Russians would have spread rapidly. Without doubt most people now knew that he had been a spy. He must be Public Enemy Number One. They would tear him apart.

Perhaps we're being too clever, he thought. Maybe

we should just land and pull Abdullah in and beat the truth out of him.

No, we tried that yesterday and it didn't work. This is the only way.

Anatoly gave the headset back to the pilot, who took his seat and began to warm up the helicopter. While they were waiting, Anatoly took out his gun and showed it to Jean-Pierre. 'This is a 9mm Makarov,' he said over the noise of the rotors. He flipped a catch in the heel of the grip and drew out the magazine. It contained eight rounds. He pushed the magazine back in. He pointed to another catch on the left-hand side of the pistol. 'This is the safety catch. When the red dot is covered, the catch is in the "safe" position.' Holding the gun in his left hand, he used his right to pull back the slide above the grip. 'This is how the pistol is cocked.' He released it and it sprang back into position. 'When you fire, give a long pull on the trigger to re-cock the gun.' He handed the weapon to Jean-Pierre.

He really trusts me, Jean-Pierre thought, and for a moment a glow of pleasure took the chill off his fear.

The helicopters took off. They followed the Five Lions River south-west, going down the Valley. Jean-Pierre was thinking that he and Anatoly made a good team. Anatoly reminded him of his father: a clever, determined, brave man with an unshakable commitment to world communism. If we succeed here, Jean-Pierre thought, we will probably be able to work together again, in some other battlefield. The thought pleased him inordinately.

At Dasht-i-Riwat, where the lower Valley began, the helicopter turned south-east, following the tributary Riwat upstream into the hills, in order to approach Banda from behind the mountain.

Anatoly used the pilot's headset again, then came to shout in Jean-Pierre's ear. 'They are all in the mosque already. How long will it take the wife to reach the mullah's house?'

'Five or ten minutes,' Jean-Pierre yelled back.

'Where do you want to be dropped off?'

Jean-Pierre considered. '*All* the villagers are in the mosque, right?'

'Yes.'

'Did they check the caves?'

Anatoly went back to the radio and asked. He returned and said: 'They checked the caves.'

'Okay. Drop me there.'

'How long will it take you to reach your hiding place?'

'Give me ten minutes; then release the women and children, then wait another ten minutes and release the men.'

'Right.'

The helicopter descended into the shadow of the mountain. The afternoon was waning, but there was still an hour or so before nightfall. They landed behind the ridge, a few yards from the caves. Anatoly said to Jean-Pierre: 'Don't go yet. Let us check the caves again.'

Through the open door, Jean-Pierre saw another Hind land. Six men got out and ran over the ridge.

'How will I signal you to come down and pick me up afterwards?' Jean-Pierre asked.

'We'll wait for you here.'

'What will you do if some of the villagers come up here before I return?'

'Shoot them.'

That was something else Anatoly had in common with Jean-Pierre's father: ruthlessness.

The reconnaissance party came back over the ridge and one of the men waved an all-clear sign.

'Go,' said Anatoly.

Jean-Pierre opened the door and jumped out of the helicopter, still holding Anatoly's pistol in his hand. He hurried away from its beating blades with his head bent. When he reached the ridge he looked back: both aircraft were still there.

He crossed the familiar clearing in front of his old cave clinic and looked down into the village. He could just see into the courtyard of the mosque. He was unable to identify any of the figures he saw there, but it was just possible that one of them might glance up at the wrong moment and see him – their eyesight might be better than his – so he pulled the hood forward to obscure his face.

His heart beat faster as he got farther away from the safety of the Russian helicopters. He hurried down the hill and past the mullah's house. The Valley seemed oddly quiet, despite the ever-present noise of the river and the distant whisper of helicopter blades. It was the absence of children's voices, he realised.

He turned a corner and found that he was out of sight of the mullah's house. Beside the footpath was a clump of camelgrass and juniper bushes. He went behind it and crouched down. He was well hidden, but he had a clear view of the footpath. He settled down to wait.

He considered what he would say to Abdullah. The mullah was a hysterical woman-hater: maybe he could use that.

A sudden burst of high voices from far down in the village told him that Anatoly had given instructions for the women and children to be released from the mosque. The villagers would wonder what the whole exercise had been for, but they would attribute it to the notorious craziness of armies everywhere.

A few minutes later the mullah's wife came up the footpath, carrying her baby and followed by three older children. Jean-Pierre tensed: was he really well-hidden here? Would the children run off the path and stumble into his bush? What a humiliation that would be – to be foiled by children. He remembered the gun in his hand. Could I shoot children? he wondered.

They went past and turned the corner towards their house.

Soon afterwards the Russian helicopters began to take off from the wheat field: that meant the men had been released. Right on schedule, Abdullah came puffing up the hill, a tubby figure in a turban and a pin-striped English jacket. There must be a huge trade in used clothes between Europe and the East, Jean-Pierre had decided, for so many of these people wore clothes which had undoubtedly been made in Paris or London and then discarded, perhaps because they became unfashionable, long before they were worn out. This is it, thought Jean-Pierre as the comical figure drew level; this clown in a stockbroker's jacket could hold the key to my future. He got to his feet and stepped out from the bushes.

The mullah started and gave a cry of shock. He looked at Jean-Pierre and recognised him. 'You!' he said in Dari. His hand went to his belt. Jean-Pierre showed him the gun. Abdullah looked frightened.

'Don't be afraid,' Jean-Pierre said in Dari. The unsteadiness of his voice betrayed his jumpiness, and he made an effort to bring it under control. 'No one knows I am here. Your wife and children passed without seeing me. They are safe.'

Abdullah looked suspicious. 'What do you want?'

'My wife is an adulteress,' said Jean-Pierre, and although he was deliberately playing on the mullah's prejudices his anger was not entirely faked. 'She has taken my child and left me. She has gone whoring after the American.'

'I know,' said Abdullah, and Jean-Pierre could see him beginning to swell with righteous indignation.

'I have been searching for her, in order to bring her back and punish her.'

Abdullah nodded enthusiastically, and malice showed in his eyes: he liked the idea of punishing adulteresses.

'But the wicked couple have gone into hiding.' Jean-Pierre was speaking slowly and carefully: at this point every nuance counted. 'You are a man of God. Tell me where they are. No one will ever know how I found out, except you, me and God.'

'They have gone away,' Abdullah spat, and saliva wetted his red-dyed beard.

'Where?' Jean-Pierre held his breath.

'They have left the Valley.'

'*But where did they go?*'

'To Pakistan.'

To Pakistan! What was the old fool talking about? 'The routes are closed!' Jean-Pierre yelled in exasperation.

'Not the Butter Trail.'

'Mon Dieu,' Jean-Pierre whispered in his native tongue. 'The Butter Trail.' He was awestruck by their courage, and at the same time bitterly disappointed, for it would be impossible to find them now. 'Did they take the baby?'

'Yes.'

'Then I'll never see my daughter again.'

'They will all die in Nuristan,' Abdullah said with satisfaction. 'A Western woman with a baby will never survive those high passes, and the American will die trying to save her. Thus God punishes those who escape man's justice.'

Jean-Pierre realised he should get back to the helicopter as quickly as possible. 'Go back to your house, now,' he told Abdullah.

'The treaty will die with them, for Ellis has the paper,' Abdullah added. 'This is a good thing. Although we need the American weapons, it is dangerous to make pacts with infidels.'

'Go!' said Jean-Pierre. 'If you don't want your family to see me, make them stay inside for a few minutes.'

Abdullah looked momentarily indignant at being given orders, but he seemed to realise he was at the wrong end of the gun for protests, and he hurried away.

Jean-Pierre wondered whether they would all die in Nuristan as Abdullah had gloatingly predicted. That was not what he wanted. It would not give him revenge or satisfaction. He wanted his daughter back. He wanted Jane alive and in his power. He wanted Ellis to suffer pain and humiliation.

He gave Abdullah time to get inside his house, then drew the hood over his face and set off disconsolately up the the hill. He kept his face averted as he passed the house in case one of the children should look out.

Anatoly was waiting for him in the clearing in front of the caves. He held out his hand for the pistol and said: 'Well?'

Jean-Pierre gave him back his gun. 'They have escaped us,' he said. 'They've left the Valley.'

'They can't have *escaped* us,' said Anatoly angrily. 'Where have they gone?'

'To Nuristan.' Jean-Pierre pointed in the direction of the helicopters. 'Shouldn't we leave?'

'We can't talk in the helicopters.'

'But if the villagers come—'

'To hell with the villagers! Stop acting defeated! What are they doing in Nuristan?'

'They're heading for Pakistan by a route known as the Butter Trail.'

'If we know their route we can find them.'

'I don't think so. There is one route, but it has variations.'

'We'll overfly them all.'

'You can't follow these paths from the air. You can hardly follow them from the *ground* without a native guide.'

'We can use maps—'

'What maps?' said Jean-Pierre. 'I've seen your maps, and they're no better than my American ones, which are the best available – and they do not show these trails and passes. Don't you know there are regions of the world that have never been properly charted? You're in one of them now!'

'I know – I'm in Intelligence, remember?' Anatoly lowered his voice. 'You're too easily discouraged, my friend. Think. If Ellis can find a native guide to show him the route, then I can do the same.'

Was it possible? Jean-Pierre wondered. 'But there is more than one way to go.'

'Suppose there are ten variations. We need ten native guides to lead ten search parties.'

Jean-Pierre's enthusiasm rose rapidly as he realised that he might yet get Jane and Chantal back and see Ellis captured. 'It might not be that bad,' he said enthusiastically. 'We can simply enquire along the way. Once we are out of this godforsaken Valley people may be less tight-lipped. The Nuristanis aren't as involved in the war as these people.'

'Good,' said Anatoly abruptly. 'It is getting dark. We've got a lot to do tonight. We start early in the morning. Let's go!'

378

CHAPTER SEVENTEEN

JANE WOKE up frightened. She did not know where she was or who she was with or whether the Russians had caught her. For a second she stared up at the exposed underside of a wattle roof, thinking *Is this a prison?* Then she sat up abruptly, her heart hammering, and saw Ellis in his sleeping bag, slumbering with his mouth open, and she remembered: *We're out of the Valley. We escaped. The Russians don't know where we are and they can't find us.*

She lay down again and waited for her heartbeat to return to normal.

They were not following the route Ellis had originally planned. Instead of going north to Comar and then east along the Comar Valley into Nuristan, they had turned back south from Saniz and gone east along the Aryu Valley: Mohammed had suggested this because it got them out of the Five Lions Valley much more quickly, and Ellis had agreed.

They had left before dawn and walked uphill all day, Ellis and Jane taking turns to carry Chantal, Mohammed leading Maggie. At midday they had stopped in the mud-hut village of Aryu and bought bread from a suspicious old man with a snapping dog.

Aryu village had been the limit of civilization: after that there had been nothing for miles but the boulder-strewn river and the great bare ivory-coloured mountains on either side, until they reached this place at the weary end of the afternoon.

Jane sat up again. Chantal lay beside her, breathing evenly and radiating heat like a hot-water-bottle. Ellis was in his own sleeping bag: they could have zipped the two bags together to make one, but Jane had been afraid that Ellis might roll on to Chantal in the night, so they had slept separately and contented themselves with lying close together and reaching out to touch one another now and again. Mohammed was in the adjoining room.

Jane got up carefully, trying not to disturb Chantal. As she put her shirt on and stepped into her trousers, she felt twinges of pain in her back and her legs: she was hardened to walking, but not all day, climbing without respite, on such rough terrain.

She put her boots on without tying the laces and went outside. She blinked against the bright cold light of the mountains. She was in an upland meadow, a vast green field with a stream winding through it. To one side of the meadow the mountain rose steeply, and here at the foot of the slope sheltered a handful of stone houses and some cattle pens. The houses were empty and the cattle had gone: this was a summer pasture, and the cowherds had left for their winter quarters. It was still summer in the Five Lions Valley but at this altitude autumn came in September.

Jane walked over to the stream. It was sufficiently far

from the stone houses for her to slip out of her clothes
without fear of offending Mohammed. She ran into the
stream and quickly immersed herself in the water. It
was searingly cold. She got out again immediately, her
teeth chattering uncontrollably. 'To hell with *this*,' she
said aloud. She would stay dirty until she got back to
civilisation, she resolved.

She put her clothes back on – there was only one
towel, and that was reserved for Chantal – and ran back
to the house, picking up a few sticks on the way. She
laid the sticks over the remains of last night's fire and
blew on the embers until the wood caught. She held
her frozen hands to the flames until they felt normal
again.

She put a pan of water on the fire for washing
Chantal. While she was waiting for it to warm up, the
others woke, one by one: first Mohammed, who went
outside to wash; then Ellis, who complained that he
ached all over; and finally Chantal, who demanded to
be fed and was satisfied.

Jane felt oddly euphoric. She should have been
anxious, she thought, about taking her two-month-old
baby into one of the world's wild places; but somehow
that anxiety was swamped by her happiness. Why am I
happy? she asked herself, and the answer came out of
the back of her mind: because I'm with Ellis.

Chantal also seemed happy, as if she were imbibing
contentment with her mother's milk. They had been
unable to buy food last night, because the cowherds
had left and there was nobody to buy it from. However,
they had some rice and salt, which they had boiled –

not without difficulty, because it took forever to boil water at this altitude. Now for breakfast there was cold leftover rice. That brought Jane's spirits down a little.

She ate while Chantal fed, then washed and changed her. The spare diaper, washed in the stream yesterday, had dried by the fire overnight. Jane put it on Chantal and took the dirty diaper to the stream. She would attach it to the baggage and hope that the wind and the heat of the horse's body would dry it. What would Mummy say about her granddaughter wearing one diaper all day? She would be horrified. Never mind . . .

Ellis and Mohammed loaded the horse and got her pointed in the right direction. Today would be harder than yesterday. They had to cross the mountain range that for centuries had kept Nuristan more or less isolated from the rest of the world. They would climb the Aryu Pass, fourteen thousand feet high. Much of the way they would have to struggle through snow and ice. They hoped to reach the Nuristan village of Linar: it was only ten miles away as the crow flies but they would be doing well to get there by late afternoon.

The sunlight was bright when they set off, but the air was cold. Jane was wearing heavy socks and mittens and an oiled sweater under her fur-lined coat. She carried Chantal in the sling between her sweater and her coat, with the top buttons of the coat undone to let air in.

They left the meadow, following the Aryu river upstream, and immediately the landscape became harsh and hostile again. The cold cliffs were bare of vegetation. Once Jane saw, far in the distance, a huddle of nomads' tents on a bleak slope: she did not know whether to be glad there were other humans around or frightened of them. The only other living thing she saw was a bearded vulture floating in the bitter wind.

There was no visible pathway. Jane was immeasurably glad that Mohammed was with them. At first he followed the river, but when it narrowed and petered out he carried on with undiminished confidence. Jane asked him how he knew the way, and he told her that the route was marked by piles of stones at intervals. She had not noticed them until he pointed them out.

Soon there was a thin layer of snow on the ground, and Jane's feet got cold despite her heavy socks and her boots.

Amazingly, Chantal slept much of the time. Every couple of hours they stopped for a few minutes' rest, and Jane took the opportunity to feed her, wincing as she exposed her tender breasts to the freezing air. She told Ellis that she thought Chantal was being remarkably good, and he said: 'Unbelievably. Unbelievably.'

At midday they stopped within sight of the Aryu Pass for a welcome half-hour rest. Jane was already tired, and her back hurt. She was also starving hungry – she wolfed the mulberry-and-walnut cake they had for lunch.

The approach to the pass was terribly daunting. Looking at that steep climb, Jane lost heart. I think I'll sit here a little longer, she thought; but it was cold, and she began to shiver, and Ellis noticed and stood up.

'Let's go, before we're frozen to the spot,' he said brightly, and Jane thought: I wish you wouldn't be so bloody cheerful.

She stood up with an effort of will.

Ellis said: 'Let me carry Chantal.'

Jane handed the baby over gratefully. Mohammed led the way, heaving on Maggie's rein. Wearily, Jane forced herself to follow. Ellis brought up the rear.

The slope was steep and the ground slippery with snow. After a few minutes Jane was more tired than she had been before they stopped to rest. As she stumbled along, panting and aching, she recalled saying to Ellis *I suppose I have a better chance of escaping from here with you than of escaping from Siberia alone.* Perhaps I can't manage either, she thought now. I didn't know it was going to be like this. Then she caught herself. Of course you knew, she said to herself; and you know it's going to get worse before it gets better. Snap out of it, you pathetic creature. At that moment she slipped on an icy rock and fell sideways. Ellis, just behind her, caught her arm and held her upright. She realised that he was watching her carefully, and she felt a surge of love for him. Ellis cherished her in a way Jean-Pierre never had. Jean-Pierre would have walked on ahead, assuming that if she needed help she would ask for it; and if she had complained about that attitude he would have asked whether she wanted to be treated as an equal or not.

They were almost at the summit. Jane leaned forward to take the incline, thinking: Just a little more, just a little more. She felt dizzy. In front of her, Maggie skidded on the loose rocks and then scampered up the last few feet, forcing Mohammed to run alongside. Jane plodded after her, counting the steps. At last she reached the level ground. She stopped. Her head was spinning. Ellis's arm went around her, and she closed her eyes and leaned on him.

'From now on it's downhill all day,' he said.

She opened her eyes. She could never have imagined such a cruel landscape: nothing but snow, wind, mountains and loneliness for ever and ever. 'What a godforsaken place this is,' she said.

They looked at the view for a minute, then Ellis said: 'We must keep going.'

They walked on. The way down was steeper. Mohammed, who had been heaving on Maggie's rein all the way up, now hung on to her rein to act as a brake and prevent the horse slithering out of control down the slippery slope. The cairns were hard to distinguish among the litter of loose snow-covered rocks, but Mohammed showed no hesitation about which way to go. Jane thought she should offer to take Chantal, to give Ellis a reprieve, but she knew she could not carry her.

As they descended, the snow thinned and then cleared, and the track was visible. Jane kept hearing an odd whistling sound, and eventually found the energy to ask Mohammed what it was. In reply he used a Dari word she did not know. He did not know the French equivalent. In the end he pointed, and Jane saw a small squirrel-like animal scuttling out of the way: a marmot. Afterwards she saw several more, and wondered what they found to eat up here.

Soon they were walking alongside another brook, heading downstream now, and the endless grey-and-white rock was relieved by a little coarse grass and a few low bushes on the banks of the stream; but still the wind hurtled up the gorge and penetrated Jane's clothing like needles of ice.

Just as the climb had become relentlessly worse, so the descent got easier and easier: the path growing smoother, the air warmer, and the landscape friendlier. Jane was still exhausted but she no longer felt oppressed and downcast. After a couple of miles they reached the first village in Nuristan. The men there wore thick sleeveless sweaters with a striking black-and-white pattern, and spoke a language of their own which Mohammed could barely understand. However, he managed to buy bread with some of Ellis's Afghan money.

Here Jane was tempted to plead with Ellis that they stop for the night, for she felt desperately weary; but there were still several hours of daylight left, and they had agreed they would try to reach Linar today, so she bit her tongue and forced her aching legs to walk on.

To her immense relief the remaining four or five miles were easier, and they arrived well before nightfall. Jane sank to the ground underneath an enormous mulberry tree and simply sat still for a while. Mohammed lit a fire and began to make tea.

Mohammed somehow let it be known that Jane was a Western nurse, and later, while she was feeding and changing Chantal, a little group of patients gathered, waiting at a respectful distance. Jane summoned her energy and saw them. There were the usual infected wounds, intestinal parasites and bronchial complaints, but there were fewer malnourished children here than in the Five Lions Valley, presumably because the war had not much affected this remote wilderness.

As a result of the impromptu clinic, Mohammed got a chicken which he boiled in their saucepan. Jane would have preferred to go to sleep, but she made herself wait for the food and ate ravenously when it came. It was stringy and tasteless, but she was hungrier than she had ever been in her life.

Ellis and Jane were given a room in one of the village houses. There was a mattress for them and a crude wooden crib for Chantal. They joined their sleeping bags together and made love with weary tenderness. Jane enjoyed the warmth and the lying down almost as much as the sex. Afterwards, Ellis fell asleep instantly. Jane lay awake for a few minutes. Her muscles seemed to hurt more now that she was relaxing. She thought about lying on a real bed in an ordinary bedroom, with street lights shining through the curtains and car doors slamming outside, and a bathroom with a flush toilet and hot-water tap, and a shop on the corner where you could buy cotton buds and Pampers and Johnson's No-More-Tears Baby Shampoo. We escaped from the Russians, she thought as she drifted off to sleep; maybe we really will make it home. Maybe we really will.

Jane woke when Ellis did, sensing his sudden tension. He lay rigid beside her for a moment, not breathing, listening to the sound of two dogs barking. Then he slipped out of bed fast.

The room was pitch dark. She heard a match scrape, then a candle flickered in the corner. She looked at Chantal: the baby was sleeping peacefully. 'What is it?' she said to Ellis.

'I don't know,' he whispered. He pulled on his jeans, stepped into his boots, and put on his coat, then he went out.

Jane threw on some clothes and followed him. In the next room, moonlight coming through the open door revealed four children in a row in a bed, all staring wide-eyed over the edge of their shared blanket. Their parents were asleep in another room. Ellis was in the doorway, looking out.

Jane stood beside him. Up on the hill she could see, by the moonlight, a lone figure, running towards them.

'The dogs heard him,' Ellis whispered.

'But who is he?' said Jane.

Suddenly there was another figure beside them. Jane gave a start, then recognised Mohammed. The blade of a knife glinted in his hand.

The figure came closer. His gait seemed familiar to Jane. Suddenly Mohammed gave a grunt and lowered the knife. 'Ali Ghanim,' he said.

Jane now recognised the distinctive stride of Ali, who ran that way because his back was slightly twisted. 'But why?' she whispered.

Mohammed stepped forward and waved. Ali saw him, waved back, and ran to the hut where the three of them stood. He and Mohammed embraced.

Jane waited impatiently for Ali to catch his breath. At last he said: 'The Russians are on your trail.'

Jane's heart sank. She had thought they had escaped. What had gone wrong?

Ali breathed hard for a few seconds longer then went on: 'Masud has sent me to warn you. The day you left, they searched the whole Five Lions Valley for you, with hundreds of helicopters and thousands of men. Today, having failed to find you, they sent search parties to follow each valley leading to Nuristan.'

'What's he saying?' Ellis interrupted.

Jane held up a hand to stop Ali while she translated to Ellis who could not follow Ali's rapid, breathless speech.

Ellis said: 'How did they know we had gone to Nuristan? We might have decided to hide out anywhere in the damn country.'

Jane asked Ali. He did not know.

'Is there a search party in this valley?' Jane asked Ali.

'Yes. I overtook them just before the Aryu Pass. They may have reached the last village by nightfall.'

'Oh, no,' said Jane despairingly. She translated for Ellis. 'How can they move so much faster than us?' she said. Ellis shrugged, and she answered the question herself: 'Because they're not slowed down by a woman with a baby. Oh, shit.'

Ellis said: 'If they start early in the morning they'll catch us tomorrow.'

'What can we do?'

'Leave now.'

Jane felt the weariness in her bones, and she was

filled with an irrational resentment against Ellis. 'Can't we hide somewhere?' she said irritably.

'Where?' said Ellis. 'There's only one road here. The Russians have enough men to search all the houses – there aren't many. Besides, the local people aren't necessarily on our side. They might easily tell the Russians where we're hiding. No, our only hope is to stay ahead of the searchers.'

Jane looked at her watch. It was two a.m. She felt ready to give up.

'I'll load the horse,' Ellis said. 'You feed Chantal.' He switched to Dari and said to Mohammed: 'Will you make some tea? And give Ali something to eat.'

Jane went back into the house, finished dressing, then fed Chantal. While she was doing that, Ellis brought her sweet green tea in a pottery bowl. She drank it gratefully.

As Chantal sucked, Jane wondered how much Jean-Pierre had to do with this relentless pursuit of her and Ellis. She knew he had helped with the raid on Banda, for she had seen him. When they searched the Five Lions Valley his local knowledge would have been invaluable. He must know they were hunting down his wife and baby like dogs chasing rats. How could he bring himself to help them? His love must have been changed to hatred by his seething resentment and jealousy.

Chantal had had enough. How pleasant it must be, Jane thought, to know nothing of passion or jealousy or betrayal, to have no feelings but warm or cold and full or empty. 'Enjoy it while you may, little girl,' she said.

Hurriedly, she buttoned her shirt and pulled her heavy oiled sweater over her head. She put the sling around her neck, made Chantal comfortable inside it, then shrugged into her coat and went outside.

Ellis and Mohammed were studying the map by the light of a lantern. Ellis showed Jane their route. 'We follow the Linar down to where it empties into the Nuristan river, then we turn uphill again, following the Nuristan north. Then we take one of these side valleys – Mohammed won't be sure which one until he gets there – and head for the Kantiwar Pass. I'd like to get out of the Nuristan Valley today – that will make it more difficult for the Russians to follow us, for they won't be sure which side valley we've taken.'

'How far is it?' said Jane.

'It's only fifteen miles – but whether that's easy or tough depends on the terrain, of course.'

Jane nodded. 'Let's get going,' she said. She was proud of herself for sounding more cheerful than she felt.

They set off in the moonlight. Mohammed set a fast pace, and whipped the horse mercilessly with a leather strap when she hung back. Jane had a slight headache and an empty, nauseous feeling in her stomach. However, she was not sleepy, but rather nervously tense and bone-weary.

She found the track scary by night. Sometimes they walked in the sparse grass beside the river, which was all right; but then the trail would hairpin up the mountainside to continue on the cliff edge hundreds of feet above, where the ground was covered with snow, and Jane was terrified of slipping and falling to her death with her baby in her arms.

Sometimes there was a choice: the path forked, one way going up and the other down. Since none of them knew which route to take they let Mohammed guess. The first time, he stayed low and turned out to be right: the track led them across a little beach where they had to wade through a foot of water, but it saved them a long diversion. However, the second time they had to choose, they again took the river bank, but this time they regretted it: after a mile or so the path led straight into a sheer rock face, and the way around it would have been to swim. Wearily they retraced their steps to the fork and then climbed the cliff path.

At the next opportunity they descended to the river bank again. This time the path led them to a ledge which ran along the face of the cliff about a hundred feet above the river. The horse became nervous, probably because the path was so narrow. Jane was frightened too. The starlight was not enough to illuminate the river below, so the gorge seemed like a bottomless black pit beside her. Maggie kept stopping, and Mohammed would have to heave on the rein to make her go again.

When the path turned blindly around an abutment in the cliff, Maggie refused to go around the corner, and became skittish. Jane backed away, wary of the horse's shuffling rear feet. Chantal began to cry, either because she sensed the moment of tension or because she had not gone back to sleep after her two a.m. feed.

Ellis gave Chantal to Jane and went forward to help Mohammed with the horse.

Ellis offered to take the rein, but Mohammed refused ungraciously: the tension was getting to him. Ellis contented himself with pushing the beast from behind and yelling *hup* and *git* at it. Jane was just thinking that it was almost funny when Maggie reared, Mohammed dropped the rein and stumbled, and the mare backed into Ellis and knocked him off his feet and kept coming.

Fortunately Ellis fell to the left, against the cliff wall. When the horse backed into Jane she found herself on the wrong side of it, with her feet at the edge of the path as it pushed past her. She grabbed hold of a bag that was lashed to its harness, holding on like grim death in case it should nudge her sideways over the precipice. 'You stupid beast!' she screamed. Chantal, squashed between Jane and the horse, screamed too. Jane was carried along for several feet, afraid to loose her hold. Then, taking her life in her hands, she let go of the bag, reached out with her right hand and grabbed the bridle, got a firm footing, pushed past the horse's forequarter to stand beside her head, tugged hard on the bridle and said 'Stop!' in a loud voice.

Somewhat to her surprise, Maggie stopped.

Jane turned around. Ellis and Mohammed were getting to their feet. 'Are you all right?' she asked them in French.

'Just about,' said Ellis.

'I lost the lantern,' said Mohammed.

Ellis said in English: 'I just hope the fucking Russians have the same problems.'

Jane realised that they had not seen how the horse had almost pushed her over the edge. She decided not to tell them. She found the leading rein and gave it to Ellis. 'Let's keep going,' she said. 'We can lick our wounds later.' She walked past Ellis and said to Mohammed: 'Lead the way.'

Mohammed cheered up after a few minutes without Maggie. Jane wondered whether they really needed a horse, but she decided they did: there was too much baggage for them to carry, and all of it was essential – indeed they probably should have brought more food.

They hurried through a silent, sleeping hamlet, just a handful of houses and a waterfall. In one of the cottages a dog barked hysterically until someone silenced it with a curse. Then they were in the wilderness again.

The sky was turning from black to grey, and the stars had gone: it was getting light. Jane wondered what the Russians were doing. Perhaps the officers would now be rousing the men, shouting to wake them and kicking those who were slow to climb out of their sleeping bags. A cook would be making coffee while the commanding officer studied his map. Or perhaps they had got up early, an hour or two ago, while it was still dark, and had set out within minutes, marching in single file alongside the river Linar; perhaps they had already passed through the village of Linar; perhaps they had taken all the right forks and were even now just a mile or so behind their quarry.

Jane walked a little faster.

The ledge meandered along the cliff and then dropped down to the river bank. There were no signs of agriculture, but the mountain slopes on either side were thickly wooded, and as the light brightened, Jane identified the trees as holly oak. She pointed them out to Ellis, saying: 'Why can't we hide in the woods?'

'As a last resort, we could,' he said. 'But the Russians would soon realise we had stopped, because they would question villagers and be told we had not passed through; so they would turn back and start searching intensively.'

Jane nodded resignedly. She was just looking for excuses to stop.

Just before sunrise they rounded a bend and stopped short: a landslide had filled the gorge with earth and loose rock, blocking it completely.

Jane felt like bursting into tears. They had walked two or three miles along the bank and that narrow ledge: to turn back meant an extra five miles, including the section that had so frightened Maggie.

The three of them stood for a moment looking at the blockage. 'Could we climb it?' said Jane.

'The horse can't,' said Ellis.

Jane was mad at him for stating the obvious. 'One of us could go back with the horse,' she said impatiently. 'The other two could rest while waiting for the horse to catch up.'

'I don't think it's wise to get separated.'

Jane resented his my-decision-is-final tone of voice.

'Don't assume we'll all do what *you* happen to think is wise,' she snapped.

He looked startled. 'All right. But I also think that mound of earth and stones might shift if someone tried to climb it. In fact, I might as well say that I'm not going to try it, regardless of what you two might decide.'

'So you won't even discuss it. I see.' Furious, Jane turned around and started back along the track, leaving the two men to follow her. Why was it, she wondered, that men slipped into that bossy, know-it-all mode whenever there was a physical or mechanical problem?

Ellis was not without his faults, she reflected. He could be woolly-minded: for all his talk about being an anti-terrorist expert, still he worked for the CIA which was probably the largest group of terrorists in the world. There was undeniably a side of him that liked danger, violence and deceit. Don't pick a macho romantic, she thought, if you want a man to respect you.

One thing that could be said for Jean-Pierre was that he never patronised women. He might neglect you, deceive you or ignore you but he would never condescend to you. Perhaps it was because he was younger.

She passed the place where Maggie had reared. She did not wait for the men: they could cope with the damn horse themselves this time.

Chantal was grizzling but Jane made her wait. She strode on until she reached a point where there seemed to be a pathway up to the cliff top. There she sat down and unilaterally declared a rest. Ellis and Mohammed caught up with her a minute or two later. Mohammed got some mulberry-and-walnut cake out of the baggage and handed it around. Ellis did not speak to Jane.

After the break they climbed the hillside. When they reached the top they emerged into sunshine, and Jane began to feel a little less angry. After a while Ellis put his arm around her and said: 'I apologise for assuming command.'

'Thank you,' Jane said stiffly.

'Do you think that maybe you might have over-reacted a little bit?'

'No doubt I did. Sorry.'

'You bet. Let me take Chantal.'

Jane handed the baby over. As the weight lifted she realised that her back was aching. Chantal had never *seemed* heavy, but the burden told over a long distance. It was like carrying a bag of shopping for ten miles.

The air became milder as the sun climbed the morning sky. Jane opened her coat and Ellis took his off. Mohammed retained his Russian uniform great-coat, with characteristic Afghan indifference to all but the most severe changes in the weather.

Towards noon they emerged from the narrow gorge of the Linar into the broad Nuristan Valley. Here the way was once again quite clearly marked, the path being almost as good as the cart track which ran up the Five Lions Valley. They turned north, going upstream and uphill.

Jane felt terribly tired and discouraged. After getting up at two a.m. she had walked for ten hours – but they had only covered four or five miles. Ellis wanted to do another ten miles today. It was Jane's third consecutive day on the march, and she knew she could not continue until nightfall. Even Ellis was wearing the bad-tempered expression which, Jane knew, was a sign he was weary. Only Mohammed seemed tireless.

In the Linar Valley they had seen no one outside the villages, but here there were a few travellers, most of them wearing white robes and white turbans. The Nuristanis looked with curiosity at the two pale, exhausted Westerners, but greeted Mohammed with wary respect, no doubt because of the Kalashnikov slung over his shoulder.

As they trudged uphill beside the Nuristan River they were overtaken by a black-bearded, bright-eyed young man carrying ten fresh fish speared on a pole. He spoke to Mohammed in a mixture of languages – Jane recognised some Dari and the occasional Pashto word – and they understood one another well enough for Mohammed to buy three of the fish.

Ellis counted out the money, and said to Jane: 'Five hundred afghanis per fish – how much is that?'

'Five hundred afghanis is fifty French francs – five pounds.'

'Ten bucks,' said Ellis. 'Expensive fish.'

Jane wished he would stop jabbering: it was as much as she could do to put one foot in front of the other, and he was talking about the price of fish.

The young man, whose name was Halam, said he had caught the fish in Lake Mundol, farther down the valley, although he had probably bought them, for he did not look like a fisherman. He slowed his pace to walk with them, talking volubly, apparently not much concerned about whether they understood him or not.

Like the Five Lions Valley, the Nuristan was a rocky canyon which broadened, every few miles, into small cultivated plains with terraced fields. The most noticeable difference was the forest of holly oak which covered the mountainsides here like the wool on a sheep's back, and which Jane thought of as her hiding-place should all else fail.

They were making better time now. There were no infuriating diversions up the mountain, for which Jane was deeply thankful. In one place the road was blocked by a landfall, but this time Ellis and Jane were able to climb over it, and Mohammed and the horse forded the river and came back across a few yards upstream. A little later, when an abutment jutted into the stream, the road continued around the cliff face on a shaky wooden trestle which the horse refused to tread on, and once again Mohammed solved the problem by crossing the water.

By this time Jane was near to collapse. When Mohammed came back across the river she said: 'I need to stop and rest.'

Mohammed said: 'We are almost at Gadwal.'

'How far is it?'

Mohammed conferred with Halam in Dari and French, then said: 'One half-hour.'

It seemed like forever to Jane. Of *course* I can walk for another half-hour, she told herself, and tried to think of something other than the ache in her back and the need to lie down.

But then, when they turned the next bend, they saw the village.

It was a startling sight as well as a welcome one: the wooden houses scrambled up the steep mountainside like children clambering on one another's backs, giving the impression that if one house at the bottom were to collapse, the whole village would come tumbling down the hill and fall into the water.

As soon as they drew alongside the first house, Jane simply stopped and sat down on the river bank. Every muscle in her body ached, and she hardly had the strength to take Chantal from Ellis, who sat down beside her with a readiness that suggested he, too, was wiped out. A curious face looked out from the house, and Halam immediately began to talk to the woman, presumably telling her what he knew about Jane and Ellis. Mohammed tethered Maggie where she could graze the coarse grass on the river bank, then squatted beside Ellis.

'We must buy bread and tea,' Mohammed said.

Jane thought they all needed something more substantial. 'What about the fish?' she said.

Ellis said: 'It would take too long to clean and cook it. We'll have that for tonight. I don't want to spend more than half an hour here.'

'All right,' said Jane, although she was not sure she would be able to carry on after only half an hour. Perhaps some food would revive her, she thought.

Halam called to them. Jane looked up and saw him beckoning. The woman did the same: she was inviting them into her house. Ellis and Mohammmed got to their feet. Jane put Chantal down on the ground, stood up, then bent down to pick up the baby. Suddenly her vision blurred at the edges and she seemed to lose her balance. For a moment she fought it, seeing only Chantal's tiny face surrounded by a haze; then her knees became weak and she sank to the ground, and everything went dark.

When she opened her eyes she saw a circle of anxious faces above her: Ellis, Mohammed, Halam, and the woman. Ellis said: 'How do you feel?'

'Foolish,' she said. 'What happened?'

'You fainted.'

She sat upright. 'I'll be all right.'

'No, you won't,' said Ellis. 'You can't go any farther today.'

Jane's head was clearing. She knew he was right. Her body would not take any more, and no effort of will would change that. She started to speak French so that Mohammed could understand. 'But the Russians are sure to reach here today.'

'We'll have to hide,' said Ellis.

Mohammed said: 'Look at these people. Do you think they could keep a secret?'

Jane looked at Halam and the woman. They were watching, riveted by the conversation even though they could not understand a word of it. The arrival of the foreigners was probably the most exciting event of the year. In a few minutes the whole of the village would be here. She studied Halam. Telling him not to gossip would be like telling a dog not to bark. The location of their hideout would be known all over Nuristan by nightfall. Was it possible to get away from these people, and sneak off up a side valley unobserved? Perhaps. But they could not live indefinitely without help from the local people – at some point their food would run out, and that would be at about the time the Russians realised they had stopped and began searching the woods and canyons. Ellis had been right, earlier in the day, when he said their only hope was to stay ahead of their pursuers.

Mohammed drew heavily on his cigarette, looking thoughtful. He spoke to Ellis. 'You and I will have to go on, and leave Jane behind.'

'No,' said Ellis.

Mohammed said: 'The piece of paper you have, which bears the signatures of Masud, Kamil and Azizi, is more important than the life of any one of us. It represents the future of Afghanistan – the freedom for which my son died.'

Ellis would have to go on alone, Jane realised. At least he could be saved. She was ashamed of herself for the terrible despair she felt at the thought of losing him. She should be trying to figure out how to help him, not wondering how she could keep him with her. Suddenly she had an idea. 'I could divert the Russians,' she said. 'I could let myself be captured, then, after a show of reluctance, I could give Jean-Pierre all sorts of false information about which way you were headed and how you were travelling ... If I sent them off completely the wrong way you might gain several days' lead – enough to get you safely out of the country!' She became enthusiastic about the idea even while in her heart she was thinking *Don't leave me, please don't leave me.*

Mohammed looked at Ellis. 'It's the only way, Ellis,' he said.

'Forget it,' said Ellis. 'It isn't going to happen.'

'But, Ellis—'

'It isn't going to happen,' Ellis repeated. 'Forget it.'

Mohammed shut up.

Jane said: 'But what are we going to do?'

'The Russians won't catch up with us today,' Ellis said. 'We still have a lead – we got up so early this morning. We'll stay here tonight and start early again tomorrow. Remember, it isn't over until it's over. Anything could happen. Somebody back in Moscow could decide that Anatoly is out of his mind and order the search called off.'

'Bullshit,' said Jane in English, but secretly she was glad, against all reason, that he had refused to go on alone.

'I have an alternative suggestion,' said Mohammed. 'I will go back and divert the Russians.'

Jane's heart leaped. Was it possible?

Ellis said: 'How?'

'I will offer to be their guide and interpreter, and I will lead them south down the Nuristan Valley, away from you, to lake Mundol.'

Jane thought of a snag, and her heart sank again. 'But they must have a guide already,' she said.

'He may be a good man from the Five Lions Valley

who has been forced to help the Russians against his will. In that case I will speak with him and arrange things.'

'What if he won't help?'

Mohammed considered. 'Then he is not a good man who has been forced to help them, but a traitor who willingly collaborates with the enemy for personal gain; in which case I will kill him.'

'I don't want anyone killed for my sake,' she said quickly.

'It's not for you,' Ellis said harshly. 'It's for me – I refused to go on alone.'

Jane shut up.

Ellis was thinking about practicalities. He said to Mohammed: 'You're not dressed like a Nuristani.'

'I will change clothes with Halam.'

'You don't speak the local language well.'

'There are many languages in Nuristan. I will pretend to come from a district where they use a different tongue. The Russians speak none of these languages anyway, so they will never know.'

'What will you do with your gun?'

Mohammed thought for a moment. 'Will you give me your bag?'

'It's too small.'

'My Kalashnikov is the type that has a folding butt.'

'Sure,' said Ellis. 'You can have the bag.'

Jane wondered whether it would attract suspicion, but decided not: Afghans' bags were as strange and varied as their clothes. All the same, Mohammed would surely arouse suspicion sooner or later. She said: 'What will happen when they finally realise they are on the wrong trail?'

'Before that happens I will run away in the night, leaving them in the middle of nowhere.'

'It's terribly dangerous,' said Jane.

Mohammed tried to look heroically unconcerned. Like most of the guerrillas, he was genuinely brave but also ludicrously vain.

Ellis said: 'If you time this wrongly, and they suspect you before you've decided to leave them, they will torture you to find out which way we went.'

'They will never take me alive,' said Mohammed.

Jane believed him.

Ellis said: 'But we will have no guide.'

'I shall find you another one.' Mohammed turned to Halam and began a rapid multilingual conversation. Jane gathered that Mohammed was proposing to hire Halam as a guide. She did not like Halam much – he was too good a salesman to be entirely trustworthy – but he was obviously a travelling man, so he was a natural choice. Most of the local people had probably never ventured outside their own valley.

'He says he knows the way,' said Mohammed, reverting to French. Jane suffered a twinge of anxiety about the words *He says*. Mohammed went on: 'He will take you to Kantiwar, and there he will find another guide to take you across the next pass, and in this way you will proceed to Pakistan. He will charge five thousand afghanis.'

Ellis said: 'It sounds like a fair price, but how many more guides will we have to hire at that rate before we reach Chitral?'

'Maybe five or six,' said Mohammed.

Ellis shook his head. 'We don't have thirty thousand afghanis. And we have to buy food.'

'You will have to get food by holding clinics,' Mohammed said. 'And the way becomes easier once you are in Pakistan. Perhaps you will not need guides at the end.'

Ellis looked dubious. 'What do you think?' he asked Jane.

'There's an alternative,' she said. 'You could go on without me.'

'No,' he said. 'That's not an alternative. We'll go on together.'

CHAPTER EIGHTEEN

ALL THE first day, the search parties found no trace of Ellis and Jane.

Jean-Pierre and Anatoly sat on hard wooden chairs in a spartan, windowless office at the Bagram air base, monitoring the reports as they came in over the radio network. The search parties had left before dawn – again. There were six of them at the start: one for each of the five main side valleys leading east from the Five Lions, and one to follow the Five Lions River north to its source and beyond. Each of the parties included at least one Dari-speaking officer from the Afghan regular army. They landed their helicopters at six different villages in the Valley, and half an hour later all six had reported that they had found local guides.

'That was quick,' said Jean-Pierre after the sixth reported in. 'How did they do it?'

'Simple,' said Anatoly. 'They ask someone to be a guide. He says no. They shoot him. They ask someone else. It doesn't take long to find a volunteer.'

One of the search parties tried to follow its assigned trail from the air, but the experiment was a failure. The trails were rather difficult to follow from the ground; impossible from the air. Furthermore, none of the guides had ever been in an aircraft before and the new experience was totally disorienting. So all the search parties went on foot, some with commandeered horses to carry their baggage.

Jean-Pierre did not expect any further news in the morning, for the fugitives had a full day's start. However, the soldiers would certainly move faster than Jane, especially as she was carrying Chantal—

Jean-Pierre felt a stab of guilt every time he thought of Chantal. His rage at what his wife was doing did not extend to his daughter, yet the baby was suffering, he felt sure: trekking all day, crossing passes above the snow line, blasted by icy winds . . .

His mind turned, as it often did nowadays, to the question of what would happen if Jane died and Chantal survived. He pictured Ellis captured, alone; Jane's body found a mile or two back, dead of the cold, with the baby still miraculously alive in her arms. I would arrive back in Paris a tragic, romantic figure, thought Jean-Pierre; a widower with a baby daughter, a veteran of the war in Afghanistan . . . How they would lionise me! I'm perfectly capable of bringing up a baby. What an intense relationship we would have as she grew older. I'd have to hire a nanny, of course, but I'd make sure she did not take the place of a mother in the child's affections. No, I would be both father and mother to her.

The more he thought about it, the more outraged he felt that Jane was risking Chantal's life. Surely she had forfeited all her parental rights by taking her baby on such an escapade. He thought he could probably get legal custody of the child in a European court on this basis . . .

As the afternoon wore on, Anatoly grew bored and Jean-Pierre became tense. They were both tetchy. Anatoly held long conversations in Russian with other officers who came into the windowless little room, and their interminable jabbering got on Jean-Pierre's nerves. At first Anatoly had translated all the radio reports of the search parties, but now he would just say 'Nothing.' Jean-Pierre had been plotting the routes of the parties on a set of maps, marking their locations with red pins, but by the end of the afternoon they were following trails or dried-up river-beds which were not on the maps, and if their radio reports gave clues to their whereabouts, Anatoly was not passing them on.

The parties made camp at nightfall without reporting any signs of the fugitives. The searchers had been instructed to question the inhabitants of the villages through which they passed. The villagers were saying they had seen no foreigners. This was not surprising, for the searchers were still on the Five Lions side of the great passes leading to Nuristan. The people they were questioning were generally loyal to Masud: to them, helping the Russians was treason. Tomorrow, when the search parties passed into Nuristan, the people would be more co-operative.

Nevertheless Jean-Pierre felt dispirited as he and Anatoly left the office at nightfall and walked across the concrete to the canteen. They ate a vile dinner of tinned sausages and reconstituted mashed potato, then Anatoly went off moodily to drink vodka with some brother officers, leaving Jean-Pierre in the care of a sergeant who spoke only Russian. They played chess once, but – to Jean-Pierre's chagrin – the sergeant was far too good. Jean-Pierre retired early and lay awake on a hard army mattress, visualising Jane and Ellis in bed together.

Next morning he was awakened by Anatoly, his Oriental face wreathed in smiles, all irritation gone, and Jean-Pierre felt like a bad child who has been forgiven, although as far as he knew he had done nothing wrong. They ate their breakfast porridge together in the canteen. Anatoly had already talked to each of the search parties, all of which had struck camp and set off again at dawn. 'Today we will catch your wife, my friend,' said Anatoly cheerfully, and Jean-Pierre felt a surge of happy optimism.

As soon as they reached the office, Anatoly radioed to the searchers again. He asked them to describe what they could see all around them, and Jean-Pierre used their descriptions of streams, lakes, depressions and moraines to guess their locations. They seemed to be moving terribly slowly in terms of kilometres per hour, but of course they were going uphill on difficult terrain, and the same factors would slow Ellis and Jane.

Each search party had a guide, and when they came to a place where the trail forked and both ways led to Nuristan, they would conscript an additional guide from the nearest village and split into two groups. By noon Jean-Pierre's map was spotted with little red pinheads like a case of the measles.

In the middle of the afternoon there was an unexpected distraction. A bespectacled general on a five-day fact-finding tour of Afghanistan landed at Bagram and decided to find out how Anatoly was spending the Russian taxpayers' money. This Jean-Pierre learned in a few words from Anatoly seconds before the general burst into the little office, followed by anxious officers like ducklings hurrying after the mother duck.

Jean-Pierre was fascinated to see how masterfully Anatoly handled the visitor. He sprang to his feet, looking energetic but unruffled; shook the general's hand and gave him a chair; barked a series of orders through the open door; spoke rapidly but deferentially to the general for a minute or so; excused himself and spoke into the radio; translated for Jean-Pierre's benefit the reply that came crackling through the atmosphere from Nuristan; and introduced the general to Jean-Pierre in French.

The general began to ask questions, and Anatoly pointed to the pin-heads on Jean-Pierre's map as he replied. Then, in the middle of it all, one of the search parties called in unbidden, an excited voice jabbering in Russian, and Anatoly shushed the general in mid-sentence to listen.

Jean-Pierre sat on the edge of his hard seat and longed for a translation.

The voice stopped. Anatoly asked a question and got a reply.

'What did he see?' blurted Jean-Pierre, unable to keep silent any longer.

Anatoly ignored him for a moment and spoke to the general. At last he turned to Jean-Pierre. 'They have found two Americans at a village called Atati in the Nuristan Valley.'

'Wonderful!' said Jean-Pierre. 'It's them!'

'I suppose so,' said Anatoly.

Jean-Pierre could not understand his lack of enthusiasm. 'Of course it is! Your troops don't know the difference between American and English.'

'Probably not. But they say there is no baby.'

'No baby!' Jean-Pierre frowned. How could that be? Had Jane left Chantal behind in the Five Lions Valley, to be brought up by Rabia or Zahara or Fara? It seemed impossible. Had she hidden the baby with a family in this village – Atati – just a few seconds before being caught by the search party? That, too, seemed unlikely: Jane's instinct would be to keep the baby close to her in times of danger.

Was Chantal dead?

It was probably a mistake, he decided: some error of communication, atmospheric interference on the radio link, or even a purblind officer in the search party who simply had not seen the tiny baby.

'Let's not speculate,' he said to Anatoly. 'Let's go and see.'

'I want you to go with the pick-up squad,' said Anatoly.

'Of course,' said Jean-Pierre, then he was struck by Anatoly's phrasing. 'Do you mean to say you're not coming?'

'Correct.'

'Why not?'

'I'm needed here.' Anatoly shot a glance at the general.

'All right.' There were power games within the military bureaucracy, no doubt: Anatoly was afraid to leave a base while the general was still prowling around in case some rival should get a chance to slander him behind his back.

Anatoly picked up the desk phone and gave a series of orders in Russian. While he was still speaking, an orderly came into the room and beckoned Jean-Pierre. Anatoly put his hand over the mouthpiece and said: 'They'll give you a warm coat – it's already winter in Nuristan. *A bientot.*'

Jean-Pierre went out with the orderly. They walked across the concrete apron. Two helicopters were waiting, rotors spinning: a bug-eyed Hind with rocket pods slung under its stubby wings, and a Hip, rather bigger, with a row of portholes along its fuselage. Jean-Pierre wondered what the Hip was for then realised it was to bring back the search party. Just before they reached the machines, a soldier ran up to them with a uniform greatcoat and gave it to Jean-Pierre. He slung it over his arm and boarded the Hind.

They took off immediately. Jean-Pierre was in a fever of anticipation. He sat on the bench in the passenger cabin with half a dozen troops. They headed north-east.

When they were clear of the air base, the pilot beckoned Jean-Pierre. Jean-Pierre went forward and stood on the step so that the pilot could speak to him.

'I will be your translator,' the man said in hesitant French.

'Thank you. You know where we're headed?'

'Yes, sir. We have the co-ordinates, and I can speak by radio with the leader of the search party.'

'Fine.' Jean-Pierre was surprised to be treated with such deference. It seemed he had acquired honorary rank by association with a KGB Colonel.

He wondered, as he returned to his seat, how Jane would look when he walked in. Would she be relieved? Defiant? Or just exhausted? Ellis would be angry and humiliated, of course. How should I act? wondered Jean-Pierre. I want to make them squirm, but I must remain dignified. What should I say?

He tried to visualise the scene. Ellis and Jane would be in the courtyard of some mosque, or sitting on the earth floor of a stone hut, possibly tied up, guarded by soldiers with Kalashnikovs. They would probably be cold, hungry and miserable. Jean-Pierre would stride in, wearing his Russian greatcoat, looking confident and commanding, followed by deferential junior officers. He would give them a long, penetrating look and say—

What would he say? *We meet again* sounded terribly melodramatic. *Did you really think you could escape from us?* was too rhetorical. *You never stood a chance* was better, but a little anti-climatic.

The temperature dropped fast as they headed into the mountains. Jean-Pierre put on his coat and stood by the open door, looking down. Below him was a valley something like the Five Lions, with a river at its centre flowing in the shadows of the mountains. There was snow on the peaks and ridges to either side, but none in the valley itself.

Jean-Pierre went forward to the flight deck and spoke into the pilot's ear. 'Where are we?'

'This is called the Sakardara Valley,' the man replied. 'As we go north its name changes to the Nuristan Valley. It takes us all the way to Atati.'

'How much longer?'

'Twenty minutes.'

It sounded like forever. Controlling his impatience with an effort, Jean-Pierre went back to sit on the bench among the troops. They sat still and quiet, watching him. They seemed afraid of him. Perhaps they thought he was in the KGB.

I *am* in the KGB, he thought suddenly.

He wondered what the troops were thinking about. Girlfriends and wives back home, perhaps? Their home would be his home, from now on. He would have an apartment in Moscow. He wondered whether he could possibly have a happy married life with Jane now. He wanted to install her and Chantal in his apartment while he, like these soldiers, would fight the good fight in foreign countries and look forward to going home on leave, to sleep with his wife again and see how his daughter had grown. I betrayed Jane and she betrayed me, he thought; perhaps we can forgive one another, if only for the sake of Chantal.

What had happened to Chantal?

He was about to find out. The helicopter lost height. They were almost there. Jean-Pierre stood up to look out of the door again. They were coming down to a meadow where a tributary joined the main river. It was a pretty spot, with just a few houses sprawling up the hillside, each overlapping the one beneath in the Nuristani manner: Jean-Pierre remembered seeing photographs of such villages in coffee-table books about the Himalayas.

The helicopter touched down.

Jean-Pierre jumped to the ground. On the other side of the meadow, a group of Russian soldiers – the search party, undoubtedly – emerged from the lowest of a mound of wooden houses. Jean-Pierre waited impatiently for the pilot, his interpreter. Finally the man got out of the helicopter. 'Let's go!' said Jean-Pierre and started off across the field.

He restrained himself from breaking into a run. Ellis and Jane were probably in the house from which the search party was emerging, he thought, and he headed that way at a fast walk. He began to feel angry: long-suppressed rage was churning up inside him. To hell with being dignified, he thought; I'm going to tell this loathsome couple just what I think of them.

As he neared the search party, the officer at the head of the group began speaking. Ignoring him, Jean-Pierre turned to his pilot and said: 'Ask him where they are.'

The pilot asked, and the officer pointed to the wooden house. Without further ado Jean-Pierre went past the soldiers to the house.

His anger was at boiling point as he stormed into the crude building. Several more of the search party stood

416

in a group in one corner. They looked at him, then made way for him.

In the corner were two people tied to a bench.

Jean-Pierre stared at them, shocked. His mouth fell open and the blood drained from his face. There was a thin, anaemic-looking boy of eighteen or nineteen with long, dirty hair and a droopy moustache; and a large-bosomed blonde girl with flowers in her hair. The boy looked at Jean-Pierre with relief and said in English: 'Hey, man, will you help us? We are in deep shit.'

Jean-Pierre felt as if he would explode. They were just a couple of hippies on the Katmandu trail, a species of tourist which had not quite died out despite the war. What a disappointment! Why did they have to be here just when the whole world was looking for a runaway Western couple?

Jean-Pierre certainly was not going to help a pair of drug-taking degenerates. He turned around and went out.

The pilot was just coming in. He saw the expression on Jean-Pierre's face and said: 'What's the matter?'

'It's the wrong couple. Come with me.'

The man hurried after Jean-Pierre. 'The wrong people? These are not the Americans?'

'They're Americans, but they're not the people we're looking for.'

'What are you going to do now?'

'I'm going to speak to Anatoly, and I need you to get him on the radio for me.'

They crossed the field and climbed into the helicopter. Jean-Pierre sat in the gunner's seat and put on the headphones. He tapped his foot impatiently on the metal floor as the pilot talked interminably over the radio in Russian. At last Anatoly's voice came on, sounding very distant and punctuated with atmospheric crackling.

'Jean-Pierre, my friend, here is Anatoly. Where are you?'

'I'm at Atati. The two Americans they have captured are not Ellis and Jane. Repeat, they are not Ellis and Jane. They're just a couple of foolish kids looking for nirvana. Over.'

'This does not surprise me, Jean-Pierre,' Anatoly's voice came back.

'What?' Jean-Pierre interrupted, forgetting that communication was one-way.

' – have received a series of reports that Ellis and Jane have been seen in the Linar Valley. The search party has not made contact with them but we are hot on their trail. Over.'

Jean-Pierre's anger about the hippies evaporated and some of his eagerness came back. 'The Linar Valley – where is that? Over.'

'Near where you are now. It runs into the Nuristan Valley fifteen or twenty miles south of Atati. Over.'

So close! 'Are you sure? Over.'

'The search party got several reports in the villages they passed through. The descriptions fit Ellis and Jane. And they mention a baby. Over.'

Then it *was* them. 'Can we figure out where they are now? Over.'

'Not yet. I'm on my way to join the search party. Then I'll get more details. Over.'

'You mean you're not at Bagram? What happened to your, ah . . . visitor? Over.'

'He left,' Anatoly said briskly. 'I'm in the air now and about to meet the team at a village called Mundol. It's in the Nuristan Valley, downstream of the point where the Linar joins the Nuristan, and it's near a big lake which is also called Mundol. Join me there. We'll spend the night there and then supervise the search in the morning. Over.'

'I'll be there!' said Jean-Pierre elatedly. He was struck by a thought. 'What are we going to do with these hippies? Over.'

'I'll have them taken to Kabul for interrogation. We have some people there who will remind them of the reality of the material world. Let me speak to your pilot. Over.'

'See you in Mundol. Over.'

Anatoly began speaking in Russian to the co-pilot, and Jean-Pierre took off his headset. He wondered why Anatoly wanted to waste time interrogating a pair of harmless hippies. They obviously weren't spies. Then it occurred to him that the only person who really *knew* whether or not these two were Ellis and Jane was Jean-Pierre himself. It was possible – even if wildly unlikely – that Ellis and Jane might have persuaded him to let them go and tell Anatoly that his search party had just captured a couple of hippies.

He was a suspicious bastard, that Russian.

Jean-Pierre waited impatiently for him to finish talking to the pilot. It sounded as if the search party down in Mundol was close to its quarry. Tomorrow, perhaps, Ellis and Jane would be caught. Their attempt to escape had always been more or less futile, in reality; but that did not stop Jean-Pierre worrying, and he would be in this agony of suspense until the two of them were bound hand and foot and locked into a Russian cell.

The pilot took off the headset and said: 'We will take you to Mundol in this helicopter. The Hip will take the others back to base.'

'Okay.'

A few minutes later they were in the air, leaving the others to take their time. It was almost dark, and Jean-Pierre wondered whether it would prove difficult to find the village of Mundol.

Night fell rapidly as they headed downstream. The landscape below disappeared into darkness. The pilot spoke constantly on the radio, and Jean-Pierre imagined that the people on the ground at Mundol were guiding him. After ten or fifteen minutes, powerful lights appeared below. A kilometre or so beyond the lights, the moon glinted off the surface of a large body of water. The helicopter went down.

It landed near another helicopter in a field. A waiting trooper led Jean-Pierre across the grass to a village on a hillside. The silhouettes of the wooden houses were limned with moonlight. Jean-Pierre followed the trooper into one of the houses. There, sitting on a folding chair and wrapped in an enormous coat of wolf fur, was Anatoly.

He was in an ebullient mood. 'Jean-Pierre, my French friend, we are close to success!' he said loudly. It was odd to see a man with an Oriental face being hearty and jovial. 'Have some coffee – there's vodka in it.'

Jean-Pierre accepted a paper cup from an Afghan woman who appeared to be waiting on Anatoly. He sat down on a folding chair like Anatoly's. They looked Army, these chairs. If the Russians were carrying this much equipment – folding chairs and coffee and paper cups and vodka – perhaps they would not move faster than Ellis and Jane, after all.

Anatoly read his mind. 'I brought a few little luxuries in my helicopter,' he said with a smile. 'The KGB has its dignity, you know.'

Jean-Pierre could not read the expression on his face and did not know whether he was joking or not. He changed the subject.

'What's the latest news?'

'Our fugitives definitely passed through the villages of Bosaydur and Linar today. At some point this afternoon the search party lost its guide – he just disappeared. He probably decided to go home.' Anatoly frowned, as if bothered by that little loose end, then resumed his story. 'Fortunately, they found another guide almost immediately.'

'Employing your usual highly persuasive recruiting technique, no doubt,' said Jean-Pierre.

'No, oddly enough. This one was a genuine volunteer, they tell me. He's here in the village somewhere.'

'Of course, they're more likely to volunteer here in

Nuristan,' Jean-Pierre mused. 'They're hardly involved in the war – and in any case they're said to be totally without scruples.'

'This new man claims actually to have seen the fugitives today, before he joined us. They passed him at the point where the Linar flows into the Nuristan. He saw them turn south, heading this way.'

'Good!'

'Tonight, after the search party arrived here in Mundol, our man questioned some villagers and learned that two foreigners with a baby passed through this afternoon, going south.'

'Then there's no doubt,' said Jean-Pierre with satisfaction.

'None at all,' Anatoly agreed. 'We'll catch them tomorrow. For sure.'

Jean-Pierre woke up on an inflatable mattress – another KGB luxury – on the dirt floor of the house. The fire had gone out during the night and the air was cold. Anatoly's bed, across the dim little room, was empty. Jean-Pierre did not know where the owners of the house spent the night. After they had provided food and served it, Anatoly had sent them away. He treated the whole of Afghanistan as if it were his personal kingdom. Perhaps it was.

Jean-Pierre sat up and rubbed his eyes, then saw Anatoly standing in the doorway, looking at him speculatively. 'Good morning,' said Jean-Pierre.

'Have you ever been here before?' Anatoly said without preamble.

Jean-Pierre's brain was still foggy with sleep. 'Where?'

'Nuristan,' Anatoly replied impatiently.

'No.'

'Strange.'

Jean-Pierre found this enigmatic style of conversation irritating so early in the morning. 'Why?' he said tetchily. 'Why is it strange?'

'I was talking to the new guide a few minutes ago.'

'What's his name?'

'Mohammed, Muhammed, Mahomet, Mahmoud – one of those names a million other people have.'

'What language did you use, with a Nuristani?'

'French, Russian, Dari, and English – the usual mixture. He asked me who arrived in the second helicopter last night. I said: "A Frenchman who can identify the fugitives," or words to that effect. He asked your name, so I told him: I wanted to keep him going until I found out why he was so interested. But he didn't ask any more questions. It was almost as if he knew you.'

'Impossible.'

'I suppose so.'

'Why don't you just ask him?' It was not like Anatoly to be diffident, Jean-Pierre thought.

'There is no point in asking a man a question until you have established whether he has any reason to lie to you.' With that, Anatoly went out.

Jean-Pierre got up. He had slept in his shirt and underwear. He pulled on his trousers and boots then draped the greatcoat over his shoulders and stepped outside.

He found himself on a rough wooden verandah overlooking the whole valley. Down below, the river coiled between the fields, broad and sluggish. Some way to the south it entered a long, narrow lake rimmed with mountains. The sun had not yet risen. A mist over the water obscured the far end of the lake. It was a pleasant scene. Of course, Jean-Pierre remembered, this was the most fertile and populous part of Nuristan: most of the rest was wilderness.

The Russians had dug a field latrine, Jean-Pierre noted with approval. The Afghan practice of using the streams from which they took their drinking water was the reason they all had worms. The Russians will really knock this country into shape once they get control of it, he thought.

He walked down to the meadow, used the latrine, washed in the river, and got a cup of coffee from a group of soldiers standing around the cooking fire.

The search party was ready to leave. Anatoly had decided, last night, that he would direct the search from here, remaining in constant radio contact with the searchers. The helicopters would stay ready to take him and Jean-Pierre to join the searchers as soon as they sighted their quarry.

While Jean-Pierre was sipping his coffee, Anatoly came across the field from the village. 'Have you seen that damned guide?' he asked abruptly.

'No.'

'He seems to have disappeared.'

Jean-Pierre raised his eyebrows. 'Just like the last one.'

'These people are impossible. I'll have to ask the villagers. Come and translate.'

'I don't speak their language.'

'Maybe they'll understand your Dari.'

Jean-Pierre walked with Anatoly back across the meadow to the village. As they climbed the narrow dirt path between the rickety houses, somebody called to Anatoly in Russian. They stopped and looked to the side. Ten or twelve men, some Nuristanis in white and some Russians in uniform, were crowded together on a verandah looking at something on the ground. They parted to let Anatoly and Jean-Pierre through. The thing on the floor was a dead man.

The villagers were jabbering in outraged tones and pointing to the body. The man's throat had been cut: the wound gaped horribly and the head hung loose. The blood had dried – he had probably been killed yesterday.

'Is this Mohammed, the guide?' Jean-Pierre asked.

'No,' said Anatoly. He questioned one of the soldiers, then said: 'This is the *previous* guide, the one who disappeared.'

Jean-Pierre addressed the villagers slowly in Dari. 'What is going on?'

After a pause, a wrinkled old man with a bad occlusion in his right eye replied in the same language. 'He has been murdered,' he said accusingly.

Jean-Pierre began to question him and, bit by bit, the story emerged. The dead man was a villager from the Linar Valley who had been conscripted as guide by the Russians. His body, hastily concealed in a clump of bushes, had been found by a goatherd's dog. The man's family thought the Russians had murdered him, and they had brought the body here this morning in a dramatic attempt to find out why.

Jean-Pierre explained to Anatoly. 'They're outraged because they think your men killed him,' he finished.

'Outraged?' said Anatoly. 'Don't they know there's a war on? People are getting killed every day – that's the whole idea.'

'Obviously they don't see much action here. *Did* you kill him?'

'I'll find out.' Anatoly spoke to the soldiers. Several of them answered together in animated tones. 'We didn't kill him,' Anatoly translated to Jean-Pierre.

'So who did, I wonder? Could the locals be murdering our guides for collaborating with the enemy?'

'No,' said Anatoly. 'If they hated collaborators they wouldn't be making this fuss about one who got killed. Tell them we're innocent – calm them down.'

Jean-Pierre spoke to the one-eyed man. 'The foreigners did not kill this man. They want to know who murdered their guide.'

The one-eyed man translated this, and the villagers reacted with consternation.

Anatoly looked thoughtful. 'Perhaps the disappearing Mohammed killed this man in order to get the job of guide.'

'Are you paying much?' Jean-Pierre asked.

'I doubt it.' Anatoly asked a sergeant and translated the answer. 'Five hundred afghanis a day.'

'It's a good wage, to an Afghan, but hardly worth killing for – although they do say a Nuristani will murder you for your sandals if they're new.'

'Ask them if they know where Mohammed is.'

Jean-Pierre asked. There was some discussion. Most of the villagers were shaking their heads, but one man raised his voice above the others and pointed insistently to the north. Eventually the one-eyed man said to Jean-Pierre: 'He left the village early this morning. Abdul saw him go north.'

'Did he leave before or after this body was brought here?'

'Before.'

Jean-Pierre told Anatoly, and added: 'I wonder why he went away, then?'

'He's acting like a man guilty of *something*.'

'He must have left immediately after he spoke to you this morning. It's almost as if he went because I had arrived.'

Anatoly nodded thoughtfully. 'Whatever the explanation is, I think he knows something we don't. We'd better go after him. If we lose a little time, too bad – we can afford it, anyway.'

'How long ago was it that you spoke to him?'

Anatoly looked at his watch. 'A little over an hour.'

'Then he can't have got far.'

'Right.' Anatoly turned away and gave a rapid series of orders. The soldiers were suddenly galvanised. Two of them got hold of the one-eyed man and marched him down towards the field. Another ran to the helicopters. Anatoly took Jean-Pierre's arm and they walked briskly after the soldiers. 'We will take the one-eyed man, in case we need an interpreter,' Anatoly said.

By the time they reached the field the two helicopters were cranking. Anatoly and Jean-Pierre boarded one of them. The one-eyed man was already inside, looking at once thrilled and terrified. He'll be telling the story of this day for the rest of his life, thought Jean-Pierre.

A few minutes later they were in the air. Both Anatoly and Jean-Pierre stood near the open door and looked down. A well-beaten path, clearly visible, led from the village to the top of the hill then disappeared into the trees. Anatoly spoke into the pilot's radio then explained to Jean-Pierre: 'I have sent some troopers to beat those woods, just in case he decided to hide.'

The runaway had almost certainly gone farther than this, Jean-Pierre thought, but Anatoly was being cautious – as usual.

They flew parallel with the river for a mile or so then reached the mouth of the Linar. Had Mohammed continued up the valley, into the cold heart of Nuristan, or had he turned east, into the Linar Valley, heading for Five Lions?

Jean-Pierre said to the one-eyed man: 'Where did Mohammed come from?'

'I don't know,' said the man. 'But he was a Tajik.'

That meant he was more likely to be from the Linar Valley than the Nuristan. Jean-Pierre explained to

Anatoly, and Anatoly directed the pilot to turn left and follow the Linar.

This was a telling illustration, Jean-Pierre thought, of why the search for Ellis and Jane could not be conducted by helicopter. Mohammed had only an hour's start, and already they might have lost track of him. When the fugitives were a whole day ahead, as Ellis and Jane were, there were very many more alternative routes and places to hide.

If there was a track along the Linar Valley, it was not visible from the air. The helicopter pilot simply followed the river. The hillsides were bare of vegetation, but not yet snow-covered, so that if the fugitive were here, he would have nowhere to hide.

They spotted him a few minutes later.

His white robes and turban stood out clearly against the grey-brown ground. He was striding out along the cliff top with the steady, tireless pace of Afghan travellers, his possessions in a bag slung over his shoulder. When he heard the noise of the helicopters he stopped and looked back at them, then continued walking.

'Is that him?' said Jean-Pierre.

'I think so,' said Anatoly. 'We'll soon find out.' He took the pilot's headset and spoke to the other helicopter. It went on ahead, passing over the figure on the ground, and landed a hundred metres or so in front of him. He walked towards it unconcernedly.

'Why don't we land, too?' Jean-Pierre asked Anatoly.

'Just a precaution.'

The side door of the other helicopter opened and six troopers got out. The man in white walked towards them, unslinging his bag. It was a long bag, like a military kitbag, and the sight of it rang a bell in Jean-Pierre's memory; but before he could figure out what it reminded him of, Mohammed hefted the bag and pointed it at the troopers, and Jean-Pierre realised what he was about to do and opened his mouth to shout a useless warning.

It was like trying to shout in a dream, or run under water: events moved slowly but he moved even slower. Before words could come he saw the snout of a machine-gun emerge from the bag.

The sound of shooting was drowned by the noise of the helicopters, which gave the weird impression that it all took place in dead silence. One of the Russian troops clutched his belly and fell forward; another threw up his arms and fell back; and the face of a third exploded in blood and flesh. The other three got their weapons raised. One died before he could pull the trigger, but the other two unleashed a storm of bullets, and even as Anatoly was yelling '*Niet! Niet! Niet! Niet!*' into the radio, the body of Mohammed was lifted off the ground and thrown backwards to land in a bloody heap on the cold ground.

Anatoly was still shouting furiously into the radio. The helicopter went down fast. Jean-Pierre found himself trembling with excitement. The sight of battle had given him a high like cocaine, making him feel as if he wanted to laugh, or fuck, or run, or dance. The thought flashed across his mind: I used to want to *heal* people.

The helicopter touched down. Anatoly pulled off the headset, saying disgustedly: 'Now we'll never know why that guide got his throat cut.' He jumped out, and Jean-Pierre followed him.

They walked over to the dead Afghan. The front of his body was a mass of torn flesh, and most of his face had gone, but Anatoly said: 'It's that guide, I'm sure. The build is right, the colouring is right, and I recognize the bag.' He bent down and carefully picked up the machine-gun. 'But why is he carrying a machine-gun?'

A piece of paper had fallen out of the bag and fluttered to the ground. Jean-Pierre picked it up and looked at it. It was a Polaroid photograph of Mousa. 'Oh, my God,' he said. 'I think I understand this.'

'What is it?' said Anatoly. 'What do you understand?'

'The dead man is from the Five Lions Valley,' Jean-Pierre said. 'He is one of Masud's top lieutenants. This is a photograph of his son, Mousa. The photograph was taken by Jane. I also recognise the bag in which he concealed his gun: it used to belong to Ellis.'

'So what?' said Anatoly impatiently. 'What do you conclude from that?'

Jean-Pierre's brain was in overdrive, working things out faster than he could explain them. 'Mohammed killed your guide in order to take his place,' he began. 'You had no way of knowing he was not what he claimed to be. The Nuristanis knew that he was not one of them, of course, but that didn't matter, because (a) they didn't know he was pretending to be a local and (b) even if they had they couldn't have told you because he was also your interpreter. In fact there was only one person who could possibly find him out . . .'

'You,' said Anatoly. 'Because you knew him.'

'He was aware of that danger and he was on the lookout for me. That's why this morning he asked you who it was that arrived after dark yesterday. You told him my name. He left immediately.' Jean-Pierre frowned: something was not quite right. 'But why did he stay out in the open? He could have concealed himself in the woods, or hidden in a cave: it would have taken us much longer to find him. It's as if he didn't expect to be pursued.'

'Why should he?' said Anatoly. 'When the first guide disappeared, we didn't send a search party after *him* – we just got another guide and carried on: no investigation, no pursuit. What was different this time – what went wrong for Mohammed – was that the local people found the body and accused us of murder. That made us suspicious of Mohammed. Even so, we considered forgetting about him and just pressing on. He was unlucky.'

'He didn't know what a cautious man he was dealing with,' said Jean-Pierre. 'Next question: what was his motive in all this? Why did he go to so much trouble to substitute himself for the original guide?'

'Presumably to mislead us. Presumably, everything he told us was a lie. He did *not* see Ellis and Jane yesterday afternoon at the mouth of the Linar Valley. They did *not* turn south into the Nuristan. The villagers of Mundol did *not* confirm that two foreigners with a baby passed through yesterday heading south – Mohammed never even asked them the question. He *knew* where the fugitives were—'

'And he led us in the opposite direction, of course!' Jean-Pierre felt elated again. 'The old guide disappeared just after the search party left the village of Linar, didn't he?'

'Yes. So we can assume that reports *up* to that point are true – therefore Ellis and Jane *did* pass through that village. Afterwards, Mohammed took over and led us *south*—'

'Because Ellis and Jane went north!' said Jean-Pierre triumphantly.

Anatoly nodded grimly. 'Mohammed gained them a day, at most,' he said thoughtfully. 'For that he gave his life. Was it worth it?'

Jean-Pierre looked again at the Polaroid photograph of Mousa. The cold wind made it flutter in his hand. 'You know,' he said, 'I think Mohammed would answer Yes, it was worth it.'

CHAPTER NINETEEN

THEY LEFT Gadwal in the deep darkness before dawn, hoping to steal a march on the Russians by setting out so early. Ellis knew how difficult it was for even the most capable officer to get a squad of soldiers moving before dawn: the cook had to make breakfast, the quartermaster had to strike camp, the radio operator had to check in with headquarters, and the men had to eat; and all those things took time. The one advantage Ellis had over the Russian commander was that he had no more to do than load the mare while Jane fed Chantal then shake Halam awake.

Ahead of them was a long, slow climb up the Nuristan Valley for eight or nine miles and then up a side valley. The first part, in the Nuristan, should not be too difficult, Ellis thought, even in the dark, for there was a road of sorts. If only Jane could keep going, they should be able to get into the side valley during the afternoon and travel a few miles up it by nightfall. Once they were out of the Nuristan Valley it would be much more difficult to trail them, for the Russians would not know which side valley they had taken.

Halam led the way, wearing Mohammed's clothes, including his Chitrali cap. Jane followed, carrying

Chantal, and Ellis brought up the rear, leading Maggie. The horse was now carrying one bag fewer: Mohammed had taken the kitbag and Ellis had not found a suitable container to replace it. He had been forced to leave most of his blasting equipment in Gadwal. However, he had kept some TNT, a length of Primacord, a few blasting caps and the pull-ring firing device, and had them stowed in the roomy pockets of his New York down coat.

Jane was cheerful and energetic. The rest yesterday afternoon had renewed her reserves of strength. She was marvellously tough, and Ellis felt proud of her, although when he thought about it he did not see why *he* should be entitled to feel proud of *her* strength.

Halam was carrying a candle lantern which threw grotesque shadows on the cliff walls. He seemed disgruntled. Yesterday he had been all smiles, apparently pleased to be part of this bizarre expedition; but this morning he was grim-faced and taciturn. Ellis blamed the early start.

The path, such as it was, snaked along the cliffside, rounding promontories that jutted out into the stream, sometimes hugging the water's edge and sometimes ascending to the cliff top. After less than a mile they came to a place where the track simply vanished: there was a cliff on the left and the river on the right. Halam said the path had been washed away in a rainstorm, and they would have to wait until light to find a way around.

Ellis was unwilling to lose any time. He took off his boots and trousers and waded into the ice-cold water.

At its deepest it was only up to his waist, and he gained the far bank easily. He returned and led Maggie across, then came back for Jane and Chantal. Halam followed at last, but modesty prevented him from undressing, even in the dark, so he had to walk on with soaking wet trousers, which made his mood worse.

They passed through a village in darkness, followed briefly by a couple of mangy dogs that barked at them from a safe distance. Soon after that, dawn cracked the eastern sky, and Halam snuffed the candle.

They had to ford the river several more times in places where the path was washed away or blocked by a landslide. Halam gave in and rolled his baggy trousers up over his knees. At one of these crossings they met a traveller coming in the opposite direction, a small, skeletal man leading a fat-tailed sheep which he carried across the river in his arms. Halam had a long conversation with him in some Nuristani language, and Ellis suspected, from the way they waved their arms, that they were talking about routes across the mountains.

After they parted from the traveller, Ellis said to Halam in Dari: 'Don't tell people where we are going.'

Halam pretended not to understand.

Jane repeated what Ellis had said. She spoke more fluently, and used emphatic gestures and nods as the Afghan men did. 'The Russians will question all travellers,' she explained.

Halam appeared to understand, but he did exactly the same thing with the next traveller they met, a dangerous-looking young man carrying a venerable

Lee-Enfield rifle. During the conversation, Ellis thought he heard Halam say 'Kantiwar', the name of the pass for which they were heading; and a moment later the traveller repeated the word. Ellis was angered: Halam was fooling around with their lives. But the damage was done, so he suppressed the urge to interfere, and waited patiently until they moved on again.

As soon as the young man with the rifle was out of sight, Ellis said: 'I said you are not to tell people where we are going.'

This time Halam did not pretend incomprehension. 'I told him nothing,' he said indignantly.

'You did,' said Ellis emphatically. 'From now on you will not speak to other travellers.'

Halam said nothing.

Jane said: 'You will not talk to other travellers, do you understand?'

'Yes,' Halam admitted reluctantly.

Ellis felt it was important to shut him up. He could guess why Halam wanted to discuss routes with other people: they might know of factors such as landslides, snowfalls or floods in the mountains which might block one valley and make another approach preferable. He had not really grasped the fact that Ellis and Jane were *running away* from the Russians. The existence of alternative routes was about the only factor in the fugitives' favour, for the Russians had to check every possible route. They would be working quite hard to eliminate some of these routes by interrogating people, especially travellers. The less information they could garner that way, the more difficult and lengthy their search would be, and the better the chances that Ellis and Jane would evade them.

A little later they met a white-robed mullah with a red-dyed beard, and to Ellis's frustration Halam immediately opened a conversation with the man in exactly the same way as he had with the previous two travellers.

Ellis hesitated only for a moment. He went up to Halam, grabbed him in a painful double-arm lock, and marched him off.

Halam struggled briefly, but soon stopped because it hurt. He called out something, but the mullah simply watched open-mouthed, doing nothing. Looking back, Ellis saw that Jane had taken the reins and was following with Maggie.

After a hundred yards or so Ellis released Halam, saying: 'If the Russians find me, they will kill me. This is why you must not talk to anyone.'

Halam said nothing but went into a sulk.

After they had walked on a little, Jane said: 'I fear he'll make us suffer for that.'

'I suppose he will,' said Ellis. 'But I had to shut him up somehow.'

'I just think there may have been a better way to handle him.'

Ellis suppressed a spasm of irritation. He wanted to say *So why didn't you do it, smartass?* but this was not the time to quarrel. Halam passed the next traveller with only the briefest of formal greetings, and Ellis thought: At least my technique was effective.

At first their progress was a lot slower than Ellis had anticipated. The meandering path, the uneven ground, the uphill gradient and the continual diversions meant that by mid-morning they had covered only four or five miles as the crow flies, he estimated. Then, however, the way became easier, passing through the woods high above the river.

There was still a village or hamlet every mile or so, but now, instead of ramshackle wooden houses piled up the hillsides like collapsible chairs thrown haphazardly into a heap, there were box-shaped dwellings made of the same stone as the cliffs on whose sides they perched so precariously, like seagulls' nests.

At midday they stopped in a village, and Halam got them invited into a house and given tea. It was a two-storey building, the ground floor apparently being a storeroom, just like the English medieval houses Ellis remembered from ninth-grade history lessons. Jane gave the woman of the house a small bottle of pink medicine for her children's intestinal worms, and in return got pan-baked bread and delicious goat's-milk cheese. They sat on rugs on the mud floor around the open fire, with the poplar beams and willow laths of the roof visible above them. There was no chimney, so the smoke from the fire drifted up to the rafters and eventually seeped through the roof: that, Ellis surmised, was why the houses had no ceilings.

He would have liked to let Jane rest after eating, but he dared not risk it, for he did not know how close behind them the Russians might be. She looked tired, but all right. Leaving immediately had the additional advantage that it prevented Halam getting into conversation with the villagers.

However, Ellis watched Jane carefully as they walked on up the valley. He asked her to lead the horse while he carried Chantal, judging that the baby was more tiring.

Each time they came upon an eastward-leading side valley, Halam would stop and study it carefully then shake his head and walk on. Clearly he was not sure of the way, although he denied this hotly when Jane asked him. It was infuriating, especially when Ellis was so impatient to get out of the Nuristan Valley; but he consoled himself with the thought that if Halam was not sure which valley to take then the Russians would not know which way the fugitives had gone.

He was beginning to wonder whether Halam might have gone past the turning when, at last, Halam stopped where a chattering stream flowed into the Nuristan river, and announced that their route lay up this valley. He seemed to want to stop for a rest, as if he was reluctant to leave familiar territory, but Ellis hurried them along.

Soon they were climbing through a forest of silver birch, and the main valley was lost to view behind them. Ahead of them they could see the mountain range they had to cross, an immense snow-covered wall filling a quarter of the sky, and Ellis kept thinking: even if we escape from the Russians, how can we possibly climb that? Jane stumbled once or twice and cursed, which Ellis took as a sign she was tiring rapidly, although she did not complain.

At dusk they emerged from the forest on to a bare, bleak, uninhabited landscape. It seemed to Ellis that they might not find shelter in such territory, so he suggested they spend the night in an empty stone hut they had passed half an hour or so earlier. Jane and Halam agreed, and they turned back.

Ellis insisted that Halam build the fire inside the hut, not outside, so that the flame could not be seen from the air and there would be no tell-tale column of smoke. His caution was vindicated a little later, when they heard a helicopter drone overhead. That meant, he supposed, that the Russians were not far away; but in this country, what was a short distance for a helicopter could be an impossible journey on foot. The Russians might be just the other side of an impassable mountain – or only a mile down the track. It was fortunate that the landscape was too wild, and the path too difficult to discern from the air, for a helicopter search to be viable.

Ellis gave the horse some grain. Jane fed and changed Chantal then fell asleep immediately. Ellis roused her to zip her into the sleeping bag, then he took Chantal's diaper down to the stream, washed it out, and put it by the fire to dry. He lay beside Jane for a while, looking at her face in the flickering firelight while Halam snored on the other side of the hut. She looked absolutely drained, her face thin and taut, her hair dirty, her cheeks smudged with earth. She slept restlessly, wincing and grimacing and moving her mouth in silent speech. He wondered how much longer she could go on. It was the pace that was killing her. If they could move more slowly she would be all right. If only the Russians would give up, or be recalled for some major battle in another part of this wretched country . . .

He wondered about the helicopter he had heard. Perhaps it was on a mission unconnected with Ellis. That seemed unlikely. If it had been part of a search party, then Mohammed's attempt to divert the Russians must have had very limited success.

He allowed himself to think about what would happen if they were captured. For him there would be a show trial, at which the Russians would prove to sceptical non-aligned countries that the Afghan rebels were no more than CIA stooges. The agreement between Masud, Kamil and Azizi would collapse. There would be no American arms for the rebels. Dispirited, the Resistance would weaken and might not last another summer.

After the trial, Ellis would be interrogated by the KGB. He would make an initial show of resisting the torture, then pretend to break down and tell them everything; but what he told them would be all lies. They were prepared for that, of course, and they would torture him further; and this time he would act a more convincing breakdown, and tell them a mixture of fact and fiction that would be difficult for them to check out. That way he hoped to survive. If he did, he would be sent to Siberia. After a few years, he might hope to be exchanged for a Soviet spy captured in the States. If not, he would die in the camps.

What would grieve him most would be to be parted

from Jane. He had found her, and lost her, and found her again – a piece of luck that still made him reel when he thought of it. To lose her a second time would be unbearable, unbearable. He lay staring at her for a long time, trying not to go to sleep for fear she might not be there when he woke up.

Jane dreamed she was in the George V Hotel in Peshawar, Pakistan. The George V was in Paris, of course, but in her dream she did not notice this oddity. She called room service and ordered a fillet steak, medium rare, with mashed potatoes, and a bottle of Château Ausone 1971. She was terribly hungry, but she could not remember why she had waited so long before ordering. She decided to take a bath while they were preparing her dinner. The bathroom was warm and carpeted. She turned on the water and poured in some bath salts, and the room filled with scented steam. She could not understand how she had let herself get this dirty: it was a miracle they had admitted her into the hotel! She was about to step into the hot water when she heard someone calling her name. It must be room service, she thought; how annoying – now she would have to eat while she was still dirty, or let the food get cold. She was tempted to lie down in the hot water and ignore the voice – it was rude of them to call her 'Jane' anyway, they should call her 'Madame' – but it was a very persistent voice, and somehow familiar. In fact it was not room service, but Ellis, and he was shaking her shoulder; and with the most tragic sense of disappointment she realised that the George V was a dream, and in reality she was in a cold stone hut in Nuristan, a million miles from a hot bath.

She opened her eyes and saw Ellis's face.

'You have to wake up,' he was saying.

Jane felt almost paralysed by lethargy. 'Is it morning already?'

'No, it's the middle of the night.'

'What time?'

'One-thirty.'

'Fuck.' She felt angry with him for disturbing her sleep. 'Why have you woken me?' she said irritably.

'Halam has gone.'

'Gone?' She was still sleepy and confused. 'Where? Why? Is he coming back?'

'He didn't tell me. I woke up to find he had gone.'

'You think he's abandoned us?'

'Yes.'

'Oh, God. How will we find our way without a guide?' Jane had a nightmare dread of getting lost in the snow with Chantal in her arms.

'I'm afraid it could be worse than that,' said Ellis.

'What do you mean?'

'You said he would make us suffer for humiliating him in front of that mullah. Perhaps abandoning us is sufficient revenge. I hope so. But I assume he's headed back the way we came. He may run into the Russians. I don't think it will take them long to persuade him to tell them exactly where he left us.'

'It's too much,' said Jane, and a feeling almost like grief gripped her. It seemed as if some malign deity was conspiring against them. 'I'm too tired,' she said. 'I'm going to lie here and sleep until the Russians come and take me prisoner.'

Chantal had been stirring quietly, moving her head from side to side and making sucking noises, and now she started to cry. Jane sat up and picked her up.

'If we leave now we can still escape,' Ellis said. 'I'll load the horse while you feed her.'

'All right,' said Jane. She put Chantal to her breast. Ellis watched her for a second, smiling faintly, then went out into the night. Jane thought they could easily escape if they did not have Chantal. She wondered how Ellis felt about that. She was, after all, another man's child. But he did not seem to mind. He regarded Chantal as part of Jane. Or was he hiding some resentment?

Would he like to be a father to Chantal? she asked herself. She looked at the tiny face, and wide blue eyes looked back at her. Who could fail to cherish this helpless little girl?

Suddenly she was completely uncertain about everything. She was not sure how much she loved Ellis; she did not know what she felt about Jean-Pierre, the husband who was hunting her; she could not figure out what her duty to her child was. She was frightened of the snow and the mountains and the Russians, and she had been tired and tense and cold for too long.

Automatically she changed Chantal, using the dry diaper from the fireside. She could not remember changing her last night. It seemed to her that she had fallen asleep after feeding her. She frowned, doubting her memory, then it came back to her that Ellis had roused her momentarily to zip her into the sleeping bag. He must have taken the soiled diaper down to the stream and washed it and wrung it out and hung it on a stick beside the fire to dry. Jane started to cry.

She felt very foolish, but she could not stop, so she carried on dressing Chantal with tears streaming down her face. Ellis came back in as she was making the baby comfortable in the carrying sling.

'Goddam horse didn't want to wake up either,' he said, then he saw her face and said: 'What is it?'

'I don't know why I ever left you,' she said. 'You're the best man I've ever known, and I never stopped loving you. Please forgive me.'

He put his arms around her and Chantal. 'Just don't do it again, that's all,' he said.

They stood like that for a while.

Eventually Jane said: 'I'm ready.'

'Good. Let's go.'

They went outside and set off uphill through the thinning woodland. Halam had taken the lantern, but the moon was out and they could see clearly. The air was so cold it hurt to breathe. Jane worried about Chantal. The baby was once again inside Jane's fur-lined coat, and she hoped that her body warmed the air Chantal was breathing. Could a baby come to harm by breathing cold air? Jane had no idea.

Ahead of them was the Kantiwar Pass, at fifteen thousand feet a good deal higher than the last pass, the Aryu. Jane knew she was going to be colder and more tired than she had ever been in her life, and perhaps more frightened, too, but her spirits were high. She felt she had resolved something deep inside herself. If I live, she thought, I want to live with Ellis. One of these days I'll tell him it was because he washed out a dirty diaper.

They soon left the trees behind and started across a plateau like a moonscape, with boulders and craters and odd patches of snow. They followed a line of huge flat stones like a giant's footpath. They were still climbing, although less steeply for the moment, and the temperature dropped steadily, the white patches increasing until the ground was a crazy chessboard.

Nervous energy kept Jane going for the first hour or so, but then, as she settled into the endless march, weariness overcame her again. She wanted to say *How far is it now?* and *Will we be there soon?* as she had when a child in the back of her father's car on those long journeys through the Rhodesian bush.

At some point on that sloping upland they crossed the ice line. Jane became aware of the new danger when the horse skidded, snorted with fear, almost fell, and regained its balance. Then she noticed that the moonlight was reflecting off the boulders as if they were glazed: the rocks were like diamonds, cold and hard and glittering. Her boots gripped better than Maggie's hooves, but nevertheless, a little while later, Jane slipped and almost fell. From then on she was terrified she would fall and crush Chantal, and she trod ultra-carefully, her nerves so taut she felt she might snap.

After a little more than two hours they reached the

far side of the plateau and found themselves facing a steep path up a snow-covered mountainside. Ellis went first, pulling Maggie behind him. Jane followed at a safe distance in case the horse should slip backwards. They went up the mountain in a zig-zag.

The path was not clearly marked. They presumed it lay wherever the ground was lower than in neighbouring areas. Jane longed for a more definite sign that this was the route: the remains of a fire, a clean-picked chicken carcase, even a discarded matchbox – anything that would indicate that other human beings had once passed this way. She began obsessively to imagine that they were completely lost, far from the path, wandering aimlessly through endless snows; and that they would continue to meander for days, until they ran out of food and energy and will-power and they lay down in the snow, all three of them, to freeze to death together.

Her back ached insupportably. With much reluctance she gave Chantal to Ellis and took the horse's rein from him, to transfer the strain to a different set of muscles. The wretched horse stumbled constantly now. At one point it slipped on an iced boulder and went down. Jane had to haul mercilessly on its bridle to get it to its feet. When finally it stood up she saw a dark stain on the snow where it had fallen: blood. Looking more closely, she saw a cut on its left knee. The injury did not appear serious: she made it walk on.

Now that she was in the lead, she had to decide where the path lay, and the nightmare of getting irretrievably lost haunted every hesitation. At times the way seemed to fork and she had to guess, left or right. Often the ground was more or less uniformly level, so she just followed her nose until some kind of pathway reappeared. Once she found herself floundering in a snowdrift, and had to be pulled out by Ellis and the horse.

Eventually the path led her on to a ledge which wound far up the side of the mountain. They were very high: looking back across the plateau so far below made her a little dizzy. Surely they could not be far from the pass?

The ledge was steep, icy, and only a few feet wide, and beyond the edge was a precipitous drop. Jane trod extra carefully, but all the same she stumbled several times, and once fell to her knees, bruising them. She ached so much all over that she hardly noticed the new pains. Maggie slipped constantly, until Jane no longer bothered to turn around when she heard her hooves skid, but simply pulled harder on the reins. She would have liked to readjust the horse's load so that the heavy bags were farther forward, which would have helped the animal's stability on the uphill climb; but there was no room on the ledge, and anyway she was afraid that if she stopped she would not be able to start again.

The ledge narrowed and wound around an outcrop of cliff. Jane took gingerly steps across the most slender section, but despite her caution – or perhaps because she was so nervous – she slipped. For a heart-stopping moment she thought she was going to fall over the edge; but she landed on her knees and steadied herself with both hands. From the corner of her eye she could see the snowy slopes hundreds of feet below. She started to shake, and controlled herself with an effort.

She stood up slowly and turned around. She had let go of the rein, and it now dangled over the precipice. The horse stood watching her, stiff-legged and trembling, evidently terrified. When she reached for its bridle it took a panicky step backward. 'Stop!' Jane cried, then she made her voice calm and said quietly: 'Don't do that. Come to me. You'll be all right.'

Ellis called to her from the other side of the outcrop. 'What is it?'

'Hush,' she called softly. 'Maggie's frightened. Stay back.' She was dreadfully aware that Ellis was carrying Chantal. She continued to murmur reassuringly to the horse as she stepped slowly towards it. It stared at her, wide-eyed, breath like smoke coming from its flared nostrils. She got within an arm's length and reached for its bridle.

The horse jerked its head away, stepped backward, skidded, and lost its balance.

As its head jerked back Jane caught the rein; but its legs slipped from beneath it, it fell to the right, the rein flew from Jane's hand, and to her unspeakable horror the horse slid slowly on its back to the lip of the ledge and fell over, neighing in terror.

Ellis appeared. 'Stop!' he shouted at Jane, and she realised she was screaming. She closed her mouth with a snap. Ellis knelt down and peered over the edge, still clutching Chantal to his chest beneath his down coat. Jane controlled her hysteria and knelt beside him.

She expected to see the body of the horse embedded in the snow hundreds of feet below. In fact it had landed on a shelf just five or six feet down, and it was lying on its side with its feet sticking out into the void. 'It's still alive!' Jane cried. 'Thank God!'

'And our supplies are intact,' said Ellis unsentimentally.

'But how can we get the animal back up here?'

Ellis looked at her and said nothing.

Jane realised they could not possibly get the horse back up on to the path. 'But we can't leave her behind to die in the cold!' Jane said.

'I'm sorry,' said Ellis.

'Oh, God, it's unbearable.'

Ellis unzipped his down coat and unslung Chantal. Jane took her and put her inside her own coat. 'I'll get the food first,' said Ellis.

He lay flat on his belly along the lip of the ledge and then swung his feet over. Loose snow flurried over the prone horse. Ellis lowered himself slowly, feet searching for the shelf. He touched firm ground, slid his elbows off the ledge, and carefully turned around.

Jane watched him, petrified. Between the horse's rump and the face of the cliff there was not room for both of Ellis's feet side by side: he had to stand with his feet one behind the other, like a figure in an Ancient Egyptian wall painting. He bent at the knees and slowly lowered himself into a crouch, then he reached for the complex web of leather straps holding the canvas bag of emergency rations.

At that moment the horse decided to get up.

It bent its front legs and somehow managed to get them under its forequarters; then, with the familiar snake-like wriggle of a horse getting to its feet, it lifted its front end and tried to swing its rear legs back on to the ledge.

It almost succeeded.

Then its back feet slid away, it lost its balance, and its rear end fell sideways. Ellis grabbed the food bag. Inch by inch the horse slipped away, kicking and struggling. Jane was terrified it would injure Ellis. Inexorably the animal slithered over the edge. Ellis jerked at the food bag, no longer trying to save the horse but hoping to snap the leather straps and hold on to the food. So determined was he that Jane feared he would let the horse pull him over the edge. It slid faster, dragging Ellis to the brink. At the last second he let go of the bag with a cry of frustration, and the horse made a noise like a scream and dropped away, tumbling over and over as it fell into the void, taking with it all their food, their medical supplies, their sleeping bag and Chantal's spare diaper.

Jane burst into tears.

A few moments later Ellis scrambled up on to the ledge beside her. He put his arms around her and knelt there with her for a minute while she cried for the horse and the supplies and her aching legs and her frozen feet. Then he stood up, gently helped her up, and said: 'We mustn't stop.'

'But how can we go on?' she cried. 'We've nothing to eat, we can't boil water, we've no sleeping bags, no medicines . . .'

'We've got each other,' he said.

She hugged him tightly when she remembered how near to the edge he had slipped. If we live through this, she thought, and if we escape the Russians and get back to Europe together, I'll never let him out of my sight, I swear.

'You go first,' he said, disentangling himself from her embrace. 'I want to be able to see you.' He gave her a gentle shove, and automatically she began to walk on up the mountain. Slowly her despair crept back. She decided her aim would simply be to carry on walking until she dropped dead. After a while Chantal began to cry. Jane ignored her, and eventually she stopped.

Some time later – it might have been minutes or hours, for she had lost track of time – as Jane was rounding a corner, Ellis caught up with her and stopped her with a hand on her arm. 'Look,' he said, pointing ahead.

The track led down into a vast bowl of hills rimmed by white-peaked mountains. At first Jane did not understand why Ellis had said *Look*; then she realised that the track was leading *down*.

'Is this the top?' she said stupidly.

'This is it,' he said. 'This is the Kantiwar Pass. We've done the worst part of this leg of the journey. For the next couple of days the route will lie downhill, and the weather will get warmer.'

Jane sat down on an icy boulder. I made it, she thought. I made it.

While the two of them looked at the black hills, the sky beyond the mountain peaks turned from pearl grey to dusty pink. Day was breaking. As the light slowly stained the sky, so a little hope crept into Jane's heart again. *Downhill*, she thought, and *warmer*. Perhaps we will escape.

Chantal cried again. Well, *her* food supply had not gone with Maggie. Jane fed her, sitting on that icy boulder on the roof of the world, while Ellis melted snow in his hands for Jane to drink.

The descent into the Kantiwar Valley was a relatively gentle slope, but very icy at first. However, it was less nerve-racking without the horse to worry about. Ellis, who had not slipped at all on the way up, carried Chantal.

Ahead of them, the morning sky turned flame red, as if the world beyond the mountains was on fire. Jane's feet were still numb with cold but her nose unfroze. Suddenly she realised she was terribly hungry. They would simply have to keep walking until they came across people. All they had to trade, now, was the TNT in Ellis's pockets. When that was gone they would have to rely on traditional Afghan hospitality.

They were also without bedding. They would have to sleep in their coats, with their boots on. Somehow Jane felt they would solve all problems. Even finding the path was easy, now, for the valley walls on either side were a constant guide and limited the distance they might stray. Soon there was a little stream burbling along beside them: they were below the ice line again. The ground was fairly even, and if they had still had the horse they could have ridden her.

After another two hours they paused to rest at the

head of a gorge, and Jane took Chantal from Ellis. Ahead of them, the descent became rough and steep, but because they were below the ice line the rocks were not slippery. The gorge was quite narrow and could quite easily get blocked. 'I hope there are no landslides down there,' said Jane.

Ellis was looking the other way, back up the valley. Suddenly he gave a start, and said: 'Jesus Christ.'

'What on earth is the matter?' Jane turned and followed his gaze, and her heart sank. Behind them, about a mile up the valley, were half a dozen men in uniform and a horse: the search party.

After all that, thought Jane; after all we went through, they caught us anyway. She was too miserable even to cry.

Ellis grabbed her arm. 'Quick, let's move,' he said. He started hurrying down into the gorge, pulling her after him.

'What's the point?' Jane said wearily. 'They're sure to catch us.'

'We've got one chance left.' As they walked, Ellis was surveying the steep, rocky sides of the gorge.

'What?'

'A rockfall.'

'They'll find a way over or around it.'

'Not if they're all buried underneath it.'

He stopped at a place where the floor of the canyon was only a few feet wide and one wall was precipitously steep and high. 'This is perfect,' he said. He took from the pockets of his coat a block of TNT, a reel of cable marked with the name Primacord, a small metal object

about the size of the cap of a fountain-pen, and
something that looked like a metal syringe, except that
at its blunt end it had a pull-ring instead of a plunger.
He laid the objects out on the ground.

Jane watched him in a daze. She did not dare to
hope.

He fixed the small metal object to one end of the
Primacord by crimping it with his teeth; then he fixed
the metal object to the sharp end of the syringe. He
handed the whole assembly to Jane.

'This is what you have to do,' he began. 'Walk down
the gorge, paying out the cable. Try to conceal it. It
doesn't matter if you lay it in the stream – this stuff
burns under-water. When you reach the limit of the
wire, pull out the safety pins like this.' He showed her
two split-pins which pierced the barrel of the syringe.
He pulled them out and put them back in. 'Then keep
your eye on me. Wait for me to wave my arms above my
head like this.' He showed her what he meant. 'Then
pull the ring. If we time this just right, we can kill them
all. Go!'

Jane followed orders like a robot, without thinking.
She walked down the gorge, paying out the cable. At
first she concealed it behind a line of low bushes, then
she laid it in the bed of the stream. Chantal slept on in
the sling, swaying gently as Jane walked, leaving both
Jane's arms free.

After a minute she looked back. Ellis was wedging
the TNT into a fissure in the rock. Jane had always
believed that explosives would go off spontaneously if

you handled them roughly: obviously that was a popular misconception.

She walked on until the cable became taut in her hand, then she turned around again. Ellis was now scaling the canyon wall, presumably searching for the best position from which to observe the Russians as they stepped into the trap.

She sat down beside the stream. Chantal's tiny body rested in her lap. The sling went slack, taking the weight off Jane's back. Ellis's words kept repeating in her mind: *If we time this just right, we can kill them all.* Could it work? she wondered. Would they all be killed?

What would the other Russians do then? Jane's head began to clear and she considered the likely sequence of events. In an hour or two someone would notice that this little party had not called in for a while, and would attempt to raise them on the radio. Finding that impossible, they would assume that the party was in a deep gorge, or that its radio was on the blink. After a couple more hours without contact, they would send a helicopter to look for the party, assuming that the officer in charge would have had the sense to light a fire or do something else to make his location easily visible from the air. When that failed, the people at headquarters would start to worry. At some point they would have to send out a search party to look for the missing search party. The new party would have to cover the same ground as the old one. They certainly would not complete that trip today, and it would be impossible to search properly at night. By the time they found the bodies, Ellis and Jane would be at least a day and a half ahead, possibly more. It might be enough, Jane thought; by then she and Ellis might have gone past so many forks and side valleys and alternative routes that they might be untraceable. I wonder, she thought wearily. I wonder if this could be the end. I wish the soldiers would hurry. I can't bear the waiting. I'm so afraid.

She could see Ellis clearly, crawling along the cliff top on his hands and knees. She could see the search party, too, as they marched down the valley. Even at this distance they appeared dirty, and their slumped shoulders and dragging feet showed them to be tired and dispirited. They had not seen her, yet; she blended into the landscape.

Ellis crouched behind a bluff and peered around its edge at the approaching soldiers. He was clearly visible to Jane but hidden from the Russians, and he had a clear view of the place where he had planted the explosives.

The soldiers reached the head of the gorge and began to descend. One of them was riding, and had a moustache: presumably he was the officer. Another wore a Chitrali cap. That's Halam, Jane thought; the traitor. After what Jean-Pierre had done, treachery seemed to her an unforgivable crime. There were five others, and they all had short hair and uniform caps and youthful, clean-shaven faces. Two men and five boys, she thought.

She watched Ellis. He would give the sign at any minute. Her neck began to ache from the strain of looking up at him. The soldiers still had not spotted her: they were concentrating on finding their way along the rocky ground. At last Ellis turned to her and, slowly and deliberately, waved both his arms in the air above his head.

Jane looked back at the soldiers. One of them reached out and took the bridle of the horse, to help it over the uneven ground. Jane had the syringe-type device in her left hand and the forefinger of her right hand was crooked inside the pull-ring. One jerk would light the fuse and detonate the TNT and bring the cliff tumbling down on her pursuers. Five boys, she thought. Joined the army because they are poor or foolish or both, or because they were conscripted. Posted to a cold, inhospitable country where the people hate them. Marched through a mountainous, icy wilderness. Buried under a landslide, heads smashed and lungs choked with earth and backs broken and chests crushed, screaming and suffocating and bleeding to death in agony and terror. Five letters to be written to proud fathers and anxious mothers at home: regret to inform, died in action, historic struggle against the forces of reaction, act of heroism, posthumous medal, deepest sympathy. Deepest sympathy. The mother's contempt for these fine words as she recalled how she had given birth in pain and fear, fed the boy in hard times and easy, taught him to walk straight and wash his hands and spell his name, sent him to school; how she had watched him grow and grow until he was almost as tall as she, then even taller, until he was ready to earn a living and marry a healthy girl and start a family of his own and give her grandchildren. The mother's grief when she realised that all that, everything she had done, the pain and the work and the worry, had been for nothing: this miracle, her man child, had been destroyed by braggartly men in a stupid, vain war. The sense of loss. The sense of loss.

Jane heard Ellis shout. She looked up. He was on his feet, not caring now whether he was seen, waving at her and yelling: 'Do it now! Do it now!'

Carefully, she put the pull-ring device down on the ground beside the rushing stream.

The soldiers had seen both of them now. Two men began climbing up the side of the gorge towards where Ellis stood. The others surrounded Jane, pointing their rifles at her and her baby, looking embarrassed and foolish. She ignored them and watched Ellis. He climbed down the side of the gorge. The men who had been scrambling up towards him stopped and waited to see what he was going to do.

He reached the level ground and walked slowly up to Jane. He stood in front of her. 'Why?' he said. 'Why didn't you do it?'

Because they are so young, she thought; because they are young, and innocent, and they don't want to kill me. Because it would have been murder. But most of all . . .

'Because they have mothers,' she said.

Jean-Pierre opened his eyes. The bulky figure of Anatoly was crouching beside the camp bed. Behind Anatoly, bright sunlight streamed through the open flap of the tent. Jean-Pierre suffered a moment of panic, not knowing why he had slept so late or what he had missed; then, all in a flash, he recalled the events of the night.

He and Anatoly were encamped in the approach to the Kantiwar Pass. They had been awakened at around two-thirty a.m. by the captain commanding the search party, who in turn had been roused by the soldier on watch. A young Afghan called Halam had stumbled into the encampment, said the captain. Using a mixture of Pashto, English and Russian, he had said that he had been guide to the fleeing Americans, but they had insulted him so he had abandoned them. On being asked where the 'Americans' were now, he had offered to lead the Russians to the stone hut where, even now, the fugitives lay in unsuspecting sleep.

Jean-Pierre had been all for jumping into the heli-copter and rushing off right away.

Anatoly had been more circumspect. 'In Mongolia we have a saying: Don't get a hard-on until the whore opens her legs,' he said. 'Halam may be lying. If he is telling the truth, still he may not be able to find the hut, especially at night, especially from the air. And even if he finds it they may have gone.'

'So what do you think we should do?'

'Send an advance party – a captain, five troopers and a horse, with this Halam of course. They can leave immediately. We can rest until they find the runaways.'

His caution had been vindicated. The advance party reported back by radio at three-thirty, saying that the

461

hut was empty. However, they added, the fire was still alight so Halam had probably been telling the truth.

Anatoly and Jean-Pierre concluded that Ellis and Jane had woken up in the night, had seen that their guide was gone, and had decided to flee. Anatoly ordered the advance party to go after them, relying on Halam to indicate the likeliest route.

At that point Jean-Pierre had gone back to bed and fallen into a heavy sleep, which was why he had failed to wake at dawn. Now he looked blearily at Anatoly and said: 'What's the time?'

'Eight o'clock. And we've caught them.'

Jean-Pierre's heart leaped – then he remembered that he had felt this way before, and had been let down. 'For sure?' he asked.

'We can go and check just as soon as you put your trousers on.'

It was almost that quick. A refuelling helicopter arrived just as they were about to board, and Anatoly judged it wise to wait a few more minutes while their tanks were filled, so Jean-Pierre had to contain his consuming impatience a little longer.

They took off a few minutes later. Jean-Pierre looked at the landscape through the open door. As they flew up into the mountains Jean-Pierre realised this was the bleakest, harshest territory he had yet seen in Afghanistan. Had Jane really crossed this bare, cruel, icebound moonscape with a baby in her arms? She must really hate me, Jean-Pierre thought, to go through so much to get away from me. Now she will know that it was all in vain. She is mine forever.

But had she really been caught? He was terrified of another disappointment. When he landed, would he find that the advance party had captured another pair of hippies, or two fanatical mountain climbers, or even a couple of nomads who looked vaguely European?

Anatoly pointed out the Kantiwar Pass as they flew over it. 'Looks like they lost their horse,' he added, shouting into Jean-Pierre's ear over the noise of the engines and the wind. Sure enough, Jean-Pierre saw the outline of a dead horse in the snows below the pass. He wondered if it was Maggie. He rather hoped it was that stubborn beast.

They flew down the Kantiwar Valley, scanning the ground for the advance party. Eventually they saw smoke: someone had lit a fire to guide them in. They descended towards a patch of level ground near the head of a gorge. Jean-Pierre scrutinised the area as they went down: he saw three or four men in Russian uniforms but he did not spot Jane.

The helicopter touched down. Jean-Pierre's heart was in his mouth. He jumped to the ground, feeling nauseous with tension. Anatoly jumped out beside him. The captain led them away from the helicopter and down into the gorge.

And there they were.

Jean-Pierre felt like one who has been tortured and now has the torturer in his power. Jane was sitting on the ground beside a little stream with Chantal in her lap. Ellis stood behind her. They both looked exhausted, defeated and demoralised.

Jean-Pierre stopped. 'Come here,' he said to Jane.

She got to her feet and walked towards him. He saw that she was carrying Chantal in some kind of sling around her neck which left her hands free. Ellis started to follow her. 'Not you,' said Jean-Pierre. Ellis stopped.

Jane stood in front of Jean-Pierre and looked up at him. He raised his right hand and smacked the side of her face with all his might. It was the most satisfying blow he had ever struck. She reeled backwards, staggering, so that he thought she would fall; but she kept her balance and stood staring at him defiantly, with tears of pain running down her face. Over her shoulder Jean-Pierre saw Ellis take a sudden step forward then restrain himself. Jean-Pierre was mildly disappointed: if Ellis had tried to do something, the soldiers would have jumped him and beaten him up. Never mind: he would get his beating soon enough.

Jean-Pierre raised his hand to slap Jane again. She flinched, and covered Chantal protectively with her arms. Jean-Pierre changed his mind. 'There will be plenty of time for that later,' he said as he lowered his hand. 'Plenty of time.'

Jean-Pierre turned away and walked back towards the helicopter. Jane looked down at Chantal. The baby looked back at her, awake but not hungry. Jane hugged her, as if it were the baby who needed comforting. In a way she was glad Jean-Pierre had struck her, although her face was still hot with pain and humiliation. The blow was like the decree absolute in a divorce: it meant that her marriage was finally, officially, definitively over, and she had no further responsibility. If he had wept, or asked her forgiveness, or begged her not to hate him for what he had done, she would have felt guilty. But the blow finished all that. She had no feelings left for him: not an ounce of love or respect or even compassion. It was ironic, she thought, that she should feel completely free of him at the moment when he had finally captured her.

Up to this point a captain had been in charge, the one who had been riding the horse, but now it was Anatoly, Jean-Pierre's Oriental-looking contact, who took control. As he gave orders, Jane realised that she knew what he was saying. It was more than a year since she had heard Russian spoken, and at first it sounded like gibberish, but now that her ear was in tune she could understand every word. At the moment, he was telling a trooper to bind Ellis's hands. The soldier, apparently prepared for this, produced a pair of handcuffs. Ellis held his hands out in front of him co-operatively, and the soldier manacled him.

Ellis looked cowed and dejected. Seeing him in chains, defeated, Jane felt a surge of pity and despair, and tears came to her eyes.

The soldier asked if he should handcuff Jane.

'No,' said Anatoly. 'She has the baby.'

They were shepherded to the helicopter. Ellis said: 'I'm sorry. About Jean-Pierre. I couldn't get to him . . .'

She shook her head, to indicate there was no need for apology, but she could not manage to speak. Ellis's utter submissiveness made her angry, not with him but with everyone else for making him like this: Jean-Pierre and Anatoly and Halam and the Russians. She almost wished she had detonated the explosion.

Ellis jumped into the helicopter then reached down to help her. She held Chantal with her left arm, to keep the sling steady, and gave him her right hand. He pulled her up. At the moment when she was closest to him, he murmured: 'As soon as we take off, slap Jean-Pierre.'

Jane was too shocked to react, which was probably fortunate. Nobody else seemed to have heard Ellis, and anyway none of them spoke much English. She concentrated on trying to look normal.

The passenger cabin was small and bare, with a low ceiling so that the men had to stoop. There was nothing in it but a small shelf, for seating, fixed to the fuselage opposite the door. Jane sat down gratefully. She could see into the cockpit. The pilot's seat was raised two or three feet off the floor, with a step beside it for access. The pilot was still there – the crew had not disembarked – and the rotors were still turning. The noise was very loud.

Ellis squatted on the floor beside Jane, between the bench and the pilot's seat.

Anatoly boarded with a trooper beside him. He spoke to the trooper and pointed at Ellis. Jane could not hear what was said but it was plain from the trooper's reaction that he had been told to guard Ellis: he unslung his rifle and held it loosely in his hands.

Jean-Pierre boarded last. He stood by the open door, looking out, as the helicopter lifted. Jane felt panicky. It was all very well for Ellis to tell her to slap Jean-Pierre as they were taking off but how was it to be done? Right now Jean-Pierre was facing away from her and standing by the open door – if she tried to hit him she would probably lose her balance and fall out. She looked at Ellis, hoping for guidance. There was a set, tense expression on his face, but he did not meet her eye.

The helicopter rose eight or ten feet into the air, paused a moment, then did a sort of swoop, gaining speed, and began to climb again.

Jean-Pierre turned away from the door, stepped across the cabin, and saw there was nowhere for him to sit. He hesitated. Jane knew she should stand up and slap him – although she had no idea why – but she was frozen to her seat, paralysed by panic. Then Jean-Pierre jerked his thumb at her, indicating that she should get up.

That was when she snapped.

She was tired and miserable and aching and hungry and wretched, and he wanted her to stand up, carrying the weight of their baby, so that he could sit. That contemptuous jerk of the thumb seemed to sum up all his cruelty and malice and treachery, and it enraged her. She stood up, with Chantal swinging from her neck, and thrust her face into his, screaming: 'You bastard! You bastard!' Her words were lost in the roar of the engines and the rushing wind, but her facial expression apparently shocked him, for he took a startled step back. 'I hate you!' Jane shrieked; then she rushed at him with her hands outstretched and violently pushed him backwards out through the open door.

The Russians had made one mistake. It was a very small one, but it was all Ellis had, and he was ready to make the most of it. Their mistake had been to fasten his hands in front instead of behind his back.

He had been hoping they would not bind him at all – that was why he had done nothing, by a superhuman effort, when Jean-Pierre started slapping Jane. There had been a chance they might leave him unrestrained: after all, he was unarmed and outnumbered. But Anatoly was a cautious man, it seemed.

Fortunately, Anatoly had not been the one to put the handcuffs on: a trooper had. Soldiers knew that it was easier to deal with a prisoner whose arms were bound in front – he was less likely to fall over, and he could get in and out of trucks and helicopters unaided. So, when Ellis had submissively held out his hands in front, the soldier had not given it a second thought.

Unaided, Ellis could not overpower three men, especially as at least one of the three was armed. His chances in a straight fight were zero. His only hope was to crash the helicopter.

There was an instant of frozen time when Jane stood at the open doorway, the baby swinging from her neck, and stared with a horrified expression as Jean-Pierre fell into space; and in that moment Ellis thought *We're only twelve or fifteen feet up, the bastard will probably survive, more's the pity*; then Anatoly sprang up and grabbed her arms from behind, restraining her. Now Anatoly and Jane stood between Ellis and the trooper at the other end of the cabin.

Ellis whirled around, sprang up beside the pilot's raised seat, hooked his manacled arms over the pilot's head, drew the chain of the handcuffs into the flesh of the man's throat, and heaved.

The pilot did not panic.

Keeping his feet on the pedals and his left hand on the collective pitch lever, he reached up with his right hand and clawed at Ellis's wrists.

Ellis had a flash of dread. This was his last chance and he had only a second or two. The trooper in the cabin would at first be afraid to use his rifle for fear of hitting the pilot; and Anatoly, assuming he too was armed, would share the same fear; but in a moment one of them would realise that they had nothing to lose, since if they did not shoot Ellis the aircraft would crash anyway, so they would take the risk.

Ellis's shoulders were grabbed from behind. A glimpse of dark grey sleeve told him it was Anatoly. Down in the nose of the helicopter, the gunner turned around, saw what was happening, and started to get out of his seat.

Ellis jerked savagely on the chain. The pain was too much for the pilot, who threw up both hands and rose from his seat.

As soon as the pilot's hands and feet left the controls, the helicopter began to buck and sway in the wind. Ellis was ready for that, and kept his footing by bracing himself against the pilot's seat; but Anatoly, behind him, lost his balance and released his grip.

Ellis hauled the pilot out of the seat and threw him to the floor, then reached over the controls and pushed the collective stick down.

The helicopter dropped like a stone.

Ellis turned around and braced himself for the impact.

The pilot was on the cabin floor at his feet, clutching his throat. Anatoly had fallen full-length in the middle of the cabin. Jane was crouched in a corner with her arms protectively enclosing Chantal. The trooper, too, had fallen, but he had regained his balance and was now on one knee and raising his Kalashnikov towards Ellis.

As he pulled the trigger, the helicopter's wheels hit the ground.

The impact threw Ellis to his knees but he was ready for it and he kept his balance. The trooper staggered sideways, his shots going through the fuselage a yard from Ellis's head, then fell forward, dropping his gun and throwing out his hands to break his fall.

Ellis leaned forward, snatched up the rifle, and held it awkwardly in his manacled hands.

It was a moment of pure joy.

He was fighting back. He had run away, he had been captured and humiliated, he had suffered cold and hunger and fear, and he had stood helpless while Jane was slapped around; but now, at last, he had a chance to stand and fight.

He got his finger to the trigger. His hands were bound too close together for him to hold the Kalashnikov in the normal position, but he was able to support the barrel unconventionally by using his left hand to hold the curved magazine which jutted down just in front of the trigger guard.

The helicopter's engine stalled and the rotors began to slow. Ellis glanced into the flight deck and saw the gunner jumping out through the pilot's side door. He had to gain control of the situation quickly, before the Russians outside gathered their wits.

He moved so that Anatoly, who was stretched out on the floor, was between him and the door; then he rested the muzzle of the rifle on Anatoly's cheek.

The trooper stared at him, looking frightened. 'Get out,' Ellis said with a jerk of his head. The trooper understood and jumped out through the door.

The pilot was still lying down, apparently having trouble breathing. Ellis kicked him to get his attention, then told him to get out too. The man struggled to his feet, still clutching his throat, and went out the same way.

Ellis said to Jane: 'Tell this guy to get out of the helicopter and stand real close with his back to me. Quick, quick!'

Jane shouted a stream of Russian at Anatoly. The man got to his feet, shot a glance of pure hatred at Ellis, and slowly climbed out of the helicopter.

Ellis rested the muzzle of the rifle on the back of Anatoly's neck and said: 'Tell him to have the others freeze.'

Jane spoke again and Anatoly shouted an order. Ellis looked around. The pilot, the gunner and the trooper who had been in the helicopter were nearby. Just beyond them was Jean-Pierre, sitting on the ground and clutching his ankle; he must have fallen well, thought Ellis; there's nothing much wrong with him. Farther away were three more soldiers, the captain, the horse, and Halam.

Ellis said: 'Tell Anatoly to unbutton his coat, slowly take out his pistol, and hand it to you.'

Jane translated. Ellis pressed the rifle harder into Anatoly's flesh as he drew the pistol from its holster and reached behind him with it in his hand.

Jane took it from him.

Ellis said: 'Is it a Makarov? Yes. You'll see a safety catch on the left-hand side. Move it until it covers the red dot. To fire the gun, first pull back the slide above the grip, then pull the trigger. Okay?'

'Okay,' she said. She was white and trembling, but her mouth was set in a determined line.

Ellis said: 'Tell him to have the soldiers bring their weapons here, one by one, and throw them into the helicopter.'

Jane translated and Anatoly gave the order.

'Point that pistol at them as they get close,' Ellis added.

One by one, the soldiers came up and disarmed.

'Five young men,' said Jane.

'What are you talking about?'

'There was the captain, Halam, and five young men. I only see four.'

'Tell Anatoly he has to find the other one if he wants to live.'

Jane shouted at Anatoly, and Ellis was surprised by the vehemence of her voice. Anatoly sounded scared as he shouted his order. A moment later the fifth soldier came around the tail of the helicopter and surrendered his rifle as the others had.

'Well done,' Ellis said to Jane. 'He might have ruined everything. Now make them all lie down.'

A minute later they were all lying face down on the ground.

'You have to shoot off my handcuffs,' he said to Jane.

He put his rifle down and stood with his arms outstretched towards the doorway. Jane pulled back the slide of the pistol then placed its muzzle against the chain. They positioned themselves so that the spent bullet would go through the doorway.

'I hope this doesn't break my fucking wrist,' said Ellis.

Jane closed her eyes and pulled the trigger.

Ellis roared: 'Ow, fuck!' At first his wrists hurt like hell. Then, after a moment, he realized they were not broken – but the chain was.

He picked up his rifle. 'Now I want their radio,' he said.

On Anatoly's order, the captain began to unstrap a large box from the horse's back.

Ellis wondered whether the helicopter would fly again. Its undercarriage would be destroyed, of course, and there might be all sorts of other damage underneath; but the engine and the main control lines were on top. He recalled how, during the battle of Darg, he had seen a Hind just like this one crash twenty or thirty feet then lift off again. This bastard ought to fly if that one did, he thought. If not . . .

He did not know what he would do otherwise.

The captain brought the radio and put it into the helicopter, then walked away again.

Ellis allowed himself a moment of relief. As long as he had the radio, the Russians could not contact their base. That meant they could not get reinforcements, nor could they alert anybody to what had happened. If Ellis could get the helicopter into the air, he would be safe from pursuit.

'Keep your gun aimed at Anatoly,' he said to Jane. 'I'm going to see whether this thing will fly.'

Jane found the gun surprisingly heavy. She kept her arm outstretched, aiming at Anatoly, for a while, but soon she had to lower her arm to rest it. With her left hand she patted Chantal's back. Chantal had cried, off and on, during the last few minutes, but now she had stopped.

The helicopter's engine turned over, kicked, and hesitated. Oh, please start, she prayed; please go.

The engine roared into life and she saw the blades turn.

Jean-Pierre looked up.

Don't you dare, she thought. Don't move!

Jean-Pierre sat upright, looked at her, then got painfully to his feet.

Jane pointed the pistol at him.

He started to walk towards her.

'Don't make me shoot you!' she screamed, but her voice was drowned by the increasing roar of the helicopter.

Anatoly must have seen Jean-Pierre, for he rolled over and sat up. Jane pointed the gun at him. He lifted his hands in a gesture of surrender. Jane swung the gun back towards Jean-Pierre. Jean-Pierre kept coming.

Jane felt the helicopter shudder and try to lift.

Jean-Pierre was close, now. She could see his face clearly. His hands were spread wide in a gesture of appeal, but there was a mad light in his eyes. He's lost his mind, she thought; but perhaps that happened a long time ago.

'I will do it!' she yelled, although she knew he could not hear. 'I will shoot you!'

The helicopter lifted off the ground.

Jean-Pierre broke into a run.

As the aircraft went up he jumped and landed on the deck. Jane hoped he would fall out again but he steadied himself. He looked at her with hate in his eyes, and gathered himself to spring.

She closed her eyes and pulled the trigger.

The gun crashed and bucked in her hand.

She opened her eyes again. Jean-Pierre was still standing upright, with an expression of astonishment on his face. There was a spreading dark stain on the breast of his coat. Panicking, Jane pulled the trigger again, and again, and a third time. She missed with the first two, but the third seemed to hit his shoulder. He spun around, facing out, and fell forward through the doorway.

Then he was gone.

I killed him, she thought.

At first she felt a kind of wild elation. He had tried to capture her and imprison her and make her a slave. He had hunted her like an animal. He had betrayed her and beaten her. Now she had killed him.

Then she was overcome with grief. She sat on the deck and sobbed. Chantal began to cry too, and Jane rocked her baby as they wept together.

She did not know how long she stayed there. Eventually she got to her feet and went forward to stand beside the pilot's seat.

'Are you all right?' Ellis shouted.

She nodded and tried a weak smile.

Ellis smiled back, pointed to a gauge, and yelled: 'Look – full tanks!'

She kissed his cheek. One day she would tell him she had shot Jean-Pierre; but not now. 'How far to the border?' she asked him.

'Less than an hour. And they can't send anybody after us because we have their radio.'

Jane looked through the windscreen. Directly ahead, she could see the white-peaked mountains she would have had to climb. I don't think I could have done it, she said to herself. I think I would have lain down in the snow and died.

Ellis had a wistful expression on his face.

'What are you thinking about?' she asked him.

'I was thinking how much I'd like a roast beef

sandwich with lettuce and tomato and mayonnaise on wholewheat bread,' he said, and Jane smiled.

Chantal stirred and cried. Ellis took a hand off the controls and touched her pink cheek. 'She's hungry,' he said.

'I'll go back and take care of her,' said Jane. She returned to the passenger cabin and sat on the bench. She unbuttoned her coat and her shirt, and fed her baby as the helicopter flew on into the rising sun.

Part Three

1983

CHAPTER TWENTY

J ANE FELT pleased as she walked down the suburban driveway and climbed into the passenger seat
of Ellis's car. It had been a successful afternoon. The
pizzas had been good, and Petal had loved *Flashdance*.
Ellis had been very tense about introducing his daughter to his girlfriend, but Petal had been thrilled by the
young Chantal, and everything had been easy. Ellis had
felt so good about it that he had suggested, when they
dropped Petal off, that Jane walk up the drive with him
and say hello to Gill. Gill had invited them in, and had
cooed over Chantal, so Jane had got to know his ex-
wife as well as his daughter, and all in one afternoon.

Ellis – Jane could not get used to the fact that his
name was John, and she had decided always to call him
Ellis – put Chantal on the back seat and got into the
car beside Jane. 'Well, what do you think?' he asked as
they pulled away.

'You didn't tell me she was pretty,' Jane said.

'Petal is pretty?'

'I meant Gill,' said Jane with a laugh.

'Yes, she's pretty.'

'They're fine people and they don't deserve to be
mixed up with someone like you.'

She was joking, but Ellis nodded sombrely.

Jane leaned over and touched his thigh. 'I didn't mean it,' she said.

'It's true, though.'

They drove on in silence for a while. It was six months to the day since they had escaped from Afghanistan. Now and again Jane would burst into tears for no apparent reason, but she no longer had the nightmares in which she shot Jean-Pierre again and again. Nobody but she and Ellis knew what had happened – Ellis had even lied to his superiors about how Jean-Pierre died – and Jane had decided she would tell Chantal that her Daddy died in Afghanistan in the war: no more than that.

Instead of heading back to the city, Ellis took a series of back streets and eventually parked next to a vacant lot overlooking the water.

'What are we going to do here?' said Jane. 'Neck?'

'If you like. But I want to talk.'

'Okay.'

'It was a good day.'

'Yes.'

'Petal was more relaxed with me today than she has ever been.'

'I wonder why?'

'I have a theory,' said Ellis. 'It's because of you and Chantal. Now that I'm part of a family, I'm no longer a threat to her home and her stability. I think that's it, anyway.'

'It makes sense to me. Is that what you wanted to talk about?'

'No.' He hesitated. 'I'm leaving the Agency.'

Jane nodded. 'I'm very glad,' she said fervently. She had been waiting for something like this. He was settling his accounts and closing the books.

'The Afghan assignment is over, basically,' he went on. 'Masud's training programme is under way and they've taken delivery of their first shipment. Masud is so strong now that he has negotiated a winter truce with the Russians.'

'Good!' said Jane. 'I'm in favour of anything that leads to a ceasefire.'

'While I was in Washington, and you were in London, I was offered another job. It's something I really want to do, plus it pays well.'

'What is it?' said Jane, intrigued.

'Working with a new Presidential task force on organised crime.'

Fear stabbed Jane's heart. 'Is it dangerous?'

'Not for me. I'm too old for undercover work, now. It'll be my job to direct the undercover men.'

Jane could tell he was not being completely honest with her. 'Tell me the truth, you bastard,' she said.

'Well, it's a lot less dangerous than what I've been doing. But it's not as safe as teaching kindergarten.'

She smiled at him. She knew what this was leading to, now, and it made her happy.

He said: 'Also, I'll be based here in New York.'

That took her by surprise. 'Really?'

'Why are you so astonished?'

'Because I've applied for a job with the United Nations. Here in New York.'

'You didn't tell me you were going to do that!' he said, sounding hurt.

'You didn't tell me about *your* plans,' she said indignantly.

'I'm telling you now.'

'And I'm telling *you* now.'

'But . . . would you have left me?'

'Why should we live where you work? Why shouldn't we live where I work?'

'In the month we've been apart I completely forgot how goddam touchy you are,' he said.

'Right.'

There was a silence.

Eventually Ellis said: 'Well, anyway, as we're both going to be living in New York . . .'

'We could share the housekeeping?'

'Yes,' he said hesitantly.

Suddenly she regretted flying off the handle. He wasn't really inconsiderate, just dumb. She had almost lost him, back there in Afghanistan, and now she could never be mad at him for very long because she would always remember how frightened she had been that they would be parted forever, and how inexpressibly glad she had been that they had stayed together and survived. 'Okay,' she said in a softer voice. 'Let's share the housekeeping.'

'Actually . . . I was thinking of making it official. If you want.'

This was what she had been waiting for. 'Official,' she said as if she did not understand.

'Yes,' he said awkwardly. 'I mean we could get married. If you want.'

She laughed with pleasure. 'Do it right, Ellis!' she said. 'Propose!'

He took her hand. 'Jane, my dear, I love you. Will you marry me?'

'Yes! Yes!' she said. 'As soon as possible! Tomorrow! Today!'

'Thank you,' he said.

She leaned over and kissed him. 'I love you, too.'

They sat in silence, then, holding hands and watching the sun go down. It was funny, Jane thought, but Afghanistan seemed unreal now, like a bad dream, vivid but no longer frightening. She remembered the people well enough – Abdullah the mullah, and Rabia the midwife, handsome Mohammed and sensual Zahara and loyal Fara – but the bombs and the helicopters, the fear and the hardship were fading from her memory. This was the real adventure, she felt; getting married and bringing up Chantal and making the world a better place for her to live in.

'Shall we go?' said Ellis.

'Yes.' She gave his hand a final squeeze, then let it go. 'We've got a lot to do.'

He started the car and they drove back into the city.

BIBLIOGRAPHY

The following are books about Afghanistan by writers who have visited the country since the Soviet invasion of 1979:

Chaliand, Gerard: *Report from Afghanistan* (New York: Penguin, 1982).

Fullerton, John: *The Soviet Occupation of Afghanistan* (London: Methuen, 1984).

Gall, Sandy: *Behind Russian Lines* (London: Sidgwick & Jackson, 1983).

Martin, Mike: *Afghanistan: Inside a Rebel Stronghold* (Poole: Blandford Press, 1984).

Ryan, Nigel: *A Hitch or Two in Afghanistan* (London: Weidenfeld & Nicolson, 1983).

Van Dyk, Jere: *In Afghanistan* (New York: Coward-McCann, 1983).

The standard reference book on Afghanistan is:

Dupree, Louis: *Afghanistan* (Princeton: Princeton University Press, 1980).

On women and children I recommend the following:

Bailleau Lajoinie, Simone: *Conditions de Femmes en Afghanistan* (Paris: Editions Sociales, 1980).

Hunte, Pamela Anne: *The Sociocultural Context of Perinatality in Afghanistan* (Ann Arbor: University Microfilms International, 1984).

van Oudenhoven, Nico J. A.: *Common Afghan Street Games* (Lisse: Swets & Zeitlinger, 1979).

The classic travel book on the Panisher Valley and Nuristan is:

Newby, Eric: *A Short Walk in the Hindu Kush* (London: Secker & Warburg, 1958).

KEN FOLLETT

The Third Twin

Pan Books £6.99

A chilling story of hidden evil, set at the forefront of modern technology, *The Third Twin* is the heart-stopping new thriller from Ken Follett.

In the course of her work, beautiful scientist Jeannie Ferrami stumbles across a baffling mystery: Steve and Dan appear to be identical twins, but were born on different days to different mothers. A law student and a convicted murderer they seem a world apart, but when Steve is accused of a terrible crime, Jeannie must question just how different they really are.

As she begins to fall in love with Steve, Jeannie finds more than her professional future threatened. Her life is also now at risk. Together Steve and Jeannie will investigate the mystery, uncover all the secrets. But some secrets were meant to be left alone . . .

'Follett is a master storyteller'
The Times